The Original Bl Adventures Second Edition
Vol. 2
In The Shadow Of My Life & Wheel Of Deception
John Roberts

Copyright © 2024 John Roberts
All rights reserved.

Chapter One

The Brother And The Dead

"Fractured skull, neck broken, signs of sexual assault although we're still running tests," Sergeant Shaun Bryant confirmed.

"Do we know who she is?" Joe Knight asked.

"We found her student card in her purse. Everything else was taken."

"Convenient."

"Quite."

"This is the second one we've found. Have they informed the next of kin?"

"Eric Gordon's arranging that once the ID has been confirmed. We're looking for one seriously messed up son-of-a-bitch here."

Joe sighed. "What type of person would rape and kill a student and then, rather than hide or bury the body, they throw it off of a bridge on to one of the busiest roads in the south?"

"To send a message?"

"To whom?"

"That's what we need to work out."

"This can't leak out."

"With all due respect, Sir, the media are all over it. We need to give them something."

"They have their story. A young girl commits suicide on the A34. That's all they need to know."

"And what about the trafficking of foreign students?"

"No comment."

"The CIA are starting to get itchy feet already. It's only a matter of time before they come over and investigate for themselves."

"That's where you come in," Joe snapped, walking over to his desk, pulling a blue folder out of a drawer and handing it over to Sergeant Bryant. "That is the file of mugshots for all the missing students across the country. Now whoever is behind this has given us one. He's obviously one for melodrama. We need to find the others before he pulls another stunt like this. Speak to their families again. Gain as much knowledge as possible on them whilst Special Branch work on taking this group down."

"And what makes you think they'll say anything to me that's not already on record?"

"Because I have an eighteen year old American girl in the morgue who needs justice. Gordon's pulling the strings to get our men in place. Until we get a formal ID on this girl, it remains classified. Am I understood?"

Bryant nodded.

"Good. I need those statements yesterday. If we can find any kind of pattern, we might be able to find out where they're going to strike next."

Sergeant Shaun Bryant left the room as Joe Knight sat back in his chair, feeling the weight of the case heavy on his shoulders. He couldn't help but think about the dead girl, who was just a year younger than his own daughter. He shook his head to clear the thought and focused on the task at hand.

He flicked through a scattering of paperwork before filing it into the bin. He pulled his phone out of his pocket and scanned through his contacts list. He stopped at Langford 27942. He jotted the phone number down onto a notepad before locking his phone and returning it to his pocket. A photo of his wife, Patricia and his daughter, Carla, stared back at him from beside his laptop screen.

"It's time," he said before picking up his suit jacket from the back of his chair and walking out of the door.

***

The early spring sunshine sparkled on the morning dew that clung to the grass of the old cemetery on the edge of The New Forest. Blake knelt beside a newly erected headstone and placed some fresh daffodils into its rose bowl. As he stood once again, he took in a deep breath and sighed. The gold writing inscribed into the marble stone had a sense of finality about it. For the past few months, he tried to dismiss the reality that Rachael was gone. That it was some kind of bad dream that he just needed to wake up from. Seeing her name on the stone however, cut him deep once more.

"I hope you understand," Blake said softly, his hand brushing against the top of the gravestone as he walked by before heading back towards his car.

As he arrived at the cemetery gates, Blake noticed a man standing by his silver Ford Mondeo wearing a dark suit, white shirt, black tie and perfectly polished black shoes.

"I'm sorry for your loss Blake," the man said as Blake approached his car.

"Joe Knight, they finally let you out from behind a desk?"

"Briefly, you caused quite a shitstorm up north."

"If they wanted Ramon's soul they should have sent a priest. Unfortunately too much was left in the hands of amateurs. So what brings you down here?"

"We need to establish protection for yourself and your family."

"Frank Jackson, the agent that Gordon sent, is already here. My family are fine. We live in a quiet little village by the sea," Blake replied.

"And yet your son and partner have almost become collateral damage in your previous two assignments."

Blake sighed. "I take it this isn't a social call Knight so what is it?"

"We need you in London. Something big's going down."

"Gordon has my number."

"And he'd have used it if it was his case."

"I'm not for hire," Blake replied as he opened the driver's door.

"Eliza Lewis."

"What about her?"

"Old friend?"

"Irrelevant."

"Scottish student murdered ten years ago and then mysteriously turns up at a local newspaper as a journalist uncovering a major news story. I understand she got under your skin too..."

"Get to the point."

"Twelve students have disappeared in the past six months. You stumbled upon one in that old underground station and we found one of them tossed from a motorway bridge on the A34 overnight."

"How has this been kept out of the media? Twelve students, surely they've been missed by families and friends."

"You'd think so but so far we've come up with nothing. The only thing found on her was a student card, Victoria Louise Dawson, eighteen years old from Shreveport, Louisiana, attending Kings Cross University, London."

"Very convenient, has the university been contacted for a formal ID?"

"A formal ID isn't possible considering how she was found but every avenue is being explored."

Blake shook his head. "I'm not your guy Joe. My team..."

"I know all about Mo and Peter."

"I can't attack a case like this alone. I need specialist people I can rely on and bounce ideas off of. People who I can trust to have my back when the shit hits the fan."

"Then we'll form a new team. Get your stuff and meet me in the blue room tomorrow morning," Joe replied, handing Blake his card before wandering over towards his own car.

Blake looked at the card. The blue room was Special Branch's undercover offices in Vauxhall, London. He watched the dust cloud rise and fall on the gravel track as Joe Knight drove away before he climbed into his car and headed back to Aunt Mary's holiday home at Lepe Beach. Blake had inherited the house after her death and he wanted it to become the family home for his new life with Paula and Michael. As he parked his car on the driveway, he saw Paula standing in the doorway.

"Where's Frank?" Blake asked as he approached the front door.

"On the beach kicking a football around with Michael," Paula sighed. "You're going back in again aren't you?"

"You spoke to Knight?"

"He asked where you were. Frank said he used to work with you."

"I'm sorry."

"For what?"

"Not being here. I should be kicking a ball around with Michael. You shouldn't need a bodyguard. How are we meant to have a normal family life when..."

"We don't have a normal family life. It's the job Blake. I knew what I was signing up for. When shit happens, you have to deal with it."

Blake leant against the wooden post at the entrance to the porch.

"Why don't we come with you?" Paula asked.

"To London?"

"Yeh, the change will probably do us all some good. We can see a few friends. Michael wants to see Arsenal play and you won't have to worry about us being isolated down here."

Blake moved forward and Paula leant into his chest wrapping her arms around his waist. Her long blonde hair brushed across his face in the breeze as he held her close. His mind was transported back a couple of weeks to that cold January night when they were alone on the London Eye together. After overcoming his doubts and fears, he finally gathered up the courage to ask Paula to marry him. Since that day, both of them had felt a closeness that they never had experienced before. A renewed focus that no matter what life was going to throw at them, somehow they would make it through.

"Okay," he said as they headed inside.

***

Later that night, a loud knocking on the front door of 124 Alfredson Road woke Emily Langford out of a deep sleep. She looked at the clock on her bedside table before staggering towards the bedroom door. She slipped on her dressing gown and wandered downstairs towards the front door.

"Who is it?" she called out as she lifted the key from the hook in the hallway.

"Mum, it's me!"

"Steven? For goodness sake, it's three a.m."

"I know, I'm sorry. I locked myself out and didn't have anywhere else to go."

Emily opened the front door and gasped when she noticed her youngest son standing there with blood all over his hands and t-shirt. "What on Earth has happened?"

"Nothing, there was a fight at Renda's Bar that got a bit out of hand," Steven replied as he entered the house. "I just need to get cleaned up. Is it ok to sleep here tonight?"

"Yes, of course. I think Blake left a couple of shirts in the spare room that should fit you. I'll make some tea."

Steven disappeared upstairs whilst Emily wandered into the kitchen to fill up the kettle and prepare their drinks. When he returned, he noticed his mum was sitting at the kitchen table staring outside at the night sky.

"Mum? Are you okay?"

"Oh Steven, I never heard you come in. Would you like some tea? she asked.

"Yes, it's okay, I'll make it…" Steven replied as Emily began to stand up from the chair before losing her balance and falling back into the chair.

Steven quickly moved to stop the chair from overbalancing and steadied her once again.

"Are you sure you're okay? I'm sorry if I woke you from a deep sleep."

"I'm okay, it's just a headache John. You go back to bed. I'll be fine."

Steven pulled his phone out of his pocket and scrolled down to his sister Jenny's number. It rang several times before going into her answerphone.

"Jen, it's Steven. I think mum's ill, call me as soon as you get this!" Steven said before cutting off the call.

Emily sat in the chair looking out at the night sky as he prepared two cups of tea before sitting beside her at the kitchen table.

"Oh, hello Steven, I didn't hear you come home. Make sure Jenny lets Milo out in the morning before she goes to work," she said before reaching for her cup of tea.

Steven held the cup to assist her as she took a sip of the tea.

"I'm not incapable of drinking a drink!" she snapped.

Steven moved his hands away slowly, not taking his eyes off of his mum's face. He noticed the right side of her face was starting to droop. He was about to speak when Emily dropped her cup spilling the hot tea across the table.

"Oh now look at what you've made me do!" Emily snapped as she tried to stand up.

"It's ok mum, wait there. I will sort it out!" Steven replied as he rushed over to pick up a cloth to clean up the spillage.

As he began cleaning up the spillage, his phone rang. He answered it without looking at the caller ID.

"You'd better not be drunk!" Jenny snapped.

"Jen, I think Mum's having a stroke, get an ambulance to the house quick!"

Chapter Two

London Calling

Flight 759 from Miami landed at Heathrow Airport just after 8am. Gabby Turner and Simon Buxton wandered through the arrivals gate and collected their suitcases from the baggage reclaim conveyor before heading outside.

"Are you okay?" Simon asked.

Gabby took a deep breath. "Yeah, I will be."

"I know London doesn't hold great memories for you."

"I can't continue living in the past, Si. Sooner or later I need to find closure."

Gabby's mind drifted away as she looked out at the dark clouds that hung over the airport. When she moved to the US to be with her father, she saw it as a new start. A clean slate. George Turner, her father, had emigrated from the UK in 1985 after he had split up from her mother, Lana. Gabby was only ten years old at the time. Her brother, James, was only eight. After the divorce, Lana had struggled to keep enough money coming into the house to support the family. Gabby was forced to grow up very quickly and look after herself and her little brother whilst her mother worked long hours in the local clubs and bars. At least twice a week, Gabby would tuck James into bed and then wait in her room for her mum to come home from work with one of the local drunks who would spend the night there before disappearing at first light, never to be seen again.

She had tried to show her mum all of the love and support that she could but it never seemed to be enough. She could see her mother was struggling and was doing her best to provide for them but kept hitting setback after setback. Jane, their neighbour, helped supervise them whilst Lana worked late but friendships became strained by Lana's antics with the local men and Jane slowly pulled away from the family until one night, the unthinkable happened.

In hindsight, it was inevitable, but Gabby could never forgive her mother for leaving her so vulnerable. It was just after Gabby's thirteenth birthday when her mother met Derek Copsewood. Everything seemed to be fine until one night when Lana was working late at the club. After ensuring that James was tucked up in bed, Derek entered Gabby's bedroom and after pinning her down he viciously raped her. When he had finished, he just walked out of the house, stepped into his 4x4 and calmly drove away. She kept replaying events in her mind, thinking she could have done something to prevent it but there was nothing she could do. As he left the room, the shock paralysed her to the bed and she felt helpless. To this day, he hasn't been tried for the crime. When her mother finally returned home just after midnight, she found Gabby crying in the corner of her room.

She explained what had happened but Lana didn't believe her. She blamed Gabby for Derek's disappearance and kicked her out of the house. One of her father's old friends, Norman, had found her walking the streets in the early hours and he took her back to his home where his wife Margaret comforted her and attempted to resolve the situation. Gabby spent the night there and explained everything to Margaret and in the morning, they made their way back across the estate for Margaret to speak to Lana and explain the situation.

They knocked on the front door but couldn't get any answer. Gabby picked up the spare back door key from under one of the flower pots in the garden and she opened the back door allowing them both to enter the house. A stale smell hung in the air. Margaret ventured upstairs into the bedrooms whilst Gabby waited for her in the kitchen. A few minutes later, Margaret returned looking pale as if she'd seen a ghost. Within minutes, police cars, detectives and ambulances surrounded the house and Lana's body was carried out in a black zipped up bag.

Gabby and James, who was still asleep in his room when Margaret had first arrived, were ushered away to stay with Norman while investigations continued. It wasn't until two days later, after numerous questions, that Margaret revealed to her that Lana had hung herself in her bedroom and investigations concluded that it was indeed suicide during the night.

Gabby was crushed. Her father was halfway around the world and she was left to look after her eleven year old brother alone. Norman had other ideas though. He managed to contact George Turner in America and explained what had happened. George flew back to the UK on the following day and began the funeral proceedings. As Lana was adopted when she was only a few months old, she had no immediate family other than her children. Margaret and Norman helped George sort everything out and two months later, James and Gabby moved to Miami with their father in a bid to begin a new life.

George worked as an electrician and had sufficiently earnt enough to support the family comfortably and although he hadn't remarried, an au pair was on hand to ensure that both James and Gabby were properly cared for whilst he was working. The new life was all Gabby had ever wanted. She needed an escape route to deal with what had been happening to her over those past few months and now she had the time, the space and the freedom to move on.

Then three years later, after an accident at work, George was killed by some faulty wiring in an old warehouse that he was working on for the American Electrical Company who had a contract with the local malls. The electric shock had blown him off of the scaffolding in the warehouse and he later died on the way to the hospital. George Turner, their father, was the only man that she had ever trusted after her experience with Derek. The compensation that they received after George's death was little consolation to Gabby who felt that she'd been cheated once again. It had paid the remaining mortgage on the family home in Miami but she still missed him being there.

Her brother James had travelled the world but Gabby had always maintained the family home that they had now lived in for the past fifteen years. It was her attempt to ensure that her father's memory would not die and that James still had a place to call home. She earned her living as an artist and a freelance writer, even having her own column in the local newspaper. She had worked so hard to build the perfect family home and keep herself on the right side of the law. She had seen first hand how fragile life could be. To go from uncertainty to stability. To see both of her parents die. Life had certainly taught her some harsh lessons but yet, she still managed to find some kind of peace from within. All that she wanted was the opportunity to be happy and free. Her writing was her output to the world, sometimes controversially, of how she saw the state of society and the feedback that she received was immense.

At that time, the only family she cared for was James. Her little brother whom she had almost been a mother as well as a sister to through the years. In the past they had been able to open up to each other, talk about everything and confide in each other. That was until Ricardo Fernandez and Alekzander Kaufmann, two diamond smugglers from Europe had gotten James involved in a get rich quick scheme that had been blown way out of control. He seemed to change almost overnight into a different person. When he returned to the family home with Rachael Evans, a friend from college who had recently left her relationship with Blake Langford, he seemed distant and preoccupied. He didn't talk anymore. He became moody. Irritable even. Before her arrival, James and Gabby always held a close bond and rarely had a disagreement. Normally brothers and sisters tend to fight like cats and dogs but not them. The changes from within the family had brought them closer.

She missed James. After Special Branch and the CIA came and investigated his involvement with Fernandez and Kaufmann, James was sentenced to five years in prison leaving her to pick up the pieces once again. The one positive she could take from the intrusion though was Simon. Simon Buxton had worked alongside CIA Agent Jason Price and had protected her from a lot of the media and legal side of having the Turner family being scrutinised across America. With his help and support, she had been able to rebuild her life and write her own version of what had happened over the years in what had loosely become her own autobiography.

Ever since she left London as a teenager, this was the first time she had returned and she was determined to banish the memories of the past for good. They climbed into the first available taxi whilst the driver loaded their suitcases into the back of the car.

"Where to?" the driver asked.

"Scatterbird Publishing House, Park Lane, please," Simon replied before turning back to Gabby. "Are you sure you're okay? We can postpone the meeting if you want to?"

"I'll be fine. I've hidden in the shadows for too long. My brother's situation has kept me as a prisoner in Miami and now I'm ready to tell my story," she replied.

Simon squeezed her hand as they looked out of the window at the M25 traffic zooming past. Gabby noticed a book that had been left in the pocket behind the driver's seat. She pulled it out of the pocket, straightened out the curled edges and looked at the front cover. It read: TALES OF A LOST SOUL by EDITH HARROW. She turned it over and saw the publishing mark for SCATTERBIRD BOOKS on the back cover.

"Have a look at this, it's our publisher," Gabby said as she handed him the book.

"Poems published in 1962," Simon chuckled. "At least we know they're here for the long haul."

"If thou could compare thee to a flower in summer bloom, thy darkened shadow shalt never assume. People just don't write like this anymore. It's like a page from a Shakespeare play."

"I'm glad they don't, I'm not one for all this Shakespearean prose."

"Maybe I should take you to Stratford one day."

"Maybe, It'll all be much ado about nothing I'm sure," Simon teased.

"Excuse me driver, could I borrow this book?"

"'Ave whatever ya like love, some daft old lady left it behind," the driver replied.

Gabby read a few more pages as they arrived outside Scatterbird Publishing House on Park Lane. Simon paid the driver and they both walked up the concrete stairs into the publishing house. Gabby's agent had arranged a tour of several bookshops to promote her new book, Diamonds Don't Dream, yet the feeling of being back in London brought back a lot of childhood memories. As she looked up at the tall buildings that surrounded them, Gabby still had an uneasy feeling that she couldn't shake off.

***

Andrew Broughton stepped outside his home just after 10am. He pulled up the hood on his black waterproof jacket as the rain began steadily falling. A red double deck bus stopped on the corner of Admirals Street and he quickly stepped on board. He exchanged his money for a return ticket from the driver before finding a vacant seat halfway down the lower deck on the right hand side. He noticed a rip in the leather upholstery and someone had written the letters W W J D in purple ink on the back of the seat in front of him. He watched as crowds of people wandered down the street rushing to their jobs, appointments or whatever their day had planned for them. Everyone and everything seemed to blur into the background as he watched the world go by. Twenty minutes later, he stepped off of the bus and headed up Harlequin Square towards The Troubled Traveller pub. He knocked on the front door before noticing a yellow post-it note that had been left on the window pane. It read:

AROUND THE BACK!!

Andrew continued down the road towards an alleyway with three metal bins lined up against the wall of the pub. The stench of alcohol and urine attacked his senses as he wandered along towards the back of the pub. He saw the landlord, Richard Parsons, unloading a truck full of beer barrels and soft drinks.

"Ah better late than never!" Richard shouted as he saw Andrew arrive.

"Sorry Dickie, I got held up."

"I'll hold you up permanently if you don't help me get this delivery sorted before opening time."

The delivery driver smiled as Andrew rolled his eyes before rolling the next beer barrel inside the pub. Between them, they soon had all of the stock inside and sent the driver on his way. Dickie wandered through towards the bar whilst Andrew removed a packet of cigarettes from inside his jacket pocket. He removed one of them before striking a match and lighting it. As he wandered around the backyard of the pub, Andrea, one of the barmaids arrived.

"Filthy habit," she cussed.

"That's rich coming from an ex-smoker!"

"When are you two going to sort out that alleyway, it bloody stinks. Puts the punters right off ya know."

"I'll see to it later."

"Is Dickie Parsnips in?"

"Yeh he's in the bar."

"You might want to wander back round the front before he opens up."

"Why?"

Andrea moved closer. "There's an old man out there sitting by the front door."

"Not another beggar, we moved three of 'em on last week!"

"No, he asked for you."

"Me personally?"

"No, the postman, is there another bloody Andy Broughton 'ere?"

"Okay, I'll go and see what he wants," Andrew sighed as he stubbed out his cigarette against the wall of the pub.

Andrea watched him as he wandered back down the alleyway. As soon as he was out of sight, she pulled her phone out of her handbag, typed out a text message and sent it before wandering inside the pub.

The rain began to fall heavier as Andrew walked around the corner towards the front of the pub. He saw a grey haired man sitting next to the entrance wearing a mud splattered yellow rain mack with beige trousers and scuffed brown shoes.

"I'm sorry mate but I'm going to need to ask you to move on. We need to open up the pub soon and have to keep the access clear!" Andrew explained.

The man turned to face him.

Andrew froze. "Oh my God, Graham?"

"I had nowhere else to go," Graham replied.

"What happened to you?"

"I've done a lot of bad things…"

"Come with me," Andrew replied as he led Graham around to the back of the pub before heading inside.

"Is he all right?" Andrea asked.

"Can you find him a towel and a hot drink please?" Andrew asked before leading Graham into the bar area.

"What's going on, we don't open for another fifteen minutes," Dickie grumbled before looking over at Graham and Andrew. "Oh all right, make him a cuppa tea."

Andrea handed them a towel before wandering back into the kitchen behind the bar. Graham slipped off his wet rain mack and Andrew wrapped the towel around his shoulders.

"Where's Paula?" Andrew asked.

"I haven't seen her for years."

"She needs to help you."

"No, she's moved on. I don't need her."

"You're her father, she needs to know that you're struggling."

"No, she wouldn't care anyway. I just need to get myself sorted again."

"How do you plan on doing that?"

"I need somewhere to stay."

Andrea walked over and placed two cups of tea on the table before leaving them again.

"What about your home?" Andrew asked.

"She sold it."

"Who did?"

"Paula."

"When?"

"Last year, just after Rachael died."

"I'm sorry. I saw the news. Surely she can't sell the home you live in without your consent."

"It was in Olivia's name."

"And as her husband you would naturally inherit after she died..."

"I've been a ghost, Andy," Graham sighed as he drank some of his tea.

"A ghost?"

"Olivia died because of me. I disappeared with Dave Francis. He had a villa in the south of France. We sailed over there and kept a low profile."

"So what changed?"

"Dave got sick. Polycythemia Vera I think they called it."

Andrew frowned.

"A rare blood cancer. It caused a blood clot that hit his heart. He was only fifty-nine."

"I'm sorry."

"I thought after Rachael had died and the dust had settled that it was time for a new beginning. Dave's family sold the villa and I was left with either finding somewhere else to live out there or coming home."

"So you came home."

"Yeah."

"And..."

"I took the bus to Vincent Street and saw a young family with a removal van moving into my home."

"Did you approach them?"

"No, of course not."

"Why not?"

"What could I say, sorry, my daughter sold my home without my permission..."

"There must be some kind of legal..."

Graham raised his hand. "After Olivia died, the courts ruled that I was missing presumed dead. The house went to Paula and Rachael. Now Rachael is dead, Paula can do whatever she wants with it."

"So she sold it."

Graham nodded.

"You need to speak to her. Where is she?"

"I don't know."

"Have you tried calling her?"

"She's changed her number."

"What about Blake Langford? He was involved with Rachael's case. Surely he..."

"The Langford's won't tell me anything."

"Have you tried?"

"We never saw eye to eye. Rachael was never good enough for Blake in their eyes. Why would Emily or John help me now?"

"You need to do something. How long have you been back in London? Where have you been staying?"

"Here and there. I wouldn't intrude normally but..."

"You've got nowhere else to go."

Graham bowed his head.

"Give me ten minutes," Andrew sighed before heading out towards the kitchen behind the bar.

Graham finished the last few mouthfuls of his tea as he watched Andrea lifting the stools down off of the tables in the bar.

A few minutes later, Andrew returned. "Come with me."

"Where are we going?" Graham asked.

"To get you some dry clothes and a shower."

"Thank you. It'll only be a couple of nights I promise."

Andrea unlocked the front door as Graham and Andrew headed for the exit.

"I hope you know what you're doing," she whispered as Andrew followed him out.

"So do I," he replied as the door closed behind them.

As they walked down the street, Graham felt grateful for Andrew's help. It had been a long time since anyone had shown him any compassion. He knew he had messed up, but now he had an opportunity to start over again.

They arrived at Andrew's flat, which was small but cosy. Andrew rummaged through his clothes and found a shirt and a pair of jeans that would fit Graham.

"These might be a little tight, but it's better than nothing," he said, handing Graham the clothes.

Graham headed to the bathroom to take a shower, feeling the hot water running down his back, he closed his eyes and let out a deep sigh. It felt good to be clean again. He stayed in there a little longer than he should have, but he didn't want to face the reality of his situation. When he returned to the kitchen, Andrew had made two cups of coffee for them.

"So, what's your next step?" Andrew asked.

Graham sighed deeply, "I guess I need to find my daughter."

"Do you think she'll talk to you?"

"I'm sure it's just a misunderstanding that we can sort out between us. That's an amazing sword by the way," Graham replied as he walked over towards where a samurai sword was hung on the wall.

"Be careful with that, it belonged to my grandfather."

Graham returned the sword to its sheath. "We ignore the old ways at our peril."

"Meaning?"

"Oh nothing, just thinking out loud," Graham replied before turning on the TV and sitting down on the sofa.

Andrew studied him momentarily before heading back into the kitchen with the empty coffee cups. Something about Graham's demeanour didn't feel quite right. He was hiding something and Andrew was determined to figure out what it was.

Chapter Three

Family Feud

Blake Langford parked his car outside his flat in Portman Terrace in Kensington before collecting the bags and suitcase from the boot of the car.

"I thought we were going to see Nan?" Michael asked.

"You will see her soon. I have to go to work but Paula's got loads of fun things that you two can do while I'm away," Blake replied as they climbed the three flights of stairs up to his flat.

As they arrived at the front door of Blake's flat, his neighbour opened her front door.

"Ah Blake, I'm glad I caught you, your sister's been trying to reach you all morning."

"Hello Helen, sorry I've been driving so I haven't checked my phone recently, did she say what it was about?"

"No but she sounded a little panicked. My, haven't you changed Michael. Must be all that country air," Helen laughed as she rubbed her hand on his head.

Blake unlocked the front door and stumbled inside with the bags whilst Paula and Michael continued to talk to Helen. He pulled his phone out of his jeans pocket and found three missed calls, two text messages and a voicemail from Jenny. The messages read: CALL ME!! He dialled the voicemail and listened.

"Blake, I'm at C&W Hospital, Steven called me at three this morning, they've taken mum in. They think she may have had a stroke. Get here as soon as you can."

Blake rushed back out the front door and moved past Paula and Michael.

"Where are you going?" Paula asked.

"Mum's in hospital, I'll call you as soon as I know anything more, love you both," Blake replied before running back down the concrete stairs to the car park below.

"Oh no, I hope she's okay," Helen said as she watched Blake drive away. "Let me know if you need anything."

"I will, thank you," Paula replied before heading inside the flat with Michael.

"Is nan going to be okay?" Michael asked.

"She's just a little bit poorly at the moment. Don't worry, your dad and the doctors will help her. How about you come and help me unpack and then I'll see about getting us some lunch."

Michael nodded before rushing away into the lounge and turning on the TV. Paula smiled as she watched him from the hallway for a moment before dragging the suitcase into the bedroom.

***

Gabby and Simon entered the front door of Scatterbird Publishing House and found tall mahogany bookshelves on each wall with a selection of books from the 1960's through to the present day. There were four booths with soft semi-circular red benches accompanied by mahogany coffee tables at their centre with a small reception desk located at the far end of the room. As they approached the reception desk, a door opened from a neatly camouflaged section of the bookcase on the back wall and a tall man dressed in navy trousers, blue shirt and a navy jacket wandered over towards them.

"Gabrielle Turner, it's fantastic to finally meet you. I'm Elliot Francis and I'll be taking care of anything you need whilst you're in the UK with us. I trust you had a pleasant flight?"

"It was long but I'm very much looking forward to meeting everyone here," Gabby replied.

"Splendid, well we've booked you into the Followers Hotel which is literally two streets away from here," Elliot explained before turning his attention to the receptionist. "Wendy, could you please ask Sebastian to take Miss Turner and her partner's luggage to their hotel so we can continue our tour."

Wendy smiled and nodded before wandering over and taking the luggage from Simon. As she walked back toward the desk, she noticed the book that Gabby was holding in her hands.

"Edith Harrow?" Wendy asked.

"Yes, I found her book in the taxi on the way here. Are you familiar with her work?" Gabby asked.

"I visited her at her nursing home last week to celebrate her birthday."

"Wow, I've only read a few pages but her prose is amazing."

"It is and even at one hundred and two, she is still as sharp today as she was then. Look after that one, there are very few still available."

"Surely Scatterbird could reproduce some of her work if it was requested?" Simon asked.

"Ah yes, in theory we could," Elliot interrupted. "The problem being around contracts and historical content being, how can I say it, offensive or questionable at best. Anyway, would you like to come on through, we have a selection of cakes, drinks and sandwiches available. You must be hungry after your long journey."

Gabby and Simon looked over at Wendy who gave them a knowing nod before they headed over to where Elliot was holding open the door for them to enter into the offices of the publishing house.

"Are you thinking what I'm thinking?" Gabby whispered.

"Keep hold of that book," Simon replied before following Elliot towards one of the offices.

Gabby and Simon followed Elliot through the door that had opened in the bookcase and down a long hallway. They passed several doors on either side before Elliot stopped in front of a large wooden door at the end of the hall.

"This is our conference room," Elliot said as he opened the door and gestured for Gabby and Simon to enter.

Gabby couldn't help but let out a small gasp as she took in the room. The walls were lined with floor-to-ceiling bookshelves filled with leather-bound books, and in the centre of the room was a long table surrounded by high-backed l leather chairs.

"Wow," Simon said, echoing Gabby's thoughts.

Elliot chuckled. "Yes, it's quite impressive. Now, let's get down to business."

Gabby and Simon spent the next few hours meeting with various members of the publishing house's team, discussing their ideas and plans for the book tour. By the time they left, Gabby felt exhausted and was looking forward to a good night's sleep.

***

Blake parked his car in the car park of Chelsea And Westminster Hospital. He turned off the ignition and took a couple of deep breaths. He could feel the stress inside tightening him up like a coiled spring. So much had happened in such a short space of time that he'd struggled to stay focused. He stepped out of the car, locked it with his key fob and then wandered into the hospital reception. There was a middle-aged woman with short grey hair finishing a conversation on the phone before turning her attention to him.

"Hello, could you tell me where Emily Langford is please?" Blake asked.

"Are you family?"

"I am her son."

"I believe she is being moved up to the ward now. Just give me a moment," the receptionist replied before wandering off down a maze of corridors.

"Blake!" Jenny called out.

Blake spun around as his sister approached him. "Where is she? What happened?"

"She's stable but the doctor said she has had a stroke. It was lucky that Steven was there so they could get to her in time."

"Steven was there, at three a.m?"

"Yeah, that was my first reaction too…"

"What was he doing waking mum up at that time of morning?"

"If he didn't she could be dead now!"

Blake ran his fingers through his hair. "Where is he?"

"Upstairs, I came down to try and call you."

"Ah Mr Langford, I see your sister has…" the receptionist said as she returned to the desk.

"Yes, thank you," Blake smiled before turning his attention back to Jenny. "If he's involved, there's bound to be more to it."

"He told me that he was at Renda's Bar, a fight broke out that he got involved with…"

"Of course he did."

"Blake!"

"Okay, okay, he was at Renda's," Blake sighed.

"He lost his wallet and couldn't get a ride home so he called in at mum's to get cleaned up and get some sleep before sorting himself out in the morning.

"So the hammering on the front door in the early hours probably startled mum enough to trigger a stroke."

"The doctor seems to think it's been building for a while. Steven said that she was okay when she let him into the house but after he got changed and went back downstairs, she thought he was Dad."

"She's called me John before. She gets easily confused..."

"She asked him to tell me to take our old dog Milo out in the morning before I go to work too."

Blake paced around the corridor. "Milo's been gone what, twenty years? Dad's been gone eight and a half."

"She'd been getting headaches recently and she went to see Doctor Mulley a couple of weeks ago. He had requested that she should go for a scan but the appointment isn't for another couple of weeks yet."

Blake and Jenny walked through the glass corridors and into the hospital ward together. The smell of antiseptic attacked their senses as the sound of beeping machines echoed around them. They walked towards the end of the corridor before turning left into the second doorway from the end of the ward.

There were six beds, three on each side of the room. Emily Langford was lying asleep in one of the hospital beds nearest to the window. Her face was pale and she looked fragile, almost as if her life had been drained from her.

Blake felt a wave of emotions rush over him as he saw his mother lying in bed; sadness, guilt and regret all washing over him at once. He wanted to reach out and hold her hand but he could only bring himself to step closer and look at her in silence. He glanced at Jenny who seemed equally sad and overwhelmed by what they were seeing before them.

Steven looked up as they approached. "I was just leaving."

"No, stay," Blake replied as Steven stood up from the chair at his mother's bedside.

"This is not the time..."

"No, it's not. Sit down," Blake interrupted.

"You can't tell me what..."

"Steven," Jenny spoke this time. "Not now."

"What did the doctor say?" Blake asked.

"They've sedated her and she just needs complete rest for now," Steven replied.

"What happened to your lip?"

Steven covered this mouth with his hand. "Nothing, a bar fight got out of control last night."

"So you thought you'd wake up our elderly mother in the middle of the night covered in blood..."

"And you never cause her any stress do you Blake! You've put the family in more danger than I ever have but Dad's blue eyed boy can do no wrong!"

At that point, a nurse approached them. "I'm sorry but you're disturbing the patients, if you carry on I'll have to ask you to leave!"

Blake and Steven both apologised as Jenny stepped in between them.

"You both have created waves over the past few years but fighting between yourselves is not going to solve anything. Mum needs us to pull together not rip each other apart," Jenny said as she held Emily's hand.

"I'm sorry about Rachael," Steven conceded.

Blake nodded.

"Must be hard being a dad and trying to save the world."

"What would you know about it?"

"I see things."

"If you've got something to say, just say it."

"I saw Rachael Evans pull this family apart before disappearing with a millionaire halfway around the world whilst you emotionally blackmailed Aunt Mary with your sob stories..."

"Steven!" Jenny snapped.

"You're so bitter about money that you'd rather put all of your anger into me rather than supporting and helping your own family. I'm not the one trying to rekindle my youth by working the student bars and taking a different man's daughter home every night. Dad was a proud man. He was and still is my inspiration to this day to be the best that I can be for myself and my family. You! You're just a pathetic excuse of a man who I'm ashamed to call my brother!" Blake snapped.

"That's it, I need you both to leave now!" the nurse demanded.

"Don't worry, I was just leaving," Blake replied before storming out of the ward.

Everyone looked over at them as Steven ran his fingers through his short ginger hair.

"That went well," Jenny sighed.

"He only cares about himself," Steven replied.

"A lot has happened to him over the past year."

"What about you? What about Mum? Does he know that he's triggered your panic attacks again after seeing that girl in the station?"

"The police are dealing with that."

"He claims to love and support his family but we're the ones sitting here whilst he runs off across London in a strop."

"Let it go."

"You know I can't do that."

"Then if anything happens to Mum, she won't be the only family member you lose," Jenny replied before walking out of the hospital ward.

Steven watched her as she left before turning back towards Emily as she laid asleep beside him. He pulled his phone out from his pocket and noticed a missed call and two text messages from his manager, Nathan Cooke, at Renda's Bar. He opened and read the two messages;

POLICE WANT TO SEE YOU ABOUT LAST NIGHT. WHERE'S TIFFANY?

He quickly typed out a message before sending it and turning off his phone. If Tiffany hadn't shown up for work today, there was a good chance that Andrew Broughton knew where she was.

Chapter Four

A Brand New Beginning

Blake drove into the underground car park beneath Special Branch and parked in his usual space. His hands were still trembling with anger as he breathed deeply to calm himself down. His younger brother Steven always seemed to have a knack for getting under his skin and today was no exception. He locked his car with the key fob before taking the lift up to the eighth floor and wandering along the corridor towards Eric Gordon's office.

"Blake, is everything okay?" Angela, Eric Gordon's secretary asked as he entered.

"Nothing I can't handle," Blake replied. "Is he in?"

"They all are."

"They?"

"You should go right in," Angela replied as she pressed a button under her desk and the light above Eric Gordon's door changed from red to green.

Blake entered the office and saw Joe Knight, Alison Pearce and Samir Khalifa all sat waiting for him.

"Blake Langford, at last," Eric Gordon said as Blake closed the door behind him.

"Quite the welcoming committee," Blake quipped. "I thought the blue room was a separate operation."

"Normally it would be until it was necessary to rebuild a team. Where have you been?" Eric asked.

"A family emergency, sorry, it won't happen again."

"We're not heartless Blake. Things crop up from time to time and that's why you need people around you who can step in from time to time," Joe replied.

"I don't need a team."

"Does the name Tiffany Mason mean anything to you?" Eric Gordon asked.

"No, why?"

"She was involved in a raid at a brothel on Harlequin Square recently," Samir replied. "A local businessman was targeted after he interrupted a payoff at Renda's Bar last night."

"Targeted? In what way?"

"It's believed he was the pimp behind the brothel and the local competition tipped off the police losing him thousands of pounds as well as, obviously, his clients ending up in a cell for the night," Samir explained.

"So where do I come into this?"

"The girl you discovered in the old station two weeks ago," Alison replied.

"The one we couldn't identify?"

"The same, we discovered someone called Hannah Jane Powell from Southampton had been reported missing forty-eight hours before you found her. After formal identification, it was discovered that she was at Kings Cross University, the same university as Victoria Louise Dawson, the American student found on the A34 last night," Alison explained.

"So they're from the same university, potentially in the same friendship groups and visiting the same bars in that area of London," Blake replied. "Does that mean that potentially all twelve missing students are from the same university?"

"Not exactly," Joe answered. "When I spoke to you yesterday we only had a definite ID on Victoria Dawson. Discovering the link to Hannah Powell was pure luck on our part. We still have ten missing students unaccounted for."

"What about this, Tiffany Mason? Have you been through missing persons reports?" Blake asked.

"Extensively but we have no other leads. Mason was at Renda's Bar last night but disappeared as soon as the police arrived," Alison replied.

"Have you followed up any foreign exchange students? With one of them being American, surely that's an option."

"Samir is working through that line of enquiry now but so far, nothing has come up. In the meantime, I need your team to find this man," Eric Gordon replied as he handed Blake a print of a middle-aged man with grey hair combed to the side with a perfectly shaped goatee.

"My team?" Blake asked.

"See this as a brand new beginning Blake. Samir will control the technical side, Joe has the contacts whilst you and Alison go in for the kill."

Blake sighed. "What do you have on him?"

"Last seen getting into a white BMW outside Renda's Bar last night after it all kicked off. Sergeant Shaun Bryant followed him to a secluded mansion in South Kensington which he hasn't yet reappeared from," Joe replied.

"Do we have a name?"

"He's known as Zodiac but there's no official name on file," Alison replied.

"Okay, Joe and Samir, you two follow up on Sergeant Bryant and find out if and when Zodiac leaves the mansion. Maybe he'll lead us somewhere. Alison and I will visit Renda's Bar and see what we can find out from last night's fight," Blake replied.

"This needs to be kept under wraps. Any new scandal after the Scotland case will create a shitstorm that none of us need," Eric Gordon advised.

The four of them agreed before leaving the office. Alison joined Blake in his car and as they left the car park, Blake called Jenny through the hands free controls in his car.

"Have you calmed down yet?" she answered.

"A little, any news?" Blake asked.

"Still the same. Steven left so I'm staying at the hospital for the night."

"Is he working tonight?"

"Not that I know of, why?"

"Something's come up at work. Did he mention anything to you about a coworker, girlfriend maybe?"

"No, he just said that a police raid at the bar got out of hand and punches were thrown. Why all the questions?" Jenny asked.

"He never mentioned anyone named Tiffany?"

"No, he doesn't tell me anything like that. Blake, what's going on? Is Steven in trouble?"

"Not yet, let me know if anything changes with Mum. Love ya sis," Blake replied before cutting off the call.

"What was all that about?" Alison asked.

"My Mother had a stroke last night and is recovering in C&W Hospital," Blake replied as he weaved his car through the busy London streets.

"I'm sorry, is that why you were late to the meeting?"

"Partly, I think I may have another angle on the events that happened at Renda's Bar last night."

"How?"

"I didn't want to mention it in front of Gordon but my brother was there."

"Will he give you a statement?"

"Unlikely, but it could be useful if I need some leverage," Blake replied as they turned into a side street just behind Renda's Bar.

"So what's the plan?"

"The brothel that they closed down on Harlequin Square is around the same distance from the university that Renda's Bar is."

"On the opposite side of the campus, yeh."

"So if they were trafficking students and potentially some of them got in too deep, Zodiac would need an escape route."

"I'm not following."

"He would need a mole in each bar to keep an eye on his investment. If the heat became too much, he would move on to the next, I guess you could call it, safe house."

"Meaning?"

"How many bars are within say a three mile radius of the campus?" Blake asked.

"At least twelve. You're looking for a needle in a haystack. The three Universities account for almost two thousand students. Most of them will use waitressing jobs to make up extra money but if they've been cut off from the bank of mum and dad then they are a prime target."

Blake opened up the glove box and pulled out two polythene bags before handing one to Alison. Each bag contained a small beige coloured ear-piece. Blake opened his bag and placed the ear-piece into his right ear. Alison did the same.

"Just in case," Blake said before stepping out of the car and heading down towards the end of the side street with Alison following close behind.

A tall man with a shaved head, dressed in a black shirt, black trousers and black shoes stood at the entrance of Renda's Bar as students began entering.

Blake checked his watch. "A little heavy to have someone on the door at six o clock on a Friday night."

Alison unclipped her dark brown hair and allowed it to flow down to her shoulders before taking Blake's arm and heading towards the door. As they arrived the doorman stood in their way.

"Student bar only, beat it," he snapped.

"I'm a senior student with a degree in ackamarackus," Blake replied.

"In what?"

Blake grabbed the doorman's arm and twisted it behind his back before leading him towards the side street. "A degree in bullshit for the uneducated. Now tell me where can I find Tiffany Mason?"

The doorman struggled but Blake twisted harder.

"Tiffany Mason?" Blake asked again.

"Fuck you."

"No, that's not an option," Blake replied before kicking the back of his leg, sending him down to the floor.

As he tried to get up, Blake pulled out his gun.

"Where is Tiffany Mason?" Blake asked.

"She never showed up."

"So she works here."

"No, she's a regular."

"Where can I find her?"

"She left with one of our guys last night."

"Who?"

"Absolutely not."

Alison grabbed his shirt and pulled him up to his feet. Blake kept his gun aimed at his chest.

"Who did she leave with?" Alison asked.

"Steven."

"Steven who?"

"I don't know, he usually helps Nathan on the weekends."

"Nathan being the landlord, right?"

The doorman nodded.

Alison pushed him away as Blake replaced his gun inside his jacket.

"Amazing what you can do when you try," Blake smiled.

"You should get outta here while you still can."

"Is that a threat?" Alison snapped.

"It's a promise."

Alison spun around bringing her foot up between the doorman's legs before striking him in the face with her elbow. The doorman crumpled to the floor before she hit him on the back of his head, sending him down to the ground.

Blake and Alison moved back to the front of the building and stepped inside Renda's Bar. The bar was dimly lit and smelt of stale beer and a mix of marijana and cigarettes. Students crowded around the bar, chatting and laughing. Blake and Alison made their way towards the back of the bar where a few booths were set up.

"Look for anyone who looks out of place," Blake whispered into his ear-piece.

Alison scanned the room, her eyes coming to rest on a young woman sitting alone in a booth. She had black hair, which was pulled back into a ponytail. She was wearing a short red dress. She looked around nervously, as though she was waiting for someone.

"Check out the woman in the red dress," Alison whispered back. "She looks suspicious."

Blake and Alison made their way over to the woman's booth and sat down across from her.

"Hi there," Blake said with a smile. "Mind if we join you?"

The woman looked up at them, her eyes wide with fear. "Who are you? What do you want?" she stammered.

"We're here to help," Alison reassured her.

"We're looking for someone," Blake replied. "We were told you might be able to help us."

The woman shifted nervously in her seat. "I don't know anything," she said quickly. "I swear, I'm just waiting for someone."

Blake leaned forward, his eyes darting around the bar. "Who are you waiting for?" he asked.

The woman hesitated for a moment before speaking. "His name is Jack," she said. "He's supposed to meet me here tonight."

"Jack who?" Alison asked.

"I don't know his last name. We just met a few nights ago. He said he could help me out with something, but I don't know anything."

Blake and Alison exchanged a glance.

"What kind of help?" Blake asked.

The woman bit her lip nervously. "I have some debts," she said quietly. "Jack said he could help me take care of them."

"Debts to who?" Alison asked.

The woman hesitated.

"It's okay," Blake reassured her.

"My father owns one of the competing student bars and I needed some cash to help me through a tough time. Now I need to find a way of paying the money back and Jack gave me some options."

"Do you know someone called Tiffany Mason?" Alison asked.

"No, sorry."

Blake handed her a card with his number on it. "If you hear anything, we would really appreciate any kind of information that you have."

"Is she in trouble?"

"Possibly, why?"

"My father may know more," she conceded.

"Who is your father and where can we find him?" Alison pushed.

The woman ran her fingers through her hair and sighed. "His name is Derek Copsewood, he's the landlord of Sam's Bar, 23 St Lawrence Square. It's on the opposite side of the campus, you can't miss it."

Blake and Alison both stood up from the booth.

"Thank you Miss..." Blake began.

"Turner, Claire Turner," she replied.

"Miss Turner, please take care of yourself. There are a lot of snakes in these bars and it's very easy for unsuspecting young women like yourself to become their prey."

"I'll keep that in mind."

Blake and Alison both wandered back to the car before driving away from the bar.

"What now?" she asked.

"I'll keep Derek Copsewood in mind but firstly, I think it's time to pay my brother a visit," Blake replied.

Chapter Five

Signs Of The Zodiac

"There's our man," Samir smiled as he watched a middle aged man with grey hair wearing a navy suit climb into a white BMW.

Samir Khalifa and Joe Knight had parked their Volvo V60 a few metres further down the road from Zodiac's mansion in South Kensington for three hours before noticing any movement within the grounds.

"What would a man of his means be trawling Student Bars around London for?" Joe asked.

"Trying to recapture his misspent youth. Why else do old dudes chase young women? They think a few extra thousand in the bank is enough to persuade the young lady that she needs a sugar daddy when really, the old man just wants his ego massaged."

"Do you think Zodiac is the key to all of this?"

"No, but I think he'll lead us to whoever is," Samir replied as he dropped the binoculars he was using onto the back seat and started the car's engine.

Zodiac drove out of his driveway before turning left and heading towards Chelsea. Samir followed three cars behind as the traffic began to build up. The BMW took a sharp left into a residential street as the traffic lights turned red. When they finally moved again, Samir turned into the street but there was no sign of the BMW.

"Son-of-a-bitch got away," Joe sighed as they crawled along the street at twenty miles per hour.

As they came to a crossroads half way down the street, cars from either side sped up before skidding to a stop either side of Samir's car leaving no room for either door to open. Samir looked over and saw Zodiac walking over from the opposite side of the road. Two Indian men stepped out from each of the cars and gathered around the Volvo.

Joe opened the window. "Now come on guys, we just took a wrong turn and ended up in the wrong place so how about we talk about this."

"Samir Khalifa!" Zodiac called out.

Samir opened the window. "I'm sure there's a more social way that we could discuss this."

At that moment, another car turned into the street and began sounding their horn. Zodiac pulled out a gun and shot the driver's front tyre. The driver jumped out of the car and ran in the opposite direction.

"Why are you following me?" Zodiac asked.

"We believe your life may be in danger."

"Bullshit, I have the best men this side of the channel so tell me another one."

"But are they loyal?"

"Is anyone?"

"Tough way to make a living, continuously having to look over your shoulder."

"I get by. The question still stands or is that suit next to you got another lie he'd like to tell?"

"Someone left a Z with a spike through it, burnt into the flesh of a young girl found dead two weeks ago," Samir replied.

"Now that is interesting, if it's true?"

"How long have we known each other?"

"Not long enough."

"I know you don't trust law enforcement after what they did to your brother..."

"Don't you talk shit about Xander!" Zodiac snapped.

"If she's one of your circle, eventually it's going to work its way back to you."

"So what are you offering?"

"I know there's some action happening in the Student Bars around here. I know your boys have been dealing..."

"You can't prove..."

"I don't care about that. That's not what I'm here for. If the girl is one of yours, it may be a prelude to a bigger attack. Is there anyone new that has been creating waves around you? Have you pissed someone off that would want to frame you?"

"There's one."

"Who?"

"As if I'm gonna tell you that."

"I've given you the girl, you gotta give me something..."

"There's this guy buying up loads of shit recently. Made my guy edgy in Renda's, name's Copsewood, Derek Copsewood."

"Anything more than that? What does he look like, where can I find him?" Samir pushed.

"Not here, meet me at 121 Gerrards View, just past Eel Brook Common, eight o'clock," Zodiac replied before beckoning for the men to get back into their cars.

Zodiac turned and walked back across the road towards a house on the corner with a red wooden door. As he opened the door he turned back and looked over at Samir and Joe. The two cars that had sandwiched them in the middle of the junction backed off and Samir drove forwards before heading back down to join the Fulham Road. Zodiac watched them leave before heading inside.

"Okay, what the hell was that? How did Zodiac know who you are and when were you going to tell me about the Z marking?" Joe stammered.

"Would you rather they blew your head off and asked questions later?" Samir asked.

"You lied."

"I told him what he wanted to hear and we have hopefully got a lead, Derek Copsewood. See what you can find out."

Joe began tapping away on his laptop. Derek Copsewood - Samir couldn't get the name out of his head. He had a feeling that this guy was more than just a drug dealer. As he drove down the road, he couldn't help but feel like there was something much bigger going on.

Joe looked over at Samir. "What's going on in that head of yours?"

"Just trying to piece things together," Samir replied. "I've got a feeling that this Copsewood guy is connected to something bigger."

"What do you mean?"

"I don't know yet," Samir said, "but I think we need to find out more about him before we meet with Zodiac tonight."

"Agreed," Joe said. "What's the plan?"

"We'll do some digging and see what we can find out about him. And if things start to get too crazy, we'll back off and regroup."

Joe nodded. "Sounds like a plan. Where do we start?"

"See what you can find out, first."

"There must be hundreds of Derek Copsewood's, who knows who it's gonna be? You still didn't answer my question..."

"Five years ago when I was with Scotland Yard, we raided one of Zodiac's storage facilities and uncovered several tonnes of Columbian pure. Zodiac, or Zachary as he was known then, led us to the ringleader, Diego Luis Hernandez. I cut him a deal and he became a useful pawn in the game."

"Your grass in other words."

"Things turned sour when I joined Special Branch and he realised that the leniency he had enjoyed before was no longer there. Today was the first time in three years that I've spoken to him."

"Did you recognise any of those men who cut us off?"

"They're his men from Jaipur. Kaja's their ringleader. Nasty piece of work. Used to be involved with the Naapaak group a few years ago alongside Raj, Karun and Vijay. Trust me, they're bad news. If you wanna keep your kneecaps, don't piss them off."

"Does Gordon know about your involvement with him?"

"Of course not, he'd throw me off the case."

"What was he talking about when you mentioned his brother?"

"Xander was caught in an underground cage fight. He killed two men and was convicted of murder. There was nothing I could do but Zodiac pleads his innocence to this day."

"So what now?"

"Now I meet him at eight."

"You're not seriously going to go? You're walking into a trap."

"Maybe, sometimes I need to look in the shadow of my life to bring the truth into the light."

Joe continued tapping away on his laptop before closing it and tossing it onto the back seat. "Sam's Bar, 23 St Lawrence Square."

"What about it?" Samir asked.

"Current landlord, a Mister Derek Phillip Copsewood."

"Too easy."

"Sometimes these things happen and I could do with a pint, let's go."

***

Sergeant Shaun Bryant entered Detective Jim Curtis' office inside Kensington Police Station just after 7pm that evening.

"Nice of you to inform me that I had Special Branch breathing down my neck," Curtis snapped as Bryant closed the door.

"You're entitled to a few days leave, Sir."

"Knight made quite a mess during my few days leave, didn't he?"

"I don't follow..."

"I keep certain individuals informed about certain happenings that will interfere with their business and you go strolling in and blow up the whole damn investigation!"

"A young woman was murdered and dumped on a dual carriageway, I could hardly stand back and ignore it."

"You should've let the local force deal with it. It wasn't on our patch!"

"The girl is from Kings Cross University, that makes it our patch!" Bryant snapped.

"The press are jumping to conclusions, I've got media appointments where they are demanding an update on a case that should have been conducted discreetly. The mayor doesn't need this during his reelection campaign."

"I'm sorry that two young women, potential murder victims, have interfered with the mayor's career path. Perhaps he should include that in his next speech in Parliament so the voters know where his priorities lie!"

"I will not tolerate insubordination in this office!"

"Cut the bullshit, you're just pissed that someone has blown the lid off of a case that, for whatever reason, you've been trying to keep in the shadows."

"Sometimes things are best kept in the darkness. When people poke their noses in where they don't belong looking for skeletons in the closet, there is often a lot of needless collateral damage!"

"Meaning?" Bryant asked.

"If nobody sees you go into battle, nobody has to see you leave."

"Is that a threat?"

"Should it be?"

"Who are you running from Sir?"

"I'm your senior officer, you should know where the line is."

"You may be my senior officer but I know the difference between someone who is being authoritative and giving specific direction and someone who is scared."

"Get out!"

"What?"

"I said get out. I'm suspending you until a suitable place can be found for you elsewhere."

"On what grounds?"

"Poor taste in friends. We all know the shitshow that Special Branch caused up north, I'm not letting the same thing happen here."

Sergeant Shaun Bryant moved towards the door before looking back at Detective Jim Curtis. "You know I used to admire you when I was working my way up through the ranks. Jim Curtis, the one with all the answers, the guy who could talk his way out of a room with no doors..."

"And your point is?"

"Now I just see a bitter old man looking to do anything for an easy life. Maybe one day you'll remember what that badge stands for."

Bryant left and slammed the door before he could respond. Jim Curtis walked over towards the window and looked out at

the car park and the bustling London streets below. The beep of his phone cut into his thoughts. He opened the message, it read:
WE NEED TO TALK, Z

***

Music boomed from 235 Quebec Road as Blake Langford arrived and parked his car against the curb on the opposite side of the road.

"Quite the party animal your brother," Alison quipped.

"Not for much longer," Blake replied as he stepped out of the car and walked towards the house with Alison a few steps behind.

As they approached, Blake noticed a group of young women drinking champagne and watching him from the garden. Three men in suits began walking over towards the front door before a tall African man stepped in front of Blake.

"Sorry pal, private party," he said, looking Blake up and down.

"Firstly, I'm nobody's pal and second, I want to speak with Steven Langford," Blake snapped.

"He ain't here, now beat it."

Blake looked around and noticed the three men from the garden had crowded around him and Alison.

"Three mistakes have been made here," Blake said as he turned back to face the African man.

"I count two, you and your girl..."

In one quick movement, Blake elbowed the man on his left in the face before charging towards the African man standing in the doorway. Alison caught the man behind her with a kick to his groin before making contact with the jaw of the man on the right with a fierce uppercut.

Blake pulled out his gun and held it against the African man's head as his three accomplices got back to their feet. "I'll ask you again, where's Steven Langford?"

"I'm here!" Steven called out as he opened the front door.

The groups of people in the garden looked in Steven's direction but he waved them away. The four men got back onto their feet before moving away into the garden.

"Can't you just say hello like a normal person?" Steven asked before leading them towards the back garden.

"Why the heavy security?" Alison asked.

"Let's just say I don't have the most understanding of neighbours."

"With your choice of entertainment I can see why."

"Life is for living so live it. But you haven't come here to slap me on the wrist for loud music have you?"

"No," Blake replied.

"So what is it? You still pissed with me because I was the one helping mother and not you?"

"Needless to say with mum's illness, I thought a house party would be the last thing on your agenda this evening."

"And yet here you are, Her Majesty's loyal servant working for Queen and country whilst lecturing me on family loyalty."

"Who's Tiffany Mason?"

"Never heard of her," Steven replied as he pulled a cigarette out of a packet and lit it.

"That's odd, she left Renda's Bar with you last night," Alison added.

"So did twenty other women, doesn't mean I know them all."

"Popular guy."

"I like to think so, sweetheart. So, has my brother worked his charm on you yet? How many more notches on the bedpost do you need? You know, he collects young enthusiastic women like you..."

"Cut the bullshit," Blake snapped.

"Oooh, touchy, see what I mean."

"I know exactly what you're doing here Steven. I could get this house shut down and all of you in cells for the night with one phone call."

"So why don't you?" Steven asked, blowing smoke into Blake's face. "Or can't you bring yourself to take your little brother down on some bullshit charges that'll never stick."

"Prostitution, however you dress it up, is illegal."

"Prove it. You and your partner come to my place, bust up four of my guys with no provocation, you need to be careful with those accusations brother."

Blake took a deep breath. "We think there might be someone looking to kill you and the women you are involved with."

Steven laughed. "Oh, that's a good one. You really think I'm gonna believe all that shit. You're the one with a target on your back. You're taking down the big time criminals and I'm risking my reputation just talking to you."

"You left Renda's Bar with Tiffany Mason last night, three hours later you turned up at mum's front door covered in blood."

"Says who? Yeah, I turned up at mum's because I lost my wallet and didn't have any way of getting back here. I got changed out of my damp clothes 'cos it had been pissing down all night. Mum had her stroke, I called Jen and the ambulance took her to the hospital. I stayed there until you showed up and then came home."

"But you'd lost your wallet so how did you get back from the hospital?" Alison asked.

"My sister lent me the money and when I got back here, Nathan dropped off my wallet as I'd left it at Renda's last night."

"So you thought you'd throw a party to celebrate, is that it?" Blake asked.

"You know nothing about me Blake. You don't know how I've had to live in your shadow all these years whilst dad praised your every move."

"We both had the same opportunities…"

"No, we didn't. You were always the favourite. Blake did this, Blake did that. It became unbearable. I was glad when the old man died. Finally I was free to do whatever I wanted without judgement or confrontation."

"Because you knew mum would never be strong enough to stop you from wasting your life away!"

"Okay, stop this, both of you!" Alison interrupted. "There is obviously a lot of family baggage that needs to be unpacked but right now we have missing students who need our help before another one is murdered so can we please stick to the matter in hand?"

Blake and Steven glared at each other for a moment before turning towards Alison.

"Tiffany left the club last night after Nath refused to pay up for the weekend."

"What happened at the weekend?"

"She provided services for a well known client but she wasn't as discreet as she should have been leading to the guy only paying half."

"Who?"

"I don't know, there's a middle man, name's Vijay Bhatt, he's bad news but the client reached out to him to make the connection."

"What did Tiffany do?" Blake asked.

"It's not what she did, she was too old for him. He was expecting another girl, an eighteen year old who had just arrived at Kings Cross looking to earn some easy money on the side. When she never showed, Tiffany took her place. The client got angry, started beating on her, cut her up pretty bad, she managed to get away and then when Nath refused to pay up, she lost it with him."

"Who was the other girl that he was expecting?"

"Victoria Dawson."

Blake and Alison looked at each other and then back at Steven.

"What?" Steven asked.

"We need to find Tiffany Mason fast. What do you know about a man called Zodiac?" Blake pushed.

"It's not him."

"What's not him?"

"Zodiac was there last night but he left before all the shit kicked off. Tiffany and Nath had a fight and then the cops raided the place and everyone scattered."

"Someone lost a great deal of money when the police arrived didn't they?" Alison asked.

"Look, I have my own side hustles but I don't shit on other people's doorsteps. Vijay had it coming," Steven admitted.

"You called the cops."

Steven bowed his head. "Tiff had already been through a lot, I didn't trust... If she had recognised Vijay as the pimp, she would have blown the whole thing open."

"So you had to silence her?" Blake asked.

"No, no, I never touched her."

"But who did?"

"She took the Circle Line towards Embankment, that's the last I saw of her."

"She took the tube?"

"I walked with her to the tube station, she'd calmed down by then and I said I'd meet up with her tonight to see if I could help."

"Help with what?" Alison asked.

"Get her out of the city for a few days. Let the heat die down."

"The blood on your clothes, that wasn't from the bar fight was it? Blake asked.

"Of course it was, how else did I get this cut on my head?"

"Not from a desperate woman fighting to escape..."

"If you believed that we wouldn't be talking..."

"Does the name Hannah Powell mean anything to you?" Alison asked.

"No, should it?"

"When and where were you supposed to meet Tiffany tonight?" Blake asked.

"She was meant to be here for Justin's birthday drinks but she never showed."

"Who's Justin?"

"My housemate, not all of us can afford two homes and a family when we're cut out of inheritance."

"So where is the birthday boy now then?" Alison asked.

"He's er, being looked after."

Blake coughed to clear his throat. "Do you have any way of contacting Tiffany? Phone number, address, anything? It could literally mean life or death."

"I don't know where she lives but she shares a house with two other women."

"Who?" Alison asked.

"Andrea Smith and Nicola Pew. Andrea works at The Troubled Traveller pub down on Harlequin Square near Camden. If anyone knows where she is then it'll be Andrea."

"Thank you," Blake replied before turning away.

"For what?"

"Putting others before yourself."

"You really can't help yourself can you?"

"Do yourself a favour Steve, tidy this shit up. You're better than this and can make so much more of your life if you just apply yourself to it."

"Does it not look good for the image if a decorated agent of Special Branch has a brother on the dark side?"

"I don't have to live up to an image or an ego, I suggest you don't try it either," Blake replied before turning and walking away with Alison a few steps behind him.

Steven watched them leave before pulling his phone out of his pocket and sending a text message. The African man at the door approached him as he placed the phone back into his pocket.

"What the fuck was that about? You should've warned me you had a brother in the pigs," Luther said.

"Forget it Luther, he knows nothing," Steven replied.

"You'd better keep it that way. We don't need any more heat on us right now, especially not from your brother. He looks like he could cause some serious trouble if we don't play this right. Are you sure you can handle him?"

Steven sighed. "Yes I can handle him, don't worry about it. He's just doing his job and doesn't know anything about our business anyway."

Luther eyed him suspiciously for a moment before nodding in agreement and walking away without another word. Steven blew out a sigh of relief and took a long swig from his beer bottle before heading back inside.

Chapter Six

Family Reunion

A loud knocking at the door of 22 Portman Terrace startled Paula as she was just finishing off washing up the dinner plates. She dried off her hands before heading over towards the door.

"Sorry I'm late, the traffic on the M25 was ridiculous," Frank said as she opened the door.

"That's okay, I thought you weren't coming up until the morning," Paula replied as Frank stepped inside.

"I wasn't but then I spoke to a friend who has managed to get us two tickets to the Arsenal/Chelsea game tonight so if Michael is interested..."

"You bet I am!" Michael called out from the lounge.

"That's really nice of you, let me pay..." Paula began.

"It's fine, my friend has a season ticket and can't make it so we're getting in for next to nothing anyway."

"Are you ready then Michael? The kick-off is in just over an hour," Paula called out as she followed Frank into the lounge.

"What have you got there?" Frank asked as he looked at the laptop screen that Michael was using.

"It's called Crystal Coding," Michael smiled. "I change these numbers here and it creates a knock on effect to the rest of the sequence so they all fall like dominos."

"This is really advanced tech, where did you get this?"

"My friends Mason and Willow play it all the time. You use it to build up coded plates and when it all joins together, it creates a virtual crystal. The bigger the numbers, the bigger the crystal."

"So, is that your login ID, MJL101GG?"

"Yeah, Michael John Langford, one hundred and first greatest gamer," Michael smiled.

"Is that so?" Frank laughed.

"Willow seems to think it's cool."

Frank gave Paula a concerned look when he realised the access that Michael had to secure coding that he shouldn't have been able to access from a regular network or server. "And what can you do when you've made the biggest crystal?" Frank asked.

"You can use the data stored inside it to build your own websites, create your own games or pretty much anything online. One day people will be using the internet for everything," Michael smiled before closing the screen down. "I'll go and get changed."

Frank watched him as he left. "Does Blake know about that?"

"Kind of. Michael spoke to him about it but Blake seems to think it's some kind of exploratory programme which uses his intelligence to build things."

"I'd keep an eye on it. In the wrong hands, something like that could create a lot of damage."

"He doesn't interact with people outside of his school friends online so I think he's safe," Paula replied.

"Have you met this Mason or Willow?"

"No, not yet."

"I'm not trying to be a killjoy but with Blake's job…"

"I know. I guess I'm just trying to give him the most normal childhood that I can. His whole life in America was being kept isolated in that house in Miami. I want him to be able to develop friendships and do things that a normal 8 year old does."

"Ready!" Michael called out from the hall.

"We'll be back around eleven," Frank smiled.

"Have fun, I'll be here," Paula replied.

Michael ran over and hugged her before leaving with Frank. As Paula wandered back into the kitchen, she noticed her phone had lit up. She opened a text message from Jenny:

HI PAULA, SORRY TO BE A PAIN BUT WOULD YOU MIND COLLECTING SOME CLOTHES AND TOILETRIES FOR MUM AND BRING THEM TO THE HOSPITAL? BLAKE NORMALLY KEEPS MUM'S KEY ON THE RACK IN HIS KITCHEN. I DON'T WANT TO LEAVE HER ALONE TONIGHT & CAN'T GET HOLD OF STEVEN OR BLAKE xx

Paula looked at the key rack next to the fridge and saw a pair of gold keys with a photo keyring attached holding a photo of Emily and John Langford from years ago. She replied to Jenny's message, picked up the keys and her coat before leaving the flat and heading towards the Underground Tube station.

***

Just after 8pm, Gabby and Simon finally arrived at The Followers Hotel. They entered their hotel room and discovered their luggage had been unpacked with their clothes hung up on the hangers in the open wardrobe.

"Well I can't complain about their efficiency," Simon quipped as he stepped into the shower room.

"Did something feel off to you earlier?" Gabby asked.

"In what way?"

"That Elliot Francis, he seemed very evasive when I asked about Edith Harrow."

"I noticed that too," Simon replied, "But it could be nothing. Maybe he just doesn't like talking about work outside of his own established group or something. You know how weird these guys can get about things."

"Maybe," Gabby said, frowning. "But something just doesn't feel right about this whole thing."

Simon sighed, walking over to Gabby and wrapping his arms around her. "I know, but let's try not to worry too much. We're here to enjoy some time away and promote your book, remember? Let's leave the mystery solving to the locals, okay?"

Gabby nodded, leaning into Simon's embrace. "You're right. I just can't help but feel like we've stumbled into something we shouldn't have."

"Hey, don't worry about it," Simon said, kissing her forehead. "We'll figure it out together. Perhaps he was ignorant of her work. It was written over forty years ago."

"Maybe I'm just tired and reading too much into it. Jet-lag is hell sometimes," Gabby sighed as she laid on the bed.

Simon picked up the remote control and turned on the TV, catching the end of a local news bulletin.

"Detective Curtis, is it true that the missing students from Kings Cross University were being targeted by drug dealers and pimps connected to the Xander Zahl case?" a reporter asked amongst a scrum of people.

"I have no further comment at this time," Detective Curtis replied as he attempted to push his way towards the entrance of the police station.

"How can students stay safe when there are known predators out there and your force is doing nothing to help them?"

"We are exploring many different avenues but any further comment may jeopardise any current investigation. We will make a statement in due course!"

"Different countries but the lies stay the same," Simon commented as he switched the TV off.

"Surely Jason should be involved in this case if there's American students involved," Gabby replied.

"It's not always as black and white as that. The world can be a shitty place sometimes and those students, whoever they are, seem to have somehow been caught in the crossfire of law and politics."

"I learnt from experience that it's just a load of egotistical men in Parliament doing as little as possible to inflate their bank balance whilst the victims suffer."

Simon laid on the bed next to her and placed his arm around her. "Are you sure you can do this? I know London holds a lot of bad memories."

"We're here now and as long as you're with me, we can face anything together."

"We have two book signings confirmed for tomorrow so what do you want to do before those?"

"Go back to Somers Town and see what's changed."

"Where you grew up?"

"Yeah, if I'm going to find closure then I need to go back to where it all began."

"Only if you're sure..."

"I'm sure," Gabby replied before wrapping her arms around him.

***

Blake Langford parked his car on the corner of Harlequin Square. The Troubled Traveller pub was only a few metres ahead of them. As they stepped out of the car, Blake couldn't shake off the feeling that Steven wasn't telling them everything he knew. But for now, they had a more pressing matter to deal with.

"What are you thinking?" Alison asked.

"That I'm too old to be trawling student bars across the Capital," Blake chuckled.

"It does feel like a wild goose chase at the moment. We're only getting fragments of information and none of it seems to be making the puzzle any clearer."

"We need to find Tiffany Mason. She seems to be the key witness in all of this."

"Do you think your brother was right about this barmaid?"

"Only one way to find out."

As they approached the bar, the doorman stood aside allowing them to enter. It was bustling with people and the sound of live music filled the air. A barmaid who Blake assumed to be Andrea, was behind the bar, serving drinks to a group of rowdy students. Blake stepped back towards the doorman whilst Alison kept a lookout for any suspicious activity.

"Is Andrea Smith working tonight?" Blake asked.

"Who's asking?"

"Blake Langford, Special Branch," he replied, flashing his ID.

"Whoa, we don't need anything heavy here!"

"Then answer the question," Blake snapped.

"Yeah, she's behind the bar. Pretty pissed as her colleague ran out on her earlier."

"Why?"

"Some homeless guy turned up and he had to sort something out for him."

"The good samaritan."

"He doesn't do anything for anyone unless he's gonna benefit from it."

Blake became curious. "Who is Andrea's missing colleague?"

"Don't know much about him, some geezer called Andy."

"Surname?"

"Sorry, I don't know him that well. He's not in trouble is he?"

"Should he be?"

"Look man, I need this job, I don't want no trouble," the doorman replied as Alison rejoined them.

"There won't be, thank you mister..." Alison began.

"Hallman, Greg Hallman."

Alison and Blake both entered the bar and noticed a blonde barmaid and an older bald headed man serving at the bar. They weaved their way through dancing students in their friendship groups and eventually arrived at the bar. Whilst they were waiting, another man entered the bar from the back door wearing a creased white shirt and black trousers.

"Took ya bloody time didn't ya!" the bald man snapped.

"Sorry Dickie, it took longer than I expected," he replied before rushing over to take the next order.

"Pull that one again, it'll take you a lot longer to find work in this industry!"

"He's all heart," Alison quipped as the barmaid moved towards them.

"What'll it be?" she asked.

"Breakfast at Tiffany's," Blake replied.

"What?"

"You are Andrea Smith, right?" Alison asked.

Andrea nodded nervously.

"I need to find out where Tiffany Mason is," Blake replied.

"I don't know who she is so if you're not ordering..."

"Steven Langford said that you could help us," Alison pushed.

"Well he's a liar, who are you? Cops?"

"Kind of, we believe her life might be in danger," Blake replied.

"Meet me out the back," Andrea replied before moving past them to take another order.

Alison looked at Blake. "Deflection or trap?"

"Not sure. I recognise the guy who turned up late from somewhere but I can't place it," Blake replied.

"Someone you've dealt with before?"

"Possibly. Let's split up, you go through the bar, I'll go around the outside and meet you at the rear entrance."

They both arrived at the back door of the pub together. A few moments later, Andrea joined them.

"I don't need any more trouble," Andrea sighed as she took a deep breath of smoke from a cigarette.

"Any more? What kind of trouble are you in?" Alison asked.

"Look, working student bars isn't as cut and dry as you might think. You meet people, you hear things, a lot of it is just macho bullshit but sometimes…"

"It isn't," Blake finished for her. "Tell me about Tiffany Mason."

"She's the one you go to for stuff to get done."

"What kind of stuff? Drugs? Weapons? Prostitution?"

"All three, makes an absolute killing during freshers week," Andrea sighed. "Who's she pissed off this time?"

"She was meant to turn up for a meeting earlier today after a raid went bad at Renda's Bar last night. She was last seen getting onto the tube in the early hours of this morning," Alison replied.

"I don't keep tabs on everyone I know."

"Do you have any idea where she might be? There have been two women murdered already and she may become the third," Blake pushed. "Would she stay at a friend's place? Or go to any other bars nearby."

"Like I said, she will go wherever the money is. If you find her pimps then you'll find her. There was a problem with a girl last week who backed out at the last minute. They say that she was an informant and that's what led to the raid at Renda's last night. She hasn't been seen since and bad news travels fast."

"Meaning?"

"If she knows that you two are sniffing around, she'll go to ground to make sure she doesn't get caught up in any kind of investigation that could damage her business."

Alison and Blake exchanged a look before turning back to Andrea.

"Do you have any contacts who might know where we can find these pimps?" Alison asked.

Andrea shook her head. "I stay out of that world as much as I can. But if you're looking for trouble, I know a guy who might be able to help you."

"Who?"

"His name is Copsewood, Derek Copsewood. He runs a bar on the opposite side of the campus. He's involved in some shady business, but he might have the connections you need."

Blake paused for a moment. "Say, for argument's sake, that I wanted to acquire some merchandise from her, where would you suggest that I look?"

Andrea sighed before opening a small handbag and pulling out a white business card with only a phone number scrawled across it. She handed it to Blake. "Now go before anyone realises where you got that from."

Alison and Blake exchanged another look. "Thanks, Andrea. We'll check it out."

Andrea turned and began heading back towards the bar before Blake called out to her.

"One more thing..." he asked.

Andrea turned to face him.

"Who's the barman who turned up late and pissed off your boss?"

"He's clean before you try to plant anything on him."

"I never said otherwise, his face just seems familiar."

"Andy, Andy Broughton," Andrea replied before heading back inside.

Blake froze as he watched the back door close.

"Are you all right?" Alison asked.

"Yeah, yeah, I'm fine, let's go," Blake replied before heading back down the side of the pub towards his car with Alison following close behind.

As they walked away, Blake turned to Alison. "Do you trust her?"

"Not completely, but I think she's telling the truth about Tiffany Mason and the pimps. And Copsewood seems to be our only lead."

"Do you think Victoria Dawson was an informant and that's why she was killed?"

"That's one explanation but it still doesn't account for why Tiffany Mason would go on the run."

They both sat inside the car and Alison dialled the number that had been written on the card.

"Just an answerphone message," she sighed before cutting off. "Now what? Do you know that Andy guy?"

Blake knew he needed to tread carefully with this case but Andrew Broughton was not a name he expected to uncover. Looking older and unshaven but Blake knew his face, the same Andrew Broughton who Paula had left eight years ago.

"Nothing important but I think we need to get back to the student halls at Kings Cross and do some digging. Tiffany obviously is involved in some kind of group picking off the new and unexpecting freshers as they arrive at the uni. Maybe we can get some answers there."

***

Paula arrived outside 124 Alfredson Road in Kensington around half past eight. The house was in complete darkness as she approached the front door and turned the key. She turned on the light in the hallway as she entered and picked up a few letters from the doormat. As she moved to close the front door however, she noticed the silhouette of someone walking up the driveway towards the house.

"I'm sorry, Emily's not home at the moment," she called out before pushing the door closed.

"I'm not looking for Emily Langford," a man's voice replied.

Paula froze before slowly opening the door again and looking out at the man.

"Dad?"

Chapter Seven

Misplaced Trust

Samir and Joe parked at the end of St Lawrence Square. Sam's Bar was situated around a hundred metres further down the road. Two doormen stood at the entrance as several students entered the bar.

"Are you sure about this?" Joe asked.

"I'm never sure about anything."

"We're going to stick out like a sore thumb in there."

Samir opened up the glovebox and lifted out a wallet full of banknotes.

"What the... Did you rob a bank?" Joe gasped.

"Two currencies in this city Joe, youth and money. Come on."

Samir wandered over towards the entrance to Sam's Bar with Joe a couple of steps behind. One of the doormen stepped in front of them. Samir peeled off a twenty and placed it into the doorman's hand. He looked down at it and then nodded in Joe's direction. Samir sighed and placed a second twenty in the man's hand before he stepped aside and allowed them to enter.

"Your round next time," Samir turned to Joe as they entered the bar with loud dance music blasting out from a laptop connected to an amplifier.

Samir walked up to the bar and beckoned the barman over. "I'm looking for Derek Copsewood."

"Second booth," the barman replied, pointing over towards three booth seats in the corner of the room.

In the second booth was a grey haired man in a grey suit talking to two men dressed in black hoodies and jeans. Samir walked over with Joe a few steps behind. The two men looked up as Samir arrived.

"You Copsewood?" Samir asked.

"Depends who's asking," the grey haired man replied.

Samir dropped a roll of twenty pound notes on the table.

Derek Copsewood beckoned for the two men to leave. The first one glared at Samir before moving away. Samir sat opposite Derek with Joe moving in next to him.

"So what do I owe the pleasure of Special Branch this evening?" Derek asked.

"Well connected man," Joe commented.

"One tries."

"You wanna get that knife away from my balls before we continue?" Samir asked.

Derek looked under the table before slowly bringing the knife up onto the booth seat next to him. "When someone comes into my bar throwing money around, it pays to be cautious."

"I hear you've been replenishing your stock recently," Samir continued.

"That would depend on what stock you were talking about. As you can see, I'm a legitimate businessman these days."

"Bullshit, you set off a chain of events in Renda's Bar the other night when a consignment of Columbian pure was intercepted by a known dealer."

"I'm afraid you're mistaken. I was caught up in a disagreement after a pimp was shortchanged by a hooker who didn't live up to expectations."

"Was this so-called hooker Tiffany Mason?"

"How should I know?"

"Ok, so where did this so-called hooker end up?" Joe pushed. Derek shrugged.

"She was involved with one of your men," Samir replied.

"Vijay knew the risks. She took a line before playing the game just like everyone else."

"So he had to silence her?" Joe asked.

"Look, Tiffany was fine when she left the bar with that other dude, Langford, I think his name is. The one who works there."

"That girl holds the key to discovering what is happening to a wider group of students going missing. Where can I find Vijay Bhatt?" Samir asked.

"He lives out near Eel Brook Common, that's all I know."

At that moment, a young woman walked up to the booth. "Carl needs you," she said before moving away.

"Is she one of yours too?" Joe quipped.

In one quick movement, Derek held the knife at Joe's neck. "Claire, my daughter, is not for hire, understood?"

Joe nodded as Derek removed the knife and picked up the roll of twenties off of the table. "Zodiac may be many things but he is no fool. He sent you after me to cover his own ass. Take my advice and check your seals, you have a leak."

Joe and Samir watched Derek walk towards the bar and disappear through the door that led to the staff areas behind. They both turned and headed towards the front door. The two men who had been talking with Derek stood next to the doorman and watched them both return to their car.

"What do you think?" Joe asked.

As they arrived at the car Samir turned to Joe. "Pretty smooth, if I do say so myself."

"Smooth?" Joe scoffed. "We just bribed a man and he threatened you with a DIY vasectomy."

"Well, it worked, didn't it? We rattled the tree, now you just need to wait and see what falls out!"

Joe rolled his eyes. "Let's just hope we can find this Vijay Bhatt and get some answers."

"He's hiding something. The way he reacted to your quip about his daughter said a lot."

"He seemed to know we were coming and he knows about Blake's brother's involvement."

"We need to tread carefully. Blake's had a conflict of interest in the past and it didn't end well. I have a feeling that Vijay is playing both sides for fools and if that's the case, Zodiac will take matters out of our hands."

Joe checked his watch. "Eel Brook Common, that's where he wanted you to meet him at eight."

"Convenient wouldn't you say?"

"A trap?"

"Perhaps. Only one way to find out," Samir replied before starting the engine and heading off towards the common.

As they drove, Samir couldn't help but feel uneasy. The more he dug into this case, the more he realised how deep and twisted it was. He knew they were getting closer to finding the truth, but at what cost?

Just before eight o'clock, Samir parked halfway down Gerrard's View and turned off the engine.

"Nice houses," Samir commented.

"Do you honestly think he'll show up?" Joe asked.

"Copsewood seemed to check out. Zodiac knows that life can get more difficult for his brother if he sends me down the wrong path."

Both men watched as an Indian man walked up the hill and entered number 121.

"At least someone's home," Joe quipped.

"Come on," Samir replied before stepping out of the car and heading over towards the house.

A small paved garden with two stone steps led up to the front door. Both men walked up to the door and knocked.

"Maybe he's shy," Joe commented.

Samir knocked on the wooden frame again before heading around the side of the house. Down a weed infested alleyway was a tall wooden fence surrounding the back garden with a splintering wooden gate that had seen better days blocking their route. Samir climbed up and reached over to release a metal bolt lock before opening the gate. As they entered an astroturfed back garden, they noticed a wooden shed at the far end. The curtains were drawn in every window of the house and Samir wandered over towards the back door. He tried the handle before pulling out a small penknife to pick the lock. At that moment, there was a loud knocking coming from the shed along with a muffled female voice.

"Cover me," Joe said as he pulled out his gun and headed towards the shed.

"What are you…" Samir protested before hearing the knocking sound again and following him closely behind.

Joe arrived at the shed door and found a large metal padlock holding a rusting metal plate in place. The muffled voice became louder.

"Stand back from the door," Joe called out.

Samir rushed over towards him. "What are you doing?"

Gunfire echoed around the area as Joe shot the lock off of the shed door. At that moment, a bright orange light flashed from the inside of the shed before an explosion sent matchstick splinters of wood in all directions knocking both Joe and Samir to the ground.

***

Detective Jim Curtis parked his navy blue Mercedes outside Pentonville Prison. A man dressed in a long black overcoat approached the car and knocked on his driver's side window. Curtis stepped out without saying a word and led the man into the prison.

Sergeant Shaun Bryant parked on the opposite side of the car park and watched from a distance. He saw the man in black stepping out from a white BMW and approach Curtis' car. Part of him wanted to follow them inside but he noticed someone was waiting in the driving seat of the BMW so he waited.

"Detective Curtis, I wasn't expecting you," the guard at the reception desk said as they entered.

"Evening Kevin, no, this is a last minute thing, I need to see Xander Zhal. You can turn the cameras off too. This is off the record."

"You know I can't authorise that."

"Can't or won't. Don't forget who got you the job here in the first place," Detective Curtis snapped.

"Who's he?"

"Mickey Mouse now open the fucking door!" the man in black snapped.

Kevin looked at Detective Curtis and then back at the man in black before pressing the door release button underneath the desk. Detective Curtis and the man in black walked through into the corridors behind that led towards the cells. After the door closed behind them, Kevin picked up the phone and called the warden.

"Detective Curtis, good to see you again," one of the prison guards said as he unlocked the gate for them to enter.

"And you Patrick, can you take us to cell seventy-six?"

"That's Xander Zhal's cell," Patrick advised.

"I know."

"Who's he?"

In one quick movement, the man in black pulled out a taser and zapped Patrick with it. Patrick's body convulsed as he fell to the ground. The man grabbed his access cards and keys before moving on through the prison with Detective Curtis following close behind.

"You didn't have to do that," Curtis snapped.

"I did, now move," he replied before pushing Detective Curtis towards the stairs that led up to the cells above.

As they arrived at the third floor and began walking along the corridor towards cell seventy-six, the warden with two armed guards began walking towards them from the opposite direction.

"Shit, Kevin screwed us," Curtis snapped.

"James Curtis, what an unpleasant surprise!" the warden called out.

Inmates began to shout as they heard the warden's voice.

"We just need cell seventy-six and then we will leave!"

"On what grounds?"

"New evidence has come to light."

"Then you would have gone through the relevant channels to ensure that seventy-six would be in attendance so spare me the bullshit. Who's the grim reaper with you?" the warden asked.

The man in black lowered his hood and raised his right hand. He was holding a metal bar with white edging in his hand.

"Zodiac?" the warden gasped. "Curtis, what the..."

"Release Xander and no one gets hurt," Zodiac replied.

"Listen Zac, you know I can't just release a serial killer to a police detective and a well known arms dealer..."

"Then I push this button and everyone is released. Do you want a riot on your hands?"

"You're bluffing. You'll never get out of here alive."

"You won't, I might. You wanna take that chance?"

One of the armed guards stepped forward pointing a revolver at Zodiac. "Get out of here before I take you down."

"Guns in a prison, bad move," Zodiac replied before bringing his left arm up knocking the gun from the guard's hand and hitting him in the chest with the metal bar in his right hand sending the guard to the floor.

The warden and his one remaining guard took three steps back. "Okay, okay, let me call it in."

Zodiac picked up the revolver and checked the chamber. It was empty. He tossed it away before he and Detective Curtis stepped over the guard who was still on the ground.

"Open seventy-six," the warden spoke into his radio. He turned to Zodiac. "You're making a big mistake."

The cell door opened and Xander Zhal stepped out.

"You too," Zodiac replied before tasing the warden and the guard.

Xander, Zodiac and Detective Curtis began heading back the same way that they had entered. As they arrived back on the ground floor, a group of armed police had gathered around them.

"On the ground! Now!" one of them shouted.

Zodiac pressed the button on the metal bar and all of the automatic locks on every cell unlocked. Immediately over thirty prisoners attacked the police officers as Zodiac used Patrick's pass to escape back towards the reception area.

Kevin, the guard at the reception desk, had disappeared. As the three of them left the prison, they saw him running across the car park. The driver of the white BMW started his engine and sped over to pick up Xander and Zodiac who both piled into the back seat. Detective Curtis went to grab the handle of the front passenger door when a bullet splintered through the side window hitting him in the chest. Curtis fell to the floor as the white BMW sped away.

Sergeant Shaun Bryant stepped out of his car and rushed across towards the prison entrance.

"Officer down outside Pentonville Prison! Suspect heading east in a white BMW ZO55IAC," Bryant shouted into his radio before crouching down to help Detective Curtis.

"What are you..." Curtis began.

"Doesn't matter, just keep the pressure on the wound."

"I've been a fool."

"What happened?"

"Xander Zhal..." Detective Curtis managed to say before taking his last breath.

Police cars and Ambulances arrived as Sergeant Bryant stepped back into his car and drove away towards Kings Cross. He needed to find Joe Knight and fast.

***

"What are you doing here?" Paula asked as she stood in the doorway of Emily Langford's home.

"After almost ten years, I thought you would want to see me," Graham Evans replied as he approached the door.

"You ran out on us! You left my mother beaten to death and alone! You made Rachael run away to America! Why the hell would I want to see you now?"

"Because you owe me."

"I owe you nothing Dad, you owe me a lot! How the hell did you know I would be here?"

"Logical equation, with your sister gone and her relationship with Blake all over the news last year, it was obvious that you'd move in on her territory. You've wanted Blake for years and with your sister out of the way, you took your chance. Very opportunistic I must say if a bit premeditated. That's a nice ring, did he buy you that?"

Paula covered her hand subconsciously. "Are you saying I planned for Rachael to die just so I could move in on her fiance?"

"You made your moves on him when she was still alive so why should death stop you?"

"Go home Dad. You're not welcome here and I don't have anything left to say to you!"

"That's where you're wrong. I wanted to go home but when I arrived at Vincent Street, I saw a new family moving in."

"And that's my fault?" Paula snapped. "You disappeared for ten years. You're still wanted by the police for Mum's manslaughter and now you turn up on my in-laws doorstep demanding what? Some kind of pity or retribution? I should call the police right now and let them take you in!"

"But you won't."

"Give me one good reason why!"

"Because you're still my daughter, whether you like it or not. I haven't touched the drink since I left ten years ago. I'm a changed man and I regret all of the things that I said and did back then. I'm old and I'm tired of running. If they send me to prison, I'll never survive it. You've lost your mother and your sister. You're clinging on to Blake because he's the only connection you have left to your life from back then."

Paula looked at him. His black hair had gone from a salt and pepper look to a silver that seemed to glisten under the porchlight. The lines on his face seemed to draw a map of a thousand journeys travelled and he had a world weariness about him that she couldn't pull herself away from.

"Okay, but not here. Emily is in the hospital and I need to get some things for her. Meet me under the clock at Waterloo

Station at ten o'clock tomorrow morning," Paula replied. "Do you have somewhere to sleep tonight?"

"I've met up with an old friend. He's letting me stay with him for a while."

"Fine, I'll see you tomorrow then," Paula replied before closing the front door.

Graham stood for a moment looking at the front door. A smile broke out across his face as he turned and walked away. He knew that he had hit a nerve with Paula and now he just needed to keep pushing to see how far she would go to help him. He walked slowly down the street, taking in the sights and sounds of the city. He thought about Paula. How she had looked deep into his eyes with an intensity that he hadn't seen before. He looked back up the street before nodding slightly and turning away, walking off without another word or glance back with a newfound sense of hope burning inside him.

Chapter Eight

The Morning After...

Blake Langford wandered into his flat around four o'clock the following morning. After a night of following up on leads, he knew that he needed to get some sleep before reconvening with his team to get a better understanding of these two victims who somehow all have a connection to his brother. He closed the door as quietly as he could before noticing a flickering light coming from the kitchen. He wandered over and saw Paula sitting on one of the high stools leaning against the sideboard with a glass of whiskey in her hands. A single candle flickering in the darkness gave the only light into the room.

"I'm sorry I had to rush off. There's a big case going on and Mum's had a stroke so I've been splitting my time between the two of them," Blake explained as he placed a hand on her shoulder.

"It's okay," Paula replied as she wiped a tear from her eye.

"What's happened? Is Michael okay?"

"Yeah, he's sleeping. Frank took him to the match earlier and stayed with him until I got back from the hospital."

Blake poured himself a drink from the whiskey bottle before sitting alongside her and placing a hand on her knee.

"Jen asked me to pick up some things for Emily whilst she remained at the hospital as she couldn't get hold of you or Steven..."

"I'm sorry, I was..." Blake began but Paula raised her hand to stop him.

"When I was there, a man came up to the door looking for me."

Blake froze. He knew that Andrew Broughton, Paula's ex-fiance had been working in one of the student bars that he had visited earlier. How the hell had he found out where Paula was going to be?

"Who was it? How did he know you were going to be there?"

"It was Dad."

"What?"

"He's back and wants to speak to me about something."

"Wait, hold on a minute, he's still on the run from the police for Olivia's death and he just randomly turns up at my parent's house when you were there."

Paula nodded. "He knows that we sold the house too."

"Because in the eyes of the law, we thought he was dead. He's been on the run for ten years..."

"I know. That's why I need to see him."

"Please be careful. Who's going to look after Michael?"

"Frank will be here. I'm meeting him at Waterloo Station for coffee. Being on neutral ground will hopefully help."

"I want to be there with you."

"No, I need to do this alone."

"Paula, there may be more to this than meets the eye. At least let me be in the shadows."

"He'll spot you a mile off. If he's clued up enough to find me at your Mum's house, he obviously knows that you'll be watching me."

Blake thought about that. Perhaps Graham Evans wasn't working alone. "Is this why you're drinking at 4am?"

"It's difficult Blake. I thought selling that house would put all of the past behind us and now it seems like it's the thing that's dragged it all up again."

Blake held her close. "Hear him out but please, keep your guard up. People just don't reappear out of the woodwork for nothing. There has to be something else going on that we don't know about."

They both finished their drinks before heading off to bed. Blake laid there with a thousand thoughts accelerating across his mind but none of them seemed to be the missing piece of the puzzle. Why now? Why had Graham Evans and Andrew Broughton reappeared after so long. And how could he tell Paula that her abusive ex-fiance was possibly involved in a case that he was investigating. He knew he had to figure out the missing connections and hoped that somehow, his team had the answers.

***

Rain steadily fell as Gabby and Simon stepped off of the bus and wandered down a tree-lined side street that led to Somers Town Cemetery. Gabby walked along the pathway before turning onto a patch of grass at the far side of the cemetery. She stopped at the fourth stone and read the memorial.

In Loving Memory Of
ALANA ELIZABETH TURNER
Beloved Mother, Sister And Wife
Called To Rest On 4th May 1990

Gabby sighed deeply. She had only been a teenager when her mother had died. Her father had emigrated to America and came home to take her and her brother James back to Miami with him. Their father had also died three years later and for the past seventeen years, Gabby had felt like a surrogate parent to her younger brother James as well as a sister. She placed a single red rose on the gravestone and noticed a message tag was still attached to an artificial bouquet of blue flowers that were already on the stone. The message read:

> Though I Never Knew You,
> I Will Always Love You For
> The Gift Of Life You Gave Me.
> CAT xx

"Who's Cat?" Simon asked.

"I don't know."

"Was your mum an organ donor? Did she donate her organs that in turn, helped someone else stay alive?"

"Si, she was a heavy smoker, an alcoholic and a drug user in the final three years of her life. Dad left for the States because no matter what he tried, he couldn't help her. She even went away for a month near the end and James and I were looked after by our neighbours. When she came back, she'd lost weight, she looked healthier for a while but she soon started using again and then…"

Simon placed his arm around her. "It's okay, you don't have to go there."

"No, it's not the abuse, oh my God, no, it can't be?"

"What?"

"Look for a recent grave of Margaret and Norman Petersen," Gabby replied as she began rushing along and scanning rows of gravestones.

After a few minutes, Simon found it.

"Margaret Elsie Petersen, July 1993 and Norman Victor Petersen, December 1994," Simon called out.

Gabby rushed over and saw an identical blue bouquet of artificial flowers but without a message tag this time.

"What's the connection?" Simon asked.

"I think I might have a half sister."

"How? Surely you would…"

"That whole time was a bit of a blur but think about it. The abuse from Derek happened in the six months before he left and

Mum killed herself. She went away for a while and Margaret and Norman looked after us. She was hiding a pregnancy. This Cat, she must have either been adopted or looked after by Margaret and Norman after Dad had taken us to the States."

"You got all that from a tag on a bunch of flowers from a grave?" Simon asked.

"Can you still access the CIA database from the UK?"

"Well yeah, but come on Gab, this isn't exactly a matter of national security. All you have is a first name that you don't even know if the name is real."

Gabby looked down at the gravestone and noticed a piece of paper had been blown against the side of the stone. She picked it up and gently unfolded the wet sheet of paper. "Take a look at this!"

"Where you are standing now is where I once was. Where I am now is where you are going to be. Stay humble and embrace life for death is eternal," Simon read aloud. "Well that's a cheery thought..."

"When is my book signing?"

"4pm at the Southbank Book Market near Westminster Bridge then a talk and book signing at the Kings Cross University Hall at 7pm."

"So we have time, come on," Gabby replied as she began heading for the exit.

"Where are we going?"

"Longfellow Crescent, my old home."

***

The party had long finished in the early hours at 235 Quebec Road and a tangle of thirteen bodies were sprawled across sofas, armchairs and beds across the house. In the back bedroom, the curtains were opened and the light of morning began attacking

Stephen Langford's eyes. As he squinted against the light, he felt a cold metal blade rest against his neck. He opened his eyes and saw the silhouette of a woman standing over him.

"Someone was asking for me at the bar last night. What do they know?" the woman's voice asked.

"Tiff, what the…"

"Answer the question!" Tiffany snapped.

Stephen looked across at the empty space next to him and then back at her. "I don't know."

"He named you as his source."

"Where's Julia?"

"She left. Who have you been blabbing to Steve? Why are they following me?"

"Look, my brother works for the government and he…"

"You've got a snitch in your family, what the fu…"

"It's not like that, I can't stand the asshole."

Tiffany pressed the knife harder against his neck. "Yet, you told him where Andrea worked and how to track me."

"It was a bluff, I didn't think you'd be going back there."

"Nathan still owes me over two hundred. Dickie owes me another five. I'm going to be hanging around for a while and you better make sure that the pigs stay out of my way or I'll hang you out to dry, got it!"

Stephen nodded and she removed the knife from his neck.

"How did you get up here? Where is everyone? What happened to those girls from the Trav bar?" Stephen asked.

Tiffany pulled out a makeup pad and opened it.

"So many questions. The less you know, the better. In the meantime…" Tiffany replied before blowing a cloud of dust into Stephen's face.

Stephen fell back into the bed unconscious.

"Shame, such a cute one too," Tiffany replied before leaving the house.

Chapter Nine

Destination, Waterloo Station

Blake watched Paula leave their flat in Portman Terrace and head towards the Underground Station. Alison Pearce, his new colleague, had just arrived and parked outside his flat.

"Hey Dad, I've just finished coding the left side of my crystal. Come and have a look at this!" Michael called out.

Blake wandered over and looked at the laptop. Huge combinations of numbers formed measurements of virtual sections of a huge crystal before sticking together like a jigsaw puzzle to create the three dimensional illusion.

"So, what are all these numbers? What do they represent?" Blake asked.

"Measurements for your piece of the puzzle. You need to get the measurement and the placement of the figures right or it won't fit and the file becomes corrupted. If that happens, you have to start all over again. Willow's annoyed that I've already got seven pieces and three of his were corrupted in the last segment," Michael explained.

Blake looked over at Frank.

"Don't ask me," Frank laughed. "I'm still in the days of tetris."

"How was the football last night?" Blake asked.

"It was okay, Arsenal should've won though. Chelsea scored a penalty in the last minute but it was never a foul!" Michael replied.

"What time did Paula get back last night?"

"A little after midnight. Said she had to go to see Jenny at the hospital, why?" Frank asked.

"Did you tell Dad about the fight we saw?" Michael asked.

"What fight?"

"Oh, just two women fighting over a man in the street."

"Ah it was cool Dad, they were pulling each other's hair and everything. One of them had purple hair and the other one had a metal chain that she was whipping the other girl with."

"Okay, maybe we need to make sure you don't go walking the streets that late at night anymore," Blake advised as the doorbell rang.

"I've seen worse on video games," Michael replied.

"That's the problem..." Blake replied as he answered the door.

"We've got a problem," Alison said as she entered.

"What's up?"

"Samir and Joe are in hospital. There was an explosion at an address in Eel Brook Common last night. After confronting Copsewood they were apparently following a lead on Zodiac, they went around the back and a shed blew up. Samir is okay but he's still in the hospital and Joe's in ICU."

"Damn, we need to tread carefully. Is he going to pull through?"

"It's too soon to know. He suffered severe burns and splintering from the shed to his arms and face."

"Joe was covering for Detective Jim Curtis and there was talk of a connection there too. It may be worth speaking to his Sergeant who was involved in the recovery of the A34 body. In the meantime, I think I found a new lead last night too but we need to move fast if we're going to catch it," Blake replied.

"Then let's go," Alison replied before heading out of the door with Blake following close behind.

"Be good Michael, I'll see you tonight!" Blake called out.

Michael rushed over and gave him a hug before rushing back to the laptop as Blake left. Alison drove out of the car park and headed back onto the main road.

"So what's this hunch?" she asked.

"We need to get to Waterloo Station by 10am."

"You're cutting it a bit fine there but I'll try. Why 10am?"

"You know the guy in The Troubled Traveller Bar last night."

"The one who came in late and pissed everyone off?"

"Yeh, he's my fiance's abusive ex-partner."

"Blake, listen, we have two murders, several missing students, pimps and drug dealers covering for each other under the guise of fresher students, two of our own in hospital and you're now putting all our resources into a family matter? I can't let you do it."

"Alison, if I'm right, this has the potential to lead us directly to one of the pimps."

"How?"

"Paula was visited by her father last night who has been on the run for the past ten years and has somehow evaded authorities..."

"This gets better..."

"He could only manage that if he had an edge. I believe Andrew Broughton is that edge."

"So your fiance is walking into a trap. Didn't you think you should've told her that before the shit hit the fan?"

"I asked her if I could join her or at least be a shadow and she refused because her father would spot me a mile off," Blake conceded.

"Well she's an intelligent woman then."

"But they won't spot you."

"Really?," Alison sighed. "You're a pain in the ass, you know that."

"So you'll do it?"

"She's not even mic'd up. How will I know what's going down?"

Blake pulled out a small lapel pin from his inside jacket pocket. When they stopped at a traffic light, he handed it to Alison who fixed it to her blouse before continuing to drive. Blake opened an app on his phone and was able to log in to see and hear what was happening from the pin.

"I've slipped one inside Paula's handbag too. Hopefully, if she catches her father off-guard, he may lead us somewhere," Blake explained.

"So where will you be?" Alison asked.

"Fred's news stand. She just needs to make contact with her father and she said they're going for coffee. We just need to see if Andrew turns up and if not, then we need Graham Evans to show us where he is hiding out. Either way, it will develop a lead."

"I see what they said was right about you," Alison replied as she parked up outside Waterloo Station and stepped out of the car.

"What's that?"

"You're annoyingly efficient," Alison smiled before heading inside the station.

"I'll take that as a compliment," Blake replied before heading towards the entrance further down the road.

***

Eric Gordon scrolled through emails as he began to understand the events of the previous night. Two agents in hospital and a riot at Pentonville Prison was enough to make senior members of parliament begin to ask uncomfortable questions. The intercom buzzed as he tapped away a report on his laptop.

"Yes," he replied.

"A Sergeant Shaun Bryant to see you," Angela, Eric Gordon's long standing secretary replied.

"Send him in, please," he replied.

A few seconds later, the mahogany door of Eric Gordon's office opened and a tall man in his late thirties with short black hair entered. He stood opposite Eric's desk.

Eric looked up from his laptop screen; "Sergeant Bryant, what do we owe the pleasure?"

"I was hoping to contact Joe Knight but he has not been answering my calls."

"Knight is currently indisposed, may I ask what it was regarding?"

"I may have some information about the riot at Pentonville Prison last night."

Eric Gordon closed his laptop. "What do you know about a man nicknamed Zodiac?"

"Nothing specific except that he is known to have dealings with a known group of drug dealers who work out of the student bars near Kings Cross."

"Known? Does he ever get his hands dirty?"

"He has his gang of brothers that do his dirty work but from conversations I've heard, Zodiac is the ringleader. There seems to be an initial introduction to some guy called Tom who makes all the arrangements."

"You seem well informed."

"Fifteen years on the streets does that to you."

"Does this Tom have a last name?"

"He's a ghost. Nobody seems to know who or where he is."

"So how does he make the connections?"

"He picks up impressionable young women in the bars and takes them to Vijay Bhatt. We sent a mole into Renda's Bar last night. He never showed up. We think he may have been scared off by a well informed couple who tried to get some information from her."

"What kind of information?"

"She said they were interested in her father, Derek Copsewood's bar on the opposite side of the campus."

Eric Gordon thought about that before changing the subject. "How did you end up at the prison?"

"I followed Detective Curtis there."

"Why did you do that?"

"He threw me off the case."

"Why?"

"That's what I wanted to find out. I believe he was covering for someone and when I followed him to the prison, it became obvious what was happening."

"And what was he doing there that late at night and without prior authorization?"

"He met with a man dressed in black that I couldn't get a clear look at but when they came out, the guy in black jumped into the back of a white BMW with someone else. When Curtis tried to get into the front, the driver shot him and then drove away."

"What did you do then?"

"I ran over to Curtis but he died moments later."

"Did he say anything?"

"Just a name, Xander Zhal."

Eric Gordon sat back in his chair. Xander Zhal had been part of an underground cage fighting group and had been convicted of several counts of murder, GBH and ABH. Just the type of person that Zodiac would need in his circle.

"Joe Knight spoke highly of you regarding his time working alongside you. We believe that there is a link to the people in Zodiac's circle and the body that you found on the A34. If you want justice for your senior officer and the family of that young girl, I need to be able to trust you out in the field."

Shaun nodded.

"Joe's partner Samir Khalifa, is currently at Chelsea And Westminster Hospital. Go to him and tell him what you've told me. He's a bit shaken up but I need you to work with him to help nail these bastards before they strike again."

"Without a credible cover, they'll see straight through us."

"Use your initiative Shaun, if you've managed to gain this much traction so far, there has to be a degree of trust in less than legitimate circles. Use your inside knowledge to help guide my team to the root of this organisation and there may be a position for you in Special Branch at the end of it. This whole operation is classified and nobody from your current posting must know any details of what you are working on."

"Agreed, thank you Sir," Shaun Bryant replied before leaving the room.

Eric Gordon pulled out his phone and typed out a message before sending it to Samir. He knew that they needed an edge to get into the inner circle of Zodiac's organisation and Bryant may well give them that.

Shaun Bryant left Eric Gordon's office. He knew he needed to tread carefully and make sure he gained Samir's trust if they were to have any chance of catching Zodiac and the rest of his group. Shaun's first stop was the hospital to visit Samir. As he entered the room, he saw Samir sitting in a chair watching over the motionless body of Joe Knight laying on the bed with his eyes closed. His face, shoulder and right arm were heavily bandaged and machines beeped incessantly. Shaun approached Samir and he slowly looked up.

"Samir, my name is Shaun Bryant. Eric Gordon sent me to talk to you."

Samir looked at up him. "What do you want?"

"I have some information about the Pentonville riot and the man known as Zodiac."

Samir looked at Joe then back at him. "What do you know?"

Shaun laid out everything that he knew, including what he had learned from Detective Curtis, as well as his own investigation from the discovery of the body on the A34 until now.

When he had finished, a priest arrived at the door and looked over at Joe. Samir and Shaun walked over towards the door.

"God bless you my sons," the priest muttered as he walked over towards Joe.

Samir took one more look back at Joe before following Shaun out of the door.

***

Paula Evans waited under the huge clock suspended several metres in the air above the hustle of commuters rushing to their destinations around Waterloo Station. Her hands felt clammy and she tried to focus on her breathing to remain calm. In her books that she often wrote, she took her protagonists on emotional adventures and was able to construct endless prose to diagnose their anxiety, yet she struggled to take the advice of her own research when it came to her own real life dramas. Thousands of thoughts flooded her mind. Ten years was a long time. Her life had changed dramatically. She now had a new fiance and an adopted son that was going through the tricky age of wanting to understand the complicated world around him. She wanted so much to protect her little bubble of a family unit that Blake and Michael had given her and the thought of Graham Evans, her father and Michael's grandfather, coming in and ripping open old forgotten deep wounds from many years ago filled her with dread.

"Paula?" Graham called out.

Paula turned around and saw her father wearing the same clothes that she had seen him in the night before outside Emily Langford's house. She moved towards him for a brief embrace before they moved away towards a coffee shop a few metres further down the station.

"Everything seems normal so far," Alison spoke into the lapel pin on her blouse.

Blake Langford handed a pound coin over to the newsagent before taking a seat on one of the metal benches a few metres further down the station from the coffee shop. "I still don't trust him, look out for anything unusual."

"The only thing unusual is you reading a newspaper in the middle of a busy station. Don't you know they have apps for those things these days?"

"Where else can I read the football headlines whilst on a stakeout?"

Inside the coffee shop, Paula ordered a Latte and a Cappuccino before taking a seat in a booth nearest to the back wall with Graham sitting down opposite her.

"Why are you here Dad?" she asked.

"After what happened with your mother, I was ashamed. I let the drink control my life and I knew that I had to do something about it. Before I knew what was happening, the police were surrounding the house, your mother was in the hospital and Rachael had disappeared. I panicked. I made my way down to Portsmouth and managed to bribe a member of the crew aboard the ferry to take me to Cherbourg. I had no idea where I was going. I just knew that I had to get away. I had to get clean. I couldn't face the shame of what I did to you all and by some quirk of fate, my old friend Dave Francis, you remember him? He used to always be at the snooker club when we were younger..."

Paula nodded noncommittally.

"Well, he was in Cherbourg at the same time."

"Running away from your problems doesn't solve anything. Rachael was unconscious and you literally beat Mum to death before you left. Her injuries led to a bleed on her brain and she died two weeks later. How the hell can anyone live with that?"

Graham bowed his head. "I know."

"I should take you down to the police station right now!"

"But you won't."

"How do you know I won't?"

"Because if you were going to do that then Blake would be charging in here by now."

"You don't know anything about Blake."

"I know what I read in the media. British agent goes over to America and cocks up an intelligence investigation into George Turner's kids who had been caught up with a diamond smuggling ring in Miami."

"Then you'll also know that he tried to save Rachael."

"But he didn't and you're the consolation prize."

"Fuck you," Paula snapped as she stood from her seat.

"Excuse me? How dare you..."

"No, how dare you make me out to be some kind of consolation prize because Rachael died! Her and Blake were over a long time ago. The destruction that you and John Langford created meant that she felt the only way she could be free was to run away halfway around the world to get away from you. If you two hadn't been such bastards to her, she'd still be alive today!"

"I guess we'll never know, will we," Graham conceded as he took a mouthful of his cappuccino.

Paula sighed deeply before reclaiming her seat. "So, you stayed in Cherbourg with Dave Francis then..." She pushed for more information.

"Obviously I couldn't come back to the UK so Dave let me stay with him at his villa in Toulouse. It was only meant to be a temporary thing but we stayed almost ten years."

"So what made you come back?"

"Dave got sick and died and his family sold the villa so I was left with finding somewhere else to live in France which wasn't possible as I was there without the right paperwork so I had to come home."

"I didn't know that Dave Francis had a family."

"His parents died but he had a son born out of a one night stand. Not sure if the mother is still around. I thought I could start afresh somewhere else but then his son, Elliot, showed up at Dave's villa with an entourage of lawyers demanding that the place be sold and my things removed within two weeks or else he would take legal action against me. Anyway, somehow he discovered that my circumstances were less than ideal and used them against me. He's a well established businessman and now runs his own publishing house here in the city and told me that if I ever set foot on any of his property again then he would make sure my connections would become public knowledge and everyone would know what I had done."

"So why did you come back to London?"

"I had no other options."

"Were you working out in France?"

"We helped out the local farmers for cash in hand jobs as well as maintaining the vegetable gardens and vineyards for a modest sum but nothing substantial."

"You said you got clean…"

"I haven't touched any alcohol for eight years."

Paula looked at him.

"I swear, it took a lot to realise where my life was heading and I felt like I'd been given a second chance at life again."

"A lot has changed in ten years Dad. I don't live in the city anymore. I have a life with my own family and I really don't need any extra drama right now."

"I'm not expecting to just walk back into your life but you have sold our family home..."

"The home that you destroyed when you killed my mother, abused my sister and walked out on us!"

Graham bowed his head. "I know I can never change what I did, but I want to make things right," he said, his voice barely above a whisper. "I have nothing left now, Paula. No family, no home, nothing. The only thing I have left is the hope that maybe, just maybe, we can try to reconcile and find some kind of closure."

Paula stared at him, her expression softening slightly. She had always thought that she would never be able to forgive her father for what he had done, but looking at him now, she could see the pain and regret etched into his face. Maybe it was time to let go of the anger and bitterness that had been eating away at her for so long.

"I'll think about it," she said finally, grabbing her handbag and standing up.

"Where are you staying?" Paula finally asked.

"With a friend in the city."

"Is this long term? Do you have any money?"

"Some. Obviously I can't just go and collect my pension like any other normal person..."

Paula picked up a napkin and wrote her mobile phone number on it. "Take this. I need to sort a few things out my end first but call me in three days and I will arrange something for you."

"Thank you, Paula. I know I don't deserve this..."

"You don't but I'm not some heartless bitch who'll let you die on the streets either. Do you have enough money to get back to where you're staying?"

"I'm not that bad yet."

"I need to go. I have my family waiting for me at home."

Graham nodded, understanding the dismissal. He watched as his daughter walked away before finishing his cappuccino and leaving the coffee shop and heading towards the exit.

"Nothing out of the ordinary," Alison spoke into the lapel. "Hang on a minute..."

"What?" Blake asked.

"He's met someone at the exit. Looks like the guy who pissed his boss off at the bar last night."

Blake quickly stood up from his seat and began heading towards the station exit, near to the London Eye. Alison moved from her position to join him at the exit. A black taxi had pulled into the layby. Graham Evans climbed into the nearside back seat, closing the door swiftly behind him, but Blake's attention was on the man climbing into the opposite side of the taxi. He looked over at Blake, making eye contact before climbing inside. It was Andrew Broughton.

Chapter Ten

Deadly Consequences

Gabby and Simon arrived at Longfellow Crescent, the street where Gabby and her brother, James, had grown up. The houses had not changed much over the years, but they looked older and less vibrant. Gabby led the way to her old house, number 24, and stopped in front of it.

"Wow, it's strange how I still remember this place so well," Gabby said, staring at the old house.

"Do you want to go in?" Simon asked.

Gabby hesitated for a moment before nodding. They walked up to the door, and Gabby rang the doorbell. The door creaked open, and they were greeted by an elderly woman.

"Can I help you?" the woman asked.

"Hi, sorry to bother you. I used to live here when I was a child, and I was wondering if I could take a look around?" Gabby asked.

The woman looked at Gabby for a moment before nodding. "Sure, come on in. I've just put the kettle on. Can I push you to a Chamomile tea?"

"That would be lovely, thank you Miss..."

"Oh, no need to be so formal dear, Harriet, Harriet Squantz. And you are?" Harriet asked as she led them into the kitchen.

Gabby looked around at the same old window frames that had recently been double-glazed. The kitchen area that had long been updated from what she remembered. She looked up at the old wooden beams that ran across the ceiling and felt a shiver run down her spine as memories that she had tried to forget came flooding back with a vengeance.

"Gabrielle Turner, my friends call me Gabby and this is my partner Simon. We're over here on vacation and I thought it would be nice to revisit some of the places where I grew up and to see how they've changed," Gabby explained as Harriet handed them both a cup of Chamomile Tea in white china cups with saucers.

"Turner, hmm, the family I brought this place from, I'm sure one of those were a Turner," Harriet replied as she led them towards the lounge.

"What year did you move here?" Simon asked.

"1990 or was it '91? Sorry, ever since my husband Vincent passed away, time seems to blur into one. There was some kind of dispute and the house was sold by someone in America but some of the moneys were held in trust in the UK. I don't remember the full details but anyway, how old were you when you lived here?"

"I was twelve when we left in 1990," Gabby replied.

"Ah so it was your family. We had some wonderful neighbours back then who adopted a young girl and had helped to look after the other children on the street too."

"Helped? In what way?" Simon questioned.

"Oh, you know, just giving them a safe space to play and socialise in. They never had any children of their own so I guess it was the closest they had to having grandchildren."

"Margaret and Norman Petersen," Gabby replied.

"Yes, that's them. Poor Margaret. She took on way too much and died in 1993 the poor soul. Norman just gave up after that. Became a recluse. We never saw him for weeks on end and when he died, the police had to break down his door to find him. They covered it up well but I think he had been gone for a week or so before they recovered his body."

"You said that Margaret took on too much. What do you mean by that?" Gabby asked.

"Well, a newborn baby at her age. If I'm half as sprightly at seventy-two as Margaret was then I'll be very happy."

"What happened to the child after Margaret died? Surely Norman couldn't look after it," Simon pushed.

"Not an it, a her. After Margaret died, Norman fell apart and the little girl was looked after by one of their friends, Edith, for a while but she was elderly too so I think the father eventually returned and took care of his daughter after that. Would you like a biscuit with your tea?"

"No, no, I'm fine, thank you," Gabby reassured her. "Did you know the little girl's name?"

"Oh, now you're asking me, gosh, it was so long ago. Catherine? No. Caroline? No. Sorry, my mind isn't what it once was."

"Did her name begin with C?" Simon asked. "Possibly the initials C.A.T.?"

"Chloe? Crystal? Cassie? Claire?" Gabby tried.

"Claire, that's it, Claire Turner."

Gabby froze. Colour drained from her face when she realised that her hunch about her mother's pregnancy was right.

"Are you okay dear? You look a little pale," Harriet asked.

"I think that, this Claire, might be my half sister," Gabby managed to say.

"Oh my, I was told that her mother had died during childbirth."

"Our mother committed suicide in the kitchen of this house."

Harriet froze. Her once warm welcoming eyes turned as hard as stone. She placed her cup of tea onto the coffee table. "I think you should both leave now."

"I'm sorry if I upset you…" Gabby tried.

"Go!"

"At least let me know who this Edith was so I can find out more about her."

"She's in a nursing home now so you'll never get to her," Harriet replied as she opened the front door.

Simon led the way with Gabby close behind him.

"Just one more thing…" Gabby asked as she stood in the doorway.

"What?"

"Claire's father who came back to look after her. Was his name Derek Copsewood?"

Harriet glared into Gabby's eyes making her feel uncomfortable. "You're playing a dangerous game my dear. If you want my advice, leave and don't come back."

"Was it Derek?" Gabby pleaded.

"Yes," Harriet replied before closing the door.

Gabby stared at the wooden door for a moment before stepping away and following Simon out of the front gate.

"What now?" Simon asked as they began walking down the road.

"Now we find my sister and I have to face my abuser."

"You don't need to do this Gab. You could be opening up a whole can of worms here that don't need to be opened."

"I need to find closure Si. I'm tired of running away from my past. If I'm going to be able to move on with my life then I need to deal with the emotional baggage that I'm carrying. Are you with me on this?"

Simon held her close. "Of course I am, I just don't want you to get hurt."

"I know, but I need to know the truth about what happened in 1990."

As Gabby and Simon headed away from Longfellow Crescent, Harriet looked out of her lounge window at the house opposite hers. The front door opened and a young woman walked over to her grey Nissan Micra. She had shoulder-length black hair tied back in a severe bun and wore black jeans and a branded black shirt for Sam's Bar. An older man stood in the doorway calling something out to her which Harriet couldn't hear. The young woman climbed into her car and drove away. The older man caught sight of Harriet watching them and waved. Harriet stepped back and pulled the curtain across.

***

Steven Langford awoke as the sound of someone knocking at the front door alerted him. The light through the window stung his eyes as his head pounded from whatever Tiffany had used to sedate him. Bleary-eyed, he peered out of the window and saw the postman waiting at the door with a parcel.

"Delivery for Mr Langford!" the postman called out.

"Can you leave it on the doorstep and I'll be down in a minute?" Steven called out.

"Okay, must have been quite a party!" the postman chuckled as he left the parcel and continued on his way.

"You have no idea," Steven sighed as he pulled on his dressing gown and opened the bedroom door.

As he opened the door, a foul stench attacked his senses, almost sending him back into the bedroom. He wandered over towards the top of the stairs.

"Justin? Julia? Luther? Anybody?" Steven called out.

The whole house was eerily quiet. As he reached the bottom of the stairs, he felt a sticky warm liquid under his bare feet. He looked down and noticed a pool of blood had formed in the hall.

"No! No!" Steven gasped as he opened the lounge door.

The entire room was filled with pools of blood. The carpet was soaked in it. Sticky red already faded, leaving the carpet black. Three mutilated bodies had been sat ghoulishly on the sofa with the word TRAITOR scrawled in blood across the wall. He ran back up the stairs and into his bedroom. The room was empty. He could still smell the sickly stench of death and it clung to his mouth and nostrils. Steven ran into the bathroom and threw up. He wiped his mouth with the back of his hand and stared at himself in the mirror.

"What the fu..." he began shouting at himself before breaking down in tears.

He rushed back into his bedroom and grabbed his phone from the bedside table. He had twenty-five missed calls and eighteen text messages. He scrolled down his contacts and called Jenny.

"You better have a damn good excuse for ignoring me for the past twenty-four hours!" Jenny snapped as she answered the call.

"They're dead!" Steven gasped.

"What? Who?"

"Everyone! They're all dead!"

"This is not funny! If you're pissed again Steven, I swear I'm going..."

"Jenny! I need Blake!"

"What?"

"I woke up and everyone is dead!"

"What are you talking about?"

"We had a party for Justin's birthday last night. I fell asleep and when I woke up, my house resembled a horror movie! I need Blake! Get him here now!"

Jenny was silent for a moment as she tried to process what Steven had just said. Then, in a hushed voice, she asked, "Are you sure? Are you absolutely sure that everyone is dead?"

"Yes, I'm sure. I just saw their bodies downstairs," Steven confirmed, his voice shaking with fear and disbelief.

"I'll call Blake right away. Stay where you are. Don't touch anything or go near the bodies, okay? Just wait for Blake and the police."

Steven nodded, even though Jenny couldn't see him. He stayed on the line until he heard sirens in the distance. "I can't..."

"You can, just wait..." Jenny replied before the phone cut off.

Steven remembered the postman and rushed down towards the front door. He picked up the parcel and rushed back up to the bedroom. As he ripped open the box he found the severed head of a young blonde woman. Scratched into the forehead was a message:

JUST ANOTHER
GAME

Steven dropped it on the floor, pulled on his jeans, t-shirt and shoes from the floor before running out of the front door. He ran around the corner, across the road and into the park, before heading towards East Putney Tube Station.

The adrenaline coursing through Steven's veins was taking over. He couldn't breathe. His head was spinning. His heart was pounding. Feeling dizzy, he stopped and leaned against a tree for support.

The pain was throbbing and deep in his guts. He dropped to his knees and clutched his stomach.

"Are you okay buddy?" a passer-by asked.

Breathlessly, Steven got back to his feet. "I'm... fine..." he managed to say before rushing over towards the shopping centre.

He saw a black taxi pull up outside to drop somebody off and quickly dived inside.

"Where to mister?" the driver asked.

A thousand thoughts scattered around Steven's mind. None of them gave any explanation of what had just happened.

"I need to know where you're going, mister..." the driver asked again.

"Portman Terrace, Kensington," Steven replied.

Chapter Eleven

Everyone Has A Secret That Can Kill

Wendy Dawkins arrived outside Badgers Nest Nursing Home in East London just after 2pm. She wandered over towards the door and rang the bell. A nurse in navy blue uniform opened the door and asked her to sign in. Wendy picked up the blue biro and signed her name and time of arrival before being led down a corridor with woodchip wallpaper walls and a green and brown patterned carpet. Several small rooms had their doors open allowing the residents to wander around as they pleased. When they arrived at room fifteen, the nurse knocked lightly on the door. An elderly lady sitting in a wooden chair next to the window at the side of a bed reading a paperback book looked over at them.

"You have a visitor Edith," the nurse stated as she stood aside for Wendy to enter the room.

"Wendy, my dear, how are you?" Edith asked as she carefully stood from her chair and they embraced before sitting down again.

"Very well thank you Mrs Harrow, I brought you a packet of mints as I know how much you like the humbugs. I must apologise that I had to have one of them as I had a terrible coughing fit earlier on the bus," Wendy replied as she took a seat opposite her.

"Oh, thank you dear and come on, none of this Mrs Harrow, call me Edith. You've known me long enough for that. So what brings you here on this miserable day?"

"I was in the area and thought I'd stop by and see how you were doing."

Edith looked at her over her glasses. "I didn't come over on the last banana boat, you have that look in your eyes…"

"One of our new authors came into the publishing house yesterday."

"Makes a change for one of them to turn up in person. I thought everything was done on the internet these days."

"This one was different. She's travelled from Miami to see us."

"Well it's good to know that Elliot is branching out internationally these days. How did the little twerp bribe this one?"

"She had a copy of one of your books," Wendy replied.

"Not to be modest, dear, but a lot of people do."

"Tales Of A Lost Soul," Wendy replied.

Edith looked at her. "No, that's not possible."

"I saw it myself. She claimed that she found it in the back of a cab that she took from the airport with her partner."

"That book hasn't been in print in over forty years. The last copy I had I gave to Lana Turner before she died. When they went through her things, the book had vanished."

Wendy pulled out a book from her handbag and handed it over to Edith. "Do you know this author?"

Edith took the book in a trembling hand and read the title. "Diamonds Don't Dream, by Gabrielle Turner." She turned the book over and saw Gabby's photo on the back cover. She dropped the book onto the floor.

"Do you know Gabrielle Turner?" Wendy asked.

"You should leave," Edith replied. "Nurse!"

"I'm sorry, I didn't mean to upset you. I thought that her having a copy of your old book was significant."

The nurse came into Edith's room and walked over towards Wendy. "Is everything ok?"

"There are some things that should never be recalled from the past! Please leave!" Edith snapped.

Wendy stood up, taken aback by Edith's sudden change of mood. She knew better than to argue with the elderly woman when she was in such a state. "I'm sorry, Edith. I didn't mean to upset you," she said softly. "I'll leave you to rest now."

Without another word, she made her way out of the nursing home and back onto the street. The rain had become much heavier. She pulled up her hood and began walking, her mind still reeling from the encounter with Edith. A grey Nissan Micra splashed water onto the path soaking her feet as it passed by. She turned around and cursed at the driver under her breath, before watching as the car turned into the nursing home's car park before continuing on her way.

As she walked, she couldn't shake the feeling that something was deeply wrong. The way Edith had reacted to the mention of Gabrielle Turner's name. The fact that she had, seemingly by chance, found a copy of Edith's long-lost book. And who was this Lana Turner? A relative perhaps? Wendy knew that Gabby had a chequered history of secrets, but this was something else entirely. She needed to know what was going on. She looked at her watch. She was too late to catch up with the first book signing at Waterloo and she needed to find out more about Gabby's past. She headed for the nearest tube station and made her way back to Scatterbird Publishing House determined to find some answers before Gabby gave her speech and signed her books at Kings Cross University Halls later tonight.

***

Blake and Alison parked their car outside Chelsea And Westminster Hospital. Both of them ventured inside.

"I'm looking for Joe Knight, he was brought in last night," Alison asked the receptionist.

"Are you family?"

Alison showed her ID. "His colleague, he came in with Samir Khalifa."

"Yes, Mr Khalifa has been discharged a few hours ago but Mr Knight is currently in ICU on the fifth floor," the receptionist advised.

Alison thanked the receptionist before following Blake towards the nearest lift.

"You go on ahead and check up on Joe. I need to call in and see how Mum's baring up," Blake advised as they stepped inside the lift.

Blake stepped off on the third floor whilst Alison continued up to the fifth.

As Alison stepped out of the lift, the smell of antiseptic hit her. She followed the signs to the ICU and found Joe's room. She could see him lying in the bed, hooked up to various machines, with an oxygen mask over his partially burnt face. His eyes were closed, and his skin was pale. She noticed further burns on his left arm, hand and shoulder.

Alison felt a lump forming in her throat. She had known Joe for years, and he was one of the toughest guys she knew. To see him lying there like this was heartbreaking. She walked over to the bed and took his hand. It was cold to the touch. She noticed a priest standing by the door making the sign of the cross before leaving.

"Hey, Joe," she said softly. "It's me, Alison. I'm here for you."

Joe's eyelids fluttered, and he managed to open his eyes slightly. He murmured something before drifting away again.

"It's okay, I'm here," she whispered.

He looked at her for a moment before his eyes drifted shut again.

Alison sat down in the chair next to the bed and watched him for a while. She didn't know the full details of what had happened but for Samir to already be out, he must have some idea.

A nurse came into the room to check on Joe. "Has he said anything?" she asked.

"He murmured something when I came in. What's with the priest? I don't think Joe's religious."

"He came in to give the last rights. Unfortunately, some don't make it," the nurse replied before leaving.

Alison took hold of Joe's right hand and sat at his bedside as the machines continued beeping methodically to keep his body stabilised.

Meanwhile, two floors below, Blake wandered through the ward towards his mother's bed. His sister, Jenny, was sitting in a wooden chair at her bedside.

"Where the hell have you been?" Jenny asked. "I've been trying to reach you for the past hour!"

"Whoa, I'm here now. What's going on? Is Mum okay?"

"Mum's fine, it's Steven..."

"Oh God, what's he done now?"

"He needs you."

"That's a first..."

"No, seriously, he woke up in his house and everyone was dead. He's freaking out. I called the police but I think he ran..."

"What's he playing at? If he's drunk or high I'm gonna..." Blake began.

"I said the same thing but I've never known him to be like this. He pleaded for me to get hold of you."

Blake sighed. "Okay, I'll go and see what's going on but first I need to know what the doctors have said?"

"Mum's stable but they're concerned about pressure on her brain so she's in an induced coma for now. Paula brought some of her things here last night."

"Yeah, I know. Was Paula okay when she came here?"

"She was pretty shaken up. She didn't stay for long. Said she needed to sort some things out. Is everything okay with you two?"

Blake pondered that for a moment. "She came face to face with her Dad last night. He turned up at Mum's house."

"What?"

"I know, it gets worse. She met up with him this morning and when he left he got into a taxi with Andrew Broughton."

"How did... You tailed her? Blake!"

"I had to. I needed to know what was happening. Too much weird stuff keeps happening and I don't know whether I'm coming or going at the moment."

"Look, I'll stay here and keep you posted if anything changes with Mum. Make sure you answer your phone! Please go and find out what the hell is happening with Steven and then go and speak to your fiance rather than stalking her. She deserves better than that."

"He's probably overexaggerating things but I get it," Blake sighed and gave his sister a quick hug before heading out of the hospital ward.

He took the lift up two floors and joined Alison at Joe's bedside in the ICU. He looked down at Joe. "Who the hell did this?"

"I don't know but we need to contact Samir and find out," Alison replied.

As she stood from her seat, Joe mumbled something under his oxygen mask.

"It's okay," Alison reassured him. "We're going to find the ones responsible for this."

Joe looked at her and mumbled something again. Alison looked at Blake before carefully lifting up Joe's oxygen mask.

"Tell... the..." he managed to say.

"Tell the, what? The nurse?" Alison tried.

"Tell the... Tell the priest to piss off, I'm not dead yet!" Joe replied before closing his eyes again.

Alison replaced the mask and looked at Blake.

"Stay strong buddy, we won't let you down," Blake replied before they both left the hospital.

Blake told Alison about what he had heard from Jenny as they made their way to the car and drove to Steven's house at 235 Quebec Drive. When they arrived, the police were already there, and there was a crowd of onlookers gathered outside.

Blake approached one of the officers and flashed his badge.

"Blake Langford, Special Branch. What's the situation?" he asked.

The officer filled him in on the details. Steven had woken up that morning to find his entire household slaughtered in his home. The killer was still on the loose, and Steven had fled the scene in a panic.

Blake surveyed the scene, taking in the bloodstained walls and floors. It was a gruesome sight, and he felt his stomach turn.

"Has anyone said anything else about what happened?" Blake asked the officer.

The officer shook his head. "All we have is the 999 call from his sister and a neighbour's account of him running away. We're trying to track him down to get him to the station for questioning, but so far, nothing."

Blake looked at the three bodies and at the word TRAITOR written in blood across the wall. He felt a shiver run down his spine. What if his visit here last night set off this chain of events?

"We also found this. Looks like it was delivered by the postman. We've sent an officer to the local sorting office to find out who delivered it," the officer continued.

Blake looked at the severed head in the cardboard box that the forensic team had already bagged for evidence.

"Just another game," Blake read aloud. "We're dealing with one sick son-of-a-bitch here."

"Everyone has a secret that can kill," Alison replied as she joined Blake in the lounge.

"That's three of the missing twelve. Someone obviously wants to make a statement. We need to get on to Gordon and find out what Samir has uncovered. When will we get any ID's on these?" Blake asked.

"They're cut up pretty bad, my guess is forty-eight hours at best," the officer replied.

Blake and Alison stepped outside the house and back into the fresh air once again.

"We seem to be one step behind every time. We need to get ahead and I think Samir knows where we need to look," Blake stated as he reached into his pocket and pulled out his phone.

Seventeen missed calls and messages from Jenny filled the screen as he scrolled through his call log. As he stopped on Samir's number, Paula called him. Blake grimaced at the timing but he knew he needed to answer the call.

"Hey, how did it go this morning," Blake answered, attempting to hide the frustration in his voice.

"Hey, we'll get to that later. I need you to come back to the flat as soon as possible," Paula replied.

"I'm kind of tied up in the middle of a multiple murder investigation right now, can it wait until later?"

"There's someone here that needs to see you."

Blake felt a shiver run down his spine. "Who?"

"Your brother, Steven."

Chapter Twelve

Tying Up Loose Ends

Sergeant Shaun Bryant and Samir Khalifa drove away from Chelsea And Westminster Hospital, discussing their plan of action.

"We need to find this killer before they strike again. Do you have any leads on who it could be?" Shaun asked Samir.

Samir shook his head. "Not yet, I have a score to settle with Zachary Zhal but I have a feeling that Blake's brother could also be involved somehow. We need to reconvene with Blake before we bring him in for questioning."

Shaun nodded in agreement. "I'll put out an APB on him, but it might take some time to track him down or at least get our shot at him."

"Why?"

"From what I heard earlier, the police are already looking at him for a murder scene out at Quebec Drive. If we stumble into their investigation, the Chief will go ape-shit!"

Samir sighed. "Collateral damage unfortunately. We don't have much time. We need to work out the connection between Steven Langford, Zodiac and Derek Copsewood. We need to find Steven as soon as possible. Lives are at stake."

As they drove through the busy London streets, Samir's phone buzzed with a text message. He glanced down at his phone and saw a message from an unknown number. It read: "Meet me at the abandoned metro warehouse on the outskirts of Somers Town."

Samir frowned. He had no idea who could be contacting him like this, but he had a feeling it had something to do with the case. He turned to Shaun.

"I just got a message. Someone wants to meet me at an abandoned metro warehouse on the outskirts of Somers Town. I think we should check it out."

Shaun raised an eyebrow. "Are you sure it's not a trap? Zodiac's already taken a shot at you and Joe."

"I can't be sure, but we don't have any other leads right now."

Shaun nodded. "Okay, let's go. But I'm going with you."

They drove to the abandoned warehouse and parked the car on a side road. As they got out, Samir couldn't shake off the feeling that something was off. It was eerily quiet. He wondered if the aftereffects of yesterday's blast were still affecting him but he tried his best to shake the feeling off.

"Let's be careful," Shaun said, drawing his gun and gesturing for Samir to do the same.

They made their way inside, scanning the empty warehouse for any signs of life. As they approached the centre of the building, they saw a figure standing in the shadows. A large spotlight lit up a circle in the centre of the room as if illuminating a stage ready for a big performance.

"Who's there?" Samir called out, his heart pounding in his chest.

The figure stepped into the light, revealing itself to be a tall, muscular man with a shaved head and a scar above his left eyebrow.

"Samir Khalifa. I've been expecting you," the man said, his voice deep and menacing.

"Who are you?" Samir asked, his gun still trained on the man.

"You can call me Reaper. I have information that you might find useful," Reaper said, his eyes flickering under the harsh spotlight in the centre of the room.

"What do you want from me?" Samir asked.

"That was an amateur mistake back in the common. I thought better of a Special Branch agent than that. Still, we don't all get to study in the F block do we?"

Samir stepped forward into the light. "What do you have and what do I have to do to get it?"

At that moment, a door opened and a young woman entered with Zachary Zhal and Xander Zhal following close behind her.

"Zodiac?" Shaun gasped.

"I have many questions for you Sergeant Bryant," Zodiac called out. "You enlisted the help of an informer in the service of Special Branch rather than pursuing me after the riot at Pentonville Prison. Why?"

Shaun looked at Samir. "You..."

Samir glared at him but didn't say a word.

"Well, one good deed deserves another," Reaper spoke now as he pushed the young woman towards Samir.

She had blood weeping from a cut on her bottom lip and had bruises around her face and neck.

"Who are you?" Samir asked.

"Her name's Tiffany Mason," Zodiac replied. "She's been playing both sides for fools to ensure that her pimps and drug pushers get in and out of the clubs unnoticed. Unfortunately she shit on the wrong person so now she's all yours."

Samir took a step forward, his gun still trained on Zodiac and Reaper. He felt a wave of anger wash over him at the sight of Tiffany's injuries and he knew he had to keep his composure.

"Let her go," he demanded.

Reaper just laughed. "We're not holding her hostage, Khalifa. She's yours to deal with now. We just wanted to give you a little gift. She has some amazing fairy tales to tell."

Samir clenched his jaw, trying to reign in his temper. He gestured for Shaun to take Tiffany outside.

"But..." Shaun protested.

"Go!" Samir replied.

Once she was out of the building, he turned back to Zodiac and Reaper.

"All right, what's this information you have for me?" he asked.

Reaper stepped forward, his eyes glinting under the spotlight. "We know who's behind the murders. And we know where they're going to strike next."

Samir felt a prickle of excitement run down his spine. "Who is it?" he demanded.

"That's for me to know and you to find out," Reaper smirked.

Samir narrowed his eyes. "What do I have to do?"

Reaper leaned in close, his breath hot against Samir's ear. "You're going to have to come with us."

Samir hesitated. He didn't like the sound of that. "Where?"

"St Katharine Docks," Zodiac spoke up. "There's a ship that's in port tonight. That's where the killer is headed."

Samir didn't have much choice. He had to find out who the killer was and stop them before they struck again. "Okay, let's go."

He followed Reaper, Xander and Zodiac out of the warehouse. Shaun and Tiffany were waiting for them outside surrounded by four Indian men. Zodiac waved his hand and the four men retreated into two cars that had been parked nearby. As they drove towards the docks, sandwiched between the two cars driven by the Indian men, Samir couldn't shake off the feeling that he was walking into a trap.

"Where the hell are you taking me?" Tiffany demanded.

"You first, who is this Reaper guy?" Samir snapped.

"I've only just met him."

"Don't lie to me..."

"What would be the point, you're just gonna kill me anyway."

"You obviously don't know us then. What was that remark about F block?" Shaun asked. "Is it a place?"

"Kinda," Tiffany snapped.

"Care to elaborate? What's your connection with the missing girls?" Samir asked.

Tiffany didn't respond.

"It's going to take a lot longer and there's gonna be a lot more collateral damage if I don't understand what part you play in this mess," Shaun continued.

"F block is a section of Kings Cross University. Now where the hell are we going?"

"What kind of section of the university?" Samir asked.

"Students with phenomenal IQ's end up there."

"Like the ones who went missing?" Shaun asked.

"Possibly, now answer my question."

"We're going to a meeting with someone with vital information," Samir replied.

"Talk about vague," Tiffany quipped.

"Do you think this Reaper could be involved with the University? Perhaps even work there?" Shaun asked.

"Anything's possible right now," Samir replied.

"What was all that about you being an informant back there?" Shaun asked.

"You believe that?"

Shaun didn't reply.

"If I was, you'd both be dead already," Samir finally replied.

"So what now? We're walking into a trap set up by one of the most wanted men in Europe."

"We're just tying up loose ends."

"In what way?"

"I don't think Zodiac is pulling the strings here."

"He busted his brother out of prison. There has to be some kind of end game for that," Shaun replied.

"I think he's just a pawn in a much bigger game. We need to find the link and discover where these missing students are being held before it's too late. Some petty crimes and a bit of drug dealing can wait until later. We need to go after the big fish."

"And what about Langford?"

That caught Tiffany's attention. "What about him? Is he dead?"

Samir looked at Shaun and then at Tiffany. "Not yet."

Chapter Thirteen

A Family Affair

Meanwhile, Blake arrived back at his flat in Kensington, his heart racing with anticipation. Alison followed him up the concrete stairs before stepping in front of him just before they arrived at the front door.

"Remember to approach this objectively, don't let family cloud your judgement," Alison advised.

"He's been getting himself in trouble for years and now it seems like he's landed himself into some deep shit that he needs bailing out of."

"But that's not your job here Blake. We need to find out if he has any connection to the ongoing investigation or if we're chasing a dead end here."

"So what do you think I should do?"

"Just be professional."

Blake nodded. He knew she was right. As much as Steven's attitude and way of life irritated him, he needed to come into this conversation objectively and professionally.

As he walked into the living room, he saw Steven sitting on the sofa, looking pale and shaken.

Blake placed an arm around Paula. "Where's Michael?"

"Frank took him out to a gaming convention."

Blake nodded before sitting in the armchair opposite Steven whilst Paula and Alison pulled up two chairs from the dining table.

"Steven, what the hell is going on?" Blake asked.

Steven took a deep breath, his hands shaking as he spoke. "I messed up, okay? I got involved with the wrong people and now they're after me."

"What kind of people?" Paula asked.

"I don't know, okay? They never told me their names or what they were into. I just did some jobs for them, delivered some packages. I didn't know it was anything illegal."

"You didn't think it was suspicious that they were paying you so much for simple deliveries?" Alison asked.

"I needed the money, okay? I'm in debt. I didn't ask questions."

Blake leaned forward in his chair, his eyes locked on Steven's. "Did they mention anything about missing students? Anything about Tiffany Mason? Or maybe Derek Copsewood?"

Steven's eyes widened in surprise. "How did you know about that?"

"We're investigating," Alison replied.

"I heard some rumours, okay? About students going missing, but I didn't think it was true. Then when I was visiting Julia..." Steven began to break down.

"Julia?" Blake pushed.

"She was a student. She was my..."

"It's okay," Alison added, handing him a tissue.

"When we were on campus, we overheard a conversation with one of the lecturers there. A Mr Bleeker, but everyone called him Reaper after he dressed up for Halloween one year."

"Do you think this Reaper is responsible for the dead bodies at your house this morning?" Blake asked.

Steven ran his fingers through his hair. "I don't know?"

"Who's the traitor? Why did someone send you a parcel containing a severed head?" Alison pushed.

"I don't know, okay! I don't know anything!"

"Then tell us what you do know," Blake replied.

Steven held his head in his hands.

"Let's work things backwards, okay..." Alison tried.

Steven nodded.

"So you woke up and found the parcel at what time?"

"About half eleven. The postman knocked on the door. I wasn't dressed so I shouted out from the bedroom window for him to leave it on the doorstep."

"We need to find out who that postman was," Blake added.

Alison nodded.

"What time did you go to sleep last night? Were you alone?" Blake asked.

"About two, the party had died down. Most people were leaving so Julia and I had a smoke and then..."

Blake nodded. "Smoke as in..."

"A spliff, okay, don't judge me..."

"I'm not. So you had a smoke, had sex then flaked out," Blake continued.

Steven nodded.

"And Julia was with you the whole time."

"I guess, I was high for Christ sake."

"But she was gone in the morning," Alison continued.

"She was..." Steven took a deep breath. "What was left of her body was on the couch."

"And the other three?" Blake asked.

Steven swallowed before talking. "Luther, Michelle and Justin."

"You slept all night? Didn't wake up to use the bathroom or anything," Alison pushed.

"I did wake up."

Blake and Alison looked at Steven.

"About seven, I think."

"Okay, was Julia still with you?" Blake asked.

"No."

"Didn't you think that was strange?" Paula asked.

"Not really, she had what she wanted and then left as usual until..."

"Until you found her..." Blake pushed.

"Yeah."

"But you didn't hear any commotion from the time you flaked out around two until the postman woke you up around half eleven besides waking up briefly to notice that Julia was gone," Alison analysed.

"There was someone else," Steven admitted.

Blake sighed deeply. "Who?"

"Tiffany Mason."

Blake ran his fingers through his hair. "You told me you didn't know Tiffany Mason! You've been sending me on a wild fucking goose chase on a mountain of lies! I should call in the police and drag your ass inside right now!"

"Blake!" Alison snapped. "Not now!"

"I shouldn't have come here," Steven began to stand from the couch.

"Sit down," Blake replied.

"What?"

"Sit your ass down. I'm sorry, okay. This case goes deeper and more personal than any of us want to acknowledge. Tell me about Tiffany. The truth this time."

"We had a fling. Things got out of hand so we cooled it. Soon after, I hear that she's working the clubs as a pimp as well as getting some of the action herself."

"You became jealous?" Alison asked.

"Yeah, I guess I did."

"What was Tiffany doing at your house this morning? Possibly even involved in a murder scene?" Blake asked.

"She wanted to know who was looking for her at the bar last night."

"Did you tell her?"

"What do you think?"

"Why did someone write "traitor" on the wall?" Alison asked. "Did they find out about your connection to Blake?"

Steven nodded.

"She said that Nathan and Dickie owed her some money and she wouldn't leave town without it."

"Dickie?" Blake questioned.

"Dickie Parsnips, Richard Parsons, it's his nickname, he's the landlord at The Troubled Traveller pub."

That caught Blake's attention. He had spotted Andrew Broughton, Paula's ex-fiance, working in that same bar when they visited there yesterday.

"So, after she spoke to you did she just leave?" Alison asked.

"She blew some weird stuff in my face..."

"What kind of stuff?" Blake asked.

"I don't know, some kinda weird stuff that knocked me out until the postman knocked on the door and I ended up in a murder scene."

"So, if she was part of the group who murdered your housemates, why didn't Tiffany kill you?" Alison asked.

"I don't know," Steven replied.

Blake thought about that for a moment before changing direction. "About these packages you delivered, did you know who was sending them? Was there anything unusual about them lately?"

"There was a package last week. The parcel came with a note. It said that if I didn't deliver it to some location, they would kill Julia. I didn't want her to get hurt, so I did what they asked."

"You didn't think to flag that up to someone? Anyone?" Alison asked.

"These are the types of people you don't routinely go round pissing them off. Sooner or later, they'll come for you."

"So, did you deliver it?" Paula asked.

Steven nodded. "I left it in the place they told me to leave it. Then I left. Two days later, I was waking up in my house with a head in a box."

"Did you recognize the head?" Alison asked.

"No, I didn't. I swear, I don't know anything about it."

"Where did you deliver that parcel to?" Blake asked.

"Some warehouse on the edge of Somers Town. Metro, I think it was called."

"I'll look into it," Alison replied.

"You must have some idea of who these people are. How did you get involved with them in the first place?" Blake asked.

Steven hesitated before speaking. "I met them at a party. They said they had some job opportunities for me. I didn't realise they were involved in anything illegal until it was too late."

Blake leaned back in his chair, a thoughtful expression on his face. "We need to find out who sent that parcel to you today and who is behind all of this. Steven, do you have any idea where they could be?"

"No, I don't. I swear."

"We need to keep digging," Alison said, standing up from her chair. "Blake, I think we should take Steven to a safe house. We'll keep investigating and see if we can find any leads."

Blake nodded.

"What kind of safe house? What are you talking about?" Steven asked.

"Off the grid. You have the police, Special Branch and half of London's worst criminals wanting a piece of you. If you want to stay alive, I need you to cooperate," Blake advised.

Steven nodded. "Was there anything else?

"Does the name Andrew Broughton mean anything to you?" Alison asked.

Paula gasped and glared at Blake. Blake looked over at her.

"You didn't..." Paula began.

"Just a line of inquiry," Blake replied.

Paula left the room and the bedroom door slammed shut.

"Shall I?" Alison asked.

"No, I will in a minute but first," Blake turned back to Steven. "What is Andrew Broughton and Derek Copsewood's connection in this?"

Steven's eyes widened in recognition. "Copsewood is the middle man. Broughton, Yes, I've heard of him. He's been around for several years.."

"Longer than that," Blake commented.

"You know him don't you? So does Paula. That's why she ran out," Steven asked.

"Irrelevant," Blake snapped.

"Did Broughton have anything to do with the missing students?" Alison asked.

"I don't know. I've never had any direct contact with him, but I've heard rumours that he's involved in some shady stuff," Steven replied.

Blake leaned back in his chair, deep in thought. "We need to find out more about this Reaper and what he's up to. It could be our missing link."

"I can try to find out more information," Steven offered, desperation in his voice.

Alison shook her head. "No, Steven. You're in too deep. We need you to remain in the safe house. You need to stay out of this. We'll handle it from here."

"But I want to help!" Steven protested.

"You've done enough, Steven. If you want to stay alive, go with Alison to the safe house. I'll catch up with you soon."

Blake stood up, signalling the end of the conversation.

Blake watched Alison and Steven leave before wandering over to the bedroom. He slowly opened the door and saw Paula laying on the bed curled up cuddling a pillow and crying. Blake sat on the opposite side and placed a hand on her arm. She shrugged him off.

"I'm sorry, I was going to tell you," Blake sighed.

"When?"

"It's just a line of inquiry. He may not even be involved."

"Don't you get it!" Paula snapped as she turned to face him. "Dad mysteriously returns after all these years and then suddenly, Alison mentions his name. Isn't it obvious? If Dad's back, there's a good chance that Andy is helping him."

Blake bowed his head.

"You knew, didn't you."

"I saw your father getting into a taxi with Andy this morning after he met you at Waterloo Station," Blake admitted.

"You bastard! You spied on me and then kept information from me. You knew how many years he abused me and you led him straight to us!"

"Paula, it's not like that. His name came up during the inquiries and I had to follow it up. Nothing more."

"Go back to work Blake. You're needed elsewhere," Paula replied before turning away from him again.

Blake placed his hand on her arm and she shrugged him off again. He slowly stood up from the bed and walked out of the door.

Chapter Fourteen
The Rabbit Hole

Jenny Langford stepped outside the front entrance of Chelsea And Westminster Hospital to take in some fresh air. For the past forty-eight hours, she had been at her mother's bedside as she recovered from a stroke.

She took a deep breath of the cool February air and exhaled slowly, feeling the stress of the past few days slowly begin to slip away. She had always been close to her mother, and seeing her in the hospital had been a shock. But now, as she stood outside and gazed up at the cloudy sky, she felt a sense of peace.

As she leaned against the hospital wall, Jenny heard footsteps approaching from behind her. She turned to see a man, tall and dark-haired with silver highlights, walking towards her.

"Excuse me," the man said. "Are you Jenny Langford?"

Jenny tensed slightly. She didn't recognize the man, and his sudden appearance made her uneasy.

"Yes," she said cautiously. "Who are you?"

"My name is Derek Copsewood," the man replied. "I'm a private investigator. I was hired to find you."

Jenny's heart raced at the mention of a private investigator. She had no idea who could have hired someone to find her, especially since she kept a low profile and didn't have any enemies. She looked at him sceptically, trying to gauge his intentions.

"Why were you hired to find me?" she asked, her voice wavering slightly.

"I'm sorry, I can't disclose that information. But I do have a message for you," Derek said, handing her an envelope. "It's from an anonymous sender."

Jenny took the envelope cautiously, her hands shaking as she opened it. Inside was a note written in a familiar handwriting. It read: "Jenny, I know about your secret. Meet me at the rabbit hole tomorrow at midnight. Come alone or your secret will be exposed."

Jenny's mind raced as she tried to figure out who could have written the note. She had a secret, one that she had buried deep inside her for years. A secret that she had worked so hard to keep in the shadows for so long. The rabbit hole was a secret entrance that led down to a disused underground station near to Kings Cross Station. Many years ago, when she was out with her friends, they used to hang out there when they were teenagers and Blake had taken her there once when they were being followed by a group of gang leaders that Special Branch were investigating. It was kind of an off the record escape room but the thought of going back there sent a shiver down her spine.

She knew that whoever had written the note had the power to ruin her life. She looked up at Derek, who was watching her intently.

"What am I supposed to do?" she asked, desperation creeping into her voice.

"I suggest you meet the person and find out what they want," Derek replied. "But be careful. Don't trust anyone."

Jenny nodded, still reeling from the shock of the note. She wondered if this was somehow connected to the investigation that Blake and Alison were working on.

"Thank you for delivering this," she said, handing the note back to Derek. "I'll take it from here."

Derek nodded and walked away, disappearing into the crowd of people who were gathering further down the road. Jenny leaned back against the wall, trying to calm her racing thoughts.

She knew that she had to meet the person at the specified time and place. But the thought of going alone filled her with dread. She needed someone to confide in, someone to help her.

Jenny pulled out her phone and started typing a message, it read;

I NEED TO SEE YOU, URGENT XX

Within less than a minute, the reply came through;

MY PLACE, 4.30PM XX

Jenny looked at her watch. She had just over two hours. She looked back at the hospital entrance. It's cold grey walls imposing over the well maintained gardens gave it an almost haunting look mirrored by the grey skies overhead. Jenny breathed deeply before heading back to her car and driving back to her flat in Chelsea. As she left the car park, Derek fired up the engine of his blue BMW before following her at a safe distance back through the city.

***

Gabby Turner arrived at the Southbank Book Market on Waterloo Bridge at half past three to get ready for her book signing session at four o'clock. Her latest novel, "Diamonds Don't Dream," was based on her own life experiences with her family's involvement in organised crime before she found love with CIA agent, Simon Buxton. She had found the writing process had been a way to give herself some kind of closure from the past. However, since arriving in London, Gabby had felt more unsettled than ever.

Simon placed an arm around her shoulders and softly kissed her cheek. "You've got this!"

Gabby smiled as he turned and walked away.

After all of the emotions she had felt since arriving in London, Gabby felt happy to finally be doing what she came here to do but she felt excited and nervous at the same time. The book market was packed with people browsing through the various stalls, but she knew deep down that her fans would be there, waiting for her to sign their copies of her book. She took in a few deep breaths and tried to dispel any nerves or emotions from her London adventure so far and focus on the job in hand.

Elliot Francis from her publishing house came over to give her some final words of encouragement but Gabby was mentally in her zone and his words didn't seem to register as she made her way towards her table that had been decorated with leaflets, promotional bookmarks, pens and mugs as well as hardback and paperback copies of her book.

As she approached her table, she noticed a man standing a few feet away, watching her intently. He was tall, with dark hair and piercing blue eyes. Gabby felt a shiver run down her spine as she noticed the way he was looking at her.

"Excuse me, can I help you?" Gabby asked, trying to hide her unease.

"I'm sorry to bother you," the man said, his voice smooth and deep. "I'm a big fan of your work. I just wanted to say hello."

Gabby forced a smile, feeling a sense of relief wash over her.

"Thank you," she replied. "It's always great to meet a fan. Would you like me to sign a copy of my book for you?"

The man nodded eagerly and handed Gabby a copy of "Diamonds Don't Dream."

"Who am I addressing this to?"

"Andrew," the man replied.

As she signed the book, she couldn't shake the feeling that something wasn't quite right about the man. His intense gaze and the way he seemed to be studying her made her nervous.

"Here you go," Gabby said, handing the book back to the man. "Thanks for coming to see me."

Andrew smiled and walked away, disappearing into the crowd. Gabby let out a sigh of relief, feeling silly for letting her nerves get the best of her. She turned her attention back to her table, ready to greet her fans and sign more books.

As she signed copy after copy, Gabby couldn't help but feel like she was being watched. She kept glancing over her shoulder, but she didn't see anyone out of the ordinary. However, as she was signing the last book, she saw Andrew, the man from earlier, walking towards her again. This time, he was holding a small slip of paper.

"I'm sorry to bother you again," he said, handing her the paper. "But I think you dropped this earlier."

Gabby frowned, confused. She didn't remember dropping anything. "Thank you," she said, taking the slip of paper. As she unfolded it, her heart dropped. It read:

"Gabby, I know about your past. Meet me at the rabbit hole tomorrow at midnight. Come alone or your secret will be exposed."

Gabby's mind raced. How did this person know about her past in London or was it a connection to what had happened with her brother James in Miami? Her new book had stirred up a lot of memories from the past. And what was their motive? And the rabbit hole? The last time she was there was when they were children. James had been messing around and discovered a door that was unlocked that led down to a disused underground station near to Kings Cross Station. When they tried to go back a few weeks later, the door had been locked. She wondered if it was still the same place that she remembered. A thousand questions filled her mind with very few answers. She looked up at Andrew, who was watching her intently.

"Do you know who wrote this?" she asked, her voice shaking slightly.

He shook his head. "I'm sorry, I don't. I just found it on the ground and thought it might belong to you."

Gabby nodded, feeling confused. She knew she had to take this seriously. She had worked so hard to leave her past behind and build a new life for herself. The last thing she wanted was for it to come back and ruining her new life with Simon.

"Thank you for returning this to me," she said, trying to keep her composure. "I'm sure it's just a misunderstanding."

Andrew nodded and walked away, disappearing once again into the crowd. Gabby sat back down at her table, her mind racing with thoughts of who could have written the note and what they wanted from her. She knew she couldn't go to the police. There were too many secrets from her past that she couldn't risk being exposed. She needed to figure out a way to handle this on her own.

As the book market closed down and the crowds began to disperse, Gabby packed up her things into several cardboard boxes. She still continued to look around for anyone acting out of the ordinary. She had wanted to bury the thoughts and memories of the past by coming back to London and facing them head-on. Now she wondered if that was a mistake too?

Simon walked over to join her. "How did it go? Looks like you attracted quite a crowd."

Gabby showed him the note.

"The rabbit hole?" Simon asked.

"It's a disused underground station. Only a select few people know about it."

"I'm coming with you."

"No, if it's to do with my family's past then I have to face it alone."

"You could be walking into anything. It's insane."

"What choice do I have? If they were able to get a message to me here then they obviously would have been watching us."

"Who gave you that note?"

"A fan called Andrew. Said he found it on the floor."

"Convenient."

"To be honest, he did come across rather..."

"Rather what?"

"Odd, I guess."

"If you won't let me come with you, at least let me look into it further," Simon reasoned.

"How? All we have is a note. The CIA won't follow that up too seriously."

"Maybe not, but Blake Langford will."

***

Andrew Broughton and Graham Evans left Kings Cross Station together before wandering down towards The Troubled Traveller Pub. Once inside, they both sat down at the bar and ordered a couple of pints.

"So, did she take the bait?" Graham asked.

Andrew nodded and pulled out his phone to show Graham a text message from Derek. "They're both meeting us at the rabbit hole at midnight tomorrow night. They think they're going alone."

Graham smiled. "Excellent. This is going to be easier than I thought."

Andrew took a sip of his pint, feeling a twinge of guilt. He had never intended for things to go this far, but Graham had convinced him that it was necessary to get Blake off their backs.

"I still don't understand why we had to bring up her past," Andrew said. "It seemed like a low blow."

Graham shrugged. "We had to do something to convince her to come. And besides, it's always good to have a little leverage."

Andrew shook his head. He felt uncomfortable with the way Graham operated, but he had gotten in too deep to back out now. Ever since Graham's reappearance, Andrew had struggled to get Paula off of his mind. If he was going to have a chance to get close to her, he needed Blake to be preoccupied and having Jenny and Gabby caught up in Derek's tangled web of blackmail and intimidation seemed to be the ideal scenario.

"What brings you two back here?" Andrea, the barmaid, asked as she cleared their empty glasses away and replaced them with two more beers.

"Family reunions," Graham replied.

"Any news on when Steven's back?" Andrew asked.

"He hasn't shown his face since he sold Tiffany out to his pig brother. Dickie was majorly pissed off as he had to cough up another three hundred to Nathan that Steven hadn't paid."

"Wait, are we talking about Steven Langford?" Graham asked.

"Yeah, do you know him?" Andrea asked.

"I know of him."

"Well I wouldn't want to be in his shoes when Tiff gets hold of him," Andrea replied before heading back towards the far side of the bar.

"When were you going to tell me that you had dealings with Blake's brother?" Graham snapped.

"It's irrelevant. They hate each other. It won't blow things with Paula and when Jenny is out of the equation, things will be a lot easier," Andrew replied.

Graham pondered that for a moment. "I hope you're right. We have a lot riding on this. If it doesn't work, we could all end up in the shit," Graham said, downing the rest of his pint.

"I know. That's why we have to make sure it goes smoothly," Andrew replied, his mind racing with the implications of what they were planning to do.

Chapter Fifteen

Setting The Traps

Jenny Langford arrived outside a student house in Finsbury just before 4.30pm. Her heart was racing after her encounter with Derek earlier. Her friend Nicola, shared a house with two other women, Andrea and Tiffany. The three of them had been to university together and then they stayed together as it was the only way they could pay the rent and stay in the capital. Nicola's older sister had studied law with Jenny several years earlier but they had all remained friends throughout the years.

Jenny knocked on the door and was greeted by Nicola with a warm hug. They headed into the living room, where Jenny told her about the strange encounter with Derek.

"I don't know what to do," Jenny said, her voice trembling. "I feel like I'm in over my head."

Nicola put a reassuring hand on her shoulder. "You need to tell Blake about this. He'll know what to do. What is this hold that they have over you? What is this secret?"

"I let someone down. Someone I really, deeply cared about. He ended up dead because of me."

Nicola sat there in silence.

Jenny thought for a moment. She knew that Blake would be furious if he found out that she had gotten involved in something like this, but she also knew that he would do whatever it took to protect his family.

"Blake's got way too much on at the moment and Mum's in hospital too."

"Oh my God, is she okay?"

"Doctor's think she's had a stroke but she is in an artificial coma at the moment whilst they monitor her brain activity."

Nicola's expression turned to one of concern. "Jenny, you need to tell Blake everything. He deserves to know what's going on."

Jenny sighed, knowing her friend was right. "I just don't know how to confront him about it. He's going to be so angry."

"Would you rather have him angry or have something happen to you?"

Jenny shook her head. "You're right. I'll call him tonight. Thanks, Nic."

At that moment, the lounge door opened and an Indian man entered.

"I'm sorry, I didn't realise you had company, I'll..." Jenny began.

"No, no, stay. Kaja, this is my friend, Jenny. The one I told you about," Nicola explained.

Kaja smiled warmly at Jenny. "It's nice to meet you. Even more beautiful in the flesh."

Jenny blushed and returned the smile, grateful for the distraction. "Likewise."

They chatted for a while, and Jenny found herself relaxing in their company. For the first time all day, she was able to forget about Derek's ominous warning and feel at ease once again.

As the evening wore on, Jenny's thoughts turned to Blake. She knew she had to tell him about what had happened, but she didn't want to burden him with more stress on top of everything else he was dealing with. But she also knew that she couldn't keep it from him any longer. He deserved to know the truth about her past. As she was about to make her excuses to leave, Kaja pulled out his phone and showed Jenny a photo of a man in his early forties wearing a military uniform.

"Do you know this man?" Kaja asked, looking at her with an intensity that made Jenny feel uncomfortable.

"No, should I?"

"Look closer, you haven't seen each other for a long time."

As Jenny looked closer at the photo, her heart skipped a beat and she felt tears well up in her eyes. "Tom?" she gasped. "But he's... dead!"

"That's what everyone was led to believe until he reappeared some time ago in Afghanistan."

"How did..."

"He said you were the only one he could trust with this information. He's a ghost but his security has been compromised. He needs your help."

Jenny's mind was spinning as she looked at the photo of Tom, a former RAF pilot who had been declared dead after his plane went down in Afghanistan. The one man she had truly loved. She had gone to his funeral, mourned his loss, and now, out of nowhere, he was back and needed her help. It was all too much to process.

"What kind of help does he need?" Jenny asked, her voice barely above a whisper.

Kaja hesitated for a moment before replying. "He's involved in something big and dangerous. He needs someone he can trust to help him get out of the country and disappear."

Jenny's heart sank. She had always harboured feelings for Tom, and the thought of him being in danger was almost too much to bear. But she also knew that she couldn't turn her back on him.

"I'll help him. But I need to tell Blake first. He's my brother, and he deserves to know what's going on," Jenny said firmly.

"No, Blake cannot know anything about this. We believe there is a mole in Special Branch. We are leading one of their operatives into a false lead at St Katherine's Docks tonight. Help us to make the deception real and we will reunite you with Tom. You have my word."

Jenny looked at Nicola and then back at Kaja. "And if I refuse?"

"Then you won't leave this room alive," Kaja snapped.

Jenny's heart raced faster, and she could feel the sweat on her palms. She knew she had to make a decision, and fast. "All right, I'll do it," she said, her voice barely above a whisper.

"Good," Kaja replied, his face softening. "We'll make sure you're safe, and we'll keep you in the loop every step of the way."

Jenny nodded, feeling a sense of dread wash over her. She knew that what she was getting into was dangerous, but she also knew that she had no choice. Tom needed her, and she couldn't turn her back on him.

At that moment, another Indian man opened the lounge door and stood in the doorway. Kaja nodded before following him outside.

A black Volvo Estate car was waiting for them as they left the house and headed back towards the docks. She looked at Nicola who's face showed no expression. She couldn't shake the feeling of unease that had settled in the pit of her stomach. She knew that things were only going to get worse from here on out, and she just hoped that she was strong enough to handle it.

***

As Andrew and Graham left the pub and headed back out into the night, Andrew couldn't shake the feeling of guilt that was gnawing at his conscience. He knew what they were doing was wrong, but he had already come too far to back out now. The thought of Blake uncovering the network of people that he and Derek had built around them and facing the consequences was too much to bear. Graham's involvement had complicated things and Andrew knew deep down, his feelings for Paula were still there. The thought of her being with Blake ripped him apart. He knew he needed to follow through on his plan to sidetrack Jenny but he saw genuine fear in Gabby's eyes earlier.

Back home in his two bedroom apartment in Tufnell Park, as the night drew on, Andrew's guilt grew stronger. He knew he had to find a way to warn Gabby about what was really going on before it was too late.

Graham was asleep in the armchair with the TV playing to itself as he slipped out into the next room and dialled Gabby's number, hoping she would answer. After a few rings, she picked up.

"Hello?"

"Gabby, it's Andrew. Listen, I need to talk to you about that note. It was a setup. They're trying to trap you."

"How did you get this number? What do you mean?" Gabby asked, her voice trembling.

"It's complicated, but just trust me. Don't go to the rabbit hole. It's a trap."

Gabby paused for a moment, considering his words. "Okay, I won't go. But who's behind this? Who's trying to trap me?"

Andrew hesitated, not wanting to reveal too much. "I can't say right now. But just be careful, okay? I'll try to find out more and let you know what comes up."

At that moment, Andrew felt something metallic hit him on the back of his head. He fell to the floor unconscious. The phone hit the floor shattering its glass screen.

"Hello? Hello? Andrew? Are you there?" Gabby called out.

She heard some heavy breathing on the line and then it cut off.

In the back corridors of Kings Cross University, Gabby stared motionless at the wall. She was about to give a speech in front of a room full of students and yet, she struggled to find the words to describe how she was feeling. How had Andrew been able to get her phone number? Why did he try to warn her? And who cut him off.

At that moment, Simon came rushing towards her. "I can't get hold of Blake but I've emailed Eric Gordon so I'm hoping he will get back to us soon. Oh my God, are you okay? You look like you've seen a ghost!"

Gabby explained about her conversation with Andrew.

"We need to cancel. We need to get you out of here," Simon insisted.

"Ah, there you are. You're on in five minutes!" Elliot Francis beamed as he approached them.

"I'm sorry Elliot but Gabby isn't feeling well. We'll have to postpone the talk..." Simon began.

"What..." Elliot gasped. "But..."

"No, no, I'll be fine," Gabby insisted.

"Gabby, you need some time..." Simon tried.

"No, I need to show them that they can't get to me."

"Who? What's she talking about?" Elliot asked.

"It's complicated," Simon replied.

"Is there anything I can do to help?"

"Yes, postpone the meeting."

"No, no, Si, let's just get it over and done with,"

Gabby replied, taking a couple of deep breaths to compose herself.

"If you're sure," Simon replied unconvincingly.

"I'm sure."

Elliot wandered out onto the stage in the University Hall and announced Gabby to the crowd. As she stepped out to a loud round of applause, Gabby's eyes were everywhere. Scanning every face in every row of the seats until she noticed Wendy,

Elliot's secretary in the fifth row and then two seats behind her was a young woman with shoulder length black hair wearing a white blouse and a black jacket. Gabby felt a shiver run down her spine as she looked closely at the woman, almost a double of her mother, Lana Turner.

Chapter Sixteen

St Katherine's Docks

Four cars followed nose to tail through the streets of London before arriving at St Katherine's Docks.

As they approached the docks, Samir's unease grew stronger. The ship they were looking for was large and ominous, with rusted metal and flickering lights. The Indian men parked the cars and stepped out, standing guard around the perimeter of the docks.

"You're not seriously going in there alone. It's suicide," Shaun advised.

Samir handed him a phone. "If I'm not out in thirty minutes, call 55582392 and give them our location."

"What will that do?"

"Alert Gordon that we're in the shit," Samir replied before stepping out of the car.

Reaper led the way up the ramp and onto the ship, with Xander and Zodiac following him. Samir followed closely behind, trying to keep his nerves in check. They entered a dimly lit cargo hold, filled with crates and boxes stacked haphazardly.

"Stay here," Reaper ordered, gesturing towards a corner of the room. "We'll come back for you once we've taken care of things."

Samir nodded, not wanting to provoke them any further. He watched as the three men disappeared through a doorway on the other side of the room.

Alone in the dark, Samir's thoughts raced. What had he gotten himself into? Was this truly the only way to find the killer?

He tried to calm himself down and focused on his breathing. Suddenly, he heard a soft shuffling sound behind him. He spun around, but there was no one there. He turned back to face the corner where he was standing, but he wasn't alone anymore. A woman with long blond hair was standing just a few feet away from him, her eyes fixed on him, her expression unreadable.

"Who are you?" Samir asked, his voice barely above a whisper.

The woman didn't reply. Instead, she slowly walked towards him, her eyes never leaving his. Samir clenched his fists, ready to defend himself if necessary.

But then the woman spoke. "You're not supposed to be here," she said in a soft, almost musical voice.

"I know," Samir replied. "But I have to find the killer."

The woman tilted her head to one side, studying him intently. "You're a brave man, Samir. But you're playing with fire."

"What do you mean?" Samir asked, his heart pounding in his chest.

"Let's just say that some things are better left alone. You should leave this investigation to the professionals," the woman replied cryptically.

Samir was confused. Who was this woman and why was she trying to warn him? Before he could ask any more questions, he heard the sound of footsteps approaching. Reaper, Xander, and Zodiac emerged from the doorway, their faces grim.

"We need to go. Now!" Reaper said, grabbing Samir by the arm and leading him towards the exit.

"What about the woman?" Samir asked.

"What woman? There's no one there!" Reaper snapped.

As they ran through the cargo hold, Samir caught a glimpse of the woman disappearing into the shadows. Was he going crazy? Was she a ghost? Was he the only one who could see her? Had the blast from before done something to his mind? Whatever it was, he had a feeling that he would never forget her face. When they were outside, the Indian men quickly got into their cars and sped away from the docks. Shaun leapt out of the car and stood at Samir's side.

Samir was shaking with adrenaline and fear, unsure of what had just happened. "What did you find?" he asked, his voice shaking.

Reaper turned to him, his face grim. "We found evidence that this ship is being used by a human trafficking ring. There were women locked up in a room, waiting to be shipped off to who knows where."

"Are they still onboard?" Shaun asked.

"No, their belongings are though."

"Someone knew we were coming," Samir replied.

"Indeed."

Samir felt sick to his stomach. He had stumbled into something much bigger than he had anticipated.

"We need to report this to the authorities," Shaun said firmly.

"No," Reaper replied, his eyes cold. "We handle things our own way. The authorities won't do anything. We have to take matters into our own hands."

Samir felt a chill run down his spine. He had just witnessed something that was beyond his understanding, and he wasn't sure he wanted to be involved any further. But he knew he had to see it through if he ever wanted to find out who was taking the missing students.

"Okay," he said, trying to sound braver than he felt. "What's next?"

Reaper looked at him for a long moment before nodding. "Next, we track down the men behind this operation. And we make them pay."

Samir nodded, steeling himself for whatever was to come. He had a feeling that this was only the beginning of a much larger and more dangerous investigation.

"We need to take care of a few things on our end but we'll be in touch," Samir replied.

Reaper nodded before joining Zodiac and Xander in the car and driving away.

"What now?" Shaun asked.

"Whatever he saw in there has him spooked. We need to get Tiffany to the safe house and then come back here alone."

"And do what?"

"I think those girls were taken off the ship and I have a feeling they're going to be brought back on too. If I'm right then I want to be here when they return. In the meantime... Oh shit!" Samir sighed.

Shaun looked around at the open rear door of their car. Tiffany had gone.

"So much for Scotland Yard efficiency," Samir cussed.

"I'm sorry, I thought..." Shaun replied before Samir waved him away.

"We'll deal with her later. I'll get a message to Blake to meet us at Kings Cross University. That seems to be a key starting point and then we'll come back when it's late."

As they drove away from the docks, Samir couldn't shake off the image of the woman with the long blond hair. Who was she and why was she warning him? He couldn't help but feel that there was more to this investigation than what he knew. He needed to do some digging of his own and see what he could find out. But for now, he had to focus on the task at hand.

As Shaun drove through the busy London streets, Samir fired up his laptop, scouring the internet for any information related to the human trafficking ring. He found some news articles about missing women and girls, but nothing that linked them to the ship at St Katherine's Docks. He was about to give up when he stumbled upon a forum where people were discussing the recent disappearances.

He scrolled through the posts, and one caught his eye. It was from a user named "Blondie." The post read;

"If you're looking into the missing students, be careful. There are some powerful people involved, and they won't hesitate to silence anyone who gets in their way."

Samir's heart skipped a beat. Could this have been the woman he had encountered on the ship? He quickly messaged "Blondie," asking for more information, but there was no response.

He leaned back in his seat, deep in thought. He knew he was treading dangerous waters, but he couldn't turn back now. He had to see this through to the end. As they pulled up to the university, Samir's phone buzzed with a message. It was from an unknown number, and the message read;

YOU'RE GETTING TOO CLOSE, BACK OFF!!

Samir's hands shook as he read the message. He knew he was being threatened, but he refused to let fear get the better of him. He was determined to bring those responsible to justice, no matter the cost. He took a deep breath and stepped out of the car, closely followed by Shaun, ready to face whatever lay ahead. As they approached the entrance, he noticed a poster advertising Gabby Turner's appearance this evening to give a literature talk and promote her new book.

"Now that's interesting," Samir said as they entered.

"Didn't know you were into romantic fiction," Shaun quipped.

"I'm not, but the Turner family have strong links to this area and to Blake. A bit coincidental that she's here tonight and our investigations have led us here too don't you think?"

"She's James Turner's sister..."

"The same James Turner who ran off with Blake's fiance and child nine years ago and created that shitstorm in the States when the Ricardo Fernandez case blew up," Samir confirmed.

As they walked through the halls of the university, Samir couldn't shake off the feeling that he was being watched. He scanned the faces of the students and professors, trying to figure out who, if any, could be involved in the human trafficking ring. But everyone seemed normal, and no one gave him a second glance. Something wasn't right, he could feel it.

***

Back in Kensington, Paula turned off the bedroom light as Michael rolled over in his bed to go to sleep. It had been a rollercoaster of emotions throughout the day and she couldn't shake the anger and distrust she now had for Blake watching over her. Frank finished tidying up the games console wires as Paula returned to the kitchen.

"Would you like a coffee?" she asked, as she filled the kettle with some fresh water.

"Yeah, yeah, okay, thanks," Frank replied as he joined her in the kitchen. "Are you okay? You seemed a bit worked up when we came back earlier."

Paula sighed. "I just don't trust Blake. He's been acting strange lately, and I can't help but feel like he's hiding something from us."

Frank raised an eyebrow. "What do you mean?"

"I don't know," Paula admitted. "It's just a feeling I have. Maybe it's nothing, but with everything that's been going on lately, I can't help but be suspicious."

Frank took a sip of his coffee, deep in thought. "You know, you're not the only one who feels that way."

"What do you mean?"

"Samir and Shaun have been investigating some things lately. They think something big is happening, but they haven't told us what it is yet."

Paula leaned against the counter, intrigued. "What kind of things?"

"Missing students, human trafficking, that kind of thing."

Paula's eyes widened. "That's terrible."

"Yeah, it is. And they think it's connected to some powerful people," Frank continued, "But they haven't found any concrete evidence yet. They're being cautious, but determined to find out the truth."

Paula nodded, her mind racing with possibilities. What if Andrew Broughton was involved. Blake seemed to think it was possible. She kept her thoughts to herself. "They can't seriously think Blake could be involved?"

Frank shrugged. "I don't know. But I think Samir and Shaun have their suspicions around members of Blake's side of the family. They're going to be meeting us later tonight to fill us in."

As they finished their coffee, Paula couldn't help but feel a sense of unease.

"Has Steven Langford been in touch?" Frank asked.

Paula looked at him. "Why do you ask?"

"Blake's brother, sometimes the waters can become muddy when family is involved. You of all people should recognise that."

"He was here earlier but then he left."

"Did he say where he was going?"

"No," Paula lied.

"You know you can talk to me if there's anything bothering you. I've known Blake a long time and I know he'll do whatever it takes to protect his family and get the job done."

"It's just difficult right now. Always having to look over our shoulders all the time in case someone comes after us."

"Hey, I'm not just here as a babysitter, if the shit hits the fan, I know which way is up."

"I know and I appreciate that," Paula sighed as her phone pinged into life.

She picked up the phone and looked at a text message.

"Shit, I have to nip out real quick, are you okay to..."

"Take all the time you need," Frank reassured her.

"I'll catch up on the football highlights."

Paula hugged him briefly. "Thank you, you're a lifesaver."

"That's what they pay me for," Frank smiled as Paula grabbed her coat and shoes and rushed out of the flat door.

After a few moments, Frank pulled out his phone and logged into a secure network. The crystal that Michael had been coding with him at the internet cafe earlier was beginning to take shape. He logged into the cell hacker dark web and typed in Paula's phone number. It came up with a message:

I NEED TO SEE YOU, SAME PLACE, 9.30pm, DAD.

Frank smiled and forwarded the message to Blake.

Chapter Seventeen

Claire Turner

Gabby's heart was beating faster than she could remember as she stood on the University Hall stage. The woman in the fifth row, who looked like her mother, was a chilling reminder of her traumatic past. She tried to focus on the crowd in front of her, but her eyes kept wandering back to the woman.

As she spoke about her literary journey and her latest book, Gabby couldn't shake the feeling of unease. When she finished her speech, she quickly exited the stage and made her way to the green room. Simon and Elliot were waiting for her, both looking concerned.

"Are you okay?" Simon asked, placing a hand on her shoulder.

Gabby nodded, trying to steady her breathing. "I'm fine. I just need a minute."

Elliot handed her a glass of water, and she took a sip, grateful for the cool liquid. But her mind was still racing with questions. Who was that woman in the audience? She looked oddly familiar. Was she a threat?

Simon and Elliot exchanged a worried look, sensing that Gabby wasn't telling them everything. They knew that she had a dark past, but she had always been hesitant to talk about it.

"Gabby, you can tell us anything," Elliot said softly, taking her hand.

Gabby took a deep breath, feeling tears prick at the corners of her eyes. "A woman in the audience... she reminded me of someone from my past. Someone who hurt me."

Simon and Elliot's expressions hardened. "Do you want us to find out who she is?" Simon asked.

Gabby hesitated for a moment. Was she overreacting? "Maybe," she said finally. "But not yet. Let's wait and see how the meet and greet goes."

"Surely, you're not going out there. You need to take a break," Simon protested.

"It's just signing a few books, nothing too taxing," Elliot reasoned.

Simon glared at him.

"Elliot's right, I'm being silly, let's go," Gabby replied, as she headed out towards the main hall where hundreds of people were awaiting her.

As Gabby made her way through the crowd towards the signing table, she tried to push the thoughts of the woman from her mind. She smiled and chatted with the fans, signing copies of her latest book and taking photos with them. But as the line began to dwindle, Gabby's eyes suddenly locked with a pair of icy blue ones that sent a shiver down her spine. It was the woman from the audience, standing at the front of the line with a menacing expression on her face.

Gabby's heart began to race as she saw the woman pull something out of her pocket. She couldn't see what it was, but she knew she had to act fast. Without thinking, Gabby grabbed the closest object, a heavy glass paperweight, and hurled it towards the woman.

The woman ducked down just in time as the glass paperweight hit the wall and shattered into pieces. The remaining crowd erupted into screams and chaos as Gabby realised what she had done.

"Oh my God, I'm so sorry... I don't know what came over me..." Gabby began.

"It's okay, I would have probably done the same if my sister turned up uninvited," the woman replied as she placed a photo on the table in front of Gabby.

Gabby studied her open mouthed. She couldn't believe what she was hearing. She picked up the photo and studied it closely. The ensuing chaos of the last few minutes seemed to disappear into background noise as she looked at the photograph of her mother, Lana Turner, her old neighbour, Margaret Petersen and a third older woman that she didn't recognise.

"It's the only photo I have of my birth mother. I was looked after by Margaret Petersen and her husband whilst I was a baby and then, after Margaret died, I was looked after by the lady on the right there, Edith Harrow. My name is Claire Amy Turner. I took my mother's name as my father was not involved in my life until my teenage years when Edith could no longer look after me," she explained.

"CAT, the initials on the flowers," Gabby whispered to herself.

Claire nodded, her eyes filled with tears. "Yes, I've been trying to find you for years. I've read all your books; I knew you had to be my sister. I just didn't know how to approach you."

Gabby was too stunned to speak. She had always suspected that her mother had hidden her pregnancy before she died, but she never expected the truth to happen like this. She looked at Claire's face, seeing the resemblance to her mother and feeling a surge of emotion she couldn't explain.

"I need to sit down," Gabby said, her legs feeling weak.

Claire helped her to a nearby chair, and they sat down together, holding hands. Simon and Elliot came over, looking bewildered at the sudden turn of events.

"What the hell just happened?" Simon asked, his eyes wide.

"I think I just met my sister," Gabby said, her voice barely above a whisper.

Elliot's mouth dropped open. "What? How is that even possible?"

"I'd always suspected that Mum went away for a while and when she came home again, she had lost weight but being a naive teenager at the time, I never put the pieces together. So, your father is..." Gabby's smile dropped as she realised the truth. "No, no, not him!"

Gabby stood up and moved away.

"Gabby, what's wrong?" Claire asked.

"I have to go!" Gabby replied as she ran towards the door leading back towards the hall.

Simon held her at the door. "Gabby, what's wrong? You're acting irrationally."

"Tell them!" Gabby demanded as she turned to face Claire. "Tell them who your father is!"

"Derek Copsewood," Blake Langford announced.

Everyone turned to face Blake as he wandered over towards them with Alison, Samir and Shaun following closely behind.

"Blake, what the hell is going on?" Gabby asked.

"Derek's daughter has been doing a bit of her father's dirty work for him leading us on a wild goose chase around London. Where is he?" Blake asked.

"I don't know what you're talking about!" Claire stammered. "What's my Dad ever done to you? He runs a pub in the square for Christ's sake!"

"Okay folks, show's over, let's give them some space," Samir called out as he ushered the remaining crowd out of the University Hall.

"Samir!" Shaun shouted as Claire ran for the exit.

Samir dived but couldn't stop her. Shaun and Alison gave chase as Simon, Elliot, Blake and Samir retreated to the corridors behind the main hall. Gabby led them to the green room where two tables with chairs were laid out with drinks and nibbles.

"Firstly, who the hell are you and what just happened out there?" Elliot demanded.

"He's a friend," Gabby replied.

"What friend would come along and destroy a publicity tour in front of some of the most influential people you're going to meet on this tour? This whole shitshow is going to be all over social media and Scatterbird Publishers are going to be a laughing stock!"

Blake walked towards Elliot who backed away towards the door. "You're right, a friend would take his friend out of the clutches of vultures like you who manipulate Fleet Street news for his own benefit. Normally I'd lay you out cold but you have an important PR mess to sort out so why don't you run along and do that before I pin your ass to the wall!"

Elliot nodded before quickly leaving the room.

"Nice to see you haven't lost your touch for diplomacy," Gabby remarked.

"What the hell just happened out there?" Simon asked.

"Who are you?" Samir asked.

"Simon Buxton, CIA. Who are you?"

"Samir Khalifa, he's Special Branch with me," Blake replied. "Look, Gabby, Samir uncovered a human trafficking ring within the student community. There was evidence of the victims being kept on a ship in St Katherine's Docks. We believe there is a connection to Derek Copsewood. He's already taken aim at my brother and I'm assuming that little stunt with his daughter was to try and bring you into it."

"But I don't know anything," Gabby pleaded.

"Have you raked up anything from the past since you've been here?"

Simon handed Blake the note that Andrew had given Gabby earlier that day. "We also visited her mother's grave and her old family home."

"The Rabbit Hole, not the same..." Blake began.

"Yeah, the one we used to go down when we were kids."

"Is it still there?"

"I don't know," Gabby sighed as she explained the weird phone call she received from someone called Andrew earlier.

Blake pulled out his phone and found a photo of Andrew Broughton from his social media page. "Is that him?"

"Yeah, how did..."

"Simon, you both need to go back to your hotel and wait there for me. Don't talk to anyone, don't meet with anyone, wait for my call, okay?" Blake demanded.

Gabby and Simon nodded. Simon had worked alongside Blake on a case in Miami and knew that he could be trusted. As they left the room, Gabby couldn't help but feel a sense of unease hanging over her. The revelation of having a sister had been overwhelming, but the realisation and the implications about her mother's involvement with Derek Copsewood and the potential danger it posed to her and those around her was too much to bear.

As they walked towards their hotel, Gabby couldn't shake the feeling that they were being followed. She turned around, but saw no one. Simon noticed her unease and placed his hand on her shoulder.

"Are you okay?" he asked.

"I don't know. I feel like someone's watching us," Gabby replied.

Simon looked around cautiously, but saw nothing out of the ordinary. "Let's hurry up and get to the hotel then."

***

"Stop! Police!" Shaun Bryant shouted as he chased Claire Turner into Kings Cross tube station closely followed by Alison Pearce.

Claire pushed her way through the crowds receiving some shouting, swearing and pushing aimed at her along the way. She ran through an open turnstile as a ticket officer shouted after her. Shaun and Alison followed as she sprinted down the escalators that led down to the train lines below. As they arrived at the bottom of the escalators, they had three options.

"Which way?" Shaun asked.

"I'll take the Piccadilly Line, you take the Circle!" Alison shouted as she sprinted down one of the corridors.

Shaun pushed his way through the crowds as he tried in vain to catch up with Claire. He arrived on the platforms but she was nowhere to be seen. He felt the cool breeze of a train approaching as he turned back towards the stairs. At that moment, he heard a mixture of screams and panic coming from the platform. He turned around and saw the body of a young woman pressed against the driver's cab at the front of the train. As the train stopped, the driver jumped out of his cab.

"Oh my God! I didn't see her, I swear!" he gasped.

Shaun Bryant rushed over. "Step aside please, I'm a police sergeant!"

The crowd began pulling their phones out to take photos but a man in a suit began ushering them away. Shaun looked down at the bloody mess as the body slumped down onto the tracks. He pulled his phone out and turned on the light.

"Shit! No! Call the police now!" Shaun shouted.

Shaun looked down on the partially amputated body of Tiffany Mason. He felt sick to his stomach as he tried to process what had just happened. This wasn't the first time he had seen a body on the tracks, but it never got any easier.

As he waited for backup to arrive, he couldn't help but think about Claire. Had she witnessed what had just happened? Was she involved somehow? He needed to find her and get to the bottom of this.

Alison arrived on the platform, out of breath and panting. "Did you find her?"

"No, but we have a bigger problem. Tiffany Mason's body is on the tracks," Shaun replied, gesturing towards the gruesome scene.

Alison's face went pale. "Oh my God, I'll call it into SB. We need to find Claire and figure out what the hell is going on."

Shaun nodded in agreement and they quickly set off to search for Claire. They searched every platform and train carriage, but she was nowhere to be found. As they made their way back towards the exit, Shaun's phone rang. It was Blake.

"Shaun, I need you and Alison to get to the hotel where Gabby and Simon are staying. Samir will ping you the address. I'll fill you in on the way," Blake said urgently.

"What's going on? Is Gabby okay?" Shaun asked.

"I'll explain on the way, just get there as fast as you can," Blake replied before hanging up.

Shaun and Alison rushed out of the station and hailed a taxi. As they sped towards the hotel, Blake filled them in on everything that had happened so far.

"We need your help to keep Gabby and Simon safe. Derek Copsewood is involved in human trafficking and we believe Gabby's mother was connected to him. We think her sister, Claire, might be in danger too," Blake explained.

"What about Tiffany Mason's body on the tracks?" Alison asked.

"That's a separate case, but we suspect it might be related. I need you two to keep your eyes peeled for anything suspicious. Copsewood is well connected and he won't hesitate to hurt anyone who gets in his way," Blake warned.

As they arrived at the hotel, Blake filled them in on the details of the plan. Gabby and Simon would be taken to a safe location while they hunted down Claire and tried to uncover the truth about Copsewood's operation.

Shaun and Alison entered the lobby of the hotel and quickly spotted Gabby and Simon sitting in the corner. They rushed over to them and instructed them to follow them out to the waiting car. As they stepped outside, they were immediately ambushed by a group of men in suits.

"Gabrielle Turner, we need to talk," one of them said, holding out a hand to stop them.

"Who the hell are you?" Shaun demanded.

"We're with the Home Office. We've been tracking Gabby's movements ever since she arrived in London," the man replied.

"Well, you're not taking her anywhere. She's under our protection," Alison said firmly.

"Listen, we don't have time for this. Gabby, we need you to come with us. It's a matter of national security," the man said, grabbing Gabby's arm.

Before anyone could react, Simon stepped forward and punched the man in the face. The other men quickly moved to restrain Simon, but he fought back with surprising ferocity. Shaun and Alison stepped in to help, exchanging blows with the men.

In the chaos, Gabby managed to break free and run towards the waiting car. The men quickly gave chase, but Shaun and

Alison managed to hold them off. They quickly got into the car and sped off into the night. As they drove towards the safe location, Gabby couldn't help but feel a sense of relief. She wasn't going insane. There really was a sinister underworld that her family was involved in but she knew she had to trust Blake. He may be a loose cannon, but she knew he was her best chance of getting out of this alive.

Chapter Eighteen

A Daughter's Love

Paula Evans stepped off of the train at Waterloo Station. She climbed the stairs and escalators up the main railway station level. Announcements echoed around the station about the Circle Line being closed immediately but the words faded into the background as she noticed her father, Graham Evans, standing outside the coffee shop nearby wearing a long dark green trench coat with a black rucksack swung over his right shoulder.

"Paula, there you are," Graham said with relief as he hugged his daughter.

"What's going on, Dad? Why did you call me here?" Paula asked, sensing the urgency in her father's voice.

"I've landed myself into a spot of bother. I have a friend who is willing to let me board his cargo ship at midnight tomorrow night. He's sailing away to Phuket for six months. Said it would be an ideal opportunity for me to see more of the world."

"So, what's the spot of bother?"

"I need three thousand pounds to pay for my share."

"And you thought I would give it to you?"

"You sold my home, where else am I meant to go?" Graham asked.

Paula sighed. She knew her father had always been unpredictable, but this was a new low even for him.

"Dad, I can't just give you that kind of money. I have bills to pay and a life to live," Paula said, trying to reason with him.

"You'll get it back, I promise. It's just a loan," Graham pleaded.

"I don't even know if I can get that kind of money in such short notice," Paula replied, feeling frustrated.

Graham's face fell. "Please, Paula. I need this. I promise I'll make it up to you."

Paula hesitated for a moment before making a decision. She knew that giving her father the money was a risk, but she also couldn't abandon him in his time of need. "Why do you always pull at the heartstrings?"

"Please, Paula. I don't have anyone else to turn to. If I don't get out of here, I'll be in serious danger," Graham pleaded.

"What kind of danger?"

Graham hesitated before answering. "Old grudges that I thought were dead and buried seem to have come out of the woodwork again."

"That's pretty vague. Anything specific?"

"The less you know about it, the better it is. I'm taking a risk even coming here to talk to you. If they think you're involved then there's no telling if they'll come after you too."

"Who? Debt collectors? Drug dealers? Who is coming after me and my family?"

"Please, Paula. Trust me, the more you know, the more dangerous this whole situation will become. I've already lost one daughter, please don't let me lose another..."

Paula sighed. "Okay, I'll see what I can do. But this is the last time, Dad. You need to start taking responsibility for yourself!"

Graham smiled and hugged her. "There's a twenty-four hour bank just around the corner. Can we go and get the money now?"

As they walked towards the bank, Paula couldn't shake the feeling of unease. She had always known her father could be reckless, but she never imagined he would be involved in something dangerous. She wondered if this was the kind of danger that could follow her too. She cursed herself for being so reckless. Blake's job had already put them both in difficult situations and now she felt like she was walking straight into another one.

When they arrived at the bank, Paula withdrew the money from her account and handed it over to her father. He promised to pay her back as soon as he could and hugged her tightly before disappearing into the night.

Paula began to make her way back towards Waterloo Station, feeling angry and frustrated with her father. As she walked, she noticed a dark figure lurking in the shadows. She quickened her pace, feeling a knot of fear in her stomach. Suddenly, she was grabbed from behind and pulled into an alleyway. She screamed, but a hand covered her mouth and a voice whispered in her ear.

"Shh, Paula, it's me. Andy," the voice said.

Paula tensed up as she heard his voice for the first time in eight years. He released her.

"What the hell do you want?" Paula snapped.

In the moonlight, she noticed dried blood in his hair towards the back of his head. "What happened to you?" she asked.

"Your father knocked me unconscious before leaving my flat and coming to meet you. He's involved with some powerful people. Drug runners, human traffickers, they're part of a huge operation that is kidnapping students around the capital."

"Whoa, hang on a minute, he was at your flat? How did he find you? What were you doing letting him in?"

"He turned up outside my pub in Harlequin Square. He was all dishevelled, looked like he'd been sleeping rough for a while and fed me a sob story about being on the run since..."

"Since Mum died and Rachael disappeared leaving us to pick up the broken crockery. Why should I trust you? How did you know I was here?"

"When Graham arrived, he came to my place to stay for a few days. Whilst he was in the shower, I placed a homing device inside the heel of his shoe," Andrew explained.

"Wait, how did you get hold of a homing device?"

"Blake's not the only one with access to toys."

"Leave Blake out of this. This is between you, me and my father!"

"How much did you give him?"

"What?"

"I saw you at the bank, how much did you give him?"

"Three thousand pounds."

"Shit, Paula, why?"

"Because I'm gullible all right! Love hurts and I'm easily manipulated as you of all people should know!" Paula snapped.

Andrew placed a hand on her shoulder. "Look, I'm sorry. I didn't mean to snap at you. I'm just worried about you. You need to stay away from your father. He's not who you think he is. He's dangerous."

"And you're my knight in shining armour coming to save the day? It wasn't long ago that you were blacking my eyes after one of your drunken binges. How the hell can I trust you?"

"Do you think you can trust anyone? Me? Blake? Did you know he was watching you and Graham at the station during your first meeting?"

Paula glared at him. She knew that Blake had Andy under suspicion as part of his investigation but she kept it to herself. "You were there too?"

"I didn't trust Graham's motives so I offered to meet him after and stayed in the shadows until you were done and then we took a cab back to the pub. You can't trust your father Paula!"

"I know that now," Paula said, tears streaming down her face. "But what can I do? I can't just leave him with half of London after him."

"Yes, you can. You need to cut ties with him before it's too late. These people he's involved with, they won't hesitate to hurt you if they think you're a threat."

Paula wiped her tears away and took a deep breath. "You're right. I need to get away from him. But I don't know how."

"You need Blake to take you out of the firing line until all of this dies down."

"Why are you doing this for me? You could have just left me out there to potentially get killed."

"Because sometimes, you don't realise what you had until you lose it."

Paula looked into his teary eyes. "You mean that?"

Andrew nodded. "I do. I never meant to hurt you, Paula. I was out of control. I screwed up. I know it. I've replayed scenarios time and time again and I know it's going to take a lot for you to trust me again, but I'm willing to do whatever it takes to prove to you that I've changed."

Paula felt her heart racing. She wasn't sure if she was ready to forgive Andy, but she knew that he was the only one who could help her now that her father had dragged her into his mess.

"Okay," she said finally. "What do we do now?"

"We need to get you out of here first. Come on."

Andy took her by the hand and led her out of the alleyway, scanning the streets for any signs of danger. When they reached his car, he opened the passenger door for Paula and got in on the driver's side.

"Where are we going?" Paula asked.

"To my place. You can stay with me until we figure out what to do next."

Paula hesitated. "Won't that be the first place Dad will go back to?"

"He left me there unconscious, my guess is he'll avoid it in case I get the authorities after him."

"I have to get Michael!"

"Michael?"

"My son, I mean nephew. Blake's son. He's at Blake's flat!"

"Alone? You left a child alone?"

"No, a friend is looking after him."

"Did you say how long you'd be gone?"

"Not specifically but he'll get suspicious if I don't return soon."

"Okay, where is that?"

"Portman Terrace, Kensington."

As Andrew drove away into the night, Graham stepped out from a nearby alleyway. His phone showed Andrew's car snaking through the London streets. He pulled a new pair of shoes and half a bottle of vodka out of his rucksack. He threw his old shoes into a metal dumpster and replaced them with the new ones before pouring the remaining contents of the vodka bottle over the old shoes in the dumpster. He flicked a match and set the shoes and the contents of the bin on fire.

At that moment, a black taxi cab pulled up at the end of the alleyway.

Graham stepped inside and sat in the front seat. "You took your time, Vijay."

Vijay rejoined a steady flow of traffic heading towards Kensington.

"Is it done?"

Graham waved a wad of twenty pound notes into the air. "Like candy from a baby."

Vijay smiled. "Where are we heading?"

"Eel Brook Common."

***

Blake and Samir sped through the streets of London on their way to the safe houses out near Enfield Island Village.

"This is getting way out of hand, Blake. How many more dead girls are we gonna rack up before we pin these bastards down?" Samir asked.

"I don't know. But we're doing everything we can to stop them," Blake replied, his eyes focused on the road.

"I just don't want to lose any more of our own in the process," Samir snapped.

"I know, Samir. None of us do. But we have to keep going. Keep fighting until we bring these guys down,"

As they approached the safe house, Blake's phone illuminated in the holder.

"Can you read it?" Blake asked.

Samir read the messages, his face falling as he took in the information.

"What is it?" Blake asked, concern etched on his face.

"It's Paula. She's in trouble. Frank pinged you a message on the secure server that Paula exchanged with her father. The second message is Paula saying her father has gotten her involved in something and now she's in danger," Samir said, his voice urgent.

Blake pulled the handbrake and performed a complete one-hundred-and-eighty degree turn in the middle of the road to a chorus of car horns and shouting coming from the cars around them.

"Shit, man, what are you doing?" Samir gasped.

"Where is she? Get me the GPS on her phone."

"No need, she said in the message that she's heading back to your flat with Andy."

Blake's grip tightened on the steering wheel as he floored the accelerator and sped in and out of cars as he raced across London towards Kensington.

Chapter Nineteen

Jenny's Secret

Reaper returned to the docks and found Kaja, Raj, Jenny Langford and Nicola Pew waiting for him near the terminal entrance. As the car stopped alongside them, the passenger window opened.

"Get in," Reaper demanded.

Raj got into the front seat with Kaja taking a seat in the back next to the two women. They exchanged quick nods before returning to their silence as Reaper drove off towards the city.

"What's the situation?" Kaja asked, trying to keep his voice calm.

"The usual. The cops are getting closer to our operations. We need to reinforce security and make sure we're not leaving any loose ends," Reaper replied, his eyes focused on the road.

"And what about the girls?" Raj asked.

"They're safe. They're being taken care of."

Kaja felt relieved at hearing this. He knew that Reaper and his men would ensure the safety of the girls under their care, but the thought of them being caught by the authorities still lingered in the back of his mind.

As they approached Camden, Reaper pulled over to the side of the road, parking the car in a deserted alleyway.

He turned to face Jenny, his gaze intense. "Did Samir take the bait?"

"Completely, now when do I see Tom?" Jenny replied.

Reaper leaned in closer to Jenny, his eyes piercing. "You'll see him when we're ready, not before. And don't forget what's at stake here. You mess this up and you'll regret it."

Jenny met his gaze with a steely determination. "I won't mess it up. I know what's at stake."

Reaper nodded, satisfied with her answer before gesturing for them to follow him out of the car. "Let's go. We have work to do."

As they stepped out of the car, Kaja noticed the distinct smell of petrol in the air. He glanced around, trying to locate the source of the smell. That's when he noticed the flames in the distance - a building was on fire.

"What the hell is going on over there?" Kaja asked, pointing towards the flames.

Reaper turned to look in the direction Kaja was pointing. "Shit, that's the holding facility. Let's go check it out."

They rushed towards the burning building, navigating through the crowded streets of Camden. As they got closer, they could see that it was an apartment building.

"We have to do something," Kaja said.

Reaper nodded in agreement. "Raj, take Jenny and Nic, get the car. We'll see if we can help anyone inside."

Raj nodded before rushing off with Jenny and Nicola in tow. Reaper and Kaja made their way towards the burning building, trying to force their way inside despite the heat and smoke. They managed to get through a door and were immediately met with flames and debris falling from above.

"We need to find anyone who might be trapped," Kaja said as he tried to shield his face from the heat.

Reaper nodded before they split up, each searching through the building for any survivors. Kaja approached a door and could hear someone coughing inside. He kicked the door down and found a young woman lying on the ground, her face covered in soot.

"Come on, we need to get you out of here," Kaja said as he helped her up.

Reaper found a man trying to climb out of a window, his shirt burning from the fire. He rushed over and grabbed the man, pulling him out to safety. The group managed to save a few more people before the fire department arrived to put out the flames. As the smoke cleared, they could see the charred remains of the building and the devastation that the fire had left behind.

"This could completely blow the entire operation. The whole movement was meant to be conducted discreetly!" Kaja snapped.

Reaper nodded. "Don't worry, they know they'll be dead if they talk. We need to find Vijay. That son-of-a-bitch has a lot to answer for."

"What about Xander and Zodiac?"

"They're on the move. Zodiac is chasing up a lead that he found in Enfield Island Village."

"What about Jenny and Nic?"

"They'll become useful later, let's go. We've got a few loose ends to tie up."

As they returned to the alleyway where the car was parked, there was no sign of Raj, Jenny or Nicola and the car had gone.

Kaja swore under his breath before calling Nicola's mobile.

"Hello Kaja," Derek Copsewood answered. "Looking for someone?"

"Where are they?" Kaja asked.

"Soon, they'll be everywhere unless my ship sails out of the docks unhindered tomorrow night with all of its necessary cargo restored. You have twenty-four hours or the bitch gets it!"

Derek cut off the call. Reaper looked at Kaja for answers.

"Copsewood's got them," Kaja said as he ran his fingers through his hair.

"Shit, now what?"

"You need to call Zodiac."

Meanwhile, Derek parked up behind The Troubled Traveller pub on Harlequin Square. The last few stragglers were leaving from the front entrance and the backyard was illuminated by a full moon. Derek stepped out of the car holding a gun in his hand. Raj followed suit as he opened the back door and beckoned the two women to step out. As they approached the back of the pub, Richard Parsons stepped out of the back door. He moved one of the dumpsters to block the rear exit before opening the trapdoor that led down to the cellar below.

Jenny and Nicola looked at Derek. "You're no private investigator," Jenny cussed.

"And you're not the kind of girl to turn the other cheek, Miss Langford. We all have our secrets. Yours just haven't come out into the open yet. Move!" Derek demanded as he ushered them towards the trapdoor.

A wooden ladder that had seen better days, led down into a dark concrete cellar below.

"Are you sure about this?" Richard asked.

"It's a temporary arrangement Dickie and you will be compensated," Derek replied.

As the two women entered the cellar, the trapdoor closed sending a plume of dust into the air as Jenny and Nicola reached the bottom. In the darkness, Nicola could just about see the outline of Jenny's face and her long blonde hair.

"Okay, you need to tell me what this is all about. What is this secret? What hold have they got over you?" Nicola asked.

"You're the one with the crazy boyfriend who led us into this mess in the first place!" Jenny snapped back.

"Kaja said he needed a blonde woman to help him get some agents off his back. He's been dabbling in some small-time smuggling and I thought that maybe we could help him. You know, just a one off."

"But it wasn't, was it?"

"I don't blame you for not trusting me Jen. I wouldn't trust me either. But I need to know what we're getting ourselves into. Who is Tom? What hold do they have on you?"

Jenny sighed deeply. "Tom was the only man I ever loved. He was my first, you know. Anyway, he got himself involved in something heavy and asked me to go to Salisbury to meet a man who was connected to the operation he and his team were involved in during their tour of Afghanistan. I remember it like it was yesterday. He was an older man, overweight, bald with grey hair at the sides and had some kind of mole on the right side of his neck. His name was Ivan Stepanchikov. I handed him a Manila envelope and then left. Twenty-four hours later, Tom and his entire team were wiped out near Qala-e-Naw. I was told that his plane was shot down and he died. I went to his funeral with his family. I grieved his loss and I closed myself off from love. The pain of losing someone you love with all of your heart. With all the intensity that comes with it. I just couldn't go through it again."

"And then Kaja shows you that photo," Nicola replied.

"Yeah. My whole love for Tom and the grieving process of the past ten years have been a lie. I need to find closure. I need to ask him why? Most of all, I need to find out if he ever truly loved me at all or was it just a game to him?"

Nicola didn't reply.

"What about you? How long have you and Kaja been..."

"A few months. Andrea met him at The Troubled Traveller and she invited me to join them when they had a lock in one night. Things just kind of led on from there but I never expected him to be involved in something like this."

"I guess we never truly know anyone anymore."

"What about The Rabbit Hole? If you don't turn up..."

"With us being stuck in here, I don't really have a choice do I? If the truth about my involvement in Tom's, I guess you could call it defection comes out, then I'm as good as dead anyway."

"Surely Blake can do something."

"Blake can do a lot of things but I doubt he'll be able to stop this train wreck."

The two women sat in silence as they heard the car engine start once again before fading away into the distance. Jenny let her mind wander back to her Mum, Emily, laying in the hospital alone. She was so hell bent on protecting her own image that she had abandoned the one person who had never abandoned her. She felt ashamed. Disgusted with herself that she could have been so shallow. She needed to find a way out and it seemed like this time, she had to do it without Blake's help.

Meanwhile upstairs in the pub, Andrea was busy wiping over the tables before placing the stools up on top of them ready for the cleaner to hoover the floor in the morning. Richard Parsons wandered in through the front door before locking the door behind him.

"That's the last few gone, I'm just going to cash up the till," he said as he wandered over towards the bar.

"Have you heard from Andy this evening?" Andrea asked.

"Not since he left with that old hobo earlier. Honestly, he'll fall for anybody's sob story these days. He's going soft!" Richard replied, counting the notes in the till.

"It doesn't mean you're soft if you try to help someone in need."

"Since when did you get all philosophical?"

"I just don't trust that Graham guy. Apparently he's the father of Andy's ex-girlfriend from a few years ago.

That caught Richard's attention. "Did he tell you that?"

"Kind of. I think he still has feelings for his ex and he sees this as an opportunity to get her back."

"By helping her Dad out of a tough spot? Come on, Andrea, if the old man is in that much trouble, there's obviously no love lost there. The guy probably abandoned the family in search of an affair and it bit him on the ass and now he's come back with his tail between his legs begging for forgiveness."

"I've never known you to be so judgemental Dickie," Andrea replied.

"When you work around students for so long, most of them with parent baggage, they're always trying to escape home life with no direction or idea where their degree is taking them. The vast majority end up flipping burgers or delivering pizza like the rest of us! A group of nobody's and a lost generation of potential entrepreneurs who end up being a burden on society."

"Like Victoria Dawson?"

Richard slammed the till drawer shut. "What about Victoria?"

"Well she came here from the States, started her studies, worked a few shifts here and then disappeared. She had dreams of being a lawyer but within weeks of starting, she stopped attending lectures and Nic saw her leaving Andy's place the morning she disappeared."

Richard walked over towards her. "Be careful who you pass judgement on. There's a lot more to some stories than you think!"

Andrea was taken aback by Richard's sudden change of tone, but she couldn't deny that there was truth in his words. She had jumped to conclusions about Graham and his motives, just like she had done with Victoria. She had never known the full story behind Victoria's disappearance, but now she couldn't help but wonder.

"I'm sorry, Dickie," she said, placing a hand on his arm. "You're right. I shouldn't judge people without knowing their whole story."

Richard softened slightly and gave her a small smile. "It's okay. We all make mistakes."

The two of them fell into a comfortable silence as they finished closing up the pub.

As they walked out into the cool night air, Richard turned to Andrea. "You know, I was thinking. We haven't had a staff night out in ages. How about we organise something with Andy and Steven for next weekend?"

Andrea smiled. "I would love that."

"Do you need a lift home?"

"No thanks, I'm going to get some food at the kebab house so I'll catch the late bus. Thanks anyway."

"No problem, see you tomorrow."

Andrea headed down the road towards the kebab house, occasionally turning around to check that Richard had headed towards the car park. When she was sure he was gone, she looped around and headed back towards the pub. She had heard voices and the dumpster being moved as she was clearing the last few glasses from tables inside the pub and she was sure that Richard was hiding something. His reaction to her mention of Victoria's name had just increased her suspicion even more. She wandered around the side of the pub and saw the dumpster blocking the rear entrance with a piece of wood wedged between the door handles of the trapdoor that led down to the basement. She pulled the piece of wood out of the door handles before pulling her keys out of her pocket and unlocking the trapdoor. The smell of stagnant alcohol attacked her senses as she opened the door.

"Andrea?" Nicola called out.

"Nic? What the hell..."

Nicola and Jenny rushed back up out of the cellar before Andrea closed the trapdoor once again.

"How did you end up down there?" Andrea asked.

"Your boss is working with someone called Derek. He's involved in something big, something dangerous," Jenny said, her voice trembling with fear.

"What kind of danger?"

"We don't know yet," Nicola replied. "But we overheard them talking about getting rid of someone who knows too much."

Andrea's heart started racing. "Who? Who do they want to get rid of?"

"We don't know," Jenny said again. "But we think it might be Tom.

Andrea felt a lump form in her throat. Tom, the man she had been seeing for the past few months. What did he have to do with any of this?

"We have to warn him," Andrea said, her voice shaking. "We have to tell him what's going on."

"Wait, hang on a minute, you know where Tom is?" Jenny asked.

"Sorry, who are you?" Andrea asked.

"This is my friend, Jenny, that I told you about. The one who's brother is in Special Branch," Nicola replied.

"Jenny Langford?" Andrea questioned.

"Yes, you must be Nicola's housemate Andrea."

Andrea nodded. A thousand thoughts ran through her mind. She knew that Tom had been involved in operations that were considered less than ethical and Jenny's name had cropped up before. Things were becoming way too complicated and she knew she had to tread carefully.

"How are we going to find Tom?" Nicola asked. "Do you know where he is?"

Andrea bit her lip, trying to think. "I have an idea. But we're going to need Richard's help."

"The same Richard who helped put us in that cellar?" Jenny questioned.

"He doesn't need to know that you're out. He's been arranging for Freshers students to link up with Raj and Karun. They work for Zodiac and he gets them into exclusive clubs as well as less ethical situations."

"Drugs you mean," Nicola replied.

"If I can convince him that I have found two more students willing to go to the party, I might be able to pinpoint where Zodiac will turn up next and in turn, that should lead us to Tom."

Jenny and Nicola exchanged a worried glance, but Andrea was already heading back down the alleyway towards the front entrance of the pub. She knew it was risky to involve Richard, especially after their conversation about Victoria, but she couldn't think of anyone else to turn to. She pulled out her phone and called him, hoping he would answer.

"Hey, what's up?" Richard answered after a few rings.

"Dickie, I need your help. It's urgent," Andrea replied.

"What's going on?"

"I can't explain over the phone, but we need to find Tom. He might be in danger."

"Okay, I'm on my way. Where are you?"

"Meet me outside Kings Cross University. Hurry."

Andrea hung up before Richard could ask any more questions. She turned to Jenny and Nicola. "Is there anywhere that you two can go where they won't find you?"

"I know a place," Jenny replied.

"Go, I'll call Nic when I've sorted things out with Dickie," Andrea replied.

"Kaja took our phones," Nicola replied.

Andrea pulled an old receipt out of her pocket and jotted down her phone number. "Give me three hours and then call me on this number."

Nicola and Jenny rushed away towards the nearest tube station.

"Where are we going?" Nicola asked.

"My parent's house," Jenny replied.

Chapter Twenty

A Warning

Blake's heart was pounding in his chest as he raced towards his flat in Kensington. Paula was in danger, and he knew he had to get to her before it was too late.

Samir sat beside him, his eyes fixed on the road ahead, scanning for any sign of Paula or Andrew Broughton.

"Are we almost there?" Samir asked.

Blake nodded, his jaw clenched. He could feel his adrenaline surging as he prepared himself for what lay ahead. A message alert from his phone cut into the silence.

"It's from Gordon," Samir said as he opened the attachment.

As he scrolled through it, it showed a tall dark haired man push a woman in front of an oncoming underground train. The graphic detail shown from CCTV pictures made Samir wince.

"Positive ID's made, Tiffany Jane Mason and Andrew Frederick Broughton. APB placed for Broughton's arrest, use all force necessary," Eric Gordon's voice echoed around the car.

"So they were connected. Tiffany, Steven and now Broughton," Samir acknowledged.

"I didn't want to believe that that scumbag was back on the scene but it's now become blatantly obvious that I overlooked some important details last time our paths crossed," Blake replied. "I just hope we're not too late."

As they pulled up in the courtyard outside Blake's flat in Portman Terrace, Blake saw a black Land Rover parked outside. Frank was here. That gave him some renewed hope. As he scanned the cars, he noticed a new green Vauxhall Cavalier that wasn't usually there. "Green Cavalier, I'm sure that's them," he said, his voice barely above a whisper.

Samir reached for his gun, readying himself for a fight. Blake nodded, knowing he had to act fast. He got out of the car and rushed up the concrete stairs towards the flat, his eyes fixed on the Cavalier as Samir followed close behind.

As they arrived at the front door, Blake noticed that the door was already open ajar. He pulled his gun and carefully opened the door before stepping inside. The whole flat was silent as he moved from the hall into the kitchen and then into the lounge. As Blake entered the lounge, he heard a groan and turned around to find Frank laid out on the floor with blood coming from the back of his head.

"Frank, what happened?" Blake asked, as he crouched down and helped his friend up into a seated position.

"Paula came home with some dude and said that they had to get away. Something to do with her father and when I advised that they wait for you, the guy struck me from behind and I was out cold," Frank explained. "I'm sorry Blake, I let you down."

Blake shook his head. "No, you didn't let me down. You did the right thing by staying here and keeping watch."

As Samir checked the flat for anyone else being there, he noticed a photo in a gold frame on the mantelpiece. He picked it up and looked at the woman with blonde hair standing next to Blake in the photo. A shiver ran down his spine. He was almost certain it was the same woman that he saw at the ship. He took the photo back into the lounge.

"Who's this?" Samir asked.

"It's my sister, Jenny, when we were at The New Forest Show a few years ago, why?"

"Just thought I recognised her, that's all."

Blake shook his head before turning his attention back to Frank. "Did you see a car or find out where they were going?"

Frank rubbed the back of his head, wincing in pain. "A green Cavalier came into the courtyard just before they arrived. Not sure for definite if it was theirs or not. I think they headed towards the Thames. Said something about a ship waiting for them at the docks."

Samir rushed to the balcony but the green Cavalier had already gone. "The bastard gave us the slip! I bet they're heading to St Katherine's Docks!"

Blake cursed under his breath. He had a hunch that the Cavalier was out of place but he stupidly ignored it. He knew he had to act fast if he wanted to catch up to Paula, Michael and Andrew. "Samir, get the car ready. We're going after them."

As Samir rushed out to get the car, Blake turned to Frank. "Can you make it out of here? I'll call an ambulance."

Frank nodded, his eyes heavy with pain. "No need to fuss, I'll be fine. Just go get Paula and Michael back.

Blake rushed out of the flat, down the concrete stairs and into the street, his heart pounding in his chest. He knew he was getting closer to them. As he got into the car and sped off towards the Docks, he couldn't help but think about what he would do when he found Paula and Michael. Would he be able to forgive Paula for keeping secrets from him and putting them in danger? Would he be able to let go of the anger and hurt he felt from Paula trusting Andrew again? The same person who had abused her and beaten her in the past. It made no sense and he needed to find out why? As they drove along the river, Blake's mind raced with thoughts of what he would say to them. He knew he had to stay calm and focused if he wanted to bring them back safely. Finally, they reached the docks where the ship was docked. Blake could see the green Cavalier parked nearby and he knew they had found the right place.

He turned to Samir. "You wait here. I'll go and check it out."

"Blake, Shaun and I were here earlier this evening. Something weird is going on in there. I think they have or are going to take some young students out of the country."

"Great time to drop that one on me. What actually happened?"

Samir explained about Reaper and Zodiac leading them here and the blonde woman warning him to stay away.

"You know how crazy that all sounds, right?" Blake replied.

"It's completely true! And I'm convinced that woman was your sister."

Blake shook his head. "That's impossible, she's at the hospital at Mum's bedside. Are you sure it was definitely her?"

"One hundred percent."

Blake nodded, his eyes narrowing in suspicion. "I don't know what the hell is going on, but I'm going to find out. You wait here and call for backup if you hear anything. I'm going in."

He got out of the car and walked towards the ship, his gun drawn and at the ready. As he climbed aboard, he listened for voices, anything, but the ship was deathly silent. He took a deep breath and headed towards the rear of the ship, his senses on high alert. He moved quickly and quietly through the ship, checking each room for any sign of Paula, Michael, or Andrew. Finally, he found Paula and Michael in the back of the boat, tied up and gagged.

"Blake!" Paula mumbled as soon as she saw him.

Blake rushed over to them and began untying them. "Are you both okay?"

Paula nodded, tears streaming down her face as Michael wrapped his arms around him.

"Thank God you came. They were going to take us away."

Blake hugged them both tightly, feeling relief flood through him. "It's alright, you're safe now. We need to hurry and get out of here though, before anyone else shows up."

As they made their way off the ship and back towards the car, Blake couldn't help but feel grateful that they were all okay. He knew that he still had a lot of questions for Paula, but for now, he was just glad to have them back in his arms. They would figure everything out later, but for now, they needed to focus on getting as far away from this dangerous situation as possible. They returned to the car and Samir drove them away through the streets of London towards the safe house in Enfield Island Village. Blake pulled out his phone and scrolled down to find Jenny's number. He called the number and straightaway, the message came through that the phone was switched off. Blake looked quizzically at his phone. Jenny never turned her phone off. He called Chelsea And Westminster Hospital and asked if Jenny was still visiting Emily Langford's bedside.

"I'm sorry Mr Langford, your sister left several hours ago," the nurse replied. "Would you like me to take a message?"

"No, it's fine, thank you for your help," Blake replied as he finished the call.

"Where's Jenny? Is she okay?" Paula asked.

"I don't know," Blake replied. "Samir, what time did you see my sister earlier today?"

"Around six o'clock, right before we joined you at the University Hall, why?" Samir asked.

"I have a feeling she's got herself involved in something she shouldn't have!" Blake replied.

"What do you mean?" Paula asked.

"A long time ago, Jenny became caught up in an undercover operation in Salisbury. I wasn't assigned to it at the time but she lost someone very close to her and never really spoke of it again after his funeral."

"You think it's connected to that?" Samir asked.

"If what you experienced earlier checks out, then I wouldn't be surprised if Ivan Stepanchikov is behind it. If I'm right, then Jenny is in this way over her head."

As Blake and Samir left the docks, Andrew started the engine on a black Audi that had been parked behind a forklift truck further down the dockside. Sat in the passenger seat was Derek Copsewood.

***

Elliot Francis arrived back at Scatterbird Publishing House just before midnight. He rubbed his tired eyes and let out a deep sigh. He couldn't believe the day he had just had. He had been chasing leads on the circumstances surrounding Gabby's latest book all day and he felt like he was no closer to the truth than he was when he started. As he walked towards his office, he noticed a light on in his assistant's office. He walked over and peeked in, surprised to find her working so late.

"Hey, what are you still doing here?" he asked, leaning against the doorframe.

Wendy looked up and smiled. "Just finishing up some paperwork. It turned into quite an eventful evening at the University didn't it? How was your day?"

Elliot rolled his eyes. "I really don't know what got into her. Day was long and unproductive. I feel like I'm chasing my tail with this latest tour. Tonight was a complete disaster and I can't seem to find anything concrete to explain why."

Wendy raised an eyebrow. "Anything I can help with?"

Elliot smiled appreciatively. "Actually, yes. I was wondering if you could do some digging on a new lead I got today. Gabby seemed to freak out with that woman who was in front of you in the hall. Can you find out more about her?"

Wendy nodded, jotting down some notes. "Sure, I'll get right on it. Was her name on the guest list?"

"Her name is Claire. I don't know her last name. Blasted doorman spilt coffee over the register, but she was with Gabby after her reading tonight. I have a feeling she knows more than she's letting on," Elliot explained.

Wendy got up from her desk and grabbed her coat. "I'll see what I can find out. You should get some rest, Elliot. You look exhausted."

Elliot smiled wearily. "Thanks, Wendy. I think I will. See you tomorrow."

Wendy watched him go. She had a million questions going around in her brain. There was obviously a connection between Gabby and Claire but she struggled to make the connection with Edith Harrow. When she visited Edith earlier, there was a strange atmosphere when she mentioned Gabby's name. There had to be a connection and she was determined to find it.

As Elliot made his way into his own office, his mind raced with thoughts of Gabby and the strange events that had been happening since the release of her latest book. He couldn't shake the feeling that something was off, that there was something he was missing. He sat down at his desk and pulled out a notebook, jotting down everything he knew so far. As he worked, he couldn't help but feel a sense of dread creep up on him. He had a sinking feeling that he was getting in over his head, that he was digging into something that he shouldn't be. Just as he was about to call it a night, he heard a noise outside his office door. He quickly closed his notebook and grabbed a letter opener, holding it tightly in his hand. The door slowly creaked open and Elliot held his breath, ready to defend himself if necessary. But it was just Wendy, peeking in through the crack in the door.

"Sorry, I forgot my phone charger," she said, holding up the charger in question.

Elliot let out a breath he didn't know he was holding and chuckled nervously. "You scared me for a second there. Take what you need, I'm done for the night."

Wendy nodded and grabbed her charger, closing the door behind her as she left. Elliot let out a sigh and leaned back in his chair, trying to calm his racing heart. He knew he needed to be more careful, but he couldn't help but feel that he was on the verge of uncovering something big. He decided to call it a night and gathered his things before leaving the office. As he walked towards the front door, he saw a dark figure lurking in the shadows. Elliot's heart raced as he recognized the man from Gabby's reading earlier that night.

"Excuse me, sir, can I help you?" Elliot asked, trying to sound confident.

The man stepped closer, his hands in his pockets. "I couldn't help but notice you've been poking your nose into things that don't concern you, Mr. Francis."

Elliot's grip tightened on his bag. "I don't know what you're talking about. Who are you?"

The man stepped forward, his face illuminated by the neon lights above. "Let's just say I'm a concerned party. You should be careful who you associate with, Mr. Francis. You never know who might have ulterior motives."

Elliot took a step back, feeling a cold sweat break out on his forehead. "Look, I don't want any trouble. I'm just doing my job."

The man laughed. "That's what they all say. Just be careful, Mr. Francis. You've pissed off a lot of people. One of them wants you dead but I'm willing to see how far you're willing to go for your reputation. You wouldn't want anything to happen to you or your loved ones."

With that, the man turned and walked out of the door and disappeared into the night, leaving Elliot standing there, shaken. He knew he needed to take the warning seriously, but he couldn't shake the feeling that he was too close to the truth to back away now.

The man watched Elliot leave the publishing house before climbing inside a blue Volkswagen.

"The mole has come up from his hole," an Indian man in the driving seat said as he showed him a GPS tracking from Enfield Island Village.

"Raj, you are a diamond," the man smiled. "How did you track him?"

"He ordered a pizza."

"Steven Langford, you are a silly boy. Let's go!"

Chapter Twenty-One

The Not-So-Safe House

Alison Pearce led Shaun, Gabby and Simon into a well maintained thatched cottage on Horncastle Way in Enfield Island Village.

"What is this place?" Simon asked.

"We have a network of safe houses in this area to keep people safe during ongoing investigations," Alison explained. "You should be okay here for now."

"For now?" Gabby asked. "I need to find out who is behind all of this. Someone is screwing with me on this tour and I'm determined to find out who and why!"

Alison sighed and looked at Gabby sympathetically. "I understand your frustration, Gabby. But we need to prioritise your safety above all else. The best thing you can do now is rest and let us handle the investigation."

Alison handed Gabby a two inch long white plastic stick.

"This has a homing device inside it. If anything happens, go down to the basement and press this red button on the stick. It will send a distress signal to Special Branch and we'll get you out of here as soon as we can," Alison explained.

"That might not be soon enough," Simon quipped.

Shaun and Alison glared at him. Gabby nodded reluctantly, but as soon as Alison and Shaun left, she turned to Simon with a determined look. "I'm not just going to sit here and wait for someone to come after me. We need to find out who's behind all of this and put a stop to it."

Simon nodded in agreement. "I'm with you, Gabby, but how do we even begin to find out who's behind this? They hold all the aces, that scene at the hotel proved it! Someone is going to extreme lengths to stop you from uncovering something. It's either connected to your book or to the people of Longfellow Crescent."

Gabby thought for a moment before an idea struck her. "Elliot. He's been investigating too. Maybe he's uncovered something that can help us."

Shaun nodded. "It's worth a shot. But we're stuck in a safe house. Any communication will compromise security."

"I still need to turn up at The Rabbit Hole tomorrow night," Gabby replied.

"And walk directly into a trap. Come on Gab, it's not worth it."

Gabby shook her head. "I have to do it, Si. It's the only way to get closer to the truth. But I won't go alone, you're coming with me."

Simon looked hesitant, but Gabby gave him a convincing look. "I need you with me, Simon. You're the only one I trust to have my back."

Simon nodded, relenting. "Alright, I'm in. But how do we contact Elliot without compromising security?"

Gabby thought for a moment before an idea struck her. "I remember Elliot mentioning an app he uses to send encrypted messages. We can use that to contact him without anyone intercepting our messages."

Simon nodded in agreement. "Sounds like a plan. Let's do it."

Meanwhile, Elliot had arrived home and settled into the leather office chair in his study. He couldn't shake off the eerie encounter from earlier and decided to take some precautions to protect himself. He pulled out his laptop and began searching for ways to increase his security. As he searched, his phone beeped with a notification. It was a message from Gabby, and it read:

We need your help. Can you meet us at The Rabbit Hole tomorrow night? It's urgent.

Elliot's heart raced as he read the message. He hadn't gone anywhere near The Rabbit Hole for years after a police sting operation led to his father being wrongfully arrested. He knew it was dangerous to get involved, but he couldn't ignore the plea for help. He quickly replied:

I'll be there. But we need to be careful. It's not safe.

Gabby replied almost immediately.

Don't worry, we have a plan. Just make sure you come alone.

Elliot wasn't sure if he liked the sound of that, but he knew he had to trust Gabby. He spent the rest of the night preparing for the meeting, checking and rechecking his security measures. By the time he went to bed, he was exhausted and anxious.

At the safe house, Simon looked out of the window and saw a car pull up outside one of the cottages further down the road. The car had a magnetic triangle on the top of it advertising JoJo's Pizza Delivery. His stomach rumbled, they hadn't stopped to eat much all day.

"I guess someone didn't get the memo," Simon chuckled.

"What do you mean?" Gabby asked.

Simon watched as he saw a tall man with ginger hair answer the door and hand over cash to the delivery guy in exchange for a pizza. "The guy at number one just ordered a pizza. To be honest, I could easily finish off a large Meat Feast about now."

Gabby joined him at the window as the delivery driver drove away and a blue Volkswagen parked in its place. Two men emerged from the car and moved around to the boot.

"Turn off the lights," Simon whispered.

Gabby rushed over and turned off the lights before rejoining him at the window. The two men pulled out two fully loaded machine guns from the boot of the car. They approached number one and knocked on the front door. Nobody answered. They knocked again. Still nobody answered. The two men stepped back down the garden path and opened fire on the house.

Simon and Gabby gasped in horror as they watched the attack unfold. The sound of gunfire echoed through the night, shattering the peacefulness of the village. Simon quickly grabbed Gabby's hand and pulled her away from the window, leading her to the basement where they had been told to go in case of an emergency.

"We have to stay here until it's safe," he whispered. "We can't risk going out there and getting caught in the crossfire."

Gabby nodded, her face pale with fear. They huddled together in the dimly lit room, listening to the sound of gunfire and shouting outside. After what felt like hours, the noise finally died down and they heard the sound of a car driving away. Simon cautiously made his way upstairs, peering out of the window to check if it was safe. He saw that the attackers were gone, but the damage had been done. The house that had been attacked was now a smouldering ruin, with smoke billowing out of the shattered windows. Simon quickly went back downstairs to where Gabby was waiting.

"It's clear now," he said. "But we need to get out of here. This safe house isn't safe anymore."

Gabby nodded, her mind racing with fear and adrenaline. They quickly gathered their things and headed towards the door, but as soon as they stepped outside they were met with the sight of two men standing in their way.

"Well, well, well," one of them sneered. "Looks like we caught ourselves with a couple of rats trying to escape."

Simon stepped forward, his fists clenched. "We don't want any trouble. Just let us go."

The second man of Indian descent, a burly figure with a thick beard, stepped forward and grabbed Simon by the collar. "You think you can just waltz out of here after what you've seen? Think again."

Gabby looked around frantically, trying to find a way out of the situation. She spotted a nearby screwdriver lying on the ground and quickly grabbed it, ready to defend herself and Simon. But before she could use it, there was a sudden burst of gunfire and the two men fell to the ground, dead. Gabby and Simon turned to see Alison and Shaun standing in the road, guns in hand.

"We came as soon as we heard the gunshots," Alison said. "We need to move now before any more of them come."

Gabby and Simon quickly followed Alison and Shaun to a waiting car, their hearts pounding with adrenaline. As they drove away from the safe house, Gabby couldn't help but wonder who those attackers were and how they had found them so quickly.

"We need to find out who those guys were," Simon said, echoing her thoughts. "And we need to do it fast before they come after us again."

Gabby nodded in agreement. She knew they had to be quick, before those attackers found out what they were doing and used it against them. She was determined to find out the truth behind the history in Longfellow Crescent, even if it meant putting her life on the line. Those men who fired the machine guns obviously discovered a connection and she was determined to find out what it was.

Samir sped past Alison and Shaun as he drove into Horncastle Way.

"Wasn't that Alison driving that car?" Samir asked.

"She must be following a lead," Blake replied before they pulled up outside the smouldering remains of the first cottage. "What the hell..."

"What happened?" Paula asked.

"Stay in the car!" Blake replied as both he and Samir rushed over towards the remains of the house.

Small smouldering fires and electrical sparks made it impossible for them to enter the destroyed cottage.

"Come on Steven, where are you? Tell me you got out alive," Blake whispered to himself.

"Blake! Over here!" Samir called out as he discovered the two dead bodies outside number five."

Blake rushed over and recognised the Indian man on the ground. He reached inside the man's jacket and pulled out a wallet.

"I've seen him before, he's one of Zodiac's men," Blake said as he showed Samir a small packet of five matches wrapped in a yellow and black cardboard wrapping with a white Z on it.

"Karun Patel, he cornered us earlier when we were on the stake-out outside Zodiac's mansion and the other guy must be Raj Omar"

"Diversion or a loaded gun?"

"Your guess is as good as mine. Zodiac won't go home. He knows that the cops will be all over that since Xander got out. Escaping on that ship would be the ideal getaway."

Blake nodded. "Then we need to make sure that it doesn't set sail. Anything on the other body?"

"Nothing."

Blake stood up and wandered back over towards the first cottage. He could see the basement door was still closed.

"Who was in number one?" Samir asked.

"My brother."

"I'm sorry Blake. We need to take Paula and Michael to HQ. There's nowhere else that they will be safe."

Blake nodded. "Alison must have come to the same conclusion with Gabby and Simon. You take them and then come back for me."

"What? Surely you can't be thinking..."

"The tunnels lead out of the safe houses and underground towards the river."

"Nobody could have survived that destruction."

"Steven's impulsive but not stupid. Take them to HQ and come back for me," Blake replied before rushing into the woodland behind the cottages.

Samir turned and headed back towards the car. Paula opened the rear passenger door. "Where's he gone?"

"To find his brother. I need to take you into Special Branch and then come back for him."

"You can't just leave him out here!"

"He's made his choice Paula, the important thing is that you two are safe so he can concentrate on bringing these bastards down before he loses all of you."

Paula reluctantly sat back inside the car as Samir drove them back towards Special Branch. A thousand thoughts raced through her mind but she knew that Blake needed to do what was right.

"Is Daddy going to be okay?" Michael asked as the streets of London passed by in a blur.

"He will be," Paula smiled, unconvincingly.

Michael looked outside lost in his own thoughts. As they entered the underground car park in Vauxhall, Samir pressed a button on the dashboard that blacked out all of the windows on the car.

"What's happening?" Paula asked.

"We're heading into the secure unit," Samir replied.

Paula's heart raced as they descended deeper into the underground complex. The darkness was suffocating, and the silence only made it worse. She knew they were safe here, but the thought of being trapped underground filled her with dread. When they finally came to a stop, Samir got out of the car and opened the door for Paula and Michael. They stepped out into a brightly lit corridor, lined with doors and cameras.

"Welcome to Special Branch," Samir said, leading them towards a nearby door. "You'll be safe here, I promise. We'll keep you protected until this is all over."

Paula nodded, still feeling uneasy. As they stepped into the room, they were greeted by a team of agents who welcomed them and showed them to their quarters. Paula and Michael settled in, grateful for the safety and comfort of the room. But Paula couldn't shake the feeling that things were far from over.

Chapter Twenty-Two

The Family Home Clues

Zodiac and Xander pulled up outside 121 Gerrard's View in Eel Brook Common. A blue and white police crime scene tape had been placed across the gate and the front door. Zodiac cursed under his breath. He had hoped to have some time to search the house before the police arrived, but it seemed he had been too late.

"What's the plan?" Xander asked.

"We need to find out what they know. The police would have seized anything useful, but there might be something they missed."

Xander nodded, and they got out of the car, making their way towards the house. The smell of smoke still lingered in the air, and the windows were shattered. Zodiac pushed past the crime scene tape and made his way inside. The house was in a mess - furniture overturned, broken glass and debris scattered everywhere. It was clear that the police had ransacked the place. The kitchen at the back of the house was splintered with shards of wood from the garden shed explosion earlier. As Zodiac made his way through the mess, he spotted a glimmer of something shiny under a pile of rubble. He knelt down and dug through the debris. It was a small, silver USB drive. Zodiac's heart skipped a beat as he pocketed the USB drive, knowing it could contain valuable information about their operations. He turned to Xander and nodded, signalling that they needed to leave before the police returned. But as they made their way back outside, two cars pulled up either side of theirs blocking their exit. Kaja and Tom stepped out of the left car and Vijay and Graham stepped out of the other.

"Going somewhere gentlemen?" Tom asked.

"Vijay, Kaja, what's going on?" Zodiac asked. "We need to get out of here before the police catch up with Xander."

Tom laughed. "They'll be too busy tidying up the mess of their pathetic safe house. I heard a rumour that you were entertaining Special Branch agents whilst I've been tidying up your mess. Maybe we should head inside and discuss things further."

"What do you want?" Xander demanded.

"We've come too far to let this operation be compromised by incompetence, inside," Tom snapped.

Zodiac and Xander exchanged a quick look before following the others inside. The house was dark and still, the only light coming from the moon shining through the shattered windows. They walked through the debris, following Tom and the others.

"I trust you have the information we need," Vijay asked.

Zodiac's heart was pounding in his chest as he reached into his pocket and pulled out the USB drive. He hesitated for a moment before handing it over to Vijay.

"There's nothing on it," Tom sneered as he looked at the drive.

"What?" Zodiac asked, confused.

Tom smirked. "Did you really think we wouldn't notice you planting a fake drive? We know you're up to something, and we're not going to let you ruin everything for us."

Zodiac's mind raced as he tried to come up with a plan. He knew he had to get out of there alive, but the odds were against him. "I'm the least of your worries here. Copsewood has taken it upon himself to pursue a famous author that he has some kind of connection to."

"I've already warned Elliot Francis of the consequences of interfering in our business."

"Elliot Francis?" Graham spoke up. "He needs to be taken down."

"Why, so you get to keep that manky old villa on the Cote d'azur?" Vijay remarked.

"No, he has contacts in The Crystal that can lead to influential people being made scapegoats for crimes they didn't commit. A few clicks and he could drop you all in the shit," Graham replied.

Zodiac saw an opportunity to turn the tables on the group. "Maybe we can work together to take down Elliot Francis. We can use his contacts to our advantage and strengthen our position."

Tom narrowed his eyes. "And why should we trust you?"

"Because we have a common enemy. Copsewood is a wildcard and we need to neutralise him before he causes any more problems for us."

The group fell into a heated discussion, weighing the pros and cons of working together. Zodiac could feel his heart racing as he waited for their decision.

Finally, Kaja spoke up. "Fine. We'll work together, but we'll be watching you closely. One false move and you're all dead."

Zodiac nodded, relief washing over him. "We'll do whatever it takes to bring down Elliot Francis."

The group dispersed, leaving Zodiac and Xander alone in the wreckage of the house. Zodiac knew they had narrowly escaped death, but he also knew the danger was far from over.

***

A police officer was standing outside the front of 124 Alfredson Road in Kensington, the family home of Blake Langford's mother, Emily Langford. Jenny Langford and Nicola Pew approached the house.

"Excuse me, what is going on? Why is there a police patrol around my mother's house? Don't you know she has been taken into hospital after suffering a stroke!" Jenny fumed.

"I'm sorry, who are you?" the police officer asked.

"I'm Jenny Langford, Emily Langford's daughter and you have no right to block off access to my family home!"

"Actually we do, I have a warrant that gives me rights to search and seize anything I deem fit from this address after your brother went on the run earlier today suspected of multiple murders at his home address!" the police officer replied.

Jenny felt a wave of shock wash over her as she heard the officer's words. Steven, her own brother, suspected of murder? She knew he was in some kind of trouble but this was serious.

"Please, can we just go inside and gather some of Jenny's belongings?" Nicola pleaded with the officer.

The officer hesitated for a moment before nodding. "Fine, but I'll have to accompany you."

Jenny and Nicola headed towards the house. As they stepped inside, they were greeted by a team of detectives who were already going through the place with a fine-toothed comb. The sight of her family home in disarray made Jenny's heart ache. It was clear that the detectives had searched every nook and cranny of the house, leaving it in a mess. As they made their way up to what used to be Steven's room, Jenny couldn't help but feel a sense of dread.

The room was a complete mess. The drawers had been pulled out with clothes strewn all over the floor. Jenny reached under the bed and found the spare mobile phone that Blake had hidden there in case of an emergency. Nicola continued looking around before something caught her eye. It was a picture frame lying face down on the ground. She picked it up and gasped. It was a picture of Steven and a woman she didn't recognize. They were standing in front of a big, white house with a beautiful garden. Nicola's heart sank as she realised that this was the house that Steven had been staying at.

"Jenny, come and look at this," she said, holding out the picture frame. "Do you recognise her?"

Jenny's eyes widened as she saw the picture of Steven and the unknown woman. "No, I don't but we need to find out who she is. She might know something about what happened to Steven that can help clear his name."

Nicola nodded in agreement. "I'll do some digging and see if I can find out anything about her."

As they made their way back down the stairs, Jenny couldn't shake off the feeling that something else was off. She looked around the house and noticed a few things that didn't belong there. There was a pair of men's shoes by the door, a set of keys on the kitchen counter. It was as if someone had been inside the house and left in a hurry.

"Excuse me," Jenny called out to one of the detectives. "Do you know anything about these shoes and keys?"

The detective looked at the items in question before shaking his head. "No, we didn't find those during our search. They must have been left here by someone else."

Jenny's heart began to race as she realised that someone else had been inside the house. Could it be the murderer? Were they still here?

"Nicola, we need to leave. Now," Jenny whispered urgently.

Nicola looked at her friend, confusion evident on her face. "What's wrong?"

"I think someone else has been inside the house. We need to go before they come back," Jenny replied.

"Everything okay?" the police officer asked.

Jenny nodded before picking up Emily's car keys from the keyholder by the door. As they hurried out of the house, Jenny couldn't help but feel like they were being watched. She looked around, but there was no one in sight. She breathed a sigh of relief as they got into the car and drove away. As they drove, Nicola scrolled through social media, trying to find out more about the woman in the picture. But every lead turned out to be a dead end. Jenny's mind raced as they made their way through the city, trying to piece together the clues. She couldn't shake off the feeling that all of this was connected somehow to Steven's behaviour earlier, the murder investigation, the strange items in the house and deep down, Jenny still had a feeling that she couldn't completely trust Nicola either.

"Someone is playing a sick game with my family! We need to find out who's behind all of this," Jenny said as they continued on their way through the streets of London.

Nicola nodded in agreement. "But how do we do that? We don't even know where to start."

"We'll start with the only lead we have - the woman in the picture. We need to find her and talk to her," Jenny replied.

"We don't even have a name Jen. How do we even know where to find her?" Nicola asked.

"I need to contact Blake but we need to be away from prying eyes. I'll drop you at your house and then go on to the hospital to check on Mum," Jenny replied.

Jenny dropped Nicola off before finally arriving at the hospital. She continuously checked over her shoulder as she walked through the corridors of the hospital. As she sat by her mother's bedside, she couldn't help but wonder how much she knew about Steven's situation. Did she know something that could help them? And what about her home being dissected by the police looking for clues to trap him? She pulled out the phone that she had taken from the house and switched it on. She typed out a message and sent it to Blake hoping that he would respond. All she could do now was wait and hope that Blake had the answer that she needed.

Chapter Twenty-Three

Brothers In Arms

Blake pushed his way through overgrown woodland behind the safe house before coming to a run down street with two blocks of garages which had graffiti spray-painted all over the walls and garage doors. Three high rise flats dominated the skyline and a burnt out car sat alongside several other rusting cars that had seen better days. Blake walked down a pathway between two of the blocks of flats which led down towards a stream with a small footbridge leading towards a building site. Three men gathered around a metal dumpster fire sharing a bottle of whiskey encased in a brown paper bag between them to keep warm.

Blake approached the men cautiously, his hand hovering over his gun, ready to defend himself if needed. One of the men noticed him and nudged the other two, gesturing towards Blake. They all stood up, eyeing him warily.

"What do you want?" the tallest of the three asked.

"I'm looking for someone," Blake replied, his eyes scanning the area around them.

The men exchanged a look before the tallest one spoke up again. "Who are you looking for?"

"A man around my height, short ginger hair, hazel brown eyes, dark rimmed glasses and wearing black jeans and a navy blue shirt," Blake said, trying to keep his voice steady.

The men laughed, their breath turning into mist in the cold air. "No one of that description would come around 'ere bruv," one of them said, taking a swig from the bottle.

Blake frowned, his thoughts racing. It was possible that they knew something and were just trying to throw him off. "Look,

I don't want any trouble. I just need to find him. People's lives might be in danger."

The tallest man narrowed his eyes, studying Blake. "Why should we believe you?"

Blake took a deep breath. "Because I'm trying to stop my brother from doing something stupid. He's in trouble and I need to find him before it's too late."

The men exchanged another look before the tallest one spoke up again. "Alright, we might know something. But it's gonna cost you."

Blake nodded, pulling out his wallet. He handed over a wad of cash to the tallest man, who counted it before nodding in approval.

"Alright, we heard that someone fitting that description was seen at the abandoned warehouse down the street. But be careful, there's some shady characters hanging around there."

Blake thanked them before hurrying off in the direction of the warehouse. As he approached the run-down building, the sound of rustling coming from the bushes nearby caught his attention. He gripped his gun tightly, ready for anything. As he entered the warehouse, the stench of decay hit him like a brick wall. He coughed, trying to cover his nose with his shirt. The place was littered with debris and broken furniture, but there was no sign of Steven or anyone else for that matter.

"Steven?" Blake called out, his voice echoing through the empty space.

There was no answer. Blake continued to search the warehouse, moving slowly and cautiously. As he made his way through the maze of broken furniture and debris, he heard a faint sound coming from one of the corners of the building. It sounded like someone was crying. Blake approached the corner carefully, his gun drawn. He peeked around the corner and saw a figure huddled in the shadows. It was Steven.

"Steven, what are you doing here?" Blake asked, his voice soft.

Steven looked up, his eyes red and puffy from crying. "Blake... I'm sorry, I'm such an idiot."

"What is this place?"

"Heartbreak Hotel."

"Seriously?"

"It's a code name for the place we go to when we're in trouble. Guess Zodiac has a soft spot for Elvis."

"Who's we? If it's part of the same group that blew up the safe house then it's not safe here!"

"I haven't been totally honest with you. I was part of a group who trade in the student bars. Young freshers coming through looking to make some easy money on the side. It was all harmless fun until recently when more questionable members joined and students ended up being murdered if they didn't tow the line. Would you like some pizza?" Steven asked, offering a half eaten pizza in a crumpled box.

Blake shook his head. "And what line is that?"

"Sex, drugs, alcohol, whatever. Usually it's just some dirty old men getting some of their kicks with an eighteen year old getting access to the funds of a sugar-daddy but things got heavy real fast. When one client didn't receive what he expected, the girl ended up on the A34."

"I know, that's part of the reason why I've been pulled in. They also took out one of my team members. What's more disturbing and what I'm still trying to work out is how does Jenny fit into all of this?" Blake asked.

That caught Steven's attention. "What do you mean?"

"Don't bullshit me here, she left the hospital and then I received a text message from the burner phone saying that she received a message to go to The Rabbit Hole tomorrow night. Gabby Turner also received a message asking her to go to The Rabbit Hole. We haven't been anywhere near that place since we were teenagers so who the hell is fucking with us Steven? What hold do they have on you and how many more people have to get killed before you stop playing your pathetic games?"

"Thanks for your support. I almost get blown to pieces by a hit team that somehow managed to find out where your so called safe houses were and all you care about is your fucking reputation!"

Blake recoiled at Steven's outburst, but he knew that his brother was hurting. He lowered his gun, trying to diffuse the situation. "Steven, I'm sorry. I didn't mean it like that. We're in this together, remember? We'll figure this out," Blake sighed.

"You're right, this has a lot to do with our past. Members of the group have been in the community for many years and hold some grudges. I don't know how to fix this. I thought I could handle it, but I was wrong. I didn't mean for anyone to get hurt. As far as Jenny's concerned, you're right. I saw one of the guys who shot up the safe house. I heard that he was back on the scene but it was all rumours until tonight."

"Who was it?"

"Tom Gibson."

Blake looked at Steven. "The same Tom Gibson..."

"Yeah, the one she helped give information to the Russians for."

"You knew about that?"

"You weren't there when Dad went ape-shit at home about her compromising your career and bringing the family name into disrepute. We all knew what she did but we also knew how you did a good job brushing it under the carpet but she still fell for him, big time. Did you know she aborted his child too?"

Blake struggled to find the words. "Why didn't she talk to me? Surely something could've been sorted out?"

"When he was pronounced dead, she lost it. Her mental health went off the scale. She felt suicidal and didn't want to carry on. She stopped eating. Lost interest in everything. Mum took her to the doctor, she then discovered she was pregnant but she was in no fit state to be a mother and didn't want to be if Tom wasn't around anymore."

"All this time she thought he was dead."

Steven nodded. "Did you know he was alive?"

"After I called in a few favours to make sure that Jenny's involvement wasn't made public knowledge, I never followed up on any of the details. The Ministry Of Defence concluded that Gibson's team were caught up in a crossfire in Afghanistan and his body was amongst the dead. There was no indication that he was alive or indeed back in England setting up the human trafficking ring that seems to have developed around the local Universities. How the hell have these young women become so desperate to trust these men?"

"He's enlisted the four main bodyguards that used to deal for Zodiac. After Xander went down after those underground cage fights, Zodiac lost his edge. He seemed to lose interest in the deals and would often no-show. That pissed a lot of people off, including his close circle. Gibson is working with Derek Copsewood and this is the big one. If they can close the deal, they have a buyer in Phuket who will take the students off of their hands and they can then sail off into the sunset. No questions asked."

"Where does Andrew Broughton fit into this?" Blake asked.

"He works at The Troubled Traveller with Dickie Parsnips."

"Who?"

"Richard Parsons, it's his nickname. Jenny's friend Nicola Pew shares a house with Dickie's barmaid Andrea Smith and Tiffany Mason. If you find them, you'll probably find another link into Gibson's group. Last I heard, Nicola was dating one of Zodiac's bodyguards, a guy called Kaja."

"Zodiac led two of my team on a wild goose chase to a ship in St Katherine's Docks. Andrew took Paula and Michael to the same ship. We're keeping a discreet eye on it as we assume they will want to use it to transfer the women but we don't know when or how they will be moving them onto it."

"They need an edge. Tiffany can probably get them that edge with her knowledge..."

"She's dead."

Steven stared at Blake. "What?"

"She was pushed in front of an Underground Train earlier this evening. One of my team was pursuing a suspect when he saw her body spread over the front of the train. I'm sorry."

Steven put his head in his hands. "No, not Tiff," he cried.

Blake stepped closer to Steven, placing a hand on his shoulder. "We'll find a way to make things right. To get justice for Tiffany and the others who have died. I've got a close friend laying in intensive care too. I need you by my side, supporting me and bringing this group down. But first, you need to tell me everything. Start from the beginning."

Steven took a deep breath, steeling himself. He began to recount everything that had happened. How he had gotten caught up in the wrong crowd, how he had started dealing drugs to get out of debt, and how he had eventually become involved with a group that traded young girls for profit. He told Blake about how he had met Tiffany through this group, and how they had become close. He explained that he had fallen in love with her, and that he had tried to leave the group, but they had threatened to kill him if he ever tried to leave. Tonight was proof that they meant what they said.

Blake listened carefully. He had never realised that his brother was in so deep.

"We have to stop this group," Blake realised. "We have to put an end to it once and for all."

Steven nodded. "I'm in. Whatever it takes."

Blake nodded, relieved to know that his brother was with him. As they stepped out of the warehouse, they were met with a sudden gust of cold wind. The sky was darkening, and the clouds overhead looked ominous. Steven shivered, and Blake pulled his jacket tighter around him.

"Let's get out of here," Blake said, leading the way. "We need to regroup and come up with a plan."

They walked in silence for a few minutes before arriving at a bus shelter. Blake called Samir and asked him to pick them up from there.

Finally, Steven spoke up. "I know someone who might be able to help us."

"Who?" Blake asked, intrigued.

"If your hunch about someone who knew about The Rabbit Hole and the Langford, Turner and Evans family connections to it, James Turner, Gabby's brother used to house share with the doorman from The Troubled Traveller Pub, Greg Hallman. If anyone knows what dirty secrets are going on in there, it's him."

"You might be onto something there. The problem we have is the police still want to question you for what happened at your home so I need to get Gordon to block the police from taking you down until this is over and we can fight your corner. So for now, we need to head back to Special Branch and get some sleep. I have a feeling tomorrow is going to be a long day."

***

Alison and Shaun led Gabby and Simon into the offices at Special Branch. The building was quiet, with only a few agents scattered around. Alison led them into a small conference room and motioned for them to take a seat. Shaun disappeared to fetch some food and drinks and to make a phone call.

"You're safe here," Alison said, her voice soft. "No one will touch you. We'll provide you with protection until this is all over."

"Thank you," Gabby said, her voice barely above a whisper. "It's funny, I had all of this trepidation about coming back to London for a book tour and suddenly, my past comes flying back and hitting me from all angles. After James went to prison and we sold the house in Miami, I thought I'd turned my back on a life of crime. How wrong was I? I don't know what we would have done without you."

"It's our job," Alison said with a smile. "Now, tell us everything. Start from the beginning."

Gabby took a deep breath and began to recount the events of the past few days. She told them about the messages she had received, about the strange reception they had received on Longfellow Crescent and about the meeting with Claire Turner at the University Hall. She had a suspicion about Elliot Francis' involvement too which Shaun agreed to follow up on. She spared no detail, knowing that they needed to know everything if they were to help. When she finished, Alison and Shaun exchanged a worried look.

"This is serious," Alison said. "It sounds like you're dealing with a powerful and dangerous group."

"We need to find out who's behind this," Shaun added. "We'll reconvene with Blake and find out what he's discovered so far and start investigating right away."

"Thank you," Gabby replied, feeling a glimmer of hope. "I just want this nightmare to end."

"We'll do everything we can to make that happen," Alison promised.

Gabby and Simon followed Alison and Shaun to a small living area with a bedroom off to the right with a lounge and dining area where they would be staying until further notice. As they settled in, Gabby's mind was racing with possibilities. Who was behind this? Why were they targeting her and her friends? And most importantly, how could they be stopped? As Alison and Shaun were about to leave, Simon pulled Shaun to the side.

"I don't mean to be disrespectful but as a CIA agent, I feel like I can use my expertise to help you find out what is connecting Gabby to this group. I know she has a very chequered past and her family left an obvious trail of destruction when they left Longfellow Crescent. The CIA and Special Branch are brothers in arms, let me help you," Simon explained.

"I appreciate your enthusiasm but the fact that you are in a relationship with Gabby makes it a conflict of interests so please, let us handle it. We can't risk both of you being targeted again so whenever you two break cover, we need to be by your side. The best thing you can do for us is to stay here, keep Gabby calm and let us know if any new information comes to light. The hit team that ambushed you earlier proves that you are both not safe in London at the moment."

"And what about the meeting at The Rabbit Hole?"

"If Gabby needs to attend, we will be right behind you both."

"If she doesn't then it will speak volumes to the people involved that we have engaged in contacting the authorities. They will all go to ground and any new leads will dry up."

"I guess it's a gamble we need to take," Shaun replied. "Get some sleep and let us take care of it."

Gabby and Simon watched them both leave. As the door closed behind them, Simon turned to Gabby.

"Are you okay?"

Gabby nodded, trying to put on a brave face. "I'm okay. I'm just worried about what's going to happen next."

"I know," Simon said, taking her hand. "But we're in this together. We'll get through it."

Gabby leaned into him, feeling a sense of comfort in his embrace. As the night wore on, they both tried to get some rest, but sleep eluded them. They were both too consumed by their thoughts, too worried about what the future held. Finally, as dawn broke, they heard a knock on the door. Simon got up to answer it, and found Shaun standing outside.

"Get dressed," he said.

"Where are we going?" Gabby asked.

"214 Orpington Road."

"Where is that?" Simon asked.

"The home of Elliot Francis."

"Why are you taking us there?" Gabby asked.

"Elliot was found dead by his housekeeper this morning. He had a knife through his heart and a page from Edith Harrow's book, Tales Of A Lost Soul, screwed up in his hand. A paragraph had been circled which read; "All ye who taketh upon ones self to deceive, will endeavour to pay the debt of life."

Gabby and Simon looked at each other. They knew they needed to find out what the connection to Edith Harrow was before it was too late.

Chapter Twenty-Four

Death For Breakfast

Alison and Shaun arrived outside Elliot Francis' house just after 9am. Gabby and Simon climbed out of the back seats and joined them outside. Blake, Samir and Steven were already there waiting for them. As they were about to head inside, a black Land Rover parked up against the grass verge and Frank stepped out from the driver's seat.

Blake walked over to meet him. "Aren't you meant to be at the hospital taking things easy?"

"They checked me over yesterday and said I was fine and I needed to have something to occupy my mind or I'll be going crazy at the office. I have an interesting development that I needed to run by you. After I had seen the doctor, I went up to see Joe Knight."

"How is he?"

"Still drugged up but he told me that before they entered the garden when the shed blew up, he noticed one of Zodiac's men entering the house."

"Samir told me the same thing but they didn't have a positive ID on the guy."

"Samir has Zodiac in his pocket. They made a deal a few years ago and Samir is letting stuff slide in exchange for inside information. The description that Joe gave me brought up a match. Karun Patel."

"One of Zodiac's men?"

"Precisely, so why didn't Samir point the finger at him. Watch your back, okay," Frank advised.

Blake nodded, his mind already racing with the implications of this new information. He turned back to the group briefly before turning back to Frank. "Thanks for letting me know. We need to focus on Elliot Francis for now, but good work. If you're up to it, I need to ask a favour."

"Shoot."

"I need you to visit Edith Harrow. She's in Badger's Nest Nursing Home. Find out about her relationship with Elliot Francis and her connection to the Turner family. Gabby in particular."

"I'm on it," Frank replied before leaving.

Blake turned and rejoined the rest of them as they entered the house, which was eerily quiet. The housekeeper was nowhere to be seen, and they could hear the distant sound of police sirens outside. They made their way to the study, where they found Elliot's lifeless body slumped in his armchair. A letter opener had been stabbed through his heart and the page from Edith Harrow's book was still clutched tightly in his hand. Alison took photos of the scene while Shaun searched the room for any clues. Steven, Gabby and Simon stood back, not wanting to disturb anything. Blake and Samir stood by the front door, keeping an eye on the perimeter.

"Anything?" Blake called out.

"Nothing yet," Shaun replied.

As they continued to search, they heard a noise coming from the kitchen. They cautiously made their way towards the sound, their guns drawn. When they entered the kitchen, they found the housekeeper, Mrs. Peters, lying unconscious on the floor. She had been hit on the head with a blunt object.

"We need to call for an ambulance," Simon said, rushing over to Mrs. Peters' side.

Blake nodded and quickly made the call. As they waited for the ambulance to arrive, they continued to search the house for any further clues. They found nothing out of the ordinary until they entered the dining room. There, on the table, was a breakfast spread laid out for two, with two plates, two cups, and two glasses of orange juice. But there was no one there to eat it.

"Someone was here with Elliot this morning," Gabby said, her eyes scanning the room for any further evidence.

"But who?" Steven asked.

"That's what we need to find out," Blake replied. "Let's keep looking."

As they continued their search, they found a note on the table next to the breakfast spread. It was written in a hurried scrawl, as if whoever wrote it was in a rush. The note read:

"I know what you did. You can't hide from me. I'm coming for you."

"This looks like a message from the killer," Alison said, examining the note closely.

"Or a diversion. Any idea who could've wrote it?" Blake asked.

"I'm not sure," Alison replied. "But we need to find out."

Just then, the ambulance arrived and Mrs. Peters was taken away for treatment. Blake and the rest of the team continued to search the house, hoping to find any further clues that might lead them to the killer. As they were searching the upstairs bedrooms, they heard a noise in the attic. They cautiously made their way up the stairs and opened the hatch to the attic. A metal ladder had been attached to the edge of the hatch and as they pulled it down to use, a small mouse dropped down from the entrance before scurrying away into one of the bedrooms.

"I guess we've found our suspect," Shaun quipped.

Nobody responded as Blake led the way up the ladder. Inside, they found a makeshift bedroom with a bed, a dresser, and some clothes. But what caught their attention was the wall that was covered in photos of Gabby and Simon. The photos were taken from various angles, and some of them were taken without their knowledge. It was clear that whoever lived in this room was obsessed with them.

"This is disturbing," Gabby said, her voice shaking. "Whoever this is, they've been watching us for a long time."

"We need to find out who this room belongs to," Blake said, his voice steady. "Keep searching for any clues."

As they continued to search the room, they found a journal on the bedside table. It was locked, but Simon managed to pick the lock and opened it.

Inside, they found a disturbing collection of ramblings and drawings. The pages were filled with violent and obscene fantasies about Gabby and Simon, and it was clear that the writer was deeply disturbed and dangerous. They also found a name written repeatedly throughout the journal: Edith Harrow.

"This is our connection," Blake said, his eyes scanning the pages of the journal. "This person is obsessed with Edith Harrow, and they're taking out their rage on anyone connected to her."

"We need to find this person before they hurt anyone else," Gabby replied.

"I agree," Blake said. "Let's get out of here and regroup. We need to put together a plan to catch this killer before they strike again."

"Guys! I found something!" Alison called out from downstairs.

They all filed into the lounge where Alison had moved a rug and there was a trapdoor that had been hidden underneath it. Simon picked up two dinner knives from the kitchen table and handed one of them to Blake. Together, they forced the trapdoor open. Underneath the floorboards was a hidden wooden basement lit with a dull light. There were four single beds and on each one of them was a young female student tied and gagged to the bed frame.

"Call it in Shaun, we've found four of them," Blake said before he and Alison entered the basement and untied the girls.

***

The front door of Scatterbird Publishing House on Park Lane creaked open before the door slammed shut behind the customer. Wendy, the receptionist, was at the far side of the room placing a folder on top of a tall bookcase when she heard the clunk of the deadlock click into place.

"Hello?" she called out.

Nobody answered. She stepped down off of the ladder that she was using and wandered over towards her desk.

"Oh, it's you."

"That's not a nice way to greet an old friend."

"We're not friends, Graham. I'm sorry Elliot isn't here today if you were hoping for another slanging match over that bloody villa. He texted me at 6am to say that he wouldn't be in and for me to open up."

"I knew Elliot wouldn't be in. Did you do it?"

"Do what?"

"Don't play dumb with me, Wendy. Did you give Edith the poisoned sweets?"

"Yes but she left them on her bedside table so I don't know when or if she will eat them."

"Let's hope for your sake that she eats it sooner rather than later. I don't like loose ends."

Graham's voice was as cold as ice, sending shivers down Wendy's spine. She had known Graham for years, right back to when he was still married to Olivia, but she had never seen him like this. His eyes were dark and his expression was cold and calculating.

"What do you want from me?" Wendy asked, her voice shaking.

"I want you to keep your mouth shut. If anyone asks, you don't know anything about Edith or the sweets," Graham replied, his tone leaving no room for argument.

Wendy nodded, a lump forming in her throat. "I won't say anything."

"Elliot has diverted the attention for a while. We lost some of our cargo but it'll all soon be over."

"What do you mean?"

"That's not your concern, just keep your mouth shut and everything will be okay, agreed?"

Wendy nodded.

"Good. And just to make sure you don't get any funny ideas, I have a little insurance policy," Graham said, reaching into his pocket and pulling out a small syringe filled with a clear liquid.

Wendy's eyes widened in fear as Graham stepped closer to her, holding the syringe out in front of him.

"What is that?" she asked, her voice trembling.

"It's a little something to make sure you stay quiet," Graham said with a cold smile. "Now, hold still."

Wendy tried to back away, but Graham was too quick. He grabbed her by the arm and injected the liquid into her veins. Wendy felt a sudden rush of dizziness and weakness, and she collapsed to the floor. Graham stood over her for a moment, watching as she writhed in pain. Then, with a satisfied smirk, he turned and walked out of the back door, leaving Wendy to suffer alone on the floor.

***

As Blake and his team were leaving Elliot Francis' house and the forensic teams entered to do their jobs, Blake's phone rang.

"That was quick. I hope you've got some good news for me Frank," Blake answered as he stood next to the front passenger door of his car.

"Not really," Frank replied. "The coroner's here. Edith Harrow died last night. Looks like she was poisoned."

"Poisoned? How? Why?" Blake asked, his heart sank at the news.

"The nursing home is still in a state of chaos as they check their procedures so nothing concrete to go on as yet."

"Damn it," Blake muttered under his breath. "We need to find out who did this. Any leads at all?"

"We're still waiting on toxicology reports, but the initial findings suggest that the poison was in a bag of mint humbugs that was found on her bedside table," Frank replied.

"Who gave her the sweets?" Blake asked, his mind racing. "Did we get any fingerprints or DNA from the packaging?"

"The officers are still processing the evidence, but I'll let you know as soon as I hear anything," Frank replied.

"What about visitor logs?"

"She had two visitors, Wendy Dawkins and Claire Turner."

Blake pondered that one. "Alright. Keep me posted," he said before ending the call.

He leaned against his car for a moment, taking deep breaths to calm his racing heart. This case was getting more and more complicated by the minute. Alison wandered over towards him.

"Any news?" she asked.

"Edith Harrow is dead. They suspect that she was poisoned by a mint humbug given to her by either Wendy Dawkins or Claire Turner. We need Gabby to visit her half sister and we need to find out who Wendy Dawkins is."

"She's the receptionist at Scatterbird Publishing House on Park Lane. Gabby mentioned her when she was talking about Elliot when they first met."

"Right, Samir and I will go to Scatterbird Publishing House, you and Shaun, find Claire Turner's home address and go there with Gabby. She's more likely to talk to you if Gabby is with you. We need to find out where the rest of the girls are before it's too late."

"Got it," Alison said, nodding. "And what about Simon?"

"Have him continue to work with the forensic team on the evidence we found here. Maybe he can find something that they missed."

Alison nodded again before turning to the rest of the team. "Alright, let's split up and get to work. We don't have much time."

As they split up, Blake couldn't help but feel a sense of unease. The killer was getting closer and closer, and he knew that they needed to catch them before anyone else got hurt. He just hoped that they could do it in time.

Chapter Twenty-Five

"The Funny Thing About Money, It Gets Shit Done"

Andrew Broughton arrived at The Troubled Traveller just after 10am. His thoughts consumed with his involvement with Paula and Michael from the previous night. He felt wrong that he had betrayed her trust like that but he needed to find out where the safe houses were and Blake had led him straight to them. As he arrived at the pub, a delivery driver was sitting in the cabin of his lorry waiting to unload a delivery.

"About bloody time, I've been waiting here over an hour," he complained as Andrew walked around the side of the pub.

"Sorry, I was under the assumption that Dickie was opening up this morning," Andrew apologised as he opened the back door.

As he wandered over to the hatch that led down to the basement cellar, he noticed that the padlock and latch that was used to keep the hatch secure had been broken off.

"Not again," he muttered under his breath as he opened the hatch.

As the hatch opened, an overwhelming smell hit him and as he looked down into the cellar, he saw the headless body of Richard Parsons.

Andrew stumbled backwards in shock, clutching his chest as he gasped for breath. The delivery driver looked over in concern.

"Are you alright mate?" he asked.

Andrew shook his head, his mind racing. He couldn't believe what he was seeing. Richard, his friend and business partner, dead in the cellar of their pub.

"We need to call the police," Andrew said, reaching for his phone.

The delivery driver looked into the cellar and nodded before dialling 999 as Andrew made his way down into the cellar to get a closer look. It was even worse than he had thought. Richard's body was lying in a pool of blood, his head nowhere to be found. Andrew felt bile rise up in his throat as he struggled to hold back his nausea. As he looked around, he saw that the cellar had been ransacked. Boxes were overturned, bottles were smashed, and the shelves were empty. The delivery driver looked down on them from above, not saying a word. The police arrived at the scene within minutes, and Andrew found himself being questioned by a detective in the pub's back office.

"Can you think of anyone who would have wanted to harm Richard?" the detective asked.

Andrew shook his head. "No, Richard was a good guy. He didn't have any enemies that I know of."

"What about financial troubles? Did the pub owe anyone money?"

Andrew thought for a moment before answering. "We were struggling to make ends meet, but we didn't owe anyone any significant debts."

"Well, we'll need to take a closer look at your finances just to be sure," the detective said. "In the meantime, do you know of anyone who may have had access to the pub's cellar?"

"No, only me and Richard had the keys to the hatch," Andrew replied.

The detective nodded before leaving the room to continue his investigation. Andrew slumped into a chair, his mind reeling. He couldn't believe that Richard was gone. It was a nightmare that he couldn't wake up from. As he sat there, he couldn't help but think about the last time he had seen Richard. They had been arguing about the pub's finances and Richard had been so stressed out that he had been on the verge of tears. Andrew had tried to reassure him, telling him that they would figure it out together, but now he wondered if that argument had been the catalyst for what had happened. A knock at the office door interrupted his thoughts.

"Excuse me, Mr Broughton, would you mind stepping into the cellar for a moment?" the detective asked.

Andrew nodded and followed the officer down to the cellar. As he stepped into the room, he saw that the forensic team had arrived and were busy taking pictures and gathering evidence.

"Is there anything you can tell us about this area?" the detective asked.

Andrew looked around, trying to recall anything that might be helpful. "This is where we keep our alcohol and other supplies. There's not much down here except for the shelves and boxes."

The detective nodded and continued to take notes. Andrew's eyes were drawn to the broken padlock on the floor. He felt a sense of anger rise in him as he realised that someone had broken into the pub and killed his friend.

"Did you notice anything strange or out of place when you arrived this morning?" the detective asked, interrupting his thoughts.

Andrew shook his head. "No, everything looked normal from the outside. The driver was pissed that there was nobody here to accept the delivery but otherwise everything was normal. It wasn't until I came down here that I saw the broken lock, the mess and Richard's body."

The detective nodded before turning towards the officer next to him who was holding up a plastic forensic bag which contained a samurai sword. "And do you recognise this?"

Andrew felt his blood run cold as the detective and police officer stared him down.

"That... That's mine," Andrew stammered.

"And do you have any idea how it ended up behind those crates over there covered in blood?" the detective asked.

Andrew's mind was racing. How could his sword be covered in blood? He had last seen it in his bedroom, safely tucked away in its sheath. He struggled to come up with an explanation that wouldn't incriminate him in Richard's murder.

"I don't know," he blurted out, hoping it sounded convincing.

The detective and police officer exchanged a look before the detective spoke again. "Mr Broughton, I'm going to need you to come down to the station with us for further questioning."

Andrew nodded, feeling a sense of dread wash over him. He knew that his sword being found in the cellar, covered in blood, made him look guilty. But he was innocent. He had to find a way to prove it. As he was led out of the pub in handcuffs, he couldn't help but wonder who had set him up. He knew that he had enemies. Had one of them decided to frame him. As the police officer led him away to the police car, Andrew looked up and saw Andrea standing in the street watching him.

"I didn't do it, I swear!" Andrew shouted.

Andrea just stood there watching him, not saying a word.

As he sat inside the police car and the driver sped away towards the station, he knew he needed an alibi for last night to prove that he wasn't the killer but he knew that Karun would never back him up. Another chess piece off of the board would be one less problem to solve when Derek took the girls away. That left only one person he could call on. One person he could trust, Paula.

***

Alison Pearce parked her car on Longfellow Crescent and stepped out of the car followed by Shaun Bryant and Gabby Turner.

"Shaun, you stay out here and let us know if anything unusual happens," Alison said as she led Gabby up the garden path of Claire Turner's house.

Gabby looked around at the street where she used to live. The curtains twitched in the bedroom window of Harriet Squantz's house, the house that she used to live in and she felt a sense of dread as they approached Claire's front door.

Alison rang the doorbell and they waited for a moment before Claire answered the door. Her face was pale and her eyes were red from crying.

"Hello Claire. I'm Alison Pearce, I work for Special Branch, and you already know Gabby Turner," Alison said, introducing herself and Gabby.

Claire looked at Gabby for a moment before her eyes widened in recognition. "Gabby? What are you doing here?" she asked, her voice trembling with emotion.

Gabby felt tears welling up in her eyes. "I'm sorry for what happened at the university hall. Can we talk? I really need to speak to you. It could be a matter of life and death."

Claire pulled Gabby into a tight hug, sobbing into her shoulder. "I'm so sorry," she whispered.

Alison watched them for a moment before clearing her throat.

"Claire, we're here to talk to you about Edith Harrow, can we come inside?" Alison asked.

Claire pulled away from Gabby, wiping her tears. "Is she okay?"

"She died this morning."

"Oh my God! What happened?"

"We're not exactly sure yet, but we believe it was foul play," Alison replied, her eyes studying Claire's reaction.

Claire gasped, gripping the door frame for support. "How? She seemed fine when I saw her. Who would do something like that?"

"We're trying to figure that out. But we need your help," Alison said, stepping forward.

Claire looked at Alison for a moment before nodding. "Okay. Come in."

The three of them stepped into Claire's living room and sat down on the sofa. Alison took out a notebook and pen, ready to take notes.

"Can you tell us everything you know about Edith?" Alison asked, her eyes focused on Claire.

Claire took a deep breath before starting. "Edith looked after me when I was a child. My mother died just after I was born and I was looked after by Margaret and Norman Petersen. After Margaret died, Edith looked after me until my father came back from travelling. I used to visit her every week and went shopping for her. When she moved into the nursing home, I still visited her regularly but work meant that I haven't been able to see her as much as I would have liked."

"Where do you work?"

"Behind the bar at my father's pub, Sam's Bar in St Lawrence Square."

"Another student bar?" Gabby asked.

Claire nodded.

Alison continued scribbling in her notebook. "Did she have any enemies? Anyone who might have wanted to harm her?"

Claire thought for a moment before shaking her head. "Not that I know of. Edith was a kind and gentle soul. She didn't have any enemies."

"What about anyone who might have had a reason to harm her? Did she have any valuable possessions or money that might have made her a target?" Alison asked.

Claire frowned, trying to think. "Well, she did have a valuable antique necklace that had been in her family for generations. She always kept it on her and was very protective of it."

"That's a good lead. Thank you, Claire," Alison said, closing her notebook. "We'll be in touch if we need anything else."

As they stood up to leave, Gabby hesitated for a moment before turning to Claire. "I'm really sorry about what happened at the university hall. I never meant to hurt you or send those people after you."

"It's okay, it must have come as quite a shock to learn that you had a half sister."

Gabby noticed a photo on the mantelpiece and walked over towards it. As she picked up the photo and looked at the picture, she saw a younger Claire standing at the top of a mountain overlooking a town below and next to her was the man who had haunted her every thought and dream since she was a teenager, Derek Copsewood. A shiver ran through her body as she relived the horror of fifteen years ago when she was laying in her bed sleeping whilst her mother, Lana Turner, had left the house to go to the shop to buy more alcohol. Derek took his opportunity and sneaked into her room and stole her innocence. Her brother James was woken up by her screams. He had tried to fight Derek off but he was too powerful and managed to lock James in his bedroom before getting in the car and driving away. In a blood soaked nightie, Gabby had sat trembling and crying in her room when her mother returned. Instead of showing concern for her daughter, Lana was furious. She blamed Gabby for Derek leaving and slapped her across the face. Gabby had slipped her coat on over her nightie and had run out of the house. She wandered the streets for what seemed like hours before Norman Petersen, their neighbour, had found her crying on a wooden bench in Vernwood Park whilst he was walking his dog. He had convinced Gabby to come home to see his wife, Margaret, who had taken care of her until the morning. When they had returned to the Turner family home, Norman managed to break into James' locked bedroom and bring him back to their house after Margaret had discovered that Lana had hung herself in the kitchen. Gabby closed her eyes tightly for a moment before turning and facing Claire again.

"Does Derek know Elliot Francis?" Gabby asked.

"They used to work together before Elliot became a publisher, why?" Claire asked.

"Where is Derek?"

"He didn't come home last night."

"So he lives here?"

Claire nodded.

"Does he visit Elliot Francis' house?"

"Sometimes, why all the questions?"

"Elliot Francis was found murdered this morning," Alison replied.

"And you think my father did it?" Claire asked.

"Your father raped me when I was fifteen years old Claire. He drove our mother to suicide and he has some creepy obsession with me displayed all over the attic of Elliot Francis' house!" Gabby fumed.

"Liar! He would never..."

"Claire, we believe your father and Elliot were involved in an operation to traffick young impressionable girls abroad to work in the illegal sex trade. Two have been murdered for not doing what they were told and making clients unhappy. Four more were found hidden in the basement of Elliot Francis' house. We need to find the rest of them before anything happens to them!" Alison replied.

Claire sat back in the chair staring at the wall. She couldn't believe what she was hearing. Edith Harrow, the woman who had looked after her when she was growing up had been killed. Now her father was accused of grooming young girls for the sex trade. "My father couldn't do that. He's a good man. I don't believe any of this," she said quietly.

"Well, I believe it," Gabby snapped.

"Gabby is telling the truth, Claire. Your father was stalking her. I've seen the photos in Elliot's attic that he has taken over the past twenty years. Somehow, he has managed to stalk her halfway around the world," Alison said.

"I can't believe this is happening," Claire said, her voice trembling. "Please find the girls and get them help. My father doesn't even know that I reached out and made contact with Gabby. That's why I ran the other night. I thought that he might have found out and sent someone after me."

"Claire, I know that this must be very hard for you to take in. Do you know of a place called The Rabbit Hole?" Alison asked.

Claire nodded. "It's an abandoned tube station near Kings Cross Station. As kids we used to play there before the police closed it off due to the high speed european trains."

"Gabby received a message yesterday telling her to go there at midnight tonight. I need you to find out if your father is planning to be at that meeting and let us know if he is."

Claire nodded as Alison wrote down her phone number on a scrap of paper and handed it to her. As they stood up to leave, Claire moved towards Gabby and held her close once more. "I'm sorry," she whispered.

"So am I," Gabby replied as she broke the embrace and followed Alison out of the door.

As they walked away, Shaun stepped out of the car and closed the door behind him. "Any luck?" he asked.

"We need a surveillance team watching this house in case Derek Copsewood returns home," Alison replied as she climbed into the driver's seat.

"I'll call it in and wait until they arrive," Shaun replied.

Gabby joined Alison in the car and the two women left, leaving Shaun Bryant wandering over towards a wooden bench that was situated next to a climbing frame, a couple of swings and a slide. He looked at the playground and wondered how a small innocent looking community could house so many secrets. He sat down on the bench directly opposite Harriet Squantz's house. Harriet watched out of her bedroom window before pulling out her phone and sending a message. It read:

Gabby has visited Claire.
They left a straggler behind.

Her phone vibrated almost immediately in reply:
You know what to do.
I'll transfer the funds after it's done.

***

Kaja drove past The Troubled Traveller Pub and saw three police cars parked outside with blue and white police tape across the entrance and the side alley. A thousand thoughts flooded his mind as he tried to figure out what had happened? He noticed Nicola's housemate Andrea walking towards the University Halls. He pulled over next to her and opened the passenger window.

"What's going on?" Kaja asked.

"The police found a body in the cellar and have arrested Andy so the pub is closed."

Kaja's mind ran through all kinds of possibilities. "That's awful! Do they know who it is?"

"Not yet," Andrea lied. "Anyway, as you're here, any chance of giving me a lift home?"

"Yeah, sure, get in," Kaja replied.

As they weaved through the London traffic, Andrea was busy texting on her phone before they reached a queue of traffic where some roadworks were being completed.

"Take a left over there," Andrea said, pointing towards a service road.

"That's a dead end."

"No, it's not, just do it."

Kaja cut across the line of traffic before turning into the service road. They drove past two cars that were parked at the side of the road with blacked out windows before looping around into a four space car park.

"See, I told you it was a dead end."

"Not necessarily," Andrea replied as she unbuttoned the top of her shirt and rubbed her hand over his thigh.

"No, Andrea, we can't. You're Nicola's friend, I can't..."

"Yes, you can. She doesn't have to know. Turn the engine off and let's have some fun."

Kaja turned the key and the engine cut out. Andrea began unzipping his jeans as his hands began exploring her body, unclipping her bra, as she leaned forwards. As she lowered her head, a bullet entered through the passenger window hitting Kaja in the side of his head.

"That was for Nicky," Andrea said as she moved herself out of the car and began walking back towards the two cars that were parked at the entrance of the service road, readjusting her clothing as she walked towards them.

She climbed into the back seat of the second car. Zodiac was sitting next to her in the back seat of the car and handed her a wad of twenty pound notes. She counted them before stuffing them inside her bra as their driver headed back through the city.

"A pleasure doing business with you Zac," she said as she settled back in her seat.

"That's the funny thing about money, it gets shit done," Zodiac replied.

Chapter Twenty-Six

Jenny's Confession

Blake Langford and Samir Khalifa arrived outside Scatterbird Publishing House and found the front door locked. Blake tried to look through the window but there was no sign of any life inside the building.

"You stay here, I'm going around the back!" Blake advised before heading down a side alley.

Blake found the back door of the publishing house and tried the handle. To his surprise, the door opened. He edged inside. The whole building was quiet. Too quiet. He pulled out his gun and moved from the back door down a corridor towards a wooden door. He turned the handle carefully before barging the door open. He found himself in the main reception room and there was a middle aged woman laying face down on the floor. He moved towards the front door to let Samir inside before going back to check on the woman.

"She has a pulse. She's been drugged. Get an ambulance here, quick!" Blake demanded.

Samir called an ambulance whilst Blake searched the rest of the publishing house. He found Elliot Francis' office and the CCTV system. He scrolled back through the recording until he came to this morning and he saw a man dressed in black entering the publishing house. He was wearing a hat and seemed to know where the cameras were as he never looked directly at them. With his height, build and the way that the man walked, Blake was in little doubt who the attacker was.

Samir joined Blake in the office. "Victim identified as Elliot Francis' assistant Wendy Dawkins. Looks like whoever topped

Elliot wanted to tie up some loose ends but didn't complete the job. Paramedic seems to think she was drugged with Rohypnol."

"The date rape drug?" Blake asked.

"The same one that was used on those four girls that were taken from Elliot's basement."

"Look at this," Blake replied as he showed Samir the CCTV footage.

"He knew he was on camera, he never looked up once."

"No but I know that man."

"How?"

"He's Paula's father, Graham Evans."

"How can you be so sure?" Samir asked.

"He walks with a limp, same height, same build, I know it's him."

"So do half of the Londoners I know, come on brother, I've heard of folks getting pissed off with their in-laws but attempted murder and assault, what's that guy ever done to you to deserve that?"

"A lot of things but that's irrelevant. We need to track him down and the one person who knows where he is kidnapped my fiance and son last night."

"Seriously, you're going after Andrew Broughton? This is more than a conflict of interests Blake."

"And what's Zodiac to you? I know he's one of your grasses so if Graham Evans or Andrew Broughton is on his payroll, tell your guy to cough them up before he gets a bullet in his head!"

Samir backed down. "Okay, okay, let's go."

As Blake and Samir returned to their car, Blake's phone rang.

"Any more news, Frank?" Blake asked as he answered.

"Nothing more about Edith Harrow but I had a call from an old buddy of mine in the met, Detective Jack Young. He's arrested Andrew Broughton for murder this morning after he found his samurai sword at the murder scene at The Troubled Traveller. All the serial numbers match so it seems to be a slam dunk case."

Thoughts swirled through Blake's mind. Only a few hours earlier, Broughton was holding Paula and Michael captive on a ship in St Katherine's Docks. "Well that's one less chess piece on the board. Who did he murder?"

"Richard Parsons, his boss at The Troubled Traveller pub. The funny thing is though, he needed an alibi for last night, so he made his call and Special Branch intercepted it."

Blake felt a shiver run down his spine. Special Branch only intercepted calls of agents and those in protective custody. "Who did he call?"

"Paula."

"And she gave him an alibi?"

"Yep, she was with him around the alleged time that Parsons met his maker."

Blake couldn't believe what he was hearing. "Are they sure of the time frame? Where is she now? I told them to keep her in Special Branch until this has blown over."

"Young has requested that she joins him at New Scotland Yard on the Embankment to complete a formal statement of events from last night."

Blake swore under his breath. "We need to track down Graham Evans and I need to tie up some loose ends with Alison before I come in. Can you keep an eye on her for me please, I just hope she doesn't do anything stupid."

"Will do," Frank replied before cutting off the call.

"Is everything okay?" Samir asked as Blake joined him in the car.

"It will be," Blake replied before driving towards Harlequin Square and The Troubled Traveller Pub.

***

Andrea and Nicola wandered through the glass corridors of Chelsea And Westminster Hospital until they arrived at the High Dependency Unit. They saw Jenny Langford sitting at her mother's bedside. Jenny looked up as they approached her. Her eyes were red and swollen and it was clear she had been crying.

"How is she?" Nicola asked softly.

Jenny shook her head. "They don't know yet. She's still unconscious."

"I'm so sorry, Jenny," Andrea said, placing a comforting hand on her shoulder.

"It's all my fault," Jenny whispered, tears streaming down her face. "She's been struggling with her balance for a while. If I hadn't convinced her that she had nothing to worry about, perhaps she wouldn't be in this condition."

Andrea knelt down beside Jenny and took her hand. "You can't blame yourself for this. You didn't know what was going to happen."

"But I should have," Jenny replied. "And I shouldn't have left her side yesterday on some wild goose chase in a vain attempt to chase after a guy who it turns out is a snake."

"We all make mistakes, Jen. When they realise that the two of you are not in that cellar anymore, hopefully they will leave you alone," Andrea replied.

Jenny shook her head. "I don't think we can count on that. They know who we are, where we live, where we work. They could come after us anytime."

Nicola looked at Jenny with concern. "Then we need to do something. We can't just sit here and wait for them to strike again."

"Starting with your boyfriend? He led us into the mess last night," Jenny snapped.

"Kaja won't bother you anymore," Andrea replied.

The two women looked at her. "How can you be so sure?" Nicola asked.

"Because I know men. Once they've had what they want, they head for the hills."

"Thanks, you're saying I'm easy..." Nicola snapped.

"No, I just think that he used you for some reason that we still don't understand and now he's cast you aside to chase whatever prize is at the end. Men are bastards like that," Andrea explained, trying not to dig herself any deeper into the hole she had created.

Nicola bowed her head.

Jenny took hold of her hand. "You're not the first to be taken in by a cute smile and a toned body Nic. But last night proved that Kaja can't be trusted."

"I just... I just thought that creep loved me," Nicola confessed.

"So now we need to find out what is going on behind the scenes. Nic told me about this Rabbit Hole. What is it?" Andrea asked.

"It's an old abandoned tube station near Kings Cross. We used to play there when we were teenagers before the police found it and sealed it up. Some guy called Derek gave me the message to go there at midnight tonight," Jenny explained.

The name Derek sent a shiver down Andrea's spine. She knew that if Derek Copsewood was involved then there was going to be trouble ahead.

"If the police sealed it up, how are you meant to get in there?" Nicola asked.

"There's another way. There's a blank door at the Eurostar terminal that leads down to it. Very few people even know it exists," Jenny replied.

"You need to be careful lurking around abandoned underground stations. There was a girl discovered dead in one of them a few weeks ago," Andrea advised.

"I know, I was one of the people who found her," Jenny replied.

Andrea and Nicola stared at her.

"What?" Nicola gasped.

"I was on a train with my brother and his fiance and the train broke down at a disused station. My brother, being the restless sod he is, decided that we should climb up the two hundred odd stairs to the surface but rather than finding an exit, we found a dead girl staring back at us."

"She couldn't have been there long if you could identify her," Andrea replied.

"She was wearing a black skirt and a pink hoodie but I'll never forget the look of her face. Have you ever seen a decomposing body?" Jenny asked.

Nicola shuddered. "No, and I don't want to either."

"Okay, we need to be careful. If Derek is involved, then we need to assume that there will be others waiting for us at the Rabbit Hole too. We need to be prepared for anything," Andrea said.

"Us?" Jenny asked. "I'm not dragging you two into that. It's my mess and I need to clean it up!"

"Or end up dead?" Andrea asked.

Jenny didn't reply.

"So what do you suggest?" Nicola asked.

Jenny thought for a moment. "We need to get some backup. We need to speak to my brother, Blake. He's been investigating a case that might be connected to all of this."

"Are you sure you can trust him?" Andrea asked.

"I trust him enough to know that he can help us. We don't have any other options," Jenny replied.

"Okay, we'll go and see your brother. But we need to be cautious. We don't want to tip off whoever is behind all of this," Andrea said.

Nicola nodded in agreement. "And we need to be armed. Just in case."

Andrea shook her head. "No way, Nic. We can't go around carrying weapons. We'll just need to be smart about how we handle ourselves."

"But what if they come at us with guns or knives or something?" Nicola argued.

"Then we run. We don't want to get into a physical fight with them. We'll call the police if we have to," Andrea replied.

Jenny nodded. "She's right. We don't want to make things worse."

Nicola sighed. "Fine. But I'm not going down without a fight."

Andrea smiled. "That's more like it. But let's try to avoid any fighting if we can."

Jenny leaned across and kissed her mother on the forehead before the three women left the hospital. As they were about to leave the ward, a nurse called Jenny aside whilst Nicola and Andrea waited by the door. A local news update was being shown on a TV in one of the side rooms. The reporter was standing outside The Troubled Traveller Pub and the headline across the bottom of the screen read:

Police looking for witnesses after brutal murder.

Nicola looked at Andrea. "What did you do after we left last night?"

"I gave Xander the key to Andy's flat. Who knows what happened next," Andrea replied.

"You..."

"Sshh! Jenny's got enough going on," Andrea smiled as Jenny rejoined them and the three women left the hospital and headed back towards Jenny's flat in Kensington.

As they walked, Jenny called Blake and asked him to meet her at her flat. Nicola continued to look around as she couldn't help but feel a sense of unease. Andrea was acting weird and she felt betrayed by Kaja and his friends. When they arrived at Jenny's flat, they found Blake waiting for them. He was tall and lean, with piercing blue eyes, short black hair and a sharp jawline. He looked up from his laptop as they entered and his face lit up when he saw his sister.

"Jenny! Are you okay?" he asked, getting up from his seat and giving her a hug.

"I'm fine, Blake. Thanks for coming," she replied, returning the embrace.

He turned to Andrea and Nicola. "And you two must be the friends Jenny was telling me about. I'm Blake."

Andrea shook his hand. "I'm Andrea. This is Nicola."

Blake turned his attention to Andrea. "I recognise you from The Troubled Traveller Pub. Were you there last night or this morning?"

"Whoa, am I on trial or something?" Andrea asked.

"No, of course not, just naturally curious when your boss gets killed and your colleague is arrested for suspected murder," Blake pushed.

Andrea felt a knot form in her stomach. She had been hoping to avoid any questions about her whereabouts, but she knew that it was inevitable. "I was there last night," she admitted.

Blake raised an eyebrow. "And what were you doing there?"

"Working until closing time and then I went home," Andrea lied.

"That's not strictly true, is it Andrea?" Nicola replied.

Andrea glared at her before confessing. "I heard someone knocking at the basement trap door so after I said good night to Dickie, I went around the back and opened the trap door. Nic and Jen were inside. They had been locked in there by Dickie and Derek."

Blake turned to Jenny in astonishment. "Jenny, can you fill me in on what's been going on? When did you leave the hospital and how did you end up in the cellar of a pub that is now a murder scene?"

Jenny recounted the events of the past 24 hours starting with the message to meet at the Rabbit Hole, Kaja and Raj taking them to the ship to fool Samir, the promise to see Tom again and then being locked inside the basement before being freed by Andrea.

Blake listened intently, his eyes narrowing as she spoke. "And where did you go after Andrea set you both free?"

"I went back to Mum's to get changed and then went to the hospital."

"Why didn't you come back here?" Blake asked.

"I don't know, my head was all over the place. The police have raided Mum's house and are looking for Steven," Jenny replied.

"I know, don't worry, he's safe. What time did you leave the basement at The Troubled Traveller Pub?" Blake asked.

"About midnight, why?"

Blake suddenly realised that if Richard Parsons was killed after midnight then Paula's alibi for Andrew Broughton was useless. "So, Richard Parsons wasn't with you?"

"No, Blake..." Jenny began.

"Are you accusing us of murdering him?" Andrea asked.

"You were there last night and there was a motive if he locked Jenny and Nicola in the basement," Blake reasoned.

"You've gotta be kiddin' me, I thought your brother was meant to help us not frame us for murder!" Nicola snapped.

Blake held up his hands. "I'm not accusing anyone. I'm just trying to piece together what happened. We need to be aware of all possibilities, including the fact that the police might suspect you."

"This is insane," Andrea muttered.

"So what do we do now?" Jenny asked.

"We need to find out who killed Richard Parsons and clear your names," Blake replied. "But first, we need to make sure that you three are safe."

"So you're saying we should just sit tight and do nothing?" Nicola asked.

"No, we need to be proactive. But we need to do it carefully. We don't want to make any mistakes that could incriminate us further," Blake said.

Andrea nodded. "He's right. We need to be smart about this. Let's start by figuring out who would have wanted to kill Richard Parsons."

"Maybe it was Derek," Jenny suggested.

"It's quite possible or maybe one of his associates," Blake added. "But we can't jump to conclusions."

"Are you sure about Derek Copsewood? Don't get me wrong, he's weird and creepy but I would've thought he's more of a pervert than a murderer," Nicola reasoned.

"This definitely sounds like something Derek would be involved in. He's been getting more and more involved in the criminal underworld lately," Blake replied.

"So what's your plan?" Andrea asked.

"I need you two to go home and if you see or hear anything from Derek or his associates, call me!" Blake advised.

"The worm on the hook until we end up dead," Nicola complained.

"With the police closing off the pub, it has created a diversion. Anyone who knew that you were in the basement last night will probably think that you were murdered so the last place they will look for you is your home," Blake reasoned. "Unless you've spoken to someone of interest since then?"

Both women shook their heads.

"I guess you're right but I still don't like it," Andrea replied.

Blake handed both of them a business card with his number on it before they left. After Jenny closed the door on them she turned back towards Blake. "Do you really think they'll be safe out on their own?"

"They should be but I'm more concerned about you. This whole investigation is turning into a family affair and they never seem to end well. First Steven, then Paula and now you."

"What do you mean?"

"Tom Gibson."

Jenny bowed her head.

"Jen?"

"Did you know?"

"Know what?"

"Don't play dumb Blake, did you know he was still alive?"

"Not until recently."

"How recent?"

"It doesn't matter, the problem we have is that you seem to still be under his spell."

Jenny felt the sting of tears build up in her eyes. "I know, I stupidly followed my heart rather than my head. I'm an idiot. I should've known better."

"I managed to cover up a lot last time but Tom betrayed you in the worst possible way. He led you and his family to believe he was dead when in fact, he was a double agent. That dossier that you handed over to the Russian informant had the details of his whole team's operation. Fourteen men were murdered on his watch. You know the details about his past. What makes you think that he would care for you and look after you again this time given the facts?"

"I thought he loved me Blake! And I loved him! More than I've ever loved any man that I've ever met!" Jenny cried. "I mourned his death. I vowed never to have my heart broken like that again and for thirteen years, I've never allowed myself to love another man in that way. Do you know how that feels? To see your family and friends in relationships, finding unconditional love, having children, the questions constantly being asked, when will you start dating again Jen? Are you sure you're not gay? Why don't you try going on dating websites? Why don't you go for a drink with this guy or that guy? For what, a couple of hours of small talk and then meaningless sex at the end before the inevitable rejection. I can't face that again. If there's even a remote chance that I can come face to face with him again, just to gain some kind of closure. To ask him why he did what he did. And if he ever truly loved me or if I was just a pawn in his sick game. I need to take that chance if I'm ever going to be able to move on with my life."

Blake held her close. "Is that why you tried to fool Samir into thinking he was chasing a false lead on the ship at the docks?"

"You knew about that?"

"He recognised your photo when we went back to my place. It didn't take long to make the connection."

"Is that why he didn't come here with you?"

"No, I left him at The Troubled Traveller gathering up whatever information that he can find."

"The ship is a diversion."

"How can you be so sure?"

"The leftover clothes and belongings were conveniently placed, don't you think?"

Blake pondered that. "Now that you mention it..."

"It all comes down to The Rabbit Hole. Why lead the police and your team to the docks and incriminate themselves. They must know that you're watching otherwise the ship would have been impounded by now."

"You're more switched on then I gave you credit for," Blake smiled. "Go on."

"Reaper and Zodiac believe that there is going to be a showdown between Derek Copsewood and Tom Gibson to get the girls out of the country. I think they want to use me as bait to distract you from the investigation."

"So you need to go in wired. We need to hear the conversation, find out where the girls are and how they plan to get them out."

"Isn't it obvious? Think about the tunnels that we used to go down as teenagers. Why would they choose the Rabbit Hole?" Jenny asked.

"Because it would lead them down to section X, the loading yard for the freight trains that would use the same high speed network as the European trains. They could hide in the freight train and then escape as soon as they get past the checkpoint at Calais," Blake pondered. "Of course!"

"All roads lead to this. You just need to work out the trail of destruction that's left behind. A lot of people were involved and a lot of money changed hands."

Blake looked at her. "What aren't you telling me?"

"I was asked by Zodiac if I would help them with a honey trap. He had a couple of people who were assisting Derek in trafficking some of the young freshers into prostitution and pornography. He wanted to get rid of them by having some women lead them astray before they disappear. I refused."

At that moment, Blake's mobile phone rang. "Hold that thought," he said as he answered the call. "What have you got for me, Frank?"

"I'm at Scotland Yard now. Paula gave her statement but it's come to light that Richard Parsons was killed later than they originally thought, making her statement redundant."

"Yeah, I found that out at my end too. Please get her back to HQ as soon as possible."

"Will do, there's one more thing though. There's just been a report called in, that Kaja Patel, one of Zodiac's men, has been found shot in the head in a car park behind a department stall near the roadworks on the Fulham Road. Seems like he went with a smile on his face if you get my drift."

"Completely, good work Frank. I'll be back at HQ soon. Don't let Paula out of your sight," Blake replied before cutting off the call.

He turned back to Jenny. "Kaja's dead."

Jenny gasped. "When? How?"

"This morning in a car park whilst receiving a blowjob by all accounts. You were talking about a honey trap? Do you know anyone who would take Zodiac up on his offer?"

Jenny shook her head. "No, but if they're attacking his men, you need to find Zodiac."

"Get your coat, we need to go to Special Branch."

Jenny collected her things and led Blake out of the flat. Blake closed the door behind him before following her down the stairs. This case was becoming more and more complicated by the minute but at least now he finally had some idea of who was responsible.

***

Meanwhile, at The Troubled Traveller Pub, Samir stepped outside the hatch of the pub cellar to get some fresh air. As he wandered over towards the dumpsters, he found a used match on the ground near to the dumpster wheel. He picked it up and noticed some yellow and black paint on the end of the match.

"Zodiac?" he whispered to himself.

He pulled out his phone and sent a text, it read:

DO YOU KNOW WHERE YOUR MEN WERE LAST NIGHT?

Chapter Twenty-Seven

Making Waves

Claire Turner picked up her handbag and keys before heading out of the house. Her mind was still spinning from her earlier conversation with Gabby.

"Going somewhere?" Derek asked as she locked the front door.

"Dad, I didn't expect you home until tonight," Claire stammered as she turned to face him.

"No, I thought I'd take the day off. Where are you going?"

"I'm just heading to Oxford Street to meet a friend for afternoon tea."

"Really, who?"

"Oh, just someone I met in the pub a few weeks ago."

"So it's a date?"

"Would I honestly be going out on a date in the middle of the afternoon dressed like this?"

"Who knows these days..."

"Why all the questions?" Claire asked.

"No reason, except I want to know why Gabrielle Turner visited you this morning?"

Claire felt a shiver run down her spine. "Have you been spying on me?"

"Answer the question, what did she want?"

"She was with a police officer, they were looking into the disappearance of the missing students."

"And what did you tell her?"

"Nothing. Just that I work in the pub and I'd keep a listen out and tell them if I heard anything suspicious. Speaking of which, if you're here, who's running the pub today?" Claire asked, attempting to change the subject.

"Vijay has it all under control. Anyway, don't be too late back. I may have a surprise for you later."

"What kind of surprise?"

"If I tell you, it won't be a surprise will it?"

"I guess not," Claire replied, giving her father a peck on the cheek. "I'll see you soon."

Derek nodded as he watched Claire climb into her car and drive away. He looked up at the house opposite them and saw Harriet Squantz approaching her front garden gate. She was holding two coffee mugs in her hands. They both looked at each other before Derek headed inside his house.

Shaun Bryant was sitting on a wooden bench on the patch of grass in the centre of Longfellow Crescent with his phone in his hand trying to keep a close watch on what was happening outside the Turner/Copsewood house. He scrolled down to Alison's number in his phone and sent a message before hearing footsteps behind him. Shaun turned around and saw a lady approaching him with two mugs of coffee in her hands.

"You look like you could do with a nice hot cup of coffee. It's not the most ideal weather for sitting and contemplating in the park," she said as she sat down next to him.

"Thank you for the offer Mrs..."

"Squantz, Harriet Squantz. I often come here during the summertime and watch the children play on the climbing frame and just to smell the freshly cut grass and take in the fresh air. London's become so overcrowded that it's often difficult to find time and space to just slow things down a little and replenish the soul, don't you think?" she asked, pushing the coffee mug into Shaun's hands.

Shaun took the coffee mug and tasted the coffee.

"White with one sugar, was I right?" she asked.

"Mmm, perfect, how did you know?"

"Lucky guess. So what brings you to Longfellow Crescent anyway? Are you visiting someone?"

"I'm afraid I can't..." Shaun began before a feeling of dizziness and sickness overcame him.

Shaun staggered to his feet before falling to his knees, dropping the coffee mug and its remaining contents onto the ground before landing face down on the grass.

Harriet looked over towards the Turner house before the silenced pop of a gunshot sounded and she fell forwards on top of Shaun after a bullet had hit her in the forehead.

A black Ford Focus pulled up at the side of the playground and a man dressed in black with a balaclava over his head walked over to where Harriet and Shaun were laying on the ground. He picked up Shaun's phone before heading back to the car and driving away once again. Derek watched from the bedroom window of his house as the events unfolded.

"Paid in full," he smiled before heading downstairs and out of his back door.

Derek followed a gravel track behind the row of houses where he lived and headed into the next street. A minute or so later, the black Ford Focus appeared. It stopped in front of Derek who climbed into the passenger seat before the driver headed back into central London.

***

Reaper walked into Waterloo Station and headed over towards the coffee shop opposite the underground terminal. He watched the escalator with interest as hundreds of men and women continued on their way to wherever they were headed. He could see the fear in their eyes. He could see how scared they were of their jobs, their futures, of the prospect of getting on the train and arriving at the destination that they would be spending the next eight hours of their life at. He watched them all ascend the escalator and felt disdain for their sheep-like existence. He was different. He was special. He carried around with him a quiet determination and an understanding that this was a dog-eat-dog world and that if you didn't watch your own back, no one else was going to. Reaper had left his home and family behind in his quest for a purpose to exist. He was in no doubt that he would have to kill again and again before he would find what he was looking for.

He noticed a young woman looking at him. She was sitting at a table with another couple. Reaper watched them closely. He could see that the woman had made eye contact with him. He could see that she was trying to work out if there was anything she recognised about him. He could see that he was an external distraction to the couple but not a threat. They returned their attention to each other and to their drinks before jumping up when the next train announcement echoed around the station. They headed on their way leaving Reaper behind in the coffee shop.

Samir Khalifa ascended the escalator and headed over towards the coffee shop. He looked around at a couple of occupied tables before he noticed Reaper. He ordered a Flat White coffee before wandering over and sitting down opposite him.

"Where's Zodiac?" Samir asked.

"Indisposed."

"Meaning?"

"He thought it was unwise to see you out in such a public place. So what's this shit that you uncovered at The Troubled Traveller?"

"When forensics were just finishing up, I found one of the team's yellow and black matches next to one of the dumpsters outside the pub."

"That's flimsy, the amount of people who go out for a smoke by those bins, it could've been anyone."

"Yes, but we both know that Zodiac's men haven't exactly been loyal of late."

"What do you mean?"

"What I mean is, Zodiac may have a mole that is feeding information about his whereabouts to Derek Copsewood."

"And?"

"Copsewood may be setting Zodiac up for a fall when he takes those girls out of the country."

"If you were so convinced of that, why haven't Special Branch impounded the ship at the docks?"

"They believe it's a decoy."

"How can you be so sure?"

"You first, where's Zodiac and Xander?"

"As if I'm going to tell you that. Xander's ass would be back in jail before we even finish this rather disappointing coffee."

"You led me to the ship so you must have had a suspicion of what was going on. We know that at least two of Zodiac's men have been acting in the interests of Derek Copsewood," Samir replied.

Reaper took a sip of his coffee before replying. "My sources tell me that Copsewood is planning on taking the girls out of the country on a freight train. They're being held in a secure location until the time is right."

"Do you have any idea where this train is headed?"

"Not yet, but I have a feeling that Zodiac knows more than he's letting on."

"What makes you say that?"

"Call it intuition, but something doesn't add up. Copsewood has too much at stake and must have an edge on Zodiac and his crew."

"If he gets Xander out of the country as well as the girls, then he can't be taken back to jail."

"That was my conclusion too. That was until this morning when Zodiac turned on one of his own."

"Who?"

"Kaja Patel."

"What happened?"

"He convinced Kaja's girlfriend and her friend to play an elaborate trick on you before locking her in the basement of The Troubled Traveller Pub."

"Hang on a minute, what trick? There were no women in the basement of that pub. I was there this morning."

"They wanted you to believe that the ship was a decoy so that ironically, Special Branch would investigate further. What they didn't expect was that Kaja would get greedy. He arranged for Jenny Langford to be locked in that basement in an attempt to destabilise the operation. Derek needs Blake Langford's attention. Zodiac knows that. So he sent one of his own to free the girlfriend and Jenny from the basement and send Kaja and his accomplice to death."

"So Richard Parsons was in on it?"

"Of course, he wanted Derek out of the way. With all the students passing through the bars and several of them disappearing for his own sexual gratification, it was bad for business. But his allegiance to Kaja bit him on the ass and Xander made sure that he paid for it."

"How did he get hold of the sword?"

"A pissed father of one of the girls, I guess. Someone paid him three grand to kill Parsons and send the poor bastard down who owns the sword."

Samir thought about that for a moment. "So what's our next move?"

"We need to find out where the girls are being held and get them out of there before it's too late. And we need to make sure that Copsewood doesn't get his hands on them."

"How do you propose we do that?"

"Simple. We follow the money. Someone had to pay Zodiac's crew to kidnap those girls. We find out who that someone is, and we can uncover the location of the girls and the train they will be transported on."

Samir nodded. "And do you have any leads on who that someone might be?"

"Not yet, but I have a few ideas. Some of the names that have been thrown around in the underworld seem to be connected to this case."

"I suppose we'll have to start digging then," Samir said with a sigh.

Reaper finished his coffee and stood up. "I'll start making some calls. We need to move quickly before it's too late."

Samir nodded and watched as Reaper walked away, disappearing into the crowds of people at the station. He knew that they had a lot of work ahead of them, but he was determined to see this case through to the end and rescue those girls before it was too late.

Reaper checked behind him to make sure that Samir wasn't following him. He stepped outside the station and climbed into a black cab taxi.

"Where to bud?" the driver asked.

"124 Alfredson Road, Kensington," Reaper replied.

***

Andrea and Nicola stepped off of the bus at the corner of Jones Lane and Alfredson Road in Kensington.

"Would you mind telling me what we're doing here?" Nicola asked. "Blake said we should go home."

"Which is precisely why we shouldn't go home."

"Why?"

"Isn't it obvious? He's just looking out for his sister. He doesn't give a shit about us. If he did, he would've made sure that you and Jenny didn't end up in that basement and I wouldn't have had to tidy up that mess."

Nicola placed her hand on Andrea's shoulder. "What do you mean to tidy up that mess?"

"It doesn't matter."

"I think it does, Andrea. You said that you were going to call Richard Parsons last night and then this morning, he ended up dead."

"Coincidence, that's all."

"Bullshit. Now you're gonna tell me what's going on or I'm calling the cops right now."

"Your boyfriend tried to hit on me, okay."

"Kaja?"

"Yes, your beloved Kaja. I got a friend to make sure that Dickie and Kaja stayed away from us for good."

"Where is he?"

"I don't know, okay. He tried it on with me, I said no and we went our separate ways. He locked you in a basement to use you as bribery to get money out of some perverted paedophile who would sell your body to the highest bidder. You're well rid of him Nic!"

"No, it was Derek! Kaja wouldn't do that!"

"Open your eyes, Nic. It's blatantly obvious what he was doing! So you can either go home and wait for the bastards to come along and kill you or you can come with me and speak to someone who can help us."

Nicola looked at Andrea, her mind racing with the information she had just been given. She knew that Andrea was right, but she couldn't bring herself to believe that Kaja was capable of such a thing. "Who are we going to see?" Nicola asked.

"A friend of mine. He can help us find out who's behind this and get us out of harm's way."

Nicola nodded slowly. "Okay, let's go see him."

Andrea led the way down Alfredson Road, nervously looking around as they turned a corner and stopped outside number 124. The police that had been present the previous night had since disappeared and all that was left was a dimly lit shell of a house that had been torn apart by the authorities.

"This is the place," Andrea said, as she wandered up the driveway towards the front door and motioned for Nicola to follow her inside.

"This is Jenny's parent's house," Nicola replied.

"Yeah, that friend of yours, Jenny, did you know that her brother, Steven, is currently on the run for several murders after he had a house party. Police found everyone dead the following morning. Had the police all over this place and his own place but of course, Blake Langford is the one we should trust, right?"

Nicola noticed the same boots and keys by the door that Jenny had noticed on their last visit that seemed out of place. "Are you saying that Blake covered up his brother's murder investigation?"

Andrea nodded.

"Why? To what end?"

"He covered up Jenny's involvement in a Russian intelligence operation several years ago. Lucky really because otherwise I would never have met Tom."

As they wandered through the house, Nicola noticed that all of the curtains were closed and there was the light of a laptop screen illuminating what looked like a study at the far end of the hall.

"Why this place? Who's Tom?" Nicola asked.

"Isn't it obvious? The police have already gone through this place with a fine toothed comb looking for dirt on Steven Langford. There's no reason for them to return and Tom can set up his base in the home of the father who forbade him to get engaged to his precious daughter. So in one of life's little ironies, little Jenny Langford became involved in a Russian intelligence investigation to wipe out an entire force in Afghanistan leaving Tom to pick up the pieces and make his move back to the UK."

When the two women entered the study, on the laptop screen was a red crystal with blue segments that had already been placed into what looked like an extremely complex puzzle. As the pieces of the crystal puzzle entered the main frame on the screen, thousands of pounds were being transferred into a collection at the bottom of the screen. The current amount was just over two million pounds. The top earner in the top left corner of the screen was MJL101GG who had already theoretically banked five million, two hundred and fifty thousand pounds.

Tom turned and faced the two women as they entered. "Phase two in progress. Soon, we will have the funds to close the deal once the final details have been ironed out. You must be Nicky, I'm Tom Gibson. I've heard a lot about you.

"What is this? What do you intend to achieve?" Nicola asked.

"Oh, nothing. Just the highest yield in crypto-currency that the world has ever seen, all courtesy of the incompetence of Special Branch."

"And the women?"

"Mere pieces of gold that can be turned as and when needed. Perhaps you'd like to join them?"

From the darkness in the corner of the room, two men took hold of Nicola, injecting her in the arm as they led her away towards the staircase in the hall that led up to the bedrooms.

"So what now?" Andrea asked.

"Now, we wait and then go to The Rabbit Hole," Tom replied as he continued to build his crystal on the laptop screen.

Chapter Twenty-Eight

Love Hurts

"Just sign here, here and here Miss Evans and then he's all yours," the police officer said as Andrew Broughton and Paula Evans waited by a desk inside Scotland Yard.

"Lucky me," Paula sighed as she signed the paperwork.

"Don't leave the country Broughton, this ain't over," one of the officers commented as they turned to leave.

"I doubt it is," Andrew replied before they left the station.

An agent from Special Branch was waiting by a car for them but Paula raised her hand and led Andrew to a wooden bench outside the station.

"Sit down," she said.

"Paula, what..."

"Sit your ass down Andy," Paula demanded as she sat on the bench.

Andrew looked at the Special Branch agent before sitting down next to her. He grabbed his stomach and groaned before leaning forward.

"Are you okay?" Paula asked.

"Yeh, sorry. Just feeling a bit nauseous and I have a stomach ache."

Paula waited for a moment until he looked at her again. "I've risked everything coming here today. I guess for some reason, I thought you were innocent and the police agreed that you were only implicated circumstantially."

"I appreciate it. I didn't deserve that after everything that I've done."

"No, you didn't. I wasn't strong enough at the time but you were a bastard when we were together and I don't know why or how I put up with it for so long."

Andrew bowed his head. "I know what I've done in the past was wrong but I want to make things right again."

"Then you can start by telling me what my father has been doing with you?"

"He turned up at the pub with apparently nowhere else to go and I gave him somewhere to stay for a few nights but he turned on me."

"Where was he staying?"

"In my flat," Andrew sighed.

"What happened?"

"I overheard a conversation that he was having with Elliot Francis and Tom Gibson. They planned to get out of the country with the girls that Derek Copsewood and his men were seducing at the pubs and sell them on to the highest bidders in Europe. Tom has a score to settle with Blake so he tried to murder his brother, Steven, by sending one of his girls to kill everyone at his house party."

"Tiffany Mason."

Andrew nodded.

"But Steven survived. He was only drugged and when he woke up and saw the mess, he ran."

Andrew nodded. "They threatened to come after you and Michael if Steven wasn't murdered but Blake had already taken him off the grid. Tom wanted Tiffany taken out so when it all kicked off at the student hall, I took my chance."

Paula gasped. "The train... you didn't..."

Andrew nodded, wiping tears from his eyes. "I had to. It was her or you. The train wasn't going to stop so I knew I had a small window to work in. When nobody was looking, I pushed her in front of the train. It looked like she just tripped and she was found at the next station."

Paula recoiled in horror. "You killed someone? You murdered Tiffany Mason?"

Andrew began coughing and holding his chest as he struggled to catch his breath. "I had no choice," his voice choked with emotion. "I was trying to protect you."

"Protect me? You murdered someone. You destroyed a family. How am I supposed to forgive you for that?"

"I know what I did was wrong, but I had no other choice. I had to act to protect you from those people."

"That doesn't excuse what you did. You need to turn yourself in and face the consequences of your actions."

"I can't do that, Paula. I can't go to prison. I'll do anything to make it up to you, but I can't give myself up."

Paula ran her fingers through her hair in frustration. "So, what happened with Dad?" she asked.

Andrew coughed again before spitting some blood onto the floor. "He hit me over the head with something at the flat, when I came around he was gone."

"With the sword to incriminate you later?"

"I don't remember..."

"Think Andy, if we can prove that Dad took the sword and either used it or gave it to someone else to use, then you can at least get off of those charges."

"I don't know, all right!" Andrew snapped before coughing once again.

"You need to see a doctor. Your eyes are looking dark and you're coughing up blood."

"I'm fine."

Paula waited a moment before continuing. "Who else has keys to your flat?"

"Me, your Dad and Andrea."

"Who's Andrea? Girlfriend?"

Andrew shook his head. "Someone I work with."

"Would she have a grudge against you? Is she likely to have wanted you in jail?"

Andrew shook his head again. "No, it doesn't make sense."

Paula took a deep breath. "Let's get the elephant in the room out of the way, if you were so concerned about my safety, why did you take Michael and me to that ship and tie us up? Why did you attack Frank? And why did you give Blake an open goal to come and rescue us with nobody interfering?"

"They were leading Blake into a trap. The only way I could stop it was to create a diversion. They were going after Steven at Blake's safe house and were hoping to get Blake too. I had to make it look like I'd kidnapped you and it was a cock-up in their execution," Andrew explained before coughing and clutching his chest again.

"Why do you want to help Blake? I thought you hated him?"

"I did it for you."

"Why didn't you just say that in the first place."

"Would you have believed me?"

Paula bowed her head. "I guess not."

"I know I treated you badly Paula. I regret it every day. I was childish, immature, an asshole, but I have always loved you."

Paula sighed, looking at Andrew with a mixture of sorrow and anger. "Love hurts, Andy. You can't just say that you love me and expect everything to be forgiven. You took a life, you put Michael and me in danger, and you've been lying to me this whole time."

"I know and I'll do whatever it takes to make it right. Just tell me what I can do."

"I don't know, Andy. I need to process all of this. I need time. You need to go to the doctors as you don't look so good."

Andrew nodded, looking down at his hands that suddenly felt like they were on fire. "I understand."

At that moment, Blake arrived in his Ford Mondeo and stepped out of the car. He walked over towards them.

"What the hell is going on?" Blake asked.

"Andy has some interesting information that may help you track down where the girls are," Paula replied.

"I should rip the bastard limb from limb..."

"Blake!" Paula snapped.

"You shouldn't even be here!"

"Tom Gibson is going to lead your sister into danger tonight at the Rabbit Hole. He wants to trap you so you don't impede him from leaving the country with twelve young students who they will sell to the highest bidders in Europe."

"Six, two have been murdered and we found four in a basement," Blake snapped back.

"In Elliot Francis' house I guess?" Andrew replied.

Blake glared at him.

"A decoy. The girls are in a warehouse somewhere in Somers Town," Andrew replied, pulling out his phone and scrolling down to a number. "Use your guys to triangulate that number from a burner phone. You'll find Tom Gibson and his team planning to move the girls tonight if he hasn't already. If you and Jenny go to the Rabbit Hole later, you're walking into a trap."

Blake looked at the phone and noticed something metallic down the side of the phone case. He looked at Andrew and noticed his skin was becoming a pale yellow. Paula reached out for the phone but he pushed her hand away.

"Don't touch it!" Blake snapped.

"It's not a bomb," Andrew replied.

"Why are you helping me?" Blake asked.

"Because I know what it's like to get shit on by people you trust. I regret what I did to Paula in the past and if I can help you to make some kind of amends for what I did, then I guess that's good enough."

At that moment, Blake's phone rang. It was Alison.

"What's happening?" Blake asked.

"The girls who we found in Elliot Francis' basement have come round at the hospital. They had been drugged whilst out for a friend's eighteenth birthday party and woke up in the basement yesterday morning. They're not the missing students."

"I think I may have found a lead here, let's all meet back at HQ to discuss."

"Agreed, but there's one more thing, Shaun Bryant is dead," Alison replied.

"What? How?"

"We don't know the full details but one of the neighbours called in and said they saw a man wearing a balaclava step out of the car and take something from one of the bodies."

"Wait, bodies? Plural? Who was with him?"

"One of the residents, identified as Harriet Squantz. Gunshot wound to the side of the head. She lived in the house that used to be owned by Gabby Turner's parents."

"That's more than a coincidence, how was Bryant killed? Did they charge into the Copsewood house?"

"Agents are still there checking everything out but there were two cups of coffee on the floor next to where the bodies were found. One of the cups smelt of almonds."

"Poisoned?" Blake asked.

"It looks like it."

"How did he not smell it or notice anything suspicious?"

"We're still trying to piece together the details, but one of our agents found an empty vial of cyanide in the bin. It looks like it was dissolved in the second cup of coffee, which was meant for Shaun. It's possible that Harriet Squantz played the sweet older lady, offering him a drink in the cold and led him to his death."

Blake swore under his breath. "Okay, let's get back to HQ as soon as possible," he sighed before cutting off the call and turning his attention back to Paula and Andrew.

"He's closing the loop and killing off the deadwood," Andrew commented.

At that moment, two ambulances pulled up outside Scotland Yard and four paramedics rushed inside. Andrew bent over and began coughing up blood and clutching his chest. He dropped his phone on the floor. Paula moved towards it but Blake pushed her away. He looked at the metal on the edge of the phone's casing and noticed that it had begun to turn rusty. At that moment, two police officers were being rushed into the ambulance clutching their chests and vomiting.

"He's been poisoned! He needs to get to the hospital!" Blake called out as he caught the attention of a paramedic.

The Special Branch agent that had been waiting by the car approached them as the paramedic took Andrew away with the two officers.

"Kevin, close off this area and get forensics to check that phone. I think someone has placed thallium into the handset. Whoever has touched it seems to have been poisoned," Blake explained before turning towards Paula who was watching the ambulances disappear into the London traffic. "Did you touch his phone?"

Paula shook her head.

"What about his hands? His face?"

"No, nothing. Blake, what's happening?"

"Tom's tying up some loose ends. He's managed to get thallium into Andy's phone which passes through skin contact. His skin was pale and coughing up blood with stomach cramps and vomiting, it's all signs of it. Swear to me that you made no physical contact with him."

"I swear," Paula replied.

"Come on, we need to get back to HQ," Blake insisted before leading Paula back to his car and driving back towards Vauxhall.

Chapter Twenty-Nine

Too Close To Home

Blake entered the conference room at Special Branch and found Alison Pearce, Samir Khalifa, Gabby Turner, Simon Buxton, his sister Jenny and Chief Eric Gordon waiting for him.

"Where's Paula and Andy?" Jenny asked.

"Paula's being checked by the medical team. Andrew Broughton has been taken to hospital along with two officers from Scotland Yard with suspected thallium poisoning," Blake replied.

"Well that's lit the fuse, what else do you all have?" Eric Gordon asked.

Blake took a deep breath before beginning his report. "It looks like Tom has been systematically eliminating the people involved in his cover-up. We know for sure that Harriet Squantz was involved, probably with Derek Copsewood and she was found dead with a gunshot wound to the head. Shaun Bryant was also found dead, suspected poisoning with cyanide."

"Copsewood has been covering up drug pushers and prostitution rings for years and now that they're all in danger of being exposed, he's taking matters into his own hands," Alison interjected.

"Exactly. And now that he's poisoned Andrew, it's clear that he's willing to take down anyone who gets in his way," Blake added.

"What's our next move then?" Gabby asked.

"We need to find Tom and stop him before he can do any more damage," Eric replied.

"How do we do that? He's disappeared without a trace," Simon pointed out.

"Before Andrew collapsed, he gave me a number of a burner phone that he said would lead us to Tom Gibson. I've asked forensics to go through it and Kevin McCoy has retrieved the phone to check if my thallium theory was right," Blake replied.

Jenny leaned forward. "But even if we find Tom, how do we bring him in without risking more casualties?"

"We need to catch him off guard," Eric Gordon replied. "He's been too careful so far. We need to find his weak spot."

"His weak spot?" Gabby asked.

"Yes," Eric nodded. "Tom Gibson is a smart man, but he's also arrogant. He's been getting away with his crimes for years and he thinks he's invincible. We need to use that to our advantage."

"How?" Alison asked.

"We need to fake a leak," Eric replied. "We need to make it seem like we've found evidence that could incriminate Copsewood and his associates. Tom will see that as a threat and he'll act accordingly."

"So we set up a trap to convince Gibson that he has traitors in his team," Blake said slowly. "But how do we make it convincing enough for him to take the bait?"

"That's where I can help," Jenny said, a sly grin on her face. "I have a few contacts in the media who owe me favours. We can leak a story to them, make it seem like we've got damning evidence against Copsewood and his men. Tom will believe it, and he'll try to destroy the evidence before we can use it against him."

"That could work," Eric nodded. "We'll need to coordinate with the media and make sure the story gets out at the right time."

"And we need to be ready to move in as soon as Tom takes the bait," Blake added.

The group nodded in agreement, their minds already working on the plan.

"But what about Andrew and the police officers?" Gabby asked. "Do we have any leads on who poisoned them?"

"Kevin is still analysing the phone with forensics, but I suspect that whoever poisoned it knew exactly what they were doing," Blake replied. "It looks like we're dealing with a professional."

"Great," Alison muttered. "So how are they managing to still get under our skin? I'm getting tired of chasing shadows all the time."

Blake looked directly at Samir. "You're quiet in the corner there Samir, any news from your end?"

Samir cleared his throat before speaking. "We've been looking into Tom's finances and we found a couple of suspicious transactions. It seems like he's been funnelling money into an offshore account."

"An offshore account?" Simon asked, raising his eyebrows. "That sounds like classic money laundering."

"Exactly. We think he's been using it to hide the proceeds from his illegal activities," Samir replied.

"So we have evidence of financial wrongdoing," Alison said thoughtfully. "That could be enough to take him down for good."

"But we need to be careful," Gabby warned. "If Tom knows we're onto him, he'll go into hiding again."

"Agreed," Eric nodded. "We need to make sure everything is in place before we make our move. Blake, keep us updated on the phone analysis. Alison, coordinate with Jenny on the media leak whilst assisting Blake in the field, Simon, you and Gabby need to keep digging into Tom's finances, use whatever you need here. Samir, work on logistics and contingency plans."

"What about Zodiac?" Blake asked.

"What about him?" Samir asked.

"He springs his brother Xander from jail with casualties whilst he was meant to be under our supervision and then suddenly everything goes silent."

"If you've got something to say Blake then say it!" Samir snapped back.

"When I'm out in the field risking my life, I need to know that my team is gonna have my back, not stab me in it!"

"Blake!" Alison snapped.

"What do you mean Blake?" Eric Gordon asked.

"I want to know what Zodiac or Zachary Zhal, whatever he calls himself now has on Samir!"

"Nothing!" Samir replied.

"Then why has he disappeared into the wilderness after leading you on a wild goose chase to be fooled by my sister that you were going after the wrong man!" Blake snapped.

Jenny bowed her head. "It was a different situation then Blake and you know it!"

"Wait, what's going on here?" Alison asked.

"Tell her Samir, tell everyone..." Blake replied.

Samir took a deep breath before speaking. "Zodiac has been blackmailing me. He has evidence of some things I did in the past that could ruin my career and my life if they were to come to light."

"What kind of things?" Alison asked.

"I...I can't say," Samir replied, his voice barely above a whisper.

"Samir, we need to know what we're dealing with here," Eric said firmly.

Samir looked around the room, his eyes pleading for understanding. "I've done some things I'm not proud of. Things that could ruin everything I've worked for. But I swear, I'm not involved with Tom or any of this."

"We believe you, Samir," Alison said, reaching out to put a reassuring hand on his arm. "But we need to know the whole story if we're going to protect you and stop Tom."

Samir took a deep breath before speaking. "It was a long time ago, when I was just starting out in the force. I was young and naive, and I got involved with the wrong people. I took bribes and looked the other way on certain cases. But I knew it was wrong, and I eventually came clean to my superiors. They gave me a second chance, but Zodiac somehow got wind of it and has been using it against me ever since."

"That's a tough spot to be in," Simon said sympathetically.

"It's not an excuse, I know that," Samir said, his voice heavy with guilt. "But I'm willing to do whatever it takes to make it right."

"We'll help you, Samir," Gabby said firmly. "We're all in this together. Hell, if you look at my family history, we're the most disfunctional family to ever be involved in any of this and we're not going to let Tom or Zodiac win."

"Did Joe Knight know about this before he got blown to pieces in one of Zodiac's safe houses?" Blake asked.

Samir's face dropped at the mention of Joe. "No, I never told Joe about any of this. He was my partner, but I didn't want to drag him down with me. I was trying to make it right on my own."

"You should have told us, Samir," Eric said firmly. "We're a team, and we're supposed to have each other's backs."

"I know," Samir replied. "I was just so scared of losing everything I'd worked for."

"We'll figure it out," Alison said reassuringly. "But right now, we need to focus on taking down Tom and protecting our team. We'll deal with Zodiac later."

The group nodded in agreement. As they began forming plans, a nagging feeling grew in the back of Blake's mind. Something wasn't adding up. Why was Zodiac so interested in Samir's past? And what did Xander Zhal have to do with all of this? He made a mental note to keep digging, to find the answers he needed. But for now, they had a plan to execute. They needed to make it seem like they had damning evidence against Tom and his associates in the hope that his paranoia would cause him to take action against his own team. Jenny would leak the story to her media contacts, and they would wait for Tom to take the bait.

As they made their preparations, Blake couldn't focus. Ever since his case in America where Mo Touro and Peter Simpson, his previous partners, had been led into an ambush by Luigi Cessotto, he had struggled to trust anyone anymore. As they were about to leave, Frank entered the room and rushed over to Blake.

"This just came through from I.T. They have triangulated that burner number that you gave us but it's come up with something unexpected," Frank explained.

Blake scanned his eyes over the paper report. "What was unexpected?"

"It seems that Tom Gibson is using crypto-currency to send thousands of small transactions into an off-shore account using a program called The Crystal."

Blake froze. "The same one that Michael was playing on."

Frank nodded.

"That's too close to home," Samir commented.

Blake glared at him.

"There's something else too," Frank added.

Blake looked at him.

"The signal that came from the burner phone and the IP address came from 124 Alfredson Road in Kensington."

"Our parents' house!" Jenny gasped.

"That's impossible, Jenny was there last night and it was still under police corden. They pulled the place apart. It has to be a VPN or something," Blake protested.

"Police corden was cut off at midnight last night. He moved quickly," Eric Gordon replied. "We need to move faster. We can't let Tom Gibson slip through our fingers again."

Blake's mind raced as he tried to process the new information. Tom was using the same program that Michael had been obsessed with and he was sending money to an off-shore account. It was all starting to make sense now.

"We need to get a team over to 124 Alfredson Road right now," Blake said, his voice urgent. "Alison and I will go on ahead. If you could provide back-up Chief it would be much appreciated."

Eric Gordon nodded.

"We need to see what Tom was doing at our parents' house and if he's still there."

"Agreed," Eric said, already reaching for his phone to call in the necessary back-up.

Jenny rushed up to Blake as they entered the corridor towards the lift. "I need to tell you something…"

Blake looked at his sister warily.

"When we went to the house last night, there was a pair of green and black hiking boots next to the shoe rack by the front door."

Blake nodded.

"None of us own those boots," Jenny continued.

"So you think Tom could've been there during the police search?" Blake asked.

"Anything's possible."

"How? Where would he hide? The police were looking for something to frame Steven with before we brought him into Special Branch for his own safety. They would've gone through the house with a fine toothed comb unless..."

"Unless what?"

"No, he wouldn't..."

"Unless what?"

"Unless he posed as an officer and was part of the team."

"He wouldn't get away with that would he?" Jenny asked.

Blake shook his head. "Nothing would surprise me with this case now. I'll keep the boots in mind but I think you're overthinking it. They probably belonged to one of the officers who was working there."

"Do police officers regularly take off their shoes?"

Blake sighed. "You've got a point but they would've found him or noticed something suspicious."

"Like this?" Jenny asked as she showed Blake the spare phone that she retrieved from underneath Steven's bed at their parent's house.

Blake shook his head in disbelief. "I forgot that damn thing was still there. Ok, come with me and Alison to the house but stay out of harm's way. If Tom is there, you could be the one that makes him talk."

Jenny nodded as they got into the lift and descended to the car park.

As they got into the car, Alison turned to Jenny. "Are you sure you're up for this? It could get dangerous."

"I'm sure," Jenny replied. "I want to help bring Tom down, and if this is what it takes, then I'm all in."

Blake looked at his sister with pride and a little bit of worry. He knew how much she wanted to be a part of the action, but he also knew how dangerous it could be. But there was no stopping her now. As they drove towards their childhood home, the tension in the car was palpable. They didn't know what they were walking into, but they were all prepared for the worst. As they approached the house, they could see that there was still police tape around the perimeter. But there were no officers visible and the house appeared to be quiet.

"Okay, we need to be careful," Blake cautioned as they parked the car. "We have no idea what we're walking into."

Jenny nodded, her eyes wide with apprehension. "I'm ready."

As they crept towards the front door, Blake noticed that the lock was already broken. He motioned for Alison to cover the back door while he and Jenny entered.

Jenny immediately looked at the shoe rack. "The boots are gone," she whispered.

Blake nodded in acknowledgement before carefully moving through the house. The family home where they had spent many happy times was deathly silent but as they moved through the living room, Blake caught a movement out of the corner of his eye. He spun around, gun at the ready, but it was just a shadow.

"Blake, look!" Jenny pointed towards the study where a laptop was sitting open on a table.

Blake approached it cautiously, his heart pounding in his chest. As he looked at the screen, he felt a knot form in his stomach. There were files on the desktop labelled with their names. He opened one and saw that it was a dossier on their team.

"This is everything on us," Blake whispered, his voice full of disbelief. "Tom's been spying on us all along. How did he get this?"

"And this," Jenny pointed to a file labelled "Family Secrets", it must be the reason that he came here. He wanted to see what he could find at our parents' house."

Blake nodded, his mind racing with possibilities. If Tom had been spying on them, he would know their weaknesses. He could use their past against them and especially after what Samir had admitted to in their conference meeting, he could use it to manipulate them into doing his bidding.

"We need to find Tom," Blake said. "He can't be far."

A noise behind them made Blake spin around quickly.

"All clear this side," Alison said as she stepped into the study.

"We need to get Frank and the team to look into this, we have a leak in our system," Blake advised.

"Samir?" Alison asked.

"Your guess is as good as mine," Blake sighed.

As they made their way towards the stairs, they heard a beep. Blake looked up and saw a black box with two lights at the top of the stairs. The left light was illuminated green but as Blake looked up, it changed to red.

"Run!" Blake shouted.

The three of them ran out of the front door as a huge explosion ripped the house apart sending debris everywhere. Car alarms rang out as Blake, Jenny and Alison laid face down on the front lawn of 124 Alfredson Road. As the dust settled, Blake struggled to his feet, coughing and wheezing as he tried to get his bearings.

"Is everyone okay?" he yelled out, his ears were ringing from the noise of the explosion and his voice was hoarse.

"I'm okay," Alison groaned, rolling over onto her back.

Jenny didn't respond and Blake's heart leaped into his throat. He ran over to her and knelt down, checking for a pulse.

"She's alive," he breathed a sigh of relief.

Jenny stirred, her eyes fluttering open. "What happened?" she groaned.

"Tom rigged the house to explode," Blake explained, his voice full of anger. "He's getting desperate."

Jenny looked over at the crumbling remains of their family home. "We need to catch him!"

Blake nodded. "We will, but first we need to get you to safety."

As they made their way to the car, Blake couldn't shake the feeling that they were running out of time. Tom was getting more and more desperate and they needed to find him before he caused any more damage. He started the engine and sped away from the destroyed house, his mind racing with possible leads.

"Did you find anything else in the house?" Alison asked, breaking the tense silence.

"Just some files on us and our family," Blake answered. "But it's clear that Tom has been spying on us for a while now."

"I can't believe he would do this," Jenny sighed. "I thought he loved me. How could he turn on us like this?"

"We need to try and draw him out," Blake replied.

"The Rabbit Hole?" Alison asked.

"It's the only card we have left to play."

Chapter Thirty

Who Can You Trust?

The lift at Special Branch arrived at the car park level. The doors opened and Samir and Simon stepped out into the cool breeze that flowed through the car park air vents.

"Where are we going?" Simon asked as they arrived at the car. "We were meant to be organising logistics for tonight."

"Just a hunch that I have. If I'm wrong, we'll still have plenty of time to sort out the Rabbit Hole later."

Simon gave him a wary look.

"What?" Samir asked.

"Were any of Blake's suggestions true up there?"

Samir swore under his breath. "If the CIA don't want to support a brother in a case in London then feel free to walk out that door. I can do this with or without you. I don't need a babysitter."

"I know, but I'm also aware that I'm here on vacation to help my girlfriend promote her book and don't plan to get my ass nailed to a wall or my head blown off in the process."

"Then trust me," Samir replied as he climbed into the driver's seat and fired up the engine of his black BMW.

Simon climbed into the passenger seat before Samir drove them out of the car park.

"Do you really think it's going to work tonight? They'll know that Gabby and Jenny will be bugged or they'll have some kind of back-up. They're not stupid."

"I don't know. Blake seems intent on exposing my past which I admit, isn't exactly as pure as it should be but I still have a few favours owed to me from certain individuals. The current situation doesn't exactly paint the Langford's in the best light either. Sister assisting Russian intelligence in slaughtering our soldiers and a brother on the run for suspected multiple homicides."

"I haven't known Blake for long but my superior, Jason Price, has known him for years. He said that he would put his life on the line for Langford and Price never praises anyone so if he's good enough for him, then I'm willing to take that chance."

"Be careful what you wish for."

"What do you mean?"

Before Samir could reply, car horns screamed out around them as a Land Rover sped into the side of the BMW crashing hard into the driver's side and flipping the car against the curb and over into the front window of a local newsagents in a shower of glass, metal and wood. Shattered glass and smoke billowed out from the car. Scared onlookers rushed away in all directions. Those that stayed, watched as two men stepped out of the Land Rover.

"It's okay, we're Special Branch! Move on please!" the driver called out as he held up a black wallet with some kind of photo ID inside it.

The Land Rover passenger moved towards the car and dragged Samir out of the wreckage. Samir staggered, trying to regain his balance before the driver placed a black hood over his head, cuffed his hands behind his back and dragged him away towards the back of the Land Rover. The driver did the same with Simon and they were both pushed into the back doors of the Land Rover landing with a thud on the metal base at the back of the vehicle. The two men climbed back into the front of the Land Rover and sped away as two police cars and an ambulance arrived on the scene.

Samir and Simon were thrown around in the back of the Land Rover as it careened through the streets of London. Samir's mind raced as he tried to think of a way out of their situation. He had been kidnapped by someone and he had a feeling it was Tom. But why would he do this? What was his endgame?

The Land Rover screeched to a halt, and the doors were thrown open. Samir and Simon were dragged out of the vehicle and led away before being pushed to their knees on a concrete floor. The hoods were taken off both of their heads, and they squinted in the glow of a bright light.

"Welcome, Samir," a familiar voice said. "It's been a long time."

Samir looked up and saw Tom Gibson standing in front of him, a smug grin on his face.

"What do you want, Tom?" Samir asked.

"I want your help," Tom replied. "I need you to help me get away from here. There are people who want to take me down and I need your expertise to help me and the merchandise escape."

Samir glared at him. "Why should I help you? So you can sell those poor girls into some sick prostitution ring abroad where they'll likely be raped and murdered. You've caused so much damage already."

"Because I have something that you want," Tom replied, pulling out a small flash drive from his pocket. "Information on your past, Samir. If you help me, I'll give you this. You can finally clear your name."

Samir's heart leaped in his chest. The flash drive could hold the key to his past, the one thing he had been searching for all these years. But could he trust Tom?

"What's your plan?" Simon asked, breaking the tense silence.

Tom smirked. "We're going to disappear. But I need your help to secure a new identity, new passports and new transport. I don't have much time, so we need to act fast."

Samir weighed up his options. He could help Tom and potentially clear his name, or he could refuse and remain in the dark about what information was available about his past. Constantly looking over his shoulder just in case another skeleton came out of the closet. "Never! I'm tired of running away. If you want to kill us, go ahead!"

Simon looked at Samir in disbelief.

"Have it your way," Tom replied before everything went black.

Samir woke up in a dark room, his head pounding with pain. He tried to move his hands and realised they were tied behind his back. Panic set in as he tried to remember how he ended up here.

"Wakey, wakey, sleepyhead!" Tom's voice came from the darkness.

"What's going on?" Samir asked, his voice hoarse.

"You passed out earlier. Don't worry, it's just a mild concussion," Tom replied, lighting a match to reveal his face.

"Why are you doing this?" Samir asked, trying to keep his voice steady.

"Because I need your help," Tom replied. "And you're going to give it to me."

"I won't help you," Samir snapped.

"Oh, but you will," Tom said, pulling out a small knife. "Or things will get very ugly for you and your friend."

Samir's heart raced as he watched Tom approach him with the knife. He had never been so scared in his life. He closed his eyes and braced himself for the worst, but to his surprise, the ropes around his wrists were cut loose and he was free.

"What's going on?" Samir asked, rubbing his sore wrists.

"I had to make sure you were serious about not wanting to help me," Tom replied, sheathing the knife. "But I have a new plan. I'll give you the flash drive and you help me disappear. But first, we need to take care of some loose ends."

"What loose ends?" Simon asked, groggily coming to.

"Your superiors," Tom replied. "We can't have them following us, can we?"

Samir's heart sank as he realised what Tom was planning. He couldn't let innocent people die because of his past mistakes.

"Stop!" Samir shouted, standing up and blocking Tom's path. "I'll help you disappear, but I won't let you harm anyone else."

Tom laughed. "You don't have a choice, Samir. You need me to clear your name."

"I'll find another way," Samir replied firmly. "I won't let you use me to hurt innocent people."

Tom's smile faded and he lunged at Samir with the knife. Samir reacted quickly, ducking and rolling away from the attack. He grabbed a nearby chair and swung it at Tom, knocking him to the ground.

Simon had managed to free himself and was now standing behind Tom, ready to help Samir.

"Hand over the flash drive, Tom," Samir said, holding the chair defensively.

Tom sneered as he tossed the flash drive in the air. Samir caught it before striking Tom with the chair.

"Let's get out of here," Simon said. "We need to disappear before he comes to."

Samir and Simon left the dark room but as they turned into the corridor, they ran into two men. Simon shouted out as he was hit from behind and fell to the floor.

"Xander? Reaper?" Samir gasped before he heard a buzzing in his ears, his muscles began to spasm uncontrollably and he felt sharp pain explode through his body until he passed out.

"Sorry buddy, nothing personal," Reaper replied as they dragged Samir and Simon away.

***

Alison, Jenny and Blake entered Special Branch before heading into the intelligence quarter.

Frank looked up from his screen. "Jeez man, you look like shit, what happened?"

"It was a trap. Gibson's gone, he blew up the house, he sent us on another wild goose chase. We need to get Jenny and Gabby ready for tonight. It's the only way we're going to get him to come out of whatever wormhole he's found. Where's Samir?"

"He left with Simon soon after you left, why?"

"I need him to hack into The Crystal and find out what the hell is going on."

"We've made some progress on that. We've taken over Michael's username on the system and one of our analysts has been continuing the cycle. Seems like Gibson has linked onto Michael's account and was working alongside him to help build the virtual crystal but he was selling particles of it to the highest bidder, in effect, money laundering," Frank explained.

"That's got to be more than a coincidence. A million profiles and he happens to hit Michael's."

Frank ushered Blake to the side of the room. "He's somehow got into the personal details of your family Blake. Stuff that he shouldn't know without inside information."

"Do you think we have a leak?"

"When was the last time he contacted your sister?"

"Just before his team got annihilated in Afghanistan around ten years ago, it was all over the news, why?"

"Are you sure?"

"She wouldn't lie to me."

"I've asked the team to check her social media in case there's any trail. Any other ideas?" Frank asked.

"Did Samir say where they were heading?"

"No, but I can track his phone if you give me a minute..."

Frank tapped away on a keyboard before the screen in front of him changed and zoomed in on London from above before zooming into street level. The screen changed and showed a black BMW on fire hanging out of a newsagent's window.

"Jamie, can you get me the radio on that incident?" Frank asked.

One of the assistants tapped away on his laptop before handing Frank a headset. Frank listened intently to the radio messages being shared between the police, fire service and paramedics at the scene.

Frank swore as he tossed the headset back onto the desk. "No sign of Samir or Simon but onlookers said that two Special Branch agents bundled the victims unceremoniously into the back of a Land Rover and sped away before the emergency services arrived."

"Did they get a car reg?" Blake asked.

"Got it," Jamie called out as he handed Frank a piece of paper.

Blake pulled out his phone and logged into the secure network at Special Branch.

"Hotel, Lima, One, Zero, Tango, X-ray, Juliet," Frank read out.

"Damn, it's a rental. Dan's Autos at 227 Newton Grove in Soho," Blake explained.

"Well, what are we waiting for, let's go!" Alison replied.

"What about Jenny?" Blake asked.

"I'll deal with her, you go!" Frank replied.

Blake and Alison rushed out of Special Branch and headed towards Dan's Autos in Soho. Frank and Jenny wandered upstairs to get ready for the meeting at The Rabbit Hole.

***

Samir woke up in a dark room, his head throbbing with pain. He was laying on his back looking up at darkness besides a few little splinters of light from somewhere above. He tried to move but realised his hands and feet were tied to metal bars which looked like railway lines. Simon was lying next to him on what seemed to be a second railway line in the partial light.

"Simon, wake up," Samir whispered.

Simon groaned and slowly opened his eyes. "What happened?"

"They got us," Samir replied, glancing around the area. "We need to find a way out of here."

Suddenly, the whole area illuminated with bright light stinging Simon's and Samir's eyes. A door burst open and Tom walked in, followed by Xander and Reaper.

"Good, you're finally awake," Tom said, smiling. "I have a proposition for you, Samir. My final offer, I guess you could call it. Help me take down Special Branch and I'll clear your name."

"I won't help you," Samir replied firmly. "Reaper? I trusted you!"

"Sorry old buddy but in this game knowing who to trust can quite literally be the difference between life and death," Reaper laughed.

"Xander, what about your brother? I gave him a clear shot to get you out of jail. Without me, you'd be rotting your ass away at Pentonville!" Samir snapped.

"Yes, it's funny how a little act of kindness can sometimes come along and bite you later on. That's why I don't have friends.

They expect loyalty and before you know it they decide to get married out of town and then you're stuck at this happy happy place that no one wants to be at, exchanging pleasantries with their family who can't stand the sight of you and who you're never likely to see again and for what? It's all a load of bullshit. At the end of the day, everyone is in it for themselves," Tom replied.

"Is that why you ran out on Jenny Langford after she had done your dirty work for you? Couldn't handle the commitment?" Samir snapped.

"Jen was an unfortunate casualty along the way. That was a regret but she will soon become useful once again. Take a look around you. Metropolitan London can be really beautiful," Tom replied.

Samir and Simon looked around and realised that they were in a disused London Underground station and were tied to railway tracks.

"Is this what you did to Hannah Powell before you hid her upstairs for Blake to find?" Samir asked.

"Oh no, she was far too beautiful to get run down by a train. She wasn't willing to follow orders but we gave her a much more pleasurable send off."

Samir spat into the gutter.

"Blake really does enjoy poking his nose into things that don't concern him, doesn't he? Just think, if he hadn't been such an adventurer, who knows when she would've been found. A bit like you two right here," Tom replied.

"These aren't even subway rails so we know you're bluffing," Simon snapped.

"Ah, he's finally found his tongue. CIA and Special Branch, two for the price of one. You are right though my dear boy, this is an old shunting yard where the trains used to be repaired so no underground trains will run along it but..."

"Overground trains will," Samir finished for him.

Xander pulled a lever and electricity pulsed through Samir's and Simon's bodies until he shut it off. Both men groaned as their muscles began to relax once again.

"If Langford tries anything stupid tonight then the signal man knows what to do. Enjoy your train-ing," Tom laughed before shutting off the lights and walking away with Reaper and Xander close behind.

"We've gotta get out of here," Samir said into the darkness.

"No shit, what have you got? A magic wand?" Simon cussed.

"No, I need to hit my left heel onto the metal but I need to get my foot free from these ties."

"What will that do?"

"There's a homing device in the heel of my shoe. If I can activate it, Special Branch will be able to track us," Samir explained as he continued to wriggle around trying to gain some kind of freedom from his restraints.

"I'm getting too old for this shit," Simon sighed.

Chapter Thirty-One

Underground Secrets

Night fell over the streets of London as Jenny Langford and Gabby Turner prepared themselves to go to The Rabbit Hole. A knock at the door of their suite inside Special Branch startled them. Jenny wandered over towards the door and opened it. Blake and Alison stepped inside.

"Any news on Simon?" Gabby asked.

"Nothing yet, Frank and his team are still trying to find him and Samir," Alison replied.

"What did you find out at the rental place?"

"Rented to a John Smith of no fixed abode. We left the officers there to close the place down. Cash in hand may work elsewhere but not here," Blake replied.

"No CCTV or anything?" Jenny asked.

"Not that we could use. They were still using VCR from the eighties."

"I can't do this without him," Gabby sighed. "Why did I let myself get caught up in this mess? I was meant to be here promoting my book not playing bloody cowboys and indians again!"

"You had no idea that your publisher was a crook, Gabby. Don't be so hard on yourself," Blake replied.

"I know, this was meant to be a fresh start after everything that happened with James. I thought that I'd found someone with Simon and now he's gone too."

Alison placed her hand on Gabby's shoulder. "We have the best team on the look-out for him and Samir. We will find them but right now we need you to focus on getting as much information as you can from tonight's meeting."

Alison handed Gabby a small cream coloured ear-piece and Blake handed the same to Jenny.

"Place this inside your ear. Jamie and Denise will guide you through the underground and will hear what you hear and you can speak to them through it. It also has a homing device fitted so if the sound stops working for whatever reason, we will still know where you are. We have a team at St Pancras, on the platforms at Kings Cross and all of the surrounding stations. The Rabbit Hole runs down towards an old siding near Angel Tube Station. When we were kids, we used to watch the builders in the yard below working on the trains. That area has been sealed up for over ten years. Be careful where you walk as the old wooden beams may have deteriorated over time," Blake explained.

"They'll expect us to go in there with backup. Where are you going to be?" Jenny asked.

"We think he's going to look to get onto the high speed European line with the hostages and escape into the tunnel towards Calais. We have plain clothed armed police at St Pancras and three of our team stationed outside the station in case they make it onto the main line," Alison replied. "Don't worry, all you need to do is go along with their plan and they should walk directly into an ambush," Alison explained.

"And if they don't?" Gabby asked.

"Then we'll have to put plan B into action," Blake replied. "Come on, let's go."

Alison and Blake led Gabby and Jenny downstairs towards the car park. Two black cab taxis were waiting for them.

"Black cabs, really?" Gabby questioned.

"Our team is multi-talented," Blake quipped. "Good luck!"

They each climbed into the back of the taxis before the drivers drove out into the streets of London.

As they left the car park, Frank came rushing out of the lift and ran towards Alison and Blake.

"Have you found them?" Blake asked.

"Not exactly but Samir has activated his homer," Frank replied.

"Samir had a homing device?"

"Standard issue in the heel of his shoe. If you weren't so image conscious..."

"Yeah whatever, where is he?"

"Looks like somewhere between Euston and Kings Cross. The satellite is picking up some kind of pharmacy or library of some kind," Frank explained.

"It's not, it's underground. There's an old workshop between Euston and Kings Cross that overground trains used for servicing during the late eighties. They closed it after the earthquake in 1988. Just the kind of place to hide some bodies," Alison explained.

"We didn't have an earthquake in London in '88," Blake replied.

Frank and Alison both looked at him.

"What?"

"Just because the media covered it up doesn't mean it didn't happen. There's two fault lines that run through Metropolitan London. Luckily we're not as susceptible to it as the US are for example but in June 1988 there was a 4.2 earthquake that caused several tunnels to collapse and significant building damage. Your father was the spokesperson to the media to claim that it was a gas explosion and that Londoners had nothing to fear," Frank explained.

Blake turned to Alison. "How did you know all of this?"

"Because my father was one of the engineers who died down there and the government covered it up. My mother ended up having to bring up three girls on her own on hush money that the powers that be saw fit to give to the victims families who knew the truth," Alison explained.

"I'm sorry," Blake replied. "I didn't know."

"Nobody did," Alison confirmed. "So let's go and get them back."

***

The first black cab arrived outside Kings Cross Station at five minutes to ten. The second black cab arrived at Angel Tube Station on Islington High Street at the same time. Jenny stepped out of her cab at Kings Cross and Gabby stepped out of hers before heading into Angel station. Gabby wandered through the entry gates before turning left and entering a side door which led to a concrete staircase. She started the descent down until she came to a door with a keypad.

"This is new. There's a door with a keypad. I don't know the code," Gabby whispered.

"Keep going down Gabby, there must be another way in," Denise replied in her ear.

"Gabby Turner?" a man called out.

Gabby spun around and saw an older man wearing a beige suit jacket, white shirt and beige trousers looking at her from the bottom of the next flight of stairs. "Who wants to know?"

"There's someone who needs to see you. Follow me please," the man replied before opening a door on the next level down.

Gabby reluctantly stepped down the stairs before following the man through the door and into a dimly lit corridor.

"We've got a match, Zachary Zhal, also known as Zodiac," Denise whispered into Gabby's ear.

Gabby's heart raced as she followed the man who she now knew as Zodiac through the dark corridor. The only sound was the echo of their footsteps against the concrete walls. She couldn't shake the feeling of unease that was creeping up on her.

Finally, they arrived at a large steel door, guarded by two burly men in black suits. Zodiac whispered something to one of the guards, who then opened the door and let her inside. The room was small and cramped, with barely enough space for a table and chairs. A man sat at the table, his face obscured by the hood of his sweatshirt. Gabby could feel his eyes on her even though she couldn't see them.

"Gabby Turner," he said, his voice low and guttural. "I've been waiting for you."

Gabby stood frozen, unsure of what to do next. "Who are you?" she asked. "And where is everyone else?"

"They're around but I thought we should be reacquainted first," the man said before standing from the table and turning towards her.

His green bloodshot eyes and red cheeks from too much alcohol over the years gave him a menacing look. The same kind that Gabby had seen all those years ago. The same look that had haunted her dreams for years since the abuse took place.

"Derek?" Gabby managed to say.

Derek grinned, revealing a set of yellowed teeth. "Long time no see, Gabby," he said, taking a step towards her. He let out a low, throaty laugh. "You remember me. I'm flattered."

"I wouldn't be," Gabby spat, her heart racing faster.

Derek was the man who had abused her when she was a child, the man who had driven her mother to suicide. And here he was, standing in front of her as if nothing had ever happened.

"Where are the others?" Gabby asked, trying to keep her voice steady.

"You're expectedly well informed. They're safe, for now, as is your beloved CIA agent, Simon," Derek replied. "But if you don't cooperate, they won't be for long."

"What do you want?" Gabby asked, dreading the answer.

"I want you to do a job for me," Derek said. "A simple job. And if you do it, I'll let your friends go."

Gabby's mind raced. She knew she couldn't trust Derek, but she also knew she couldn't let anything happen to Simon, Jenny or the students because of her. "What kind of job?" she asked, trying to buy herself some time.

Derek smiled, revealing his yellowed teeth once more. "Just a little delivery. You'll take a package to a man named Vladimir Vasilievich in Moscow. He'll give you further instructions."

Gabby weighed up her options. She knew this was risky, but she also knew she had to play along, at least for now.

"Fine," she said. "I'll do it."

Derek's smile widened. "Good. I knew you'd see it my way. You leave tonight. Don't try to run or your friends will pay the price."

"What is the package and how do I get to Moscow?"

"You'll join me and my associates on the midnight train to Paris. You'll head to Moscow from there."

A million thoughts flooded Gabby's mind as she tried to remain focused. "What is the package?"

"You!" Derek replied.

Gabby turned and tried to push the door open again. One man grabbed her before someone tased him, sending him to the floor in pain.

"Come on, this way!" a woman's voice called out as Gabby ran into darkness through a side door and headed further down into the underground.

"Stop them! And bring me my daughter!" Derek shouted as three men chased after them.

***

Meanwhile, Jenny had entered Kings Cross Station and headed towards the St Pancras International side of the station before turning into the public toilets opposite the Eurostar terminal. She went into the far end cubicle and closed the door. She pulled out a small pen knife and cut around the sealant on a drain cover that had been hidden under a new floor covering on the cubicle floor. Once the seal was broken, she slid the knife down the side of the cover and levered it open. She stepped down into the trapdoor, closing it behind her as she descended lower underground.

"Okay, I'm in," she whispered.

"We're with you Jen," Jamie replied into her ear-piece.

"Has Gabby arrived yet?"

"She's inside, just focus on your own journey. You and Blake know those tunnels better than most."

"I'm not a teenager anymore though," Jenny smirked as she followed a maze of dimly lit tunnels underneath the station.

She eventually arrived at a wooden staircase that led down towards a service platform below. As she walked along the wooden bridge towards the top of the staircase, she noticed a man wearing jeans and a dark blue shirt standing at the top of the stairs.

"Hello Jenny," he called out.

Jenny froze. "Who are you?"

"You don't remember me? I guess Blake never really introduced us," the man replied as he walked into the partial light.

"Graham?" Jenny asked. "You're Paula's...."

"Yes, I'm Paula and Rachael's father."

"What are you doing here?" Jenny asked.

"I'm here to help you."

"Help me? Why? Does Paula know that you're back in London?" Jenny asked, trying to buy some time.

"We've met again but this is not about me or my family. There's someone here to see you. Come on. Mind your step, these old wooden staircases are a bit rickety."

Jenny's heart pounded as she followed Graham down the staircase. She couldn't believe he was here, especially after everything that had happened with Paula and Rachael. She couldn't help but feel a sense of distrust towards him. As they reached the bottom of the staircase, Graham led Jenny through a dimly lit corridor and into a small room. The room was sparsely furnished, with only a wooden bench in the centre. A man in a suit was already sitting on the bench, his face obscured by shadows.

"Who are you?" Jenny asked warily.

"We met a long time ago but I see you no longer recognise me. My name is Ivan," the man replied in a thick Russian accent. "I thank you for your service last time and I must call on you once again. I understand you have experience in the underground tunnels of London."

Jenny's mind raced. Was this the same Ivan Stepanchikov she had given the dossier to all those years ago that led to Tom's team being killed in Afghanistan? If so, he had put on a significant amount of weight, had definitely aged a lot and it looked like his nose had been broken and reshaped. She tried to calm her nerves. "What do you need me to do?" she asked.

"There's been a breach in our security system and we need to transport some valuable cargo through the underground tunnels.

You will lead the way and ensure that we reach our destination safely," Ivan explained.

Jenny couldn't believe what she was hearing. "And if I refuse?"

"Then there is a dossier on its way to 10 Downing Street detailing your brother's plan to assassinate a member of The Royal Family at midnight tonight. As you know, a dossier like the ones you dealt with before can be very impactful."

Jenny knew that Special Branch would intercept it whether it was a hoax or not. "I'll do it," she said firmly.

"Good. We'll be here soon to collect you," Ivan replied, rising from the bench. "And remember, your life, and the lives of those you care about, depend on it."

"When do I get to see Tom?" Jenny asked.

"Soon," Ivan replied before walking away.

Jenny watched silently as Ivan and Graham left the room, leaving her alone in the dimly lit space. She took a deep breath knowing that all she could do now was wait.

Chapter Thirty-Two

Making The Right Call

Blake and Alison rushed through Euston Railway Station and headed towards the Underground Station. They came to a service door that was guarded by a man wearing a high visibility jacket and trousers with a tool-belt strapped to his waist.

"Special Branch, I need access to section four," Alison said to him, flashing her ID.

"Hey, I've got no authorization to let you two down there. It's unsafe."

"I'm sorry, what's your name?" Blake asked.

"Dean, Dean Kingsley," the man replied.

"Let me tell you this Dean, Dean Kingsley, if you don't let us down there right now, you're going to have a terrorist attack on your hands with cops swarming around you like flies on shit, do we understand each other?" Blake snapped.

Dean nodded before reluctantly punching an access code into the keypad which released the door. Alison and Blake both rushed inside before the door closed again.

"I admire your restraint," Alison quipped when they were inside.

"Because I didn't pull a gun on him? That doesn't tend to go down too well these days," Blake replied.

"How long before he calls that in?"

"Hopefully not before we've found what we're looking for. Where to now?"

Alison led them down a corridor towards a shed which had a metal plate and a new padlock on the door.

"This is new," Alison said as she moved around the shed and continued down the corridor.

"The bigger question is how did they get it down here? The underground isn't exactly accommodating."

"You've obviously never bought flat-pack furniture," Alison laughed.

They arrived at an empty platform with two railway tracks at the far side of the platform.

"That's not underground rails," Blake commented.

"No, we're close," Alison replied as she headed towards a metal door on the opposite side of the platform.

She pushed it as hard as she could.

"It's locked, doesn't look like we have any way of getting past it," Alison replied.

Blake walked over and attempted to kick the door open twice but it didn't budge. "That metal must be inches thick. Is there any other way?"

"Only from Euston Square but we'll have to go all the way back on ourselves, unless..."

Alison looked over towards the tracks. Blake followed her lead.

"Are these tracks live?" Blake asked.

"Possibly. They used to be."

Blake started searching around and found a small metal pipe at the back of the platform.

"You're not going to hold that on the line are you? You'll electrocute yourself," Alison explained.

"No, I'm testing an old theory," Blake replied as he walked over to a puddle of water that had collected in the corner of the platform and rolled the metal pole in the puddle to make it wet.

Blake walked over towards the rails and dropped the pole down onto the middle rails. There was a brief spark and the pole rolled away. "Exactly what I thought, the middle rails are live, the edge rails are earthed. If we need to get through to the next station, we need to walk along the tracks and keep away from the two centre rails."

They both climbed down onto the tracks. Blake pulled his phone out and used the light to guide them through the darkness. After what felt like an age, they eventually arrived at another platform. They climbed up and saw a lever on the wall. As Blake pulled the lever, the whole platform illuminated. They heard someone groaning down on the rails.

"It's them!" Alison called out as she jumped back down onto the rails.

"Don't touch us. The track is live!" Simon called out.

Blake stood on the edge of the platform. Both Simon and Samir were tied onto the tracks with metal chains around their wrists and ankles. "He's right, we need to isolate the power."

"Over by the lever you just pulled. Tom managed to control the current there."

Blake wandered over towards the lever and found a second smaller lever behind it. "I've found another lever."

"Try it!" Simon shouted.

Blake pulled the lever and heard a loud buzzing before Simon and Samir both shouted out. He quickly shut it off again.

"Not... that... one...!" Samir gasped as he tried to take in some air.

Blake continued looking for anything else that could shut off the power. As he did, he heard some noise in his ear-piece. He stopped.

"Please repeat!" Alison called out as she held her ear.

"Alison, it's Denise, Gabby is on the move, repeat, Gabby is on the move, hostiles in pursuit," Denise said into their ear-pieces.

At that moment, they all heard a rumbling in the tunnel.

"Oh shit, no! Blake, whatever you're doing, you need to do fast!" Samir shouted out.

"That's a train, we need to short circuit the system!" Alison replied.

"Both of you, listen to me!" Blake shouted as he came to the edge of the platform. "The two centre rails are live. I'm going to shoot out the chains that are holding you to the centre rails. Alison, you shoot out the earthed line chains."

"You're gonna send a metal bullet into a live rail Blake, do you know what that will do?" Samir asked.

"We don't have a choice, ready!" Blake replied.

Both Simon and Samir closed their eyes as the train became louder.

"On my count, three, two one, fire!" Blake shouted.

Blake fired two quick shots at the centre rails snapping the chains around their arms before doing the same to their ankles, sending a fountain of sparks into the air. Alison simultaneously fired at Samir's wrist and ankle on the earthed side before moving across and doing the same for Simon. The rumbling became louder and a light appeared further down the tunnel. A train horn echoed around the tunnel creating a deafening sound. Samir leapt up onto the platform edge. Blake grabbed hold of his shirt pulling him clear as the train sped through the station and onwards into the darkness.

The platform was silent once again as Blake helped Samir up onto his feet.

"Thank you," Samir gasped as he tried to calm the adrenaline that was running through his body.

"Alison! Simon!" Blake called out.

"We're here!" Simon called out from the opposite side of the tracks.

They both carefully climbed across the tracks and up onto the platform.

"What's going on? Where's Gabby?" Simon asked.

"Special Branch are tracking her but she's on the move in the tunnels with hostiles in pursuit. We need to move fast," Alison replied.

"So what's the plan?" Samir asked.

Alison looked over and saw a metal ladder attached to the back of the platform which led up towards some kind of trapdoor in the ceiling above. "Now we go up."

***

Gabby raced through the tunnels following her saviour as she heard the shouts from the men chasing them.

"Quickly, in here!" the woman said as she grabbed Gabby and pulled her into what seemed like a storage cupboard.

The sound of men running past and disappearing into the darkness gave them both a moment to breathe. Gabby pulled her phone out of her pocket and held it up to light up where they were. There was a control panel with hundreds of switches in front of her and they were standing on a metal grid with train tracks beneath them.

Gabby raised the light up and looked at who had led her here. "Claire?"

"I'm sorry I didn't believe you before. I didn't think my father was capable of such awful things. His mind is poisoned. We need to keep moving. They'll double back soon when they realise we didn't head into the station. Come on," Claire replied as she began to lead Gabby away from the control panels.

"Where are we going? The Rabbit Hole is back that way!"

"If you go there you'll just be a number on a delivery note. I found the paperwork in my father's briefcase. Tom Gibson has agreed a deal with the Russians and you are the top prize."

"I need to go back there. Jenny Langford is still in there."

"She'll need to fight her own battle. If you come with me, we can escape through the freight station and get out onto Pancras Road."

"Why are you helping me?" Gabby asked.

"You're my sister, come on, let's go!"

Gabby followed Claire through a maze of tunnels until they eventually arrived at an opening that led out onto a platform. A black train with a front cab that resembled a bullet was at the station. Porters were loading stacks of wooden boxes on trolleys into the coaches behind the main cab.

"We need to stop them. I'm willing to bet that the missing students are on that train," Gabby whispered.

Claire led Gabby onto the platform and approached a group of porters loading boxes onto the train. One of them, a tall man with a thick Eastern European accent, approached them.

"Excuse me, I'm looking for a shipment to Moscow," Claire said.

"Ah, yes. That is us. You have the payment?" the porter replied.

Claire nodded and handed over a thick envelope. The porter counted the cash and nodded in satisfaction. He signalled for the other porters to load the last of the boxes onto the train.

"Come on, we need to move fast," Claire whispered to Gabby.

They climbed onto the train and found a compartment to hide in. As soon as they were inside, the doors closed with a loud thud and the sound of locks clanked before the train fell silent.

"Wait, we've trapped ourselves here. If Derek wants to take us away, we've done his job for him."

"Not if the cargo doesn't arrive," Claire replied.

"Where did all that money come from?"

"Dad's pay-off, he won't miss it. Come on, we need to find those students."

As they walked through the carriage, Gabby noticed someone walking towards the window to look in from the outside. "Get down!"

Gabby and Claire both laid on the floor as the man looked inside the carriage before moving on.

"Reaper, so he's back," Claire said as she got back to her feet again.

"Who's Reaper?"

"Bad news, he's got influential friends in the government and was involved in Dad's financial affairs last year when he nearly lost the licence of the pub. I'm sure there was some kind of deal made as he's been hanging around like a bad smell. Come on, let's go."

Gabby got back to her feet before following Claire into the next carriage. She knew that she had to try and find the missing students and get them off the train but she still had a nagging feeling that she was walking into a trap.

Chapter Thirty-Three

Love Coming Down

"Blake, where are you? Gabby's gone dark, I repeat Gabby's gone dark, we've lost all communication with her," Denise spoke into Blake and Alison's ear-pieces.

"Do you have her tracker?" Blake asked.

"Last picked up at the far side of St Pancras Station. Looks like some kind of loading bay or storage yard."

"Can you get a satellite fix?" Alison asked.

"Coming into range now."

Alison, Blake, Samir and Simon had climbed up the ladder from the abandoned station and were now inside a tunnel that ran parallel to the railway line below with Euston to the left and Kings Cross to the right.

"Can you see anything?" Blake asked.

"Looks like some kind of bullet train. Definitely not commercial," Denise finally replied.

"That's gotta be where they're keeping the students. If this all goes pear shaped with Jenny and Gabby, they can still escape the city," Alison replied.

"So what now? Where's Gabby?" Simon asked.

"On the train. Alison, Simon, you go to the train, find out who or what is on it and stop it from leaving," Blake replied.

Alison and Simon disappeared down the tunnel towards Kings Cross Station.

Blake looked at Samir. "It's time to go to work," he said.

"What's your plan?" Samir asked.

"We go to the Rabbit Hole and blow this place to hell."

Samir nodded and followed him down the tunnel towards Euston Station.

***

A metal door creaked open and Ivan Stepanchikov stood in the doorway. "Tom will see you now."

"Such hospitality," Jenny quipped as she moved towards him.

As Jenny went to move past him, Ivan's hand came up out of the darkness and slapped her across her face. Her ear-piece disappeared onto the floor as she gasped and turned back to face him.

"Women should know their place," he spat as he pushed past her.

Jenny looked down at the floor but couldn't see the ear-piece in the dim light. She knew that she was on her own now and just had to hope that Blake was able to find her. She followed Ivan through the tunnels until they finally arrived at The Rabbit Hole. Jenny walked into the open space that had six circular tunnels heading off in different directions. Around sixty metres above them was a drain cover which created an almost prison-like shadow inside the chamber. A large parasol umbrella deflected any rainwater that would splash down through the drain cover and underneath the umbrella was a man sat at a desk tapping away on a laptop. Jenny recognised his broad shoulders and muscular frame although his dark brown hair now carried a hint of grey highlights.

"Hello Jen, it's been a long time," Tom said.

Jenny approached Tom with a calm and collected demeanour, trying to hide her fear and anxiety. "Tom. I wish I could say it's good to see you again, but under the circumstances..."

Tom chuckled, turning to face her. His grey eyes staring into her soul like they used to on those romantic nights of yesteryear when she would let herself be swept away with his charm and bravado. "Yes, I can imagine. But we have a lot to catch up on, don't we?" He gestured for her to take a seat in one of the chairs on the opposite side of his desk.

Jenny hesitated before sitting down, glancing around the dimly lit chamber. "I'm not sure how much catching up we'll be doing."

Tom studied her with a serious expression. "You're here for the students, aren't you?"

Jenny nodded.

"I see." Tom rubbed his chin thoughtfully. "It's a shame you never showed this kind of remorse and care when you sent a whole regiment of soldiers to their deaths by handing over that dossier to the Russians. Detente indeed."

"You used me. I thought that you loved me but it was all a lie!"

"I did love you Jen. You were the only one who ever spoke to my heart. I felt alive with you. What we had, I will never forget."

"But you were still too busy going up in the world and plotting behind my back!"

"Sometimes we're too focused on going up that we fail to see love coming down. Such a tragedy but through tragedy and circumstance, it has brought us back together and maybe we can right a few wrongs along the way."

"I doubt that."

"You know, Jen, I always knew you were trouble. But I never expected you to be involved in something like this."

"Like what?" Jenny asked, her heart racing with anticipation.

Tom leaned back in his chair, steepling his fingers. "Like interfering with things that don't concern you such as trying to take down my operation."

Jenny swallowed hard, trying to keep her composure. "I'm not trying to take down your operation, Tom. I'm just trying to save those girls. They're innocent teenagers for Christ's sake. What sick, perverse men have you been working with? What happened to the old Tom. The one I loved. The gentleman who would do anything to make a woman happy? Is he still in there? Whatever happens, I'll make sure that you'll never use me again!"

Tom raised an eyebrow. "And how do you plan on doing that?"

Jenny hesitated, not sure how much she should reveal. But she knew she had to tread carefully. "I have some people on the outside, working to shut down your organisation."

Tom chuckled. "Is that so?"

Jenny nodded. "We're doing everything we can to stop you, Tom. And we won't stop until those girls are free and you pay for your betrayal."

Tom's expression darkened. "I'm afraid that's not going to happen, Jen. Despite what your dear brother has promised, no one can stop us now."

"What do you mean?"

Tom leaned forward, his eyes boring into hers. "I mean that you're in way over your head, Jen. You have no idea what you're getting yourself into."

Jenny leaned in closer, her eyes narrowing. "Try me."

Tom smirked. "Oh, I intend to. But not here. I have a proposition for you, Jen. One that could benefit us both."

Jenny raised an eyebrow. "Go on."

Tom stood up, walking around the desk to stand in front of her. "I need someone with your skills, Jen. Your connections. Your knowledge of the city. Hell, you practically grew up in this dump! I'm willing to make a deal with you. Help me with my operation, and I'll let the students go."

"If the end goal isn't getting the girls out of the country and into prostitution then what is?"

"That is for me to worry about. There's a lot more money to be made on the continent than just selling off some skirt to the highest bidder. Help me out of this glorified outdated scrap heap with the merchandise on board and I will make things very comfortable for you."

Jenny's heart raced. "And if I refuse?"

Tom shrugged. "Then you'll never see those girls again and you'll be an unfortunate addition to my list of people to be eliminated."

At that moment, a man came rushing over towards them from one of the tunnels wearing a high-visibility jacket and trousers. "Sir, there's been a development," he said breathlessly as he stood at Tom's side.

"Go on," Tom replied as he turned to face him.

"Special Branch agents are in the system, they're claiming that they are preventing a terrorist attack!"

"And I suppose you let them down here."

The man nodded nervously.

Tom let out a loud sigh. "Jen, meet Dean. Dean, say goodbye to Jen," Tom said before pulling out a gun and firing it, sending a bullet directly into Dean's forehead.

Jenny gasped in horror as she watched the man fall to the ground, blood pooling around him. She instinctively made a lunge at Tom but he stepped back and raised a hand to stop her.

"Now, now, Jen. Don't be foolish," he said calmly, tucking his gun away.

Jenny stared at him in disbelief. "You just killed him!"

Tom shrugged. "He won't take it personally, he was a liability. And I can't have anyone interfering with my plans. We're gonna have a beautiful future together. Just like you always wanted. The fairytale wedding, house in the countryside and kids playing in the fields. The whole nine yards."

Jenny felt sick to her stomach as she realised the extent of Tom's ruthlessness. She knew she had to get out of there, and fast. "That was with the Tom Gibson I used to love. He died long ago, I'm leaving," she said firmly.

Tom raised an eyebrow. "You're not even going to hear me out? That's the trouble with you Langford's, always too trigger happy."

"I've heard enough," Jenny replied, her voice shaking with anger. "I'm not going to help you with your twisted operation."

Tom chuckled. "Suit yourself, Jen. But don't say I didn't warn you."

Jenny turned to leave, but Tom's voice stopped her in her tracks. "Oh, and one more thing."

She turned back to face him warily. "What?"

"Your curiosity brought you back to me. It's that bond we still hold from years ago. So I'll give you fair warning. You might want to watch your back," Tom said, with a sly smile. "You never know who might be watching."

Jenny didn't waste any more time. She ran out of the chamber as fast as she could. She couldn't believe what she had just witnessed. Tom was a cold-blooded murderer and he had no qualms about killing anyone who got in his way. She knew she had to warn Blake about the danger they were in. She took out her phone to call him, but before she could even dial the number, she felt a sharp pain at the back of her head and everything went black.

***

Alison and Simon crawled through tunnels that eventually led them to the freight platform at the far side of St Pancras station. They looked down on the freight train below them and noticed two men standing on the platform.

"Zodiac, I might've guessed," Alison said as she searched for an exit out of the tunnel.

"You know them?"

"One of them has been on our radar for a while. Somehow, he keeps giving Samir the slip."

"What about the other guy?"

Alison shook her head. "Never seen him before but if Zodiac is here, keep a lookout for his brother Xander. He won't be too far away and he's on the run from prison."

"What did he go down for?"

"The usual, GBH, attempted murder and extortion."

"Nice fella then," Simon quipped.

Alison didn't respond.

"Looks like armoured plating on that train. It must be inches thick. If Gabby and the girls are on there, how the hell are we going to stop it?" Simon asked.

Alison frowned, trying to come up with a plan. "We'll have to figure it out. But first, we need to get closer and see if we can find any weaknesses in their system."

They continued to crawl along the tunnel, watching the two men on the platform closely. As they got closer, they noticed that the men were heavily armed and wearing bulletproof vests. It was going to be a risky move to get past them.

"We need a distraction," Simon whispered. "Something to draw their attention away from us."

Alison noticed a metal grid in front of them. She used a knife to release the grid and saw a thick pole holding up the structure that led down to the platform. An idea formed in her mind.

"If we can slide down the pole undetected then maybe we can get close enough to disarm them."

Simon nodded, scanning the area for anything they could use. He noticed a stack of crates nearby. "We'll use those," he said, pointing to them.

Alison looked at him sceptically. "How?"

"We'll knock them over," Simon said, a sly smile forming on his lips as he slipped a silencer on to his gun. "It'll make enough noise to draw their attention away from us."

"Can you make that shot from here?" Alison asked.

Simon looked at her like she had just farted in a lift. "The CIA do give us some training."

"Okay, do it," Alison replied as she got herself into position to slide down the pole.

Simon aimed through the gap and hit the second crate in the stack of three sending them all toppling over. As the two men walked over to investigate, Alison and Simon slid down the pole and managed to get themselves onto the opposite side of the train. They watched through the gap between the carriages as the two men returned to their original positions.

"Now what?" Alison asked.

"These old trains have an escape hatch in the floor of the front cab. If I can get underneath the train and somehow manoeuvre it, I can get onto the train and stop it from leaving."

"Do it. I'll try and work on Zodiac and his accomplice."

Alison watched as Simon made his way towards the front of the train before she moved towards the back. She knew it was a risky strategy but they had to stop the train from leaving the station.

Chapter Thirty-Four
Hello Old Friend

Blake and Samir emerged out of the tunnels and arrived at The Rabbit Hole. The old drain cover way above at street level allowed the light of the moon to give an ominous glow inside the chamber. A wooden table with a parasol in the centre of the chamber was all that remained from how Blake remembered it.

"This is where you hung out as kids?" Samir asked.

"When you're young and rebellious you tend to do stupid things. Unfortunately some of us never grow out of that phase."

"Touche brother," Samir smirked.

Blake walked over to the table and saw a sheet of paper with an arrow drawn on it pointing left. "I guess we go this way," he said, heading towards the left tunnel.

"You know we're walking right into a trap, don't you?" Samir asked.

"What choice do we have? If we want to find those missing girls and rescue Jenny and Gabby, we need to find out who or what is behind this."

They followed two more arrows until they could hear running water. They followed the tunnel down until they arrived at a huge sewerage drain. Sewer water was running rapidly several metres below them leaving a putrid smell in the air. High above, there was a storm drain that had constant waves of water seeping through it at regular intervals. Blake looked over at the far side and saw Jenny, Nicola and Andrea tied to the wall.

"Hello old friend, it's been a long time!" Tom called out. "Why don't you join the party?"

Blake looked directly opposite from where he was standing and saw Tom standing on a platform next to Graham Evans, Xander Zhal and Vijay Bhatt.

"Why are you doing this Tom?" Blake asked. "Didn't Jen help you enough last time? Her mistake allowed you to disappear into the shadows. You had the perfect end game. The perfect escape. So, why not stay dead? Why come back now?"

"Oh I may have gone off the grid for a while but there was always an irritant poking his nose into my affairs. Now we have a common interest. You."

"Then take me and let the girls go."

"I can't do that Blake. Go back on a promise, it would be bad for my reputation. As you can see we're at the overflow for the river Thames here. In bad weather, this storm drain takes the excess water and diverts it away from the city. You took Graham's daughters away from him. You put Xander behind bars for a crime he didn't commit and you implicated Vijay in this ongoing investigation after you sent Samir onto one of his guardian angels."

Blake looked at Samir.

"Oh, didn't he tell you, he works for Zodiac too," Tom chuckled.

Samir shook his head. "No, no, you know that's not true."

At that moment, Derek Copsewood burst in behind where Tom, Graham, Vijay and Xander were standing.

"She's gone, we can't find her. Looks like she had help," Derek explained breathlessly.

Tom beckoned him forwards. Derek warily moved towards him.

"I gave you one job," Tom snapped. "One job! And you couldn't even do that."

In one quick move, Tom brought his fist up catching Derek with an uppercut to his chin sending him backwards over the metal barrier and down into the sewer drains below. A maniacal scream echoed around the sewer before his body disappeared into the huge flowing pool of water below.

"You bastard!" Andrea shouted out. "He never did anything to you!"

"Just tying up some loose ends," Tom smiled. "Now Blake, you have a choice, save your sister and her friends or save the students. Either way I'm going to be leaving you and heading out of this Godforsaken dump you call a metropolis."

"What was it Tom? What turned you into the bitter and twisted psychopath you are today?" Blake asked.

The four men took a step backwards towards the tunnels behind them.

"It was you Blake, you and your father chasing down all those lost causes. I knew that if I was to get into your head, I'd have to get close. John Langford couldn't let it go that his family had assisted a terrorist attack and wiped out half of a regiment of soldiers. You thought that between you it had been covered up but getting into your head was only half the battle, but your sister, she was even easier. The clock's ticking Blake, make a decision."

Tom pressed a button on a control in his hand. Blake and Samir both pulled their guns out and fired but the four men disappeared into the tunnels behind. Blake looked up and saw four dark green hexagonal boxes on the wall opposite with a flashing red light and a timer on both.

"He's gonna blow that wall. If that goes, the river will flood the chamber and possibly the tracks below!" Blake shouted. "We have to get up there!"

Samir and Blake dashed towards the wall, their guns still in hand. They could hear the sound of rushing water growing louder as they approached the boxes. Samir noticed that the boxes had small keypads on them.

"Blake, look! There's a keypad. We might be able to disarm it," Samir shouted over the noise.

Blake nodded and ran towards the keypad, his fingers quickly tapping in a series of numbers. Nothing happened. Suddenly, they heard footsteps behind them. They turned around to see Derek climbing out of the sewer drain below. His face was covered in dirt and blood, but he was still alive.

"We have to get out of here before it's too late," Derek gasped.

"We need to disable the bombs Derek, do you know the code?" Samir shouted.

"Two, five, seven, nine!"

Blake punched in the code and the timer on the box slowed down until it finally stopped.

"Got it!" Blake yelled triumphantly.

They moved to the other boxes and disarmed them before climbing down to release Jenny, Andrea and Nicola.

"Do you know where the girls are?" Samir asked.

Andrea nodded, "Follow me!"

***

At the freight train, gunshots echoed around the station and screams could be heard in the background. As Alison arrived at the back of the train, the engines boomed into life with a thunderous roar. She looked around the side and saw five men join Zodiac and his accomplice on the platform. The doors of one of the carriages whooshed open and all seven men stepped inside. Alison climbed up the back of the train and pulled herself up onto the roof. The engines roared louder as the train began to move out of the station.

"Blake, Blake, can you hear me," Alison spoke into her ear-piece hoping that Blake could hear her over the noise. "The train is leaving. The train is leaving!"

Meanwhile, inside the freight train, Claire and Gabby had made their way towards the back of the train. As they arrived at the second to last carriage, they came up against a locked door. They heard gunshots and shouting coming from further down the train.

"This must be it!" Gabby said as Claire crouched down and removed a metal clip from her hair. "What are you doing?"

Claire removed the small plastic cover just below the door release and found a small circuit with several wires. She released the brown and blue wires before using her metal clip to connect them. A small spark flashed and the door opened.

"How did you do that?" Gabby asked.

"Misspent youth, come on," Claire replied.

The carriage was dark and had blacked out windows with only a strip of light either side of the walkway down the middle of the carriage to light the way. Gabby pulled out her phone and lit up the carriage. They both gasped as they saw ten young women laying on the floor barely conscious wearing ripped clothes and looking very pale.

"We've got to get them out of here!" Claire said.

"Claire! Look out!" Gabby shouted as one of the girls launched herself at Claire grabbing her hair and pinning her to the floor.

Gabby grabbed hold of her attacker and pulled her off of Claire. "Stop! We're here to help you!"

"You're one of them!" the girl shouted as she continued to try and fight Claire who had regained her balance.

At that moment, the rest of the girls stood up around them.

"What's going on?" Claire asked. "I thought they drugged you all."

"That's what the deal was. We do favours for the Russian, he doesn't drug us. Who are you?" the attacker asked.

"We're working with Special Branch to get you off of this train," Gabby replied.

Claire looked at her confused. At that moment, the train began to move.

"We need to get you off now!" Gabby said.

In a split second, the girls immediately dropped to the floor once again. Gabby and Claire looked towards the exit and saw a large heavy built man looking back at them. He smiled before closing the door.

***

Blake, Samir, Jenny, Andrea, Nicola and Derek all ran through Kings Cross Station towards the St Pancras International Station.

Blake rushed over to security. "Special Branch, I need to borrow this train!" he said, showing his ID.

"What? I've got five hundred passengers waiting to embark!" the security guard protested.

"And we've got a terrorist to catch!" Samir added.

The security guard looked at them. "Just you two," he said.

Samir and Blake looked back at Jenny, Derek, Nicola and Andrea.

"We'll come back for you," Blake said before rushing through the station towards the train with Samir close behind.

Blake and Samir pushed their way through the crowds and up the travelators to the main Eurostar platform. The engines of the huge train were ticking over as they arrived at the driver's cab.

"Special Branch, we need to borrow your train!" Samir shouted.

"What the...." The driver managed to say before Samir and Blake climbed inside.

Blake fired up the engines which roared in response.

"You're over revving," the driver explained.

"What's your name?" Samir asked.

"Ahmed."

"Ahmed, we're in pursuit of a terrorist. Can you drive this thing and catch him before he gets to the Eurotunnel?"

Ahmed nodded nervously.

"Welcome to the team!" Blake said as he patted him on the back.

Ahmed took the controls and the train roared into life as it headed out of the station. "I don't get paid enough for this!"

"Neither do we, act accordingly," Samir quipped.

As the train joined the main railway line, they could see a black bullet train on the rail next to them up ahead.

"Faster Ahmed, faster!" Blake shouted as they began gaining on them.

Adrenaline was coursing through Blake as he saw the train getting closer and closer. He knew he had one chance and he had to take it.

Chapter Thirty-Five

Plans Derailed

Ahmed sped up the train until they were almost level with the freight train. Blake watched as Alison managed to find an opening and slip into the third carriage from the roof of the train. Gunshots fired out of the driver's cab of the train as it looked like Simon was fighting with the driver.

"Brace yourselves, I'm going to derail it!" Blake called into his ear-piece.

With a determined expression, Blake pulled out his gun and aimed it at the freight train. Simon and the driver fell out of the cab landing on the gravel and rolling several metres further down the tracks narrowly avoiding the oncoming Eurostar Train.

"What the hell are you doing?!" Ahmed yelled.

"Trust me," Blake replied before firing a several shots at the tracks in front of the freight train.

The sound of metal clanging against metal echoed through the air as the train derailed on the buckled track, sending it crashing into a ditch. Blake and Samir jumped out of the Eurostar and ran towards the wreckage. They could hear the sound of screams and cries for help coming from the train.

As they approached, they saw a man in blue jeans and a white t-shirt emerge from the wreckage, holding a young woman by the neck.

Samir recognised him instantly. "It's over Xander! Drop the girl and surrender!"

Xander laughed and tightened his grip on the girl's neck. "That's rich coming from the guy who enabled all of this to happen! You think you can stop me? I have explosives on this train, and I'll blow it all to hell if you come any closer!"

"You'd never blow up a train that your brother is still on! Give it up, it's over!"

"Not between you and me!"

Blake and Samir exchanged a look before nodding at each other. They knew they had to act fast if they wanted to save the hostages and stop Xander from doing anything stupid. Taking out their guns, they moved closer to Xander and the girl, keeping their eyes on him at all times.

"Come on Xander, it's over. Let the girl go," Blake said, his voice steady and calm.

Xander's eyes flickered between Blake and Samir, his grip on the girl's neck tightening. "I'll kill her, I swear it!"

"You won't get away with this," Samir said, his gun trained on Xander.

Xander laughed. "Do your colleagues realise they have a snake in the grass, Samir? How you and my brother colluded together over the past few years. No, no, I'm on my way to France and a new life. The explosives on this train will take out half of London, and you can't do a damn thing to stop me."

Blake and Samir shared a look.

Taking a deep breath, Blake stepped forward, his gun steady in his hand. "You're bluffing. Drop the girl and surrender."

Xander hesitated for a moment before suddenly pushing the girl towards Blake and making a run for it. Blake caught the girl and watched as Xander disappeared into the distance.

Samir chased after him with Blake close behind. Their footsteps echoing as they crunched along the gravel at the side of the railway tracks. As they got closer, they could see Xander's figure becoming more defined. Suddenly, Xander turned around and aimed a gun at them. Blake and Samir quickly took cover behind a nearby tree as the shots continued to rain down on them. Samir blindly fired two shots back.

"We need to take him out," Samir said, reloading his gun.

Blake nodded, his heart pounding in his chest. They had to stop Xander before he could cause any more damage. Taking a deep breath, Samir emerged from behind the tree and fired a shot at Xander. Xander fell to the ground, his gun clattering onto the gravel beside him.

Samir and Blake walked over towards him. Samir's shot had caught him in the chest.

"Your secret will come out. Nobody stays hidden forever," Xander said before taking his last breath.

Blake looked at Samir.

"I told you what happened Blake. If you don't believe that then I'll hang up my weapon today," Samir sighed.

Blake placed his hand on Samir's shoulder. "I believe you. Now let's go and tidy this mess up."

Samir smiled briefly before they headed back towards the train. By the time they arrived back at the freight train, police had arrived on the scene and Simon had pinned the driver onto the floor.

"Where's Alison?" Blake asked.

"Still inside the train!" Simon replied.

Blake and Samir cautiously entered the wreckage of the train from the second carriage. As they walked through the carriage, they heard a groan coming from one of the seats. Blake moved towards the seat, gun ready in case of attack.

"You don't need the gun Blake, I'm dead already," Graham Evans said as he held his hand against a bloodstained shirt that was pressed against his abdomen.

"Not dead enough for me. Where's Alison?" Blake snapped holding the gun under Graham's chin.

"Your agent is with Ivan, through there," Graham replied, using his eyes to guide Blake in the direction of the next carriage.

Blake stepped back and looked at Samir. "Keep an eye on him, I'm going through."

Samir nodded and stayed with Graham as Blake continued through the carriage. The carriage was split into seats on the left and piles of wooden crates tied into the side of the carriage with metal chains on the right. He could hear the faint sound of breathing coming from one of the seats. He approached each row, gun raised and ready to shoot. He heard someone groan and spun around. Alison was lying on the ground between a pile of broken crates and broken glass. A strong smell of whiskey hung in the air. Her clothes were torn and her face was bruised. Blake rushed to her side, checking if she was breathing. Relief flooded him as he felt her pulse under his fingers. He picked her up, cradling her in his arms. She was so light, so fragile. He felt a wave of protectiveness wash over him. This was all his fault. He should have never sent her and Simon onto the train alone.

As he carried Alison towards the door, Blake was knocked to the floor. He felt a huge pain in his ribs as someone rugby tackled him to the ground. Alison's body landed against the emergency exit door as Blake turned to face his attacker.

Ivan pinned Blake to the ground and began landing punches to his ribs. Blake managed to bring his knee up between the legs of his attacker, momentarily sending him rolling away before another huge fist landed against the side of Blake's head.

Blake's vision blurred for a moment, but he quickly regained his focus as Ivan pulled out a knife. Ivan attempted to plunge it into Blake's chest, but Blake managed to block the attack with his arm, causing the knife to graze his skin.

Blake gasped in pain as he kicked Ivan off of him and scrambled to his feet. Ivan lunged forward again, but Blake was ready this time, dodging the attack and landing a powerful punch to his jaw.

Ivan stumbled backwards, but quickly regained his balance and charged at Blake once again. Blake grabbed his arm, twisted it behind his back and slammed him face-first into the ground.

Ivan laid there, groaning in pain, as Blake checked on Alison. She was still dazed, but he could feel her breathing steadily against his chest. He lifted her up once more and headed towards the door.

At that moment, he heard Ivan laugh. He turned to face him.

"This is what happens when women don't do as they are told," Ivan called out.

Blake placed Alison back down onto the floor before turning to face him. Blake realised that Ivan had managed to get hold of his gun and was aiming it at Blake's chest.

"At least I'll have the chance to take down the great Blake Langford," Ivan spat. "For Queen and country Blake?"

Blake looked left and right but quickly realised he had nowhere to take cover.

"No, for me!" Alison shouted out before firing her gun.

The shot hit Ivan in the centre of his chest and he fell backwards into the crates of whiskey. Blake walked over to him to check he was dead.

"Are you okay?" Alison asked.

"Am I okay? I thought you were dead!"

"I'm not going to let a few scrapes stop me from killing a sexist misogynist asshole like that," Alison replied as she carefully got back onto her feet, grimacing a couple of times.

"We need to get you to the ambulance," Blake advised.

"No, we need to find the girls. I think they're at the back of the train."

"Everyone okay?" Samir asked as he entered the carriage. He looked at Alison. "Jeez, what happened to you?"

"Come on, we need to move. Where's Graham Evans?" Blake asked.

"Police have him. They're moving in so we need to move fast."

Samir and Blake entered the next carriage with Alison close behind. The carriage was full of wooden crates with the words EXPLOSIVES and AMMUNITION written in red on the sides of the crates.

"He wasn't bluffing then," Samir commented.

"It's like a terrorist supermarket. It's obvious it wasn't just the girls they were trafficking into Europe," Alison replied.

They continued through the next two carriages with the same crates stacked up inside them. Finally, they arrived at another passenger carriage.

Samir managed to open one of the cargo doors just wide enough for him to squeeze through. "Give me three minutes, I'll get in the other side, you take them from this side."

"And if they see you?" Alison asked.

"Then at least I'll be a diversion," Samir replied before jumping out of the train.

Blake and Alison crouched down behind the door that entered the next carriage. They heard raised voices but couldn't understand what was being said. Blake risked a look inside the next carriage through the small window in the door but couldn't see anybody.

"Zodiac," Blake whispered.

"So where's Gibson?" Alison asked.

Blake heard Samir through his ear-piece.

"Let's go," Blake said as he opened the door and shot two warning shots into the roof of the carriage. "Everybody down!"

Zodiac stood with his arms raised. "Situation analysis, hopeless. I have the weapons and the girls. You shoot me and this detonator will send the whole of London off of the face of the earth."

"Where's Gibson?" Blake asked.

"He's around," Zodiac smiled. "Didn't Samir tell you, he was the one who arranged my brother's untimely release from prison so this whole operation could be completed. Copsewood had the contacts to bring the girls in but your colleague was so much easier, so willing to save face."

Samir appeared from behind Zodiac and struck him on the back of the head, sending him to the floor and the detonator rolling down the carriage. Alison picked up the detonator and ran out into the previous carriage and squeezed through the gap in the cargo door that Samir had created. She fell to the floor outside. Simon rushed over to help her.

"The detonator!" Alison shouted.

"What?" Simon asked before seeing a metal pole rolling back towards the railway track.

Simon leapt on top of it and grabbed hold of the detonator before helping Alison back to her feet.

"Bomb squads are on their way. Get it as far away as you can," Simon said as he rushed towards the back of the train.

Meanwhile, inside the train, Zodiac regained his balance and faced Samir. "You have no idea what you're getting yourself into. I could've made you a very rich man instead of a poor dead one."

"Maybe, but I'd rather fight for what's right than work for a small-time criminal," Samir snapped.

"See you in the crystal," Zodiac replied as he dropped two smoke bombs onto the floor and headed toward the cargo carriage.

Blake struck out blindly but only managed to hit into a passenger seat. The carriage filled up with smoke which stung their eyes.

"Stay low!" Blake shouted.

Samir and Blake crawled back towards the cargo carriage. Shouts of female voices echoed outside as they made their way out of the train. When they were outside, the fresh air helped them regain their vision once again. Simon and a police officer were helping the girls escape from the rear carriage of the train. Gabby and Claire Turner were sitting at the side of the tracks but there was no sign of Zodiac or Tom Gibson.

"Son-of-a-bitch gave us the slip!" Blake cussed.

Samir scanned the surrounding area with a frown on his face. They had failed to capture Zodiac and that meant he was still out there, planning his next move. This wasn't over yet. Simon rushed across to join them.

"We need to find Gibson," Simon said, his eyes darting around looking for any sign of movement.

"I agree," Samir replied. "But we need to be careful. Zodiac may have other traps set up for us."

Blake nodded. "We'll split up and search the area. Be on the lookout for any suspicious activity."

The group split up, each taking a different direction. Samir headed towards a nearby alleyway, his hand hovering over his gun. He had a feeling that someone might be hiding there. As he approached the entrance to the alleyway, he heard a faint noise coming from inside. He moved cautiously, his senses on high alert.

Suddenly, a figure jumped out from behind a dumpster, brandishing a knife. Samir reacted quickly, dodging the blade and catching his attacker with a strong fist to his chin. Zodiac fell to the floor but quickly rolled away and got back to his feet.

"Give it up Zac, it's over," Samir said, his gun trained on Zodiac's chest.

"It's never over, Samir. When the world discovers Blake's family's dirty little secret, he'll have nowhere to run."

"What are you talking about?"

"It's beautiful, Samir. The inheritance and the crystal. His son's already involved and sooner or later, he'll learn that his perfect little family is not so pure after all."

Samir had heard about Michael and Frank working on a program called "The Crystal" but how did it link back to Blake? "Let me take you in. Tell Special Branch what you know. I can protect you."

Zodiac laughed. "As if I'm going to believe that. Xander and I have other plans..."

"Xander is dead."

Zodiac glared at him. "You're lying."

"He died running away trying to save his own skin."

"How do you know?"

"Because I killed him," Samir replied.

At that moment, a black Volkswagen pulled up at the end of the alleyway. Zodiac and Samir both glared at each other.

"Don't forget Samir, I know what you did. So you have a choice. Kill me now and never have to worry about me talking to anyone. But you'll always be the outcast. Always be the black sheep of the team. No one will ever trust you again. Or you can let me finish what I started and Blake Langford will never hold the higher ground over you again."

Samir watched as Zodiac walked towards the car. His gun never moved from aiming at Zodiac's chest. Zodiac continued to slowly walk backwards before turning and stepping into the car. The driver sped away as Samir lowered his gun. He knew this was far from over.

Chapter Thirty-Six

More Questions Than Answers

Six hours later, Alison, Samir, Simon and Blake were standing in front of Eric Gordon's desk at the Special Branch offices.

"At least most of the girls were released unharmed," Eric Gordon surmised.

"They are likely to need a lot of psychological support in the coming months Sir, however, after examining the contents of the freight train, I don't think the girls were the only target here," Alison explained.

"I don't follow. I thought we had uncovered that Derek Copsewood and Zodiac were targeting young students to traffick them to the highest bidders in Europe," Eric replied.

"That may have been their initial plan, but we found evidence that they were also trying to smuggle something else out of the country," Samir added.

"What is it?"

"We don't know yet. We found explosives and ammunition for rocket launchers and machine guns but this whole Crystal thing seems to be a highly valuable and dangerous item. They were willing to kill for it," Simon explained.

Eric Gordon looked at the group of agents with concern. "So what do we do now?"

"We need to find Tom Gibson," Blake replied. "He holds the key to all of this."

"What about the ship at St Katherine's Docks? Someone went to a lot of effort to try and throw us off the scent," Alison added.

"Detective Jim Curtis is all over it. Seems to be, like you said, an effort to divert attention away from the real crime here," Eric Gordon replied.

"And what are we doing about the crystal?" Eric asked.

"Frank and the team are working on it. Whatever it is, it seems to be linked to whatever Gibson was going after," Blake replied.

"How did your son access it so easily and engage with Gibson online?" Eric asked.

"We're still investigating," Samir replied. "There is a chance that Michael's account was compromised deliberately and that Blake's family was the target."

Blake nodded in agreement. "Where does this leave my family now?"

"Investigations need to continue. Paula, obviously caught up in it with Andrew Broughton and her father. Jennifer, her past relationship with Tom Gibson makes her a target and she will need protection and Steven is still being investigated after the bloodbath at his shared accommodation. The reality is, until Gibson is taken down, you're always going to be looking over your shoulder Blake," Eric Gordon explained.

At that moment, Angela, Eric Gordon's secretary, entered the room. "Sorry to interrupt but I thought you may want to know, Graham Evans has been released without charge and Derek Copsewood is still missing presumed dead."

"Do they know where Graham Evans is heading to?" Blake asked.

"No fixed abode in the UK but I'll ask the team to keep a close watch for anything unusual," Angela replied.

"Thank you Angela," Eric Gordon replied as she turned and left the office.

"And still nothing on Zodiac?" Simon asked.

"No, Samir chased him from the train wreck but lost him in the back alleys of Kings Cross," Eric Gordon confirmed. "The good news is that Joe Knight is out of intensive care and will be out of hospital soon. His insight could be helpful in tying up some of the loose ends."

"Where does this leave Gabby?" Simon asked.

"She's free to return to the US as are you. I'm sorry that you became caught up in all of this but I'm sure Jason Price will be in touch if anything changes."

Alison's mind was reeling as she listened to the updates. The case had taken so many twists and turns, and yet it felt like they were no closer to finding all of the answers they needed. She couldn't help but think about the young girls who had been taken, and the trauma they must be experiencing even after the event.

"I think we need to maintain our focus on finding Tom Gibson," Alison spoke up, breaking the tension in the room. "He's the one who seems to be at the root of all of this and if we take him out, the deck of cards will hopefully fall. He's the only one who can tell us what this Crystal is and why it's so valuable."

"I agree," Eric Gordon nodded. "But we need to be careful. The trail has gone cold and Gibson is a dangerous man, he has many influential friends in many governments who would protect him and he's proven that he will do whatever it takes to protect his interests."

"I'll go back to Michael's computer and see if there's any way to trace where Gibson is," Blake replied.

"And I'll continue working on the explosives and ammunition we found in the freight train," Samir added.

As the team left Eric Gordon's office, Angela called out to Blake.

"There's a phone call for you, it's Jenny!" she called out.

Blake took the phone and listened for a moment. "I'm on my way," he said before handing the phone back to Angela and sprinting away down into the car park below the Special Branch offices.

Blake rushed across London before entering Chelsea And Westminster Hospital. When he arrived on the ward, he saw Jenny and Steven waiting by the entrance. Steven had his arms around his sister as she cried on his shoulder.

"What's going on?" Blake asked.

"She's gone Blake, mum died about ten minutes ago," Steven replied.

Blake froze. The news hit him hard and for a moment he felt as if the world had stopped turning. They had lost their mother, the woman who had always been there for them, the one who had watched over them alone after their father's death. Tears welled up in his eyes, but he fought them back, trying to be strong for his siblings.

Jenny turned to face him and Blake held her close.

"I should've been here," Jenny sighed.

"You did what you needed to do. Mum would have understood that," Blake replied.

"I thought we had more time."

Blake didn't reply and just held her close.

"We need to make arrangements," Steven said, his voice low. "I don't know where to start."

Blake nodded, taking charge as he broke the embrace with Jenny. "I'll take care of it. You two go home and rest. I'll call you later."

As his siblings left the hospital, Blake felt a wave of grief wash over him. He had lost his mother and he didn't know how to cope with the pain.

"Mr Langford," a nurse called out, breaking his thoughts.

Blake nodded as he followed the nurse into a side room.

"I'll be just outside," she said as she left him alone in the room.

Blake walked over to the side of the bed and placed the palm of his hand on his mother's forehead before running his fingers through her gold and grey hair.

"I'm sorry I wasn't there when you needed me. I guess I've been on this never ending rollercoaster and never knew when it was time to step off. I will be better from now on and try to make you proud of me and Michael. Say hi to Dad for me," Blake whispered before turning and heading back towards the door.

As he opened the door, he turned around for one final look across at Emily Langford before turning and walking away.

Blake had seen many people die during his work and by his own hand over the years but when it was his own family, he never could quite find the same detachment that he had built up professionally. He walked out of the hospital and into the busy streets of London, surrounded by hundreds of people but he felt lost and alone.

***

Later that same day, at the Eurostar terminal at St Pancras International Station, Andrea Smith and Nicola Pew stepped onto a train heading for Paris with Graham Evans and Zodiac following close behind. They took their seats and looked out of the window not saying a word to each other as the train pulled away from the station. Passengers gasped as they saw the freight train still being lifted from the track by cranes as they passed by. Nicola removed a bottle of red wine from her bag along with four plastic wine glasses.

"Les Chouacheux, Jean-Claude has influenced your taste already" Zodiac commented as she poured the four glasses of wine.

"To new beginnings," Andrea smiled.

They raised their glasses in a toast and took a sip. Andrea felt a strange sense of relief wash over her as the train sped through the English countryside. She knew that they were leaving a lot of unfinished business behind, but they had done all they could for now. They were on their way to Paris, where a new chapter of their lives would begin.

As the train approached the channel tunnel, Andrea leaned over and whispered in Nicola's ear. "Are you sure you're ready for this?"

Nicola nodded, her heart racing with anticipation. She had been waiting for this moment and nothing could stop her now. "After what happened with Kaja, this is exactly what I need."

Andrea smiled. "I hope you're right."

The train emerged from the tunnel into the French countryside and Nicole felt a wave of excitement wash over her. They were heading towards Paris, the city of love and she was finally going to meet Jean-Claude, the man who had caught her attention over social media for the past few months but she hadn't dared to allow herself the opportunity to come to France to meet him.

Andrea led the way as they disembarked at Gare du Nord and made their way to a waiting car. The driver loaded their bags into the boot of the car and they sped away towards Toulouse.

Four hours later, they stopped at the top of a hill overlooking a lush green valley below.

"Why are we stopping?" Nicola asked.

"Jean-Claude wanted to meet you here so you could see the sunset together," the driver explained.

Nicola smiled at Andrea who returned the smile.

The driver opened the door and ushered Nicola out of the car. The driver led her down a dirt track in between miles of overgrown hedges and trees until they came to a clearing at the top of a cliff that overlooked the valley below. The driver walked back to the car as Nicole approached the cliff. She saw a man standing on the edge of the cliff. He was wearing ripped blue jeans and a white shirt that was blowing freely in the breeze.

"Hello Nicola," he said as he turned to face her.

"Tom?" she gasped. "What are you doing here?"

She noticed a scar that had appeared down the left side of his face.

"What happened to you?" she asked.

"This is what happens when you trust too many people. Kaja has left an unpaid debt that needs to be settled. Come closer, take a look at this beautiful sunset."

Nicola slowly approached the edge. "I don't understand, I was meant to be meeting someone. What do you mean Kaja has an unpaid debt? Where is Jean-claude."

"Jean-Claude can have many faces behind a screen," Tom smirked. "You let Jenny Langford get away. Andrea made sure that Kaja paid for his role in undermining my operation and now you will have the same penalty."

Nicola looked around to see if there was anyone or anything that she could use to protect herself but found nothing. She saw Tom reach inside the top of his jeans underneath the white shirt and pull out a gun.

"Tom, let me explain..."

"You've said enough," Tom replied before firing the gun at her chest.

Nicola's body fell from the top of the cliff and rolled down into the valley below. Tom watched her as she fell before heading back to the car that was waiting at the top of the mud path. He climbed into the passenger seat and the driver sped away.

Chapter Thirty-Seven

Secrets Never Die

Two weeks later, Blake, Jenny and Steven all gathered around the graveside at Collier Cemetery as Emily Langford was lowered into the ground to be reunited with her husband John Langford. Paula and Michael waited nearby as Blake, Jenny and Steven dropped a rose each into the grave. As they walked away, Michael took hold of Blake's hand and walked between him and Paula.

"Do you think Mum will meet Nan on the other side?" Michael asked.

"I'd like to think so," Blake smiled.

His work so often hinged on a split-second decision where life and death are on the line but Blake rarely acknowledged the impact of his actions until it concerned his own family. The reuniting of the students with their families was a joyous occasion. Tom Gibson was still missing and Blake wondered what the consequences of that would be for Jenny in the future. He just hoped that when or if Gibson reappeared, he would be there to protect her. If anything good had come out of this case, he knew that he was a lot closer to his siblings than he had ever been before. This needed to be his new focus if the family unit was to survive.

As if she had read his thoughts, Paula held him close. "We'll get through this," she whispered to him.

"I know we will," Blake replied.

As he stepped back, he noticed a black Bentley parked at the cemetery gates with Chief Eric Gordon standing by the passenger door. Blake looked at Paula and then back at the car.

"Do what you have to do. We'll be waiting for you," she said.

Blake crouched down and hugged Michael and then hugged Paula once more before wandering over towards the parked Bentley. Jenny and Steven wandered over to join Paula and Michael. Together they walked back towards the waiting cars in the cemetery car park.

Blake slid into the back seat of the Bentley and found Alison sitting alongside him with Samir in the driving seat. Eric Gordon sat in the front passenger seat as Samir drove them away.

"What's new?" Blake asked.

"No sign of Derek Copsewood. He's gone to ground and no more charges are coming the way of Steven Langford so he's in the clear," Eric Gordon confirmed.

"What about Zodiac?"

"None of his associates have sprung up since the crash but there was a suspected sighting at a villa near Toulouse," Alison confirmed.

"The same one that was in dispute with Elliot Francis' family and Graham Evans?" Blake asked.

"The same one, we're heading to the Eurotunnel now," Samir confirmed.

"One more thing, French authorities recovered the body of a young woman below a tall cliff-face overlooking Limoges. The French authorities have ID'd her as Nicole Pew," Alison explained.

"Limoges is a straight run from Paris to Toulouse. They were obviously heading for a rendezvous point at Elliot Francis' villa."

"It seems that way," Eric Gordon replied.

"Good, then we'll know where to find them, let's go," Blake replied.

***

Meanwhile, on the opposite side of London, Simon Buxton alongside Gabby and Claire Turner watched on with several others as Edith Harrow was given her send-off at Hounslow Crematorium.

"I guess this is the closure we both needed," Claire said as they left the crematorium.

"Unfortunately, he's still out there somewhere but I guess I can find comfort in the fact that you're okay," Gabby replied as she handed Claire the copy of Edith's book that she had found in the back of the taxi when she first arrived back in London. "Here, I'm sure she'd have wanted you to have it."

"I guess some secrets never die do they," Claire sighed as she took the book from Gabby.

"Some secrets are better kept in the past. That way they can't damage our future. Take care sis," Gabby replied as she embraced Claire.

After a brief moment, Gabby and Simon headed towards their rental car and left to go to the airport. Claire spoke to a couple of Edith's carers from the nursing home before wandering over towards the selection of flowers that had been laid out in her memory. Amongst the flowers was a small bouquet of blue artificial roses with a small message tag attached to them.

Claire turned the card over and read the message;

I could never have repaid the debt that I owe you. The gift of my daughter's life will haunt me forever. DC

Claire looked up at the skies above the crematorium. "Where are you Dad?" she whispered but no one answered.

She left without saying another word. Deep down, she knew it wasn't over.

***

Later that day, Samir, Alison and Blake arrived outside Chateau Delphine, just outside Toulouse. They approached the front door and rang the doorbell. After a moment, they heard a bolt slide back and the door opened. A short man with black hair, wearing a plain black t-shirt and matching shorts with a hoop earring in his right ear answered.

"Good evening, is Mr Evans home?" Blake asked.

"Monsieur Evans does not live 'ere anymore," the man replied.

At that moment, they heard a car engine start and tyres screeching from the side of the villa. Samir sprinted back towards the car and chased the car down some twisty roads towards a village in the distance. Blake and Alison pushed past the man and entered the villa.

"Excusez-moi Monsieur, Madame, you 'ave no right to be here," the man protested.

As they wandered through towards the back of the villa, they discovered a swimming pool with three sun loungers set up alongside it.

"Expecting company?" Blake asked as he continued on his way through into the kitchen.

"You 'ave no right..." the man continued.

"We have so shut up," Alison replied as she flashed her Special Branch badge.

As Blake entered the kitchen, he saw Andrea, Graham and Derek sitting at a dining room table. Alison and the man followed him into the room.

"Monsieur Derek, I sorry..." the man began.

Derek raised his hand. "It's okay Claude, I'm tired of running. Take me in, Blake. I deserve whatever comes my way."

Blake looked at him puzzled. "That's it?"

"I was foolish to believe that I could find happiness in another life out here."

"And what is here?" Alison asked.

"My home," Graham replied.

"I thought you were being evicted from here by Elliot Francis' solicitor," Blake questioned.

"Yeah, about that, in one of life's little ironies, Francis signed the place over to me just before he died. Funny how things work out like that, eh?" Graham smirked.

"Hilarious," Blake cussed before turning his attention back to Derek. "Why did you help me in London?"

"I'm not a barbarian Blake, yes I've used women in the past and I'm not proud of what I've done but I would never kill them. Gibson took things too far."

"And Nicola Pew?"

"An unfortunate occurrence."

"Where's Tom Gibson?"

"He took off as soon as you arrived," Derek confirmed.

Alison arrested Derek and led him back outside. Samir returned in the car.

"He got away," Samir sighed.

"It's okay, he can't run forever. We've got one of them. Let's go home," Blake replied.

"What about Graham?"

"His time will come."

As they drove away, Andrea and Graham stood in the doorway of the chateau and watched them leave.

"So, what now?" Andrea asked. "I can't stay here forever."

"When he discovers the truth, he'll have nowhere to turn. It's just a matter of time," Graham replied as he began walking down the side of the chateau with Andrea close behind him.

On the far side of the back garden, there was an old wooden shed. Graham approached the shed and opened the door. Inside, they saw Zodiac tapping away on a laptop.

"What's he doing here?" Andrea asked.

Graham ignored her. "They've gone," he said.

"And so have you," Zodiac replied as he shot Andrea with a tranquiliser gun.

She staggered for a moment and Graham caught her as she fell. Zodiac helped lift her inside the shed before leaving and locking the door behind them.

"Let's go, Reaper is waiting," Zodiac said as they walked away.

***

At 9am the following morning, Blake drove his silver Ford Mondeo into Portland Terrace car park before heading back up the concrete stairs to his London flat. Michael came running out to meet him, wrapping his arms around his father's waist.

Paula wandered over towards them. "Did you get Gibson?" she asked.

"No, not yet," Blake sighed. "He took off before we had the chance but he'll slip up eventually."

"And Dad?"

"He's keeping a low profile in the south of France. I don't think we'll be hearing from him again anytime soon."

Paula nodded.

"Are you okay?"

"Yeah, I guess it's better this way," Paula sighed. "At least he won't be coming back to the UK anytime soon.

Michael rushed back into the lounge to play as Blake moved towards Paula.

"He can't run forever Paula and he needs to pay for what he did to you, Rachael and Olivia."

"I know. I guess sometimes the past really can come back and bite you when you least expect it. I'm sorry for being so weak and letting him extort money from us."

"He played on your love for him to get what he wanted. All you're guilty of is loving your father when he didn't deserve it."

Paula held him close and they held the embrace for a moment.

"This came in the mail for you," Paula said as she broke the embrace and handed Blake a brown envelope.

Blake looked at it but didn't recognise the handwriting. When he opened it, there was an A4 sheet of paper inside with a key. Blake looked at the key before opening up the folded paper. It had gold headering from Goodman, Parker & Knowles inc. on the paper and all that was written on it was a number:

405

"What is it?" Paula asked.

"I'm not sure, I think the company owns some safe deposit boxes in London but as far as I know, nobody uses them anymore," Blake replied before he and Paula headed towards the kitchen.

For the rest of the day, the key and the mysterious letter played on Blake's mind. He laid awake that night wondering if he'd somehow missed something on his previous case and if this was the missing piece that he needed. He hated leaving loose ends in a case and the disappearance of Zodiac and Tom Gibson bothered him. After a restless sleep, he finally climbed out of bed and headed to the bathroom. He splashed some water on his face and got dressed. As he walked back into the bedroom, Paula stirred from her sleep.

"Where are you going?" she asked.

"I need some answers. I'll be back soon," Blake replied as he leant over the bed and kissed her forehead.

Three hours later he was standing at the reception desk of Goodman, Parker & Knowles inc. on Regent Street. A man in a freshly pressed white shirt and grey tie greeted him at the desk before leading him into a back room where all the safe deposit boxes were kept. He found box number 405 and used the key to open the box.

"My apologies for your loss, Mr Langford. Mrs Langford was a wonderful lady," the man said.

Blake smiled and nodded as the man presented him with the box before leaving the room. He opened up the box and found three gold and diamond rings inside, a necklace, a Rolex watch and an old black and white photograph. He picked it up and looked closely at it. There were two men and two women in the photo which looked like it had been taken on Lepe Beach. There were also three children playing in the sand in front of them, two boys and a young girl.

Blake looked at the man standing in the corner and recognised that he was his grandfather Edward Langford. Therefore, the children playing must be his father John, his uncle Fred who died in 1977 and his aunt Mary who he inherited his beachside home from. He looked at the other adults. The woman next to Edward Langford looked a lot like Blake's grandmother Mavis. Hundreds of questions spun in Blake's mind. Why would his mother keep an old photo of her in-laws long after his father had died? And why would it be kept securely locked away in here?

He looked closer at the other couple in the photo and then he dropped the photo. The second lady in the photo was Dana Handanowicz, his grandmother on Emily Langford's side of the family but the man next to her was not his grandfather William. Blake turned the photo over and on the back was the date;

14th July 1948

Blake looked at the photo once again. Could the Handanowicz and Langford families have known each other over twenty-five years before his parents John Langford and Emily Handanowicz got married. John was eight years older than Emily so this must have been taken before she was born. Blake did the maths quickly in his mind and worked out that his mother was born a year after this photo had been taken. Something was still troubling him though. It felt like way more than a coincidence. And who was this mysterious man in the photo and why had his mother kept the photo all this time?

Blake placed all of the belongings into a bag and left the room determined to find out why, after his mother's death, she sent him one last clue to figure out his family's history. He cursed the fact that the family home had been destroyed and a lot of his parents' possessions and photographs had gone up in smoke. He had a suspicion that this photograph held the answer to a lot of questions though and he was determined to figure out who the mysterious man in the corner was.

Chapter Thirty-Eight

A Mother's Love
Thursday 2nd October 2008

Blake Langford breathlessly crossed the finish line and glugged a mouthful of water down as his team completed the assault course at RAF Upper Heyford. The cool liquid provided welcome relief as the former air force base provided the ideal facilities for Special Branch to push their agents through endurance tests that would serve them well as they travelled around the world.

"You improved your time from last year," Alison Pearce smiled as she showed him the times for their team.

Samir and Joe eventually caught up a few moments later. The training facility was just what Blake needed after taking some long overdue leave from Special Branch. His last case, investigating the trafficking of students in and out of London, had taken its toll on him. Having the break allowed him to come back refreshed and ready to take on a new challenge.

"I see you can move your ass when you want to," Joe laughed.

"Kicking a football around a field with my son keeps me young. Anyway, you're not doing too bad yourself for being three months out of hospital."

"It'll take more than an exploding shed to keep me down."

"Speaking of which, have you found any leads from Zodiac or Reaper?"

"We're still looking into it but nothing so far," Samir replied.

"What about The Crystal?" Blake asked.

"All major operations have been shut down but that doesn't mean that there won't be any streams going in from the dark web," Joe replied.

"Keep me posted if you find anything," Blake said before picking up his towel and heading towards the changing rooms.

Joe and Samir watched him as he left.

"Do you think he's ready to come back?" Samir asked.

"Grief can change a lot of people but I've known Blake for a long time. He's like a dog with a bone. As soon as he grabs hold, he won't let go. Come on, two more circuits then we'll go for a beer," Joe replied before running back to the start line.

Samir watched Blake and Alison leave before following Joe to the start line. He felt uneasy about their alliance but knew he had to keep them close if he was to find out how much they knew about his involvement in The Crystal.

Alison met Blake outside after he had changed his clothes and returned to the car park. They walked from the main entrance together. "I didn't want to mention it in front of the other two but I think Joe is pushing himself too hard," she said as they arrived at Blake's car.

"In what way?"

"Trying to prove himself again. Samir led him into a dangerous situation that almost cost him his life."

"You don't trust Samir?"

Alison sighed. "It's not that, it's just…"

"We all have skeletons in our past that we'd rather hide away from. Samir admitted his mistakes. It takes a lot to admit to bribes in front of Eric and not be concerned for your future in Special Branch."

"Joe told me that Samir and Zodiac were friends. He was willing to cut Zodiac a deal in exchange for information. That deal led them to the house where Joe was almost killed."

"Do you think it was deliberate or did Zodiac lead them into a trap?" Blake asked.

"I don't know. Maybe I'm reading too much into this but something is off. I'm not sure what it is but I just have this feeling."

"Personally or professionally?"

"What do you mean?"

"Samir and you were close for a while."

"That was a long time ago, Blake. He's changed."

"In what way?"

"The job makes us all a lot harder. It takes a lot longer to let people in."

"Does having Samir in the team make you feel uneasy?"

"I loved him once. Now he's more like a brother. He's good at his job and can be a valuable asset. I just don't know if I'd trust him to have my back if I was in trouble. He led Joe into that garden and the explosion left him severely burnt. We split when I realised that he'd rather save his own skin than mine."

Blake thought about that for a moment. "What are you doing this afternoon?"

"I have to visit my mother in Basingstoke. It's her birthday tomorrow and I promised I'd go and see her."

Blake thought of his own mother who had died from a stroke only six months ago.

Alison noticed his demeanour change. "I'm sorry Blake, I didn't..."

"It's okay, it just doesn't seem real sometimes."

"A mother's love is never forgotten."

Blake pulled out a photo from his jacket pocket and showed it to Alison. There were two men and two women in the photo which looked like it had been taken on Lepe Beach many years ago. There were also three children playing in the sand in front of them, two boys and a girl. "Soon after Mum's death, I received a key to a safe deposit box in London. This photo was inside the box."

"I didn't realise anyone still used safe deposit boxes anymore," Alison replied as she looked at the photo. "Is this your grandparents with their children?"

"The two boys are my father John and his brother Fred. The girl is Edith Wise, my mum's older sister who died in 1956. My father's parents are there and so is my grandmother on Mum's side but nobody seems to be able to identify the man with his arm around my grandmother," Blake explained.

"Could've been a family friend?"

"Family friends didn't hold each other like that in 1948."

"How do you know when it was taken?"

Blake turned the photo over and showed the date on the back.

"Do you think there's more to it than that?" Alison asked.

"The family solicitor has asked to see Jenny, Steven and myself tomorrow for the reading of Mum's will. Apparently, there was a delay due to the contents of the will and the need to find out everyone who is due to inherit from it."

"Surely it should just be you three as Emily's children."

"Apparently not but none of us ever knew the contents of my parents' wills when they wrote them around the time of their marriage in 1977. Anyway, Steven can't make it so it'll just be Jenny and me going."

"I'm sure it's just a formality. You know how these solicitors like to drag things out for maximum fees."

Blake nodded. "If you're concerned about Samir, I could ask Eric Gordon to consider moving him off of the team."

"If he can keep the partnership professional then so can I."

"Trusting your team can be the difference between life and death."

"Then I hope I can trust all three of you when it counts," Alison smiled.

Blake replaced the photo in his pocket. "I guess you're right. I'll see you soon."

Alison headed over towards her car as Blake climbed inside his. He knew what Alison was saying was logical but something was still eating away at him. He just wasn't sure what.

***

The following day, Blake and his sister Jenny, arrived at Cartwright And Sons Solicitors on Bond Street, London. After a short wait, they were ushered inside one of the offices and sat opposite a large mahogany desk.

"Here we have the last will and testament of Emily Avis Jane Langford along with a scroll that was given to Cartwright Solicitors when the will was made," Julia Cartwight explained as she handed Blake the scroll.

Blake unrolled the scroll to reveal a letter dated August 12th 1977. A crumpled piece of yellow paper fell out of it and landed next to Jenny's foot. She carefully picked it up and noticed that it seemed to form part of a map.

"This was written the day before our parents were married," Jenny said as she read the scroll.

"Yes, your father, John Langford, was also present at the time. Your mother thought it important that the exact details of her will were kept quiet until she had passed away. Obviously, other interested parties will have been contacted after her death," Julia confirmed.

"What other parties? Us two and our brother Steven are her only living relatives!" Blake replied.

"That's not strictly true Mr Langford. You see, the will includes a benefaction that came from her late father. She was entitled to just over sixteen and a half percent of this benefaction if it was ever claimed."

"I don't understand. When our grandfather, William Handanowicz, died, the estate was split between the family."

"William Handanowicz was not Emily's father. The will contains a HM25 clause in it."

"What's a HM25 clause?"

"Harvey Matchbox twenty-five is a clause where a large benefaction is split through several members of the extended family. The benefaction comes from a sum of money that was written off in 1940. That money, if found, would be split six ways between the surviving relatives of your mother, Emily Handanowicz, now Langford, Evelyn Handanowicz, Victor Wise, Frederick Langford, Mary Langford and Patricia Hughes."

Blake sat back in his chair struggling to piece the information together. "Who put the benefaction in place?"

"Someone by the name of Jack Walter Smith, who died August 21st 1948."

"Does this mean Jack Smith was our grandfather?" Jenny asked.

"That scroll confirms that when Jack Smith died in 1948, the gold that was robbed from a bank in Portsmouth in 1938 and then written off two years later, was left as inheritance to his children. The problem was, the gold was buried and eight pieces of the map were given to relatives to keep safe. You have the first piece of the map. If you find the other seven pieces, it will give you the location of the gold."

Blake laughed. "I'm sorry but I'm not buying this treasure map fairytale. What the hell is going on here and even if this is true, how come nobody else has uncovered this in the past seventy years?"

"You're right to be sceptical Mr Langford but I have been doing some digging myself and it all seems to line up," Julia confirmed.

"How much gold is there?" Jenny asked.

"Nobody knows for sure, but the estimated value of what was taken by my calculations would be in the region of three million pounds."

Blake shook his head. "My family come from a long line of law-abiding people, Miss Cartwright. I worked my way through the police force, so did my father, my grandfather and my great-grandfather. Are you saying that they covered this all up? And if so, why?"

"All I have is what Emily Handanowicz placed on file in August 1977 right before her marriage to your father, John Langford."

"Why was this all contained in our mother's will?" Jenny asked. "Why haven't the other beneficiaries had the same information that we have?"

"Emily was very protective of her family. She took on the burden to protect not just her three children but the entire family. Now that her secret is out, it's only a matter of time before the rest of the beneficiaries will come knocking. Until then, the estate will be held in trust until everybody's whereabouts and connection to this benefaction have been accounted for."

"But my mother, Emily, my uncle Fred and aunt Mary are all dead," Blake explained.

"That may be so but the remaining few are still alive. Mary and Fred had no children. You are Emily's children hence the benefaction was triggered after her death and you stand to inherit her share."

"So what do we do now?" Jenny asked.

"If I were you, I'd speak to as many family members and friends of the family that you can and try to figure out what really happened in 1938 which led to Jack Smith leaving his fortune to your family ten years later," Julia replied.

***

In a rundown two bedroom basement flat in south-east London, Tom Gibson walked out into the back garden as rain fell heavily. He wandered over to a brick shed and unlocked a silver padlock. He opened the door and tossed a carrier bag of food into the dimly lit space. Pleading eyes came from a young woman caged behind steel bars at the back of the shed. She quickly gathered the food out of the bag and began to eat the stale bread he had given her. Her eyes bloodshot from crying and a combination of sedatives gave her a vacant appearance. Tom closed the door and locked the padlock once again before heading back inside the flat.

He began tapping away on a laptop, connecting investors to crypto-currency in a program known as The Crystal as the front door slammed shut.

A blonde haired woman appeared in the doorway of the lounge. "Any news from Andrea?" she asked.

"Nothing," Tom lied. "I'm sure she'll let us know when she's back."

"You have a letter here."

He turned to face her as she handed him the brown envelope with Cartwright And Sons Solicitors printed on it. He opened it and smiled as he read the letter.

"What is it?" she asked.

"Of course," Tom smiled as he quickly searched for obituaries on his laptop. He turned the screen to face her.

"Emily Langford?"

"Don't you see what this means Jade?"

She shook her head.

"Emily Langford was the missing piece. She held the second piece of the map. With her death, the inheritance moves to Blake. It was only a matter of time. When he discovers his whole life was built on a lie, it'll finish him!"

Jade moved towards him. "Don't you think this obsession with the Langfords is going too far?"

Tom glared at her. "I was never good enough in John Langford's eyes for his precious daughter. They stole what was rightfully ours. Our inheritance, our futures! How the hell can you defend them?"

"Jenny Langford was my friend in Uni. She'd never deliberately go out and hurt anybody."

"Yet she failed to tell you that she was your cousin."

"She probably didn't know."

"Probably," Tom huffed. "That family covers up more than a corrupt politician!"

"I don't believe that."

"Money changes people."

"No, it changed you. If it wasn't for Samir letting Zodiac go, he'd have taken you down with him."

"Zodiac knows what to do. If Emily had the declaration in her will then her brother James must have the next piece."

"Aren't you getting too old for all this Indiana Jones stuff? How do you know if there really is treasure to be found?" Jade asked.

"Jack Smith was my grandfather. He robbed a bank in 1938 and got away with it. After the war, he planned to give it all to my mother Patricia but he died before he had the chance to. She had to grow up in foster care because Blake Langford's great-grandfather couldn't keep his nose out of her business.

Those bastards have been corrupting the police force for four generations. Playing the self-righteous detectives and sergeants throughout whilst their wives were sleeping around. My grandfather survived the war, he had his fun and then the Langfords killed him to make sure his secret remained hidden. Not anymore."

"Your mother was in foster care from when she was a baby. How the hell do you know if she was even telling the truth?"

Tom reached inside a drawer under his desk and pulled out an old metal cigarette case. He opened it and inside was a lock of light brown hair. "When my mother was given up for adoption, Jack gave her a lock of his hair in this cigarette box. It was proof that she was his daughter. It has since been DNA tested. It is our blood line Jade! He planned to come back for her. Then the bombing started. He went off to fight in the war and my grandmother, Ada, was killed in one of the blasts near Portsmouth. When he returned, injured from battle, he found out that she had been killed. He slept with two of the nurses who cared for him before deserting. When he returned to the south coast, he found out what really happened the night his daughter, Patricia, was given up and it cost him his life. It was the talk of the city for many years after. That's why she came back to London and I vowed to make amends one day."

Jade watched as Tom held a photo of his mother in his hands and traced the outline of her face with his finger. She turned and left him heading towards the bedroom. She had also received a letter in the mail. She had recognised her grandfather's writing immediately. She opened it and read the letter before picking up her phone and scrolling through her contacts until she arrived at Victor (Grandad). Her finger hovered over the call button for a moment before she closed it down again. She knew she needed to get close to Tom to find out how much he knew about the family legacy but visiting her grandad would open up a lot of deep wounds from her past that she wasn't ready to face.

She slipped the letter back into the envelope and hid it in the bottom drawer of the cabinet in the corner of the room. Thousands of questions flooded her mind. If the money really was hidden somewhere, how could they find it and how could she stop Tom from blowing it all on crypto-currency. She opened her laptop and began searching for significant dates from 1938. She needed to go back in time...

Chapter Thirty-Nine

A Time For Letting Go
Saturday 27th August 1938

"For goodness sake Jack, sit down! You're wearing a hole in the floor!" Charlie snapped as they heard the screams of childbirth coming from the bedroom upstairs.

"It's the wrong time, Charlie. We've got the big one on Saturday and Ada having the baby early has thrown a spanner in the works," Jack replied as he continued pacing up and down the lounge area.

"We go ahead as planned whatever happens. We have one chance to make this work and I won't let anything get in the way of our future!"

"And what about Ada?"

"She needs to make a choice. You knew that before you got yourselves into this mess. You take her and live out your lives here or you take a chance and leave a mark on this world."

At that moment, the sound of a newborn baby crying echoed down the hall. Jack looked over at Charlie who walked over towards the back door.

Jack checked his watch. "Seven o'clock tomorrow night, I'll be there to set it up."

Charlie nodded before leaving the house.

Jack took a deep breath before heading upstairs. He stood for a moment outside the bedroom door before gently knocking. A moment later, the door opened and he saw Ada holding a baby in her arms whilst the midwife continued to help her mother, Joan, with the towels and blankets.

Jack knelt down beside the bed and looked at the baby in Ada's arms.

"She has your eyes," she smiled.

"She?" Jack asked.

"Yes, Patricia Ivy Smith."

Jack smiled as he held them both closely to him. He knew they needed to savour this moment as it may well be one of their last together as a family. After a couple of minutes, he excused himself from the room and headed out of the house.

Wandering through the busy streets of Portsmouth, he headed towards The King's Hat pub next to the guildhall. As he entered, the smell of tobacco and stale beer attacked his senses. He saw a man in a black trench coat standing in the corner drinking beer from an overflowing glass. Jack walked over to the bar and exchanged his money for a pint of bitter before joining the man in the corner.

"Everything as agreed?" the man in the trench coat asked.

"Charlie knows what to do," Jack replied as he enjoyed a mouthful of ale.

"Bob takes over from the night guard at four o'clock. We'll have about half an hour to get inside before the rest of them arrive."

"That should give us enough time."

The man in the trench coat looked over Jack's shoulder as two police officers entered the pub. "You ought to be careful about the company you keep," he snapped before slamming his glass onto the bar and walking out of the pub.

One of the police officers walked over towards Jack who calmly finished his pint.

"You think it's acceptable to be here when your wife is giving birth do you?" the officer asked.

Jack turned around to face him. "Your wife and daughter are fine without me."

"Never a truer word said in jest. Get home where you belong Smith or I'll make sure you don't get anywhere near my grandchild."

"Calm down Ern, I was just leaving," Jack smirked as he pushed his way through the crowd and left the pub.

One week later, just before four o'clock on the morning of Saturday 3rd September 1938, a huge explosion echoed around Portsmouth City Centre. Dust filled the air as the walls of the City Bank fell and shattered into small pieces of brick and concrete. Police cars, fire engines and ambulances arrived to remove people who were caught up in the blast and to extinguish the flames from the explosion. Witnesses claimed that a bomb had just exploded inside the bank and two men and a woman had been seen climbing into a truck and speeding away from the city. In three minutes, it was over and gone. As the dust settled, police officers were left to try and piece together what had just happened.

***

When Joan Hughes entered the grocery store later that morning, she was met with stunned silence by the shopkeeper behind the counter.

"Is something wrong Iris?" Joan asked.

"Where have you been? The police have been trying to find you all morning."

"I was at home. Nobody came around. Oh no, has something happened? I need to find Ernest...."

At that moment, Joan heard a baby crying. Iris opened the door that led into the stockroom behind the counter and beckoned her daughter to come into the shop. As she approached, Joan looked at the baby in her arms and gasped.

"No! No! Where's Ada?"

"We were hoping that you could tell us," Iris replied.

"There must be some simple explanation... Some reason. They would not leave Patricia behind."

"It's obvious isn't it."

Joan looked at Iris.

"He's gone back to his old ways. The bank. The explosion. We all heard it on the wireless this morning. You should never have let your Ada hook up with a man like him. You know what they say..."

Joan moved towards Iris' daughter and took Patricia into her arms. "No, what do they say?"

"Once a thief, always a thief. Your Ada was silly to think that she could change his ways."

"Jack Smith is a most respectable man and he has always provided for my daughter in their marriage. This is just a misunderstanding. Good day to you..." Joan snapped before storming out of the shop.

"What did I say?" Iris asked after she had left.

"Some people just don't want to hear the truth mama," her daughter replied.

Joan stormed back into the family home and found her husband Ernest standing in the kitchen still wearing his coat as he looked out at the back garden.

"You knew, didn't you!" Joan snapped.

"It's just part of our inquiries for now..."

"You were out all night! Tell me Ern, where are they?"

Ernest turned to face her and saw Patricia in her arms. "Where was she?" he asked.

"Where are they? Why aren't you out there looking for our daughter and Jack?"

"My superior thinks that because I am Ada's father, I should be excluded from the investigation. Where was Patricia?"

"Iris Jones had her in the grocery shop," Joan admitted as she tried to fight back her tears.

Ernest thought back to the previous weekend when he saw Jack Smith in the local bar drinking with someone he didn't recognise. Surely they couldn't have been planning the bank robbery whilst Ada was having the baby, could they? He battled with himself weighing up whether to tell Joan about their short exchange but decided to keep that information to himself.

"What can I do to help?" he finally asked.

Joan looked at him through tear-filled eyes. "Find our daughter," she replied before heading upstairs with the baby in her arms.

Ernest watched her leave before picking up his hat and coat and leaving the house, looking for answers but not expecting many to arrive.

One Year Later...

Joan and Ernest Hughes were sitting at the dining table with their one year old granddaughter Patricia when a message from the Prime Minister, Neville Chamberlain, interrupted the music that was playing on the radio. As he told the nation of Hitler's failure to respond to British demands to leave Poland and that the UK will be at war with Germany, a feeling of dread overwhelmed them.

"Do you know what today is?" Joan asked.

"Sunday," Ernest sighed as he tried to lose himself in the headlines of the newspaper he was reading.

"It's been one year since Ada and Jack went missing."

Ernest's face turned red. The lines of too many red wines traced a roadmap on his cheeks. "I think we have bigger things to worry about than some small-time crook and our selfish excuse of a daughter running away from their responsibilities!"

"How can you be so cold?"

"I'm forty-five years old Joan! I should be enjoying the fruits of my labour. Playing bridge at the Golf Club, going fishing down on the beach and now it looks like we're about to head into another battle that nobody can win. I had enough of that when I was a young man."

"Well I'm sorry that the world didn't ask for your permission before joining a fight for freedom!"

Ernest stood up from his chair. "Any more lip like that and I'll..."

"You'll do what? I've had it with you Ern. Ever since Ada disappeared you've changed."

"What do you expect when your only daughter runs off with some low-life and you're powerless to stop it?"

"And why do you think she ran away with him in the first place?"

Ernest raised his hand and struck Joan across her face, sending her into the dining chair before she regained her balance.

"You have no right to speak to me like that! All I've ever done is work hard to provide for this family and for what?"

"There's more than just you hurting in this family, remember that before you lash out again," Joan replied before picking up Patricia and heading out of the house.

She had been planning this moment for a while. Ernest's outburst had finally given her the courage to follow it through. Joan had already packed a small suitcase full of clothes for herself and Patricia and had taken it to a friend's house the previous day. She walked towards Southsea seafront before heading down Palmerston Road towards the shops. She turned into a sideroad where her friend, Florence and her husband, Ron, lived.

Joan entered the house with Patricia in her arms. As the door closed behind them, Ron led her to the dining table where three sheets of paper were laid out.

"Are you sure about this?" Florence asked.

"I can't keep her in that environment and with the war starting, she has a better chance away from here," Joan sighed as she signed the papers.

Ron collected the signed documents from the table and placed them into an envelope.

"What now?" Joan asked.

"You'll stay here for tonight, there is a train leaving for London at ten minutes past nine in the morning. We need to be on that train. We will head towards Hammersmith to finalise all of the details. It's a time for letting go, Mrs Hughes," Ron replied.

Florence led them both to a spare bedroom with a double bed that had been made up with soft blankets and a selection of cuddly toys laid out on the bed. For the rest of that evening, Joan played and held her granddaughter close before they both fell asleep together as night fell. The following morning, Florence waved them goodbye at the railway station as Ron, wearing a long trench coat, joined them both on the train to London. From that moment on, Joan knew that their lives would never be the same again.

Chapter Forty

One Hand Out Of The Grave
Friday 31st October 2008

If Blake Langford had broken a mirror, he wouldn't have expected the misfortune that had come his way. He drove his silver Ford Mondeo up the slight incline of his driveway towards Southward Cottage, his home that overlooked Lepe Beach, before parking his car behind a blue Nissan Note belonging to his sister, Jenny. He stepped out of his car and headed inside taking note of a spherical dent with accompanying scratches on the rear bumper of his sister's car.

"Good morning, looks like somebody had a disagreement with something outside," Blake said as he entered the dining room where Jenny and Paula were sitting at the table enjoying some coffee.

"Nothing gets past you does it?" Jenny smiled as she hugged Blake.

"Having a fight with the lamp post again?"

"It wasn't there when I reversed it!"

Blake laughed as he poured himself a cup of coffee. "I'm sure it just appeared out of nowhere. Seriously though, do you want me to try and do something for that dent?"

"No, it's okay, Dan will take care of it."

"Oh, who's this Dan then?" Paula asked.

"Just a friend..." Jenny smiled. "Anyway, the police have allowed us to go back into mum's house and recover what we can from the explosion."

Blake's expression changed. "I doubt there's much left to salvage after what happened."

Whilst Blake and Jenny's mother, Emily Langford, was ill in hospital, Tom Gibson, the leader of a student trafficking group in London had planted a bomb in the Langford family home. Blake, his colleague Alison Pearce, and Jenny had been lucky to escape before the bomb exploded, mostly destroying the entire house. The general feeling was that Gibson had set up the bomb to target Blake. Jenny and Tom had been in a relationship several years earlier which Blake felt, still had an influence on how that assignment ended. Tom Gibson, Ian Bleeker and Zachary Zhal were still out there running free in Europe. Blake hated loose ends and knew that it was only a matter of time before their paths crossed again.

"They're looking to demolish and rebuild it but they've put some scaffolding in place to allow us to search through anything that we can salvage," Jenny explained.

Even though years of training had given Blake the tools he needed to cope with most things, he had struggled to compartmentalise what had happened to him and his family over the past year or so. After the death of his fiance Rachael Evans, he discovered that he was a father and had an eight year old son whom he barely knew before then losing his mother to a severe stroke that caused her to have a brain haemorrhage, he felt like the world was conspiring against him and there was little or no clue as to where he should turn next. "I'm not interested in any of it," he snapped. "Mum and Dad are gone and the house is just an empty shell of what it once was."

Jenny lifted a small dented metal box out of a bag and placed it on the table.

"What's that?" Blake asked.

"Photos from when Mum and Dad were kids. Our photos from years ago. Somehow they survived the blast. Thought maybe you'd want to reminisce..."

"What's the point Jen? What's done is done. We can't bring them back so there's no point in rehashing the past!"

Jenny opened up the box and pulled out a black and white photo of a man in a suit standing next to a pregnant woman at a railway station.

"Blake, look at this," Paula said.

Blake looked down at the photo.

"Isn't that the same man who was in the photo that you found?" Paula asked.

Jenny looked at them both. "What photo?"

"A few months ago after the Gibson case and our trip to France, I received a letter in the mail from Goodman, Parker & Knowles in London," Blake explained.

Jenny gasped. "Mum's safety deposit box!"

"You knew about it?"

"Yeah, she had used it for years to store away valuable jewellery and money when times were tough. What was inside the box?"

Paula stood up from the table and walked over towards a wooden cabinet in the corner of the room. She opened a drawer and pulled out a small plastic bag and an old black and white photo. She brought them over to the table and laid them down alongside the photo that Jenny had selected. The new photo showed two men, two women and three children on Lepe Beach in 1948.

"Mum's engagement ring, dad's old Rolex watch, I think that might be Grandma Handanowicz's ring and I'm not sure of the other one," Jenny explained.

"Where does the Handanowicz name come from?" Paula asked.

"Mum's parents were Dana and William Handanowicz, our grandparents," Blake replied. "They died a long time ago."

"That's not an English name. I never knew your mother had foreign parents," Paula replied.

"No, our grandad was originally from what used to be Yugoslavia but he settled here after the war. Mum, aunt Evelyn and our uncle Jim were all born in Southampton," Jenny explained as she took a closer look at the two photos. "Oh my God!" she gasped.

"What?" Paula asked.

"That's Dad's parents, Edward and Mavis Langford alongside Grandma Dana Handanowicz and that other man," Jenny replied.

Blake nodded. "That's what I noticed. The Langfords and the Handanowicz's at least knew of each other in 1948."

"Wait, Mum wasn't born until 1949 so who are the children in this photo?" Jenny asked.

"Dad, uncle Fred and aunt Mary," Blake confirmed. "Dad was nine years older than Mum. Fred and Mary must have been around six at the time."

"That means your Dad was born in 1940 and Mary and Fred were born in 1942. Wasn't your grandad fighting in the war back then?" Paula asked.

"Our Grandad, Edward Langford was a local police detective and he didn't get drafted until the beginning of 1942. From what I remember of their stories, Aunt Mary and Uncle Fred were twins and they were born whilst Grandad was away," Blake explained.

"Your grandmother must have been through so much during that time. The bombing and being pregnant as well as looking after your Dad."

"She was a nurse and helped look after the war wounded so I guess she had like minded people around her to help at the time."

"So where is Grandad Will?" Jenny asked.

"I've been doing some research online and it looks like our Handanowicz grandparents didn't get married until April 22nd 1949," Blake replied.

"And mum's birthday was August 16th 1949," Jenny gasped.

"Maybe they realised that she was pregnant and then quickly arranged the wedding so they wouldn't be frowned upon for having sex before marriage. Back then, there was a social stigma around unmarried mothers, wasn't there?" Paula asked.

Blake nodded as he looked at both photos and turned them over. On the back of the beach photo it read 14th July 1948 and the photo from the train station was dated 24th March 1948. There was a smudge below the date on the train photo which he looked closely at but couldn't quite make anything out of it.

"So Dana was pregnant in the train photo and not in the beach photo," Paula said as she tried to work out the dates.

"Are there any photos of Grandad Will before Mum was born?" Blake asked.

"Not here but they may have gone up in smoke. Why?" Jenny asked.

"I'm thinking that Grandad Will might not have been our biological grandad," Blake replied.

"How do you get that from a random photograph?" Jenny asked.

"Back in 1948, you wouldn't lay a hand on a woman that you were not married to in public. He has his arms around Grandma in both photos."

"That's pretty flimsy Blake, he may have been a close friend and Grandad Will might have been taking the photo."

Paula picked up the railway station photo and walked over towards the study. She turned the desk lamp on and studied the smudge underneath the date. "I think I've got something!" she called out.

Blake and Jenny joined her in the study.

"It's very faint but I think that is a J, something, something, K and then a space before an S," Paula pointed out.

Blake and Jenny took a closer look.

"It's got to be the name of a person or a place," Jenny said.

"The obvious name for the time would be John or Jack but John or Jack S isn't going to get us far," Blake sighed.

"There might be someone who would know," Jenny replied.

"No, we're not going there!" Blake snapped.

"He's Mum's sole living relative from that generation Blake!" Jenny pleaded.

"I'm not going all the way out to Greece to track down Uncle Jim in his private villa simply for a little bit of fact-finding for a family tree. That man is poisonous. He'd walk over anyone to chase a fiver in a force-ten gale!" Blake fumed.

"Aren't you just a little bit inquisitive?" Paula asked.

"Why should I be? Mum and Dad are both gone. Let them and whatever they got up to in the past rest in peace with them," Blake sighed.

"But why did Mum find that photograph important enough to lock away in a safety deposit box? There has to be more to this Blake! Maybe the map is connected to it in some way," Jenny replied.

"What map?" Paula asked.

Blake took a deep breath. "Just some fairytale story that the solicitor tried to sell us the other day."

"They must have had a reason to bring it up."

"I need some air," he replied before heading out of the back door and walking down the wooden steps at the far end of the garden towards the stony beach below.

Paula and Jenny stood by the door and watched him leave.

"He's too stubborn for his own good, just like Dad," Jenny sighed.

"What did your Uncle Jim do that was so bad?" Paula asked.

"Nobody knows the full story but it almost cost Dad his job at Scotland Yard. There was a huge family row about twenty years ago and then Uncle Jim just sold up and left. Last we heard he had a villa out in Rhodes, one of the Greek Islands."

"Was Jim your Mum's only sibling?"

"No, she had Evelyn, her twin sister and an older sister too, called Edith, but she died when she was only a teenager in 1956."

"I'll talk to him. He'll come around eventually," Paula replied.

"I hope so," Jenny said as she returned to the dining table to finish her coffee. "How are you bearing up?"

"Me? I'm fine. Just trying to get on with things again. After Dad fled the country with our money, there's not much left to say anymore."

"You can't blame yourself Paula. He played on your sympathy and even though what he's done over the years was wrong, he's still your father and deep down you still love and care for him."

"Yeah, and look how that turned out. I know there's a lot going on with your family since Emily passed away but mine seems to be as disjointed as ever too."

"I would have done the same thing in those circumstances. You can't change the past, only learn from it."

"I guess you're right. Sorry, I've just had a lot on my mind lately," Paula sighed.

"Andrew Broughton?"

"His funeral was two weeks ago and I just can't seem to get him off of my mind. Crazy huh? I have everything I want here with Blake and Michael and yet I'm still tied in knots with a guy who physically and mentally abused me ten years ago."

"It's not crazy at all. We can't help who we fall in love with."

"But why do I always go for the high maintenance ones?"

"Is Blake high maintenance?"

Paula shook her head. "I don't know Jen. I'm so confused about everything right now. There's deaths and betrayals every way we turn at the moment and I'm struggling to know whether I'm coming or going."

Jenny didn't reply.

"I know his job takes priority and occasionally Michael and I would become collateral damage, I just didn't think it would be this hard."

"Blake loves you both and will do anything to protect you. You just need to trust that when things get rough, he will make the right decision."

Paula walked over towards the window and looked out at the beach. "I know all of this but why am I still unsure of myself? Why do I have my ex ingrained in my memory and why am I full of distrust for Blake?"

Jenny joined her at the window. "Only you can answer that. When Tom returned after fifteen years, I still had that fantasy in my mind of the dreams we shared when we were together. But that's all they were, dreams. Sometimes you need to love someone enough to let them go. Tom will always have a place in my heart but he'll never hurt me again. You need to decide how to move forward. With the ghost of Andy and what might have been or with Blake. Only you can decide."

Paula thought about what Jenny had said. She knew that Blake was still fighting his own thoughts and emotions about her sister Rachael's death and the guilt he carried for not being able to save her. She felt the same about Andy. If only she had been there, maybe he wouldn't have been poisoned. The flip of a coin. Whichever way she looked at it, there were pros and cons on both sides. Andy's death had hit her harder than she ever wanted to admit. It filled her with thoughts that she had never felt before. Doubts and fears that had been buried for so long. She knew she needed to face up to them sooner or later and whatever the consequences were, she would have to accept them. But right now, she still didn't know which way to turn. So much had gone wrong recently and her confidence was at an all-time-low. She just hoped that somehow, she still had a chance to fight for what she truly wanted when all was said and done.

"Where's Dad gone?" Michael asked as he entered the room.

"He's just gone for a walk, is everything okay?" Jenny asked.

"Yeah, I just thought we could have a rematch on the Playstation."

"Well how about you show me," Jenny replied as she led him away.

Paula watched them leave. She knew that Michael was beginning to feel the tension in the house between her and Blake. He'd been through so much at such a young age after losing his mother and relocating from Miami to The New Forest in the UK but there was still that nagging doubt in her mind and she struggled to figure out who or what could change it.

***

Later that night, a man walking his cocker spaniel through the fields of the New Forest National Park heard a muffled sound like somebody trying to scream. His dog darted towards East Boldre cemetery.

"Spike! Come here!" the man called out as he swung his torch around in all directions trying to find out where his dog had run off to.

He heard his dog barking and whining. He shone his torch up to see a sign displaying the cemetery's name on the gate that had been left open. "You would pick this place on Halloween night!" he grumbled.

Using his torch to light up the muddy pathway, the man followed the whines and barks of his dog into the cemetery.

"Spike! This is not funny! Where are you!" he snapped.

At that moment, he noticed his dog sitting beside a grave, whining.

"There you are, come here boy!" the man called out but the dog wouldn't move.

"Spike! Come on, here boy!" He tried again.

The dog remained seated next to the grave. The man walked towards him. "What's gotten into you?"

As he approached, the dog barked at him. "What's wrong?"

As the man waved his torch around he stood frozen to the spot. Next to where Spike was sitting was an unmarked grave and from the centre of it pointing to the sky was somebody's arm and hand.

Chapter Forty-One

Alfred Langford
Wednesday 6th September 1939

Joan Hughes returned home on Wednesday morning and noticed eight bottles of milk had been left in the porch with a note from the milkman. Thoughts flooded her mind as Ernest would always take the milk in and pay the milkman in advance. She thought about the argument on Sunday, her trip to London to leave Patricia at the adoption agency and the lonely night she had spent at Florence and Ron's house last night.

The bruising on her face had only just started to fade and she knew when she told Ernest that she had given up Patricia, he would likely lash out again. Tears stung her eyes as the reality of her tough decision began to hit her. She knew Patricia would be better off away from here but now she needed to find the courage to face her husband's fury. She slid her key into the lock and opened the front door. The smell of stale tobacco and alcohol caught her attention as she wandered through the kitchen and into the dining room before entering the lounge.

The morning sun shining through the curtains gave the room a green glow. A pile of letters had been left unopened on the arm of the sofa and a glass with a small amount of whiskey inside it had been left on the coffee table. Joan tutted to herself because a coaster hadn't been used and the glass had left a watermark on the table. She placed a coaster underneath the glass and then smiled at herself for the absurdity of her pickiness given the circumstances they found themselves in.

"Ernest?" she called out. "Ern? Are you home?"

The house was deathly silent. Joan felt a cold sweat overwhelm her body as she carefully began climbing the stairs. As she reached the top, she heard someone breathing heavily.

"Ern?"

At that moment, an ironing board flew past in front of her and clattered into the wall at the top of the stairs.

"What on earth..."

"Where the hell have you been?" Ernest slurred.

Joan looked towards the bathroom doorway and saw Ernest leaning against the doorframe. He was wearing a ripped shirt, trousers with a belt hanging loosely from the waist and looked as if he hadn't shaved for a few days.

"What happened?" Joan asked.

"Answer the question!"

"I had to get away for a few days."

"You've been with him haven't you!"

"Who?"

"You know who, that bloody copper who goes to The King's Hat!"

"Alfred Langford? He's married and we've only spoken a couple of times. How dare you..."

Ernest lunged at her but Joan managed to step back before he slumped down in the doorway of their bedroom. "You should... know your place," he grimaced.

"No, you should understand that I'm the only one looking out for us whilst everything else is falling apart!"

"What's that supposed to mean?"

"In case you haven't noticed, there is a war going on and rather than doing anything to help, you're drowning in whiskey hoping that it all goes away. Look at the state of you. Call yourself a Police Officer? You're pathetic."

Ernest stood up and attempted to walk towards her. He lost his balance and hit the door of Patricia's bedroom open. He looked inside the room before turning back to Joan. His eyes were bloodshot and piercing. "Where is she?"

"Safe."

"Where is she? Tell me!"

"Safe! Away from you and away from the coast."

Ernest swung his fist in her direction and made contact with her cheek before falling against the doorframe of their bedroom. Joan staggered back to her feet and began heading towards the stairs. Ernest crawled towards the chest of drawers in the bedroom and removed his gun from the bottom drawer. As she reached the hallway, Joan turned around and saw him standing at the bottom of the stairs aiming the gun at her.

"You won't leave this house alive," Ernest spat as he began to move towards her.

"What happened to you? What happened to the man I married?" Joan replied, trying with all her strength to keep her voice calm.

"We were fine. We were happy until you let Ada go off with that lowlife common criminal. Then to top it all, my wife becomes the city whore and takes turns at my colleagues."

"Jack Smith was a good man. He worked on his father's farm land for years!"

"He's a petty thief! A criminal. A shoplifter. He robbed the City Bank and is now on the run with our only daughter! Now tell me, where is Patricia?"

"At the adoption agency. You'll never see her again!"

Ernest froze for a moment, unsure of how to react. "No, no, why? Why would you do that?"

"Isn't it obvious! You're out of control Ern!"

Ernest fired the gun at the ceiling sending a shower of wood and plaster sprinkling all over the room.

"You had everything a woman could want! A family, a home, a husband, I gave you everything!" he fumed, his face turning red and his eyes piercing as they glared at Joan.

She tried to open the front door but the lock had jammed.

"Don't even think about escaping!" he shouted as he staggered towards her.

Joan quickly looked around and found a glass ashtray on the sideboard. She picked it up and threw it at Ernest. The ashtray hit him on the side of his head with a sickening crack. He fell to the floor with blood seeping from a cut at the side of his forehead.

"Oh my God! No! Ern!" Joan gasped as she rushed towards him. "I'm so sorry, I didn't mean..."

As she crouched down beside him, Ernest grabbed her arms and swung his whole body weight on top of her to pin her to the floor.

"No wife of mine is going to walk out on me alive!" he cussed as he wrestled with Joan on the floor.

Joan saw the gun on the floor next to them. As if reading her mind, Ernest reached for the gun. She brought her knee up and made contact between his legs. He momentarily let go of her, giving Joan the opportunity to get up. Ernest reached for the gun but she kicked it towards the front door. She tried to run towards the door but he grabbed her ankle, sending her crashing to the floor, hitting her head on the sideboard in the hallway. As she regained her senses, Ernest was standing over her. Blood was dripping from the cut on his forehead leaving a large bloodstain on his shirt.

"You just couldn't leave things alone could you? You had to chase your freedom. You are my wife and that means you do what I tell you to! You knew that! You knew that!"

Joan nodded nervously as he aimed the gun at her head.

"Things could have been so different Joan. We could've been happy..."

"We still can be..." she stammered.

"Not now, once I've taken care of you, I'll pay a visit to your little friend and make sure he knows the pain of betrayal."

Joan noticed an umbrella that had been left beside the front door just behind where Ernest was standing. She needed a distraction and that could be it.

"And then what Ern, if the police find out what you've done you'll be spending the rest of your life rotting in jail!"

"Who are they going to believe, a copper wet behind the ears or me?"

At that moment, Joan kicked out causing the umbrella to fall. The noise distracted Ernest long enough for her to grab his arm and knock the gun out of his hand. He wrestled and tried to overpower her but she found strength from somewhere to push him away and tried the door again. The door opened and they saw a police car driving down the road towards the house. Ernest grabbed her hair and dragged her back before slamming the door shut. Joan backed herself against the wall. He lunged at her once more. She dodged him and kicked his kneecap, sending him down to the floor once more. As she tried to get to the door, he grabbed her leg once more and pulled her down on top of him. Joan clawed at his face, drawing blood from his cheek. Ernest smiled menacingly as he brought the gun up between them. She saw it and grabbed the barrel of the gun and pulled with all of her might to aim it away from them.

Another shot fired into the ceiling sending more wood and plaster sprinkling around the room. Ernest managed to cock the gun once more and held her head close to him. With all her strength, Joan caught his hand with her fist sending the gun towards his chin and suddenly, it fired once more.

There was a sudden deathly silence in the house. Joan began gasping for air as she exhaled a breath she hadn't realised that she was holding. She looked down at Ernest's body and the pool of blood that was coming from his head. She vomited on the floor at the sight and the stench coming from his body. A loud knocking at the front door caught her attention.

"Hello! Mr Hughes? Mrs Hughes? It's the police!" Alfred Langford called out.

A feeling of panic ran through Joan's body as she saw her husband's body laying on the ground.

"Mrs Hughes? Joan? Are you all right?" Alfred called out again.

Joan carefully climbed over Ernest's body and opened the door. She was thankful to see a friendly face and quickly ushered Alfred inside. As he entered though, his friendly expression quickly hardened.

"Oh my God. I need to call this in. Joan, what happened?" Alfred asked.

Joan fell to her knees and cried. "It was an accident! I didn't mean to kill him! How did you know?"

"Someone called the station because they heard a gunshot. Tell me everything that happened."

Joan told Alfred Langford everything including her journey to London to give up Patricia to the adoption agency and Ernest's increased violent outbursts since their daughter's disappearance. Alfred listened intently, nodding, taking notes in his notebook and trying not to interrupt until she was finished.

When she had finally finished, two more police cars appeared outside.

"They're going to arrest me aren't they? I'm going to spend the rest of my life in jail for protecting my granddaughter," Joan sighed.

Alfred took a deep breath and looked down at the gun on the floor. He picked up a cloth from the kitchen table and walked over towards the gun. Using the cloth, he picked up the gun and placed it in Ernest's right hand before returning the cloth to the kitchen table.

"Why? What..." Joan gasped.

"That's where the gun should have been. Ernest Hughes was an arrogant bastard who should have been put in his place a long time ago. As far as anyone else knows, there was a family argument and he committed suicide. Do you think you can stick to that story?"

Joan looked down at Ernest's body and then back at Alfred. "Why are you doing this for me? He's one of your own. You should be throwing the key away."

"I once had a friend in a similar situation to yours. Nobody was willing to help her and she ended up dead because of it. If you're willing to support this, I will make sure that nothing happens to you. You did what you needed to do to protect your granddaughter. You deserve a chance to see what you did was right."

A knock at the door interrupted their conversation.

"I need an answer Joan..."

She nodded before heading over towards the door. A police detective with two more officers were waiting for them. Joan walked out whilst Alfred Langford told the detective the new version of what had happened. When he finished briefing the detective, he wandered over towards the waiting ambulance. Joan was sitting on the edge of a wall talking to a nurse.

"Do you have anywhere to stay until we have cleaned up your home?" Alfred asked.

"I can stay with friends, thank you Officer Langford," Joan replied.

"Well, I hope things work out for you Mrs Hughes and my condolences for your loss," Alfred replied before heading back towards his car and driving away.

Alfred Langford gave Joan one final glance as he drove away from the house. He had a feeling that this wouldn't be the last he would see of the Hughes family.

Chapter Forty-Two

Picking Up The Pieces
Saturday 1st November 2008

Blake Langford inhaled deeply as he parked his car outside the charred remains of his family home at 124 Alfredson Road. He had driven up to London from his home on the south coast to where he shared many family memories with his sister Jenny, who was sat alongside him, and their brother Steven along with their parents and grandparents. Now however, the house looked like a decaying shell that was slowly falling to pieces in front of him. He felt numb. There was no longing, no attachment to the bricks and mortar that had been the home of the Langford family for so many years.

"Are you okay?" Jenny asked.

"Yeah, there's just been too many weird things going on lately. I'm struggling to piece it all together. If mum had some kind of family secret, why didn't she tell us?"

"I guess there are some things we need to keep to ourselves until we're ready to confront them."

"Or until it's taken to the grave."

"She wouldn't want us to mull over what might've been. Out of tragedy, at least you and Steven are talking again."

Blake smiled at the thought of his brother. They had been at each other's throats for years but after Steven had woken up to a house full of murdered students, Blake had been the only one who had stood by him and helped to prove his innocence.

"He's gone off the radar lately. Have you heard from him?" Blake asked.

"He's gone on some kind of silent retreat. Somewhere in Cambodia. A spiritual healer has convinced him to go into a monastery for thirty days to help him find himself again."

Blake looked at his sister shocked. "Are we talking about the same person here? Our brother, the gobshite of the nightclubs who can barely keep his mouth shut for two minutes, has gone away on some woo woo pilgrimage to what.... Find Jesus?"

"Grief takes people on different journeys Blake. Sometimes, you need to face the truth and admit that you need help."

"Why do those who insist on giving advice never seem to take it themselves?"

"Meaning?"

"Tom Gibson?"

"What about him?"

"Knowing that he's still out there somewhere."

"I grieved for Tom a long time ago. The man I knew and loved was not the man I saw at that underground station."

"I just don't want you to rush into another relationship on the rebound..."

"The rebound from what Blake? I discovered that the man I loved from ten years ago is in fact a callous bastard who faked his death, led his team into a death trap and is now trafficking young girls across Europe. As far as I'm concerned, he's dead to me and he has been for a long time. What I have with Dan now is just a close friendship and in time, who knows?"

"I'm just worried about you..."

"Coming from the guy who's recently proposed to the love of his life's sister..."

"You know that's different. Rachael and I were over long ago."

"Yet you're standing at her graveside at every opportunity you get."

"Sometimes the heart takes a while to catch up with the brain. We do stupid things in the name of love and then get burnt because of it."

"So you should understand that the feelings I had for Tom are now over and I'm ready to move on. You share a beautiful son with Rachael and you and Paula will be great parents for him as he grows up. Don't let the chip on your shoulder prevent you from being there for Michael and making the best of what you have. I'm still picking up the pieces of my life but in the end, we all need to find closure and move on."

Blake looked over at their family home. The windows were all boarded up and the white PVC front door had now been replaced with a dark grey metal one. He wondered what their father, John Langford, would have thought of the situation they now found themselves in.

"Did mum ever speak much to you about her family before she married dad?" Blake asked.

"Not much more than what we all knew. Grandma Dana married Grandad William in 1949 and they had mum a few months later before Uncle Jim came along in 1951. Have you thought any more about contacting him? He's the only one who could possibly know why that photo was in the box."

Blake shook his head. "Sometimes we just need to let things be and after what Jim did to Dad, I don't want to bring up any more bad memories. We've had enough aggravation already. The photo was taken three years before he was born anyway. Chances of him knowing anything are very slim."

Jenny nodded noncommittally.

"Grandma Dana was married before she met Grandad William though, wasn't she?" Blake asked.

"She was married to someone called Gerald but he died during the war. He was Edith's father but she died in 1956 of

Pneumonia. Do you think Mum was trying to tell us something with that photo or was she just keeping hold of it for sentimental reasons?"

"It's probably nothing and I'm just overthinking it but why did she keep that specific photo in her safe deposit box? Even the guy at the depository seemed to be familiar with mum and gave his condolences for her."

"I know she did visit there regularly because her friend, Sandra, commented on it a while back," Jenny conceded.

"Do you think she may have information about why mum was so meticulous about that box?"

"I guess it wouldn't hurt to ask."

Blake pondered that for a moment. "I'll keep it in mind. I guess we can't put it this off any longer," he sighed as he opened the car door and headed over towards the house with Jenny following close behind.

They collected several boxes of ornaments and whatever they could salvage from the charred remains of the house and placed them in the back of the car. After the bomb had exploded and blown out most of the front of the house, Blake had arranged for scaffolders and builders to attempt to make the remains of the building as secure as possible but the reality was, it would have to be completely demolished and rebuilt.

Blake was usually very good at compartmentalising things but the memories of his childhood and his parents lives in this house over the years panged him anew as he looked at what the remains of the building had become. As they locked the door and returned to the car, Blake noticed a black BMW had pulled up on the opposite side of the road.

"Trouble?" Jenny asked as she nodded in the direction of the car.

"I don't think so," Blake replied as he wandered over towards the car.

As he approached, Joe Knight stepped out from the driver's seat. A roadmap of veins and shrapnel scarring on the left side of his face told the story of a shed exploding during a stake-out with Samir Khalifa a few months ago. Blake still felt guilty for sending them to the address where they were pursuing a lead on a known criminal called Zodiac but after a lengthy stay in hospital, Joe was back in the field again and Blake was pleased to see him.

"I see they can't keep a good man down. Good to see you Joe," Blake smiled as he shook his hand. "What brings you here?"

"Thanks, Blake. Unfortunately, I wish it was under better circumstances. Gordon needs you to come in. Some weird stuff has been flagged up from Hampshire Constabulary."

"Hampshire?"

"Yeah, last night a man was walking his dog through a graveyard and gave himself a fright."

"What rational man would wander through a graveyard on Halloween night anyway?"

"Your guess is as good as mine but when his dog ran over to an unmarked grave, he discovered a hand sticking out of it," Joe replied.

"Halloween prank taken too far?"

"That's what the police thought until they dug deeper shall we say."

"Meaning?"

"They dug into the grave and discovered a young woman who had recently been buried alive."

"And the hand was her failed attempt to escape?" Blake asked. "That's a rough way to die."

"The plot thickens, early indications show that the young woman could well be Andrea Louise Smith."

That took Blake by surprise. "The same Andrea Smith that was staying at the chateau in Toulouse with Graham Evans?"

"The same."

"But how? Why? I thought she was on the red list. If her, Gibson, Zodiac or Evans returned to the UK they'd have been flagged up."

"That's the thing, there is no record of any of them returning to the UK since they left after the trafficking case went south."

"It doesn't make any sense. Whose grave was she buried in?"

"The grave at East Boldre cemetery was unmarked and there seems to be no paper trail. All we know is that it apparently belongs to someone who died in the 1980's but so far, the authorities have been unable to get permission to exhume the body for identification."

"Why? Surely if the body is a John or Jane Doe then there are no connected relatives to the deceased, therefore no red tape."

"You'd think so but the undertaker, a Mr Paul Crowther, refuses to give up the paperwork that was processed by his father whom he inherited the company from. Without the legal paperwork, the authorities cannot proceed with the dig any further."

"So, have the French police contacted Graham Evans?" Blake asked.

"He claims that Andrea left the chateau around a month ago and was meeting up with some friends in Monte Carlo. He hasn't seen or heard from her since."

"And they bought that?"

"They had no reason to suspect otherwise. The final will of Elliot Francis left the estate to Graham Evans so he is legally, as far as the French authorities are concerned, living at the chateau alone."

"Except he isn't. Gibson and Zodiac are still out there and he probably knows where they are."

"The trail's gone cold Blake. Derek Copsewood isn't giving anything up despite facing ten years behind bars. The only chance we had to get them was on that freight train and they slipped through our fingers."

Blake swore under his breath. He had been tracking a student trafficking ring across London led my Derek Copsewood, Tom Gibson and Zachary Zhal, better known as Zodiac but despite him and his team rescuing the missing students and Derek Copsewood giving himself up, Gibson and Zodiac managed to escape. He had a feeling that Andrea's body turning up in a grave nearby to his family home on the south coast was more than just a coincidence.

"So, what do we do now?" Blake asked.

"Given that you're familiar with the area, Gordon is sending your team to the cemetery at 0900 hours tomorrow morning to meet with the local vicar and the forensic team later in the day."

Eric Gordon was head of Special Branch and often had inside information that Blake knew he needed if he was to try and untangle what had happened over the past few months.

"Okay, I'll be there but keep me informed about Graham Evans. I need to know everything he does. He could well be the key to all of this," Blake replied.

"Our man in Paris is on his way there now," Joe confirmed. "It's good to see you again Blake."

"Likewise," Blake smiled before returning to his car on the driveway of the remains of his parents home.

Jenny was waiting inside the car for him.

"Well?" she asked as Blake sat in the driver's seat.

"Andrea Smith is back in the UK. Are you still friends with her older sister?" Blake asked.

"We went to uni together but I haven't spoken to Jade for a couple of years. I guess I could message her on social media. Is everything okay?"

Blake wasn't sure how much information he should tell his sister but at the same time, he knew the media would be all over it sooner rather than later. He took a deep breath. "There's been no official ID, however, a body has been discovered in East Boldre Cemetery in The New Forest. There's a strong possibility that it could be Andrea. Alison, Samir and I have to go there tomorrow morning to continue the investigation."

Jenny gasped, holding her hand over her mouth. "No, not Andrea too. He's tying up loose ends!"

"What do you mean?"

"Tom, he's finishing us off one by one. Nicola was murdered near Paris and now Andrea. It's only a matter of time before he comes for me."

"I don't think that's his plan Jen."

"Why?"

"Because if he wanted to kill you, he would have done it at The Rabbit Hole."

The Rabbit Hole was a disused London underground station that Jenny, Blake and a few friends used to go to as teenagers to hang out until the police sealed up all of the entrances. Jenny received a message to go there and that was where she had learnt the truth about Tom Gibson's betrayal. She hated him for it. As she thought about what Blake had said, she soon realised that the hunter had become the hunted.

"What can I do to help?" Jenny asked.

"Contact Jade but do not let her know too many details about the investigation. There has to be a connection with the Smith family and The New Forest. Something we're not seeing."

"We are the connection Blake. Aunt Mary's house at Lepe. The same house that Dad grew up in and it was owned by his parents, our grandparents. We may have grown up in London but our roots are down in Hampshire."

Blake pondered that for a moment. Jenny had gone to Plymouth University with Jade Smith almost fifteen years ago. She knew Andrea Smith after regularly visiting Jade at her parents' home in Putney, south London. Andrea had been to university with Nicola Pew and Tiffany Mason and had often met up for drinks with Jenny in the bars around Kings Cross University over the years. Now that all three women were dead, Blake could understand his sister's fears but he needed her to reach out to Jade to find out if there was any further connections between the Smith family and whoever was in the unknown grave in East Boldre.

"Okay, I'll drop you off at your place, can you try and make contact with Jade and let me know what you can find out. I'll head back to Lepe tonight. If you still feel uneasy about being in London then come and stay with us for a while," Blake replied.

Jenny agreed and they drove back through the busy London streets towards her flat in Kensington before Blake returned to the south coast. A thousand questions flooded his mind as he drove down the rain-soaked M3 motorway towards Southampton but no obvious answers seemed to be coming through. He knew there had to be a connection with his previous assignment, he just needed to figure out how Andrea Smith fitted into all of it.

Blake arrived home just after 9pm. He let himself in the front door and saw a flickering of candlelight coming from the lounge. He slowly pushed open the door and saw Paula curled up on the sofa hugging a pillow and finishing the last mouthful of red wine from her glass. He sat down beside her and placed his hand over hers. She pulled it away.

"I'm sorry I've been preoccupied lately," Blake said as he moved closer to her.

He noticed her eyes, so often bright, were now red and glistened with unshed tears. She stared at the flickering flame of the candle barely acknowledging that he was there.

"Is Michael asleep?" he asked.

"He's at Dexter's for the night," Paula replied.

Blake moved to place his arms around her but she pulled away again.

"Don't."

He moved away reluctantly. "What's wrong?"

Paula didn't respond.

"Did Jenny upset you yesterday? Have I done something?"

She shook her head.

"I need to know what's wrong so I can try and make things right again."

Paula took a deep breath. "That's just it though isn't it?"

Blake looked at her.

"You always need to fix things Blake. Whatever happens you always need to fix it. Never fear, Blake Langford is here!"

"Is that a bad thing?"

"It is when the thing you're trying to fix is the one thing that can't be fixed."

Blake frowned. "You're talking in riddles Paula, what's happened? What have I done wrong?"

"Nothing. You've done nothing."

Blake waited.

"I never asked for this life. To always be looking over my shoulder in case some crazed criminal comes after me. To be the surrogate mother to my nephew. To be in my sister's shadow for the rest of my life."

"Rachael died and nobody could have seen that coming. Yes, I used to love your sister but that was nine years ago..."

"And yet you still slept with me!"

Blake was taken by surprise at her sudden outburst. "We were both in a situation where we needed somebody!"

"Is that how you justify it?"

"My father died that morning. I was up to my neck in aggravation at work. There was a suspicion that Rachael had been sneaking off with one of her college friends and I needed a release. I drank myself into stupidity to escape the reality of my world crashing down around me!"

"So I'm stupid now? Is that what you're saying? That I'm some kind of stupid mistake!"

Blake shook his head. "No, no, I'm not saying that at all."

"If you can sleep with me whilst being engaged to my sister, how can I trust you with anything now?"

"It takes two Paula."

She laughed in disbelief. "That's your excuse?"

"You had just been beaten up by Andrew Broughton and turned up at my flat and practically threw yourself at me. I'd just finished a bottle of Jack Daniels and could barely understand what was happening."

"So it's my fault now then?"

"No, I'll accept my part in it. Yes, we did sleep together. Yes, I willingly made love to you at a time when in the cold light of day we shouldn't have done it. No matter what you think, I cared for you then and I..."

Paula waited.

"And I love you now," he finally replied.

Paula moved towards him and they held each other close. "I'm sorry," she whispered.

"So am I."

"With so many things going on and raking up the past I just don't know what's going on anymore."

They broke the embrace. "There are a lot of things at play here that don't make any sense. But I promise, I will do whatever it takes to keep you and Michael safe," Blake said.

"I don't want to be, just safe, I want time with you. The three of us as a family. Burying so many people lately makes you realise that life isn't that long and you need to make the most of it."

"Andrew's death has hit you hard hasn't it?"

"Have you been talking to Jen?"

"No, but I know you and I know what it's like to lose someone you used to love."

Paula looked at him.

"Rachael will always be in my heart but my life, my future and my love is right here with you. Likewise, I know deep down that Andrew still has a place in your heart but I hope that we can both move on together and create a beautiful future together."

Paula hugged him again. "You're an asshole aren't ya," she laughed into his shirt.

"I'll take that as a complement shall I?" Blake smiled.

They blew out the candles and headed off to bed. Blake knew that he had a lot of things he needed to juggle at the moment but being there for his family was still important. He'd made many mistakes over the years, he just hoped that he had learnt from them and the consequences of his decisions in the future were less than what had gone before.

Chapter Forty-Three

Mr Smith
Saturday 21st August 1948

A tall middle-aged man wearing a brown suit, mustard yellow shirt, light brown tie and brown shoes stepped off of the train at Southampton Terminus Station just after 11am. He took a deep breath of fresh air, embracing his freedom, after being stuck in a sweaty crowded carriage for the past couple of hours before taking in his surroundings.

He recognised the road that led towards dock gate number three from a newspaper report he had read from earlier in the year when King George VI and Queen Elizabeth had visited to see Cunard's renowned Atlantic liner, Queen Elizabeth. It was a big event for the city which was still recovering from the after effects of the second world war.

The man carried his brown leather suitcase that had seen better days with a newspaper tucked under his arm. He wandered over towards the ticket office as his train left the station to continue its journey along the coast towards Bournemouth.

"Good morning, sir," the man in the ticket office beamed.

The man in the brown suit noticed a nameplate in front of the ticket office gentleman. It read "Kenneth Bates." "Good morning, could you kindly inform me when the next train to Lymington is scheduled to depart?" he asked.

"You've just missed the morning one. The next train is due at one o'clock," Kenneth replied.

The man in the brown suit let out a sigh. "Oh well, that will have to suffice. May I purchase a second-class one-way ticket for the one o'clock train to Lymington, please?"

Kenneth promptly stamped a ticket before exchanging it for several shillings. "Would you like to store your suitcase in the cloakroom until your train arrives, sir?"

"Yes, that would be greatly appreciated, thank you."

Kenneth picked up a sheet of paper and a pen. "May I take a name, please, sir?"

"Smith, Jack Smith," the man in the brown suit responded.

"Thank you, Mr. Smith," Kenneth smiled as he handed Jack his cloakroom receipt before placing his suitcase in the wooden storage rack behind him. "Enjoy your time in our city."

"I'm sure I will," Jack smiled before turning away from the ticket office.

He placed his newspaper on a wooden bench at the side of the waiting room before heading outside where he noticed two buses had stopped on the opposite side of the road. The midday heat was stifling so he crossed the road and headed towards the bus stop and the shade of some overhanging oak trees.

After the first bus had left, Jack noticed that the remaining bus was heading towards Lepe Beach. He pulled a crumpled piece of paper out of his pocket and read an address that had been scribbled down on it many years ago. He realised that the bus would bring him closer to where he wanted to be than the train would.

As the last passenger at the bus stop climbed aboard, Jack quickly moved to join them, cursing the fact that his luggage was still in the cloak room at the railway station. He would deal with that later. He exchanged a few coins for his bus ticket before moving towards the back of the bus where an open window generated a cool breeze as the bus travelled away from the city centre.

***

Southward Cottage overlooking Lepe Beach with the Isle Of Wight in the distance was the home of Mavis and Edward Langford. Enjoying a rare day off from the police force, Edward Langford sat in a deck chair reading a newspaper whilst his children, John, Frederick and Mary played in the sand.

"Daddy, come play with us," Mary squealed excitedly.

"Come now, children. Your father's had a demanding few weeks. Let him have his rest," Mavis replied, offering Edward a glass of lemonade.

"Have you heard from Dana lately?" Edward asked.

"She's coming over with Edith soon. It's been a struggle for her since Gerald passed. I wish we could do more," Mavis sighed.

"All we can do is hope for Gerald's military pension to come through, or she'll have a tough time making ends meet."

"I couldn't bear to see her and her daughter without a home."

"We're not a charity, Mavis. Sadly, misfortunes befall good people. Besides, her father does quite well at the bridge club near Portsmouth. He's been swindling those navy cadets for years. I'm sure he's stashed away a tidy sum."

"You're all heart, Ed," Mavis quipped as she wandered back toward the house.

"Ow! Mary, don't flick sand into my eyes!" Frederick shouted.

"Ow! Don't kick me!" Mary responded.

Frederick pushed her out of the way.

"Mummy, Fred kicked me!" Mary cried out, scurrying towards Mavis.

"Frederick, brush yourself off. You know better than to bury yourself in the sand. Go find your brother," Mavis advised.

"He's off collecting shells for Edith," Frederick replied.

"Johnny has a soft spot for her," Mary teased.

"Even if he does, playing in the sand won't set the table for lunch. Frederick, find your brother and Mary, help set the table," Mavis instructed.

"Alright," they both sighed before heading off in opposite directions.

Further down the beach, John Langford gathered shells from amongst the rocks before following a stony path leading away from the shore and toward a small woodland at the top of the hill. At the summit, he spotted his friend Edith and her mother, Dana, engaged in conversation with a man wearing a brown suit and brown shoes. John didn't recognize the man, but it seemed like they were having a heated discussion. He concealed himself behind a tree until the voices quietened down. After a minute, John peeked out and saw the man handing an envelope filled with money to Dana before walking away.

John watched the man as he left before emerging from his hiding spot behind the tree.

"John! Delightful to see you!" Edith called out, rushing over to him. "What are you doing so far down the beach?"

John showed her the red bucket he was carrying. "I was collecting shells..."

Edith quickly sorted through them and selected an intriguingly shaped one. "Oh, I adore this one. Can I have it?"

"Of course," John beamed.

"Thank you, John. You're the best."

"Come along, you two, or we'll be late for Mrs. Langford's luncheon," Dana urged.

The two friends skipped along the beach, with Dana following a few steps behind. John stole a few glances back at Dana, pondering the man who had given her the money. Something didn't seem right, and his father's advice echoed in his mind, prompting him to question the situation if it seemed amiss.

"Who was that gent your Mum was talking to?" John asked.

"What gent?"

"I spied someone leaving your twosome as I arrived," John pushed.

"Oh, I don't know. Someone my Uncle Frank dispatched to aid us."

"I didn't know you had an Uncle Frank..." John began as a damp lump of sand smacked his face.

"Freddie!" Edith giggled, tossing sand back at him.

"Now, now, Edith. Don't get your dress mucked up with sand before luncheon. It'd be most disrespectful," Dana advised.

"What've you got here?" Frederick asked, tipping shells onto the sand after grabbing John's red bucket.

"Hey careful! They're fragile!" John protested.

"The only thing fragile here is you," Frederick retorted, kicking sand in John's face.

"Leave him be, he found this most amazing shell for me!" Edith replied.

John hurriedly placed the shells back into his bucket before rushing on ahead as they strolled back towards the Langford family home.

"Why are you so hard on him?" Edith asked Frederick as they arrived outside Southward cottage.

"He's too soft. If I don't toughen him up then the world will eat him alive."

"Ah, there you are Dana. We were wondering where you'd got to. Mavis has put on a delightful spread," Edward called out before leading them up the wooden steps to the picnic table on the lawn at the back of the cottage.

After lunch, the four children went to play in the sea whilst Edward reclaimed his deckchair and Mavis and Dana sat on a blanket that had been laid out on the sand. At that moment, Edward noticed a man in a brown suit staggering along the beach. He was coughing into a handkerchief and looked extremely hot. As he approached, Edward stood from his deckchair and walked over to him.

"Afternoon Sir, are you alright? You seem a little lost," Edward asked.

"I am rather, I was hoping to find somewhere to have a drink and some shade. It's so very hot today," the man replied, glancing towards Mavis and Dana.

Both women stared warily in his direction.

"Office wear isn't the best for the summer is it?" Edward chuckled. "The old cafe is a couple of miles the other way but Norman, poor old chap, hasn't opened since the war. Why don't you join us for a drink, Mister..."

"Williams, Vincent Williams," the man lied.

"Well Mr Williams, I'm sure my wife may be able to find a cold beer from indoors," Edward replied, placing his hand on the man's shoulder and leading him over to where they were all sitting.

After some awkward conversation, Mavis and Edward went back inside, leaving Dana and the man in the brown suit outside.

"What are you doing here Jack? I told you to leave. If they find out..." Dana began.

"They won't. I need to know that our son is safe. I haven't got long left. Where is he?" Jack asked.

"I told you, I gave him up for adoption at the hospital. I don't know who is looking after him now. The accusing eyes after Gerald's death would have been too much. Everyone would know that I had been unfaithful..."

"I need to see you later."

Dana sighed. "Meet me at Honeypot House, about two miles down the coast on Lepe Road. Now go, before they realise who you really are."

As Jack stood up to leave, Edward wandered back out of the house with a camera.

"My word, I haven't seen one of those cameras in years," Jack beamed as he examined Edward's camera.

"It belonged to my older brother, Robert. He gave it to me just before the war. I thought it would be nice to have a photo to remember this moment by."

"Oh, Mr Langford, I'm sure Mr Williams will want to be getting on his way," Dana tried.

"Nonsense, there's always time for a photograph," Jack replied.

"Come along children, time for a photograph," Mavis called out as the children came running over from where they were playing on the beach.

John looked at Jack suspiciously.

"Can I take the photo? I've got my own camera at home and I've taken some lovely photographs of the birds in the trees," Edith beamed.

"Okay, but please be careful Edith, it's an old and fragile camera," Edward replied, handing her the camera.

The children knelt down on the sand in front of Dana, Edward and Mavis ready for the photograph.

"Come on Mr Williams, join us," Edward called out.

"Oh, I wouldn't want to intrude," Jack replied sheepishly.

"Not at all; it'll be a reminder of the pleasant day we've all had."

Jack walked over and stood next to Dana as Edith took two photographs of them all together. As the day wore on, Dana excused herself and began walking back down the beach with Edith. Edward wandered back inside the house to listen to the radio in the lounge. The three children were building mountains with piles of stones that they had collected from further down the beach whilst Mavis began tidying up the glasses and cups from the picnic blanket.

"Alone at last," Jack whispered to her.

"You shouldn't be here Jack. Edward is no fool. If he ever found out who you really are, he'd kill you," Mavis replied.

"I had to see you one last time."

"It's over Jack. What we had, it's in the past. I'm married to Edward. We have a family and a home together. He's a good man and I'm not willing to give all of that up!"

"I'm not asking you to."

"Then why are you here pretending to be someone you're not?"

"I had to visit the doctor in London. It's not good news I'm afraid."

"What did they say?" Mavis asked.

"They think I have tuberculosis. There's no cure. I have to deal with fever, coughing and I don't have as much energy as I used to. Funny, after being sent home from battle, a damn virus takes me out."

"Why are you telling me all this?"

"You took good care of me when I came home. You helped me get my life back. Proved to me that I could still be a man…"

"Don't."

"Don't what?"

"I made a mistake. A stupid mistake. Now go."

"Or else what?"

Mavis glared at him. "If you break up my family, I'll kill you myself."

Jack raised his hands in mock surrender. "I guess I'll be on my way then."

Mavis watched him as he stood up from the picnic blanket and dusted the sand off of his clothes.

"Nice kids, shame about their mother. Good day Mrs Langford," Jack said before walking away.

Mavis watched him as he staggered down the beach and away into the distance.

"Where did Mr Williams go?" John asked as he rushed over towards his mother.

"He had an urgent appointment," Mavis replied before turning her attention back to the picnic blanket. "Come John, help me clear the cups and plates back to the kitchen, there's a good lad."

"I don't think Mr Williams is a nice man," John commented as he helped his mother carry the picnic items back towards the cottage.

"What makes you think that?"

"I saw him arguing with Mrs Wise earlier today."

"Were you eavesdropping when you shouldn't have been Jonathon?"

"I wasn't dropping any eaves Mum, honest. I was collecting my shells and I heard loud voices and saw it was Mr Williams and Mrs Wise."

"Did you hear what they were saying?"

John shook his head. "He did seem to be angry with her about something though."

Mavis pondered that for a moment. "Let's keep this between ourselves okay? Nobody else needs to know. All right?"

"What about father?"

"Especially not your father. He's got enough to worry about. Tomorrow morning, we will go to Mrs Wise and ask her if everything is okay. Until then, we say nothing more. Am I understood?"

John nodded before following his mother into the kitchen with the plates and cups. His curiosity was still beginning to think up possibilities about the mysterious Mr Williams. Did his mother know something about the man and Mrs Wise that she didn't want him to know about? Whatever it was, he was sure that Edith would have the answer. He just needed to work up the courage to ask her.

Chapter Forty-Four

Uncovering Secrets
Sunday 2nd November 2008

Blake woke up early from a restless sleep and wandered into the study at his beachside house in Lepe. A grey metal box was on his desk. He scrolled the combination lock before opening it. He had spent the previous evening attempting to map out his own family tree to try and figure out some of the answers to the questions the photo of the mysterious man at the beach had created.

As he flicked through some old photos, he found a photo of his mother, Emily, when she was a teenager alongside her mother Dana and her younger brother Jim. There was another man in the photo that was standing behind Emily that Blake seemed to recognise. Blake pulled out the 1948 photo that he had found in Emily's safe deposit box and laid it alongside this new photo that he had found. He studied the faces of the man behind Emily and the mystery man from 1948. There was definitely more than a family resemblance between the two men. Were they father and son? And if so, what connection did they have with Blake's mother's side of the family?

Blake rubbed his hands over his face in frustration. It seemed like the more he looked at the old photographs, the more confusing everything became. He opened his laptop and began looking at the records for deaths in Hampshire from 1984. He scrolled through pages of names until he found what he was looking for.

**DANA SYLVIA HANDANOWICZ
DIED 17TH APRIL 1984
AGED 69 YEARS**

LOVING WIFE OF WILLIAM DAVID HANDANOWICZ
MOTHER OF EMILY MAY, JAMES HAROLD, EDITH WINIFRED AND EVELYN JOAN.
BURIAL SITE: RECORD INCOMPLETE

Blake read the obituary before beginning a search on the Special Branch database but there was no record of an Evelyn Joan Handanowicz. He knew his grandmother was married before she met his grandfather William Handanowicz. Her previous husband was Gerald Arthur Wise who had died during the second world war. He found his record and also the record of Edith Winifred Wise. He remembered his mother talking of her older sister Edith who had died of pneumonia when she was only sixteen in 1956 but she had never mentioned anyone called Evelyn.

Blake tried searching for Evelyn Joan Wise and still found no matching records. He racked his brains trying to remember his grandmother's maiden name but it just wouldn't come to him. He searched for his grandfather's death record from 1987 in the hope that he would find Evelyn Joan's name there too but as he read his grandfather's obituary, nothing became any clearer.

WILLIAM DAVID HANDANOWICZ
DIED 22ND DECEMBER 1987
AGED 75 YEARS
LOVING HUSBAND OF DANA SYLVIA HANDANOWICZ
FATHER OF EMILY MAY AND JAMES HAROLD.
BURIAL SITE: CREMATION AT SOUTHAMPTON CREMATORIUM

"What are you looking at?" Michael asked as he wandered into the study.

Blake turned around as his son approached him. "Hey, I thought you were still asleep."

"No, I had a nightmare."

"Oh, what was it about?"

"I dreamed that I woke up and you and Aunt Paula were gone."

"Is that why you didn't want to stay at Dexter's all night?"

"I'm sorry, I didn't mean to call you out late."

"It's okay, I hadn't been home long anyway."

Michael looked at him disbelievingly.

"We're not going anywhere, Michael. We're a team, remember, and we always will be," Blake smiled.

"Don't make promises you can't keep."

"What makes you think that I won't keep them?"

"Mum always promised that she'd never leave."

Blake felt a pang in his chest. His failure to save Rachael after a previous Special Branch case in Miami went wrong still haunted him to this day. "Your mum didn't choose to leave you. I'm sure if there was anything that could have prevented what happened, she would've taken that chance."

"I guess."

"I'm not going anywhere and neither is Paula."

"Then why are you looking for dead people?"

Blake closed his laptop before turning back to him. "It's just something I'm working on for my job. It's nothing to worry about. No one is going to die."

"But Nan did."

Blake bit down on his bottom lip. "I know but your Nan was very ill and unfortunately, when people get old, they will eventually die. She's not in any pain anymore."

"Is that why you're trying to figure out her life story now that she's gone? Why couldn't you ask her about it when she was here?"

Blake thought back to his argument with Paula last night. "Sometimes, we get so caught up in doing our own things everyday, we forget to listen or be curious about our family and friends until…"

"Until it's too late."

"Yeah," Blake sighed.

Michael looked over at the photos that Blake had laid out on the desk. "Is that Nan?"

"Yeah, they were taken a long time ago."

"And is that Uncle Vic?" Michael asked, pointing to the man standing behind Emily in the photo.

Blake looked at Michael. "Do you know this man?"

"Kinda."

"Michael, if you know who he is, it's really important that you tell me. Did Nan go to visit him with you?"

"Only once."

"When?"

"Just after Mum's funeral. You and Aunt Paula were speaking to people who had come along and Nan said that she would bring me back here with Aunt Jenny."

"So Jenny knows who he is too?"

"No, Aunt Jenny drove on ahead and we visited some kind of place for old people, Priestfields, I think it was called. Anyway, we saw an old man with a walking stick and Nan gave him a brown envelope."

"And then what happened?"

"They spoke for a few minutes and then we walked back down the road for a while until one of the men in the big black cars saw us and gave us a lift back here. He gave me some buttercrunch too. They were the best buttercrunch I've ever had since we came to the UK."

"Buttercrunch?" Blake asked.

"Tofu or whatever you call it here. Sticky sweets or candy."

"Toffees."

"Yeah, I think that's what Nan called them."

"Are you sure that guy is the same guy you and Nan went to see at Priestfields?"

Michael looked at the photo again. "Kinda sure, he's a lot older now but he had that mark on his cheek and wore those thick glasses. Nan said his name was Uncle Vic. Does that mean he was Nan's brother?"

Blake pondered that for a moment. "No, your nan only had one brother. His name's Uncle Jim and he lives in Greece."

"If he's her brother, why didn't he come here for Nan's funeral?"

"Michael?" Paula called out. "Is everything okay?"

"Yeah, Dad was just explaining that Nan had a brother and I wondered why I haven't met him yet?"

"Sometimes when people live far away, they can't always get to places that they want to be. Come on, shall we get some breakfast? How about I make us some eggs and toast."

"Only if I can break the shells!" Michael replied as he headed towards the kitchen.

"Deal," Paula smiled as he ran past her. She looked over at Blake who mouthed "thank you" to her. She smiled before following Michael into the kitchen.

Blake's phone cut into his thoughts as a message from his colleague, Alison Pearce, lit up the screen. Two hours later, he parked his silver Ford Mondeo outside East Boldre Cemetery in The New Forest. He stepped out of his car and walked over towards the cemetery gates.

"We seem to be making a habit of meeting in these places," Alison said as she approached him.

"What do we have?" Blake asked as he walked alongside her towards the grave.

"They removed Andrea Smith's body from the grave but the local police are still trying to negotiate with the undertakers regarding the paperwork for the plot."

As they arrived at the graveside, Samir Khalifa was talking to one of the forensics team. He wandered over towards them. "Forensics say she was alive when she was buried and suspect that she died of suffocation when she was covered over with the dirt," Samir explained.

"Drugged?" Blake asked.

"They're still running tests but I'm guessing so. Nobody would willingly let someone bury them alive," Samir concluded.

"What's the deal with the undertaker?"

"Crowther and Jones, apparently, even though the grave has been unmarked, there is a paperwork trail to a family in London. Until they have written consent from that family, they refuse to allow the coffin below where Andrea was buried to be exhumed," Alison explained.

"How long has the body been down there?"

"Twenty-six years," Samir replied.

"For God's sake, the coffin and body would've disintegrated by now. All that's gonna be left is the skeleton, surely," Blake snapped.

"Do you wanna tell them that?" Alison asked. "Whoever is down there is obviously someone's relative. You wouldn't want a member of your family dug up just to complete some paperwork would you?"

Blake ran his fingers through his hair. "I guess you're right. Samir, can you tag along with the investigating officer and let us know what forensics finds out."

Samir nodded and wandered over towards the police officers on the opposite side of the cemetery.

"What are you thinking?" Alison asked.

"We need to fill in the gaps of what Andrea Smith has been up to since we left her in France with Graham Evans," Blake replied as he began heading back towards his car with Alison close behind him.

"The local police have tried to contact her parents already but haven't been able to track down either of them. We'll just be doubling up on their investigation."

Blake thought about that for a moment. He knew Andrea had an older sister called Jade but he wanted to see how much information Jenny could get out of her first. "What about the man with the dog?"

Alison pulled a notepad out of her pocket. "George Harding, retired, lives in Priestfields near Blackfield. He gave the police a statement when he found the hand and after the paramedics checked him over, he went home."

"Then, Priestfields seems like a good place to start. Let's go," Blake replied.

He had driven past Priestfields Assisted Living complex many times and after his conversation with his son, Michael, earlier, it seemed like an ideal time to visit the complex.

***

Jenny Langford walked through Tottenham Court Road Underground Station in London before heading out onto Oxford Street. After a few minutes, she found a cafe called Chequered Flag next door to a huge department store. It had a Formula 1 racing theme throughout with signed photos of racing drivers from over the years alongside metal models shaped like various racing circuits from all over the world. At the corner table at the back of the cafe sat a woman dressed in black with auburn her hair tied back in a large black hair grip. Jenny wandered over towards her before taking a seat on the opposite side of her table.

"I wondered when you'd come out of the woodwork," she said as Jenny sat down.

"I'm sorry Jade, I meant to keep in touch but I..."

"Was too busy leading my sister into trouble."

"It wasn't like that. She knew who she was dealing with in those student bars."

"It doesn't matter now anyway, does it? It's over."

"I'm sorry."

"For what?" Jade asked.

Before Jenny could answer, a waitress approached them. They both ordered latte's and Jade ordered a slice of carrot cake.

"You know, Andrea was always playing with fire," Jade continued. "But somehow, your family, my family, we always seemed to cross swords."

"I don't want to fight."

"Neither do I, yet here we are. Two old friends sharing a coffee and catching up on old times when the people we love are missing or barely cold in the grave."

"I realise this must be hard for you but we need to try and understand what's been happening over the past couple of years if we are going to have any chance of figuring out what happened to Andrea."

"You still don't know, do you?" Jade asked.

"Know what?"

"Your mother's will. Do you know what's inside it?"

Jenny wasn't sure how much Jade knew so decided to play it safe. "She wrote the same will that my father had. Everything goes to the surviving spouse and when they are both gone, it gets split equally between Blake, Steven and myself."

"That's what you were led to believe."

"What do you mean?"

"Did your Mum ever mention Uncle Vic?"

Jenny shook her head.

"Victor Gerald Wise is your Mum's older half brother. Your grandmother had him in 1940 but he was sent away for adoption when the bombing started in London."

"No way, Grandma Dana only had Edith before she met Grandad William, then they had Mum and Uncle Jim. Edith was only sixteen when she died. The dates don't add up."

"Edith died just before her seventeenth birthday. Victor was only a year younger than her but he was practically orphaned by the war. His father was killed and his mother abandoned him."

"How do you know all of this?"

"Because Victor Wise is my grandad."

Jenny gasped. "Wait, are you telling me that we are related?"

Jade nodded.

"You wait over twenty years to spring that one on me! Why didn't you tell me before?"

"I only found out about it myself a few years ago."

"How many is a few?"

"Your Mum, Emily, had been exchanging letters with my grandad, Victor Wise, for a few years. After your father died, she finally decided to meet with him. She told him that she lost touch with her younger brother James and her twin sister, Evelyn, after they disappeared years ago and that he was the only relative she had left from her generation."

Jenny sipped her latte as she processed what Jade was telling her. Her mother rarely spoke of her siblings and whenever they came up in conversation, the subject was quickly dismissed. "I can't believe she never told us about him."

"It was a different time back then. Being a widow with two children in tow tended to leave women in a desperate situation. It was very much a man's world. There was no childcare and she couldn't work to make ends meet either."

"But she kept Edith?"

"Yeah, that's one thing that Grandad couldn't understand. Why not give them both up if she couldn't look after them?"

"Then after the war, Grandma met Grandad, Will, and they married. Mum came along…"

"Four months later," Jade added.

"Yeah. So her and grandad must have conceived Mum and Evelyn before they were married. Given the time, there must have been a rushed wedding to cover up any scandal."

"Except William Handanowicz was only discharged from the military three months prior to their marriage. I checked the records."

"So unless Mum and Evelyn were born very premature, which probably meant that it was highly unlikely that they would have survived, especially being twins back then…"

"There's a chance that William Handanowicz was not your biological grandad."

Jenny ran her fingers through her hair trying to piece everything together. "So, let me get this right, Grandma Dana had Edith and Victor before the war. Victor is given up for adoption, Edith dies in 1956. After the war she had Evelyn, my aunt, Emily, my mother, and James, my uncle who is now living somewhere in Greece. Why would she put herself into a situation with four children around the war and where is Evelyn now that all of this has blown up?"

"Nobody knows. Not meaning to state the obvious here but the rhythm method is no longer a recommended contraception for a reason. It was never a topic of conversation but do you honestly believe all of the women remained faithful whilst their men were out risking their lives for King and country?"

"I guess not," Jenny replied. She had heard snippets from her parents about someone called Evelyn but had never known the full story. "Why would they break up the family like that? Surely there must have been a way to sort their differences out!"

"This was just after the second world war. Every family was struggling on rations and a huge depression so money was tight. Quite often, families had to make a choice. Whatever the differences they had, for some reason, it's taken your mother's death to bring it all out into the open again."

Jenny paused for a moment. "So, Victor Wise is your grandad on who's side?"

"My mother's side. Both of my parents died in a motorbike accident three years ago. I never really understood the family history until we began sorting through all of their things."

"And what did you find?"

"A whole lot of nothing. My grandfather never contacted us after mum died so it was just Andrea and me against the world."

"So what did you do next?"

"What do you mean?"

"I haven't seen you for a few years, do you have a family, boyfriend?"

"Oh, no, nothing like that. I work as an accountant for one of the large firms in the city. Tell me, if Andrea hadn't gone missing, would you have contacted me?"

Jenny suddenly realised that Jade had no idea of what had happened to her sister. "I'm sorry, I've been battling with a few mental health problems recently which has led me to lose contact with a lot of people I care about. Tell me, when did you last speak to Andrea?"

"Around a month ago. She was staying somewhere in France until the heat died down in London. She got kicked out of that student house she was renting with those other two students so some guy offered her a place to stay. I didn't ask what kind of arrangement they had but knowing her..."

Jenny nodded. "Jade, I need you to come with me."

"Why? Where to?"

"Have the police contacted you?"

"No, why?"

Jenny took a deep breath. "There's a chance that your sister is dead."

A smirk of disbelief appeared on Jade's face. "No, no, you're wrong."

"Andrea became involved in a Special Branch operation and was killed by someone connected to Tom Gibson."

A look of realisation crossed Jade's face for a moment. "You're lying. Tom would never touch her. How the hell..."

"How do you know what he would do?"

"I've met him before, he couldn't possibly..."

"Jade, listen to me, Tom is tying up loose ends. Andrea's housemates Tiffany Mason and Nicola Pew are both dead. Now Andrea has disappeared, it's only a matter of time before he comes after us. I need you to come with me to see my brother."

"No."

"Jade, please, your life is in danger if they think you're involved."

"I'm only involved because you've dragged me into something..."

"He's got his claws into you hasn't he? I can see it in your eyes. He's got you running scared."

"Jen, you have no idea what you're getting yourself involved in. Our family history is going to blow up in a big way..."

"Our family history? What are you talking about?"

"Your Mum's will has opened up a can of worms and now none of us are safe!"

"What are you scared of Jade?"

She bowed her head.

"Blake can protect you."

"How?"

"I used to be you. I loved Tom Gibson with all my heart. My love for him blinded me to what was really going on and without Blake's help, I'd be behind bars if not dead by now."

"It's not like that, it's complicated."

"Then uncomplicate it for me. What hold does Tom Gibson have over you?"

Jade stood up from the table. "You're playing a dangerous game Jen. My advice, tidy up your mother's affairs and get the hell out of London."

"And if I don't?" Jenny replied, standing up to face her.

"This thing goes way deeper than you could ever understand. Leave London or you won't live to see the consequences," Jade replied before walking out of the cafe.

Jenny sat back down once again feeling her whole body shaking. She took a few deep breaths to calm the adrenaline that was running through her. She left some cash on the table before heading back outside and following the path towards the tube station.

She knew that she needed to find out exactly what was in her mother's will. The solicitor had been extremely vague when her and Blake had attended the reading. All of the information and this HM25 clause seemed to revolve around some unknown family history that she was struggling to piece together. And where did Evelyn and Jim Handanowicz fit into all of this? She took the train to South Kensington before making her way towards the remains of 124 Alfredson Road, her family home where she hoped that she could find something to help answer the million questions that were clouding her mind.

Chapter Forty-Five

Edward's Discovery
Sunday 22nd August 1948

A loud knocking at the front door woke Edward Langford from a restless sleep. He fumbled for a match and relit a candle that he had placed on the chest of drawers at the side of his bed before going to sleep last night. The knocking became more insistent as he wandered down the stairs.

"All right, all right, I'm coming!" he called out as he unlocked the door.

As he opened the door, he saw his Sergeant, Peter Hastings waiting on his doorstep illuminated by the headlights of a police patrol car on the driveway.

"Sorry to disturb you, Sir, but Honeypot House on Lepe Road went up in flames during the night. It seems like a deliberate act," Peter explained.

Edward gasped, knowing Dana Wise and her daughter, Edith, lived there. "Any survivors?" he asked.

"None Sir. The fire department has only just got it under control."

"What's wrong?" Mavis asked as she began to walk down the stairs towards them.

"Nothing, I just, er, I need to assist Hastings with a case. I'll just get dressed and gather my things," Edward replied as he closed the door on Peter. "Go back to bed, the children will be up soon."

Mavis nodded before returning upstairs. Edward quickly changed into a white shirt, black trousers and black shoes before sliding a black suit jacket around his shoulders. He collected his keys and wallet from the fireplace before joining Peter Hastings outside. As Hastings drove down the Lepe Road and the smouldering remains of Honeypot House came into view, Edward had a feeling of dread come over him. He stepped out of the car and approached the house.

"Good morning Sir," Officer George Wells greeted as Hastings and Langford approached. "Looks deliberate. We have found an oil can and remnants of cloths or blankets near to the front door."

"Any survivors or witnesses?" Edward asked.

"No Sir, in the middle of the night down here, hardly anyone ventures out in the darkness."

"Whoever set the fire must have gained access to the house or at least had some help to feed the rags through the front door," Peter Hastings reasoned.

"We thought it might have been that Sir but there's no sign of a letterbox in the front door," Officer Wells replied.

"So, whoever started the fire must have been inside the house."

"It would appear so, Sir."

Edward looked over towards the fence at the front of the property and saw a metal post box on top of a wooden stick. He walked over to it and opened the flap at the front. Five letters had been placed inside by the postman from a few days ago. As he looked at the first four letters, they all had FINAL DEMAND written on the front of the envelopes but the fifth letter was a handwritten envelope. On the back was a return address for the C.A.S. in London.

"Have you found something Sir?" Hastings asked.

"Possibly. Do you know anything about C.A.S. in London W1?" Edward asked.

"It's the Children's Adoption Service, for war orphans. Why? Who lived here?" Peter inquired.

"Dana Wise and her daughter Edith. How long does it take for a child to be adopted if the mother can't pay her way?"

"It depends. It could be a few days to a few weeks, Sir."

Edward opened the adoption letter, revealing Dana's intent to give up her eight year old son.

"Was she giving up her daughter for adoption?" Hastings asked.

"No, her son," Edward replied.

"I didn't know that she had a son."

"Neither did I. It looks like he has been at the adoption agency since birth and this was a letter confirming that she still wanted this arrangement. We need to find Dana and Edith Wise. When did the fire start?"

"It was called in at around two in the morning," Officer Wells responded.

Edward looked at his watch. It was ten minutes past five and the sun was beginning to rise in the distance as he looked up at the surrounding trees of The New Forest. "They've had at least a three hour headstart but they couldn't have gone far."

***

As the day wore on, the search teams found no sign of Edith or Dana Wise in the surrounding areas. Edward Langford and Peter Hastings returned to the Police Station to file their reports alongside the police officers that had been involved in the search and at Honeypot House.

"Did you find out anything from those letters?" Peter Hastings asked.

"Only that Dana Wise was six months behind on paying her gas and electricity and they were about to cut her off. It's this adoption letter that puzzles me though," Edward replied.

"How so? A lot of single mothers unfortunately have had to put their children into the hands of the adoption services. They would rather let them go than give them a life where they could end up on the streets."

"Her husband, Gerald Wise was one of the first to get drafted and was killed in the war. Dana Wise gave birth to her daughter Edith in 1939. This new child that has been discussed in this letter is only eight years old."

"So she got pregnant whilst her old man was away fighting," Hastings surmised.

"He was already dead. She was working as a military nurse looking after the war wounded."

"It was a tough time for us all, Sir. Most of the men I know sowed a few seeds over the years..."

"I saw Dana Wise with her daughter Edith only yesterday afternoon. She was a good friend of my wife, Mavis, but as far as I am aware, nobody knew about her son. If the adoption was done recently, where has the boy been in the meantime? It doesn't make sense. They joined us for luncheon along with a mysterious well dressed man who was strolling along the beach. Had a bit of a cough and was very sweaty. Not really dressed for the occasion," Edward explained.

At that moment, there was a knock on Edward Langford's office door.

"Come!" he ordered.

Officer George Wells entered the office. "Sorry to interrupt Sir, we may have had a breakthrough with the Honeypot House fire. A gent dressed in a brown suit has been found leant against ol' Norman's beachside cafe."

"Vincent Williams?" Edward asked.

"Do you know him, Sir?"

"Sort of, he stopped by my home yesterday afternoon."

"Well, we might need you to formally identify him Sir as nobody else seems to have the slightest idea who he is."

"What do you mean?"

"He's dead. No identification on him. No wallet. All he had on him was a train ticket for yesterday afternoon, a bus ticket, a comb, a packet of cigarettes and some matches."

Edward pondered Officer Wells' reply for a moment. The bus ticket he could understand but why would he need a train ticket for yesterday afternoon when he was at the beach? "What connection does he have with the Honeypot House fire?" Edward finally asked.

"Harry Partridge, the vicar, apparently saw the man walking nearby the house yesterday evening. Could be nothing but it's quite a trek from Honeypot House to Norman's cafe in the dark if you don't know the area too well."

"Thank you officer," Edward replied, dismissing Officer Wells before standing up and retrieving his suit jacket from the coat stand. "Come along Hastings, we need to go back to the beach."

***

Two police officers were standing guard at opposite ends of the stretch of Calshot Beach near to the building that previously belonged to Norman's Cafe. Edward Langford and Peter Hastings arrived in their car and wandered over towards where the body was laying on the beach.

"What the devil is going on here?" a man's voice called out.

Edward turned around and noticed Norman Whitehouse, the owner of the cafe, was fast approaching them. The police officer attempted to block his way.

"It's okay Jones, let him through," Edward advised as he approached the back of the cafe.

"Good God!" Norman gasped as he saw the man's body leant against the wall.

"Were you here last night Norman?" Edward asked.

"Of course not, the place hasn't reopened since the war. Don't you realise the rent they want to charge me now! Three times what I used to pay and the council won't listen to reason."

"Then why are you here now?"

"One of the villagers said that the police were interested in the place so I thought I'd come down and see what all the fuss was about."

"I see. Do you recognise this gent?" Edward asked.

Norman shook his head. "Never seen him before. Can't be local."

"No, he wasn't dressed for the beach and seemed a little out of place in the countryside."

"Probably worked in the city and took the bus out here for some sea air. You know what those city folk are like."

"Indeed. Do you still have the key to the cafe?"

"Am I under suspicion?"

"Of what?"

"I've got a dead body on my cafe doorstep."

"Should you be under suspicion?"

"No, of course not."

"Then answer the question, do you still have the keys or not?"

"Yes but it's due to be taken over by someone else in a few days so I shouldn't use them."

"Open the door," Edward replied.

"What? Why?"

"Norman, I'm investigating a possible murder here and I don't have time to ask the same question twice. Can you please unlock the door and let us inside your cafe?"

Norman nodded reluctantly before approaching the door and unlocking it. As he opened the door, it was obvious that somebody had been sleeping inside the cafe. Three blankets and pillows made from straw were laid out on the floor with empty tin cans left on the tables.

"I didn't know, I swear..." Norman pleaded as Edward and Peter entered.

"When did you last visit the cafe Mr Whitehouse?" Peter asked.

"About three weeks ago. I received a letter from the landowner telling me that I had to remove all of my things from here by next week or they would be thrown out by the new owners. Surely, you can't think the dead gent has anything to do with that?"

"I'm not ruling anything out," Edward replied.

At that moment, a knock on the door interrupted them.

"Excuse me Sir, forensics have finished and they're ready to move the body," Officer Jones explained.

Edward nodded. "What have they found so far?"

Officer Jones handed over an unused train ticket from Southampton to Lymington dated August 21st 1948, a receipt for the cloak room at Southampton Railway Station, a packet of chewing gum, a packet of cigarettes with matches and a bus ticket from Southampton to Lepe also dated August 21st 1948. Edward opened the packet of cigarettes and found a note folded around three of the cigarettes inside the packet. He unrolled the note and it had one word written on it;

FERTIG

Edward handed the note to Peter before studying the cigarettes closer.

"Any idea what fertig means?" Peter asked.

"It's a German word meaning finished or the end of something. I'm more interested in this though. Who would hide Lucky Strike cigarettes inside an Old Gold packet?" Edward asked.

"A lot of people tend to buy cheaper cigarettes and hide them inside the packet of a more expensive brand to make them look wealthier than they are," Norman explained. "It used to happen all the time."

"Except this time, we have expensive cigarettes inside a cheaper packaging," Peter replied.

"Maybe he was confused," Norman suggested.

"Everything seems peculiar with this gentleman," Officer Jones replied.

"How so?" Edward asked.

"It seems like he was almost trying to hide his wealth. All of his clothes have had the tags removed. He seemed to be a strong, well built man but besides the yellow cigarette stains, he had no calluses on his hands so he wasn't a manual worker. Missing sixteen teeth and it seems he drank some alcohol before he died. When they get him to the hospital, they should be able to tell us more."

"Other than the vicar who I will pay a visit to, do we have any witnesses who saw him on the beach late last night or early this morning?" Edward asked.

"Nobody has come forward yet Sir but we are asking all of the locals for their whereabouts in the past twenty-four hours," Officer Jones confirmed as they watched the man in the brown suit's body being loaded into the ambulance.

"Well, keep me informed. In the meantime, Hastings and I need to visit the church," Edward replied as he headed back towards his car.

As he arrived at his car, he turned back towards the group. "Oh, one more thing, Norman. Clean this place up and keep the door securely locked. You never know who is lurking around here."

As they watched Edward Langford and Peter Hastings drive away, Officer Jones noticed a black car approaching. As he walked over to stop them from parking on the verge, he recognised Officer Wells in the driving seat with a young man sitting beside him.

"Officer Wells, Detective Langford and Sergeant Hastings have just left," Officer Jones said as they stepped out of their car.

"That's okay, Charlie, I heard there were some squatters in the cafe and have come to investigate," Officer Wells replied.

"But Detective Langford..."

"Will continue the investigation so when the body has been loaded into the ambulance, you can stand your men down."

Officer Jones nodded before moving away. Officer Wells' passenger stepped out of the car and they both wandered over towards the cafe. Norman stepped outside and noticed them approaching before swiftly turning back inside again. Officer Wells and his passenger followed Norman back into the cafe and closed the door behind them. A few minutes later, Officer Wells left the cafe alone, closing the door behind him and led the rest of the officers away from the crime scene.

Chapter Forty-Six

A Message From The Grave
Sunday 2nd November 2008

Blake Langford parked his car outside the Priestfields Assisted Living Complex.

"So this is the halfway house," Alison said as they stepped out of the car.

"What do you mean?"

"Halfway between independent and dead. You know, you grow up as a teenager and think you know everything then suddenly the world kicks you in the ass before everything goes in reverse. You lose your freedom and independence and then eventually you're back in nappies again before you return to dust."

Blake laughed. "What's made you so cynical?"

"Life, I guess."

"Well, I suppose you could put it that way. At least with living here they still have some degree of freedom left before they get put into a nursing home."

"It's hard to imagine us in a place like this in thirty years' time."

"Speak for yourself, I wanna slide into my grave on the back of a motorbike shouting "What A Ride!"" Blake laughed.

"Seriously though, we seem to be dealing with a lot of deaths lately. Sometimes I wonder if it's all worth it?"

"It's the job and unfortunately, it can get a bit morbid at times."

"I didn't sign up for exhuming bodies from graveyards and having arms sticking out of graves. I prefer to live with the living and when I'm dead, I wanna stay with the dead."

"At least you can't say we don't have variety in our day, come on," Blake replied before stepping out of the car and wandering over towards the entrance with Alison following close behind.

He pressed the intercom button on a metal plate that displayed the numbers zero to nine. After a few seconds, a crackly voice answered.

"I'm here to see Mr George Harding," Blake said.

"Who?"

"George Harding."

"Then you need to call his room number."

"Look, I work for Special Branch, London, we have a few questions for Mr Harding."

At that moment, Blake noticed a man wearing white jeans, a white shirt and a straw hat approaching the glass entrance door. He pressed a green button on a display panel on the inside before opening the door.

"Do you have any ID?" he asked.

Blake showed him his ID.

"And hers?"

Alison sighed before pulling her ID out of her jeans pocket.

The man studied it for a moment before handing it back to her. "You look different."

"So did you six years ago," Alison quipped.

"Can we see Mr Harding now?" Blake sighed.

"Yes, yes, come in. You can't be too careful these days. Can I get you both to sign into the visitors book and then I'll take you up to him."

Blake and Alison both signed their names into the visitors book before following the man in white upstairs. After negotiating a maze of corridors, they eventually arrived at room thirty-three. They could hear the sound of horse racing commentary coming from inside. The man in white gently knocked on the door and waited. They heard someone shouting amongst the ferocious horse racing commentary as the race reached its conclusion, but nobody came towards the door. The man in white knocked again. Still no response. Blake moved forward and knocked loudly on the door.

"You can't hit these doors that hard, they break very easily," the man in white protested.

At that moment, they heard a latch being unlocked before the door opened and a grey haired man dressed in a white vest and beige trousers was standing there.

"No need to break the door down Ernie, I heard ya the first time!" George Harding said as he looked at Blake and Alison. "Who are these two?"

"Mr Harding, I'm Blake Langford and this is my colleague Alison Pearce, we need to ask you a few questions," Blake replied.

"Well you'd better hurry up, I've got thirty quid on the next race at Newbury," George replied as he turned and headed back inside his apartment.

Alison and Blake followed him in.

"If you need anything..." Ernie began.

"We won't," Blake replied before closing the door on him.

"Where's your dog Mr Harding?" Alison asked as she sat down on the armchair next to his sofa which had a half eaten packet of cheese and onion crisps and two empty cans of coke strewn across.

"Spike's downstairs with Maud. Her and Vic get a bit lonely so I let them look after him when I watch the racing. Made two hundred already today. If this one comes in I'll have enough for that new halogen heater I've been wanting to buy for a good while."

"Mr Harding, when you made your rather gruesome discovery, what were you doing in East Boldre cemetery late at night especially on Halloween?"

"I went to tend my late wife's grave and took Spike for a walk and lost track of time. The bloody mutt ran off and when I found him, he'd discovered the hand sticking outta the grave."

"And what did you do when you saw it?"

"I thought it was some kids playing silly buggers so I went over and grabbed hold of it."

"You grabbed hold of the hand?" Alison asked.

"Yeah, I thought some silly sods had left it there as some kind of sick joke."

"And what happened when you discovered it was real?"

"I put Spike back on the lead and we walked back down the road to the old phone box on the corner and called the police," George replied.

"You don't have a mobile phone?" Alison asked.

"Oh, that bloody thing," George replied, pointing to an old mobile phone on the coffee table. "It keeps bloody losing signal and turning itself off. Even when you try and text someone, it changes the word you type and you have to do it again and again until it gets it right. Tried to tell someone about the duck I saw at the pond the other day and almost got myself into all kinds of trouble. Modern technology is bloody crap these days."

"Did you notice anyone else around whilst you were waiting for the police?" Blake asked.

"No, I told the police officer all of this. Why are you rehashing it all again?"

"Did you tell them that you touched the hand?" Blake pushed.

George paused for a minute. "Come to think of it, no. No, I didn't. Oh Christ, they're gonna think I bloody killed her ain't they!"

"Not if you explain what happened," Alison tried to calm him down.

"It felt warm," George sighed as he leant back on the sofa.

"Warm?" Blake asked. "On Friday night it was raining and cold. Are you saying that she might have still been alive when you grabbed her hand?"

George began to shake and he brought his hands up to his mouth. "Oh my God, I killed her. I killed the poor girl."

"No, you didn't. The people who buried her there killed her," Alison replied. "You found her and with your help, we're going to make sure that whoever did this to her will go to jail for a long time."

At that moment, someone knocked at the front door. Blake wandered over and opened it.

"Oh, you're not George," an elderly man with white hair and a goatee said as a cocker spaniel bounded inside.

"No, you must be Vic," Blake replied.

"Yes, how did..."

"George told us all about you. May I ask you a few questions?" Blake asked.

Vic looked closely at Blake before answering. "Are you the police?"

"Kind of. I wanted to ask you about what happened to George on Friday night and also about Emily Langford."

Vic glared at him. "What about Emily? She has nothing to do with this!"

Blake closed the door behind him leaving Alison and George inside the apartment. Vic's eyes widened as Blake reached inside his jacket pocket.

"What are you doing?" Vic asked nervously.

"You met my son, Michael Langford, a few months ago," Blake replied as he showed Vic the photograph from Emily's safety deposit box. "I'd like to know who this man in the photo is."

A realisation crossed Victor's face. "Blake Langford?"

Blake nodded.

"Not here, come with me," Vic replied as he led Blake down the corridor and down a flight of stairs before stopping at room twenty-one.

Vic fumbled with the key before finally managing to open the door and leading them inside. Blake closed the door behind them as Vic stood in his kitchen. Blake noticed that the apartment was surprisingly spotless and the smell of disinfectant and bleach hung in the air.

"Expecting someone?" Blake inquired.

"I always thought that death would bring a familiar face back into my life. I just didn't think it would be my nephew's," Vic replied.

"I only have one uncle and he lives in Greece."

"Your grandmother had five children Blake. Edith, myself, Evelyn, Emily and James. One with Gerald Wise, one with William Handanowicz and three with Jack Smith. Unfortunately, Emily, Evelyn and I were cursed to be the bastards of the family. I'm just thankful that William stood beside mother in the end. Not many self-made men in those days would have taken on that kind of responsibility but he loved her dearly."

Blake froze. How did this man know about Edith and Evelyn and why had his mother never told him about her older brother? "That's not possible. The war. Gerald Wise was killed fighting in world war two. William Handanowicz is my grandad. He was Emily and Jim's father. And who is Jack Smith?"

"Jack Smith was my father. He was also Evelyn and Emily's father. Your grandmother had two flings with him at opposite ends of the war. I guess she must have loved him or he gave her a bit of excitement that she craved. He is the man in the photo. Take a seat," Vic replied as he wandered over towards a small dining table and sat down on one of the chairs.

"That's not possible. William Handanowicz was my grandad," Blake replied as he pulled out the opposite chair and sat down.

"I was given up for adoption just after I was born in 1940. You have to remember Blake that the war was going on. Your grandmother worked as a nurse helping the war wounded when they came back from battle minus limbs and whatever else had happened to them. Gerald Wise was killed early-on in the war leading my mother, Dana Wise, your grandmother, to send me away for mine and her own safety. It was a different time back then. Things were not as socially accepted as they are these days. If it ever came out that I was her bastard child after Gerald had been killed, she would have been cast aside. A leper. Damaged goods. Being a widow with her legitimate daughter by her side gave her a chance within the community."

"How do you know all of this? You were only a baby when all of this was going on."

"In 1967, I finally met my biological mother, your grandmother, Dana Handanowicz. She told me everything. I was made to stay away from the rest of the family but back in January 2000, I received a letter from Emily Langford, your mother. We began regularly writing to each other from then until the day she died."

Blake shook his head in disbelief. His mother had kept this secret all of her life and he had never known any of this. "So what happened during the war?"

"Your grandmother met a man who had been brought into her care suffering from what they called "shell shock" back then. His name was Jack Smith. She cared for him and helped him back to full health. Knowing that her husband, my father, was dead, my guess is that they ended up having a relationship."

"Why would she have risked being a social outcast back then? Surely any sexual relationship outside of wedlock was frowned upon."

"We're all human Blake. In our younger years we don't always make the right decisions. One night stands were still a thing back in the forties, it just wasn't in the public knowledge as it is these days."

"So, she gave you up but then fell pregnant again with Jack's child, my mother."

Vic nodded. "Children, not child Blake. Your mother had a twin sister called Evelyn. William Handanowicz married Dana Wise knowing that the children she carried were not his."

"So he was my step grandfather and nobody knew. What happened to Jack Smith?"

"He died of tuberculosis. His body was found on Calshot Beach in the summer of 1948."

"Found? Did he just collapse on the beach?" Blake asked.

"Your grandfather, Edward Langford, was the DCI in charge of the case. He managed to piece together who Jack Smith was from a railway ticket found in his pocket on the day he died."

"How do you know all of this?"

Vic stood up from his chair and opened up the top drawer of a metal filing cabinet that was in the corner of the room. He pulled out an A4 ring binder folder that was full of plastic wallets containing handwritten letters. Blake felt a lump in his throat as he recognised his mother's handwriting when Vic opened up the folder.

"Your Mother told me everything," Vic said as he sat back down.

He turned to the back of the folder and in the last plastic wallet was a small blue envelope. Vic removed the envelope from the plastic wallet and handed it to Blake. Blake opened the envelope and removed a letter from inside it. It read;

Dearest Victor,

I feel my time is near and I must pass the burden of truth to you. The Smith secret is safe in Lindos but I fear Dana may yet have a part to play. Jade will leave a white carnation on the grave of the unknown soldier if the secret is out. Only then must you contact Blake. He will know what to do.

May God help us all.

Emily

Blake laid the letter on the table and looked at Victor. "When I came here, you said that you thought death would have a familiar face but not mine. What did you mean by that?"

"Jack Smith was injured during the war and was medically evacuated but that's not the whole story. In 1938, a bank was robbed in Portsmouth city centre. The thieves got away with over three-hundred-thousand pounds worth of gold. After two years of searching, the bank wrote off the gold. Around the same time, a Mr J. Smith was medically evacuated from the front line and disappeared. His last recorded sighting was at a manor house in The New Forest called Holbury Manor. The nurses there assisted with the rehabilitation of soldiers returning from the war. Many people have suspected that the Smith family money is still out there somewhere and they will do anything to uncover its location."

"I gave up looking for buried treasure when I left school. If the money was there, someone would have claimed it by now."

"Your mother seemed to think that James knew where it was located."

"Then he would have spent it by now. Uncle Jim led my father to lose several thousands of pounds on a dodgy investment and when it all went pear shaped, Jim ran off to Greece with the remaining money."

"Blake, there are still people out there that would kill for this money. It's in my family line and it's in yours. Whoever is going after this will know that and it will turn both families into targets."

"How much money are we talking about?"

"Like I said, in 1938, it was estimated to be around three-hundred-thousand pounds in value."

"So, with the rate of inflation, in today's money, it's got to be worth..."

"Over eleven million pounds," Vic finished for him.

Blake took a moment to let it sink in. He struggled to comprehend that his mother would keep this from him and then send him this letter via Victor after she had died.

"In the letter, she said about the grave of the unknown soldier. Was that the grave that George stumbled upon?"

"No, the unknown soldier's resting place is in the shadow of All Saints Church in Dibden, a few miles from here. No one can be certain but it is the suspected resting place of Jack Smith."

"What's stopped you from pursuing this for yourself?" Blake asked.

"I'm an old man Blake. I live a simple life. I have no need for money or possessions anymore."

"What about the rest of your family?"

"My daughter Anne and her husband died in a motorbike accident three years ago and my granddaughters don't come anywhere near me anymore."

"And what about Evelyn?"

Victor looked at him. "You don't know, do you?"

"Know what?"

"Evelyn disappeared on the same day your parents got married. That's why she was wiped from the family memory. There were very few photographs and everyone wanted to forget she ever existed."

Blake bowed his head. "I'm sorry, I only found out about Evelyn after doing some digging through the obituaries this morning."

"That's not a surprise. There was a huge fallout just before your parents wedding in 1977. Evelyn and Frederick left the church and then there was the accident."

"When Dad's brother Fred died?"

Vic nodded. "Nobody knew what really happened but she just disappeared and never spoke to the family again."

"How did Dad fail to find her? He was the police sergeant at the time. There must have been a lot of unanswered questions!"

"He knew what happened but he let her run rather than face the consequences over what happened."

"But there was a chance that she was involved in his brother's death!"

"Not everything is that cut-and-dry Blake. You know that. Remember, she was also your mother's twin sister."

Blake ran his fingers through his hair. "Wait, let me get this straight, Grandma Dana had my mother Emily and Evelyn as twins and Grandma Mavis had my aunt Mary and uncle Fred as twins at opposite ends of the war. That's a massive coincidence."

"Especially as all four of them shared the same father," Vic replied.

"What?"

"Emily and Evelyn were born in 1949. Fred and Mary were only eighteen months older than your father, John Langford who was born in 1939."

"Are you saying both Dana and Mavis had affairs with the same man? Jack Smith?"

"It seems to be that way, yes."

Blake looked at the photo again before turning back to Victor. "That photo seems to show that both of my grandmothers on the Handanowicz and Langford sides were friends in 1948. My father, John, would have only been eight years old by then and Mum wouldn't have been born. Dad was thirty-seven when they married. Mum was only twenty-nine. The two families were somehow connected for over thirty years before then," Blake reflected, shaking his head in frustration. "There has to be a connection and everything is pointing to Jack Smith."

Vic bowed his head. "You have to remember that technology was nowhere near as advanced as it was today and I may be completely wrong with this but I'm going to say it anyway."

Blake looked into Victor's eyes. "You know the real reason why Evelyn disappeared after Fred died don't you?"

Vic nodded. "They were beginning to have a relationship together until..."

"Until what?"

"This is all hearsay as it was never proven at the time and I guess now we'll never know."

"Know what?"

"They discovered that they had the same father."

Blake sat back in his chair trying to process everything that Victor was telling him. What were the odds of one man having twins with two different women eight years apart? Pretty slim even with today's technology. "This can't be right."

"I've questioned it all myself thousands of times."

"All of my grandparents were cremated so there's no way to prove it either way so all of this could just be a wild goose chase."

"If you believed that, you wouldn't have come here to see me today. Your mother sent you a message from the grave Blake. She wanted you to figure out who Jack Smith was and how he links back to you today. There are a lot of people who know about the Jack Smith legacy. They will stop at nothing to get their hands on it. This is your family's genuine birthright. The Handanowicz and Langford families combined."

Blake pondered that. "I guess we'll never know because Dana and William Handanowicz were both cremated over twenty years ago."

"William was."

Blake looked at him. "On the obituary, Dana Handanowicz, my grandmother's file showed, burial site, unknown. I remember being at my grandparents house after her funeral as a child with my brother and sister because Steven ended up in hospital after hitting his head on the fireplace."

"Dana Handanowicz was not cremated on that day. She had a separate funeral with the Smith/Wise side of the family and was buried in East Boldre cemetery in The New Forest."

Blake shook his head. "No, no, that's wrong..."

Victor didn't reply.

"Then who the hell did we cremate in 1984?" Blake snapped.

"I don't know," Vic replied. "If you find that out, you may find the missing piece of the puzzle."

At that moment, a knock at the door interrupted them. Victor wandered over and answered it. After some muffled conversation, Alison walked through into the kitchen area where Blake was sitting at the table.

"Everything okay?" Alison asked.

"Just another line of inquiry but I think we're done here," Blake replied.

"You'll have to forgive ol' George, he is one for the melodrama," Vic chuckled.

"Thank you for your time Mr Wise, I'll be in touch," Blake replied as he shook Victor's hand.

"Be careful Blake, they know you're coming," Vic replied as they headed towards the door.

Just as Victor was about to close the door, Blake turned to face him again.

"One more thing," Blake asked.

Victor looked at him.

"Who are your two granddaughters?"

"You'll never get anything out of them."

"But I may be able to protect them."

Victor sighed. "Jade Lucy and Andrea Louise."

"Jade and Andrea Wise?" Blake asked.

"No, Smith," Victor replied before closing the door.

Alison looked at Blake. "He doesn't know?"

"No, and for now he doesn't need to," Blake replied as they walked away.

"If she's his granddaughter, he has a right to know. It's only a matter of time before it all comes out anyway."

"I think I may have found the link to all of this but we need to speak to the undertakers first."

"Joe came up with nothing from them."

"But I may have an angle that Joe didn't," Blake replied as he climbed back into his car.

Alison joined him in the passenger seat. "And what angle is that?"

"That grave that Andrea Smith's body was found in may belong to my grandmother."

Alison looked at him. "What? How?"

"That's what I need to find out, let's go."

Chapter Forty-Seven

Forgive Me Father For I Have Sinned
Sunday 22nd August 1948

"Lovely service Vicar, much obliged," one of the parishioners said as she left St David's Church in Lepe.

"You're most welcome Mrs Brown," Harold Partridge, the local vicar replied.

Mavis Langford hurriedly walked up the stone path towards the entrance of the church.

The vicar noticed her heading towards him. "Ah, Mrs Langford, I thought I missed you at morning worship, is everything all right?" he asked.

"Please Vicar, I don't have much time. I need to confess to you to help myself get past this awful tragedy."

Harold looked at her for a moment. He had always looked out for Mavis and seeing her in such a muddle gave him cause for concern. He nodded. "I'll meet you there in ten minutes."

Mavis rushed into the church whilst Harold continued to say goodbye to the remaining parishoners as they continued on their way out of the church. After the last parishioner had left, Harold closed the doors of the church and walked over towards the confessional box. He sat in his seat and took a deep breath. Thoughts flooded his mind. What on Earth could have made Mavis so worried that she needed to speak to him so urgently? He carefully removed the wooden slate on the wall next to him and through a wire mesh window, he saw her sat in the opposite side of the confessional box, her hands shaking on her lap.

"Forgive me Father for I have sinned," she started, her voice shaking with emotion.

"May God grant you forgiveness and peace," Harold replied.

"I don't think what I have done will find forgiveness, Father."

Harold waited a moment until she was ready to continue.

"I fear I may have contributed to the death of my friend."

Harold took a deep breath. "In what way do you think you contributed?"

"There was a gent who visited us yesterday. Someone who I thought I would never see again."

"An old friend?"

"No, no, just… Just someone I used to know," Mavis sighed.

"Someone from the village?"

"He was brought to our medical tent during the first attacks eight years ago."

Harold bowed his head. "When the bombings started at the beginning of the war."

"Yes, he had a broken arm and was struggling to focus on anything. The nurses thought he suffered shell-shock. He was in our care for six months before disappearing."

"Did he go back into battle?"

"Nobody knows. I never saw him again until yesterday."

"What happened yesterday?"

"We all had luncheon out on the beach. The sun was shining and the children were playing in the sand. Everything felt like it was going to be all right again until he showed up."

"What did he do?" Harold asked.

"He pretended to be someone else."

"Why would he do that?"

"He must have realised that Ed would work it out. He's a police detective, not much gets past him."

"And yet he failed to notice this man was not who he claimed to be."

"Dana and I covered it up well."

"Why would you not want your husband to know who this man really was?"

"My husband is a good man, Father... I never... I never meant to do it but... Oh dear Lord, what am I saying?"

"Take your time," Harold reassured her.

"He was such a strong, friendly character and we were out in the tents everyday trying to help. Our children were kept in bunkers, watched over by a select few who couldn't wrap bandages or were sick at the sight of blood. It was a silly, stupid mistake..."

Harold didn't respond.

"You understand that, don't you, Father? We didn't know if our husbands would make it back or not. It was a difficult time for us all."

"The Lord has no judgement Mrs Langford. If you have sinned then you have the right to repent."

"I don't want my sins to flow down to my children, Father. They are innocent. They love Ed so much. He is their father in almost every sense of the word."

"If you confess your sins before God, He will guide you on the path to righteousness upon hearing your confession."

"But will he forgive adultery, Father?"

Harold took a deep breath. "Is this your confession Mrs Langford?"

"I was weak. I know I shouldn't have been but Edward had been gone for weeks. We never knew if we would survive and..."

Harold waited.

"It just happened and now I have to live with the consequences. I have the reminder everyday of what I've done and I can't even begin to tell Edward what happened. I'm so ashamed, Father."

"You should not torture yourself Mrs Langford. The start of the war was a trying time for us all. If you can admit and repent for your sins, God will grant you his forgiveness. Let yourself be free of this burden and ensure that you never sin again."

"But how can I look into my children's eyes and tell them their father is dead?"

Harold paused for a moment. "Edward Langford has died?"

"No, Jack Smith is dead. He is Mary and Fred's father," Mavis admitted.

They both sat in an uncomfortable silence for a moment before Harold finally spoke again.

"Are you sure Edward Langford is not their father? Could you have become pregnant before he left for the war?"

Mavis sobbed. "I've worked out the dates, the twins were born exactly nine months after Jack and I..."

Harold nodded. "Do you believe that your secret has been discovered and that is why Mr Smith has died?"

"I... I don't know. He looked ill yesterday. Very pale and sweaty."

"It was a hot summer's day yesterday, Mrs Langford. Did he have any health problems?"

"He claimed that the doctor had told him that he had tuberculosis and that there was no cure. He said that he wanted to see me one last time before he died."

"Did you tell him that he was the father of two of your children?"

"Of course not."

"Why?"

"It was none of his business."

"It is if it was ever proven that he was their father."

Mavis shook her head. "I shouldn't have come here, I'm sorry."

"Mrs Langford, I'm sorry, I didn't mean to pry," Harold replied.

Mavis sighed deeply. "I made a stupid mistake, Father, and because of that, he came back to Lepe and lost his life."

"He would have died anyway without the right medical care. At least you were able to give him some kind of closure before he passed on. If you truly repent your sins and ensure that from this day forward, you will never sin again, you may find forgiveness in the love of God."

"And if he was murdered because of our secret?"

"That is not for us to judge unless you were the one who ended his life. If that proves to be true then you need to be honest with your husband. He is a good detective and he will find out the truth one way or another."

Mavis thought about that for a moment before stepping out of the confessional booth. Harold followed her back towards the nave of the church. They both knelt before the cross and said a silent prayer together before heading for the exit. As Harold opened the door, Detective Edward Langford and Sergeant Peter Hastings approached the church.

"Mavis, what are you doing here? Who's looking after the children?" Edward asked.

"After everything that happened this morning I missed morning worship so I came down to say a few prayers with Father Partridge before picking up some bread and oats whilst Frances from Thyme Cottage next door is watching over them for me. What are you doing here?"

"Just continuing our inquiries into the fire and the man on the beach. Frances? Is that Arthur and Iris' daughter? The one with the mole on her chin. She's only just finished school!"

"She's seventeen Ed, I was running the family home at that age. I'm on my way home now. Good day Father," Mavis snapped before walking away.

Harold watched her leave momentarily before turning his attention to Edward and Peter. "What can I do for you both?"

"What was the real reason she was here?" Edward asked.

"She came to say a few prayers at the altar, just like she said, Mr Langford. It's such a terrible thing isn't it?"

"What is?" Peter asked.

"Well, the house fire… Everyone is talking about it," Harold stammered.

"News travels fast. What else are they talking about?" Edward asked.

"I'm not at liberty to say."

"Why don't we step inside and have a conversation about it," Edward replied as he walked into the church with Peter and Harold following closely behind.

"You must hear a lot of things in your confessional Father," Peter began.

"Anything that is shared before the presence of God shall be kept within the confessional. I have taken a vow of trust…"

"And I've taken a vow to keep the people of this village safe! I have a suspected arson attack on a friend's house and a potential murder victim on our local beach so if you know anything about either of them, I'd be glad to hear it," Edward replied.

"Can you tell us your whereabouts yesterday evening, Father Partridge?" Peter Hastings asked.

"I was here until around four o'clock and then I went to visit Jim Gibbs. He's recently had a few health problems and I dropped off a basket of fruit to him and his family."

"And where did you go from there?"

"After that I walked down the old Lepe Road as I was going to visit Sheila and Derek Johnson at Sundial House."

"You said you were going to see them. Did you?"

"No, I saw a gent in a brown suit and yellow shirt wandering down the road. I don't think he was local. He was leaving Honeypot House and took the old dirt path through the woods up towards the shops."

"Did you follow him?" Edward asked.

"Yes, he went into Tom Allan's fruit and veg shop."

"And then what?" Peter asked.

"He disappeared."

"What do you mean he disappeared? He must have gone somewhere."

"I waited for a few minutes and then I carried on my way back here."

"Were you suspicious of him?"

"You can't be too careful these days."

"Meaning?"

"The war changed a lot of people."

"So, after he went into Tom Allan's fruit and veg shop, you never saw him again."

Harold shook his head.

"Did you go back to Mr and Mrs Johnson's house after your detour?" Edward asked.

"No."

"Why not?"

"I changed my mind. It was getting late and I wanted to get some tea before having an early night."

Edward and Peter looked at each other seemingly satisfied with Harold's explanation of events.

"If you think of anything else, please give the station a call," Edward said before heading towards the door with Peter Hastings following closely behind him.

Harold released a breath he hadn't realised that he was holding as they walked away.

"Oh, one last thing, Father," Peter said as he arrived at the door.

Harold looked at him warily.

"Have you heard about anyone camping out in the cafe on Calshot Beach recently?" Peter asked.

"Norman's old cafe?"

Peter nodded.

"No, nothing. Isn't that meant to be closed down? Norman hasn't reopened since the war. Why?"

"Just a thought, good day, Father," Peter replied before following Edward Langford out of the door.

Harold rushed into his vestry and watched as Edward and Peter walked down the path towards the church gate. He knew he needed to keep the vow of his confessional to God but his hands began to shake uncontrollably as he thought about the events of the past 24 hours. He knew he needed to be careful who he spoke to. One wrong word could open up a lot of secrets that a lot of people would rather keep hidden.

As Edward and Peter arrived back at their patrol car, Peter unlocked the drivers door and climbed inside before leaning across to unlock the passenger door. Edward sat alongside him and closed the door.

"Do you trust him?" Peter asked.

"Do you?"

"He seemed nervous."

"I know."

"Do you think Mavis had something to do with it?"

"To do with what?"

"His nerves. I've seen better liars in the courthouse."

"I don't know. Why would he follow a gent that he'd never met before towards the shop and then not even speak to him or follow him into the shop?" Edward asked.

"You know how nosey some of the locals can be, Sir. You only have to change your hairstyle and the whole village knows about it."

"You're right Hastings, maybe I'm overthinking it. Let's call it a day, hopefully tomorrow will give us a better idea of what's happening."

Peter started the car and drove away from the church and down the Lepe Road towards Edward Langford's house. As the car disappeared out of sight, a man wearing black trousers and a white shirt stepped out from an alley behind two houses that were on the opposite side of the road from the church. He walked up the pathway and knocked on the church door. After a couple of minutes, Harold opened the door.

"Hello Father Partridge," the man smiled.

"Officer Wells, George," Harold smiled. "I've already spoken to your superior. I've got nothing more to say."

"Forgive me Father for I have sinned," Officer George Wells replied before pushing past Harold and closing the door behind him.

Chapter Forty-Eight

Dana Handanowicz
Sunday 2nd November 2008

Blake Langford knocked on the front door of Crowther's Funeral Services on Sunday evening. A man dressed in a white shirt with a black waistcoat, black trousers and polished black shoes answered the door.

"We're closed, nobody's here," he said as he opened the door ajar.

Blake flashed his ID. "Blake Langford, Special Branch, London, is your boss here?"

"I told you, no one's here. Come back tomorrow."

Blake put his foot in the way of the door to stop the man from closing it. "I'm sorry, I didn't catch your name Mr..."

"No, you didn't," the man snapped.

"Well, Mr "No, you didn't," if I need to file a report that you have obstructed an investigation into your funeral home, I'm sure that would be a major problem for the locals looking for an honest and reputable funeral director to assist them in their time of grief. Do yourself a favour and open the fucking door."

The man looked over Blake's shoulder at Alison before letting out a sigh and opening the door.

"There you are, it's amazing what you can do when you try," Blake smiled as he entered the funeral home with Alison following close behind.

"What do you want?" the man asked as he closed the door behind them.

"The unmarked grave at East Boldre cemetery," Alison began.

"There's several..."

"The one that had the arm of a young woman sticking out of it on Friday night!" Blake snapped.

"We had nothing to do with it!"

"I'm sorry, Mr..." Alison began.

"Anderson, Chris Anderson," the man replied.

"Mr Anderson, our investigation shows that your company was the funeral director when the grave was originally occupied in 1984. Is that correct?" Alison asked.

"If you say so."

"Can you check for us please?" Blake asked.

Chris walked over and turned on a desktop computer in the corner of the room. After tapping on a few keys, he brought up the record.

"It seems that the original owner of the plot, Miss Patricia Smith, is no longer active so we need to follow the family line. She had a sister Dorothy, who is deceased so the next in line would be her daughter, Jade Smith of Arlington Grove in Ealing, West London. She's the person you need to speak to regarding the identity of the deceased as she still has seventy-six years on the plot," Chris explained.

"Mr Anderson, can I ask you, if for argument's sake, the arm of that young girl who had been buried alive in one of your graves happened to be your own daughter, or your own sister or mother, what would you do if an undertaker was pulling your chain rather than helping the investigating team solve the case?" Blake asked.

"I would make sure that I followed the relevant channels correctly and not display threatening behaviour towards the one person that could potentially help me solve the case," Chris smirked.

Blake approached the desk but Alison stood in his way.

"Let's go," she said as she ushered Blake towards the door. "Thank you for your help Mr Anderson."

Chris Anderson watched them leave before pulling his phone out of his pocket and typing out a text message. He looked out of the window and watched Blake's Ford Mondeo kick up some of the gravel at the front of the funeral home before sending the message. He looked out at the traffic on the main road for a moment before heading back over to the desk. He opened the report once again before deleting the file and closing the PC down. He waited for the screen to turn black before picking up his coat and heading out of the door.

***

"You know the one thing I hate about this job..." Blake complained as they headed back towards his home at Lepe Beach.

"The wonderful travel opportunities it presents?" Alison smirked.

Blake half smiled. "Some bureaucratic jobsworth who thinks he's being clever by impeding an investigation by using the red tape to his advantage. Client data protection crap, what a load of..."

"Okay, I get it, he's being a dick but not everything gets sorted out with fighting either," Alison countered.

"I guess you're right. Did you get much out of George Harding?"

"Apart from the winning horse at Newbury this afternoon, not much. Took his dog out for a walk, discovered a dead body and called the police. No idea who the grave belonged to or who Andrea was. Seems to be someone who just keeps himself to himself and doesn't want any fuss."

"They're usually the ones you need to watch out for."

"What about you? Did the other guy tell you much?" Alison asked.

"A lot more than I ever expected," Blake replied as he told Alison about his conversation with Victor.

As they arrived outside Blake's family home at Lepe Beach, his phone lit up with Joe Knight's number displayed on the screen. Blake turned off the ignition and answered the call.

"We have a breakthrough!" Joe said as Blake answered.

"So have we. The grave seems to be registered to Jade Smith," Blake replied.

"Correct but I've managed to dig through the paperwork, unofficially of course, and it's brought up something interesting. The occupier of that grave was thought to have been cremated by the family and in 1984 with the ashes scattered in the memorial garden in South Kensington. However, there was a rift between the families and a Miss Patricia Smith and Mrs Dorothy Farlington paid Leonard Crowther of Crowther's Funeral Services a substantial amount of money to have the body transported to The New Forest and have her buried in that unmarked plot."

"If they were so hell bent on having the body in the cemetery in East Boldre then why not have the gravestone memorial too?" Blake asked.

"No one except for certain members of the immediate family were meant to know of the location of the grave."

"So they paid Leonard Crowther for the anonymity," Alison added.

"Precisely."

"Who is the body in the grave Joe?" Blake asked.

"Dana Sylvia Handanowicz, died 17th April 1984," Joe replied.

Blake felt a shiver run through his body. "No, it can't be!"

"I've got the paperwork right in front of me."

"There has to be some mistake."

"The only way to be sure is to exhume the body and take DNA tests with her surviving relatives but so far, Jade Smith has been unresponsive."

"She's not Dana Handanowicz's relative."

"The paperwork claims that Dana would be her aunt," Joe replied. "What makes you so sure that she isn't?"

"Because Dana Handanowicz is my grandmother. She was Emily Langford's mother," Blake replied.

At that moment, Alison's phone rang. She pulled it out of her pocket and saw a coded message from Special Branch.

"We'll call you back," Alison said as she cut off Blake's phone and answered her own phone.

"Scrambler D, F, Twenty-Seven, Nine, G," she said into her phone.

The screen flickered pink and grey before connecting to a secure line.

"Alison, is Blake with you?" Eric Gordon asked.

"I'm right here," Blake replied.

"I need you both on the first plane out of Gatwick tomorrow morning flying to Diagoras in Rhodes."

"With all due respect Sir, we may have had a breakthrough in the East Boldre graveyard case," Blake replied.

"Samir and Joe can hold it until you come back. There was a mass shooting at a villa near Monolithos this evening. Greek authorities seem to believe that they were targeting one of the patients from a mental health facility called Kolopsia House until someone gunned them down."

"Do they know who the gunmen were?" Alison asked.

"Zachary Zhal and Ian Bleeker."

Blake looked at Alison in disbelief. Zachary Zhal, better known as Zodiac and Ian Bleeker, better known as Reaper, had escaped after an attempt to traffick young students out of London and into Europe was intercepted by Blake and his team.

"That can't be a coincidence," Blake replied.

"No, and neither are the others involved which is why you need to head out to Rhodes as soon as possible. One of the people involved who the Greek authorities arrested asked specifically for your help."

"Who was the person involved and who were Zodiac and Reaper targeting?" Blake asked.

"The patient was Evelyn Joan Handanowicz and the person protecting her was her brother, James William Handanowicz."

Blake couldn't believe what he was hearing. The Handanowicz family had suddenly reappeared from all angles and now it seemed that they had somehow become involved in a criminal organisation.

"Are you still there Blake?" Eric Gordon asked.

"We're here," Alison replied for him. "We'll be at Gatwick first thing in the morning."

"Angela will send over the details. This body in the cemetery seems to hold the key to all of this. You need to tread carefully as there is no telling how deep this organisation is involved and we can't let the media get hold of any more than they already have," Eric Gordon replied.

"Agreed, thank you Sir," Alison replied before ending the call.

She turned to Blake. "We need to start figuring out what the hell happened in your family's past."

Blake nodded.

"What relation are Evelyn and James Handanowicz to you?" Alison asked.

"They are my mother's brother and sister. I've never met Evelyn as she disappeared in 1977. James took a loan off of my father in 1984 to help set up a hospice, I guess you could call it, to help people with mental health difficulties. Obviously, back then, it wasn't as widely talked about as it is today but Dad saw that Uncle Jim wanted to make a difference and gave him fifty-thousand pounds to set it up."

"Then what happened?"

"I was only a child when it all went down but for some reason, he couldn't get the hospice or the support that he needed so he abandoned the idea. When Dad asked for his money back, Jim fobbed him off until Dad and another police officer turned up at Jim's home to collect the money. When they entered, they realised that he had disappeared and Dad discovered that he had flown out to Athens the day before. They never spoke or saw each other again."

"I'm sorry."

"For what? Dad learnt a big lesson that sometimes your family can screw you over more than your enemies. He was advised not to give Jim the money but he did it anyway."

"Did it affect your parent's marriage?"

"I guess so. Dad was a lot more guarded around financial matters and anytime Mum wanted us to spend time with anyone on her side of the family, he would always have other plans so he never had to socialise with them as often."

"So when Paula gave her father that money, you saw history repeating itself?" Alison asked.

"You can't hold a grudge with someone just because they were blinded by their love for a relative can you? Jim put a wedge between my parents and their relationship. I'm not going to let Graham Evans do that with mine and Paula's."

At that moment, the outside light turned on by the front door and they noticed Paula standing in the doorway.

"Come on, let's go in. I have a feeling tomorrow is going to be a long day," Blake sighed as he stepped out of the car and headed towards the house with Alison following close behind.

***

It was getting late and Jenny Langford was still picking through the remaining debris of her parent's house at 124 Alfredson Road, Kensington by torch light. She found an old red and grey metal case that contained some paperwork. The lid had buckled in the explosion but somehow, the contents were undamaged.

As she searched through the paperwork, she found some old solicitors letters, some handwritten letters still in their opened envelopes, tied together with string and an old photo album. As she sifted through them, she couldn't help but feel a sense of intrigue. These were fragments of her family's history, pieces of a puzzle she had never known existed. One particular letter caught her attention. It was addressed to her late grandfather, William Handanowicz, dated decades ago. Jenny's heart quickened as she read its contents, a plea for help from someone named Evelyn Handanowicz. The letter spoke of danger and an impending threat to their family.

Realising the significance of her discovery, Jenny decided to dig deeper into her family's past. With each photograph and letter, a clearer picture emerged. The story unfolded like a gripping tale of secrecy and betrayal. She learned that Evelyn Handanowicz, her aunt, had disappeared in 1977. She had uncovered something dangerous, something that powerful people sought to keep hidden. But what was it? What was the big secret?

She opened an A4 brown envelope and pulled out a sheet of paper that had turned yellow over time. As she read the print on it, things began to fall into place. She had found the death certificate of Jack Walter Smith, who died August 23rd 1948. The same day the photo that her mother, Emily, had left in the safe deposit box had been taken. Whatever secrets were hidden in these letters and photos, Jenny was convinced that Jack Smith was the one who linked it all together.

As she collected up her things, she heard the metal front door creak open and clank against the remains of the hallway downstairs. Jenny froze. She knew she shouldn't have been in the building whilst it was still unstable but something in her gut told her that whoever had just entered the house shouldn't have been there either. She placed her hand over her torch giving her just enough light to see where she was walking but not enough to give away that she was there. Her senses were going into overdrive. She heard footsteps as someone walked through the debris downstairs. A drawer opened followed by the rustling of some keys.

Jenny's heart raced as she strained to listen to the sounds below. Who could be in her family's old house? And what were they looking for? She clutched the stack of letters and photographs tightly, her mind racing with possibilities. Her instincts told her to stay hidden, but curiosity compelled her to investigate further. She cautiously descended the creaking stairs, each step careful and deliberate. The beam of her torch pierced through the darkness, revealing a figure hunched over a dusty desk in what used to be her father's study.

As Jenny approached, she noticed the stranger rifling through papers and files. Their back was turned towards her, obscuring their face. She could hear laboured breathing, a mixture of excitement and urgency.

Determined not to let fear paralyse her, Jenny took a deep breath before stepping forward. "Who are you?" she demanded, her voice steady despite the adrenaline coursing through her veins.

The intruder froze, before slowly turning to face her.

Jenny gasped. "Jade?"

"Guilty as charged," Jade replied.

"What the hell are you doing searching through the remains of my family home?"

"The same thing as you. Looking for clues to the family secret."

"I don't understand, what is your interest in my family's past?"

Jade leant against the doorframe of the lounge. "Jack Smith."

"Who's Jack Smith?"

"The man who started this whole deception. Why do you think Tom was at that bar in Soho when you two got together? Why were your parents so against your relationship together? Why was your father so eager to cover up your involvement in Tom's misdemeanour with the Russian agent?"

Jenny thought back to ten years ago when her relationship with Tom came to an end. He had told her that he was in trouble and that he needed her to go to Salisbury to meet a Russian agent called Ivan Stepanchikov. Unbeknown to her, she had handed him a dossier containing the details of Tom's regiment's next assignment in Afghanistan. The regiment were ambushed and were all killed. Jenny was led to believe that Tom Gibson was amongst the dead until he returned to London six months ago.

"My father was a good man and a brilliant police detective. He did what he needed to do to protect his family!" Jenny replied.

"But he left one final detail out of that story."

"What?"

"Tom Gibson is your second cousin. Andrea and I are too," Jade admitted.

Jenny sat down on the arm of an ash covered armchair. "No, how? What are you talking about? You have no connection to my parents or grandparents. They never spoke of it."

"Jack Smith is our mutual great-grandfather. Your mother left clues. Photos, letters, none of it leads us to the location of the family's inheritance though."

"What inheritance? Tom destroyed this house! There's nothing left but a charred hollowed out shell!"

"Jack and his wife Ada robbed a bank in Portsmouth in 1938. They got away with the money and were never caught. All that we know is that it's buried somewhere in Hampshire. The map of where he hid the money was split into several pieces and hidden. If we can find the pieces of the map, we'll find the gold."

"Don't you think we're both too old for fairytales. Next you're going to tell me that a dashing prince is going to come along and sweep me off my feet and take me away to an enchanted land," Jenny replied.

"Both of our families have been keeping this secret for generations. Your mother has given you the opportunity to uncover the truth. Don't waste it Jen. There's people in the shadows willing to kill for it."

Jenny sighed. "Come with me to The New Forest tomorrow. We might be able to find out more there."

"So you believe me?"

"I don't know what or who to believe anymore but Blake and his team are dealing with a case in The New Forest and it could lead to helping us find out what the hell is going on."

"I received a letter and a phone call about a grave plot in East Boldre cemetery. I didn't even know anything about it," Jade admitted. "Apparently, they want to exhume the body for DNA testing and it belongs to a distant relative."

"Do you know who?"

"No, they won't tell me unless I actually go there in person."

"Meet me here tomorrow morning at 10am. We'll go down and see what we can find out."

Jade nodded. "I'm sorry."

"For what?"

"Intruding in your family home."

"Hopefully we can get some answers tomorrow," Jenny replied.

Jade smiled awkwardly before making her way through the debris and out of the front door. Jenny watched her leave. She felt bad for not telling her what she knew about her sister, Andrea's, whereabouts but deep down, she knew that Jade couldn't be trusted. She just hoped that when the coffin was exhumed from the unmarked grave in East Boldre cemetery, the identity of the body would give them some answers.

Chapter Forty-Nine

Secrets Of A Sinner

Sunday 22nd August 1948

Police Officer George Wells pushed past Father Harold Partridge and entered the church. Harold watched as the last couple of parishoners walked away towards the main road before closing and locking the church doors. As he walked back into the church, Officer Wells was standing in front of the altar.

"It is a tad unusual for a police officer to come to my confessional. I did not realise you were catholic," Harold said as he approached him.

"Let's cut the small talk Harold, we both know why I'm here."

"I'm not sure that I understand."

"The young men at Norman Whitehouse's Cafe on Calshot Beach."

"I know nothing about them."

"Indeed. I had an interesting conversation with one of them. His name was Maximillian Friedrich Ekkehard. Is this ringing any bells Father?" Officer Wells asked.

Harold bowed his head. "Weakness of the flesh is a sin that I am unfortunately guilty of."

"This is not a straightforward sin though is it Father? Are you aware of the Criminal Law Amendment Act of 1885? Any act of male to male sexual activity shall be seen as gross indecency! I should take you in and throw you into jail right now!"

"Then why won't you?"

"Because you can still be useful. You may have betrayed the trust of those young men but whilst Detective Langford is investigating the death of the man on the beach, it has cast a shadow on Norman's dealings with the Germans."

"Meaning what?"

"Langford and Hastings won't stop until they discover who that man really is and what connections he has to the area. If they attempt to blame the Germans for his death then it blows that case wide open."

"One of them is already making eyes with a young lady in the village. They're not exactly being discreet."

"Arthur King knows what to do. He's keeping a close watch on his daughter and Christoph knows what will happen if he steps out of line."

"So why do you care so much about these men?" Father Partridge asked.

"A fellow officer identified the man on the beach as Jack Walter Smith. He was a defector during the war. He helped those four men get into the country undetected and used the local women to ensure that he never went back into battle."

"If you know who the man is then you can close the case."

"My fellow officer knew Mr Smith before the war. He helped him rob a bank in Portsmouth ten years ago. Smith then ran off with the gold and no one heard from him again until he turned up injured in a hospital in Fareham in 1942."

Harold Partridge began making the connections in his mind after Mavis Langford's confession earlier but he said nothing.

"New money is coming into the area. Someone is buying Whitehouse out of the cafe. The men need somewhere safe to stay. I'm sure you can make room in your little cottage to accommodate them," Officer Wells continued.

"But, what if they are seen? What about my parishioners when they come to visit?"

"What would happen if your parishioners knew that you were having sexual activity with a young gent that has recently come to the area? I don't think they would ever trust you again and I have a big mouth Father."

Harold bowed his head. "Indeed."

"Cheer up Father, you still have your freedom," Officer Wells smiled before heading towards the door.

"You won't get away with this George. Sooner or later, fate will cross your path."

Officer Wells stopped by the door and looked back at him. "Yours too Father, yours too," he said before leaving the church.

***

Later that day, there was a loud knocking on the front door of Harold Partridge's cottage, a short walk away from St David's Church. He ignored it at first as he furiously rushed to pack a suitcase full of clothes, handkerchiefs, talcum powder, a comb, a notebook and a couple of pens. As the knocking became more intense, he made his way to the front door.

"Finally, I thought you'd never answer," Norman Whitehouse said as he entered and closed the door behind him. "We don't have much time."

"What do you mean?" Harold asked.

"Bad news travels fast. I'll explain more as you pack."

"Pack for what?"

"Do you want to remain a free man?" Norman asked.

"Of course but..."

"Then listen to me. Those men at the cafe are getting restless. Rumour has it that one of them is courting Miss King at Thyme Cottage. It's not going to take long before the whole village is questioning where they all came from. One of them has been able to live at the institute in Totton but if the others follow, their cover will be blown."

"What does all of this have to do with me?"

"We all know as men it can be awfully lonely at times..."

Harold Partridge bowed his head.

"I met briefly with Max at the cafe earlier," Norman continued. "I told him that it was over. That he needed to leave the village and you would never see him again. If news gets out that you have been, you know..."

Harold nodded.

"I don't trust that copper, Wells, I think his name is. He's been sniffing around too much. The sooner I can sell that cafe, the better. For now, you need to come with me."

"Where are we going?"

"Somewhere safe. Somewhere where nobody can get to us. My driver will be here in twenty minutes so you had better hurry up and pack whatever you need."

"Why are you helping me?"

Norman sighed. "When Audrey passed away, I did some stupid things. Things that I'm not proud of. I found comfort in a bottle of whiskey and in a young man called Hans. I broke it off. Now he's threatening to tell everyone everything unless I help him settle here in England. You're not the only one with secrets that should never be told."

Harold nodded before heading back upstairs to continue packing. When the car stopped outside his cottage, he took one last look around it before heading out of the front door. Norman took his seat behind the driver whilst Harold opened the passenger door. As he was about to climb inside the car, he noticed a young man with blonde hair and blue eyes standing by the edge of the woodland that led up to the church. He was wearing a green shirt with baggy trousers and scuffed trainers. Harold made eye contact with him and the young man raised his hand and made a sign of the cross across his chest. Harold nodded before sitting in the car and the driver drove them away from the village.

***

Police Officer Charlie Jones stood behind a large oak tree nearby the vicar's cottage. He watched as Norman Whitehouse and Harold Partridge left in a car he didn't recognise but his attention was caught by a young man who was watching from the woods on the opposite side of the clearing. Jones waited and watched as the young man approached the cottage. He recognised him from when he had attended Norman's cafe on Calshot Beach when Jack Smith's body had been discovered. The young man removed a key from his pocket and unlocked the door before disappearing inside. Jones waited. He'd grown suspicious over Officer George Wells' involvement in this case and the young man coming here had confirmed his suspicions. He waited. Ten minutes. Twenty. Thirty. He was beginning to think that the young man would never leave until a car's headlights cut into the darkness.

Jones stayed out of sight as the car stopped on the gravel driveway. The driver stepped out of the car all dressed in black. He approached the front door of the cottage and let himself inside. Jones moved to try and get a better position. He looked at the car registration number but it was not one that he recognised.

At that moment, the silhouette of a man appeared in the bedroom window illuminated by candlelight behind him. He looked directly at Jones who felt a shiver run down his spine. The man looking back at him was Officer George Wells. He closed the curtains and moved away from the window. Jones waited a moment longer in case either one of the men left the cottage but there was no sign of any further movement from inside the cottage. Jones headed back through the woods towards the shops and returned to his car.

"Evening Officer," a woman's voice called out from behind him.

Jones spun around. "Oh, good evening Miss King," he stammered.

"I'm sorry, I didn't mean to give you a fright."

"No, no, I'm sorry, I, er, I had my mind on other things."

"Nothing too worrying I hope."

Officer Jones took his chance. "Has the young gentleman you've been courting with been around recently?"

"As a matter of fact, he has. He was tending to father's rose bushes earlier. Why?"

"Has he been staying locally?"

"How should I know?"

"Miss King..."

"Frances, please Charlie. No need to be so formal. Is he in trouble?"

"Should he be?"

"Not that I'm aware of."

"Then he has nothing to worry about."

"I'm confused, why all of the questions?" Frances asked.

"Has he been visiting the vicar recently?"

"No, why?"

"Just following up on some inquiries, that's all."

"If this is to do with that gent who was found on the beach then you can forget it. Christopher is a good man and he wouldn't hurt anyone."

"How can you be so sure?"

"Because I am."

"Do you know where he goes each night?"

"I don't stalk him if that's what you mean. He's free to come and go as he pleases."

"So where was he on Saturday night?" Jones asked.

"With me."

"All night?"

"All night."

"And your father's okay with that?"

"I know where your mind is going with that and the answer is no, we didn't. We sat out in the garden looking at the stars and talking so if you're trying to pin this murder on anyone, leave Christopher out of it!" Frances snapped.

"Who said it was a murder?"

Frances looked at him for a moment. "What else could it be?"

"People die from natural causes all the time."

"I don't like coincidences Officer Jones and I'm sure you don't either. If you want to look for clues about what happened to the gent on the beach, I suggest you begin looking closer to home."

"Meaning?"

"George Wells is one of the most untrustworthy people I have ever had the misfortune to meet. If you're looking for a scapegoat, I suggest you begin with him. Good evening to you Officer Jones," Frances snapped before walking away.

"Good evening Miss King," Jones smiled before sitting inside his car.

As he started the engine, a thousand thoughts flooded his mind. He knew that Frances King had information about who was living out of Norman Whitehouse's cafe and their connection to Officer George Wells. He just needed to find out what that connection was.

***

Edward Langford sat on a wooden chair in the back garden of Southward Cottage looking up at the moon as it shone down and glistened on the waves of the sea in the distance. His children had long gone up to bed and he was savouring the last few drops of Johnnie Walker whiskey that he had been swirling around his glass for several minutes. He hated coincidences and too many of them had been happening recently. Mavis Langford walked up behind him and placed her arms onto his shoulders. He moved his head slightly towards her.

"Did you find out who did it?" she asked.

"I'm working on it. Whoever he was, he was certainly a complicated character."

"What do you mean?"

"Most people try to increase their social standing, he was looking to decrease his."

"I don't understand."

"He was a wealthy man and he tried to hide it."

Mavis felt a shiver run through her. She knew that Edward would eventually discover Jack Smith's true identity and she would have a lot of explaining to do.

Feeling her tense up, Edward turned to face her. "What did you need to see the vicar for earlier?"

"I told you that already."

"Tell me again."

"I missed morning service so I rushed down at the end so we could say a few prayers together."

"Without the children?"

"You know how restless they get..."

"So you left them with the girl next door."

"Frances is seventeen, she's old enough to be responsible..."

"Did Father Partridge seem nervous to you when you were with him?"

"No, not that I noticed."

"He didn't have anything on his mind."

"Even if he did, I doubt that he would discuss it with me."

Edward nodded. "I guess you're right. I suppose I should be focusing more on Norman Whitehouse anyway."

"What's Norman done wrong?"

"Nothing as far as I'm aware but the body was discovered outside his cafe and when we entered the building, it looked like some people had been camping inside it."

"You shouldn't judge people for that Ed. A lot of innocent folk lost their homes and their families during the war. Who knows what the poor souls have been through."

"I don't begrudge any man an honest living Mavis. If he is willing to put in the hard graft to earn his crust then he should be able to have a roof over his head and food on his table. It's these freeloaders I struggle to deal with expecting everything to be given to them. Anyway, I've left it up to Wells and Jones to move them on. Hopefully with new owners coming into the village we won't have to deal with this calamity for much longer."

"You're all heart Ed."

"Don't you want our children to grow up in a safe environment?"

"Of course I do but just because someone has fallen on hard times does not mean they are suddenly bad people."

"What about Dana Wise?" Edward asked.

"What about her?"

"Did you know she had an eight year old son?"

Mavis opened her mouth but no words came out.

"Did she give birth whilst you were both in service at the hospital? And if so, where is that child now?" Edward asked.

"I don't know."

"You don't know where the child is..."

"I don't know if she was pregnant or not. Gerald was one of the first enlisted when war was announced so..."

"It's not uncommon for war widows to cling onto the first man that they find to give themselves some kind of future security and prospects," Edward persisted. "If she had indeed given birth, there would surely have been some obvious signs of that."

"I guess so but I never noticed it. If she was, then she managed to hide it very well."

"And what about Edith?"

"What about her?"

"Where was she during the war? She was obviously too young for service..."

"She stayed with the elderly maids who looked after the children whilst their mothers worked in the hospitals treating the wounded. Why suddenly all of these questions?"

"Did Dana Wise know this gent before he arrived at our home on Saturday afternoon?" Edward asked.

"Not that I'm aware of."

"You're not aware of much are you dear? Are you sure he wasn't treated at some point in your hospital?"

"We saw hundreds of gents with all kinds of injuries coming back from the war. How am I meant to remember one out of many hundred who passed through."

"The vicar seems to believe that he was loitering around outside Honeypot House last night before it caught fire. You know how much I hate coincidences."

"Then perhaps you should be interrogating the vicar rather than me."

Edward stood up and walked back inside the house. "Indeed," he sighed as he placed his glass in the kitchen sink before heading towards the stairs. "Maybe a good night's sleep may answer a few questions. Are you coming?"

"I'll be there soon," Mavis replied as she locked the back door and tidied up the kitchen area.

Edward nodded and continued on his way upstairs to bed. He knew Mavis was withholding some information that he needed. He just needed to figure out why.

Chapter Fifty

Murder In Monolithos
Sunday 2nd November 2008

A red Vauxhall Cavalier entered the gates of Eurydice Villa overlooking Monolithos Beach and parked on a driveway lit with solar powered stick lights at either side of it creating a landing strip for its owner. Jim Handanowicz stepped out of the driver's seat and walked around to open the passenger door allowing his sister, Evelyn, to step out of the car before closing it behind her. He collected a bag of groceries from the boot of the car and they headed towards the front door. As they entered, Jim headed towards the kitchen to prepare some food whilst Evelyn wandered over towards the lounge. At that moment, he heard her scream. Jim dropped the groceries on the kitchen sideboard and rushed into the lounge. Ian Bleeker and Zachary Zhal were standing in the corner of the room dressed in black. Zachary held a gun to Evelyn's head.

"I wondered how long it would be before you turned up," Jim said calmly as he entered the room. "Let her go, this doesn't concern her."

"It concerns your whole family Jim," Ian replied.

"You know these people..." Evelyn gasped but Zachary hardened his grip on her shoulder.

"What do you want, Reaper?"

"The map."

"What map?"

"The map your sister gave you to hide as part of the Jack Smith inheritance."

"I don't know what you're talking about."

"Tom Gibson was denied a huge inheritance by your family. He owes a lot of money to a lot of influential people in Moscow."

"If Gibson was so concerned about his inheritance, why did he send you?"

"Paper trails tend to get messy. I can glide across Europe and not even cause a ripple."

"Give them what they want Jim," Evelyn said.

Jim glared at her.

"Where is it?" Zachary asked.

"In my handbag over there," Evelyn nodded towards a black bag that was on the coffee table.

Zachary pushed her towards the bag. "Then get it!" he snapped.

Evelyn walked over to the bag, placed her hand inside it, picked it up and turned to face the two men. She fired two shots in quick succession through the bag before removing the gun from it and standing over them. Ian looked up as she stood over him. "No one threatens my family," she said before shooting him in the head.

Jim rushed over towards Zachary as he took his last breath. "How the hell did you do that?" he asked.

"Shooting tin cans in the garden at Kolopsia House," Evelyn replied calmly.

"We need to get you out of here. If anyone heard those gunshots, the police will be here in no time."

Evelyn calmly placed the gun back inside her handbag before heading out of the front door towards the car. Jim swung the car around and headed out of the main gate before taking the coastal road along the western side of the island towards Kolopsia House.

"Who were those men?" Evelyn asked as they travelled.

"Zachary Zhal and Ian Bleeker, also known as Zodiac and Reaper, two killers who work for a Russian mafia boss that I had dealings with back in the day."

"You told me you left all that behind you."

"I have, mostly."

"You're a terrible liar."

"You haven't exactly covered yourself in glory either."

"Are you angry with me?"

"No, of course not but where did you get that gun?" Jim asked.

"Under the sink."

"What sink? At the care home?"

"No, Father kept his old revolver under the sink behind the toilet bleach. I've been looking after it. It's one of the few things that I managed to bring with me from home."

"Eve, that was in 1977. Are you sure you haven't bought another one since then?"

Evelyn pulled the gun out of her handbag. "It still has the WS on it. It's our father's old Webley And Scott revolver."

"We need to get rid of it," Jim said as he pulled into a layby overlooking a stony beach far below the cliff-face. "If they find the gun, the police will know what's happened."

"Maybe they should."

"What do you mean?"

"I'm tired of running Jim. Mother's affair cost me a life with Fred Langford and I will never forgive her for that betrayal."

"But what about everything we've achieved? The new life we created out here..."

"The life that you've created."

Jim bowed his head. "I did what I thought was right."

"I know you did and I appreciate that. Take me back to the home Jim. I'm tired and it's been a long day."

"The police will come for you."

"Let them and if they do, call your nephew. He'll know what to do."

"Blake? We haven't spoken since he was a child. Why would he help us?"

"Because you have what he needs. Take him to the map and let him figure it out."

Two police cars sped past them as they sat in silence for a moment. Finally, Jim restarted the car and continued on to Kalopsia House. Evelyn placed the gun back inside her handbag and headed inside. Jim watched her leave before turning the car around and heading back home.

***

Back in London, Jenny Langford stepped out of her family home at 124 Alfredson Road and headed back to the main Fulham Road past the Picturehouse towards Redcliffe Road. The white pillared porches brought back memories of when she used to visit her mother's friend, Sandra Hayes, when she was a teenager. She approached the front door of number 24 and a doorbell echoed inside the building as she pressed it. A few moments later, an elderly man answered the door.

"Can I help you?" he asked, looking at Jenny over his black rimmed bi-focal glasses.

"Yes, I was hoping to see Mrs Hayes."

"Who?"

"Mrs Hayes, Sandra Hayes. I am Emily Langford's daughter."

"Hayes? Don't know no Hayes."

"She used to live here..."

"Who is it Albert?" a woman called out from somewhere inside the house.

"Someone looking for Greys!" Albert replied.

"No, no, Hayes, Sandra Hayes," Jenny corrected.

"Okay Albert, you go finish watching the snooker," the woman said as she approached the door from behind him. She had a blue and white striped tea-towel draped over her shoulder and was wearing a yellow and blue apron. She looked at Jenny up and down for a moment. "Sorry about him, he gets easily confused. Who were you looking for?"

"Mrs Sandra Hayes," Jenny replied. "She was close friends with my mother, Emily Langford."

"Ah yes, terrible business. I'm afraid you're out of luck if you want to find Sandra."

"Why's that?"

"Because she died three weeks ago."

Jenny's mouth opened but no words came out.

"She had moved in with her daughter and they were renting this place to us. With only our pensions to live on, it's almost impossible to acquire any real estate in the city these days so we took the opportunity to look after this place until such times..."

"What happened to Sandra?" Jenny asked.

"The police are still investigating."

"The police? Why? Did somebody kill her?"

"They don't know, it's just..."

"Just what?"

"She froze to death."

Jenny looked at her confused. "How?"

"Her son-in-law owns a restaurant in Chelsea. They were under the impression that she was meeting an old friend for dinner. After closing time, he locked up as normal and went home but Sandra wasn't there. His wife had received a text message that she was going back to her friend's house after they had eaten and would be staying the night. When the son-in-law's colleague opened up the following morning, they found her frozen to death inside the walk-in freezer at the back of the restaurant."

"Oh my God, that's terrible. She was locked inside overnight."

The woman nodded.

"Who was the friend that Sandra met that night?"

"Nobody knows her real name but the reservation for the meal was made under the name of Frances King."

***

Back in Monolithos, Jim Handanowicz drove up the incline of his driveway towards his villa before rushing inside and locking the doors behind him. He used a rug from the lounge and rolled Ian Bleeker up in it before dragging his body out of the back door and across the patio towards a small vegetable patch on the right side of his back garden. He rushed upstairs and removed a rug from the landing area and repeated the same treatment for Zachary Zhal. Thousands of thoughts flooded his mind as he furiously cleaned the marble tiles of his lounge with bleach and a mop until he was satisfied that all traces of blood had been removed. As he stepped out onto the patio outside, he noticed a red smear of blood had created a ghoulish pattern on the paving slabs. Hosing the patio down with water and scrubbing hard with a brush gave him a sense that he was finally getting things under control. He picked up a petrol can from his garage and doused the two rugs that contained their victims inside with the liquid before striking a match and setting them alight.

Standing on a soaked patio, Jim Handanowicz drank a generous glass of whiskey as the bodies of Ian Bleeker and Zachary Zhal burned in front of him. He looked at the fire burning menacingly and relentlessly. He felt nothing. No guilt. No shame. No emotion. To him, this was just business. He had spent many years evading the attention of many who had crossed his path. He heard sirens in the distance and soon, the telling flash of blue lights illuminated his front garden. As the flames began to recede and turn into ashes, Jim walked down the side of his villa and down towards his front gates. As he opened the gate, a police detective followed closely behind by a male and female officer approached him.

"James William Handanowicz?" the detective asked.

"That's what the birth certificate says," Jim replied.

"Is that meant to be funny?"

"I don't know, is it? Who are you and why are you invading my property."

The detective removed a sheet of paper from his pocket and unfolded it before handing it to Jim. "I'm Detective Aris Sotiropoulous Stathakis, there were gunshots heard coming from your property earlier this evening followed by smoke caused by a significant fire in your garden."

"I was shooting cans and it's not illegal to burn off excess garden waste last time I checked."

"So you won't mind if my officers take a look around."

"Do I have a choice?"

"Not really."

Jim Handanowicz moved aside and allowed the police to enter the villa.

As night gave way to day, Detective Stathakis stood opposite Jim in his lounge. "Mr Handanowicz, my officers have found the partially cremated remains of two men in the vegetable patch of your back garden."

Jim didn't reply.

"James William Handanowicz, I'm arresting you on suspicion of murder. You have the right to remain silent, anything you say can and will be used against you in the court of law."

Jim stood up and stared into the eyes of Detective Stathakis. "Get Blake Langford," he said.

"Who?"

"Blake Langford, Special Branch, London. I will not make any comment until he is here."

"You're not in the place to make demands, do you realise the seriousness of these allegations Mr Handanowicz."

Jim nodded. "Call Blake Langford," he said before walking out of the villa and heading towards the waiting police car outside.

***

A nurse entered room 215 at Kolopsia House and saw Evelyn Handanowicz sitting on the edge of the bed with her back towards her.

"Is everything okay, Evelyn? I've just bought some hot cocoa here for you," she said as she placed a mug on the side table. "Did you have a good evening with your brother?"

Evelyn didn't reply.

The nurse walked around the bed towards her and noticed the gun in her hands. "Maybe I should take that," she said.

Evelyn shook her head. "No, it's all that I have left of home."

"Guns are dangerous Evelyn. Maybe I should put it away until we start shooting cans again."

"Guns aren't dangerous. It's the people who pull the trigger that are the problem."

The nurse looked at her uneasily.

Evelyn placed the gun under her pillow before laying down on the bed. The nurse walked back around towards the door. "You're not planning on using that gun are you Evelyn?"

She didn't respond.

"Do I need to be concerned?" the nurse asked again.

"I murdered two men tonight."

The nurse froze. "What did you say?"

"I just squeezed the trigger and pop, pop, they were gone," Evelyn smiled.

"Evelyn, you know if this is true, it could cause a whole lot of trouble."

"Call Blake Langford."

"Who?"

"Blake Langford, he'll know what to do," she said before closing her eyes and falling asleep.

The nurse watched her for a moment before leaving the room. When she returned to the nurse's station in the hall, she told her colleague what Evelyn had said.

"Evelyn Handanowicz hasn't said a word in four months," her colleague said.

"I know but she told me she has killed two people and she has a gun under her pillow."

"Evelyn has schizophrenia and serious psychological issues. She probably dreams of killing someone every day. That gun is merely a family heirloom. Do you honestly think her brother would take her out for days away if he thought she was dangerous?"

Evelyn's nurse nodded noncommittally.

"Relax, Evelyn Handanowicz is harmless," she replied before walking away.

Chapter Fifty-One

A Suitcase With A Secret
Monday 23rd August 1948

Edward Langford left Southward Cottage, his family home overlooking Lepe Beach, just after six o'clock on Monday morning. Peter Hastings was waiting for him in their patrol car and began driving them into the city centre.

"We may have had a development in the case of the man on the beach," Peter said as they began driving down the Lepe Road.

Before he had a chance to continue the conversation, a tall blonde haired man talking to the eldest daughter of Edward's nearest neighbour at Thyme Cottage caught their attention.

"Stop a moment," Edward said before stepping out of the car and walking over towards the gate.

"A bit early for a stroll Frances," Edward commented.

Frances King was walking around the front garden with a young man he didn't recognise. "No strolling this morning Detective. Christopher is doing some gardening for us whilst father recovers from a bad back," Frances smiled. "Is Mrs Langford all right? She seemed rather flustered when she arrived here to pick up the children yesterday."

"Flustered? In what way?"

"Oh, I didn't mean any disrespect Sir, she just seemed to be in a hurry. Like she had been running or something."

"You know Mavis, she often is rushing around doing things at the last minute," Edward replied before turning his attention towards Christopher. "I don't think we've been formally introduced, I'm Edward Langford, I live in Southward Cottage, just up the hill from here."

Christopher walked towards the gate and shook his hand. "I've heard of you Detective Langford. You're a village hero."

"Well, I wouldn't go that far," Edward smiled. "Your accent isn't local..."

"No, I was born in Amsterdam, raised by my grandmother after my parents died during the first war."

"I'm sorry to hear that."

"Don't be, my grandmother was a wonderful woman. She taught me well."

"You'd better not be trying to recruit my gardener Mr Langford!" Frances' father, Arthur, called out from his front door.

"Well our hedge could do with a trim," Edward replied.

"Maybe Christopher could call round and take a look..." Frances suggested.

"Our flower beds and lawn have never looked so good," Arthur added.

"If you wouldn't mind I'd be..." Edward began.

"Of course, I have a couple of jobs to do for the vicar and then I'll call round this afternoon if that suits?" Christopher replied.

Edward nodded. "Perfect, we'll see you then."

Edward returned to the patrol car and Peter continued to drive into the city centre. Frances and Arthur watched them leave before turning towards Christopher.

"You need to be careful what you say to the Langfords," Arthur advised. "His father was a police officer before the war and if they get a hint of anything, they'll be on you like a tonne of bricks."

"I don't understand why people would turn against Christoph, he's done nothing wrong," Frances argued. "If anything, he's helping the community with their gardening, mending Mr Baker's bike, Mrs Holder's mangle and fixing the shelves in Mr Wallis's shop."

"That counts for nothing if they find his passport. You can stay in our barn until you find somewhere else to live but only you. The rest will have to go elsewhere, am I understood?" Arthur asked.

"Understood, thank you Mr King," Christopher replied as he wandered around to the back garden to start tending to the flower beds.

***

Detective Edward Langford stared out of the window of the patrol car as Sergeant Peter Hastings drove them into Southampton City Centre. Christopher's comment about him being a local hero began nagging at Edward's mind. His father Alfred was also a police officer before the war and had helped many of the people of Portsmouth to get justice against those who had suffered at the hands of others. He could cut through the years to the night in 1942 when the bombs rained down on Portsmouth's Naval Base. Although he was too old to be called up for battle, Alfred Langford was heavily involved in motivating the troops until one of the German bombs landed on the building where he was stationed. Edward never had the chance to say goodbye to his father and his mother had died of a heart attack last year. If he could become half the police officer his father was, Edward Langford knew that he would have made him proud.

As Peter Hastings parked the car outside Southampton Railway Station, Edward's mind returned to what Hastings had previously mentioned before their meeting with Christopher.

"What are we doing here?" Edward asked as he stepped out of the car.

Peter Hastings joined him in front of the station. "The train ticket that Officer Wells and the forensic team found on the body of the gent on the beach had a locker number on the back of it."

Edward nodded. "And..."

"That locker number belongs to the cloakroom here at the station. Mr Kenneth Bates was working at the ticket office on Saturday and his boss has arranged for him to meet us here this morning so we can take a look at whatever was stored in the locker."

"Did Mr Bates take a name when our man dropped off his luggage?"

"The name in the book was Mr Smith, Jack Smith."

Edward thought about that for a moment. He recognised the name Jack Smith. He had read over some old paperwork recently about a Jack and Ada Smith who disappeared after a bank robbery in Portsmouth in 1938. They had left a newborn baby behind who had been adopted by a couple near London.

Edward and Peter entered the bustling train station, their eyes scanning the sea of people making their way through the station. Spotting a man with thinning hair and a worn-out suit standing near the cloakroom area, they approached him.

"Are you Mr. Bates?" Edward asked, extending his hand for a handshake.

The man nodded nervously, wiping his palms on his trousers before shaking Edward's hand. "Yes, that's me. Are you the police officers investigating the locker?"

"We are," Peter replied, introducing them both. "We'd like to take a look at what was left in there."

Mr. Bates fumbled through his pockets for a key and handed it to Edward. With a quick nod of gratitude, Edward made his way to the cloakroom whilst Peter stayed with Mr. Bates, engaging him in small talk to put him at ease. As Edward turned the key and unlocked the locker, he felt a rush of anticipation. The door swung open, revealing a worn brown leather suitcase.

Edward lifted the suitcase out of the locker and laid it on a wooden bench. He carefully unfastened the rusty clasps before opening the case. The musty smell of mothballs hit him as he opened it. Inside he found a pair of scissors, a dressing gown, a laundry bag with an unused flannel and soap inside, underpants, slippers, trousers, shirts, toothbrush, handkerchiefs, envelopes, coat hangers, a cigarette lighter, two ties, a shaving brush, a razor, a towel, pencils, scarf and a coat. Nothing unusual at first until Edward took a closer look and noticed that all of the labels and tags had been removed from the clothing. There was nothing to identify who this mysterious Mr Smith was and it seemed as if he had covered his tracks very well.

The lack of progress frustrated Edward and he slammed the lid of the suitcase closed. As he did though, he noticed that the top of the suitcase was lopsided. It felt heavier on the right corner than on the left. He opened it again and ran his hands over the inside of the case. He traced with his fingers what seemed to be the outline of some kind of book or paperwork.

Edward removed his penknife from his pocket and cut the inside covering of the suitcase. Inside, he found a collection of old photographs, letters and newspaper clippings. The photographs revealed a young couple with striking features, Jack and Ada Smith. They were smiling in some pictures, while others captured them in intense discussions or far-off contemplation. Edward studied their faces, feeling an uncanny familiarity that stirred his curiosity. The letters were filled with affectionate words, describing the deep love shared between Jack and Ada. They spoke of dreams, aspirations, and their desire for a better life outside the constraints of society. Edward's eyes widened as he read one particular letter from Ada, describing their plan to flee to America after the bank robbery. Looking back at the young dreams from before the war gave Edward food for thought. The war had left devastation in its wake in so many ways.

The newspaper clippings told the story of the bank robbery in vivid detail, revealing how Jack and Ada had managed to escape authorities despite a nationwide manhunt. The articles praised their cunning and audacity, labelling them as modern-day Robin Hoods. Edward couldn't help but admire their resourcefulness and determination, even if their actions were unlawful. Realising that he was onto something significant, Edward meticulously examined each photograph and scrutinised every word in the letters. As he delved deeper into the contents of the suitcase, a puzzle began to form in his mind. The pieces fit together with uncanny precision, painting a picture of an extraordinary story waiting to be unravelled. If this was indeed the same man who had joined them for luncheon two days ago, it was absolutely extraordinary how he had kept his identity a secret for so long.

It became clear to Edward that Jack and Ada Smith's disappearance wasn't merely a case of fugitives eluding capture; it was a carefully orchestrated vanishing act. Their trail had gone cold, leaving the world to believe they vanished without a trace. But now, with the discovery of this old suitcase, Edward knew that there was much more to this story than met the eye. As he continued to look at the papers, he then found an obituary notice cut out from a newspaper in 1940. Ada May Smith, died 22nd December 1940, aged just 24 years. Edward sighed. All of the hopes and dreams of a young couple just two years before came to an end at the start of the war. As he was about the close the suitcase and take the items back to his office, a yellow official looking form fell out of the bundle and onto the floor.

Being an ex-military man himself, Edward Langford recognised the form immediately. It was the discharge papers for a Mr J Smith, medically discharged on September 30th 1940 after suffering shell-shock from artillery and mortar fire. He was cared for by the red cross in Fareham, Hampshire. This piqued Edward's interest. During the war, his wife Mavis and her friend, the missing Dana Wise, both worked in Fareham's red cross hospital as volunteer nurses helping injured servicemen and those affected by the war to recover. Yet, when Jack Smith visited them on Saturday afternoon, neither of them seemed interested in him or acknowledged knowing him.

Edward pondered that for a moment. Perhaps he was reading too much into it but it was definitely a line of inquiry that he would keep in mind. He placed the paperwork inside the suitcase before closing it and taking it back to the police station for further investigation. Dana's disappearance with her daughter was completely out of character and Edward felt that Jack Smith may have had something to do with it before his death. Whatever happened next, he knew he needed to talk to his wife, Mavis Langford and find out if she remembered anything about Jack Smith from their time together in Fareham.

Chapter Fifty-Two

All Rhodes Lead To The Langfords
Monday 3rd November 2008

In a two bedroom rundown flat in south-east London, cigarette smoke lingered in the lounge as Tom Gibson looked over some old letters and photos from his past. His mother, Patricia, had kept a diary from his birth in 1970 through to 1987 when she had decided to move to Greece. There had been no warning. No conversations took place. All that was left was a letter telling him that the family home was being repossessed and he had two weeks to find somewhere else to live.

Tom found himself scared and alone at seventeen years old. With no father-figure to look after him, he found a new kind of brotherhood when he joined the Royal Air Force. It became his escape route from the harsh reality of how his life had changed since his mother's disappearance. The training was hard. The days were long. But they made him into the man he was today. Despite everything he had gone through, he still kept this metal box of memories with him. Still searching for the day he could find redemption and take back what he felt was his family's legacy.

"You're up early," Jade called out as she stood in the doorway of the lounge.

"I couldn't sleep," Tom replied as he collected up the diaries, letters and photos and placed them back inside the metal box.

"I met up with an old friend at the Chequered Flag cafe yesterday."

Tom looked over at her as she walked towards him and sat on the opposite end of the sofa.

"She said that you may know where my sister is," Jade continued.

"And who might this friend be?"

"Jenny Langford."

Tom glared at her. "Why were you talking to her?"

"Tell me Tom, where is Andrea? I know she was involved with one of your friends. Is she still alive?"

"She was the last time I saw her."

"What's that supposed to mean?"

"Trust me, your interest in the Langford's is just as great as mine. Andrea got too involved in a Special Branch operation and she's hiding away in the south of France until the heat dies down. Until then, I want you to stay away from Jenny Langford. Is that understood?"

"What hold does she have over you? Whenever her name is mentioned you get all defensive."

"A lot of people don't want to discuss failed relationships from their past."

"No, it's more than that. You and Jenny were over years ago. What are you not telling me?"

"It's complicated."

Jade moved towards him. "If we're going to work together on this, I need to know what you're thinking. If one of us is on the wrong page, we could both end up in trouble."

Tom sighed deeply. "My mother once told me about stories she had been told when she was growing up in foster care in London. There was a rumour that my grandparents robbed a bank in Portsmouth back in 1938. They got away with everything. From what I've found out by doing some research, it could be worth over a million pounds in today's money. She told me that Ernest Hughes, who would have been my great-grandfather, was involved in my mother being given up for adoption."

"So, where do the Langfords fit in?"

"Ernest was influenced by a close friend. That friend was Blake's great-grandfather, Alfred Langford. He was the first officer on the scene after my great-grandfather, Ernest Hughes, committed suicide."

"Do you believe he committed suicide?"

Tom shook his head. "Neither did my mother. Whenever she tried to get more details about that time, everyone clammed up. Didn't want to talk about it. They changed the subject."

"Your mother was given up for adoption. How did she know about her biological parents or grandparents? Also, not a lot of people like to talk about suicide."

"It was the talk of the town throughout my mother's childhood. There were always whispers about the girl that Ada and Jack left behind. If Alfred Langford hadn't convinced Joan and Ernest Hughes to give up their granddaughter, my mother, for adoption, then I'm convinced that Ernest wouldn't have died the way he did."

Jade sighed. "What proof do you have of that?"

"None. Just a feeling, deep down inside. Why else would they just give up their granddaughter? Their daughter Ada had just run off with Jack leaving them with a baby to look after. Surely they would have still wanted some kind of connection to Ada through my mother."

"The war was about to start. Maybe they thought she would be safer elsewhere."

Tom shook his head. "My mother felt that it was important enough to look into her past before she left and I'm going to do all that I can to make sure I claim what's rightfully mine."

"This all happened seventy years ago Tom. A lot of water has gone under the bridge since then."

Tom stood up and walked over towards the window to look out at the dawn skyline over London. "Don't you see... The Langfords have always been there. I was never good enough in John Langford's eyes for his precious daughter Jenny. When she was meant to go down for helping a Russian spy, Blake and his father, John Langford, covered it up. When Blake's brother Steven woke up to a house full of murdered students, Blake once again was there to make sure that the charges went away. And now, we find out that their family history isn't so pure after all. When Emily Langford's true identity comes out, Blake will have nowhere to run. Our families are all intertwined whether he likes it or not. That shadow will follow him everywhere. His reputation will be ruined and I will finally claim my birthright and disappear from this drab and dingy city forever."

Jade sighed as she walked back towards her bedroom. "I hope you're right."

As he heard the bedroom door close, Tom opened his laptop and logged into his secure network. Special Branch had seized control of funds tied up in The Crystal network that he had been building but so far, they hadn't found the loophole on the dark web where he had built his own secure application and thousands of users were trading money for crypto-currency. He smiled to himself as the current user profiles stood at four hundred thousand and rising rapidly. Soon, he would have enough money to investigate his family's legacy and this time, he won't let anyone stand in his way. He checked his phone. No messages. Thoughts rushed through his mind. Surely Ian Bleeker and Zachary Zhal, two of his closest allies would have made contact by now. As he logged off of the secure network, a newsflash appeared on his search engine.

GREEK POLICE DISCOVER TWO DEAD BODIES AT THE VILLA OF A WEALTHY BUSINESSMAN ON THE ISLAND OF RHODES

As he read the report, Tom swore under his breath. He had sent Reaper and Zodiac, to trace down and kill two beneficiaries of the stolen money who had emigrated to the Greek islands. He closed the laptop and tossed it onto the sofa in disgust before heading towards the bathroom for a shower. He knew that if the identities of the two dead bodies came out, Blake would not be too far behind to chase up a lead and he needed to be ready.

***

Alison Pearce and Blake Langford landed at Diagoras Airport in Rhodes just after 1pm that afternoon. As they cleared customs and walked through the small and rather basic looking airport, they saw a man with grey hair and moustache, wearing a pale blue shirt and jeans holding up a piece of cardboard with the words Langford/Pearce written on it.

"So much for being discreet," Blake sighed as he wandered over towards him.

The man looked at his phone briefly before turning his attention to Blake and Alison. "Ah, Mr Langford, Miss Pearce, welcome to Rhodes. I am Christos Antonopoulos Papadopoulos but my friends call me Cap. I work with Detective Aris Sotiropoulos Stathakis. He told me to meet you here and take you straight to Kalopsia House in Monolithos. Follow me please."

Blake and Alison followed Cap out of the airport towards a rusting Vauxhall Astra that had seen better days.

"If he's Cap, does that mean we're working with Detective Ass?" Blake whispered.

Alison slapped his chest. "I'd rather call him Cap than his full name. Anyway, it sounds like you're going to be in the firing line when you see your uncle again."

"I can't wait," Blake replied as he climbed into the front passenger seat alongside Cap whilst Alison sat behind them.

As they drove through the busy streets towards Monolithos, Blake noticed a lot of the local people carrying large sacks and placing them on to the backs of trucks at the side of the road.

"What are they carrying in those sacks Cap?" Blake asked.

"Now the tourist season is mostly over, the locals help the farmers to collect all of the olives from the olive trees around the island. They are then used to make olive oil, soap and all kinds of different things."

"It still feels quite warm here compared to a lot of places in Europe," Alison added.

"We have very mild winters. Sometimes we only have a few days of rain each year. Most British people choose to retire here as they are fed up with the weather in London or they want to get legally stoned," Cap smirked.

"Really?" Alison gasped.

"It's one of the few places where you can legally buy cannabis for whatever you need it for. My brother Steven once brought some sun cream back to London without realising that it had cannabis oil in it," Blake explained.

"What happened to him?"

"He gave it up but was fined and had a suspended sentence for it. Luckily Dad was able to smooth things over but he gave him hell for it for years after."

"Just another reason why Faliraki is the party capital of the island," Cap replied. "Here we are."

Cap drove the car up a narrow gravel track which climbed up a steep hill towards a large house overlooking the beach and sea in the distance. As they stepped out of the car, there was an elderly lady sat on a stool with a wooden table in front of her selling locally produced honey for three euros per jar. She was muttering something in Greek that they struggled to hear.

Blake looked over at her and noticed her calloused hands were shaking as if she was shivering yet it was still relatively warm in the afternoon sun. As he was about to approach her, he heard someone call his name. Blake turned to see a tall middle-aged man with short black hair, clean shaven, wearing a white shirt with black trousers and shoes approach him with a young woman with brown hair tied back in a severe clip wearing a similar black and white suit following close behind.

"Blake Langford, so glad to finally meet you. I'm Detective Aris Stathakis, this is my assistant Lauren Prince, she will deal with the admin for us," Aris said as he shook Blake's hand completely ignoring Alison. "We have a most delicate matter inside, Miss Handanowicz is refusing to speak to anyone and we thought a family member may help to encourage her cooperation."

Blake stepped back for a moment. "Well I'm sure with the help of my colleague, Special Branch Agent Alison Pearce, we will try and assist wherever we can."

"Splendid, let's go inside," Aris replied before turning and heading back towards the entrance.

Blake and Alison looked at each other briefly before Lauren Prince walked towards them.

"Careful what you say to Aris, he's a bastard," she said before swiftly following him inside.

"I gathered that already," Alison replied.

***

Dark rain clouds gathered above The New Forest as Samir Khalifa and Joe Knight arrived at East Boldre cemetery. Two black estate cars filled with equipment and four gravediggers arrived soon after them. Joe and Samir led them through the cemetery to the unmarked grave where the body of Andrea Smith had been discovered. The gravediggers quickly moved to get their tools and pulleys into position to begin exhuming the coffin.

"I can think of better places to be on a Monday morning," Joe said as he watched the men begin digging.

"Unfortunately, the job isn't always glamorous," Samir replied.

"Have you sorted out your phone yet?"

"What do you mean?"

"I messaged you this morning to meet for breakfast but it never went through."

Samir removed his phone from his pocket and noticed that it had been turned off. He tried to turn it on but nothing was happening. "Battery's dead, I'll see if I can use the in-car charger."

Joe nodded in acknowledgement before talking to one of the gravediggers. Samir rushed back to the car and plugged his phone into the charger. He started the engine to get some power from the car's battery and his phone lit up. After a couple of minutes, a text message came through. It read:

YOUR FRIENDS ARE GETTING TOO CLOSE. MEET ME AT THE SECOND ISLAND TREE AT HATCHET POND, 10AM MONDAY.

Z

Nothing made sense. Samir and Joe had both seen the reports coming out of Greece that Zodiac and Reaper had been murdered. So how was Zodiac still messaging him and arranging to meet? Samir checked his watch. It was already 9.20am. He had forty minutes to get to the pond and find the second island tree. A thousand thoughts flooded his mind. He recognised the phone number and Zodiac always signed off his messages with the letter Z.

During a previous case, Zodiac had threatened to uncover Samir's past indiscretions and cost him his job in Special Branch if he failed to co-operate. After chasing him away from Kings Cross station in London, Samir had him cornered in an alley. He knew he should have taken him down then but he let Zodiac get away. What he couldn't work out though was what did he have to do with this new case? Where was the connection?

Samir checked the time of the message. 7pm last night. That was around the same time that Blake and Alison had been at the funeral home. Around the same time that the report had come through from Greece about Zodiac and Reaper's deaths. He hated coincidences but couldn't shake the feeling that the two could be linked.

He reversed off of the grass verge and headed back into The New Forest towards Hatchet Pond. He knew he needed answers and the only way he was going to get them was to face it head-on. When he arrived at Hatchet Pond, there were a lot of people out walking their dogs and he noticed three fishermen had taken up their positions on the left side of the lake. He looked around for any obvious signs for the second island tree. It began to rain and several people immediately pulled on a see-through plastic mack over their clothes.

Samir smirked to himself. He always found it amusing that companies could sell what was essentially a rubbish bag with holes cut out of it for the arms and people would actually pay for it.

"Nice weather if you're a duck," a lady's voice called out from behind him.

Samir turned around and saw a grey-haired lady with rosy red cheeks wearing a thick black coat with her hood up to keep the rain off of her hair. She had a dog lead wrapped around her wrist and Samir noticed a Spaniel sniffing the grass a few steps behind her.

"You're not from round here are you?" she asked.

"Is it that obvious?"

"Unless you're fishing or dog walking, no one comes out here in the winter. The summertime, my word, you can barely find a space to lay a picnic blanket down."

"Maybe you could help me," Samir smiled at her.

"If it's money, all I have is a roll of dog poo bags on me..."

"No, no, nothing like that. I'm supposed to be meeting someone here at the second island tree..."

"Ah yes, such a romantic spot for young lovers. You picked a rubbish day for it though..."

"No, no, nothing like that. I was meant to be meeting a man about something."

The lady looked at him sceptically. "Well it takes all kinds in this modern world I guess. It's just over there," she replied, pointing towards a tree that stuck out on what looked like a small island on the right side of the pond.

"Thank you and enjoy the rest of your walk," Samir smiled as he began walking towards the right side of the pond.

The lady watched him for a moment before continuing on her way. Samir checked his watch again. He had ten minutes to get to the island. He began jogging along the muddy gravel path that circled the huge pond. As he jogged around the first set of trees and hedges, he misplaced his foot and sank into a quagmire of mud and stagnant water. He swore loudly as he pulled himself out of the bog. His shoes had filled up with water and his trousers were filthy and soaking wet. He dusted himself off before carrying on.

As Samir approached the tree on the small island, he saw a figure standing under it, their back turned towards him. The rain intensified, creating a curtain of droplets between them.

"Zodiac?" Samir called out, his voice slightly echoing across the water.

The figure turned slowly, revealing a man in his mid-forties with sharp features and steely eyes. He smirked at Samir before speaking. "Samir Khalifa, always so punctual. I knew you wouldn't be able to resist my little invitation."

"You're not Zodiac, who are you? And why drag me out here in this weather?" Samir asked.

The man laughed. "My name is Chris Anderson. Your colleague called in for a friendly chat at the funeral home yesterday afternoon and then suddenly, Zodiac and Reaper are dead. Which begs the question, if you knew Z was dead, why did you come?"

"I don't like loose ends."

"And yet you let Zodiac, a known criminal go when you had him cornered. Interesting..."

"What do you want and what is your connection with Zodiac?"

"Ah, you see, I've stumbled upon something that might interest you. Something that could change everything."

"What could you possibly have that would interest me?"

Chris pulled out a burgundy urn from inside his jacket and handed it over to Samir. "Zac wanted to give it to you himself. Kind of a parting gift from his employer but he asked me to keep hold of it in case anything happened to him and lo and behold..."

"It did," Samir finished for him.

He turned the urn around and noticed a small gold plaque on the front of it. He looked closer at the inscription. It read:

JACK WALTER SMITH
DIED: 21st AUGUST 1948
Aged 41 Years

"When you uncover the secrets of the unmarked grave, you'll realise its significance," Chris said before turning and walking away.

"That's it?" Samir asked.

"That's it for my part. Good day, Mr Khalifa. Don't cock it up."

Samir carefully opened the urn and looked inside. There were the ashes of presumably Jack Walter Smith but amongst them was a gold key and a small business card. He looked at the card. It had a tracing of some kind of map on it. He placed the card and the key inside his back pocket before closing the urn again. The rain was still falling heavily and the tree was no longer giving him much shelter. He closed the urn and held it inside his coat before heading back to the car.

When he sat back inside the car, he placed the urn in the passenger footwell. His phone had several missed calls and messages on it. Samir ignored it and headed back to East Boldre cemetery, determined to figure out the connection between Jack Smith and the unmarked grave.

Chapter Fifty-Three

Mistaken Identity
Monday 23rd August 1948

On Monday afternoon, Detective Edward Langford arrived home just after 4pm. As he approached the house, he noticed his neighbour's gardener Christopher collecting up the hedge trimmings into a wheelbarrow.

"Ed, come and take a look at this!" Mavis called out.

As Edward walked into the front garden, his son, Fred, kicked a football that flew through the air towards them. Christopher moved forward and headed the ball back in Fred's direction.

"Wow, that was amazing. Do you play football Mister..." Fred called out.

"A little, when I was younger," Christopher replied.

"Be careful with that ball, if you break anything there will be big trouble!" Edward said as he joined them. "Well Arthur wasn't wrong, fabulous job Mister..."

"Fischer, but please call me Chris."

Edward pulled out a wad of notes from his pocket and handed over ten pounds to Chris.

"Thank you so much. Are you sure?" Chris asked.

"You've done a mighty fine job there and I don't mind paying for good work. I'm sure the vicar will be most satisfied too."

"I didn't get to see the vicar..."

"Oh, why was that?"

"The church was locked up and there was no answer from his cottage so I came here to work for Mrs Langford and yourself."

"How peculiar, was Harold okay when you saw him yesterday?" Edward asked, turning his attention to Mavis.

"He was fine. You saw him after I did. Did he seem okay to you?" she asked.

Edward hesitated for a moment. "Yes, he seemed perfectly fine when I saw him," he replied slowly. "But if Christopher here couldn't find him today, that's certainly odd."

Mavis exchanged a worried glance with Edward. "Perhaps we should go check on him ourselves," she suggested. After their discussion yesterday, Mavis knew that the vicar would have had some concerns over her involvement with Dana's disappearance. "I'll stay with the kids, you two can go."

"Yes, let's do that," Edward agreed. He turned to Christopher. "We'll try his cottage again. Maybe we can find him there."

Christopher nodded and the two men set off through the woods.

As they walked, a sense of unease settled over Edward. He couldn't shake the feeling that there was something he was missing. As they arrived at the cottage, he noticed that the front door was slightly ajar. He exchanged a glance with Christopher before cautiously pushing the door open and stepping inside. Christopher followed closely behind.

The interior of the cottage was dimly lit, with a sense of abandonment hanging in the air. Edward's eyes scanned the room, quickly noticing that something was amiss. Books were strewn across the floor, furniture was overturned and there were signs of a struggle. Edward moved further into the cottage, his heart pounding in his chest. He approached the study. The door stood partially open, revealing a scene of chaos within.

The room had been ransacked, papers scattered everywhere and the shelves were emptied. A broken photo frame lay on the floor, its shattered glass reflecting light from a nearby window.

At that moment, they heard a noise from the hall. Both men turned around and saw someone run out the front door.

Christopher chased the man into the woodland behind the cottage. Christopher was gaining steadily before he leapt and tackled the man to the ground.

He rolled the man over to face him. "Stefan?" he gasped.

"Christoph?"

"What are you doing?"

"Surviving. The police killed the man on the beach."

They heard footsteps in the distance.

"Go, I'll cover you," Christopher said as he groaned and rolled onto the floor.

Stefan ran into the woodland as Edward caught up with Christopher.

"What happened?" Edward asked.

"Sorry, I tripped."

"Did you see where he went?"

Christopher shook his head. "No, sorry," he gasped.

"Are you okay?"

"Yes, just winded, that's all."

They both walked slowly back towards the cottage. Inside the hallway, Edward found a set of keys with one long black key on it. After the police arrived to check over the house, Edward and Christopher walked up to the church. As they arrived, they noticed a man sitting next to the entrance dressed in black shorts and a black t-shirt.

He looked up at them as they approached. "Christoph?" he called out.

"I'm Christopher, do I know you?" Christopher asked.

"What do you mean? We were at the..."

"I'm sorry, I don't know who you are," Christopher interrupted.

At that moment, Officer George Wells arrived. "Sorry I'm late Max, here, on your way," he said as he handed the man five pounds.

Max looked at the three of them before walking away. Edward and Christopher exchanged a puzzled look, unsure of what just transpired. Officer Wells approached them with a hint of embarrassment on his face.

"Sorry about that," he said, scratching his head. "Max is a bit confused lately. Claims to know people he's never met before. Helped the vicar out a few times with odd jobs and such."

Edward narrowed his eyes at Officer Wells. "Is this related to the vicar's disappearance?"

The officer hesitated for a moment, then sighed. "I can't say for certain, it was rumoured that the vicar had been spending a lot of time with the young lad for, shall we say, unorthodox purposes, but our investigations proved fruitless. Who knows, there's a suspicion that it might be some sort of memory loss or confusion going around in the village. Everyone seems rather strange at the moment. We're investigating it, but it's been quite baffling so far."

"We just chased someone from the vicar's cottage, could it be connected?" Edward asked.

Officer Wells nodded. "It's possible. We don't have all the answers yet, but we're looking into every lead we can find."

"Why did he claim to know me?" Christopher asked.

Officer Wells looked at Christopher. "Like I said, he is a confused young man," he replied.

Edward glanced at the black key he found at the vicar's cottage. He slid the key into the lock and turned it. The lock clunked as it unlocked before Edward twisted the handle and allowed the door to creak open. A strong musty smell hung in the air as they entered. Edward and Christopher cautiously stepped into the dimly lit church, their footsteps echoing through the empty pews. Officer Wells followed closely behind them. The air inside was heavy with silence, broken only by the occasional scurrying of small creatures or the distant rustle of wind outside. As they made their way further into the church, Edward's eyes were drawn to a flickering candle at the front altar. It cast dancing shadows upon the walls, creating an eerie ambiance that made his skin prickle.

"Hello?" Edward called out tentatively, his voice swallowed by the vastness of the space. There was no response, only a faint echo that bounced back to him.

As they moved towards the vestry, Christopher noticed scratch marks on the floor leading towards the door. He nudged Edward and pointed to the floor. Edward nodded before cautiously approaching the vestry door. He carefully turned the handle and opened the door.

All three of them gasped when they looked inside. A man dressed in the vicar's robes was sitting in a chair with a metal candlestick holder impaled into his chest. As they looked closer, they could see burn marks where the lighted candles had singed the clothes as they entered the man's body. There was a hood covering the man's face. Edward moved closer and lifted the hood expecting to see the face of Harold Partridge but as he revealed the face, the vacant eyes staring back at him were of a man he had never met before.

Christopher struggled to stop himself from vomiting and rushed out of the church. Edward placed the hood back over the face of the victim.

"Officer Wells, please call the station and ask Sergeant Hastings and the forensic teams to get here as soon as possible," Edward said as he stepped away from the body.

"Yes Sir. Do you know who he is?" Officer Wells asked.

Edward looked down and noticed a significant amount of blood in the groin area of the body as well as the chest. "No, I've never seen him before," he sighed. "Do you think the rumours were true about Harry and the young lad?"

"Nobody could be certain and no complaints were made. He was just acting rather odd."

Edward thought about that. Was this murder meant for Harold Partridge and if so, had the killer murdered the wrong person? "We need to find Harry as soon as possible."

Officer Wells nodded and rushed away to find a telephone. Edward walked back through the church and out of the main entrance. He looked around at the empty cemetery but there was no sign of Christopher.

One hour later, Sergeant Phillip Hastings and the forensics team arrived at the church. Officer Wells and Edward told them what had happened earlier and how the body was discovered. After his colleagues had taken over, Edward Langford began walking away from the church and back through the village towards Lepe Road. Christopher hadn't returned since the gruesome discovery had been made and it had raised a suspicion in Edward's mind. A lot of people struggled with the sight of a dead body but to run away from a police investigation completely made him question whether it was just fear or something more.

Guiding his way through the country roads by torchlight, Edward made his way to Thyme Cottage, his neighbour's house. He walked up the main path and knocked on the door. He heard footsteps approaching followed by the sound of several bolts unlocking. Eventually, the door opened ajar allowing a slither of light to escape onto the porch.

"Yes?" Arthur answered.

"Arthur? It's me, Edward."

"What are you doing calling round this late?"

"I was concerned about young Christopher and wondered if you had seen him?"

"No, haven't seen him since he went to your place and trimmed your hedge. I hope you paid him well. He does a marvellous job."

"Of course I paid him," Edward sighed. "So, you haven't seen him?"

"No, not since lunchtime."

"Okay, thanks anyway. My apologies for disturbing you."

Arthur closed the door shrouding the porch in darkness once more. Edward turned on his torch once again before continuing on his way home. He still had some nagging questions in his mind from earlier that he wanted to speak to his wife, Mavis, about. He had a suspicion that she knew more about this, Mr Smith, who had visited them yesterday than she was telling him. When he arrived home, the whole house was in darkness.

Edward let himself inside the house as quietly as he could. He made his way upstairs and peered inside the bedrooms. Everyone was sleeping. He knew he needed answers but they would have to wait until morning. He got himself changed in the dark before stumbling into bed. Mavis stirred momentarily before turning over and going back to sleep.

Edward stared up at the ceiling. Thoughts swirling in his mind. Too many weird things were happening and he needed to find some answers and fast. He eventually drifted off, hoping that he would have a clearer focus in the morning.

***

A black Ford Anglia crunched across a gravel courtyard near Portsmouth Naval Base just after midnight. A man stepped out of the driver's seat before springing the seat forwards to allow Reverend Harold Partridge to exit from the back seat.

"Where are we?" Harold asked as he looked up at a tall stone building illuminated only by the light of the moon.

"You will be safe here," the driver said before leading Harold towards the front door.

The driver rang the doorbell which chimed like an old church bell echoing around the courtyard. A few moments later, the front door opened and a nun stood in the doorway.

"Harold Partridge," the driver said.

The nun stepped aside allowing them both to enter. The main hall was illuminated with candles placed in holders every few metres. Harold looked up and noticed three levels of accommodation above them.

"I'm sister Mary Chamberlain," the nun said as she led them further inside the building. "You will be under our protection until it is safe to return to your parish."

"Safe? What do you mean, safe? I haven't done anything," Harold protested.

Sister Mary raised her eyebrows. "We all know that is not true don't we, Harold."

Harold bowed his head. "He was just some company. Oh Lord, what have I done?"

"That will be all Sidney," she replied.

The driver turned and left as Sister Mary led Harold towards a room on the ground floor of the building. She stopped outside room twenty-three and handed him a key.

"Am I a prisoner here?" Harold asked.

"You can take walks in the grounds and interact with others in a similar position to you here. We do have children living in this facility so be mindful of that wherever you go. I shall see you in the morning. Good night, Mr Partridge," she said before walking away.

Harold watched her leave and looked at the door of his room. He placed the key into the lock and turned it. The door creaked open. Inside was a single bed, a bedside table with a lighted candle illuminating the room. Next to it was a small glass with a jug of water beside it. To the left of the room was a bathroom which had a toilet, a small sink and a bathtub inside it.

Harold closed the door behind him and sat on the edge of the bed reflecting on what had happened in the past twelve hours. Mavis Langford's confession, the visit of Detective Edward Langford and Sergeant Phillip Hastings, Officer Wells' warning to stop associating with the three young men who had recently arrived in the village and then this. Norman Whitehouse had persuaded him to go for a drive with his friend Sidney. After a drive through Portsmouth city centre, Norman had been dropped off at The Kings Hat and Sidney continued on to wherever this place was and now it seemed as if he was to be a prisoner in this concrete tomb. He walked over towards the window and found a postcard on the window sill. He brought it over towards the candlelight. It was a black coloured card with a gold crucifix on it. As he turned the card over, it read:

ST. ANNE'S CONVENT, PORTSMOUTH

Chapter Fifty-Four

Evelyn's Secret
Monday 3rd November 2008

Blake Langford stood outside room number 215 in Kalopsia House in Monolithos. As he stepped inside, he saw an elderly lady sitting in an armchair looking out at the garden with a jungle of trees leading down towards the beach and sea in the distance. Aris, Lauren and Alison waited in the doorway as Blake approached her. He noticed a wooden stool in the far corner of the room. He picked it up and placed it near to where the lady was sitting before sitting on it next to her.

For a moment, she ignored his presence before slowly turning her gaze towards him. Blake felt a pang of adrenaline running through him and his heart skipped a beat as he looked into her eyes. He felt as if his late mother was suddenly staring back at him and it caught him off-guard.

She nodded as if reading his mind before turning her attention back towards the window. Blake took a couple of deep breaths to compose himself before speaking.

"You don't know me and unfortunately, I never had the opportunity to get to know you," Blake spoke softly, barely above a whisper.

She looked directly at him but still never spoke a word.

"I am Emily Handanowicz's son and I believe your life may be in danger since her death four months ago," he explained.

"Just you," she said before turning back towards the window.

Blake stood up and walked over towards the door. "She'll only speak to me alone."

"That's not going to happen, I'm investigating a double murder here..." Aris protested.

"The nurse who looks after her has said that she hasn't spoken to anyone other than her in four months. If Blake can get her to open up and tell us what's going on, let him talk to her," Lauren replied.

Aris glared at her before turning back to Blake. "All right but I want a full report..."

"You'll get one," Alison interrupted.

Blake smiled at her before closing the door on them and returning to the stool next to the elderly lady.

She continued to look out of the window. "What day is it today?" she asked.

"It's Monday the third of November," Blake replied.

She lifted a necklace from underneath her jumper which had a gold ring attached to it. "Do you know it's thirty-two years today since Frederick Langford asked me to marry him?"

Blake gasped. Frederick Langford was his father's brother. He had died in 1977 shortly after his parents were married but he never knew the full details about his Uncle Fred's relationship with Evelyn. "I'm sorry, I wasn't aware of that," he admitted.

"Not many people were. It lives on now only in my memory. You have your mother's eyes."

"Aunt Evelyn, I'm sorry that things turned out the way that they have. Until recently, I never knew that you were here. When Mum died four months ago, she left a photograph in a safe deposit box in London. I think it holds the key to a family secret. One that those men came after you for."

Evelyn nodded. "Emily knew everything. I was very much ignorant to what our parents were up to. All I knew was that I had been cruelly tricked out of being with the love of my life. Fred was my soulmate. He was everything to me. When I was admitted here in 1984, my brother, James, made sure that I had everything that I needed but he refused to supply the one thing

I yearned for, the truth. I was kept in the dark for so long until a distant cousin came to see me."

"Who was it?"

"Ada and Jack Smith's daughter, Patricia. She came here in 1987 and told me everything. As usual, these family reunions never last and we lost touch but suddenly, everything began to make sense."

Blake took a moment to take in what Evelyn had told him. "When mum's will was read, we discovered that after her estate was split between myself, my brother and my sister, there was something left called Harvey Matchbox Twenty-Five. This was left to you, Victor Wise and James Handanowicz. What is Harvey Matchbox Twenty-Five?"

"Jack Smith's legacy," Evelyn replied.

"Who is Jack Smith?"

"Did you know on January 6th, it will be twenty-nine years since they took me away?"

"Away from where?"

"Not now Jim, I'm tired."

"Aunt Evelyn, who is Jack Smith?"

"Jack Smith? Ah, yes, Jack Smith was your grandfather. Mine, Emily's and Victor's father. Your grandmother began a wheel of deception during the war. I guess someone wants to take back what's rightfully ours."

Blake shifted in his stool as he noticed a gun hidden underneath Evelyn's jumper.

"I'm not here to take anything from you. I just want to help. I need to understand what is going on here."

"That's what that bastard said at Jim's house right before I put a bullet through his head. He never saw it coming. Zodiac, he called himself, pah! Who really believes all that bullshit!"

"You killed him, not Jim."

"Of course I did. No one suspects a mental old hag do they."

"How? I thought you never left this place."

"I'm not a prisoner. Back in 1989, I remember Victor came with Anne and we sat in the garden drinking and reminiscing. That was twenty-one years ago last July. That was the last time I saw my brother."

"How did you get to Uncle Jim's Villa?"

"He took me there yesterday. After it all happened, he brought me back here and left. Then that dosey copper started poking his nose into my affairs and I hear that Jim's been arrested."

"Give me the gun and I promise I will take care of everything."

"How do I know I can trust you? The last Langford I trusted ended up dead."

"Because I am your twin-sister's son. I may be half Langford but I am also a Handanowicz or Wise or Smith, whatever you call yourself. I am half of your blood line. You trusted Emily to do the right thing. Even after her death, she sent me a clue to figure out the truth. Let me do that and tidy up this mess, not just for me but for you, for Uncle Jim, for Mum's memory."

Evelyn reluctantly removed the gun from under her jumper and handed it to Blake. "Now what?" she asked.

"I need to help Uncle Jim but I need to know why Zodiac and Reaper came after you. What is their connection? Is it me or does it involve Tom Gibson?"

"How do you know Tom Gibson?"

"He came up in a previous case."

"Is that all?"

"Yes."

"You're a terrible liar."

"Okay, he used to be in a relationship with my sister. We recently stopped him from trafficking young women and weapons out of London."

"Why did they break-up?"

"He faked his own death. He used my sister to enable a Russian task force to kill his entire regiment in Afghanistan."

"Looking out for himself. Like father, like son."

"What do you mean?"

"It was the 3rd of September 1938 when Jack Smith and his wife Ada abandoned their child. The bank robbery was more important to him than the life of his daughter who then spent most of her childhood being passed around foster parents and orphanages during the war."

Blake stared at her in shock. "How many children did Jack Smith have?"

"Six that I know of."

"Did Mum know?"

Evelyn nodded. "Emily knew. We all did. Our mother Dana admitted it all before she died. William Handanowicz was not your biological grandfather, Jack Smith was."

Blake sat there struggling to process what Evelyn was telling him. There was a good chance that the man in the photograph that his mother had put in that safe deposit box was actually Jack Smith, his grandfather.

"So where does Tom Gibson fit into all of this?" he finally asked.

"His mother was Patricia Smith. The child that Ada and Jack gave up in 1938. The same Patricia Smith that came to see me in 1987."

"Dad knew..."

Evelyn didn't reply.

"That's why he never wanted Jenny and Tom together. It had nothing to do with him being in the military. Tom and Jenny were cousins!"

Evelyn nodded. "If you've recently crossed swords with Tom, you've kicked the hornet's nest. Emily's will uncovering heirs to Jack's money will create a storm that nobody is going to come out of unscathed."

"I spoke to Victor Wise yesterday. He told me that he wanted no part of the will. If Tom feels like there is an inheritance for him, he'll try and remove anyone who opposes him for it."

"Which is why I had the gun. I knew they would come sooner or later. Jim and I are the final two pieces of the puzzle. I may have been locked up in this place for nearly thirty years but my memory is as sharp as a packet of pins. They are coming for the money and they won't stop until they find it."

"Something that happened to a baby girl seventy years ago has triggered a fight for inheritance today..." Blake shook his head in disbelief. "Don't worry, I'll make sure he gets what's coming for him."

Evelyn glared at him. "Don't be a fool Blake."

It was the first time that she had said his name ever since he walked into the room. "You knew I was coming didn't you. You knew I wouldn't let this go."

"You're my sister's son. You have that fighting spirit. What Jack Smith did was wrong and many people have died chasing the money, the legend of it. All I'm saying is don't be an idiot. We don't need any more family in the graveyard yet."

Blake handed her back the gun. She looked at him warily.

"I will make sure that Tom can't hurt you and I'll smooth things over with Uncle Jim. He came out here in 1984 for a reason and I think that reason was to make sure that you were okay. Now I'm making that same promise. Until then, look after yourself and don't trust anyone."

"You too. If Jim asks about me, tell him to check the right foot."

Blake looked at her confused for a moment.

"He'll know what you mean," she reassured him. "Good luck."

Blake smiled before leaving the room. Finally things were beginning to form in his mind. He struggled to believe how Jack Smith had fathered six children around the time of the second world war. He had four names, Patricia, Victor, Evelyn and Emily. Blake had a feeling that the identities of the final two could help him piece the rest of the puzzle together. For now, he needed to find out where Jim Handanowicz was being held and fight for his release. He knew he needed to tread carefully. Jim had betrayed the Langfords in the past but this time, Blake was sure that he held the key to figuring out Emily Langford's will.

***

Back in the UK at East Boldre Cemetery in the New Forest, Jenny Langford and Jade Smith joined Special Branch agents, Samir Khalifa and Joe Knight as a coffin was lifted up by a small crane out of the unmarked grave.

"What happened to your trousers?" Joe asked.

"I got splashed by a passing car," Samir lied.

"Must've been quite a puddle."

"It was," Samir replied before approaching the coffin.

"After so long, I'd have thought that the coffin would have disintegrated by now," Jenny said.

Jade nodded, her eyes fixed on the old wooden coffin. "It's a miracle it's still intact," her voice barely above a whisper.

The agents carefully opened the lid, revealing the skeletal remains inside. Jenny felt a chill run through her as she gazed down at the bones. A nagging doubt in her mind made her feel uneasy about what was about to be uncovered. She couldn't help but wonder who was buried here and what was their connection to her family, if any? Or was it someone else entirely? The mystery was like a dark cloud hanging over them and now they could hopefully uncover the truth.

Samir Khalifa had previously worked with forensics teams and he carefully examined the bones, his gloved hands prodding and inspecting each fragment. After what felt like an eternity, he finally spoke up. "These remains appear to be that of a woman in her late sixties, perhaps early seventies," he said, his voice steady.

Joe Knight frowned. "Something doesn't add up here."

Jenny noticed a metal plaque had fallen off of the side of the coffin as they removed it from the grave. She knelt down and picked it up. When she read the name inscribed on it, she felt a shiver run down her spine. "Oh my God!" she gasped.

Everyone turned to look at her as she turned the plaque towards them.

"It's my grandmother, Dana Sylvia Handanowicz," she said.

The revelation stunned everyone. Jenny's grandmother, Dana Handanowicz, buried in an unmarked grave where Andrea Smith's body was discovered. How could this have happened and the Langford family knew nothing about it? Questions began to swirl in Jenny's mind. Why would her own family go to such lengths to hide the truth? How did her grandmother's remains end up here?

"Could that plaque have been planted in the grave?" Jade asked.

Joe looked at the coffin lid. "No, it was originally screwed on the coffin or at least an identical plaque was before it came loose over time and fell off."

Samir carefully examined the plaque. "This changes everything," he muttered under his breath. "We need to find out why Dana Handanowicz's body was hidden here without any official records. We'll take the body back to the lab and check the dental records just to be sure but if it is Dana, we need to find out the connection."

"Do you think Tom Gibson had something to do with this? Could he have orchestrated this entire cover-up?" Jenny asked.

Samir nodded. "It's certainly a possibility he was either involved or knew who was. Tom is desperate for the inheritance and we know he'll stop at nothing to get it. But we can't jump to any conclusions just yet."

Jenny clenched her fists in anger and frustration. "We can't let him get away with this!"

Joe placed a comforting hand on her shoulder. "Don't worry, we won't rest until we uncover the truth and find who's responsible."

"And what about Blake?"

"I just hope he's finding out the answers he needs in Rhodes."

Samir looked at the remains once more before closing the lid of the coffin. He had seen many dead bodies during his career but it never became any easier. "We need to take these bones back for further analysis," he said. "I'll get our chief of forensics, Kevin McCoy, to take a look. Maybe there's something more we can learn from them."

As they prepared to leave the cemetery, Jenny's mind raced with questions. Why would her grandmother be buried in an unmarked grave after the rest of the family had believed that both her and her husband, William, had been cremated?

Nothing made sense anymore. And what secrets did Dana Handanowicz hold that someone was willing to kill for? And not only kill but also place the victim in the grave they knew potentially held secrets to the past. She knew that finding answers would not be easy and she knew that she couldn't completely trust Jade, but she was prepared to do whatever it took to uncover the truth. As they arrived back at the car, Joe Knight called after them. Jenny and Jade both turned to face him.

"Can you both join me at the mortuary for the identification?" Joe asked.

"What identification?" Jade asked. "We've already seen the corpse."

Joe looked at Jenny who turned to face Jade. "The reason Special Branch got a court order for this grave to be dug up was because a young woman had been buried alive in it," Jenny explained.

"The missing woman on the news, oh my God! Why didn't you tell me? Wait, why do we have to go and identify her?" Jade asked.

Jenny bowed her head.

"There is a chance that she may be your sister, Andrea," Joe replied.

The colour drained from Jade's face. "No, no, you're wrong. She's in France."

"If you could come with us then we will know for certain," Joe insisted.

"You knew didn't you!" Jade snapped.

Jenny nodded.

"Why didn't you tell me?"

"I tried but you didn't want to listen. At least now we can be sure either way. It's only a possibility at the moment."

"Bullshit! You led me here under false pretences!"

Jenny didn't reply.

Jade ran her fingers through her hair in frustration. "Hang on, I need to make a call," she replied as she walked away from them.

She scrolled through her phone to find Tom's number. It went straight to voicemail.

"If my sister is dead then you are too!" she said before cutting off the call.

She turned back towards Joe and Jenny who were standing by the car waiting.

"I honestly thought I could trust you!" Jade snapped. "What am I doing here? This is madness!"

"We don't know for definite that it is her," Jenny replied.

"Have you seen her?"

Jenny shook her head.

"Please Miss Smith, come with me and we can hopefully answer all of your questions there," Joe replied.

Reluctantly, she climbed into the back of Joe's car. Jenny followed them in her car away from the cemetery and along the single-track forest roads towards the mortuary. Jenny knew that when Jade discovered Andrea's fate, things would blow up very quickly. She just hoped that Tom wasn't the one who put Andrea in the grave but she had a nagging doubt that he was.

Chapter Fifty-Five

A Letter From The Dead
Tuesday 24th August 1948

Edward Langford was awake early on Tuesday morning and headed down towards Norman Whitehouse's cafe on Calshot Beach. Something was bothering him ever since his visit on Sunday evening. He needed to take a closer look at the cafe before trying to piece together Jack Smith's final few hours. He parked his car next to a brown Austin before heading down onto the beach. As he arrived, he was surprised to find Officer Wells already there supervising a group of men who were removing the remaining fixtures and fittings from inside the cafe.

"Good morning George," Edward called out as he approached.

Officer Wells turned around to face him. "Oh, hello Sir, I didn't expect to see you down here today."

"I always find that an early morning walk helps me focus on things a little better. What brings you down here? Aren't you supposed to be following up on the postmortem of Jack Smith?"

"Officer Jones is taking care of that. Ol' Norman Whitehouse called me up late last night, he's been caught up with some business in Portsmouth so he gave me the keys to let the lads in this morning to empty the cafe out."

"I never knew you and Whitehouse were that close."

"We're not. Just doing my bit for the community, Sir."

"Would you mind if I had another look inside?"

"No, no, of course not. I'll join you," Officer Wells stammered as he led him towards the entrance.

"So who is taking the place over from Whitehouse?"

"Don't really know, some guy called William Handanowicz. He works at the City Bank in Southampton. Some kind of genius with investments or something like that."

"If he's working in the city, why does he want to buy some old cafe out here?" Edward asked.

"Who knows? He made Norman an offer he couldn't refuse so he sold it."

As they entered the cafe, Edward watched as the men worked methodically removing the remaining tables, benches and work surfaces from the cafe. One of the men lifted up a bench and carried it on his shoulder towards the exit. He had short brown hair and wore a beige buttoned-up shirt with matching trousers that looked as though they had mud or dirt splattered across one of the legs.

"Excuse me, do I know you?" Edward asked the man.

He nervously looked at Officer Wells before turning back to Edward. "No, no, I'm from out of town."

"Where out of town?"

"Tooton," he replied.

"Tooton, not Totton?"

He didn't reply.

"What's your name?"

"Steven."

"Steven what?"

"Steven Thomas."

Edward smiled. "Sorry, my mistake. You reminded me of someone I used to know. On your way."

Steven quickly continued on his way out of the door.

Edward turned back to face Officer Wells. "Do you know any of these guys?"

"No, the new owner sent them in. Why?"

"That guy I just spoke to looks a lot like the guy Christopher and I chased out of Harold Partridge's house yesterday."

"Are you sure? Did you get a good look at him?"

"No, it all happened so fast. I need to find Christopher. He would recognise him."

"Christopher, is he the gardener?" Officer Wells asked.

"Yes, do you know where he lives?"

"No, sorry. My rhododendrons need some pruning though so if you find him, send him my way."

Edward stepped outside with Officer Wells close behind him. "If you hear anything from Norman Whitehouse or if this, William Handanowicz, makes an appearance, will you let me know."

"Of course, good luck with the case," Officer Wells replied as he watched him leave.

Edward Langford looked all around the beach and the field that led towards the woodland in the distance as he left but there was no sign of the man who called himself Steven. He was about to turn back towards his car when he noticed something black on the road. He walked over and picked it up. It was a man's wallet. As he opened it up, he found some banknotes, coins and a membership card for 101 Casino in Portsmouth. What really intrigued Edward though, was hidden amongst the banknotes. As he removed them from the wallet, he found a military discharge paper folded up inside. It confirmed that the owner of the wallet was Stefan Thomas Weber, who was recently discharged from the German Armed Forces.

***

Mavis Langford was hanging some washing out on the clothesline when the postman arrived.

"Good morning Mrs Langford!" he called out.

"Good morning Terrance! If it's bills you can keep it!" she replied as he handed her several letters.

"If I had a shilling every time I'd heard that..."

"You'd never have to work again, I know. What's new?"

"Nothing much. Shame about Mrs Wise's house down the road..."

"I know, it's so out of character for her to just disappear like that."

"Are the police any closer to discovering where she went?"

"Not as far as I know but Ed doesn't tell me anything."

"What about that man on the beach?" Terrance asked.

"What about him?"

"Well he turned up dead didn't he."

"Oh, yes, yes, he did."

"Did you know him?"

"No. Well, not really. Oh, listen to that, the kettle's on, must dash," Mavis replied before rushing back inside the house.

Terrance watched her as she rushed back inside before continuing on his way. When she was inside, she quickly sorted through the letters until she came to an envelope with handwriting that she recognised.

"No, it can't be," she said to herself.

"We're off to the beach!" Fred said as he rushed past with fishing nets and buckets followed by John carrying a bowl of crabs.

"Don't go too far, remember Mary has her dance class this evening," Mavis called out.

"How could we forget..." John sighed before heading out of the back door.

Mavis sat on the chair and opened the letter. As she read it, tears fell from her cheeks down onto the envelope in her lap. It was from Dana. Her and Edith had left during the night and fled to Portsmouth where they had been looked after in a convent. She explained about her affair with Jack Smith when she was caring for him during the war. The son that she gave birth to, named Victor, who she then had to give away to the nuns to look after and how she hoped to be reunited with him once more. After their meeting on the beach on Saturday afternoon, Jack had told her that it was no longer safe to stay in the village and had given her two gold bars, worth over three hundred pounds each, to help her start a new life.

Mavis sat in stunned silence, the letter clutched tightly in her hand. Her mind raced with a whirlwind of emotions as she tried to process the shocking revelations from Dana's confession. The familiar sounds of her home faded into the background as she delved deep into the memories of the past.

She remembered the war vividly, the uncertainty that shrouded their lives and how Dana's kindness had touched so many hearts in the village. But this revelation of betrayal and clandestine love shattered the image she held of her dear friend. The weight of secrets buried for years now bore down heavily on Mavis's shoulders.

Every time she looked into the eyes of her twins, Mary and Frederick, she saw Jack staring back at her. Just like he had done on the beach only a few days ago. How could she tell her friend, the man who gave her her son, Victor, was also the father of Mary and Frederick. It had been a stupid fling. A one night stand. Edward had been working nights for over a month and he was just some company for her. She never expected to see him again, let alone, care for him during the war and now the story of his relationship with Dana, her best friend, cut her anew.

She knew if Edward ever discovered this secret that she held, their marriage would be over and what then? What about the children and the family home they had built up over the years.

All gone due to one moment of weakness. She folded up the letter and wandered upstairs into the bedroom. There was a loose floorboard in the corner next to the ottoman. She removed it and placed the letter and its envelope under the floorboard before replacing it once again.

"Hello!" a voice called out from downstairs.

The shout startled Mavis. She stood up quickly and hit her head on the side of the bedpost. Cursing quietly to herself, she wandered back downstairs.

"Hello?" the voice called out again.

"Hello Christopher," Mavis replied as she walked down the stairs. "Sorry for taking so long, I had to spend a penny."

Christopher looked at her confused.

"Use the toilet," she elaborated.

"Oh, right, okay, sorry."

"What brings you here this morning? Is everything okay?"

"I was looking for Mr Langford, is he home?"

"No, he went out early this morning and hasn't been back yet."

"Oh, okay. Maybe I'll call back later."

"Is something wrong? Anything that I can help with?"

"No. It's just… After seeing the vicar in the church yesterday, I thought that I should mention that I often saw him and a young man visiting the institute just outside the village. There may be a connection between them."

"The vicar visits many of us regularly to spread the word of God, that's not unusual. Did you ask him who the young man was when you saw him yesterday?"

"I couldn't."

"Why?"

"Because he was dead."

Mavis gasped as the front door opened and Edward Langford entered. "Did you know and you didn't tell me?" she asked.

"Know what?" Edward replied.

"The vicar is dead."

Edward gave Christopher a stern look. "You were asleep when I arrived home last night and I needed to follow up on an investigation at first light so when did I have the chance to tell you anything?"

"Is it true?"

"There was a murder at the church last night but it wasn't Harold Partridge."

Both of them looked at Edward.

"It was someone else who was locked in and murdered in the vestry. Harold's disappeared and I found this by the beach this morning after I scared away someone at Norman Whitehouse's cafe."

Edward dropped the wallet on the kitchen table. Christopher felt a shiver run through him. He knew who the wallet belonged to but tried not to let it show.

"Where did you go yesterday after you ran out of the church?" Edward asked.

"I went home. Sorry, I'm not very good in those situations. After what I saw, I had to get away. I'm not used to seeing dead bodies like that," Christopher replied.

"And where is home? Nobody in the village seems to know where you live."

"I'm staying at the institute about three miles from here. Just until I can earn enough money to buy a home of my own."

"Why all the questions Ed? Surely you can't suspect Christopher of being involved in all of this," Mavis replied.

"The man who dropped this wallet this morning whilst running away from the cafe on Calshot Beach looked very much like the man who managed to get away from us in the woods yesterday. Do you think you could recognise him again?"

"I didn't get a clear look at him. I was running through the woods and caught my foot on a tree stump. I fell and winded myself and he got away. You saw that because you were behind me."

"I saw the guy disappear into the woods whilst you were on the ground but I didn't see you fall. Where did you say you were from again?"

"Amsterdam in the Netherlands."

"And how did you end up here?"

"I came here after the war to find work."

"Do you have your papers?"

"Not with me, why?"

"Where are they?"

"Back at the institute. Have I done something wrong?" Christopher asked.

"Ed, what's going on? Christopher came here today to tell you about the vicar visiting a young man at the institute," Mavis replied.

Edward held open the discharge papers he had found inside the wallet. "Discharge papers for Stefan Thomas Weber from Dusseldorf, Germany. Either someone is housing the enemy or he was one of the squatters in the cafe where Jack Smith's body was found."

Mavis froze. How did Edward discover Jack's real identity so fast? "Who's Jack Smith?" she asked nervously.

"The gent that we were meant to believe was Vincent Williams. The man who shared luncheon with us at the weekend and who old Harold Partridge saw with Dana Wise on the evening before she disappeared who then turned up dead on the beach!" Edward replied.

"Did she have a daughter with her?" Christopher asked.

"Yes, why?" Edward asked.

"Because I saw a man in a brown suit lead a woman and her daughter to a car late on Saturday night. He handed over a lot of money to the driver and then they drove off."

"Where was this?"

"Outside the house that burnt down. Well, it was still okay when they left."

"And where did the man in the suit go after they drove away?"

"He walked back towards the house."

"Was he alone?"

"He was and then a car arrived. An Austin, I think it was."

"Did you see who got out of the car?"

"No, I wasn't paying much attention. I didn't even think about it until Frances, sorry, Miss King, told me about the house fire."

"What about the car?"

"What do you mean?"

"What colour was it? Anything unusual about it?"

"How's he meant to remember that? There's hardly any streetlights down there," Mavis interrupted.

Edward glared at her.

"I think it was brown or black but it was very dark. I only had my torch to light the way."

A loud knocking at the front door interrupted their conversation. Edward walked over and answered it. As he opened the door, they saw their neighbour, Frances King, holding a brown envelope.

"Ah, Frances, we were just talking about you," Edward said.

"Nothing bad I hope. Chris, I've been looking for you. Is there any chance you could help with my bush later, it needs trimming?"

"I'll call round in a while after I've finished helping Mr and Mrs Langford," Christopher replied.

"What brings you here dear?" Mavis asked.

"Oh, Terrance delivered this to the wrong house. It's addressed to you Mrs Langford. I don't know what's gotten into him lately. How difficult is it to put some letters in a mailbox or post them through the right doors?" Frances sighed.

Edward took the letter from her. "Well, thank you for delivering it to us Miss King, I'm sure you have a busy day ahead so run along now."

Frances looked at Mavis and Christopher for some support. Finding none, she swiftly turned and walked away as Edward closed the door behind her.

"That was rather rude," Mavis said.

"She'll live," Edward replied, looking at the envelope. "Since when have you been using the CityBank in Southampton? Have you been hiding money away from me?"

"No! I don't know anything about CityBank," Mavis snapped as she snatched the letter out of Edward's hand and opened it.

She removed the letter from the envelope and read it. On CityBank headed paper, it was a statement of earnings from a gold depository in the bank which was opened in 1940. It showed the measurement of four pounds and four ounces of gold deposited on 31st December 1940 which had now been valued at three hundred and one pounds, placed in a trust fund for Mavis Joan Langford by Mr J. Smith.

The colour drained from Mavis' face. She dropped the letter and raced to the kitchen sink to be sick. Edward picked it up and read it. He walked over to Mavis and gave her a cup of water. After a few minutes, she turned to face him.

"I want the truth this time, who is Jack Smith?" Edward asked.

Mavis began to cry. "He was someone Dana and I cared for during the war."

"Did you recognise him on Saturday?"

"Not at first. I didn't want to embarrass Dana so I just played along with her that we thought he was a stranger."

"A stranger doesn't leave you that kind of money Mavis and now Dana has disappeared with Edith. How long before whoever is behind this comes after you?"

"Maybe I should leave," Christopher said as he headed for the door.

"Yes, I'll speak to you soon," Edward replied before turning his attention back to Mavis. "I need to know what happened during the war. It may give me the answer to who killed him on the beach."

Mavis wiped her eyes. "After we heard that Gerald had died. Dana felt very lonely. She was struggling. Her sister couldn't look after Edith anymore so she had to send her to the chapel where the nuns were looking after the children whilst we looked after the wounded. John, Mary and Fred were there too so it made sense that they were all together. Dana was a marvellous stitcher. She saved a lot of the men who would have bled to death if she hadn't helped them."

"What's the connection between Dana and Jack Smith? Does it have anything to do with the boy she sent into foster care?"

"How do you know about that?"

Edward didn't respond.

"Dana had a short romance with Jack Smith. When he found out that she was pregnant, he left. As far as I know, she never saw him again until Saturday. Dana continued to work in the medical tents and buildings for as long as she could and then her sister, Enid, looked after Edith whilst she had the baby and then..."

"Then she took care of that," Edward finished for her.

"Yes, she took care of that," Mavis sighed. "Within a week, she was back in the medical tent acting like nothing had ever happened."

"You know this gives Dana Wise a reason to kill Jack Smith don't you?"

"She wouldn't. She couldn't. She loved him."

"And he left her. A widow. Pregnant and alone. A broken heart can sometimes be a dangerous thing to have. I have witnesses to say that she was seen with Jack on Saturday evening. Then, suddenly, her and Edith disappear and Jack Smith ends up dead on the beach. You know how much I hate coincidences."

"Did it look like Jack was murdered?"

Edward sighed. "To be honest, no. The postmortem will tell us more but it looks like he died naturally."

Mavis bowed her head.

"The bank would have sent this letter after they had discovered that Jack Smith had died. He must have left that gold in his will but why leave it to you and not Dana?"

"I don't know."

A knock at the front door interrupted them. Edward wandered over and as he opened the door, he found Sergeant Peter Hastings waiting for him.

"Sorry to bother you Sir, there's been another body found in the woods," Hastings said.

Edward ran his fingers through his hair. "Any idea who it is?"

"No Sir, he was found hanging from a tree with no wallet or identification on him."

Edward turned back to Mavis. "We'll continue this later," he said before heading out of the door.

Mavis sat on the chair at the kitchen table looking at the letter once again. Reading the numbers over and over again. Trying to figure out why he had decided to put the gold in trust. She had never told him about Mary and Fred. She knew she needed to keep Edward away from the truth but letters from the departed were becoming a major problem.

Chapter Fifty-Six

The Right Foot
Monday 3rd November 2008

Blake Langford and Alison Pearce followed Detective Aris Stathakis into Lalysos Police Station. He whispered something to the officer at the reception desk before leading them down a corridor to a room at the back of the station. As they entered, they noticed a table with two chairs either side of it and an old style cassette tape recorder had been left on the table.

"Am I under interrogation or something?" Blake asked.

"No, no, of course not. We just need to make sure that we have everything correct before we proceed. Please, take a seat," Aris replied before taking a seat on the opposite side of the table with Lauren Prince sitting alongside him.

Blake and Alison reluctantly took their seats opposite them.

"You know they have CD's these days too," Alison quipped.

"I don't think this is the appropriate time for jesting Miss Pearce," Aris snapped.

"And I don't think this is an appropriate time for wasting our time. We came over here to find out why two men involved in a Special Branch operation tried to kill two of your local residents," Blake replied.

"I agree. I'm just as eager as you are to find out why this has happened but I was unaware that both of the people in question are in fact related to you. Don't you think that is a conflict of interests that needs to be addressed?" Aris asked.

"Work with me or against me, I don't care. I just want to find out what's going on with Jim Handanowicz and then I'm outta here. I've got bigger fish to fry than some up-tight detective on some map dot in the Mediterranean having an ego trip!"

Aris looked at Alison. "Is he always this aggressive? No wonder the family fled the country."

Blake was about to respond but caught a stare from Lauren which told him otherwise. "Fine, have it your way but you have the wrong man in custody."

Aris glared at him. "What do you mean? My officers arrived at James Handanowicz's villa and found two dead bodies. When we arrived, he had blood on his clothes which matched the victims."

"But what if he didn't trust the Greek police?" Alison asked. "And why wouldn't he..."

"He's not a Greek national," Blake interrupted. "He was born and raised in England before moving here in 1984. Sure, he's worked here for the past twenty-five years and looked after his sister, Evelyn, whilst she was locked away in that facility in Monolithos but he is still a British citizen in a foreign land. You arrested him on the flimsiest of evidence so you can either charge him in the next few hours or he is a free man. You decide."

Aris sat back in his chair. "Okay, you managed to get Miss Handanowicz to talk when no one else could, maybe I should give you some rope here. I will let you talk with James Handanowicz but if you try anything to get him or Evelyn out of the country whilst this investigation is going on, I swear, I'll track you down."

Blake leant forward towards Aris. "Bring James Handanowicz to me, press record on your little tape recorder then piss off and let me do my job."

Aris glared at him. Blake held his gaze. Neither of them flinched for a moment before Aris stood up and stormed out of the room. Lauren gave Blake a little smirk before following Aris out of the door.

"Smooth Langford, real smooth. I don't want to come all the way out to Greece to get myself thrown into jail," Alison snapped.

"You won't, he's clutching at straws, he knows nothing," Blake replied.

After a few moments of silence, the door swung open and James Handanowicz was escorted into the room by two uniformed officers. His face carried a mix of confusion and apprehension as he glanced at Blake and Alison.

"You called for me?" James asked, sounding slightly nervous.

Blake nodded, gesturing towards the empty seat next to him. "Please, have a seat."

James hesitated for a brief moment before complying and taking the offered seat. His eyes darted around the room, clearly aware of the tension in the air. "I often wondered when the Langford juggernaut would roll into my beautiful island. For some reason, I didn't expect my nephew would be the executor of my downfall."

"Whatever dealings you had with my father are irrelevant, James. Or do I call you Uncle Jim?"

"Jim is fine. No need for false sentimentality. We all know that John Langford would have poisoned his family against us anyway. Emily was too weak to speak up. Scared of losing her privileged lifestyle."

"My mother, your sister, Emily Langford, is dead!" Blake snapped.

Jim bowed his head. "I know, I'm sorry. She was a wonderful woman."

Blake let that hang for a moment before continuing. "You underestimate my father. He told us the whole truth about what happened in 1984 and let us decide for ourselves what we thought of you."

"And?"

"Initially, I thought you were a callous bastard who had taken my parents for a ride on some sob story to extort money from the family but, when looking at the facts, you came over here and supported your sister, Evelyn Handanowicz, with her medical needs and looked after her for the past twenty-five years. For a man to give up his life to help his sister with her mental health issues, he can't be all bad."

Jim sighed. "So I assume you're here to interrogate me about those bodies they found at my home."

"Partly yes," Blake replied, his tone softer than before. "We're trying to get to the bottom of this. But before we dive into it, there's something you need to know."

Jim raised an eyebrow curiously. "What is it?"

Blake leaned forward, fixing him with an intense gaze. "You're not the only one who's been keeping secrets, Jim. There's more to this case than meets the eye. We suspect there's a connection between those bodies found at your villa and a powerful criminal organisation operating across Europe."

Jim's eyes widened in surprise. "I-I had no idea about any criminal organisation. I've been minding my own business, taking care of Evelyn. I wouldn't get involved in anything like that."

Blake nodded sympathetically. "I believe you, Jim. But sometimes, circumstances force us into situations we never anticipated. We need your help to uncover the truth."

Jim took a deep breath, his shoulders sagging with the weight of the ordeal he found himself in. "Alright, what do you need from me?"

"We need you to tell us everything you know about your sister's time at the Monolithos facility," Blake said, leaning back in his chair.

As Jim recounted the years from when he arrived in 1984 and found Evelyn crying on the floor in her rundown shack that she was living in at the time, the ups and downs of her care whilst he also attempted to earn a living as a bricklayer, there was nothing obvious there that stood out to Blake as being significant to the case. He waited for Jim to finish before playing his trump card.

"Does the name Jack Smith mean anything to you?" Blake asked.

He saw the colour drain from Jim's face.

"Not here," Jim replied.

"We don't have much time Jim," Alison spoke for the first time. "Emily's will has opened up a lot of questions and we think it may have been linked to why those men came after you."

"Get me out of here and I'll tell you everything," he replied, looking at Alison.

"What about the right foot?" Blake asked.

"Get me out of here and I'll tell you everything," Jim repeated.

Blake sighed as he leant back in his chair. "It might not be as easy as that right now. They still suspect that you murdered two men in your home."

"Circumstantial is all they have, come on Blake, you know the drill," Jim pleaded.

At that moment, Detective Aris Stathakis burst into the room. Blake and Alison immediately stood up, about to argue with him but he raised his hand in anticipation of their response.

"He's free to go," Aris said.

All three of them looked at Aris confused.

"We've had a confession and currently have no grounds to hold Mr Handanowicz any longer but don't leave the country, this is not over," Aris continued.

"I doubt it is," Jim replied.

"Does the deal still stand?" Alison asked.

"What deal is that?" Aris asked.

Jim nodded. "You two only."

Alison and Blake both nodded in agreement.

"What deal?" Aris asked again. "I told you Langford, if he even looks at an airport or boat I'll..."

"You'll what? You had your chance and failed, now let the Special Intelligence Branch of Great Britain help a British citizen to get justice for a crime he didn't commit!" Blake snapped holding Aris' gaze.

"You have no right to speak to me like this!"

"Then do your job, detective and find out as much as you can about Reaper and Zodiac!"

"And what good will that do?"

"At least you'll be earning your pay."

Aris glared at him. Both men stood unflinching for a moment.

Blake's face broke out into a smile. "You know what, you've been wasting my time. Ever since we arrived on this island, we've been tidying up your mess..."

Aris's face turned scarlet. "I'll have you thrown off the case!"

"Aris, listen, I've got five fingers and guess what, the middle one's just for you," Blake replied.

"Get him out of my sight!" he snapped before storming out of the interrogation room.

"That went well. I guess it's time to go," Alison replied as she led them out of the room and after Jim had collected his belongings, out of the police station.

As they wandered down the road, Blake heard a woman call after them. They turned and saw Lauren Prince rushing to catch up with them. Alison approached her as she handed over some paperwork.

"The confession came from Evelyn Handanowicz. She told them she killed the men and Jim had nothing to do with it. With her mental state, the judge will probably rule on her being mentally incapacitated," Lauren explained.

"Why are you helping us?" Alison asked.

"I'm not a Greek national. I moved here from London ten years ago. I want to help you get the answers you need but Aris is a bastard. Once he realises that Evelyn's confession won't hold, he'll come after Jim again."

Blake took the paperwork and quickly flicked through it. "What part of London were you from?" he asked.

"Sutton, just off the old Cheam Road," Lauren replied.

"I know it well."

"You helped my uncle with that arson attack on the church back in '97."

Blake thought for a moment. "The First Church Of Christ? Albert Prince?"

Lauren nodded. "You helped my family catch the ones responsible for the fire, it's my turn to help you."

Blake smiled. "Albert was a good man. Thank you. To be honest, we could use a car..."

Lauren reached into her pocket and pulled out a car key. "My red Fiat is parked near the gate at the side of the station, I won't need it until later."

Within minutes, Jim was driving them along mountainous roads across the island heading towards Lindos. "What did Evelyn tell you about Jack Smith?" he asked.

Blake repeated the conversation he had with Evelyn at the care home about her and Emily being fathered by Jack Smith and the fall-out it caused when it all came out.

Jim shook his head. "Evelyn never got over Fred," he sighed.

"Uncle Fred? Dad's brother?" Blake asked.

Jim nodded. "It was your parent's wedding day back in 1977 when it all happened. There had been rumours that Evelyn had found herself a man and that he would be at the wedding. Nobody realised until the week before that it would be Fred Langford."

"So what happened? It's not unusual for two sisters to marry two brothers," Alison asked.

"That's the problem, Fred was her brother. Well, half-brother at least."

Blake shook his head. "I don't understand. My grandmother on mum's side, Dana Handanowicz, had a fling with Jack Smith during the war and he fathered my mother Emily and her twin sister Evelyn. Mavis Langford, my grandmother on dad's side, had Fred, Mary and John with my grandad Edward Langford."

"Was Edward Langford called up during the Second World War?" Jim asked.

"Yes, he was always showing us his medals when Jenny, Steven and I were kids."

Jim nodded. "William Handanowicz and Edward Langford were both called up and fought for their country and when they came home, there were new babies waiting for them."

Blake shook his head. "You mean Jack Smith slept with both Dana and Mavis whilst..."

Jim nodded. "It was all covered up, you know how taboo sex outside of marriage was back then."

"So were my parents related?"

"No."

"How can you be so sure?"

"John Langford was Edward Langford's son. Mary and Fred were Jack's. That's why Evelyn and Fred couldn't be together. They shared the same father."

The pieces of the puzzle were finally falling into place for Blake. "My father said that Fred sped away from the church after a huge argument."

Jim nodded. "He lost control of the car and hit a tree somewhere near Winchester. He was dead on impact. Evelyn never forgave herself."

"Did she know about Jack?" Alison asked.

"She found out when they had the argument outside the church before Emily and John's wedding. Fred gave her the ring that he was going to propose with before speeding off and having his accident. Unbeknown to him, Evelyn was also pregnant with his child at the time."

Blake gasped. "What happened to the baby?"

"She had a miscarriage, two months after he died. From that moment on, her mental health has been in decline. The services back in the late 70's and early 80's were nothing compared to what's available today. They thought she was mad. Hallucinating. Schizophrenic even. At one point, they had her in a straight-jacket and kept her isolated for three weeks. That was why I needed the money. To help her get the support she needed. Nobody in England was willing to help. The doctors here had given up on her. I found out about a man on the island called Stelios Christodoulopoulos who ran wellness clinics and helped people with deep mental health problems. He was the one who opened the care facility in Monolithos where Evelyn stays now."

Blake bowed his head realising his anger towards Jim had been misdirected. "Is he still running the facility?"

"No, he died three years ago. The place has been going downhill ever since."

"Is she too ill to live outside of the care home?" Alison asked.

"She comes out on day trips and stays the occasional night with me but she gets overwhelmed and very reactive if she's away from the facility for too long. They have her on a strict timeline for her medication and I don't think she would be able to organise that for herself in the outside world," Jim explained.

As they turned a corner, they saw a beautiful bay far below the cliff and the road that they were travelling on. To their left was the deep blue sea lapping against a small sandy beach and in front of them was a huge rock with a stone footpath twisting its way from the base all the way to the top. Jim parked the car on the top of the cliff and handed some Euros to the parking attendant before leading Alison and Blake down a steep hill at the side of the cliff.

"Where are we going?" Blake asked as families rushed past them heading towards a market at the base of the cliff.

"You wanted to know about the right foot. First, we have to climb to the top of the acropolis," Jim replied.

As they followed Jim down towards the base of the cliff, they discovered cobbled paths that snaked their way between hundreds of market stalls selling everything from olive oil, traditional greek alcohol, souvenirs of the local area, cheaply produced football shirts, sponges from the mediterranean sea and various greek salads and moussaka. The smell of the freshly cooked food made Blake feel hungry. They had barely eaten anything since they had left London almost twelve hours ago.

Relentlessly, Jim led them out of the market and up the stone steps and pathways that circled the huge rock several times before they arrived at the summit. A couple of times, Alison lost her balance and Blake helped her up to the next section. There was no handrail or anything to guard somebody falling over the side and plummeting hundreds of metres onto the rocks and shallow sea below.

Jim looked at his watch. "We need to be quick, the sun sets in one and a half hours and you don't want to climb back down in the dark."

Blake looked around at the top of the acropolis. There were several well preserved ancient statues standing tall on top of the rock. Behind them was the cliff face that led back up to the main road but in every other direction was deep blue mediterranean sea. If he hadn't been so involved in the case, Blake thought it would be an idyllic place for a family holiday in the summertime.

"So what are these statues and how are they relevant?" Alison asked.

Jim looked around and noticed the final few tourists were beginning to leave and make their way back down towards the market. "These statues signify the Greek Gods and rulers from thousands of years ago. Come with me."

Alison and Blake followed Jim over towards the statue on the far side of the acropolis. They stopped at the feet of the statue. Jim looked around once more before removing a chisel from his pocket. He picked up a rock and used it to hammer and chisel away the stone of the right foot of the statue.

"What are you doing? This statue is thousands of years old. You're destroying history!" Alison gasped.

Jim hit the rock onto the chisel a few more times before the side of the right foot shattered and revealed what looked like a bronze pipe. It was around an inch wide and about three inches long. He removed the pipe and handed it to Blake.

"Inside there is part of the map of where Jack Smith left his fortune," Jim smiled. "Find Dana's part and you'll locate the family inheritance. This is what those men were after but Stelios and I completed some patch work for the acropolis in 1985.

Before we cemented it over, I hid the pipe inside hoping that nobody would ever find it."

"So why have you given it to me?" Blake asked.

"Emily took her secret to the grave before entrusting you to figure it out. Too many people are dying because of Jack Smith's mistakes Blake. You have a chance to end it all."

Blake looked down at the pipe and then back at Jim.

"Ti kaneis ekei?" a man shouted out from behind them.

"Go! I'll take care of them!" Jim said, handing Blake the car key and ushering them away.

"I'm not leaving you here," Blake replied.

"Na stamatisei!" the man shouted as he lunged towards Alison.

Jim moved between them and caught the man with a strong punch to the right side of his face. The man turned and took a swing at Jim who dodged before landing another blow on the man's jaw.

"Don't argue! Go now!" Jim shouted.

Two more men appeared and began rushing towards Jim. Blake took his opportunity and shoulder barged one of them against one of the statues. The man fell to the ground winded.

He handed the pipe and key to Alison. "Get back to the car. I'll catch up with you," he said as the third man launched a kick towards Blake's ribs.

Blake blocked it before following up with a kick to the man's standing leg that sent him down momentarily. He quickly got up and charged at Blake who ducked down and flipped his attacker over his shoulder. The man's momentum took him off-balance and over the side of the acropolis. They heard a scream followed by a sickening thud below. Blake looked over at Jim as the remaining two men were lining up to bring him down. Jim looked at Blake before turning and jumping off the edge of the rock.

Blake rushed to the edge and saw Jim land in the sea below and begin to swim away. He shook his head in disbelief before turning and realising that the two men were now heading his way. Blake turned and quickly rushed back down the cobbled stone steps back into the market below. As he rushed past a stall selling traditional Greek Ouzo, someone grabbed his shirt and pulled him inside. He was about to lash out before realising that it was Alison who had pulled him in. The two men rushed past the stall and into the market.

"Kalispera," the owner of the stall called out.

"Yamas," Blake replied before heading back towards the main path.

"You English?" the stall owner asked.

"Yes, how did..." Alison began.

The stall owner handed over two shot glasses of ouzo. "Take this and there's a shortcut behind here that takes you back to the hill."

They both drank the ouzo and thanked the stall owner before rushing down an alleyway filled with rubbish bags and a couple of children playing with a football before heading back up the hill.

"Where's Jim?" Alison asked as they arrived back at the car.

"He went for a swim."

"Seriously?"

"He leapt off the rock and swam away."

"So what do we do now?"

Blake looked over and noticed the two men that had been chasing them halfway up the hill. He took the car keys and climbed into the car. Alison joined him in the passenger seat.

Blake calmly reversed the car and headed out of the car park following the road that Jim had driven them down earlier.

"There seems to be a lot of people protecting whatever it is that mum's will has opened. We need to find out what's inside that tube and get it back to London," Blake replied.

"Where are we heading?"

Blake pulled over to the side of the road and searched for Monolithos on the satnav. "The only place we can go, Jim's villa."

Chapter Fifty-Seven

A German, A Police Officer And A Woman Scorned

Tuesday 24th August 1948

Sergeant Peter Hastings led Edward Langford down the mud path into the woods between the church and Harold Partridge's cottage. Officer George Wells was speaking to Christopher whilst the forensic team worked on securing the area.

"You're turning up like a bad penny today George," Edward commented as he looked up at the body hanging from the tree. "Wasn't he the guy who ran away from the cafe this morning?"

"Never seen him before," Officer Wells replied.

"Come on George, you were supervising the workers for Norman Whitehouse at the beach cafe this morning. You must have had some idea of who they were!"

"I told you, the new owner sent those men in to empty the place out."

"Who sent them? Who did they work for?" Sergeant Hastings asked.

"William Handanowicz, the guy who paid Whitehouse for it. Why am I suddenly getting questioned?" Officer Wells asked.

"Because this man has discharge papers from the German military so either you or this Handanowicz guy have been helping a German or those squatters we discovered are being killed off," Edward replied.

"How dare you suggest that I'd help a Kraut!" Officer Wells fumed. "Those bastards killed my parents!!"

"Which gives you a motive! Go back to the station Officer Wells, I'm relieving you of your command," Edward replied.

Officer George Wells glared at Edward, then at Sergeant Hastings before storming away towards the church.

Edward wandered over towards Christopher who was still looking up at the body hanging from the branch. "Do you recognise him?"

Christopher nodded. "I'm almost certain he was the one I chased..."

"I thought you were going to see Frances after you left my house. What brought you down here?"

"I was heading towards the bus stop when I saw what had happened."

"Where were you planning to go?"

"Back to the institute."

Edward sighed. "I'm sorry if I made you feel uncomfortable earlier but I need to look into every possible lead I can find."

"I understand."

"What did Officer Wells say to you?"

"Just asked if I knew who the man in the tree was."

"Did you tell him?"

"No."

"Why?"

"Because I don't trust him," Christopher replied.

"You don't trust a police officer?"

"Like you said, he keeps turning up like a bad penny."

"Have you got something to tell me Christopher?"

He looked at Edward. "The man in the church we saw yesterday..."

Edward nodded. "The one who was murdered..."

Christopher nodded. "His name is Hans Schwartz. He stayed at the institute for a while and then disappeared. When I recognised him yesterday, I panicked. I thought you'd think that I was helping them if I told you who it was."

"Did Mr Morris, the head of the institute, know?"

"No. He claimed to be someone else but, like you, I discovered who he really was."

"And what did you do?"

"I asked him to tell me the truth. He did and I told him I would report him unless he left straightaway."

"And did he?"

Christopher nodded. "He said he needed to see someone in the village first and then he would leave."

"Do you know who it was?"

"He went to the vicar's cottage."

"You followed him?"

"I didn't trust that he would do what he said."

"So what happened?"

"I met Frances King."

"What was she doing at the vicar's house?"

"She wasn't. She was walking back from the grocery store when her bags split open. I helped her carry her groceries back to her house."

"And then what?" Edward asked.

"I met her father and began helping around the village."

"You didn't think about going back to check if Hans had left?"

"Frances was very persuasive."

Edward nodded. "I'll need you to come to the station with me so we can complete the paperwork."

Christopher nodded. "I'll be there later."

***

Officer George Wells climbed into his car and slammed the door. As he started the engine, he felt a cold blade against his neck.

"Langford knows about us!" a man's voice said.

"Max, calm down. He knows nothing," Officer Wells replied.

"Stefan and Hans are both dead. How long before he finds out about Christoph and me?"

"He won't. Christoph won't tell them anything."

"I know Christoph won't but what about you?"

"What about me?"

"Remember, I know what you did at Honeypot Cottage. If Langford finds out that you helped Smith before he died, you will be finished. I can destroy your career anytime I want to."

"It doesn't matter now. Langford has taken me off the case."

"Then you're of no use anymore," Max replied before slashing the knife across George's throat.

Blood covered the steering wheel and dashboard of the car as George frantically tried to stop the bleeding. Max calmly stepped out of the car and walked away.

**

Frances King stepped out of the grocery store carrying two bags of shopping. She noticed Christopher standing at the bus stop on the opposite side of the road.

She wandered over to him. "Going somewhere?"

"I need to go back to the institute," Christopher replied.

"You don't need that place..."

"I do. Mr Langford knows about Stefan and Hans. It won't take him long to work out the rest."

"You seem to forget I have something of yours. If father finds out, he'll kill you."

"That's your problem now."

Frances raised her hand to slap him around the face but he grabbed her wrist. "You need to remember who saved you from being thrown into prison. I can end you anytime I want to."

The sound of a diesel engine interrupted them. Christopher looked over her shoulder at the bus approaching in the distance. "Let me go, Frances. It's better for everyone if I'm gone."

"Not everyone, just you," she cried before rushing away towards the woods.

The driver stopped the bus as Christopher watched her leave. He climbed on board and paid his fare before taking a seat halfway down on the left hand side of the bus. As he watched the village pass by in a blur, he knew this was far from over.

***

It was just after 6pm when Detective Edward Langford and Sergeant Peter Hastings returned to the police station. Officer Jones was at the front desk as they entered whilst a flurry of activity continued in the offices behind him.

"I have the forensic reports regarding the man on the beach for you Sir," Officer Jones said as they arrived.

"Thank you Jones, any sign of Officer Wells or Christopher Fischer yet?" Edward asked.

"Have you not heard about Officer Wells Sir?"

Edward looked at him. "No, what's he done now?"

"He's dead."

"What?"

"He was found dead in his car with his throat cut outside St David's Church this afternoon."

"What time was this?" Sergeant Hastings asked.

"It was reported at three o'clock."

"Around an hour after we found the body in the woods," Edward replied. "Do you have any idea who called it in?"

"Frances King," Officer Jones replied.

"We need to bring Miss King in for questioning," Sergeant Hastings said.

"She's only seventeen years old. We can't interview her without her father here too," Officer Jones replied.

"Then bring them both in. She could help us answer a lot of questions," Edward said before heading into the back offices.

***

Later that evening, Officer Stone brought Arthur and Frances King into the police station. Sergeant Peter Hastings led them towards an interrogation room near the cells at the rear of the station. After a few minutes, Detective Edward Langford joined them.

"What is the meaning of all this Edward? You drag us down here in front of the whole village like we're some kind of criminals!" Arthur fumed.

"I apologise for that Arthur but we think there may be some links between the cases of the man on the beach, the fire at Honeypot Cottage, the three recent murders and the men working at ol' Norman Whitehouse's cafe," Edward explained.

"How the hell are we meant to know anything about all that? I'm laid up most of the day whilst Frances keeps the house tidy and keeps an eye on the gardener."

"It must be difficult," Sergeant Hastings said.

"What?" Arthur asked.

"For Frances, I mean. Not having your mother around at such a young age."

"We get by."

"Frances," Edward spoke this time. "I want you to know that you are not in any kind of trouble and whatever you tell us here will not leave this room."

"Pah, you've got others listening in who love a good story Langford. Whatever we say will be round the village by sundown," Arthur replied.

Edward kept his focus on Frances. "Trust me to make things right. Tell me what you know about Christopher Fischer."

Frances began to cry.

"What is the meaning of this?" Arthur snapped. "He's just a gardener trying to make an honest living for Christ's sake! What are you suggesting Langford? That my daughter would frolic with the likes of him? How dare you degrade my family! This meeting is over."

"Mr King, I suggest you either take a seat next to Frances or leave the room and I will find another appropriate adult to be with her," Edward replied.

"Oh, it's Mr King now is it? Well, let me tell you this Detective Langford, my daughter is not some cheap tart who sleeps with anyone she can get..."

"Will you stop it both of you!" Frances shouted.

Both men turned to face her.

"Father, I think you should leave," Frances said, her voice barely above a whisper.

"What are you talking about?" Arthur asked.

"Please, I need to do this alone."

"But he'll twist everything you say. You'll have to watch every word in case you say something wrong."

"You can wait outside Mr King," Sergeant Hastings replied as he stood to lead him out of the room.

Reluctantly, Arthur followed him out of the door and down the corridor towards the waiting room.

"We do have a female officer, PC Joan Barnes, working here today. Would you like her to be with you?" Edward asked.

Frances nodded.

Edward sent Officer Stone away to find PC Barnes before leaving them alone to talk for a while. When Edward left the room, he could hear Arthur King arguing with Sergeant

Hastings in the waiting room. He walked down the corridor to join them.

"Go home Arthur. I will make sure that Frances is driven home and taken right up to your front door after we have finished our meeting," Edward said.

"No you won't. You'll plant something on her. You'll make her confess to some kind of crime she didn't commit and then what'll happen to me? I'll be in that house all alone!"

"I think you need to realise that Frances is your daughter, not your slave. Not your late wife, Maud. She is your daughter. She has her own life and can make her own decisions."

"Pah, she wouldn't last five minutes out in the real world. She's just a kid and you're keeping her here illegally!"

"She is free to go whenever she wants to."

"Then let her go, now!"

"When we have spoken to her in a civilised manner and answered a few questions, she will be taken home by one of my officers so if you want to help your daughter, go home and wait for her," Edward replied.

Arthur considered arguing for a moment before bowing his head, turning and walking out of the station. Sergeant Hastings followed Edward back to the interview room.

"Thanks for that," Hastings said as they arrived at the door.

"It's not over yet," Edward replied before they entered the room.

***

Meanwhile in Lepe Village, Mavis Langford was tidying up the back garden of Southward Cottage whilst Mary played on the swing at the bottom of the garden and John and Fred kicked a football around.

"You make sure you don't damage your father's rose bush or there will be trouble!" Mavis called out to them.

"Of course we won't mom," Fred replied as he tackled John once again.

As Mavis entered the house, she heard somebody knocking at the front door. As she opened the door, she noticed a short man with brown hair, unshaven and wearing black shorts and a black t-shirt. "Can I help you?" she asked.

"Is Mr Langford home?" he asked.

"No, he's at work at the moment, you can…"

"Good!" the man snapped before pulling a knife out of the pocket in his shorts and pointing it at Mavis.

Mavis stepped back. "Now, don't do anything you might regret."

"Your husband killed two of my friends. He chased the vicar away. He chased Christoph away. Now he's going to know what it's like to lose everyone he cares about!" the man replied as he stepped forward and closed the door behind him.

"There's no need for violence. I'm sure whatever has happened, there must be a simple explanation for it. What's your name?"

"Name's not important."

"You're a friend of Christopher's. The gardener? Maybe he can help you."

At that moment, they heard a squeal and then some laughter from the back garden.

"Who else is here?" the man asked.

"No one, no one, it's just kids next door. Please don't hurt them," Mavis replied.

The man moved forwards. Mavis grabbed a vase and threw it at him. It hit his arm before dropping and smashing on the floor.

He dropped the knife momentarily before quickly picking it up again.

"That was stupid!" he said before launching himself at Mavis.

Out in the back garden, John heard the vase smash. Fred and Mary were playing tag by throwing the ball at each other. Whilst they were distracted, John headed back inside the house. He heard someone arguing with his mother in the hall. He crouched down on his knees and crawled into the kitchen.

"What do you want from us?" Mavis shouted.

"I told you, he's taken everything and everyone away from me. Now I'm going to show him what it feels like!" the man replied.

John managed to crawl towards the cupboard under the kitchen sink. His father, Edward, had shown him where he hid a revolver in case there was ever an emergency. He opened the cupboard and removed the revolver that had been stuck to the underside of the sink.

John could hear the man shouting in the next room. He took a deep breath, pulled the hammer back to load the bullet and then walked from the kitchen into the hall. The man was slashing wildly at Mavis who blocked him firstly with a wooden chair and then a coat stand. He caught her arm and drew blood from a deep cut. John took a deep breath, aimed and fired. The gunshot echoed inside the house as the bullet hit a mirror on the wall shattering it into hundreds of small pieces that fell to the floor like confetti.

The man laughed and turned towards John. "You're dead, kid!" he smirked.

John quickly pulled the hammer back and fired again as the man rushed towards him. This time the bullet hit him in the centre of his chest sending him to the floor. Mavis froze as she saw what had happened. John walked over towards the man and kicked him. Suddenly, the man's arm came out and grabbed his ankle. John fell to the floor furiously kicking out at the man with his free foot in an attempt to get away. The man held onto John's ankle before Mavis picked up a wooden clock from the mantlepiece and smashed it over the man's head. He released the grip on John's ankle and Mavis moved him away. Fred and Mary quickly arrived to see what all of the commotion was about. Mavis moved them all into the kitchen and closed the door behind her.

"Mum, you're hurt!" Mary cried.

"It's just a scratch, it's fine," Mavis replied as she quickly picked up a towel, soaked it in water and applied it to the wound on her arm.

"What were you doing John!" Fred shouted.

"Freddie, leave John alone. I want you and Mary to go and tidy up your things in the garden and then go and read in the dining room until we can contact your father. Come along, hurry up," Mavis insisted.

Mary and Fred reluctantly wandered back outside before Mavis turned her attention back to John.

"How did you know that gun was there?" she asked.

"Dad showed me. He said if there was an emergency, then I should use it," John explained.

"You could have gotten yourself killed, you silly boy."

"You're welcome," John replied.

Mavis glared at him for a moment before softening her stare. "Thank you. How did you know how to use it?"

"You don't think father and I only go fishing for twelve hours do you?"

"I guess not. This is strictly between us, okay. Do not mention any of this to the other two."

John nodded in agreement.

"My purse is on the side by the stove. Take some coins, go to the telephone box and call your father. Don't speak to anyone. You go there and you come straight back, you hear?"

John nodded before picking some coins out of his mother's purse and heading towards the telephone box. He walked out of the back gate and around the house to the front garden. As he stepped outside the gate, he saw Arthur King walking down the road from the bus stop.

John began walking up the hill towards the telephone box. "Good evening Mr King," he said as he passed Arthur in the street.

Arthur ignored him and didn't reply.

John turned around and watched him walk back down towards his house. Something wasn't right. He ran the rest of the way to the telephone box. He needed his father to come home fast. Things were getting out of hand.

Chapter Fifty-Eight

The Dead Can't Talk

Tuesday 4th November 2008

A loud knocking on the front door of Jim Handanowicz's villa in Monolithos woke Blake from a restless sleep. Alison slept soundly on the sofa whilst Blake had pulled two armchairs together to create a makeshift bed for himself however the stiff neck he was experiencing this morning made him regret that decision. She stirred as the knocking became louder.

"What time is it?" she asked.

Blake looked at his watch as he headed towards the front door. "Quarter-to-six," he replied.

Alison groaned and forced herself to wake up as Blake answered the door.

"Detective Stathakis, what an unpleasant surprise," Blake quipped.

"Where is he, Langford?" Aris Stathakis snapped.

"Who?"

"Don't play games with me. You had that all planned didn't you? Take James Handanowicz to Lindos and then let him jump down into the sea and swim away to a waiting boat that will take him out of the country where we can't touch him!"

"I'd like to take the credit for such an amazing story but I don't have a clue what you are talking about! James took us to Lindos because he was convinced that we would find something important at the Acropolis!"

Aris pushed past him and walked into the villa closely followed by Lauren Prince.

"Shouldn't you be invited in unless you have a warrant to search the premises?" Blake asked as he closed the door behind them.

"Don't play dumb with me Langford, where is James Handanowicz?"

"I don't know."

"What's going on?" Alison asked as she joined them in the hall.

"Detective Ass here thinks we had something to do with Jim's disappearance yesterday," Blake explained.

"We're as much in the dark as you. He led us to the acropolis and then dived off the edge. I'm amazed he didn't kill himself in the process," Alison explained.

"James Handanowicz is a well known scuba diving instructor on the island. He's a very good swimmer and he knew we were onto him for the murder of Ian Bleeker and Zachary Zhal," Lauren added.

"I didn't want to do this but you leave me no choice," Aris replied as he handed Blake some papers.

Blake scanned his eyes over the fine print. "You're deporting us?"

"Yes. You've aided a fugitive and blown this murder investigation wide open. If you weren't working for Special Branch, I'd arrest you both and throw you into the cells right now but I've been overruled," Aris admitted.

"Overruled my ass, you don't have any evidence that proves we helped Jim Handanowicz escape. We settled his bail and he led us to Lindos to find something," Blake replied.

"And what were you looking for?"

"Something valuable to our family."

"In a prehistoric acropolis? What on Earth did you expect to find there? The report said that the three of you damaged one of the ancient ruins before being chased away back through the market."

"Okay, let's say for example that we did help Jim leave the country, why did your colleague, Miss Prince, lend us her car to get to Lindos in the first place?" Alison asked.

"All police officers have trackers on their cars," Lauren admitted. "We tracked the car to Lindos and then the head of security at the acropolis saw James climb aboard a boat a mile or so off-shore. The coastguard tracked the boat all the way to Marmaris in Turkey where they lost him."

"James Handanowicz didn't kill Reaper or Zodiac. They were looking for something that they thought James had in his possession. The piece of the puzzle that would lead them back to the UK to uncover some kind of mysterious secret. Both men were involved in a human trafficking investigation in London earlier this year that went wrong for them. I'm starting to think that it was a cover for something bigger that is yet to happen," Blake replied.

"What do you mean? James Handanowicz had the blood of those men on his clothes. They were killed right here in this villa! And this whole puzzle story, this isn't some kind of kids fairytale, this is a real murder investigation and I won't tolerate mistakes!" Aris snapped.

"James Handanowicz wasn't alone when those men came here and you never found the gun did you?" Alison replied.

"No," Aris admitted.

"So how can you prove that James Handanowicz is the murderer?" Alison asked.

"Because we found the gun yesterday."

Blake felt a shiver run down his spine. Had Evelyn been searched and they found the murder weapon on her? "Where?" he asked.

"At the nursing home but you already knew that, didn't you, Langford?"

"What's that supposed to mean? Evelyn Handanowicz was visiting Jim when the men broke in and she admitted to shooting them. Given her mental health condition, there's no way that any of this would stand up in court. She would be acquitted due to diminished responsibility and would continue to need psychiatric care for the rest of her life!" Blake replied.

"Yes, the wheel of deception turns quite conveniently to get James Handanowicz out of trouble and she gets away with a murder she was incapable of doing."

"What are you talking about? She admitted to Blake that she had done it and Jim tried to hide the evidence! Ask her yourself," Alison replied.

"We can't," Aris admitted.

"She won't talk to you or any of your team because she doesn't trust you. Says a lot for your police force on the island," Blake said.

"She won't talk because she's dead!"

The whole room fell silent for a moment before Blake launched himself towards Aris. "You son-of-a-bitch! What did you do to her!" Blake shouted as he grabbed Aris's shirt.

Alison dived in between them. "Blake! Stop! He's not worth it!" she shouted at him.

After a moment, Blake released his grip on Aris's shirt before stepping away running his fingers through his hair in frustration.

"Evelyn Handanowicz committed suicide an hour after you left the home in Monolithos," Lauren admitted.

"So, who did she confess to?"

"She spoke to me after you left."

"After being mute for so long? No, no, she wouldn't..." Blake began.

"She had the murder weapon inside her clothes when you were talking to her. She knew she was either going to be caught or James would be arrested. Either way, she would be forever alone. She put the gun in her mouth and fired it before anyone could stop her," Aris replied.

Blake stood in the doorway leading towards the lounge. He'd placed both hands on the doorframe and stared down at the floor, struggling to comprehend what Aris had told him. His mother's twin sister. The woman he had never known apart from the occasional mention in conversation during his childhood. There had to be a connection to the piece of the map they had found at the acropolis and his family but for now, he knew he needed to keep that information to himself. "So, what now?" he asked.

"Now I need you both to leave Rhodes and never come back. Your participation in this investigation has caused a lot of unrest between us and Turkey and we will do everything we can to bring James Handanowicz back to the island to face justice," Aris replied. "You have twenty-four hours."

Blake nodded. "And what about Evelyn?"

"She is a Greek citizen with no immediate family. She will be given a traditional Greek funeral and will be buried on the island."

"Like hell she will. I'm not letting my aunt's body be tossed into an unmarked grave in some island ghetto for paupers who have nothing!"

"You seem to forget that you are no longer welcome here Mr Langford so you have no say in what happens to the citizens of this island."

"She does have a family and I will pay for her body will be flown back to London and she will be buried in the same cemetery as her twin sister!"

"Very well, I will make the arrangements and when our investigation is complete, we will release the body," Aris replied before heading towards the door. "Oh, by the way, did you find what you were looking for at Lindos?"

Blake shook his head. "No, but I'm sure it's only a matter of time."

"You don't have much time left," Aris replied as he opened the door and walked out.

"Neither do you pal, neither do you," Blake said softly as he closed the door behind them.

***

Meanwhile, at a rundown two bedroom basement flat in south-east London, Jade Smith rushed towards the front door and inserted her key. She tried to turn the lock but it wouldn't budge.

"Tom! I know you're in there, you lying son-of-a-bitch! Open this door!" Jade fumed as she hammered on the door.

She tried her key again before attempting to shoulder-barge her way in. The door refused to move.

"Gibson! I'm gonna kill you!" she shouted as she kicked the door.

"Are you okay dear?" an elderly woman asked.

Jade looked up and saw her at the top of the stairs that led down to the basement flat. "It's okay, sorry. My partner has locked me out of our flat and I can't get back in."

The elderly lady carefully made her way down the stairs towards her. "Why don't you let me try? Sometimes these old wooden doors just need a little jiggle."

Jade stepped back and allowed the lady to try. She wiggled the key and then gave the door a firm hit with her forearm and surprisingly, it opened.

"How did you…" Jade began.

"Just need to know the right combination that's all," she giggled as she moved aside.

As Jade stepped forwards, she felt a sharp prick on her arm and then suddenly everything went black.

"Get her inside quick!" the lady said as she closed the door behind them.

Two men quickly manoeuvred Jade into a seat in a glass cell on the left side of the room. They strapped her arms and legs to the chair with leather restraints before injecting her again to wake her up. The two men then left the glass cell and stood by the door next to the elderly lady.

When Jade woke up, she realised where she was and immediately noticed Tom in a similar glass cell next to her. The flat had been emptied and what looked like a sprinkler system had been fitted to the top of the glass cells they were now trapped inside.

"Did you honestly think you could betray me and get away with it?" one of the men said.

"I told you Dmitri, I'll get you the money," Tom replied. "Just let her go."

"Money isn't as important as knowing who to trust and why would we want to let you go, the fun has only just started?" the elderly lady replied.

"Who are you and what the hell is going on?" Jade asked.

"You mean he didn't tell you? He's been banking all of this money in the hope that he'd uncover the location of Jack Smith's treasure whilst ripping off my family."

"Wait, you're Dmitri's Mother?" Tom asked. "What has any of this got to do with you?"

"My name is Frances Vasilievich but your parents knew me as Frances King. I believe you had some dealings with my ex-husband, Vladimir. You already know Dmitri and this is my eldest son, Timmy. John Langford took away Timmy's birthright when he chased after that Handanowicz family and now we will get what's rightfully ours!"

"I don't know what you're talking about! I have nothing to do with the Langfords!" Tom replied.

"Of course you don't. Patricia never had the guts to follow her instincts even after I gave her the information she needed."

"You poisoned my mother's mind with tales of her family before she was adopted?"

"She was already poisoned and now you have the chance to prove your loyalty to the cause. I have two pieces of the map. Jack Smith's treasure is buried somewhere near to Holbury Manor in The New Forest. During the war it was a place of recuperation for injured war heroes. Jack stayed there during the war after he deserted before returning to London. It's only a matter of time until the secret is out."

"You seem to have all the information so why do you need us?" Jade asked.

"You two share the Smith bloodline," Timmy replied.

"Fortunately we only need one of you. Tom, with his guilt over his mother's legacy and Jade, the one cast aside from the Handanowicz line by a grandfather who disowned his side of the family," Frances continued.

"Enough of this bullshit, why are we tied to these chairs?" Jade asked.

"You've heard of the phenomenon of snakes shedding their skin to remove parasites," Dmitri explained. "The same can be said here. I had dealings with a snake who failed to deliver the goods a few months ago. In the sprinkler system on top of these glass cells is sulphuric acid. On the table in front of you are scalpels and a tube that opens out onto a set of scales beneath the cells. In a moment, your restraints will be released and you will have two minutes to shed your skin. The one of you who places the most skin on the scales below will be saved and will join us on our quest for the gold."

"And the loser?" Tom asked.

"Our sprinkler system will cover them in sulphuric acid leading them to a slow and painful death."

"What kind of sick mind comes up with this?" Jade asked.

"A mind similar to the one that led his military colleagues into an ambush for a huge Russian pay-off. Isn't that right Thomas?" Frances asked.

Tom bowed his head. Seventeen years ago, he was in a relationship with Jenny Langford. He asked her to pass a dossier onto a Russian informant who she met over lunch in Salisbury, unaware that it contained details of the RAF mission into Afghanistan. The Russians used the information to murder Tom's entire regiment whilst Tom was safely smuggled into Moscow on a fake passport.

"In any case, it's got to be better than being buried alive," Frances added, breaking Tom's thoughts before leading Dmitri and Timmy out of the flat.

As they shut the door, the restraints on the chairs released. They both leapt out of their seats, shouting and hitting all sides of the glass prison they found themselves in but nothing seemed to work. A digital clock illuminated on the wall in front of them counting down the two minutes.

"You bastard, what the hell have you done!" Jade shouted.

"Stop complaining and find a way out of here!" Tom replied as he frantically hit every piece of glass in an attempt to escape.

Jade watched the clock ticking down for a moment before looking at the knives and scalpels on the table. She took some deep breaths before walking over and picking up the scalpel.

She looked at the clock. Only one minute left. She rolled up her sleeve and began to cut her skin. Clenching her fist as pain ripped through her arm. She systematically removed chunks of her skin in a pool of blood. Dropping each piece into the tube.

Tom watched her trying not to vomit. He looked at the clock counting down. He looked at the knives. He picked one up. Then he placed it back down again. He screamed. He punched the glass cell wall. He picked up the knife again. Thirty seconds remaining. He began slicing chunks of skin from his arm screaming with every cut. Twenty seconds. Fifteen. Ten. Nine. Eight Seven. He frantically began cutting himself as it counted down. Six. Five. Four. Three. Two. One. Zero.

Deathly silence. Both Jade and Tom looked at each other. It was as if time had stood still. Pools of blood and skin were spread over the metal tables.

"No, no, this was a fucking setup?" Tom raged.

At that moment, the sprinkler systems began spraying inside both cells. They both screamed as acid poured down burning their skin. The sounds of sirens outside caught their attention for a brief moment before it was all over.

Two police officers stepped out of their car outside the flat. A concerned neighbour had heard screams and had called the police to investigate. When they barged open the flat door, a gruesome discovery awaited them. Amongst the blood and the acid, a putrid stench hung in the air as the burnt and scarred bodies of a man and a woman laid inside two glass cells. Jade Smith and Tom Gibson were dead.

Chapter Fifty-Nine

Hello Old Friend
Wednesday 25th August 1948

It was just after midnight in the early hours of Wednesday morning when Sergeant Peter Hastings joined Edward Langford outside Southward Cottage. An ambulance had arrived to remove the body and a paramedic tended to the cut on Mavis Langford's arm. Edward was by her side as the paramedic wrapped a bandage around the cut.

One of the forensic team members handed Sergeant Hastings a wallet. When he opened it, he found a German passport folded inside it with the name Maximillian Friedrich Ekkehard displayed next to a photo of a much younger man in it. He walked over and handed the passport to Edward.

"So Officer Wells knew who he was..." Edward said as he looked at it.

"It seems to be that way, Sir. Whatever Wells, Harold Partridge and Norman Whitehouse were trying to cover up, it looks like they were trying to house the enemy."

"We need to find Partridge and Whitehouse. We were lucky this time but they might be the Germans next target. We need to find Christopher Fischer too. Ask Officer Jones to assist the forensics in tidying this place up. Where are the children?"

"Upstairs in their bedrooms. Do you want me to call in PC Joan Barnes to be with them?" Hastings asked.

"No, it's okay, I'll do it," Edward replied before climbing the stairs up to the children's bedrooms.

Meanwhile outside, the paramedics had finished bandaging the wound on Mavis Langford's arm and Officer Jones walked over towards her.

"The forensic teams are almost finished Mrs Langford and then we can let you and your family get back to normal," he advised.

Mavis nodded in acknowledgement.

"Do I remember seeing you in the red cross tents in Fareham during the war?" Officer Jones asked.

Mavis looked at him. "Most of us were."

"I seem to remember you…"

"My husband…"

"And his father were very good police officers. Alfred Langford caused a lot of heartache for a mutual friend of ours."

"I don't know what you're talking about."

"I was there the night Ada Hughes gave birth to Jack's first born. It was old Alfred Langford that convinced Ada's mother to give the baby up and made it look like her father committed suicide."

"I don't know anything about that."

"Your twins look a lot like him, Mavis. Jack told me stories of how he had his fun during the war after Ada died. Never believed it until now. I know your secret. You keep your old man off of my case and I'll keep my mouth shut. By the way, did Jack tell you where he buried the gold?"

"What gold?"

"Come on, he said he'd make sure that you and Dana were all right but then he died before anyone else knew where he'd hidden it."

"You're Charlie Jones aren't you? You helped him rob the bank in Portsmouth in 1938."

Officer Jones smiled.

"How did the police overlook that?" Mavis asked.

"It's amazing what money can buy you these days isn't it."

"Forensics are done, Detective Langford wants you to finish up here and then meet us back at the station to file the report," Sergeant Peter Hastings said as he approached them.

"On my way Sir," Officer Jones replied before heading back into the house.

Mavis bowed her head.

"Is everything okay Mrs Langford?" Hastings asked.

She nodded quickly trying to avoid eye contact. "Yes, everything's fine Peter. Everything's fine," she replied before heading back inside the house to find Edward and the children.

***

Eight Years Later...
Saturday 25th August 1956

John Langford stepped off of the bus and headed down the Lepe Road walking past his parent's home at Southward Cottage before entering Thyme Cottage where Frances King was finishing hanging some washing out on the line.

"John!" a seven year old boy shouted before charging towards him and wrapping himself around John's legs.

"Let him come into the house Timmy, for goodness sake," Frances smiled as she kissed John on the cheek.

John ruffled Timmy's hair and attempted to walk whilst Timmy held onto his leg. They heard loud coughing and spluttering coming from inside the house. "Is he still no better?"

"You know what he's like. Doesn't want to see a doctor even though he's coughing up blood."

"Frances! Where's my tea?" Arthur shouted.

"On the way Dad," she replied, rolling her eyes as she finished hanging the clothes on the washing line.

John wandered into the kitchen and began preparing three cups of tea. As Frances hung the last pair of shorts on the line, she noticed the postman approaching the gate.

"Good afternoon Terrance, Anything for us today?" she asked.

He glared at her and threw three letters over the gate and onto the grass.

"There's no need to be like that! What have I done?" Frances asked.

"You gave birth to a kraut's child," Terrance snapped before continuing on his way.

Frances crouched down and picked up the letters before heading inside. She placed them on the dining table as John came over with the cups of tea. He handed one of them to Arthur before turning back towards her.

"Are you okay?" John asked.

"They'll never forget will they?" Frances sobbed. "We'll have to move away. The stares. The whispers. Timmy's never going to be able to play with the other kids in the village."

"Terrance Trilby again? He should keep his bloody nose out of other people's business!"

"He's right though isn't he?"

"Christopher did a lot of things to help people in this village. He helped father find out who murdered the man on the beach. He tended everyone's gardens and he helped uncover old Harry Partridge's secret. People in this village have very short memories when they want them."

"And long ones too!" Arthur shouted out. "She should've kept her bloody legs shut!"

Frances began to cry and ran up the stairs towards the bedroom.

Timmy came rushing into the kitchen. "Is mummy crying?" he asked.

John crouched down in front of him. "She's just a little bit upset, that's all," he explained. "Are you going to show me your stick collection?"

"Yes!" Timmy replied as he led John back outside.

As they were building wigwams with sticks in the garden, John noticed a truck heading down the road towards the rebuilt Honeypot Cottage on the corner of the woods. The truck stopped outside the cottage and a husband and wife stepped out alongside their teenage daughter, two younger daughters who John guessed were around eight years old and a small boy who looked a little younger.

There was something about the teenage girl that John recognised. Her shoulder length brown hair, her dark features and the way she was ushering the children towards the house.

"It's another demand letter," Frances called out, interrupting his thoughts. "What are you looking at?"

"Oh, just the new family moving into the new Honeypot Cottage. Who is the letter from?"

"Dad hasn't been able to make the rent payment for the past three months. If we don't repay what we owe, they're going to move us out of the house."

John dug around in his pockets and pulled out some notes.

"Where did all of that money come from?" Frances gasped.

"I had an advance on my wages at the police training school. I have three pounds here. Use it to keep the housing officer happy for now and I'll get the rest as soon as I can."

Frances wrapped her arms around his neck. "I don't know what I'd do without you John Langford. You're the only one who never turned their back on me."

"Frances! What's for dinner?" Arthur shouted out.

Frances reluctantly broke the embrace.

"I'd better call in at home. I'll see you later tonight," John smiled as he left the front garden.

As he turned to walk back up the hill towards Southward Cottage, he heard someone call his name. He turned around and saw the teenage girl he'd noticed earlier rushing towards him. She was coughing and looked pale as she approached him but John recognised her immediately.

"Edith?" John asked.

"Yes, it's me. It's so good to see you again. You've changed so much," she replied before wrapping her arms around his neck.

John reluctantly returned the embrace before stepping back. "It's been over eight years, what happened to you? Where did you go?"

Edith coughed and held her chest momentarily.

"Are you okay?" John asked.

"Yes, just a bit of a cough, that's all. We went to a convent in Portsmouth where a group of nuns looked after us. I was able to finish my education there and mother met William. They've been married for four years now and I have two younger sisters and a younger brother. William owns that cafe down on the beach so we thought we'd move back here so he can keep a closer watch on it now that Norman Whitehouse is retiring. But enough about me, what about you?"

"I finished school and Father pushed me through the police training program so I can become a police officer if I pass my exam next year. His dream was to have three generations of Langfords in the force and now he's got it."

"But what's your dream John?"

"What do you mean?"

"You said it was your father's dream to have three generations of Langfords in the police force but is that really what you want?"

"Of course it is. I wouldn't have signed up for it if it wasn't."

"What about girlfriends? Or moving out into your own place."

"I'm sure that will happen in time."

At that moment, John noticed Frances standing at the front gate watching them.

"Anyway, nice to catch up. I guess I'll be seeing you around," John said before rushing away towards his parents house.

"Yes, I guess so," Edith sighed as she watched him leave.

As she turned to head back home, she noticed Frances standing at her gate.

"Edith Wise isn't it?" Frances called out.

"Yes, and you're Frances King, the woman who gave birth to a German's child out of wedlock."

"Good news travels fast."

Edith coughed again before continuing. "Not really. My stepfather owns a business in the area so he needs to know who he is dealing with."

"Just stay away from John Langford if you know what's good for you."

"Or what? John's an old friend. We grew up playing on the beach and making memories together."

"Right before your mother burnt the house down and fled the village like some criminal!"

"My mother did what she had to do to protect her children. If your father had done the same you might not have ended up in the situation you're in!"

"My situation has nothing to do with you. Just stay away from us and stay away from John!"

"You seem to forget that John and I have history together."

"From when you were ten years old, you're both fully grown adults now."

"I know, that's what makes it more exciting doesn't it. I'll be seeing you Frances," Edith smiled before heading back towards Honeypot Cottage.

"Frances! Where's my bloody medicine?" Arthur shouted from inside the house.

Frances waited at the gate for a moment watching Edith walk away before reluctantly heading back inside. She didn't trust her or her family and their return to the village would only mean trouble for her relationship with John.

***

John entered Southward Cottage just as his mother, Mavis, was serving the evening meal.

"Ah, perfect timing John. Can you take the cutlery and lay out the dining table for me?" Mavis asked.

"Of course, is father home yet?"

"No, you know him. He won't be home for hours. I'll leave him a plate of stew on the stove."

"Where are the others?"

"Fred is outside building a treehouse with his friend Sean and Mary is in her bedroom finishing some homework. Can you call them in on your way through, there's a good lad."

When the family sat down at the table to eat their evening meal, they were interrupted by someone knocking at the door. Mavis stood from the table and wandered over to answer it. When she opened the door, she gasped in surprise.

"Hello old friend," a woman's voice said.

"No, it can't be," Mavis replied.

John rushed over to join his mother at the front door. Standing in front of them was Dana Wise.

Chapter Sixty

Blake Makes The Connection
Wednesday 5th November 2008

Samir Khalifa was waiting at Gatwick Airport when Alison and Blake returned from Rhodes. As they walked through the arrivals gate, he approached them with two police officers beside him.

"What have we done now?" Alison sighed.

"Samir, what's going on? I thought you and Joe were tying up loose ends in East Boldre," Blake asked.

"We'll come to that. This is Sergeant John Burrows and Officer Kingsley Amos," Samir replied.

"Mr Langford, Miss Pearce, could you please follow us this way?" Burrows asked as he led them towards a room near to the exit.

When they were inside, Blake turned to Samir. "What the hell's going on?"

"Mr Langford," Burrows began. "We understand that Special Branch has an ongoing investigation into a Mr Thomas Edward Gibson."

"Amongst others, yes."

"Official records show that Mr Gibson is currently residing in the south of France with his cousin, a Miss Jade Elizabeth Smith."

That took Blake by surprise. "Cousin?"

"Second-cousin to be precise," Amos added.

"Is this the same Jade Smith who's sister Andrea was found in the grave in East Boldre?" Alison asked.

"The same. Formal identification was completed by Mr Khalifa and his partner, Joe Knight, when they attended the mortuary with Jade Smith and a Miss Jennifer Eleanor Langford on Monday evening," Burrows replied.

"What's Jenny got to do with this?" Blake asked.

"Nothing as yet, Mr Langford, however, after the identification, Miss Smith returned to south-east London and visited a rundown flat on Tuesday morning around 11am according to eye-witnesses."

"There's no crime in that," Blake replied.

"No, except a neighbour heard screams coming from the flat a few minutes later. When Officer Amos and his colleague arrived on the scene, they discovered two mutilated bodies trapped inside glass cells covered in acid."

Blake shook his head. He had heard about some torture methods that had been used after an alleged betrayal of Russian informants but this was the first time he had come across it in his own line of work. "Was it Tom Gibson?" he asked.

"We're still trying to identify the victims from dental records but it seems to be Gibson and quite possibly Jade Smith," Burrows confirmed.

"So, where do we come into this?" Alison asked.

"Jade Smith was involved in your investigation into the woman, Andrea Smith, who was buried alive. Our team also found evidence that led them into investigating a hidden inheritance involving the Smith, Handanowicz and Langford families. The laptops have been seized and are being analysed as we speak. There were also links to the dark web, more specifically, a program known as The Crystal."

"The Crystal was shut down after Tom Gibson and his men were stopped from trafficking students and weapons out of London six months ago," Alison replied.

"Officially it was closed down but there have been continued investments on the dark web to fund terrorism," Amos explained.

"This inheritance that you're talking about," Blake replied. "When was it discovered?"

"Its whereabouts were unknown until recently when a safety deposit box was reopened at Goodman, Parker & Knowles inc. on Regent Street."

Blake took a deep breath. The day after his mother's funeral, he received a letter in the mail containing a key to a safety deposit box at Goodman, Parker & Knowles inc. When he went to open it, he had uncovered some photos of people he didn't recognise alongside his grandparents from 1948. There had to be a connection.

"Is something wrong Mr Langford?" Amos asked.

Blake shook his head. "No, just thinking about things. Safety deposit boxes are rarely used these days so if one is opened, how is that information used?"

"Usually no information is shared however, when you opened the box belonging to the late Emily Avis Jane Langford, it automatically sent out letters to all beneficiaries of the Jack Smith legacy," Burrows explained.

"And do they all know each other?" Alison asked.

"No, but it wouldn't take a genius to work it out if you were involved in the families," Amos replied.

"If you already knew that I opened the box then why all this cloak-and-dagger bullshit?" Blake asked.

"Because more and more people connected to that box have died or had an attempt on their life!" Burrows replied. "We need to find out who is behind this and stop them before they strike again."

"Hang on, back up a minute here," Alison interrupted. "You said that the bodies you suspect belong to Tom Gibson and Jade Smith were found locked in glass cells covered in acid. Obviously they didn't encase themselves there of their own free will so did your so-called eye-witnesses notice anyone else coming or going from the flat around the time the screams were heard?"

"Only an elderly lady who was walking past with two middle aged men, probably her sons," Amos replied.

"And have you traced them?" Blake asked.

"Not yet, no."

"Well don't you think that's a good place to start?"

"We don't tell you how to do your job Mr Langford so please refrain from telling us how to do ours," Burrows replied.

"Maybe it's time to pool our resources," Samir suggested.

"What do you have in mind?" Amos asked.

"Alison and Blake headed out to Rhodes after someone tried to murder Evelyn and James Handanowicz. If what you say is true about the Jack Smith legacy, there's a good chance that Evelyn and James would stand to inherit something."

Amos nodded.

"Therefore, it seems that somebody is trying to kill off those who stand to inherit to take the money for themselves."

"Yes, we realise that Mr Khalifa. The Greek police have already informed us of Mr Langford's involvement in their case..." Burrows snapped.

"The two men sent to kill Evelyn and James worked for Tom Gibson!" Blake replied. "Ian Bleeker and Zachary Zhal, also known as Reaper and Zodiac, were big players in the trafficking of young students in the capital. If you took more care of the vulnerable people in your city, we wouldn't have to keep tidying up your mess!"

"Our mess? We weren't the ones who let a murder suspect escape a Greek island during an investigation!"

"James Handanowicz was innocent! The men who came after him were shot by Evelyn Handanowicz!"

"Who conveniently committed suicide after telling you what you needed to know. Almost like it was planned..."

"What are you insinuating?" Blake asked.

"Oh stop it, both of you!" Alison snapped. "The reality is, we have a serial killer who is somehow manipulating the system and targeting anyone who stands in their way. Does anyone know who would have some kind of vendetta against the families now that Zodiac, Reaper and Gibson are dead?"

"The Smith family were linked to the murder of several of Zodiac's acquaintances which could have made Andrea and Jade targets," Samir replied.

Blake glared at him.

"How do you know this?" Burrows asked.

"A previous investigation."

Burrows turned his attention to Blake. "Jade and Andrea were close friends with your sister, Jennifer."

"Meaning?"

"Her life could be in danger. They've already taken out both of her friends and their grandfather."

"What about their parents?" Alison asked.

"Both Smith parents were killed in a motorcycling accident three years ago. Victor Wise was their only living relative remaining," Amos replied.

"What do you mean, was?" Blake asked. "I spoke to him at the weekend!"

"Victor Wise was found dead yesterday morning in his assisted living complex near The New Forest. Early reports show that he took an overdose," Burrows confirmed.

Blake held his head in his hands.

"If you know anyone who has a vendetta against your family, now is the time to tell us Blake."

"I come from four generations of Langfords who have worked in law enforcement in one way or another. We've been responsible for putting hundreds of people away. It could be any of them," Blake admitted.

"We have advised your sister to stay with your family on the south coast. Eric Gordon has doubled up your security. Frank Jackson will be supported by Andre Park until things calm down. In the meantime, I suggest you work out who is coming after your family and stop them," Burrows replied.

When they left the airport terminal, Samir led them towards the car park. "Joe managed to track a signal from Special Branch to Goodman, Parker & Knowles inc. yesterday. Someone has inside information and we need to shut it down."

"I didn't mention it in there but my father once spoke of a woman named Frances King. She lived next door to my grandparents when my dad was growing up. Before he married my mother, he had a brief relationship with her. After he broke it off, she was borderline schizophrenic, stalking him, calling him, leaving him letters, she was obsessed with him. She was part of the reason why the family moved to London just to get away from her," Blake explained.

"Do you think she could be involved?" Alison asked. "Your parents were married for a long time."

"They married in 1977 but when I was fishing with my father one night off of Lepe beach when I was a teenager, I remember he told me how he had avoided going there for so long. It was one of the best fishing spots on the south coast but he was scared to go back in case Frances showed up and saw him there."

"So how did you come into possession of the cottage?" Samir asked.

"My grandparents died in the late 80's under suspicious circumstances which were probably connected to the King family. My father's sister, Mary, bought his share of the house and stayed there until she died in 2004. In her will, she left the house solely to me which pissed off my siblings to the extent that we didn't talk for three years."

"Why wasn't it split between the three of you?" Alison asked.

"I guess it was mine and my father's escape from the pressures of work and life. Several times per year we would go and stay with Aunt Mary and spend many nights fishing off of Lepe Beach. He told me that the beach somehow made him feel closer to his parents. I never really knew my father before then. He'd always been a private man. Much like my grandfather. They never shared their thoughts and feelings. Whatever difficulties you had in life were your own and it was a sign of weakness to show them to others."

"A lot of older people were like that."

"But when it was just the two of us, we had deep conversations that we'd never have had if we were at home or at work. I really got to know him as a man as well as a father."

"And this is when he told you about Frances?" Samir asked.

Blake nodded. "I may be completely wrong but not much unsettled my father, John Langford, but she really got under his skin."

"Did they have a serious relationship together?" Alison asked.

"Briefly, I think. She was ten years older than my father and was the next door neighbour whilst he was growing up. She had a child out of marriage, I think the father was German, and dad kind of took on the father role after leaving school, even though he was only nine years older than the child. I guess he felt sorry for them as the family became social outcasts."

"Having any kind of a relationship with the Germans after the war was frowned upon so I can see why he tried to help. What happened? Was the social stigma the reason they split up?"

"No, father's childhood girlfriend who moved away eight years earlier returned and a love triangle developed and he ended up leaving Frances for his old girlfriend."

"No wonder she was pissed then," Samir replied as they arrived at the car.

As they sat inside, Alison began logging into Special Branch's internal network to begin searching for the connection. "What was the woman's name back then?" she asked.

"King, Frances King," Blake replied. "Although there's a chance she may have been married."

"Who was the girl your father left her for? Was it your mother, Emily?" Samir asked.

"No, her older sister, Edith..." Blake paused for a moment. "Of course."

"What?" Alison asked.

"Edith Wise. Dana Handanowicz was originally married to Gerald Wise. Victor Wise told me about Edith breaking up Dad and Frances when she returned to Lepe. If Frances knew about the huge inheritance then she would have felt cheated out of the money. If it's not her then it's got to be her relatives."

"Blake, if that's true and she had this German's child in 1948, she must have been at least late teens, early twenties then, that makes her almost eighty years old! How the hell can an eighty year old arrange a coup like this?" Samir asked.

"Do you know the name of the child?" Alison asked.

"Tommy or Timmy, something like that," Blake replied. "She was seventeen when the baby was born. Her mother was killed during the war and she had to look after her father and a newborn baby at that young age. I guess that's why Dad tried to help her."

"That would still make her late seventies now. When my grandmother was in her seventies it took her all her effort to fart," Samir said as he joined the motorway heading back into London.

"That explains why you're full of hot air then, it's hereditary."

Samir gave a sarcastic laugh. "Whatever that deposit box contained, it seems to have created a shitstorm that nobody seems to be able to work out."

"You said Joe found a signal coming out of Special Branch to Goodman, Parker & Knowles inc. Any idea who made contact?" Blake asked.

"It's bouncing off of the firewalls but it seemed to come from one of the main offices. Joe has based himself in The New Forest in the hope that he can rattle the undertaker and the locals and try and get some answers there. We'll head in to see Gordon and find out if we have anything new," Samir replied.

"I think I may have found something," Alison said as she leant forward from the back seat to show Blake her phone.

"Obituaries?" Blake asked.

"Arthur Stafford King, died 5th September 1960, from Lepe, Hampshire. Beloved father of Frances Irene King and grandfather of Timothy Mark King. His grave is at All Saints Church cemetery in Hythe. That must be the same family."

"He's buried in the next village so that makes sense but as far as I'm aware, she was still there until at least 1977."

"Maybe she took over the house after her father died?" Samir added.

"How can you be so sure on dates?" Alison asked.

"My parents got married on August 12th 1977. From that date on, dad never heard from Frances again."

"Maybe she realised that now he was married, she was fighting a lost cause and moved onto someone else," Samir replied.

"It's possible but if she was that much of a stalker, a marriage certificate isn't going to stand in her way," Alison reasoned.

They soon arrived at Special Branch headquarters. Samir parked his car in the underground car park and the three of them headed up in the lift to the eighth floor. They walked along the corridor and entered the second from last door on the left.

"We thought you'd never get back," Angela, Eric Gordon's secretary, said as they entered the office.

"We had a welcoming committee at the airport," Blake replied. "Any news from the undertakers?"

"Not yet but we've traced your family tree through records back to 1882 to highlight any connections with the infamous Jack Smith."

Blake walked over and looked at Angela's screen.

"It seems that both of your grandparents, Dana Handanowicz and Mavis Langford both gave birth to Jack Smith's children as well as someone called Ada Hughes," Angela explained.

"Are you suggesting my parents could have been siblings!"

"No, John Langford was born in 1938 and was Edward Langford's biological son. Mary and Frederick Langford were fathered by Jack Smith in 1942."

"That's what Victor Wise said," Blake replied as he ran his fingers through his hair. "My grandfather was fighting in the war in '42."

"I'm sorry Blake."

"What about the Handanowicz side?"

"It seems that Dana Wise as she was originally known had two children, Edith and Victor. Edith's father was Gerald Wise who she was married to but he died in the war. Victor Wise was born in 1941. A year after Gerald Wise was enlisted."

"So Jack Smith fathered Victor in '41 and then Mary and Fred in '42."

"The photograph you discovered in the safety deposit box was from 1948. The man in that photo is Jack Smith, twenty-four hours before he died," Angela explained.

"So he was still with the family in 1948. How the hell did my grandfather not make the connection, he was a police detective for Christ's sake!"

"Sometimes, if we're too close to the subject, we become blind to things. You of all people should know that."

Blake nodded. "Point taken."

Angela clicked onto some old newspaper reports from 1948 of a burnt out house in Lepe. "The report says that Honeypot Cottage had been destroyed in a suspected arson attack on 15th July 1948."

"The day after the photo was taken."

"Dana and Edith Wise had disappeared, presumed dead, until they returned to live in the rebuilt house eight years later. Dana had a new husband, William Handanowicz, a successful businessman and two seven year old daughters with her, Emily and Evelyn Handanowicz and a four year old son, James Handanowicz."

"And there's nothing to suggest that Emily and Evelyn were William's children?" Blake asked.

"The timings don't add up. It wouldn't have been possible as Dana and William were not married until 1950."

"Even back then there was still the chance of sex before marriage," Samir reasoned.

"When your mother passed away Blake, a DNA test was done on the order of Eric and it proved a match for Jack Smith being her father," Angela admitted.

"How did Special Branch get DNA from Jack Smith? He's been dead for sixty years!" Blake snapped.

"He died in 1948 but his eldest daughter is still alive in witness protection."

"Who is she?"

"I'm not at liberty to say."

"Angela..."

At that moment, the buzzer sounded and the light above Eric Gordon's room changed from red to green. Alison, Samir and Blake reluctantly entered, more confused than ever.

Chapter Sixty-One

Edith's Secret
Saturday 22nd September 1956

John Langford entered Southampton Hospital just after 6pm on Saturday evening. Dana was waiting outside a treatment room as they approached.

"What happened?" John asked as they arrived.

"The doctor thinks she has pneumonia. She's been coughing and struggling to breathe for weeks."

"And you've only just decided to bring her to the hospital now?"

"There's been a lot of things going on in the past few months, John. We thought coming back to the village and being in familiar surroundings would help Edith recover."

"But it didn't, did it?"

"She asked for you to be here. Going in there angry isn't going to help anyone."

"If you hadn't run away all those years ago..."

"We'd be in the same situation we're in now," Dana replied. "Don't make this any more difficult than it already is!"

"What do you mean?" John asked.

At that moment, the doctor came out of the room where Edith was being treated. They both approached him.

"She's stable for now but her breathing is very shallow. We will need to run some more tests before we know how bad the pneumonia is," the doctor explained.

"Can we see her?" John asked.

"Yes but keep it brief. She needs as much rest as possible."

John looked at Dana. She nodded. She had spent the past month rebuilding her friendship with John's mother, Mavis, and knew that he still held a close bond with Edith.

John entered the room and was immediately greeted with wires and tubes coming out from all angles and making all kinds of noises. Edith smiled briefly before coughing once again.

"It's okay, don't try to talk," John said as he held her hand. "The doctors are doing all that they can to help you."

"It's too late for that," Edith sighed.

"Don't say that."

"It's true. I've been ill for so long now. It's just a matter of time until..."

John bowed his head. Edith squeezed his hand. He looked up at her. She was staring directly at him.

"I want you to do something for me John," she said.

"Anything, what is it?"

"In my bag, over there, is a brown envelope. Can you get it for me?"

John picked up the bag and brought it over to the bed before sorting through its contents. He found the brown envelope and removed it from the bag.

"Keep it safe for me. Don't let anyone else read it or know about it."

"What is it?" he asked.

"Our family's legacies. The truth about why we had to disappear in '48," Edith replied before coughing again.

John handed her a tissue which she coughed blood into. "What do you mean, our family's legacy?"

"No matter what, our families will be entwined forever. If anything happens to me, I want you to open the letter and then keep it hidden forever."

"Edith, you're not making any sense."

"Please John," she coughed again. "If you ever loved me, promise you'll do this one thing for me."

John nodded. "I promise."

He stayed at the hospital for a while longer before heading back home. As he walked up the hill towards Southward Cottage, he noticed Frances standing at the front gate of her house waiting for him.

"Where have you been?" she asked as he walked by.

"Working."

"Until this late?"

"It's a big case. Where's Timmy?"

"Inside, father's reading him a story. I heard Edith got rushed into the hospital."

"Did she?"

"But you already knew that didn't you!"

"What's your problem Frances?" John snapped.

"My problem John is the fact that my partner is spending more time with that tart down the road than me!"

"Don't ever call her that again! We've been close friends since we were children and if I want to catch up with an old friend from time to time then I will!"

"And what about us," Frances cried. "What about Timmy and me?"

"What about you?"

"Don't you care about us too?"

"Of course I do, it's just…"

"You care for Edith more."

John bowed his head.

"Just go John," Frances snapped. "Go. Be with her, just get the hell out of our lives!"

John turned and began to walk away. Frances called out his name but he ignored her. He carried on walking until he arrived at Southward Cottage, his family home. He walked up to the front door, let himself inside and closed it behind him.

**

Two days later, John was attending a call with his colleague, Officer David Oldman, from someone who discovered a pile of rubbish that had been dumped down by the river near Beaulieu. As they were collecting statements from the local residents, Edward Langford parked up next to them. Sergeant Hastings stepped out of the car and wandered over towards them. He took over the line of questioning from John and urged him to go over to the car.

John opened the passenger door and sat inside the car alongside Edward. "I thought you were avoiding me?"

"Just trying not to interfere," Edward replied. "We need to go."

"Go where? I'm in the middle of an investigation."

"Hastings can cover it until you get back."

"No Father, what's going on?"

"We had a phone call from the hospital, Edith Wise died this morning."

John sat back in his chair. A shiver ran through his body and tears stung his eyes. He took a couple of deep breaths. "When? How?" he asked.

"She died peacefully in her sleep this morning. Her lungs just couldn't go on anymore. I'm sorry, I know you and Edith were close for a long time. Dana and William Handanowicz are still at the hospital if you want to see her."

John nodded.

Edward started the car and drove away to the hospital. Both men never spoke another word on the journey there. When John walked into the hospital ward, he felt a feeling of emptiness he had never experienced before. People were rushing around him going from place to place but it all seemed to disappear into the background as he became consumed in his own little zone.

"John?" a woman's voice interrupted his thoughts.

He turned around to see Dana Handanowicz looking at him.

"Are you sure you can do this?" she asked.

John nodded.

Together, they walked along the corridor and entered a small side room at the end of the hospital ward. Laying lifeless but this time without all of the wires and tubes he had seen before was the one girl he knew deep down, had stolen his heart from when he was just a young boy. Now, at nineteen years old, he looked at Edith's body, at peace in the hospital bed and his heart broke anew. He felt a pain deep within that he knew he could never explain. So many dreams, so many memories together came flooding back but he knew, no matter what he did, there was no way to bring her back. Edith Wise, his first love, had gone.

John spent a few minutes at her bedside before leaving the hospital once again. He walked for what seemed like an eternity, not meeting the glances of anybody or acknowledging any kind of conversation or distraction. He walked into the city centre before sitting down on a wooden bench outside a pharmacy.

He looked around watching everybody else rushing to wherever they were headed, carrying on as if nothing had happened and to them, nothing had happened. Life goes on as normal. Nobody stopped to consider the wishes and dreams of those who had died and John felt a bitterness deep inside. He felt like he and Edith had been cheated out of a life they had always dreamed of and his anger burned deep inside him.

As he leant on the arm of the bench, he felt something in his inside jacket pocket. He reached inside and found an envelope.

His heart panged anew as he recognised Edith's handwriting on the front of it. He opened the envelope and read the letter inside;

Dearest John

If you're reading this, it means I'm no longer with you and though it makes me sad to think of this, I know you will go on and live those dreams we had together for me.

I know we will never be able to reclaim those missing years. I never expected to have to flee my home for the safety of my family but the war should have taught me that nothing is ever certain anymore. Not even the love of a family. You see, I have three siblings who share the same father as your siblings too. Our mother's, no matter how much they deny it, could not resist the charm of a serviceman in their care during the war.

Jack Smith was a scoundrel. He made his fortune robbing banks from before the war and used the gold to charm his way into the arms of the lonely willing women who stayed at home when their husband's went off to war.

Mother could never live with the shame of having a child out of wedlock and my elder brother has found a new life in London. She was not done there though and now Evelyn and Emily will carry on his family genes to the next generation too. If William had not been so understanding, who knows where we would have ended up?

Jack gave mother two gold bars to disappear from Lepe and never return. When I became ill, I asked her to give me one last wish and that was to see you one last time. At least we had the chance to say goodbye and I will always love you John Langford.

Take care of Evelyn, Emily, Fred and Mary. They must never know how deep the family ties run but our love will live on forever.

With all my love, now and forever,

Your Edith

XX

John read the letter several times, barely believing the words that Edith had written. Both of their mothers had had affairs during the war and it was with the same man that his father, Edward, had discovered on the beach, the day after he had joined them all for luncheon. It all made sense now. Seeing Jack Smith handing over money to Dana before she had come along to join them on the beach. Their disappearance. How he longed for those missing years now. There must have been a way for them to have resolved the situation.

He placed the envelope back inside his pocket and headed towards the railway station. He stopped at the bank just outside the station and withdrew enough money to see him through for a while before buying a one-way ticket to London Waterloo. As he climbed aboard the train, only taking with him the clothes he was wearing, John Langford knew he needed to get away, he needed somewhere to start over again. As the tall buildings and busy streets of Southampton disappeared into the distance, he took a deep breath and relaxed for the first time in a long time. He felt at peace with his life. Edith had wanted him to live his life and dreams like they had imagined when they were young and now John was determined to do just that.

***

"Open the door! I know you're in there!" Frances shouted as she hammered on the door of Southward Cottage. "Come out and face me you coward!"

"What on Earth is going on?" Edward Langford asked as he approached his front door.

"Your son has been ignoring me!"

"I'm not surprised with the way you are acting. When you decide that you can act like a lady, you can come in. Until then, be on your way."

"But..."

"No buts. My son has been more than kind to you considering your situation."

"He gets compensated for it!"

"Indeed, what I mean is there are a lot of people in this village that have very long memories."

"Just because some people are prejudiced doesn't mean I should live my life in fear!"

"Of course not but likewise, hammering on the door of a man ten years younger than yourself demanding his attention isn't a good look for a young lady either."

"This is not over!" Frances fumed before storming away back down the driveway.

"I doubt it is," Edward replied before heading inside.

As he entered the cottage, an eerie silence greeted him.

"Hello!" Edward called out but there was no reply.

He walked through the cottage and into the kitchen where there was a note left on the dining table.

GONE TO CHURCH.
DINNER IS IN THE OVEN.

Edward frowned. Ever since old Father Harold Partridge had been discovered frolicking with two young German men, most of the villagers had left the congregation in their droves. Harold had since moved on and a new vicar by the name of Rupert Bradley had taken over from him. He thought of Edith Wise and her untimely death. Since leaving John at the hospital, he hadn't heard from him for the rest of the day. He reheated his dinner before settling down to read the newspaper and enjoying some time alone. Around an hour later, the family all returned home.

Mary and Fred rushed off to get ready for bed whilst Mavis made a pot of tea.

"Have you seen John this evening?" she asked.

"No, I haven't seen him since I dropped him at the hospital at lunchtime," Edward replied.

"You didn't go in with him?"

"He's not a child anymore, Mavis. There are some things that a man should do on his own."

She didn't reply.

"How was church? Has the new reverend managed to convince the naysayers back?"

"It's not like that and you know it. However you dress it up, what Harold did to those poor men was illegal."

"Is it illegal to love somebody?"

"You know what I mean!"

"Times are changing, Mavis. Maybe the world needs to too."

"Too much is changing if you ask me. That blasted Frances turned up at the church looking for John again. Caused quite a stir."

"Well she's desperate isn't she. I told him she'd be nothing but trouble. He's too caring for his own good."

"Can you have a word with her?"

"I tried earlier when she was trying to break the door down."

"She was here too?"

Edward nodded. "If John doesn't report in, she goes loopy. No wonder Christopher left her."

"You really can be heartless at times!"

"If a woman is going to put herself in that situation then she needs to deal with the consequences."

"She lost her mother during the war, her father uses her as a slave and the gardener took advantage of her and left her pregnant and alone. I hardly call that a situation she created on her own."

"So you think John is right to keep going around there and helping her?"

"Oh, I don't know. I'm worried about him. He was very close with Edith. Her death could take its toll on him and he should be concentrating on his career rather than women."

"I'm sure he'll make the right decision in the end," Edward replied before heading out towards the back garden.

Meanwhile next door at Thyme Cottage, the doorbell echoed around the house.

"Frances!" Arthur shouted from the living room.

"Don't shout, I've just got Timmy settled," she replied as she headed towards the front door.

"If it's that Langford lad you can tell him to get lost! Calling round at this hour. Only one thing he's after..."

Frances slowly opened the front door and saw a man dressed in black waiting there.

"Father Partridge, I thought you had left the village," Frances said.

"I had, I did, I mean, well, I heard you needed some help so I thought I'd call by."

"How thoughtful," Frances smiled ruefully.

"Who is it?" Arthur asked.

"Just a friend," Frances replied as she stepped outside.

"I heard about Edith Wise. Terrible situation," Harold continued. "Have you heard from John?"

"No, not today."

"It must be tough, being cast aside for a teenager like that."

"What do you mean?"

"Oh, John and Edith were always so close. It was obvious when her family returned that she would turn his head."

"Is that so?"

"Oh, don't get me wrong, you really are a most wonderful woman Miss King, I just, er..."

"Just what?"

Harold didn't reply.

"Actually, there is something you can help me with," she said as she led Harold towards the garden shed.

"Oh, right, okay, what is it?"

"I've been having a bit of trouble with a clamp in the garden shed. It seems to be a little stiff."

Frances opened the door and picked up the torch that had been left on a workbench inside the shed. "After you," she insisted.

Harold stepped inside and in one quick movement, she struck him on the back of his head, sending him falling to the floor inside the shed. She shone the light on him briefly to check that he was unconscious before locking the door and returning to the house. As she closed the front door, she heard her father calling out again.

"It's okay, no one will disturb us anymore," she replied.

Chapter Sixty-Two

Misplaced Trust
Wednesday 5th November 2008

"In forty-three years of working for the British Government, I don't think I've ever come across a case where my lead investigator has risked everything for a fairytale!" Eric Gordon snapped as Alison, Blake and Samir entered his office and sat down. "Where is James Handanowicz?"

"Escaping an unfair justice system in the Greek Islands when all he was doing was protecting his sister," Alison replied.

"Yes, this family affair of the Langfords seems to have thrown up a history of betrayal and red herrings."

"I didn't realise my family tree was public knowledge," Blake replied.

"Don't you think we fully vet every operative that ever enters this room Blake? This is threatening to blow up into something that could seriously undermine Her Majesty's Government!"

"I don't follow Sir, how does a body sticking out of a grave and a double murder in Rhodes constitute a problem for the Government?" Alison asked. "Blake and I were just following a lead."

"When the coffin was exhumed from the cemetery, there was a noticeable difference to how the corpse was expected to be," Eric explained.

Alison and Blake both looked at Samir. "When I examined the body, it was remarkably well preserved," he explained.

"The coffin was lead lined, therefore preserving the body and its hidden contents which was discovered when it was brought to the undertakers for further examination."

"What was hidden in the coffin?" Blake asked.

Samir removed the card he found in Jack Smith's urn earlier and placed it on the desk. "I removed this when I examined the body," he lied.

Blake picked it up. "It's a piece of the map. How was it so well preserved?"

Samir shrugged.

"Dana Handanowicz, the woman whose body was in the coffin was used by her husband to hide a secret. William Handanowicz had the access codes to a nuclear bomb that was buried just after world war two in the UK. When Joe Knight went back to the undertakers to inspect the coffin and retrieve the codes, they were gone. Today, we received a letter demanding the gold that was hidden in Holbury Manor as payment for not setting that bomb off," Eric Gordon explained.

"Where is the bomb?" Alison asked.

"Underneath an oil refinery on the south coast near to The New Forest."

"The same refinery that pumps gas across the entire south of England," Blake gasped. "If that goes off, it'll kill millions and wipe out the whole of London and half of the country!"

"Indeed," Eric Gordon nodded.

"How the hell did William Handanowicz have the codes?" Samir asked.

"Because he was my senior officer in Special Branch until he retired in 1982. When I took over the office, there was no mention of it until after his death in 1987. An internal investigation discovered that he had indeed taken the codes to the grave with him."

"Was William Handanowicz's grave searched?" Alison asked.

"He was cremated," Blake replied.

"So was Dana Handanowicz," Samir added.

Blake glared at him. "So how do we stop this bomb?"

"There is an underground bunker inside the refinery that goes five hundred metres below ground. If you can access that, you could find the bomb and defuse it but you need to find those access codes."

"That's like looking for a needle in a haystack. Where do we even start?" Samir asked.

"Our friend the undertaker would be top of the list. Where's Joe Knight now?" Blake asked.

Eric Gordon pressed his intercom. "Angela? Angela?"

No response.

Eric checked his watch. "That's odd," he said as he walked towards the door.

As he opened it, the office was empty. Eric walked through and checked the toilet area before coming back to his office.

"Where is Ada Hughes' daughter?" Blake asked as Eric returned to the office.

"What do you know about the Hughes family?"

"Angela had been doing some digging before we arrived but clammed up when Blake asked where she was," Alison replied.

"Please Sir, she may be our missing connection," Blake replied.

"Patricia Hughes is in witness protection for her own safety."

"Yet Angela knew all about the Jack Smith connection. Who is Patricia hiding from?" Samir asked.

"The same people who killed her son and her niece."

"Patricia Hughes is Tom Gibson's mother," Alison replied.

Eric nodded.

Blake felt a shiver run through him. If his father John knew about the Jack Smith connection, that was why he did everything in his power to break up Tom and Jenny. He knew there was a chance that they were cousins. He rushed into the outer office and began tapping away on Angela's laptop.

"What are you doing?" Alison asked.

"If we can pick up the signal from Angela's mobile phone, we can find out where she's going!"

"You mean this mobile phone," Samir replied as he lifted up a phone that had been left by the coffee machine.

Blake swore under his breath. "Where is she going Sir? There was a signal from here to Goodman, Parker & Knowles inc. Who sent the message to release all of the information?"

"Angela released the information to the solicitors as per the freedom of information act," Eric admitted.

"In doing that, my family is now at risk. Whoever killed Gibson will now be heading for Southward Cottage!"

"Your family have protection Blake. Frank and Andre are there. They will know that and won't attack. They want the gold that Jack Smith robbed from CityBank in 1938. Tom Gibson would have had a section of the map, you have the pieces from Victor Wise and James Handanowicz, the final piece would have been left with Mavis Langford."

"But Mavis has died," Alison replied.

"Her belongings were moved after she died. Aunt Mary took over the house and Grandma's things were donated to Francesca Audrey's Hospice in Lymington," Blake said.

"That's where you'll find Patricia," Eric Gordon replied. "She will have the final piece."

***

A red FIAT 500 pulled up outside Francesca Audrey's Hospice in Lymington. Frances Vaselievich stepped out of the passenger seat and closed the door. She walked around to the drivers' side and as the window wound down, the driver handed her a small vial with clear liquid inside it.

"Make me proud," she said before walking towards the entrance.

The car drove away leaving an eerie calmness outside the home as day gave way to night time. She pressed the doorbell and waited at the door until a nurse came and answered it.

"Can I help you?" the nurse asked.

"Yes, I'm here to see Patricia Hughes," Frances replied.

"Are you a relative?"

"An old friend."

"I'm afraid visiting time is over for today."

"Oh, I've come a long way and you wouldn't see an elderly lady out in the cold in this weather would you?"

The nurse looked at her quizzically for a moment before sighing and stepping aside. "I guess thirty minutes wouldn't hurt," she said as she closed the door behind Frances.

"Bless you dear," Frances replied as she slipped off her coat.

"If I could get you to sign in for me..."

Frances picked up the pen and signed a false name in the book.

"May I take your coat?" the nurse asked.

"No, no, it's okay, I'll keep hold of it. Where is Patricia?"

"This way," the nurse replied as she led Frances through the hospice.

When they arrived at the day room, there were two elderly women and an elderly man sat in armchairs watching snooker on the TV whilst two other women were standing in, what looked like a kitchen area, making themselves a drink. Frances recognised one of the women in the kitchen area and she in turn, recognised Frances.

"Mrs Hughes, you have a visitor," the nurse called out.

Patricia kept her eyes firmly on Frances whilst fiddling with something in one of the drawers. "I thought visiting time was over."

"Is that a way to greet an old friend Pat?" Frances asked as she approached her.

The second lady in the kitchen area moved away leaving them alone.

"What do you want, Frances?" Patricia asked.

"I just came to see an old friend as I was in the area."

"Don't you live abroad now?"

"I did until my divorce and then suddenly, I no longer felt welcome behind the iron curtain anymore."

Patricia watched her as she approached the work surface where she had placed her coffee cup. "I came here to end my days in peace. Whatever Thomas has done is on him now. I've washed my hands of it all."

"You see, that's where you're wrong," Frances whispered.

"What do you mean?"

"You have something I need."

"I gave up the family legacy long ago. We're both too old for fairytales."

"Tom died for that fairytale..."

In one quick movement, Patricia removed a dinner knife from the drawer and stabbed it through the top of Frances's hand impaling it to the wooden work surface.

"Mrs Hughes! What on Earth?" the nurse gasped as she rushed over to attend to Frances's bleeding hand.

"Miss King was just leaving," Patricia replied as she began to walk away.

Frances stuck out her leg and tripped her up sending her down to the floor, hitting her head on one of the cupboards. Two more nurses rushed in to attend to Patricia whilst the knife was removed from Frances's hand and a bandage was wrapped around it to cover the wound.

"That woman is the devil!" Patricia shouted as she was led away.

The nurse who had attended to Frances picked up her handbag from the floor but as she did, a small vial of clear liquid fell out of it. "What's this?" she asked as she picked it up.

Frances raised her uninjured arm and hit the nurse in the throat with the side of her hand in a vicious karate chop. The nurse staggered backwards, dropping the vial of liquid on the floor which shattered on impact. Frances rushed towards the exit before being confronted by two men who grabbed hold of her arms and led her into a side room, closing the door behind them.

***

Joe Knight was waiting in his blue Vauxhall Astra outside Crowther's funeral home as Paul Crowther locked the front door and began heading towards his car.

Joe stepped out of his car and walked towards him. "Mr Crowther?"

"Who wants to know?"

"Joe Knight, Special Branch, may I have a word?"

Paul looked at him up and down. "I hope they paid you well for that."

"For what?"

"Looking like that in the name of Queen and country, I'd be amazed if your wife ever looked at you in the same way again."

"My appearance has nothing to do with this case. When Dana Handanowicz's body was exhumed, there was something hidden in the lining of the coffin. Something of importance to national security. When we returned to inspect the coffin, it had been removed so either you or one of your work colleagues have the information that we need."

"What information? All we received was a rotting corpse."

"We both know that's not true."

"Prove it," Paul smirked.

"Interfering with a Special Branch investigation will cost you a lot."

"Listen, all that was in that coffin was a rotting corpse of a woman who died almost thirty years ago. To be honest, her face looked in better condition than yours."

Joe grabbed his shirt and pinned him against the side of his car. "No, you listen to me you piece of shit, I know you're hiding something and you're looking to sell it to the highest bidder but this goes way deeper than you could ever understand."

"Everything all right Paul?" a passer-by asked.

"All good, just a misunderstanding..." Paul replied, "...Ain't it cop?"

Joe reluctantly released his grip on his shirt.

"As long as you're all right," the passer-by replied, looking at Joe and then back at Paul.

"You lot need to get your priorities right here. A young woman has been left buried alive and all you and your colleagues are doing is harassing me and my staff! If you don't back off, I'll get a restraining order put on the lot of ya!" Paul snapped.

"It's because a young woman was buried alive in a grave that your company was responsible for that we are investigating you in the first place. Dana Handanowicz was believed to have been cremated by her family and then her body turned up in an unmarked grave at the centre of an investigation!" Joe replied.

"Families are always at war during a time of grief. Money changes people. Even the most placid and laid-back individuals would chase a fiver in force ten gale if they thought it would give them status over someone else."

"So is this a regular occurrence amongst undertakers then? Kind of a buy one get one free on the funerals?"

"I don't know what deal they cut with my father and I don't want to know. As far as the records show, Dana Handanowicz was buried in that plot but a headstone was never ordered. If the family didn't have the money to pay for one, it wasn't unusual for there to just be the small metal plaque in the ground and any sod can pull that up and nick it. So until you have concrete evidence against me or my company, why don't you piss off and do some real police work scarface and stop wasting my time," Paul snapped as he stepped inside his car.

Joe wanted to react but forced himself to calm down. He knew Crowther wanted a reaction from him so he could get him thrown off the case. He reluctantly headed back towards his car as Paul drove away. As he climbed inside, he found a message from Alison. It read:

GO TO FRANCESCA AUDREY'S HOSPICE IN LYMINGTON, WE MAY HAVE FOUND JACK SMITH'S DAUGHTER, PATRICIA SMITH.

***

A red FIAT 500 pulled up outside Southward Cottage overlooking Lepe Beach. Dmitri and Timmy walked up the driveway past a blue Nissan Note with a spherical dent in its rear bumper and a green Volkswagen that had shiny alloy wheels reflecting the moonlight. As they arrived at the front door, they heard the crackle and bangs of fireworks coming from the back garden as a rainbow of colours illuminated the sky above the cottage. Dmitri pointed for Timmy to head around to the side gate whilst he headed towards the front door. As Dmitri reached for the doorbell, the front door opened and a tall man of African descent with wide shoulders and strong arms dressed in a navy blue shirt and jeans answered.

"Can I help you?" Frank asked.

"Yes, I was looking for Mr Langford," Dmitri replied.

Frank stepped forward and closed the door behind him. "I'm sorry, he's not home right now."

"Oh, that's a shame," Dmitri replied before pulling a knife from out of his sleeve but Frank was too quick for him, aiming a kick to his stomach before landing a right uppercut underneath his chin to send Dmitri to the floor.

At that moment, Michael came rushing out of the side gate and was immediately grabbed in a headlock by Timmy who was waiting by the gate. Michael struggled as much as he could but Timmy held a knife to his neck as he stepped back towards the front garden.

He saw Dmitri laying on the floor with Frank standing over him picking the knife up. "Drop it! Or the kid gets it!" he shouted.

Frank dropped the knife and began slowly walking towards Dmitri. "Let the kid go," he said.

"Where's Langford?" Timmy asked.

"Not here, let the kid go!" Frank replied as he continued to slowly move closer to them.

"Stop! Don't come any closer. I'll kill him, I swear!"

At that moment, Andre charged from the back gate knocking Timmy and Michael to the floor in a rugby tackle. Michael managed to free himself and ran back towards the gate. Timmy kicked, punched and scratched with all of his might and managed to wriggle free of Andre's grasp. Andre leapt on him again but missed as Timmy began running back down the driveway.

"Stay with the family!" Frank shouted as he gave chase down the driveway before heading up the hill and into the woods.

***

Meanwhile, at Francesca Audrey's Hospice in Lymington, the two men who had escorted Frances into the side room locked the door before turning to face her. Frances reached inside her bag for a small spray bottle that looked like a bottle of perfume.

"Is it here Hugh?" she asked.

The man on the right walked over to the mantlepiece and picked up a small gold clock and handed it to her.

"What's going on here?" the second man asked as he approached Frances.

"The less you know, the better," she replied before spraying the man in the face with the contents of the perfume bottle.

The man stepped back before falling to the floor.

"You weren't meant to kill him!" Hugh snapped.

"It's chloroform, it'll wear off," Frances replied before smashing the clock on the floor.

Amongst the pieces of plastic, metal and screws was a small folded piece of yellow paper. Frances carefully picked it up and opened it.

"Five down, three to go," she smiled. "Take his keys and let's go."

Hugh knelt down and removed the second man's keys from his belt before opening the fire exit and leading Frances out into the car park.

Chapter Sixty-Three

Rats
Sunday 23rd September 1956

In the early hours of Sunday morning after Frances's father, Arthur King, and her son Timmy were in bed, Frances wandered into the kitchen and picked up a knife, a jar of honey and a packet of sesame seeds before quietly sneaking out of the back door. Shining her torch on the ground, she walked down the garden path and unlocked the shed door. Squeaking and rustling noises came from the back of the shed as she entered and closed the door. Harold Partridge was still laid out cold on the floor.

Frances tossed a few sesame seeds into the cages at the back of the shed and several rats scurried to collect them. Her father had built a metal workbench around the edge of the inside of the shed where he used to craft wood and metal before he became ill. The legs of the workbench were cemented into the ground giving it a solid base for completing heavy work.

Frances picked up some rope and tied Harold's arms and legs securely to each of the legs of the workbench before waking him up. She splashed his face with some water a few times. When he opened his eyes, he saw a silhouette of a woman standing over him and realised he had been restrained.

"What's happening? What's going on?" Harold asked frantically.

"You took something away from me and somehow, you got away with it," Frances replied.

"What do you mean?"

"You know what I mean."

Harold tried to move his head and grimaced at the pain from the blow he had received to knock him out. "What do you want, Frances?"

"I want you to suffer like I have. Why did you come here?"

"I wanted to help you."

"Liar."

"I'm not proud of what I did..."

"Sleeping with those young men, you should be rotting in jail."

"I know, I know what I did was wrong. I want to make it up to you. Let me help you."

"If you'd just left them alone, Christoph would still be here and my child would have had a father."

"I can help you find him," Harold replied.

"How? After you were exposed by the police and his three friends were killed, there's no chance that he would come back. He's probably back in Germany if not dead by now!"

Harold didn't reply.

"It doesn't matter anyway," Frances sighed as she picked up a handkerchief and used it as a gag.

"What are you doing?" Harold gasped before she forced the material into his mouth.

"You destroyed my life and now I'm going to destroy yours," she replied as she picked up the knife.

Harold's eyes darted everywhere as he groaned and tried to talk through the gag. Frances used the knife to cut open his shirt before undoing his belt and removing his trousers and underwear. She then opened the jar of honey and used the knife to spread the honey over his stomach and down towards his genitals.

Harold tried to wriggle himself free from his restraints, kicking and pulling as hard as he could but he could not break free. After she had finished with the honey, she sprinkled a whole packet of sesame seeds over him. Harold watched with a mix of fear and confusion until he heard the squeaking and rustling coming from the back of the shed. One by one, Frances opened the seven cages that housed the rats. They scurried down onto the floor and climbed over Harold's body, feverishly attacking the honey and seeds. Frances soaked a blanket in a bucket of water before placing it over the top of the rats as they gorged on the honey and seeds. The wet blanket created a weighted covering that kept the rats contained on his stomach and they slowly ate him to death. Frances watched for a moment as Harold thrashed against the rats before quietly leaving the shed and locking him inside before returning back into her family home.

Later that morning, Sergeant Peter Hastings arrived at Southward Cottage as Edward Langford was building a wooden bench in the garden.

"Good morning Sir," Hastings called out as he approached the house.

"Good morning, what brings you here today?"

"Sorry to bother you on your day off Sir, I just wondered if you have seen John this morning?"

"No, he didn't come home last night, have you tried next door?"

"Yes, no answer there either."

"That's odd, Arthur rarely leaves the house these days," Edward replied as he began walking towards the driveway with Hastings following him.

"Perhaps he needed some time to himself after yesterday."

"I'd have thought that would be the last thing he wanted. In times of grief, a man needs his family's support around him."

"What's that?" Hastings asked as he jogged down the hill towards Thyme Cottage.

A plume of black smoke rose into the air with a decaying smell lingering on the breeze. Edward and Hastings rushed towards the side gate of the house.

"Mr King! Mr King! Are you all right?" Hastings shouted.

They tried the gate but it was locked. Hastings attempted to climb over and reach the latch on the opposite side but kept sliding down.

"Stand clear!" Edward shouted before shoulder barging his way into the garden.

The wooden gate splintered open and bashed hard against the side wall of the house as Edward stumbled into the garden with Hastings following close behind. Inside the garden, they saw Arthur King sitting on a garden chair drinking a cup of coffee as his garden shed burned to the ground.

"Arthur! What the hell are you doing?" Edward gasped. "Hastings, get some water from the outside tap!"

"No, leave it!" Arthur replied.

"You're going to set fire to the hedges and the fence!"

"The shed must be destroyed!"

Hastings filled a bucket of water and threw it over the fire. Flames continued to engulf the shed as a fire engine siren echoed in the distance. Between them, Hastings and Edward threw buckets of water over the hedge, fence and shed, in an attempt to control the blaze, before the firemen came to put it out completely. Edward and Hastings led Arthur back inside the house.

"What on Earth were you thinking, setting your shed on fire like that?" Edward asked. "You could've killed someone or created a bush fire!"

"Rats!" Arthur replied.

"What?"

"Rats. We had rats everywhere. Tons of them."

"Where's your daughter and grandson Mr King?" Hastings asked.

"They went to church earlier this morning. They are too pure to have death for breakfast."

At that moment, one of the firemen walked over towards them. "Excuse me Sergeant, I think you should see this!"

Edward looked back at Arthur. "Don't go anywhere," he said as he followed Hastings back out into the garden.

The fireman picked through the charred rubble of the shed with a metal pole before poking something solid. As Hastings and Edward arrived, he used the pole to move charred pieces of wood and hidden beneath the rubble was a partially cremated skeleton of a man.

Arthur approached from behind them. They turned and faced him. "I'm sorry," he said as he bowed his head.

Hastings walked over towards him and placed handcuffs onto his wrists. "Arthur King, I am arresting you on suspicion of murder. You do not have to say anything but anything you do say may be used in evidence."

Edward and Hastings led Arthur away whilst the firemen finished off what they needed to do. When they arrived back at Hastings's car, he called in the incident and waited for his colleagues to arrive before taking Arthur to the police station. As Hastings drove away, Frances and Timmy began walking down the hill towards their home.

"What's going on?" Frances asked as she approached.

"Your father has been arrested," Edward replied.

"What? Why?"

"For suspected murder and attempting to conceal the body by setting his shed on fire with the body inside."

Frances gasped. How had he known that Harold Partridge was in there? Her father was still asleep when they left for church earlier this morning. "No, no, there must be some mistake!"

"My advice to you is to find a good solicitor, you're going to need one," Edward replied before walking back to his house.

21 Years Later...
Saturday 30th July 1977

John Langford drove his black Ford Cortina back down the old Lepe Road towards his parents' house for the first time in over 20 years. His fiance Emily Handanowicz, was by his side as they parked their car on the driveway of Southward Cottage. His parents, Mavis and Edward, a little greyer but still full of life, greeted them as they arrived with his sister, Mary, following them closely behind.

"It's so good to see you here again," Mavis said as she embraced them both. "Come in, I've made some cake for you."

As the three women headed inside, John remained outside with his father. "Is she still here?" he asked.

"She's become a recluse since Arthur was convicted of murder and died in jail. Her sons have moved away and nobody sees her anymore," Edward replied.

"Sons?"

"She had a brief relationship with some foreign fella but he's hardly ever here. No surprise really. She always manages to scare them off eventually."

"I still don't think it's a good idea for us to be married in the village, Dad. There's so many bad memories here for so many of us."

"You and Emily were brought up here. It means a lot to her that you're getting married in the local church and I've made sure that Frances King will be kept away so nothing can ruin your big day."

John nodded. "How are you keeping these days? Leaving the force is a big change."

"Retirement isn't too bad. I get to go fishing more and your mother has a grocery list of jobs she wants doing everyday so it keeps me busy. But enough about me, this is about you and Emily, so come on, stop worrying and let's go inside."

When they were inside the house, they discovered that Mavis had put on a huge spread of cakes, sandwiches and drinks for them.

"Has anyone heard from Fred?" John asked as he sat alongside Emily.

"He's coming down next weekend with his girlfriend from London. It's so exciting, our boys beginning their own families," Mavis replied.

"Where did he meet her?"

"The same place you and Emily met up again, she goes to Kings Cross University. Fred has a new plumbing business that keeps him busy all over London. He's just signed a contract for the new football stadium at Wembley."

"The difference is we already knew each other from childhood," John replied.

"So did they," Emily laughed.

"You know who she is?" John asked.

"I should do, she's my twin sister Evelyn."

John felt a shiver run down his spine as Emily told him. "What? When? How long have they been together?"

"A couple of months now but it seems to be going well," Emily replied. "Are you okay? You look a little pale."

"I'm fine, just a little tired, that's all. Probably from the long drive."

Emily nodded before continuing to chat with Mary, Mavis and Edward but John knew he needed to speak to his brother as soon as possible.

Later that day, John stood out in the back garden looking out at the deep blue sea with the Isle Of Wight in the distance.

"You didn't say much at luncheon. Is everything okay?" Mavis asked as she approached him.

John turned to face her. "Did you love him?"

"Who?"

"You know who, Mum, Jack Smith."

Mavis gasped. "How did..."

"We need to stop Evelyn and Fred from being together."

"You knew this whole time and you didn't tell me."

"Why do you think I never came home? There's so many secrets hidden here. In London, Emily and I have our own little bubble where no one can hurt us. We come back here and all hell breaks loose."

"That's not fair. Emily knew they were together and decided to tell you today to keep it as a surprise. I take it she doesn't know..."

John shook his head. "It would break her heart to find out that William was not her real father."

Mavis placed her hand on his shoulder. "I love your father very much John. You're living proof of that. When the war broke out and Ed went off to fight, I thought I'd never see him again. I was convinced it was a fool's errand and he would be killed in battle. I had one moment of weakness and from that, we gained Mary and Fred. Your brother and sister who have been there for you through thick and thin. Kept in touch with you when you ran away after Edith's death. And who supported you when you began dating Emily."

"But you kept the wheel of deception going."

Mavis nodded. "I'm not proud of what I did, John. God knows if I could turn the clock back, I would. As luck would have it, they were born premature and survived. Your father believes that I fell pregnant just before he left for the war. Don't destroy that one piece of hope that he held through the battle and what inevitably led him home after. He's been their father in all but blood throughout their lives. Don't destroy that now."

John took a deep breath as he looked out to sea. Hundreds of thoughts clouded his mind. "What about Dana?"

"That's her story to tell, not ours. When Frances began making trouble for them after Edith died, they sold up and moved away again."

"Edith told me everything before she died."

"So what brought you back into the Handanowicz family? Do you see Edith in Emily?"

John shook his head. "Nothing will bring Edith back and Emily is her own person. She's special and she was there when I needed someone to be there. She never gave up on me and I'll never give up on her."

"Then there's nothing more to be said."

John turned and walked down the side of the house and out into the front garden. He continued down the driveway and up the hill towards the woods. He looked up at the remains of the old treehouse that he used to play in with Mary and Fred as a child, the little stream that ran through the woods down to the sea, the old oak tree where lovers and friends carved their names into its trunk. It all felt like a lifetime ago that he used to run through the woods carefree and alone.

He came to the cut-through that brought him out next to St David's church. The same church that he would be marrying Emily inside in two weeks time. He wandered into the cemetery that led up to the church before walking down towards the far side near to where the honeysuckle grew and found a small grey marble headstone. He crouched down next to it and read the inscription:

IN LOVING MEMORY OF
EDITH HILDA WISE
DIED SATURDAY 22ND SEPTEMBER 1956
AGED 17 YEARS
WHEN ALL OUR DREAMS TURN TO ASHES
THE LORD WILL LEAD US HOME

John felt tears sting the backs of his eyes as he read the words. For so long, he had wanted to visit her grave and had always found excuses to not come here. Now reading the stone in front of him, Edith's loss had a sense of finality to it.

"I hope you understand," he said softly as he kissed the tips of his fingers on his left hand and placed his hand on the stone as he walked away.

As he arrived at the church gate, he took one last look back towards where Edith's grave was.

"John?" a woman's voice called out.

He spun around towards where the voice came from and he saw a middle-aged woman wearing black walking towards him.

"Long time no see," she smiled at him.

John recognised her smile immediately and wished that the ground would swallow him whole. Walking towards him was Frances King.

Chapter Sixty-Four

Secrets From The Past
Wednesday 5th November 2008

Frank Jackson chased Timmy through the woods towards the open field next to St David's Church in the distance. Fireworks crackled in the night sky and a huge bonfire in the centre of the field gave the sky an eerie glow as they rushed through the woods. A crowd of people had gathered to see a firework display as Frank weaved his way through the crowd trying to find Timmy.

He heard someone shouting out up ahead and saw Timmy dart out of the crowd and head towards the church. Frank chased him through a narrow cut-through in the hedge and across the cemetery towards St David's Church. A lady holding a tray of Remembrance Poppies stood in the doorway. Timmy hit the tray out of her hands sending poppies and badges falling like confetti all over the floor. Frank quickly manoeuvred and leapt over them as he entered the church.

A curtain on the far side of the altar swished in the breeze and Frank immediately headed towards it. At that moment, he heard the clunk of a door closing and the vicar entered the church from his vestry.

"Can I help you at all?" the vicar asked.

Frank flashed his pass. "Frank Jackson, Special Branch in pursuit of suspect. Did you see anyone come in here?"

"No, I didn't. What..."

"Where does this door lead to?" Frank asked, pointing towards the curtain.

"Up to the bell tower and the balcony, why?"

Frank didn't reply and rushed through the door climbing round and round the spiral staircase. The bells began to ring out for eight o' clock and the sound was deafening as it echoed around the tight space but he continued to climb. Eventually, he made it to the top of the church. He rushed towards the left side, noticing the crumbling brickwork at the edge of the balcony. The church was in need of serious repair and he knew he needed to be careful. He stopped and listened.

Fireworks crackled and banged in the distance and he could hear the muffled tones of people talking and celebrating in the next field around the bonfire. He slowly continued moving around the edge of the balcony, listening for any kind of noise until Timmy came charging at him. Frank quickly ducked back behind the corner as Timmy made contact with his arm almost knocking him off balance. He placed his foot on the crumbling wall and launched himself at Frank once again. Frank caught him with his right arm diverting his face into the wall. Timmy staggered back momentarily stunned as blood began gushing from his nose. He charged at Frank once again but Frank dodged him. His momentum took him towards the edge. As he reached down, one of the bricks came loose and fell to the ground around fifteen metres below.

"You don't have to do this!" Frank shouted.

"Langford took everything from us!"

"What's your name? I'm sure we can sort something out."

"Timmy!" a voice called out from behind him.

Timmy turned and saw the vicar at the top of the staircase. As he turned the brickwork on the wall his foot was on, crumbled away. His foot slipped and he fell backwards.

"No!" the vicar shouted.

Frank leapt forward and managed to grab hold of his hand.

"I'm slipping!" Timmy screamed.

"Hold my legs!" Frank shouted.

The vicar rushed over and held Frank's legs as he tried to grab hold of Timmy with his second hand but he was just out of reach. He could feel Timmy's hand slipping from his grasp.

"Help me!" Timmy shouted.

The vicar held on to Frank as he took one last chance, he reached as far down as he could and managed to get his second hand onto Timmy's wrist. With all of his strength, Frank pulled as hard as he could and managed to pull him back up onto the balcony. Frank rolled over onto his back before standing up again as Timmy got back on his feet.

"Why did you save me?" Timmy asked.

"No one deserves to die that way," Frank replied. "What did the Langfords do to you?"

"John Langford walked out on us when I was only a child. He used my mother and then threw us away like a piece of rubbish!"

Frank turned to the vicar. "How did you know who he was? Is he local?"

"No," the vicar replied.

"So how did you know me?" Timmy asked.

"Because my name is Christoph Fischer. In 1948, I had a brief relationship with your mother, Frances King, before foolishly running away from my responsibilities. I'm not proud of what I did and I hope you can forgive me."

Timmy looked at him in disbelief.

"I'm your father," Christoph admitted.

"No, no, that can't be right. Mum said you were dead!"

"Maybe I was to her. I came here as a prisoner-of-war. I managed to escape with three friends and we hid out in the old cafe down on the beach in 1948. The local vicar at the time helped us out along with the owner of the cafe until one day, a police officer killed a man on the beach. Suspicion suddenly came upon us and one by one, my friends were killed. I ran away because I thought I would be next but I was spared. I discovered a convent in Portsmouth where I was able to train as a vicar and was placed in this parish ten years ago."

"So you must be, what... eighty years old now?" Timmy asked.

"Eighty-one. I'm afraid I'm not as sprightly as I used to be."

"No, no, this is wrong, everything is wrong. We were meant to uncover the Langford's treachery and we've uncovered our own instead."

"What do the Langfords have?" Frank asked.

"The map to Jack Smith's gold!" Timmy replied.

"You don't honestly believe that old fairytale do you?"

"It's there, I know it is!"

"It's not Tim. I met Jack Smith. He was nothing but a lying, cheating scoundrel who used women to get his own way in life," Christoph replied.

"Then all this was for nothing. The deaths, the constant searching, all for nothing," Timmy gasped.

"What deaths?" Frank asked.

"It doesn't matter now. It's over for us."

"It doesn't need to be," Christoph replied. "You can repent your sins. You can be born again."

"You may believe that old cobblers but mother will never let it go. It's consumed her life and in turn it has consumed mine," Timmy replied before walking towards the edge of the balcony.

"Timmy, what are you doing?" Christoph asked.

"She'll never let it go! Never! Forgive me, father," he replied before throwing himself off of the balcony.

"No!" Frank shouted as he launched himself towards him but he was too late.

Screams echoed from the cemetery below as Timmy's body fell to the ground.

***

Meanwhile, Hugh, the security officer from the hospice and Frances were driving along the country roads towards Lepe Beach. Two ambulances and a police car overtook them in a blur of flashing blue lights. Frances felt a feeling in the pit of her stomach that something wasn't right. She pulled out her phone and called Timmy. No answer. She tried to call Dmitri, no answer.

"What's wrong?" Hugh asked.

"Follow that ambulance!" she replied.

"What about the Langfords?"

"We'll get to them later!"

As they arrived at St David's Church, a large crowd had gathered in the cemetery and surrounded the right side of the church. Paramedics rushed through the crowd with a stretcher as police attempted to clear the area. Frances climbed out of the car and waited near the ambulance. After what seemed like an age, the paramedics wheeled the stretcher down the path before lifting it into the back of the ambulance. As they lifted the stretcher, she managed to get a glimpse of who was laying on it, it was Timmy.

***

Joe Knight arrived at Francesca Audrey's Hospice accompanied by two police cars. He saw a forensic team dusting for fingerprints on a side fire exit door and two nurses talking to one of the police officers at the front door.

He walked over towards them and flashed his ID. "Joe Knight, Special Branch, what happened?"

"Someone came to visit one of the residents but ended up getting her hand stabbed with a knife and then assaulting a member of security before leaving with another security guard," the officer replied.

"Do we know who she was?"

"She signed the book as Rose Wilton but the resident she came to see said her name was Frances King."

"Who was Frances King coming to see?"

"Patricia Hughes."

Joe thought about that for a moment. Frances had obviously made the connection between Tom Gibson's family and the Langfords and was looking to tie up some loose ends. "Was Mrs Hughes the one who stabbed her with the knife?"

"Yes, why?"

"I think I may know where she rushed off to. What about the security guard, who was he?"

The officer turned towards the nurse.

"Hugh Johnson, he'd only been working here for a couple of months," she replied.

"Does he live locally?" Joe asked.

"He used to help the vicar at St David's Church near Lepe chop wood for the locals to use for their fires in the winter."

"Would the vicar know where he lives?"

"No, they had a falling out quite a few years ago. The cutting shed at the back of the vicar's property is rented out by a local businessman who oversees it now."

"Who's the local businessman?"

"Andre Lewis, he bought Thyme Cottage on the old Lepe Road, next door to where old Mary Langford used to live a few years back but he's struggled to find any residents to live there."

Joe rushed back to his car and headed towards Lepe. Andre Lewis had recently been recruited by Special Branch and was being trained by Frank Jackson. If he had brought the old King family home next door to the Langfords, Blake and his family were likely to be the next targets.

***

A police car was parked outside Southward Cottage as Andre led Dmitri towards the car and pushed him into the back seat. He finished talking to the police officers who then left and drove Dmitri away. As they left, a red Vauxhall Vectra pulled up outside the house. Andre wandered over towards it as the driver's window rolled down.

"Get in, we don't have much time," Angela Barnes said.

"What about Frank?"

"Leave him, we have to go now."

Andre walked around towards the passenger side and climbed into the front seat before Angela sped away into the night. A few minutes later, Blake arrived and parked his car on the driveway. He rushed up to the front door and headed inside the house. As he opened the door, Paula, Jenny and Michael all rushed towards him.

"What's happening? What's going on?" Paula asked.

"Where's Frank and Andre?" Blake asked.

"They both went after two men who turned up at the house. One of them grabbed Michael!" Jenny explained.

"And they both left you all alone!" Blake fumed. "Where did they go?"

"Frank chased one of them into the woods whilst the second one was knocked out in the garden. The police have just taken them away," Paula explained. "What the hell is going on Blake?

We've had more police and ambulances down here tonight than I've ever seen!"

Blake was reluctant to tell them the full story and just held them close. Suddenly, the front door opened and he immediately spun around pulling his gun from his belt before stopping himself from firing. "Frank, you scared the hell out of me!"

"We've got bigger problems, where's Joe and Alison?" Frank asked.

"Joe's gone to Francesca Audrey's Hospice and Alison and Samir have gone to the oil refinery. Where were you? Why did you leave my family alone?"

"Timothy Vasilievich has just tried to commit suicide by jumping from the balcony of the church after discovering the vicar is his father. Turns out he was on a revenge mission that his mother has spent his and her entire life masterminding against your family."

"Who's Timothy Vasilievich?"

"Before his mother got married to Vladimir Vasilievich, he was known as Timothy King, Frances King's son."

Blake felt a shiver run down his spine. Frances King was the woman who had stalked his father throughout his teens and twenties before finally giving up on him when he married Emily Handanowicz. "That's our connection! Where is he now? Is he still alive?"

"Barely, paramedics have taken him away but it doesn't look good."

"Where's Frances King now?"

"Nobody knows. Police were called to Francesca Audrey's Hospice so maybe Joe can fill you in on that."

Blake thought about that for a moment. It all made sense. The vendetta that Frances King had against the family because his father left her after they had briefly been in a relationship back in 1956. "The map! It's got to be!" he said before rushing upstairs.

"Blake! What are you talking about?" Paula asked as she rushed after him.

Blake grabbed a pole from the bedroom and opened the loft hatch before pulling a metal ladder down and climbing up into the attic. He used his phone for a torchlight and quickly rummaged through some boxes before he found an old leather briefcase. He carried it back down the ladder before heading back downstairs and placing it on the dining table.

"Who keeps briefcases anymore?" Jenny asked.

"This is what Aunt Mary kept after Dad moved out and after our grandparents died," Blake explained as he moved the dials to the right combination before opening the case.

"How did you know..."

"Dad's date of birth. He told me about this when we used to go fishing."

"How do you remember that? It must have been fifteen years ago!"

Blake pulled out a handful of envelopes and handed some to Jenny, Paula and Frank before opening one himself.

"What are we looking for?" Paula asked.

"Our Grandfather kept all of these letters hidden from Dad so he wouldn't have to deal with them when he married our mother. Frances sent him letters constantly from 1956 until 1977. We're looking for the letter from 12th August 1977," Blake replied.

"There must be over two hundred letters here! It's a needle in a haystack!" Jenny complained.

"And I found the needle," Frank replied as he handed Blake the letter.

Paperclipped to the letter was a receipt for the transfer of two 6lb gold bars transferred to Miss Francis King as well as a small folded piece of yellow paper.

As Blake opened it and placed the two pieces of paper he had recovered in Rhodes, he noticed a familiar outline. "It's in Holbury Manor. Of course," he said. "This is Mavis Langford's piece of the map."

"Where's Holbury Manor?" Jenny asked.

"It's a residential area now but the old Manor House was used as an emergency hospital during the war. The same place where little Frances King, who was only a teenager when the war broke out, helped out with her mother, Dorothy King, before she was killed in the bombings. Jack Smith buried it right under her nose. If we find the rest of the map, we'll find the gold," Blake replied.

"Gold? What gold?" Paula asked.

"The Langford and Handanowicz family legacy. Jack Smith robbed a bank in 1938 and stashed the gold away in The New Forest. For the past seventy years, no one has known where it was hidden and it's been written off."

"So, if it was worth a lot in 1938, it's got to be worth..."

"Millions," Frank replied. "And Frances King is willing to kill whoever gets in her way of claiming what she believes to be hers after she was rejected by Blake's father."

"So, how do we find the missing pieces of the map?" Paula asked.

"Are we millionaires Dad?" Michael asked excitedly.

Blake shook his head. "No, people have died for that gold. It's blood money. It's not ours or anyone else's to keep. We need to find Frances King."

"She'll kill you as soon as she lays eyes on you," Frank replied. "It's too risky."

"That's why we need to come at it from a different angle. Where's Andre?"

At that moment, there was a knock at the door. Frank drew his gun and cautiously approached. He carefully opened it ajar before relaxing and opening it fully and letting Joe Knight enter the house.

"We've got trouble," Joe said as he walked over to Blake.

"I know, we need to locate Frances King and Andre," Blake replied.

"Have you met your next door neighbour whilst you've been living here?" Joe asked.

"No, the place has been empty for the past couple of years, why?" Paula asked.

"The ID we've got from the Hospice of the security guard that helped Frances King escape is Hugh Johnson. He works for a local businessman chopping wood in the cutting shed located on the back of the vicar's property up near the church however he has been recently seen coming in and out of your neighbour's house Thyme Cottage."

"So this Hugh owns the cottage next door?" Paula asked.

"The same cottage where Frances King lived until 1977," Blake replied.

"And according to records, the property was bought for four-hundred-and-seventy-thousand pounds three years ago by Andre Lewis."

Chapter Sixty-Five

Forbidden Love
Saturday 30th July 1977

"What do you want, Frances?" John asked as he began to walk away from the church.

"Is that any way to greet an old friend?"

"Our friendship was over a long time ago."

"I hear you're now with Edith's sister. How does she feel about being the consolation prize?"

"Better than having a murderer as a father and a son by a kraut."

"You never complained when you were getting your leg over."

"We were different people back then. Some of us move on whilst others stay trapped in the past."

"The past will always haunt you, John Langford. Every time you look into her eyes you'll see Edith staring back at you. If you'd given us the chance, I could've made that all fade away for you."

"I'm sorry to hear about your father and I hope whoever the new guy is makes you happy. Now do yourself a favour and stay away from me and my family."

"You know father wasn't a big loss anyway. He was a liability for the last few years of his life and then became useful in the end."

"What do you mean?" John asked.

"He went down for a crime he didn't commit. Ironic really that it was your old man who convicted him. Made our family even more of an outcast than before until I met Vladimir."

"I don't understand, your father killed someone and then tried to burn the body before it was discovered in the shed at the bottom of your garden."

"That's what the official report said but in the end, a father will do anything to protect his children won't he. I made sure that the old vicar paid for past crimes. Vlad said I even have a knack for getting what I want. I'll be seeing you John," Frances replied before continuing on her way.

***

The following weekend, Mary, Mavis, Edward, John and Emily all gathered outside Southward Cottage as Frederick drove his car onto the driveway before stepping out with Evelyn by his side. John stood back as they all smiled and greeted each other. He knew he needed to tell Fred the truth but he also knew it would break the family apart. As they all headed inside, the postman stopped and leant his pushbike against the hedge before handing John three letters.

"Looks like quite a party," the postman smiled before continuing on his way.

"That's an understatement," John replied as he flicked through the letters and noticed one addressed to him.

He walked down the side of the house and headed into the back garden where Edward was beginning to start the barbecue.

"Ah, there you are John, could you please give me a hand with this? Blasted thing doesn't seem to want to light," Edward asked as he looked over at him. "What have you got there?"

John handed him two of the letters and Edward took the third one from his hand too.

"She's at it again, I warned her," Edward said.

"Warned who? The letter was addressed to me," John replied.

"Yes, and so have dozens of others too. Your mother said she was going to put a stop to all of this."

"A stop to what?"

"Frances King or whatever her name is now. Every week we would receive a letter from her declaring her love for you and how you broke her heart. Even after she went off with that foreign bloke."

"She's definitely persistent."

"Yes. Awful woman. First a German and then a Russian. Probably because no English gent would put up with her antics. No, you're well rid of her."

"I saw her."

"What? When?"

"Last week after I visited Edith's grave. She was in the village walking back from the shop."

"But she's moved away. What on Earth is she doing back here?" Edward asked.

"Probably heard about the wedding," Mary replied.

"It's rude to eavesdrop into others conversations, young Mary," Edward snapped.

"Then you shouldn't be talking loud enough for others to overhear. Come on, this is meant to be a celebration of the family being back together again. You're not going to let some village idiot ruin it are you?" Mary asked.

"I agree," Edward replied before placing the letters in his back pocket. "Now, can you help me light this?"

John lit a small piece of balsa wood on fire and managed to get the barbecue burning before Edward began cooking sausages, burgers, bacon and corn on the cob.

Later that evening, Emily and John walked down the wooden stairs from the back garden before wandering along the stony beach as the sun began to set.

"What are you thinking?" Emily asked as they walked hand-in-hand.

"Nothing much," John sighed.

"You've been distracted today. What's wrong? Surely, you're not still thinking about work."

"No, no, nothing like that."

"You've worked tirelessly for years John, you deserve some time to relax."

"I know," he smiled. "I guess I'm so used to being on the go all the time and always looking over my shoulder, it's a hard habit to break."

"It's this place isn't it?"

"What do you mean?"

"I know I was only ten when we left here but our families have been tied to this place for so long, it almost seems like there's a curse when we come back here."

John nodded. "I always enjoyed fishing off of the beach when I was a nipper. Now I just feel detached from it."

"Is that why you went to London rather than following Edward through the police academy down here? You just needed to get away."

"Something like that. I've always wanted to face up to my problems and I guess in this case, I ran away from them."

"But we don't have to run anymore. Everything's going to be fine. We'll have a lovely wedding and we can finally be Mr and Mrs Langford," Emily smiled.

John smiled back at her. "You're right. I'm overthinking things."

As they watched the sun set over the waves of the sea, John knew that he needed to let go of the past for the sake of his marriage however, a nagging worry still troubled him. When they climbed the wooden steps back up to the back garden of Southward Cottage, Frederick was waiting for them.

"John, I'm glad I caught you, can I have a word?" Fred asked.

Emily looked at John who nodded. "I'll see you inside," he said.

As Emily headed into the house, John leant against the back gate. "Is everything okay?" he asked.

"Dad told me about Frances."

"What about her?"

"She's still sending those letters."

"You knew about them?"

Fred nodded. "She just won't let you go."

"That's all in the past now Fred. As soon as we're married, Emily and I will put as much distance between us and this place as we can."

"Her parents were pretty adamant that they wanted the wedding here."

"I know and we will do what they ask but the sooner we can get away, the better. What did you want to speak to me about anyway?"

Fred reached inside his pocket and pulled out a small burgundy box. He opened it and showed John a huge diamond ring. "I'm going to ask Evelyn to marry me," Fred smiled.

"Don't you think it's too soon? You've only been together a few months," John replied.

"I thought you'd be happy for me. She's going to be your sister-in-law next weekend anyway and we've known each other most of our lives."

"I am happy for you Fred, honestly, I am but…"

"Worried I may steal your thunder next weekend?"

"No, it's not like that..."

"Of course it is. Same old John Langford, always thinking about himself."

"No, Fred, there's a lot of things to consider..."

"Like what, your feelings. Can't have your little brother stealing some of your spotlight whilst you and Emily get married. Does she know she's only got you because her sister died?"

John grabbed Fred's shirt. "You know that's not true! I love Emily and I'm going to marry her and spend the rest of my life with her. She is not a consolation prize!"

"Let go of my shirt John," Fred said calmly.

He took a deep breath before releasing his brother's shirt.

"You've got issues John. Issues that you need to get a hold on before you put that wedding ring on or your marriage is doomed before it even gets started," Fred replied before walking away.

One Week Later...

John Langford was standing in front of a mirror in his old bedroom at Southward Cottage. His grey suit, white shirt and navy tie with a white rose in the lapel of his suit jacket gave him the confidence boost he needed. He took a deep breath before heading towards the door.

At that moment, Fred walked in. "All set?" he asked.

"As I'll ever be," John smiled.

"Look, John, I'm sorry about what I said about Edith and Emily last week. I was out of order."

"Fred, I need to tell you something," John said as he walked over and sat on the edge of the bed.

Fred joined him. "What's wrong? Feeling nervous?"

"A bit but there's something you need to know."

"What?"

"You can't marry Evelyn."

Fred smirked. "Why? You're marrying her sister?"

"That's because we have different parents."

"What do you mean?"

"You share a father with Evelyn Handanowicz," John replied.

"What are you talking about? No, Edward Langford is our father and William Handanowicz is hers."

John shook his head. "No Fred, Evelyn's mother Dana and our mum both had affairs with a man called Jack Smith during the war. He is father to both of you."

Fred stared at him without saying a word.

"I'm sorry Fred," John said as he placed his hand on top of his brother's but he moved it away.

"No, no, this can't be happening. How long?"

"How long what?"

"How long have you known?"

"Edith told me."

"She must have been mistaken. That's over twenty years ago! You knew and you never said anything! Does Dad know?" Fred asked.

"I don't think so."

"You're lying."

"Mum admitted it to me when I came back here two weeks ago. Evelyn is your half-sister."

Fred shook his head. "No, no, this can't be happening. Mum would have told me! She knew we were..."

"Let's get through today and we can sort things out."

"I can't do this," Fred replied before rushing out of the room

"Fred!" John called after him but he ran out of the house.

Edward Langford rushed upstairs to the bedroom. "Is everything okay?" he asked. "What's up with Fred?"

"He had to rush off to see somebody."

Edward looked at his watch. "He's cutting it a bit fine."

John took a deep breath. "It's fine Dad, let's go," he said before leading his father back downstairs and out towards the waiting car.

***

Meanwhile, at St David's Church, Mavis Langford rushed inside to make sure that all of the last minute arrangements had been made and people were beginning to arrive. As she walked down the aisle however, she noticed a woman dressed in red with a black hat sat near to the exit. She walked over towards her and grabbed her arm, leading her away from the crowd towards the vicar's vestry.

"What the hell are you doing?" the woman snapped.

"I could ask you the same thing Frances. You are not welcome here so why don't you do us all a favour and leave!" Mavis snapped.

"I'm not leaving your family until I get what I'm owed."

"We owe you nothing."

"I know about Jack Smith and I have a big mouth. You know I'll use it if I have to."

Mavis felt a shiver run down her spine. "Who?"

"Don't play dumb with me Mavis. He had half the village back in the forties. Wouldn't it be a shame if it all came out in front of everyone here today. Your precious little family. A pillar of the community. You'd be ruined. No one would ever trust you or your family ever again."

"No one would believe a two-bit whore like you!"

"Do you want to take that chance?"

Mavis looked around at the crowd of people entering the church. "What do you want?"

"The gold of course."

Mavis bowed her head.

"How much do you value your pride?" Frances asked.

"Okay, I'll give it to you."

"And the map."

"What map?"

"Don't give me that rubbish. The map of where the rest of it is."

"I don't have any map. I don't know what you're talking about."

"That's a shame. Maybe I need to tell everyone out there about your little affair."

"Frances, listen to me," Mavis sighed. "Leave now and never contact John again and I'll give you what you want. Meet me at the vicar's cutting shed at 6pm today."

"I have your word on that?" Frances asked.

Mavis nodded.

"You'd better not back out..."

"I won't."

"I'll see you at six then," Frances replied before turning and heading out of the church.

Mary saw her mother in the corner of the church and rushed over towards her. "Are you okay? What was that about with Frances?"

"I will be," Mavis smiled. "Nothing to worry about. Come on, they'll be here soon."

Mavis wandered back outside the church once more as Mary watched her from the altar. She knew something wasn't right and was determined to find out what it was.

Chapter Sixty-Six

Suspicion
Wednesday 5th November 2008

A red Vauxhall Vectra parked outside 391 Hampton Lane as Paul Crowther climbed into the back seat.

"Do you have it?" Angela asked.

"Do you have the money?"

Andre handed over a briefcase from the front seat. Paul opened it and flicked through the notes before reaching inside his jacket and pulling out a brown envelope. As he handed it to Angela, two silenced gunshots popped inside the car. Paul slouched down on the back seat as Andre pulled the suitcase back into the front seat.

"I do hate seeing good money go to waste," Andre smiled as they continued on their way towards the oil refinery.

Meanwhile, at the refinery terminal, Alison Pearce and Samir Khalifa arrived in their green Land Rover and were met with armed guards at the entry gate.

"Authorisation to see Colin Sanderson," Alison said as she showed her ID. "Alison Pearce, Special Branch."

"And him?" the guard asked.

Samir showed his ID. The guard studied it before handing it back and waving a hand to his colleague.

"Report to the first office on your left," he said as the barrier raised and they were waved through.

As Alison drove into the grounds of the refinery, she had a suspicion that something wasn't quite right.

"Did you notice something back there?" she asked.

"Like what?"

"The guards on the gate. I asked to visit Colin Sanderson and yet he didn't even check my name against the daily log. This place could be a major coup for any terrorist plotting to cause chaos and yet he let us through with barely a passing glance. Something's not right."

"Do you think they know about the bomb?" Samir asked.

"Doubtful but we need to be alert. I did notice their accents though."

"In what way?"

"Normally people on the south coast have that country farmer twang. I don't think their accents were necessarily local or even English."

"We do live in a multicultural country, Ali. I'm living proof of that. After 9/11 I couldn't go for a piss in peace without someone inspecting it but it's calmed down a lot lately."

Alison parked the car in a parking space numbered thirty-six. "I guess you're right. All this running around chasing undertakers and older generations is making me paranoid."

Samir placed his hand on hers. "As long as we're together, it'll be fine."

She pulled her hand away. "Don't make it complicated."

"What do you mean?"

"I don't want us screwing up because you've got one eye on my ass rather than the terrorists," Alison smiled before stepping out of the car.

"I'd never dream of it," Samir smirked as they headed towards a metal container that housed an office.

Alison knocked on the door and waited for a moment until a middle-aged bald headed man with tufts of grey hair at the sides wearing navy overalls that struggled to contain a huge beer gut answered the door.

"What?" he asked.

"Colin Sanderson?" Samir enquired.

"He's with the foreman, be back in about half hour. Whadda ya want?"

"To stop a nuclear bomb from exploding but I see you have other priorities so we'll make our own way down to the workshops," Alison replied as she turned to leave.

"Wait, wait, hold on a minute. You from the asbestos department?"

"Should we be?" Samir asked.

"They found some asbestos on the far side of one of the units down there. Foreman went ape-shit as they had to close two of the units down."

"No, we need to speak to the foreman and Colin Sanderson as we believe there is a nuclear bomb hidden inside one of your chimneys down here," Alison explained.

"Yeah and I'm Elvis Presley. Jeez, who let you clowns in here?"

"Pietro on the gate," Samir replied.

"We don't have anyone called Pietro on the gate."

"I'm sorry, what was your name?" Alison asked.

"Stanley, Stanley Froggatt."

"Well Mr Froggatt, I suggest you check your security, you may well already have a leak."

Stanley glared at her for a moment before backing up and lifting some navy overalls and two hard hats from a coat stand in the corner of his office. "You'll need these," he said as he ushered them inside the office.

When they had changed into the overalls, Stanley pressed an intercom. "Lurch, take these two new recruits down to the heat exchanger and radio Sanderson to meet them there," he said.

A minute later, a tall man with short black hair and thick dark rimmed glasses arrived at the door and led them away from the office and down through a metal tunnel towards a larger building further down the hill. After a few minutes, they arrived on a platform overlooking a workshop where at least twenty men were adjusting metal clamps and hydraulic machinery that was then passed onto a conveyor belt that led somewhere else.

"Looks like a mad scientist's tea party," Samir whispered as they continued on their way through a maze of metal corridors.

Eventually, they stopped at a noisy substation where there were two channels of liquid moving in opposite directions.

"This is the heat exchange," Lurch said as he pointed down towards the two channels of liquid. "The machine separates oil from the water and then it is pumped out of here, through the system and eventually, after it has been treated, into the pipeline."

"And any excess is burnt off through the chimneys at the far end of the site," Samir replied.

"Indeed. Ah, Mr Sanderson," Lurch smiled as a man with short blonde hair in tight curls, piercing blue eyes and flushed red cheeks came towards them.

"You two must be the two agents that have been sent on a wild goose chase from London," Colin Sanderson replied as he shook both Alison's and Samir's hands.

"If this place goes up, I'm sure it won't be a wild goose chase then," Alison said, looking at Sanderson's perfectly starched light blue shirt collar that poked out from his overalls.

"Thank you Lurch, I'll take it from here," Colin said dismissing him before leading Alison and Samir onward through another maze of corridors. "As you can see we have the most stringent procedures in place and we are equipped for any kind of attack."

Colin stopped at a metal door and tapped a code into a keypad before removing a large metal bolt that held the door shut. As it creaked open, he removed a metal bar from inside his overalls and hit Samir on the back of his head. Samir fell forwards into the darkness. Alison swung around attempting to land a punch on him but he avoided it and bundled her inside the darkened room too before closing the door once again.

***

Meanwhile at Southward Cottage, Joe and Frank rushed out into the woods in search of Andre Lewis whilst Blake remained at home with Paula, Jenny and Michael.

"You need to tell us everything Blake. What have these people got against us?" Jenny asked.

"When Dad and I used to go fishing off of the beach, he used to tell me about how he had to move away to get away from Frances King. She was obsessed with him. They had a fling when Dad was eighteen but after he left her, she never let it go. Years later, just before grandma Mavis died, she told him that she had given Frances two gold bars worth hundreds of thousands of pounds in 1977 to keep her away from Dad so he could have a chance of making his marriage to Mum work."

"And it did. They were married for twenty-two years until he died in 1999," Jenny replied.

Blake nodded. "The problem is, I think Frances King believed that Mum only had the two bars. When Mum's will was read, it proved that the map of where the rest of the gold was hidden had been split into eight different pieces. We have three of them and I'm guessing that either Frances King or her family have the other five pieces. They need our three pieces to find out where the gold is."

"But we've already worked out that the gold is in Holbury Manor," Paula added. "Surely, even with a partial map, they would have worked that out too."

"Holbury Manor backs onto The New Forest. Back in 1938, the Manor spread a lot further than it does now. Basing it on that, there are over a hundred trees in that Manor that it could be buried under or near."

Michael looked at the map. "Roman numerals," he said.

"Where?" Jenny asked.

"On the map."

Blake picked up the map and looked at it. "You're right. The trees all have roman numerals by them on the map. It has to be some kind of key."

"I've got a Forestry Encyclopedia upstairs," Michael replied as he rushed up to his room and searched for the book.

A few minutes later, he returned with the book open on a page that showed a black and white photo of an old Manor House.

Blake looked at it. "There it is. It's been changed a lot since 1938 but there used to be an arrangement with the previous landowners that all trees had a number engraved in their trunk."

Jenny pieced the sections of the map together. "You're right, the section we are looking for is between LXXIII, LXXIV and LXXV."

"Seventy-three, seventy-four and seventy-five," Michael replied.

"So if we find those trees, we'll find the gold," Paula gasped.

"It seems like it," Jenny replied.

"Hang on a minute, this gold has been buried for over seventy years. Surely someone would have found it by now," Blake said as he looked at the map.

"Only one way to find out," Paula replied.

At that moment, there was a knock at the front door. Blake pulled his gun from its holster and carefully approached the door. Rain was tapping away on the window and irritated Blake as he attempted to listen for any kind of noise from the other side of the door. As he carefully opened the door, he saw an elderly woman in a long navy blue coat standing in the doorway.

"Hello dear, I'm sorry it's so late, I was looking for Mary Langford," she said.

"I'm sorry, Mary Langford died six years ago," Blake replied.

"Oh my, I feel so foolish. I didn't know."

Blake replaced the gun in his holster but still remained in the doorway. "How did you know Mary?"

"We were old friends from when I used to live in the village. I don't suppose I could trouble you for a hot drink could I? It's so cold out tonight."

Paula joined Blake in the doorway. "I'm sure that would be okay," she said.

Blake glared at her for a moment before turning back to the woman in the doorway. "Yes, come on in Mrs..."

"Wilton, Rose Wilton, thank you dear," she said as she entered the cottage. "My, my, this place has changed over the years."

"Dad!" Michael called out as the woman slipped her coat off and removed a gun from her inside pocket.

Blake turned to face her and as she opened her coat, there were three pieces of C4 explosives and wires strapped to her chest.

"Don't do anything stupid Langford," she said.

"Frances King, we finally meet," Blake said.

Paula rushed over towards Michael and moved him away.

"Don't! I press this button on my chest and we'll all be pieces of debris in the ocean behind us," Frances snapped.

"What do you want?" Jenny asked.

"My inheritance of course. Mavis Langford convinced me that there were only two gold bars from Jack Smith's raid on the bank and then I met Tom Gibson and his mother, Patricia Hughes. We had a very enlightening conversation. And in one of life's little ironies, when Emily Langford died, the floodgates opened."

"What connection do you have to my mother?" Blake asked.

"She took John and the inheritance that was owed to my family away from me. I was always there in the background Blake. I took the opportunity to gain vengeance on Edward Langford and I knew that all I needed to do was wait. Wait for the opportunity to face you and your family once again."

"What do you mean?"

"My ex-husband, Vladimir Vasilievich was expecting a consignment of weapons and young students in Moscow until you interfered with Gibson's plan to smuggle them out of London."

"Gibson's still on the run," Blake replied.

"Not any more. He paid his debt and now it's your turn."

"If I'm the one you want then let my family go."

"It was your family who sent me on this vendetta that has consumed my entire life Blake. Your family don't know what it's like to have to fight for everything. What us normal folk have to do so the pound and the clock on the wall doesn't own them and drive them into an early grave. I'm here to give my children what they missed out on and you're going to take me to it."

"You seem to be forgetting something. One of your children are in the hospital after trying to commit suicide and the other is in a police cell."

"Liar! He was pushed! And when I'm finished with you, I'll find out exactly who was responsible and take care of them too!"

"This vendetta of yours needs to end. Not just for my family but for the sake of your own as well."

"You're just like your father, smug and think you're better than everyone else."

"My father was a good and honest man. He worked hard all of his life and provided for his family. The only reason he moved us to London was to escape a psychopath like you!"

"He could never face up to his responsibilities."

"More like you were looking for a meal ticket after your German lover ditched you!"

"Don't make this harder on yourself and your family Blake. I know you have the rest of the map and if you want your family to live, you will join me at Holbury Manor and uncover the gold."

Blake looked over at Paula, Jenny and Michael.

"Give her what she wants Blake," Jenny said.

Blake sighed. "How the hell are we meant to find a coffin full of gold in the middle of the night in The New Forest. It's pitch black for Christ sake!"

"Focus Blake!" Frances snapped. "If you want your family to live, you'll do whatever it takes."

Blake looked over at them again before picking up his keys and heading out of the door with Frances following closely behind.

Chapter Sixty-Seven

The Truth Hurts
Saturday 12th August 1977

As the bridal car arrived outside St David's Church, Edward Langford rushed up the path towards the entrance and then scurried down the aisle towards John.

"Fred's still not here!" Edward gasped. "What did you say to him back at the house?"

"Nothing that he didn't need to hear."

"You can't get married without a best man."

"Then I need you to do it Dad."

"Me? I don't have a speech ready or anything."

"You don't need to. Just being here is enough," John replied as he placed the ring in his father's hand. "Please Dad, I need you for this."

Edward looked around at everyone entering the church before nodding. "Okay, I'll do it," he said as he stood alongside his son facing the altar.

Meanwhile outside, Emily Handanowicz stepped out of the bridal car with her sister Evelyn and mother Dana by her side. She looked up at the church and took a deep breath.

"Are you ready for this?" Dana asked.

Emily smiled. "Definitely."

As they were about to walk up the path, they heard someone call out Evelyn's name. As they looked down the path towards the woods, they saw Frederick Langford running towards them.

"Fred, what are you doing out here? You should be inside with John," Evelyn asked as she approached him.

"Is it true?" Fred asked.

"Is what true?"

"Is Jack Smith your father?"

Evelyn looked at him confused. "Of course not, you know who my father is. What's brought this on? Have you been drinking?"

"Tell her the truth Dana!"

"Fred, what are you talking about?" Dana asked.

"John told me what happened with you and my mother and a young soldier during the war!" Fred snapped.

Evelyn turned and faced her mother. "What happened during the war?"

"Nothing!"

"Tell her the truth Dana!" Fred shouted.

"You have to realise, it was a difficult time for all of us. We didn't know if we would survive."

"Mum! What happened?"

Dana bowed her head. "I met a man called Jack Smith. He helped me after Gerald passed away."

"Gerald passed away in 1940. That was eight years before Emily and I were born."

"Yes, you have an older brother called Victor who was born in December 1940. Jack was his father too."

"What?" Emily asked this time. "I have an older brother and you never told me!"

"The bombs were raining down on us. We were scared and didn't know if we would survive from one day to the next. I did what I had to do," Dana cried.

"You gave him up," Evelyn replied.

Dana nodded.

"But this was eight years before we were born so William Handanowicz is our father isn't he?" Emily asked.

Dana didn't respond.

"Mum?" Evelyn asked.

"Tell her Dana!" Fred snapped.

"Can we do this after the wedding?" Dana asked.

"No, Emily and I have a right to know and I want to know now!" Evelyn replied. "Is William Handanowicz our father?"

Dana shook her head. "No, Jack Smith is."

"Are you saying that John Langford is my half-brother?" Emily asked.

"No, he was born long before Mavis had anything to do with Jack. He's definitely Edward Langford's son. It's the twins, Fred and Mary, who are Jack's but she managed to convince Edward that he got her pregnant just before he left for war."

"You've both been living a lie this whole time! Jack Smith fathered two sets of twins, me and Emily and Fred and Mary!" Evelyn snapped. "Why didn't you tell us!"

"I couldn't. It would hurt too many people!" Dana replied.

"And what about us? We're your daughters!"

Fred turned and walked back towards his car. Evelyn ran after him.

"Fred, wait!" she shouted.

"It's over Evelyn," Fred sighed as he arrived back at his car.

"We can work this out. There has to be a way."

Fred reached inside his pocket and handed her a small burgundy box. "I was going to give you this later but it seems irrelevant now."

"Don't say that! It's got to be a mistake! There has to be a way around this. Emily is marrying John so we can make it work. Please Fred, don't do this!"

Fred sat in the driver's seat. "The difference is, John is a true Langford. He's the only true bloodline in my family. Whatever anyone says now, we can't be together. I can't marry my half-sister."

Evelyn stepped back as he slammed the car door shut and sped away down the road into The New Forest. She held her stomach as a pinching pain rolled through her body. As she watched the car disappear into the distance, she opened the box and found a huge diamond ring inside. Tears stung her eyes and she felt an anger rise up inside her. All those dreams. All those promises they made to each other. Gone. In a moment of weakness, her parents had lived a lie that had cost her the love of her life.

Emily rushed over towards her. "Are you okay? What the hell just happened?"

"Mother knew and she didn't tell me," Evelyn sighed through her tears. "She knew and she didn't tell me! How could she do this to us?"

Dana rushed over to join them. "Evelyn, calm down, we have a wedding to get through first. We'll talk it over later."

"Talk it over? Talk it over! You knew I'd fallen for Fred. You knew things were getting serious between us and you didn't tell me! What kind of mother does that to her children!"

"We need to call off the wedding," Emily replied.

"No we do not. You and John will be married today, come what may. We'll deal with this misunderstanding later," Dana said as she began to lead Emily back towards the church. She turned to Evelyn; "If you had any loyalty to this family, you'll tow the line and be there for your sister and not try to ruin her special day."

Evelyn froze as she watched her mother usher Emily towards the church. "You don't care about us at all do you. All you care about is your bloody reputation!" she snapped.

"Evelyn, drop it. We'll deal with it later!" Dana replied.

Evelyn turned and walked away.

"Where are you going?" Dana asked but Evelyn kept walking away.

"Evelyn!" Dana shouted but she ran into the woods and disappeared between the trees.

At that moment, William Handanowicz came rushing down the path towards them. "Come on, quickly now, you're running late and everyone is getting worried," he said.

As he took hold of Emily's arm, he noticed that she had been crying.

"Are you okay? What's happened?" he asked.

"Nothing Dad, everything is as it should be. Let's go," Emily replied as she walked into the church with William holding onto her arm and her mother, Dana, walking close behind her.

As the wedding march rang out around the church, the people from the village, the family and friends that had gathered for the wedding, seemed to fade into the background as Emily focused on John standing by the altar. As they took their vows, Emily knew that there was a lot more happening behind the scenes than her smile let on to the world. She just hoped that her and John would be strong enough to survive it.

***

At quarter-to-six that evening, Mavis Langford left the local community hall where the wedding reception was being held for Emily and John Langford's wedding and headed down the dirt track through the woods towards the vicar's house. As she made her way through the woods, she kept checking behind her to make sure she wasn't being followed until someone calling out her name startled her.

"Mrs Langford!" a woman's voice called out.

Mavis swung around quickly, almost losing her balance and putting her hand out onto a tree trunk to steady herself.

"Sorry, I didn't mean to give you a fright."

"That's okay Elsie, it's been a pretty busy day all told."

"Well congratulations to the young couple. I hope they are very happy together. Tell them to come by my shop when they get back from their honeymoon. I have some lovely fruit cake that they can have for half the price."

"I'll be sure to tell them that, thank you," Mavis replied.

"Shouldn't you be at the wedding reception yourself?"

"I was, I just, er, needed to pay the vicar for the service and then I'll be heading back."

"Ah, that explains it. Well, mind how you go Mrs Langford and I'll see you soon," Elsie replied before continuing on her way towards the shops.

Mavis released a deep breath that she hadn't realised she was holding. She needed to remain calm. She pulled out an envelope from her handbag which confirmed the transfer of ownership of the gold that Jack had left her in 1948. She had wanted Emily and John to have it as a wedding gift and felt guilty that they would no longer have any claim on it but if it meant keeping Frances King out of John's life for good, it was worth it. As she approached the vicar's cottage, she noticed a tall man, in his twenties, walking down past the side of the house. He was wearing a blood-stained apron and a scruffy pair of grey trousers and a black t-shirt.

Mavis stood at the end of the garden path looking at the cottage unsure of what to do next. She slowly approached the front door before she noticed a rustling in the hedge at the side of the house. As she approached the hedge, a black cat darted out in front of her and sprinted across the lawn and into the woods. She took a deep breath to calm her nerves before walking around the side of the house. As she turned into the back garden, she saw the man again but this time, he was standing next to Frances King.

"I didn't think you were going to show up," Frances called out as Mavis approached.

"Who's he?" Mavis asked.

"You don't recognise my son, Timmy?"

"I haven't seen him for a few years. Looks a lot like his father doesn't he?"

Frances glared at her. "That's irrelevant."

"What have you been doing to get all of that blood over you Timmy?" Mavis asked, dreading the answer.

"Helping the old vicar out. The farmer gave him one of his cows so I helped him slaughter it so he can sell the meat."

"I see. Where is the vicar?"

"Indisposed so we won't be interrupted. Do you have the gold?" Frances asked.

Mavis handed over the envelope to her.

"What is this?" Frances asked.

"Transfer of ownership to you of the two gold bars invested in CityBank since 1948 by Jack Smith. Now I want your word that you will leave my family alone and get the hell out of this village."

Frances read through the paperwork before folding it and replacing it back inside the envelope. "A deal's a deal. Come along Timmy, we have a long journey ahead of us," she said as they pushed past Mavis and walked away.

"Where are you going?"

"I don't think that's any of your concern is it?"

"I guess not," Mavis replied as she watched them leave.

When they were finally out of sight, Mavis fell to her knees. She wondered if it truly was over. If Frances really would stay away from John. She had no guarantee but she knew she had done what she needed to do. As the sound of a car engine fired up in the distance before driving away, Mavis stood up and walked over towards the cutting shed. The previous vicar, Harold Partridge, had a wood saw installed inside the shed and would often collect wood from the forest and cut it down to manageable sizes before distributing it to the local residents for their fires in the winter. Something about Timmy's demeanour didn't sit right with her and his explanation about a cow hide seemed fanciful to say the least.

She tried the door of the old cutting shed but it was locked. She moved around to the side to try and look through the window but it was covered in green algae and moss.

"Mr Black! Dennis?" she called out as she walked all the way around the shed.

When she arrived at the back of the shed, there was a crack in the window on the far side with a small hole in the bottom right corner. The moss and algae had blocked out any chance of seeing what was inside but a strong potent smell seemed to be wafting out from the small hole in the window. Mavis looked around and found a small rock on the ground. She picked it up.

"Sorry Father," she said before hitting the damaged window with the rock.

The remaining glass smashed and opened just enough of a gap for Mavis to see inside the shed. The smell was horrendous and made her gag and step away for a moment. Taking a deep breath of fresh air, she risked one more look inside and then screamed. On the wood saw bench laid the vicar and the wood saw had cut through his skull and had sawn his head in half.

***

Three hours later, Emily and John Langford were waving to their family and friends as they headed off to The Grand Hotel overlooking Bournemouth beach for their first night together as husband and wife. As Edward Langford was about to head back inside the community hall, a police car pulled up outside. Mavis froze as she saw Edward's old sergeant, Peter Hastings, who had taken over as detective after Edward's retirement, step out of the driver's seat with a new sergeant following close behind.

"Peter, what a pleasant surprise. I'm afraid you've just missed the happy couple, they've just left," Edward beamed.

"Congratulations on your son's marriage Ed but that's not why I'm here," Hastings replied.

Mavis rushed over to join them. "Is everything okay?" she asked.

"When did you last see your son, Frederick?" Hastings asked.

"Just before we left the house for the wedding around lunchtime. John said that they had a few words and Fred rushed off to do something but didn't elaborate on what," Edward replied.

"We haven't seen Evelyn either come to think of it," Mavis added. "Did they leave early for some reason?"

"There was a road traffic accident this afternoon on the main road through Winchester. A Ford Cortina registered to Frederick Langford flipped up-side-down and hit a tree. I'm sorry Ed but I'm going to need you to come down to the station to identify the driver who I think may be your son Frederick," Hastings replied.

Edward sat on the step outside the community hall holding his head in his hands. "No, no, this can't be happening. The boys only had a few words this morning. What the hell is going on? And where's Evelyn?"

"She ran off with Fred just before the wedding," Dana replied as she joined them outside.

"Was Fred the only one in the car?" Mavis asked.

"Yes, he was on his own," Hastings confirmed.

"You need to find your daughter Dana!" Mavis snapped. "If she's been involved in the death of my son, I'll be coming for you."

"If your son wasn't so hell bent on revealing the truth, none of this would have happened!"

"What's she talking about?" Edward asked.

"Tell him Mavis! Tell everyone!" Dana snapped.

Mavis glared at her. "There's nothing to tell!" she snapped before turning towards her daughter. "Mary, finish up here for me, your father and I need to go with Detective Hastings to sort out whatever this misunderstanding is."

As Edward joined Hastings and his sergeant in their car, Mavis approached Dana. "You need to be careful what you say. You're not as pure as you think you are."

"If you had told me that Fred and Evelyn were together in London, maybe I could have put a stop to it before it got this far."

"Where is your daughter?"

"She ran off after Fred confronted her about Jack just before the wedding."

"How did he know?"

"John told him."

"Why would he do that right before his own wedding?"

"Because Fred was about to propose to her."

Mavis bowed her head. "We need to find her before she blows the lid on all of this."

"It's too late for that. Frances King already knows. If she lets it slip..."

"Frances won't be a problem anymore," Mavis replied.

"How can you be so sure?"

"Trust me on this."

Dana looked at her warily before nodding. "Okay, I'll find Evelyn. She's probably gone to cool off for a while."

"Mavis!" Edward called out.

"I've got to go. Let me know when you find her."

Dana nodded as Mavis rushed over towards the waiting police car and they drove away into Southampton City Centre.

Chapter Sixty-Eight

Holbury Manor
Thursday 6th November 2008

The fireworks had finished long before Joe Knight and Frank Jackson headed up to St David's Church. A police officer walked away from the vicar as they approached.

"Mr Fischer!" Frank called out.

"Can this wait? It's very late and I'm behind on everything," the vicar replied.

"I'm sorry the attempted suicide of your illegitimate son has inconvenienced you..."

The vicar walked up close to Frank. "I'd prefer it if that information was kept quiet if you don't mind. Mud sticks around here."

"So you won't mind if I ask you a couple of questions and then I'll let you get on with your business," Frank continued.

The vicar nodded.

"Do you know Mr Hugh Johnson?"

"Should I?"

"He recently bought a fair amount of property in your parish," Joe added.

"Ah yes, he rented Thyme Cottage for a short time I recall."

"Mr Fischer, I believe you and the previous owner of Thyme Cottage were more than friends."

"That was a long time ago and I've repented my sins for that!"

At that moment, Joe's mobile phone rang. He wandered out of the church to take the call leaving Frank alone with the vicar.

"Does Frances know you're back in the parish?" Frank asked.

"Of course not. She's rarely here anymore. When Andre bought that cottage, he rented it out to workers down at the oil refinery."

"Did Hugh Johnson or Andre Lewis work at the refinery?"

"They both did, I believe. They were both temporary workers down there for a while. Why do you ask?"

"Thank you for your time Mr Fischer," Frank replied but as he was about to leave, Joe came rushing back in.

"That was Paula. Frances King has taken Blake by gunpoint to Holbury Manor. She's wearing a suicide vest and is threatening to blow herself up if Blake doesn't help her find the gold," Joe explained.

Frank turned back to the vicar.

"Oh no, no, no, no, I left that life a long time ago," the vicar said.

Frank walked towards him. "Father, we need your help here. Mr Fischer. Christoph. You were her first love. You are the father of her oldest child who is fighting for his life in hospital. You're the only one she'll listen to."

The vicar pulled out a crucifix from underneath his robe, held it in his hand and closed his eyes. He muttered a few words to himself before looking at Frank once again and nodding. Joe led Frank and the vicar out of the church and back towards the main road where they had parked the car. They knew they only had a small window of time to get to Holbury Manor before Frances did something crazy.

***

Blake had picked up a shovel and torch from the garden shed and placed them into the boot of his car before moving around to the driving seat. Frances sat in the passenger seat alongside him keeping the gun pointed at him at all times. He looked at the explosives strapped to her chest and felt a shiver run through his body. He knew he needed to tread carefully and think before he spoke or she could easily kill them both.

"I think we'll get on a lot better if you put that away," Blake said as he started the engine.

"Ah yes, the typical Langford wit. I'm sorry but I gave up trusting your family a long time ago."

"What did my father do to you that was so bad? When the entire village turned their back on you because you had a child with a German prisoner-of-war, he helped you. Gave you his first wages when he started working. Tried to help you look after your sick father."

"I made sure he was well compensated for it."

"Not many eighteen year old men would put their lives on hold like that but my father cared about others who were struggling."

"He was a manipulative selfish man who only ever looked out for himself. As soon as Edith Wise came back to the village, he couldn't drop us quickly enough. Then when she died, he ran away to London because he couldn't face up to what he did. He never came back to Lepe again until he married Edith's sister and the only way her parents would go to the wedding was if they married in the local church."

"But you never stopped pursuing him did you?" Blake asked.

"Your grandmother made a deal with me that she would sign over her share of Jack Smith's gold if I left and never came back. I'd already planned to move out to Moscow with Vladimir anyway so that was a nice little sweetener to add to the deal."

"And when the police discovered what happened to the vicar and how you had blackmailed my grandmother, Mavis Langford..."

"They stopped the transfer. I'll never forget the smug look on Mavis's face when I saw her a few years later. That didn't last for long though."

"Both of my grandparents died in 1984," Blake replied as he parked the car in a small gravel car park at the side of Holbury Manor.

"I know, I was there," Frances smiled.

Blake felt an anger rise up inside him and he had to force himself to hold it deep within. John Langford had been convinced that his parents' deaths had been linked to Frances King but there was never enough evidence and the case had gone cold.

"I see the apple hasn't fallen far from the tree. That same red mist that John had when he discovered my involvement in that little accident."

"He knew you killed them," Blake snapped.

"Prove it! There was never enough evidence to convict. You see Blake, I have ways of getting what I want and no one is going to stand in my way. Not even you. Now get that shovel and start counting trees."

As Frances stepped out of the car, Blake weighed up his options. If he drove away, she could potentially shoot the car or blow something up that would harm the local residents. If he went into the Manor, he risked her either shooting him when they found it or blowing him up too. He stepped out of the car, hoping that Paula or Jenny had called Joe or Frank for back up. For now, he knew he just had to stall Frances for as long as he could.

He turned on the torch and carried the shovel into Holbury Manor. There was a small children's playground near the car park made out of reshaped tree trunks. As they continued into the manor, Blake shone the torch around the trees but couldn't find any kind of markings or numbers on them.

"How the hell are we meant to find the right tree in the pitch dark. We don't even know for sure if they had numbers on them," Blake said as he continued to look at the tree trunks.

"There are significantly less trees now than there were when the gold was buried in 1938," Frances replied.

"Was there any kind of markings to signify what kind of tree it was on your part of the map?"

"What do you mean?"

"Did it show oak trees, ash, willow trees, anything that's going to help us here?"

Frances looked at the photo of her section of the map on her phone. "It looks like they are next to some kind of stream or pond."

"The fishing pond on the northern side of the manor?" Blake asked.

"It's possible."

Blake continued on down the mud paths deeper into the woodlands of Holbury Manor with Frances following closely behind. He knew his best chance of survival would be to get them away from the main road and the car park and hope that whoever came looking for them could disarm the explosives. They eventually arrived at the fishing pond which was surrounded by tall oak trees.

"If my research into this was correct, the numbers were scratched into the trunks of the trees after they had been planted and grown for twenty years," Blake said as he shone the torch at the oak trees.

"So?"

"So, the majority of these trees around the pond would have been planted around 1900, therefore they would have been numbered around 1920. The average oak tree grows between four and five centimetres per year. It's now 2008 so the piece of trunk that was inscribed is now at least four metres higher than it was in 1920," Blake replied.

"Then you'd better get climbing!"

"There is no way that we are going to be able to identify all these trees. It's going to take all night!"

"Focus Blake! You give me my inheritance and you can carry on living with your family."

He shone the torch up at the tree before then beginning to climb. The wind and rain made it difficult to climb and Blake slipped a couple of times before making it onto a strong branch. He used the torch to look for a number but couldn't see anything. He continued to climb as the wind blew the branches back and forth making each manoeuvre harder than the last. He finally made it over halfway up the oak tree when he saw some roman numerals carved into the trunk.

"LXX, seventy," Blake smirked to himself. "Michael was right."

"Have you found anything?" Frances called out.

"It's not this one," Blake replied as he carefully climbed back down.

"What do you mean?"

"This is number twenty!" Blake lied. "We need to keep moving."

Frances looked at the map on her phone. "This doesn't make sense. The gold was buried within the triangle of trees near to the pond and the stream."

At that moment, Blake slipped and fell the last couple of metres landing onto the mud path and rolling away into a hedge that had grown in a semi-circle around the pond.

He swore loudly as he hobbled back to his feet. "I think I've twisted my ankle."

"You'll live. Come on, this way," Frances demanded as she continued towards where the pond became a stream deeper into the woods.

Blake hobbled along behind her flashing his torch into the trees above in hope that someone would notice them.

Meanwhile, at the car park on the opposite side of the Manor, Joe, Frank and Christoph stepped out of Joe's car and began heading into the woods. Joe used a GPS tracker to try and log on to Blake's phone signal but it was very weak amongst all of the trees around them.

"Up ahead!" Christoph said as they followed the path.

As Frank looked across an open section of field, he saw torchlight flickering through the trees ahead of them. "Put that away," he said to Joe. "The old war hero found them the old fashioned way."

Christoph smiled as they followed the stream and the mud path towards the fishing pond. When they came to a clearing, they saw Frances and Blake on the opposite side of the pond.

"It's here!" she called out.

"What is? You can't even read the numbers down here," Blake replied.

Frances shone the torch from her phone onto the trunk of a tree next to the pond. "LXXV, you lied to me Blake. If this is tree seventy-five then there is no way in hell that the one over there is twenty!"

"Roman numerals are not my strong point."

"Bullshit Langford! You're just like your father, doing everything you can to stop me from getting what's rightfully mine!"

"Okay, okay, just calm down Frances. It's okay. But think about this logically, how do you know that this wasn't engraved into the trunk more recently by someone. Lovers often engrave their initials into trees."

"Who has the initials LXXV? Quite a stretch wouldn't you say?"

Blake didn't reply.

"This is it. Look at the trees around us. A perfect triangle. This is where he buried it. In the centre of this triangle. Now dig!"

Blake looked at her for a moment.

She shot a bullet into the darkness but Blake held her gaze.

"Next time it won't miss, now dig Langford!"

Blake picked up the shovel and began to dig into the mud.

"Ich liebe dich, meine Prinzessin," a man's voice called out.

Frances turned around and shone the torch from her phone in the direction of the voice. "Who's there?"

"I always said that to you back in the day, Frances."

"Christoph?" she gasped.

Christoph walked forward and held his own torch to light up his face. "Hello Frances. It's been a long time."

"No, no, you were..."

"No, I survived, despite your best efforts. And I met our son, Timmy."

"What did you do to him?"

"Nothing, he fell from the church balcony, he's in hospital but he's alive. You need to let the past go Frances," Christoph said as he slowly walked towards her.

She pointed the gun at him. "No, no, stay away from me. Don't come any closer!"

Blake slowly backed away as Christoph continued to walk towards her.

"This isn't your fight Frances. It never was. How many more lives are you going to destroy chasing the gold?" Christoph asked.

"You know nothing about me or my family. You ran out on us. You never saw the abuse and neglect my family had because you were a kraut!"

"I know and in my pain and guilt, I found God and have come back to the parish to repent my sins. Ich liebe dich, meine Prinzessin," Christoph said as he placed his hand over Frances' hand on the gun. "Let love in and let the pain go."

She stared at him for a moment before embracing him. As he held her close, a loud buzzing sound echoed around the Manor followed by a huge flash and a mighty explosion that boomed all around. Five trees uprooted and fell in all directions. A huge sonic boom radiated from the Manor. Car alarms rang out in the distance interrupting the silence of the night and all of the streetlights from the main roads short circuited out. In a few seconds it was over as shards of tree branches, leaves and hedges settled in the woodland but there was no sign of life in the darkness.

Chapter Sixty-Nine

The Russians Are Coming

Sunday 13th August 1977

Mavis and Edward Langford arrived home in the early hours of Sunday morning. Southward Cottage, what once was a loving family home suddenly felt cold and lonesome. Edward picked up a bottle of malt whiskey and poured himself a generous glassful before sitting down in the armchair.

"You shouldn't blame yourself," Mavis broke the silence.

"I should've followed my gut. I knew something had happened between Fred and John and I should have gone looking for him."

"And what would that have done? John would've been left standing on his own on his wedding day in front of everyone. His whole family, running off on a wild goose chase."

"How can you act like this?"

"Like what?"

"Our son is dead, Mavis! Fred has died and I could have stopped it!"

"How? He had a few crossed words with his brother, ran off in a huff, had a few drinks and wrecked his car. Even if you had gone after him, would he have listened to you?"

"What did he find out?" Edward asked.

"How should I know? I'm not a mindreader."

"No, no, John said he told him what he needed to know and then Dana went for you at the hall. What was so bad that Fred went off in a rage and killed himself?"

"His girlfriend was his half-sister!" Mavis snapped. "Call yourself an ex-police detective and you never saw what's right in front of your eyes!"

Edward stood up and walked towards her. "Run that by me again."

"Evelyn and Emily have the same father as Mary and Fred."

"You had an affair when I was fighting for our lives in the war!" Edward fumed.

"It was a moment of weakness. We didn't know if you were all coming back. Gerald Wise didn't!"

"And that's supposed to make things right is it? Don't worry about poor old Ed getting himself blown up for King and country as long as ol' Mavis can take one for the team!"

"It wasn't like that and you know it! The war was a stressful time for all of us!"

Edward turned away from her for a moment before spinning around and punching her in the face with a fierce uppercut. Mavis fell backwards against the wall before sliding down to the floor.

"You slept with another man whilst I was risking my life for our freedom! You've made me live a lie for over thirty years!" Edward shouted.

"Dad! What the hell are you doing?" Mary shouted as she rushed down the stairs towards her mother.

"Maybe you should ask the village whore down there!" Edward snapped. "Is our marriage a goddamn joke to you? For pity's sake Mavis!"

"Dad, what the hell is going on? Why are you acting like this?" Mary pleaded.

Edward picked up the whiskey bottle and looked down at Mavis. He threw the bottle at the wall. It shattered on impact before leaving its contents behind. He picked up his coat and stormed out of the house, slamming the door as he left.

Mary helped Mavis back to her feet and into the armchair.

"What happened? I've never seen Dad so angry," Mary asked.

"He found out about Jack and your brother has died in a car accident," Mavis replied before bursting into tears.

Mary held her mother close, unsure of what, if anything, she could say to make sense of anything. Her mother had confided in her and now she felt a sense of duty to protect her from the fallout with her father. She just needed to figure out how.

Meanwhile, Edward Langford stormed through the woods in a rage hitting branches and reeds out of his way as he pushed his way through towards a clearing nearby to the vicar's house. As he arrived, he noticed two young men loading items into the back of a truck. As he approached them, they stopped and looked over at him.

"Can I help you?" the taller man asked.

In the half-light, Edward struggled to see his face clearly. "Is the vicar moving out?"

"He asked us to help move some things for him."

"At this hour?"

"Early bird catches the worm and all that."

"Where is the vicar? I'd like to speak with him."

"He's not home."

"So he's not home but he's allowed you two to empty his cottage for him," Edward replied before he felt a sharp pain in the back of his head and everything went black.

In the half-light, the second man had moved behind Edward and struck him on the back of his head, sending him down to the floor.

"Quick, move him inside," the second man said.

"You idiot Dmitri, he's Edward Langford, people will come looking for him!"

"Relax Timmy, we'll be long gone before they find him. Mother has already sorted out the cargo for us so take those last few bits and let's go."

Later that morning, the local parishioners along with Dana, William and James Handanowicz arrived at St David's Church but there was no sign of the Reverend Dennis Black. As the locals began to ask about the vicar's whereabouts, Dana, William and James wandered back through the woods. As they arrived at the vicar's cottage, they noticed tyre tracks on the front lawn and the door was left open ajar.

William approached the front door and as he opened it he saw a body laying on the floor.

He turned back to Dana and James. "Call the police and an ambulance, quick!" he shouted.

They rushed away towards a phone box as William entered the house. As he turned on the lights, he realised who the body was.

"Edward?" William gasped.

Edward began to stir and tried to move.

"Stay still, the police and ambulance are on their way."

"What happened?" Edward asked.

"It looks like you've had a severe head injury. Just stay as still as you can until the ambulance arrives."

Edward tried to move again but groaned in pain.

"What were you doing here? Where's the vicar?" William asked.

"I don't know. Someone was emptying the cottage last night. I tried to speak to them and ended up like this."

"What time?"

"I don't know, around midnight."

After a few minutes, blue flashing lights reflected around the hall of the cottage as the police and ambulance team arrived. The paramedics rushed in to help Edward whilst the police looked around the cottage for any significant clues as to what happened on the previous night.

Detective Peter Hastings arrived with Sergeant Stuart Newman soon after the ambulance had left with Edward Langford inside it. The police officer leading the investigation walked over towards them.

"Good morning Sir, looks like a burglary gone wrong," he explained.

"I'll be the judge of that, Harris. Edward Langford lost his youngest son yesterday and is now found at the vicar's house unconscious. Have they discovered the whereabouts of Evelyn Handanowicz yet?" Hastings asked.

"Not yet, we are still investigating."

"What's the story with the Handanowicz family?"

"Dana, William and their son James attended morning service. After the vicar failed to attend, they came here looking for him and that's when they found Edward Langford's body in the hall," Officer Harris replied.

"From what I heard from the wedding reception yesterday, the Langford's and Handanowicz's had a rather heated discussion over money and their children courting together," Sergeant Newman added.

"Surely you don't think William Handanowicz had anything to do with this, do you Sir? He's a wealthy local businessman," Officer Harris asked.

"I'm not ruling anything out at the moment. Ask forensics to check the place over, particularly by the hall and front door," Hastings replied.

At that moment, a second officer rushed over towards them. "Excuse me, Sir, I think you need to take a look at this," he said.

Hastings, Newman and Harris all followed the second officer around the side of the house and into the back garden. The shed door had been broken open by one of the officers and a strong pungent smell hung in the air. Hastings removed a handkerchief from his pocket to cover his nose and mouth as he entered the shed. Laying on the workbench in front of them was the body of Reverend Dennis Black. The mechanical wood saw had sliced through his skull and cut right through to his neck leaving a huge ghoulish bloody mess where his head had once been.

Sergeant Newman rushed out of the shed and began vomiting into the rose bush outside. Harris and Hastings followed him out.

"Officer Harris, arrest William Handanowicz and take him in for questioning. We now have a murder investigation on our hands," Hastings said before heading back towards the front of the house.

As Sergeant Newman and Officer Harris continued closing off the vicar's cottage to the public, Peter Hastings walked up the mud path through the woods towards Lepe Road. He looked across the road at Thyme Cottage, the former home of Arthur King and his family for many years.

His father used to be a member of the Dibden Golf Club, a few miles down the road from Lepe, and most Sundays, he would play a round of golf with Arthur before going into the clubhouse to join the rest of the family for an afternoon cup of tea and a cucumber sandwich. Then the war came and everything changed. The bombing cost the lives of Peter's father Joseph and Arthur's wife Anita whilst Arthur had shards of metal in his right leg after an explosive device had blown up nearby leaving him with shell-shock and needing a walking stick to maintain his balance.

Arthur never spoke to Peter again after the war until he was taken into custody in September 1956 by Officer Charlie Jones. He had set fire to his garden shed in what he had said was an attempt to kill a rat infestation that had gotten out of control. When the flames were put out, the half cremated skeleton of Harold Partridge, the previous vicar before Dennis Black was appointed, was found amongst the debris.

Arthur died in prison three months later but right up to his death, he pleaded his innocence. Now looking at the empty shell of a house that remained since his daughter and her two sons had emptied it out into a removal van yesterday, Peter couldn't help but wonder where it all went wrong for the King family and if he could have helped them in any way.

He walked up the hill towards Southward Cottage and knocked on the front door. After a few minutes, Mavis answered.

"Oh no, Peter, what's happened? Is Edward okay?" Mavis asked

"You manipulative bitch!" Dana Handanowicz shouted out from the road as she stormed up towards the house. "It wasn't enough to take my daughter away, you had to take my husband too!"

"What are you talking about?" Mavis asked.

Dana launched herself at Mavis but Peter stepped in between them. "Please ladies, calm down. Fighting between each other won't get us anywhere!"

"How dare you come around to my house shouting at me after what's happened!" Mavis snapped.

"What do you mean, my husband has been arrested for a crime he didn't even do!" Dana replied.

Mavis looked at Peter.

"We're just making inquiries at the moment!" Peter said as he tried to maintain a distance between them.

"So where's Fred?" Dana asked. "My Evelyn has disappeared without so much as a single word of goodbye!"

"Fred didn't come home," Mavis replied.

"Oh that's right, stormed off in a huff did he, after he found out his mother was a whore!"

"Frederick Langford is dead, Mrs Handanowicz," Peter replied.

Dana froze. "What?"

"He died in a road traffic accident yesterday afternoon," Mavis replied. "Peter, where is Edward?"

"In hospital. He was discovered unconscious at the vicar's cottage this morning by Mr and Mrs Handanowicz," he confirmed.

"What did you do to him?" Mavis shouted as she launched herself at Dana.

Peter once again stood in between them. "Calm down you two. Nothing is going to be solved by trying to rip each other to pieces. We need to find out what happened to Edward, Evelyn and the late Reverend Black and Frederick Langford. Mavis, when did you last see Edward?"

"Around midnight last night after we came back from identifying Fred," she replied.

"What happened after you arrived home?"

"We had a fight and he stormed out of the house."

"Is that how you received those bruises on your face?"

Mavis bowed her head. "My husband is a good man, Peter. You know him well enough to know that."

"When he left here after your fight, was he still angry?"

"I guess so. He usually goes for a walk to cool off and then comes back an hour or so later but last night..."

"He didn't," Peter finished for her.

Mavis shook her head.

"Did Edward have any kind of disagreement with Reverend Dennis Black that you knew of?"

"No, none at all. Why?"

"Reverend Black was found murdered this morning in his cutting shed at the bottom of his garden. We're trying to figure out if it is connected to Edward being knocked unconscious in the hallway of the vicar's cottage."

Mavis felt a shiver run through her body. She had seen the Reverend's body yesterday evening and hadn't reported it. Now the police were suspecting that Edward had a role to play in it. She felt tears sting the backs of her eyes. "Ed had nothing to do with it!" she cried.

"Mavis, you said yourself that Edward was angry and in a foul mood last night," Peter persisted. "Could he have potentially lashed out last night as he did to you?"

"I know he's not a murderer and deep down, so do you!"

"But he was out late last night and then the body was found this morning," Dana added.

"The reverend was already dead before Edward went there!" Mavis confessed.

"What?" Peter asked.

"I met Frances King or whatever her name is now at the cottage yesterday evening. I was looking for the reverend and when there was no answer at the cottage, I went to his shed and found his body on the workbench."

"Why didn't you call the police?" Peter asked.

"Because I was being blackmailed by Frances. The only way I could get her away from John was to sign over my share of the gold."

Dana gasped. "You did what?"

"What gold?" Peter asked.

"The gold given to Dana and myself by Jack Smith, the father of our children. It was the only way to get rid of her and from the looks of it, she packed up and cleared off overnight."

"How did she get another house so quickly?" Dana asked. "Was this all planned?"

"She's married to a Russian millionaire called Vladimir Vasilievich," Peter replied. "I believe she was planning to leave the village anyway, with or without your money."

Both women looked at him. "How did you know that?"

"He's the father of her youngest son, Dmitri. He has his own yacht anchored off the coast in Weymouth. Chances are, that's where she's headed but she never wanted to give up the family home until recently."

"When William and I went to the vicar's cottage this morning, there were tyre tracks on the front lawn. It looked like some of the furniture had been taken. Perhaps Edward interrupted them and got knocked out before they left," Dana replied.

"It's certainly a possibility. Did Frances say where she was going?" Peter asked.

Mavis shook her head.

"Either way, I'm going to need you both to come down to the station to make statements and if what you say is true, we need to find Frances King."

Chapter Seventy

The Frogman's Hatch
Thursday 6th November 2008

Blake opened his eyes to discover that he was covered in a shower of wood chippings, leaves and mud. His hearing sounded like he was under water and the flashing blue lights from the car park on the opposite side of the manor created a disorientating glow. As he staggered to his feet, he noticed the destruction around him. Frances had pressed the detonator and had taken the vicar, Christoph Fischer, with her. Joe Knight and Frank Jackson rushed over towards him.

"Are you okay?" Joe asked as he helped Blake to his feet and brushed off the debris from his clothes.

"I think so."

"You have more lives than a cat!" Frank laughed. "She could have easily killed you."

"She almost did," Blake replied as he looked at the roots of one of the uprooted trees. "What's that?"

As the three men approached the tree, they discovered a metal box that looked like an old treasure chest.

"No, it can't be," Joe gasped.

Frank grabbed hold of one side of the chest and Blake held the other side. As they lifted it out of the hole, they were surprised how light it was and almost overbalanced and fell backwards onto the mud.

"I thought treasure chests were meant to be heavy," Frank commented.

"We need to get it out of here before the police discover what we've found," Joe replied.

In the distance, they could hear the barking of police dogs and shadows of police officers appeared across the open field of the manor with their torches as the blue flashing lights illuminated several silhouettes rushing towards them.

"Come on, this way," Frank said as he led them down a mud path towards a road at the back of the manor.

When they eventually made it back to the car park, there were two police officers standing in between Frank's and Blake's cars.

"You two stay out of sight, we'll get Langford's car later," Frank said as he left Joe and Blake with the chest and walked over towards his car.

"I'm sorry Sir, this area has been closed off due to a possible terrorist attack," the police officer said as Frank approached.

"A what?" Frank asked, raising his hands in mock disbelief. "Do you honestly think a terrorist would strike out in the middle of the sticks out here when they could blow the shit out of London only an hour or so up the road?"

"We had reports of an explosion in the forest and we have to investigate."

"So how does that stop a brother from driving home?"

"How do we know that you weren't the one who set off the explosive device?"

"Would I honestly be dumb enough to come and talk to you if I was out here blowing stuff up?"

"Then what were you doing out here in the middle of the night Mr..."

"Hardy, Ivor Hardy, well if you must know, there's a young lady over in the next street and she needed some attention if you know what I'm saying and it's not going to look good if I'm heading home with a police caution after tending to her needs shall we say..." Frank replied.

The officer looked at him for a moment before smirking. "On your way Mr Hardy," he replied.

"Thank you Officer, I'll remember you when I write my memoirs," Frank smiled as he let himself back into his car.

"I hope you won't," the officer replied as Frank shut his door and drove out of the car park.

As he turned the corner, Blake and Joe climbed into the back seat with the chest and Frank sped away.

"How the hell did you get away with that?" Joe asked.

"Local forces don't want the aggro so I fed him a story about a one night stand," Frank smiled.

"And he believed you?" Blake asked.

"There's still some mileage left in this ol' body yet," Frank laughed.

"I thought the local police forces had a filtering system to keep the idiots away from the front line," Joe replied.

"Unfortunately nothing is idiot proof anymore as whenever you think you've cracked it, someone finds a better idiot," Frank said as he drove through the country roads back towards Southward Cottage overlooking Lepe Beach.

"Idiots or not, we don't have much time. Sooner or later they're going to trace Blake's car back to us so we need to move fast," Joe replied.

When they arrived outside Southward Cottage, Blake and Joe carried the chest inside the cottage and placed it on the floor.

"Where's Frances?" Paula asked.

"She blew herself and the vicar up at the manor so we need to move fast to find the connection between her and what Vladimir Vasilievich have planned next," Blake replied as he began to pick the lock on the chest.

"What's that dirty old thing?" Michael asked.

"That is your father Michael, please have a bit more respect," Frank quipped.

Blake rolled his eyes. "It's something we've found buried underground."

"Wow, is this real pirate treasure Dad?" Michael asked.

"Don't touch it Michael, you never know what's inside it," Paula replied.

After a few minutes, Blake finally managed to release the lock. As he opened the chest, a plume of dust escaped into the air causing everyone to take a step back. He looked inside the chest and found a sheet of paper with a drawing showing a map of tunnels. In the top right corner of the paper, someone had written the code:

98 72 46 79 21

"I don't understand, she was convinced that the treasure was in Holbury Manor," Jenny said as she looked at the piece of paper.

"That map was the old extraction tunnels in the village from during the war," Blake said as he rushed into the study toward the old bookcase in the corner of the room.

The old mahogany door creaked open as Blake scanned his finger across the spines of the old books until he came to Ark Of Triumph, by Denis Bright. He opened the old book and found a map of tunnels on page fifty-five. He brought it back into the hall and compared it to the piece of paper that was inside the chest.

"How the hell did you remember that?" Jenny asked.

"Dad used to talk about what used to be down in the village before they turned it into the refinery in 1951. Those are the original tunnels. If we find them, we possibly find the gold," Blake replied.

"We have a bigger problem here," Joe said as he logged into the secure network of Special Branch on his phone.

Everyone looked at him.

"Alison and Samir are walking into a trap. That code isn't just any kind of reference number. If Vladimir Vasilievich is involved, that could well be the activation code for one of the old Soviet nuclear bombs that were used in the 1930's," Joe explained.

"Meaning?" Paula asked.

"If the gold is down there, it could also be guarded by an unstable nuclear bomb. If that goes off underneath the oil refinery with all of their pipes that run from here right across the country, you could end up wiping out the whole of the UK," Joe replied.

"We need an edge," Blake said as he scanned the map of the tunnels in the book. "Frogman's hatch, of course."

"You're not thinking what I think you're thinking," Jenny gasped.

"The old hatch at Ashlett Creek," Blake replied. "It's our only way past security."

"Blake, that hatch hasn't been used in over thirty years. It's only visible at low tide and it's about ten metres off-shore," Jenny said.

"Wait, what's the frogman's hatch?" Frank asked.

"When our parents used to visit Aunt Mary when we were kids, they used to take us to a local village pub in Ashlett Creek. People used to launch their fishing boats and kayaks from the little slipway at high tide but when the tide went out, in the distance, you could see a small metal drain cover that apparently led to a tunnel underneath the refinery," Jenny explained.

"Apparently?" Joe questioned.

"Nobody knew for sure but that was the story we were told," Blake replied. "If we want to sneak in and help Samir and Ali then it's our best chance. When is the next high tide?"

Paula rushed over towards a noticeboard in the kitchen and removed a small piece of cardboard with the tidal times written on it. "Quarter-to-eight in the morning," she said.

Blake looked at his watch. "We've got five hours."

"Blake, you don't even know if this will work. The water level is higher now so how do you even know if it hasn't rusted shut?" Jenny asked.

"I have to try Jen. It's the only way."

"Then I'm coming with you," Frank replied.

***

Angela Barnes arrived at the entrance to the oil refinery. Andre stepped out from the passenger seat and warmly embraced Pietro before handing over the briefcase full of money. The barrier was lifted and Andre rejoined Angela in the car as they headed inside the refinery. As they drove down the hill towards the heat exchange, Angela noticed the green Land Rover that belonged to Alison Pearce.

"Something wrong?" Andre asked.

She shook her head. "No, everything is as it should be," she replied as she parked her car and they both headed over towards a large building that overlooked a network of pipes that disappeared underground several metres further down the road.

Angela and Andre entered the large building, its interior dimly lit and filled with the hum of machinery. They were greeted by a man in a lab coat, his face obscured by shadows.

"Welcome," the man said in a low voice. "I trust all loose ends have been tidied up."

Angela nodded. Without a word, the man led them through a maze of corridors and staircases deep into the belly of the refinery. As they walked, Angela's mind raced with thoughts of

Alison and Samir walking into danger. She knew she had to act fast to warn them, but she also couldn't risk blowing her cover.

Finally, they arrived at a heavily guarded door. The man typed in a series of codes and the door creaked open to reveal a vast chamber filled with rows of computer servers and monitors.

"This is where our transaction will take place," the man said as he led them inside.

"Angela Barnes," a man with a strong Russian accent called out.

Angela turned to see a tall overweight bald man wearing a military uniform with several medals attached to the lapel.

"It's been a long time since we met in Moscow," he continued.

"Vladimir Vasilievich, I should've known that you'd be pulling the strings," Angela replied.

"You too," he replied as he pressed a button to turn on a screen which showed Alison and Samir in a darkened room. "You seem to have led your team of agents into a trap with relative ease. Funny how one bad apple can rot the entire fruit bowl."

"What do you mean?"

"Samir Khalifa, so eager to save his own skin that he'd even lead the woman he loved astray for his own ends."

Angela's heart sank as she watched the live feed of Alison and Samir in captivity. She knew she had to think fast to come up with a plan to save them without blowing her cover.

"You don't need to concern yourself with them Vladimir, we can work something out," Angela pleaded, trying to keep her voice steady despite the rising panic within her. "Blake will bring you the gold."

Andre looked at her in disbelief. "You're a double agent?"

Vladimir Vasilievich chuckled, a cold and menacing sound that sent shivers down Angela's spine. "Oh, I have no doubt we can come to an agreement, Angela. But first, you must prove your loyalty to me."

"What do you want me to do?" Angela asked.

"I want you to retrieve an item for me from a secure vault within this facility. It's a small price to pay for the lives of your colleagues, wouldn't you agree?"

Angela nodded, her mind already racing with possible escape routes and plans. "I'll do it."

Vladimir nodded before leading her through the labyrinthine corridors of the refinery towards the secure vault. Her mind was a whirlwind of thoughts as she tried to formulate a plan to retrieve the item while also finding a way to warn Alison and Samir.

As they approached the heavily guarded vault door, Angela's heart pounded in her chest and her palms became sweaty. She knew that whatever lay inside was of utmost importance to maintain her cover and she had to retrieve it without raising suspicion.

The guards scanned her credentials and allowed her access into the vault. The room was filled with rows of lockers, each secured with intricate locking mechanisms. Angela's eyes scanned the room, searching for the item she needed to retrieve. Finally, she spotted it. A small metal box tucked away in the corner of the vault. With steady hands, she input the code Vladimir had given her and opened the box. Inside, nestled on a bed of velvet, was a shimmering diamond. As she reached up to take the diamond, a loud whirring sound echoed around her and suddenly the floor gave way underneath her, sending her down a large metal slide into a damp algae covered pit below. She could hear water sloshing against the walls of this newfound tomb that she had become encapsulated inside and soon realised that she was in an underwater bunker.

She looked around to find some kind of escape route but found nothing. She cursed herself for trusting Andre and Vladimir but she knew she had to find a way out and somehow work out where they were holding Alison and Samir.

Meanwhile at the heat treatment centre, one of the assistants, carrying a small laptop, was checking the radiation shields when he walked along the corridor and tapped a code into a keypad. The door lock clicked open before mechanically removing a large metal bolt and opening the door. As he walked through the door, Alison kicked the laptop from his grasp whilst Samir struck him on the back of his head, sending him to the floor.

The door quickly slammed shut behind him foiling their plan for escape. At that moment, a red light began flashing and a piercing alarm began to ring out. The assistant was groggy but managed to look up at them.

Alison slapped him around the face to bring him around again. "What is that alarm?" she asked.

"Why did you hit me?" he asked.

"We thought you were somebody else, now tell us what's going on!" Samir replied.

"Oh hell, no!" the man said as he staggered to his feet. "Quickly, we need to go!"

He stumbled and had to use the wall to maintain his balance.

"Go where?" Alison asked.

"That's the burner alarm!"

"What's the burner alarm?" Samir asked.

"They're going to burn off the excess fuel. If we don't get out of here, this is going to turn into your own private crematorium!"

the man screamed as he hammered on the door but nobody answered.

"Can't you override it on your laptop or something?" Alison asked.

The man looked up. "There's only one way out," he said as the roof three hundred metres above them opened up showing the night sky. "Come on, this way!"

Alison and Samir followed him as they began climbing a series of ladders that led up to the top of the chimney. Each ladder had been drilled into the concrete structure of the chimney and was around twenty-five metres in length. There were thirteen small platforms between each ladder as the three of them climbed as fast as they could. The noise of the generators below them became louder and louder and they could feel the heat rising from deep within.

"Don't look down!" Samir shouted as he followed Alison up higher and higher.

"We're not going to make it!" Alison called out.

"We will just keep going!" the assistant replied as he led them higher and higher inside the chimney.

Their arms and legs ached from the constant climbing. Reaching and pulling themselves up ladder after ladder. The heat from below sapped their energy as they began to sweat. On the last ladder, condensation had begun to form on the rungs. Alison reached for the next rung and her hand slipped. She gripped as hard as she could with her right hand as she lost her footing and was hanging from the ladder by one arm.

"I'm slipping!" she shouted.

Samir reached out and tried to push her leg back towards the ladder. She swung her hand wildly trying to grip one of the rungs when she felt someone grab her wrist. She looked up and saw the assistant help her to take a firm hold onto the ladder. They finally managed to reach the top as smoke began to billow out of the chimney.

"Now what?" Alison asked breathlessly as she looked down on the vast drop below them.

The assistant held onto the metal rail as he walked around the edge of the chimney towards some ropes and metal clips. "What goes up must come down," he said.

"We're abseiling back down!" Samir gasped breathlessly.

"Unless you'd rather take the kamikaze route! Come on quick before the fire starts!"

Samir looked at Alison. "I'm getting too old for this shit," he sighed.

Chapter Seventy-One

John Misses The Boat
Sunday 13th August 1977

At 1pm in Weymouth Bay, Frances, Timmy and Dmitri arrived in a removal van loaded with items from Thyme Cottage and some from the vicar's cottage. Timmy drove the van into a yard full of large metal storage containers. He parked it next to a container marked MC74921RU before stepping out and handing the keys and a roll of banknotes to a man wearing a beige t-shirt and matching shorts. The man inspected the banknotes before nodding in approval and signalling four other men to start unloading the van into the metal container.

Frances and Timmy then joined Dmitri as they climbed into a white Ford Cortina and drove down towards the marina where a small escort boat would take them out to the biggest yacht in the bay, SSJ St Petersburg VV. The sea was smooth in the summer sun and as they approached the yacht, a middle-aged man in a white suit looked down on them as they arrived.

Frances rushed up the steps at the side of the yacht to meet the man on the top deck.

"Any problems?" he asked.

"None that I can't handle," she replied as she handed him the envelope that Mavis Langford had given her the day before.

"One day you'll be a very rich lady," he smiled before placing it inside his suit jacket pocket.

***

Meanwhile, John and Emily Langford stepped out of a taxi outside Southward Cottage before rushing inside. Mary and

James were already there waiting for them. Mary quickly told them everything that had happened whilst they had been gone.

"So Detective Hastings took all four of our parents in for questioning?" Emily asked.

"Dad's in hospital after being knocked out at the Vicar's house last night but Detective Hastings has got it into his head that they had something to do with it," Mary explained.

"No, it wasn't them. When we were in church yesterday, I saw mother having a very stern conversation with Frances King at the side before practically dragging her out of the church," John replied.

"You don't think she's tried to frame our parents to get back at you do you?" Emily asked.

"Anything's possible with her. Mary, where does Dad keep his briefcase?" John asked.

"Under the desk in the study, why?"

John rushed through into the study and picked up the briefcase. "If my guess is correct, this might give us a clue," he said as he furiously tried different combinations. "Damn it, do you know his combination?"

"Two, five, one, zero, one, two," Mary replied.

John turned the dials, moved the clasps and the case opened. "How did you..."

"Dad's date of birth, 25th October 1912. He uses that for everything that needs a combination lock."

Inside the case were two pens, two notebooks, a tie, a can of talcum powder and a bundle of at least fifty letters held together with elastic bands.

"Here it is," John said as he removed the letter with a postmark on it from August 4th 1977.

Emily looked into the briefcase. "What is all this?"

"Letters from Frances King to John. She kept sending them even after she got married to some Russian millionaire," Mary explained.

"Why would she do this?"

"She's been obsessed with him ever since they had a relationship when he was eighteen."

"That's twenty years ago."

Mary nodded. "That's why he had to move away and didn't want to come back here but your parents insisted and now the floodgates have opened again."

"Got it, read this," John said as he placed the letter on the table.

It read:

Dearest John,

It appears that the fight is over and I have lost. I will never forget the years we had together. The times we make believed our future would end in a beautiful white wedding and we'd sail off into the sunset. Now I guess that dream belongs to someone else.

I have sold Thyme Cottage and I am going to join my husband on his new venture far away from here. Too many familiar surroundings remind me too much of you. If you feel the need for closure, I will be in Weymouth Bay until 6pm on the 13th. If I don't see you there, I guess I'll have to let you go.

Yours always

Frances

"6pm, that gives you four hours," Mary said.

"You're not seriously thinking of going after her are you?" Emily asked.

"It makes sense. She has obviously tried to frame our parents and blackmailed mother for the gold. I need to go to Weymouth and bring her in for questioning!" John replied.

"If you're going then I'm coming with you," Emily said.

"It's too dangerous Emily," Mary replied.

"I'm not letting my husband go after that psychopath alone!"

"Then we all go," James replied.

John looked at Emily and then at Mary and James before closing the briefcase. "Come on, we don't have any time to waste!" he said as he led them out towards his car.

John knew he was clutching at straws but he needed answers and Frances was his obvious connection.

***

At Southampton Police Station, Detective Peter Hastings joined Sergeant Ted Newman and William Handanowicz in the interrogation room.

"You're wasting your time here, I had no reason to kill the reverend or injure Edward Langford!" William protested.

"Our sources have said that you and Mr Langford had some differences of opinion over the marriage of your children, Emily Handanowicz and John Langford. Would you care to clarify those?" Hastings asked.

"Our situation isn't normal. I knew what I was getting into when I met Dana. She had recently been widowed, had a young daughter and was pregnant with twins whilst she was at the convent in Portsmouth but somehow we connected in a way that I've never connected with anyone before."

"This convent, am I right in believing this was St Anne's?"

William nodded.

"And how did you gain access to this place?"

"I was doing some charity work to raise some money for them. Dana volunteered to make the teas and coffees at the event. We started talking and learnt that we had a lot in common."

"Such as?"

"Detective, sometimes in life, you need to hit the reset button. When life becomes unbearable, you need an outlet or you will just bottle things up over and over again and it will eventually consume you. As a middle-aged man who had focused solely on my business ventures throughout my twenties and thirties, I felt that the opportunity of love had passed me by."

"Until you met Dana."

William nodded. "She told me about her husband Gerald who had died fighting in the war leaving her a widow. Then she told me about the charming gent, Jack Smith, who visited her several times during the war. How she had fallen for him but both times he betrayed her. Left her pregnant, firstly with a son that she had to give up for adoption in 1940 and then she was pregnant again in 1948 with twins after they had had, I guess you could call it a one night stand before his death."

"The twins, Emily and Evelyn, you raised as your own," Hastings confirmed.

William nodded. "I loved Dana and thought we could make it work. And we did. We had James in '51 and finally had our own little family. Then, when Edith became ill, her dying wish was to return to Lepe. To be with her friends once again before she passed away. Little did I realise what a tangled web Jack Smith had left behind."

The interrogation room fell silent as William's words echoed in the air. Detective Hastings exchanged a knowing look with Sergeant Newman before turning back to William.

"You're suggesting that this man, Jack Smith, had quite the impact on your wife's life," Hastings observed.

William nodded slowly. "It's like a shadow from the past has caught up with us. Dana's past with Jack Smith seemed to resurface when we returned to Lepe. She was haunted by memories she had buried deep within her heart and Frances King knew what she had to do to cause maximum pain."

Detective Hastings leaned forward, intrigued. "And you believe this connection to Jack Smith somehow led to the events that unfolded recently?"

William's eyes darkened with sorrow. "I can't be certain, but it's as if the sins of the past have woven themselves into the present. Dana was a strong woman, but the weight of her history with Jack Smith... it was a burden she couldn't shake off."

Sergeant Newman cleared his throat, breaking the heavy atmosphere in the room. "Where does Frances King fit into all of this?"

"She knew about the pay-offs," William replied.

"What pay-offs?" Hastings asked.

"Jack Smith robbed a bank in 1938 in Portsmouth. The gold was never found and it had been written off. When he returned in 1948, he gave Dana and Mavis Langford two gold bars each. Dana cashed it in and used the money to pay for her stay in Portsmouth. It wasn't until after she left that she discovered that her home had been burnt down. The money that she had wanted to use to help with the children's education ended up paying to rebuild Sundial Cottage instead. That was why we returned to the village."

"Why did Mavis Langford receive the gold from Jack Smith?" Sergeant Newman asked.

"Because Jack Smith is the father of Mary and Frederick Langford," William replied.

Detective Peter Hastings sat back in his chair. Everything was beginning to make sense. The argument between the families, Fred leaving the wedding and having the accident that cost him his life. "I'm assuming Frederick Langford and Evelyn Handanowicz did not know about their paternity."

"Not until yesterday, no. We knew that Evelyn had been dating a young man at university but until recently, we didn't know who he was," William admitted.

"And Frances King used this information to her advantage?" Sergeant Newman asked.

"She was dating John Langford soon after he left school. When our family returned to the village, John left her to be with Edith."

Sergeant Newman looked at Hastings confused.

"Edith Wise passed away in 1956," Hastings confirmed. "Frances never let it go that John had picked Edith over her."

"Mavis Langford was so keen to save face that she gave her gold bars that Jack Smith had given her to Frances in an attempt to bribe her and keep her away from John now that he had moved on and married Emily," William replied. "My advice to you, if you're looking for someone with a motive to kill the reverend and injure Edward Langford, Frances King and her family would be a good place to start."

"We can't," Hastings sighed.

"Why?"

"Because she moved away last night. Packed everything up and headed off to Russia to be with her husband," Sergeant Edwards confirmed.

Detective Hastings felt a sinking feeling in his gut as he processed the latest revelation. Frances King, the woman at the centre of it all, had slipped away just when they were getting close to unravelling the truth. He exchanged a glance with Sergeant Newman, both silently acknowledging the setback.

"Well, that complicates things," Hastings muttered under his breath. But he was not one to give up easily. "We need to find a way to track her down. Newman, get in touch with our contacts at the border control. We need to know if any flights or shipments have left for Russia recently."

As Sergeant Newman hurried out of the room to make the necessary arrangements, Detective Hastings sat back in his chair, deep in thought. The pieces of the puzzle were scattered before him, waiting to be put together. Frances King's sudden departure only affirmed his suspicions that she held the key to unravelling the mystery behind the Jack Smith case that Hastings and his Detective at the time, Edward Langford, had stumbled upon in 1948.

"So what now?" William asked.

Hastings stood from his chair. "Now I need to speak with Dana Handanowicz and Mavis Langford but thank you for your cooperation Mr Handanowicz. You may well have answered the questions from a cold case that we've been working on for almost thirty years."

***

John Langford parked his car in the marina at Weymouth Bay. In the distance he saw a huge yacht far out at sea. He opened the boot of the car and found a pair of binoculars hidden under a windbreaker and a cool box. He looked out and could just make out the name on the side of the yacht, SSJ St Petersburg VV.

"That has to be it," John said as he rushed over towards the lock building.

Two men were standing high up on a platform as the lock gates that allowed boats in and out of the marina began creaking open and closed. John shouted out to the two men but they couldn't hear him over the creaking and whooshing of the water in the lock. He began climbing up the steel steps towards their platform.

"Hey! You can't come up here!" one of them shouted down to him.

John pulled out his ID. "Officer John Langford, Met Police, do you have any boats that could take me out to the SSJ St Petersburg?"

"That boat belongs to Vladimir Vasilievich," the man replied.

"I know who it belongs to, can you get me out there?"

"You're too late pal. They set sail half an hour ago. By the time you get out there, they'll be out on the open sea. Too dangerous."

John walked back down from the lock building towards his car as he watched the yacht disappear out of sight.

"You tried John," Emily said as she held him close.

"There has to be another way."

"How? She's married to a millionaire, she'll be protected come what may. All we can do is head back home and try to figure out how to get our parents out of custody," Mary replied.

"That's it, Mary you're a genius," John gasped as he quickly climbed into the driving seat.

"I am?" Mary asked, confused.

"They've moved house right?"

Everyone nodded.

"There's no way they would have got all of their belongings onto that yacht so it would have to go into the freight containers," John explained.

Emily sighed. "But John, there must be hundreds of freight containers in the port. How on Earth are we going to find out which one Frances has used?"

"Because every container has a reference number and the last two letters of the reference number are linked to the country they are heading to. All we need to do is find the containers with their reference number ending in RU."

"Needle in a haystack," James sighed.

"Maybe, but we have to try," John replied before starting up the engine and heading towards the freight shipping terminal.

Chapter Seventy-Two

Who Can You Trust?
Thursday 6th November 2008

As Blake and Frank arrived at Ashlett Creek, Blake's phone rang. He checked the caller ID before answering.

"Any news Sir?" Blake answered.

"Angela Barnes has been tracked to the oil refinery north of your position. The Prime Minister and the Ministry Of Defence have been in touch and have received demands from Vladimir Vasilievich for the release of funds from "The Crystal" totalling one hundred million pounds," Eric Gordon confirmed.

"Joe is working his magic to keep that door closed, however, we seem to have a bigger problem than just a potentially unexploded world war bomb under the refinery. When we uncovered what was buried at Holbury Manor, it gave us the code for a nuclear bomb as well as the location of the gold inside the tunnels that were there before the refinery was even built. Jack Smith was certainly clever."

"Our records show that when he stayed at Holbury Manor House during the war, he met an architect called Herbert Thomas. That would account for how he was able to know the layout of the tunnels and potentially stash away the gold whilst still having access to it."

"It was local history books that led us here but do we have any idea where the original maps were located?"

"Underneath the floorboards of the old manor house."

"Surely they would have been discovered by now?" Blake asked.

"You'd have thought so but the house burned down in 2006 and was then rebuilt. The old maps presumably went up in flames."

"Accident or deliberate?"

"Your guess is as good as mine."

"Have safety measures been put into place if things go south?" Blake asked.

"The oil companies won't want to shut off the supply completely however contingency plans are in place. If you come face to face with Vasilievich, say goodbye from us," Eric Gordon replied. "Good luck Blake."

As Blake cut off the call, a loud boom echoed around the area and a chimney in the distance shot a large flare of flames into the night sky.

"What are you thinking?" Frank asked.

"That the sea is going to be bloody cold tonight," Blake replied.

"Let's do this," Frank said as they waded out into the water and began to swim out towards the hatch.

The icy cold water attacked their muscles as they swam against the waves until they were around ten metres offshore. Treading water for a moment, Blake took a deep breath before going underwater. Mostly by touch rather than sight, he found the hatch. It was a concrete structure out of the seabed with a metal underwater hatch that had rusted over the years. Blake came back up for air before signalling for Frank to join him underwater. Together they pulled and pushed as hard as they could to open the hatch door. They both came up for air once more before going down again and finally managing to open the hatch.

Angela had begun to explore the tunnels of her underwater bunker when she heard a clanking and groaning of a metal hatch being opened. As she turned to look back from where she had come from, a huge wave of water suddenly flooded the pipes sweeping her up off of her feet and onwards through the tunnels.

The force of the water was overwhelming, pulling her with such ferocity that she lost control of her movements. Debris swirled around her, creating a disorientating whirlpool of chaos. Her heart raced with fear as she struggled to find something to hold onto in the dark, murky waters. A loud boom of a door or hatch slamming shut echoed around the tunnels. Desperately gasping for air, Angela's mind raced with thoughts of being swept away into the unknown depths of the tunnels. Just as panic threatened to consume her entirely, her hand brushed against a metal railing embedded in the wall. With renewed determination, she grasped onto it tightly, clinging for dear life as the relentless current tugged at her.

Finding strength she didn't realise that she had, Angela managed to anchor herself to the railing, her knuckles turning white from the intensity of her grip. The water continued to rage around her, but she held on. With each passing moment, she could feel a glimmer of hope beginning to stir within her. Summoning every ounce of strength she possessed, she slowly began to pull herself along the railing, inch by painstaking inch. The water surged against her, pressing hard against her body as if trying to tear her away from her lifeline. But she refused to yield, her muscles burning with exertion as she fought against the relentless current.

Time seemed to blur as she forged ahead through the flooded tunnels, her willpower propelling her forward in the darkness. The only sound was the rush of water and her own ragged breaths echoing off the walls. She couldn't see where she was going, but she clung to the hope that there would be an end to this watery labyrinth. Just as she felt her strength waning and doubt creeping into her mind, a faint glimmer of light appeared in the distance. It beckoned to her like a beacon of salvation, a promise of escape from the watery depths that threatened to consume her. With renewed determination, Angela quickened her pace. As she pulled herself up onto a metal platform above the water, she felt a hand reach out of the water and grab her.

She screamed for a moment before realising that it was Blake and Frank pulling themselves out of the water.

"What the hell are you two doing here?" she asked as she helped them out of the water.

"I could ask you the same question," Blake replied. "What were you doing running out of Gordon's office like that?"

"Andre has the codes. I needed to make sure that I was down here before he entered the refinery but Vladimir Vasilievich was one step ahead. He revealed that I was a double agent. He led me into a trap which then led me down here."

"We could have worked together and helped you."

"And then we'd all have been trapped. If Gordon had spoken to Andre about my involvement, my cover would have been blown long before we had gained any new intelligence. I had to go it alone. Vladimir already suspected Samir of being a double agent. I had to convince him of my loyalty but ultimately, I mis-stepped."

Blake pondered that for a moment before pulling out a small earpiece from his wetsuit and placing it in his ear. "Joe, can you hear me? Joe?"

"I've got you Blake but you're a long way from the source," Joe replied as he tracked them on his laptop from Southward Cottage.

"We got washed downstream," Blake replied. "We've found Angela."

"Did Andre get hold of the codes from the undertaker?" Joe asked.

Blake repeated the question.

"Yes and then he shot him," Angela replied.

"Did you see the codes?" Frank asked.

She shook her head.

"Joe, the whole place is flooded, I'm going to need a way out," Blake replied.

"From where you are there should be a tunnel that leads up to the surface near to the heat treatment unit. From there you can access the main well where it looks like the bomb has been buried."

"I can't see anywhere. We're running around blind down here."

"What about Alison and Samir?" Angela asked.

"They are safe. When the flares went off, they managed to abseil down a chimney with a radiation specialist," Joe confirmed before consulting the map on his laptop, plotting out the best route for Blake, Angela and Frank to take.

"Okay, listen up," Joe instructed through the earpiece. "Head straight down the tunnel you're in now for about fifty metres until you reach a junction. Take a right there and keep following that path until you see a ladder leading up. It will bring you to the surface near the heat treatment unit. Once there, you should be able to access the main well where the bomb is located."

Blake relayed the instructions to Angela and Frank as they prepared to navigate through the flooded tunnels towards their escape route. The water still raged around them, but with a renewed sense of purpose and direction, they pressed forward determinedly. Each step was a battle against the relentless current, but they refused to give up. As they followed Joe's guidance, their surroundings gradually shifted from the dark, claustrophobic tunnels to a slightly more open space. The rushing water began to recede, allowing them to move more freely as they pressed on towards the surface.

Every muscle in their bodies ached from the exertion, but the trio pushed onward, driven by the urgency of their mission. Angela could feel her heart pounding in her chest as they neared the ladder that would lead them to their destination. With a shared look of determination, they braced themselves for the final ascent.

One by one, they began to climb the ladder, water dripping from their sodden clothes as they ascended towards the light above. Finally, with aching limbs and breathless anticipation, Angela emerged from the tunnel onto the surface near the heat treatment unit.

The harsh light of a floodlight blinded her momentarily, but as her eyes adjusted, she could see the vast expanse of the refinery laid out before them. Smoke billowed from various structures, the air thick with the acrid scent of industry. In the distance, the looming shape of the main well stood ominously.

"We need to move quickly," Blake said. "The bomb could detonate at any moment."

Angela nodded, her heart racing as she followed Blake and Frank towards the main well. Each step felt like a countdown to disaster.

Inside the main well, the air was thick and suffocating, the sound of their footsteps echoing off the metal walls. They moved cautiously through the dimly lit space, their senses on high alert for any sign of danger. Angela's hands trembled slightly as she scanned their surroundings, her eyes darting nervously from one shadowed corner to the next. Suddenly, a faint beeping noise cut through the silence, sending a jolt of fear coursing through Angela's veins. She froze in place, her heart pounding in her chest as she tried to pinpoint the source of the sound. With mounting dread, she realised that the beeping was coming from a darkened alcove across the chamber.

"Over there," Frank pointed, his voice barely more than a whisper in the oppressive stillness of the well.

Without hesitation, Blake and Angela followed his gaze, their eyes locking onto a small, ominous-looking device nestled among a tangle of wires and circuitry.

"It's the bomb," Blake said.

"And look at what's behind it," Frank replied as he shone the light from his phone over around a hundred solid bars of gold.

"Son-of-a-bitch entangled it in the bomb. There are metal claws holding the gold bars in place. If you remove any of it or input the wrong code, the claws will destroy the gold. The only way to get to it is to either disarm the bomb or..."

"Blow it up," Angela gasped.

"It'll kill millions," Frank gasped as he looked behind it and noticed a huge drop that went as far down as the eye could see. "Jack Smith literally buried it in the centre of the earth. There's no telling how far down that goes."

At that moment, the whole area lit up and Vlaidimir Vasilievich, Andre Lewis and Colin Sanderson entered the main well. Angela, Blake and Frank rushed to the side of the well to hide in the shadows.

Andre handed a piece of paper to Colin. "The world's greatest cash card. It better not be rejected!"

"When this is released into Crypto, nothing can stop us," Vladimir replied.

"What do you mean Crypto?" Andre asked.

"Once this is invested in The Crystal, we will be unstoppable!"

"Crypto is dead. Special Branch closed it down. Wiped millions off of its value. Why would you risk everything we've gone through for online currency?"

"My wife, Frances, ran rings around them. They took her inheritance away from her and now I will reclaim what is rightfully ours. Do you honestly think you could launder ten million in gold bullion?" Vladimir snapped. "The kremlin can cover up a lot but that much merchandise hitting the market in one hit is a tall order for anyone."

Colin removed a sheet of paper from an envelope and read what was written on it out loud. "Death is a mirror, reflect on that. Everybody will die one day, just give them time."

"What is the code?" Vladimir asked.

"It's written in Roman Numerals. I need time to figure it out."

Andre sighed and snatched the paper away from him. "If you want something done right, do it yourself."

The note read: **XII XCVII LXIV XXVII LXXXIX**

"You get this wrong and we lose everything," Vladimir replied.

"Look XII is twelve. C is one hundred but a ten before it makes it ninety so the second number is ninety-seven. L is fifty plus fourteen is sixty-four. The fourth number is twenty-seven and the fifth number is eighty-nine," Andre said as he worked out the numerals.

"It's a riddle," Frank whispered. "Their numbers are a mirror image of the code. They'll set it off."

"If you enter those numbers, you will blow us all away," Blake called out.

Andre spun around as Angela, Blake and Frank stepped into the light.

"Well, well, Blake Langford. What an unpleasant surprise," Vladimir sighed.

"If you input that code, you will blow us all off of the face of the earth!"

"What would you know? Your family are part of the reason why we're all here! If your father hadn't left Frances King when she was a young and vulnerable single mother..."

"Then she wouldn't have ended up with you."

"Let's not split hairs here. Our paths would have crossed sooner or later. Blake Langford, the government's loyal terrier, a meagre wage for risking life and limb for what? A pat on the back, good job old boy, now onto the next. I could make you a very rich man instead of a poor dead one. Your grandfather learnt that before his untimely demise."

"The code was buried with Dana Handanowicz. Why would somebody go to such lengths to protect the code for it to be wrong?" Andre asked.

"Because the code we have uncovered is different from your code," Frank replied.

"And what if your code is wrong?" Colin asked.

"Do you really want to take that chance?" Blake asked.

Vladimir stared at him for a moment. "Frances always said you Langfords never know when to keep your nose out of things. I'm going to disarm the bomb and take the gold out of here. You've interfered with my plans for the last time."

Blake's jaw tightened as Vladimir reached for the bomb, his mind racing for a plan. Without hesitation, he lunged forward and tackled Vladimir to the ground. The bomb and the gold bars rolled backwards on what looked like some kind of wheeled trolley that it was situated on towards the huge hole behind it.

Angela and Frank sprang into action, restraining Andre and Colin before they could react.

"You're not getting away with this," Blake snapped, pinning Vladimir to the floor.

Vladimir struggled beneath Blake's firm grip, his face contorted with fury. "You fool! You have no idea what you're meddling in."

Blake kept the pressure on. "I know enough to stop you. Are a few gold bars worth the lives of millions of innocent people?"

As Vladimir's resistance faltered, a cold voice cut through the tension in the air. "There's no need for violence here!"

Blake looked up and saw Samir standing in the doorway.

Chapter Seventy-Three

Through The Years

On Sunday 13th August 1977, the flashing lights of police cars illuminated the night sky as officers swarmed around the shipping container MC74921RU heading towards St Petersburg just before midnight. Items from the Reverend Denis Black's cottage, Frances King's Thyme Cottage as well as a severed hand had been discovered inside the container. Three security guards and two supervisors from the shipping yard were taken into custody and there had been a worldwide APB put out for Frances King and her family. Whether it was through fear or money, no new information came forward and the local police had to close the case.

John, Emily, James and Mary all returned to Lepe where they were reunited with their parents, Mavis and Edward Langford and Dana and William Handanowicz. Evelyn Handanowicz never returned.

Edward and Mavis Langford lived out the rest of their lives at Southward Cottage until their deaths in 1984 Mary Langford then inherited Southward Cottage where she stayed until her death in 2002.

Dana and William Handanowicz moved back to Portsmouth after relations with the Langfords became fractured over the years. Dana Handanowicz died in 1984 with William following in 1987.

Emily and John Langford returned to London where John worked for the Met Police Force until his retirement in 1997. During this time, they welcomed the births of their three children, Blake William Langford, Jennifer Eleanor Langford and Steven Alexander Langford. John died after a short battle with lung cancer in 1999. Emily followed in 2008.

After disappearing before her sister's wedding in 1977, Evelyn Handanowicz battled anxiety and depression for seven years after emigrating to the Greek Island of Rhodes.

James Handanowicz approached John Langford in 1982 about creating a safe space for war veterans and people with mental health issues. James had studied psychology at University and had managed to raise over one hundred thousand pounds towards the new centre. A derelict hospital wing in Croydon became available and James began transforming it into a new mental health facility to help the local people.

As time rolled on, mental health specialists began asking for more money and the centre looked tired. The dream of helping people in need began to falter and the companies who had sponsored the project in the early days began to pull away. James became desperate and approached John Langford with the possibility of him becoming a partner in the business.

With his dealings in law enforcement, James convinced John that his knowledge and expertise would be invaluable in securing the future of the centre.

In January 1984, John invested fifty-thousand pounds into the Handanowicz Centre For Mental Health. A steady flow of patients continued to flow into the facility however the money was disappearing fast. Without John's knowledge, James placed the centre on the market, made the entire staff redundant and sold the business by May 1984. He fled the country with the money from the sale of the business and disappeared. For four years, John Langford used all of the options he had at his discretion as a Police Detective but there was no trace of James Handanowicz.

In September 1984, James Handanowicz joined his sister Evelyn on the Greek Island of Rhodes where they worked on an olive farm together. Evelyn never fully got over the death of Frederick Langford and was admitted and sectioned to a mental health facility in Monolithos at the end of 1984 where she stayed until her death in 2008. After her death, James Handanowicz fled from the island and his location is currently unknown.

On the night of his death in 1984, Edward Langford sat on Lepe Beach with a flask of coffee and a fishing rod in his hand. He looked out as the sun began to set on the horizon and wondered where all of those years had gone. Years where he had been a young, energetic, enthusiastic police detective. All of the secrets that had crossed his desk. All of the lies and deceit that became the norm after the second world war. He thought about Frederick. How he had mourned his loss. How Mary had lived a life of solitude with her interests in birdwatching rather than any kind of relationship with the opposite sex. And then there was John. Determined and strong-willed enough that he would go far in whatever he did. He noticed his wife Mavis approaching him on the beach and she sat beside him in a fold-out chair. Together, they watched the sun go down and he placed his hand on top of hers.

"We did all right in the end, didn't we?" Edward asked.

Mavis smiled. "I think so," she said.

Edward wasn't sure if he heard the two pops. He wasn't sure if he felt himself slouch down in his chair. In a moment, it was over. Two lives so entwined through all of their ups and downs, had taken their last moments together under the setting sun. Mavis and Edward Langford had been shot dead before the engine of a Ford Escort roared away into the distance as it sped away from Lepe Beach.

Chapter Seventy-Four

The Water Bomb
Thursday 6th November 2008

Inside the main well at the oil refinery, Samir stood in the doorway with Blake, Angela and Frank to his right and Vladimir, Colin and Andre to his left.

"Samir Khalifa, what an unpleasant surprise," Vladimir spat as he moved towards the bomb.

Samir aimed his gun. "I wouldn't do that if I were you."

"Looking to take it for yourself Khalifa? After all, you know all about treachery and deception don't you? Haven't you told Langford about your little adventure whilst your colleague supervised the rising of the dead?"

"What does he mean?" Blake asked.

"I've been your guardian angel Blake. Keeping a close eye on my investment whilst Tom Gibson attempted to get under your skin like some disease that needed to be destroyed," Vladimir replied.

"You killed Gibson?" Angela asked.

"No, chalk that one up to Frances. She knows all of the ways you can torture a human body for maximum pain before they die."

"Interesting role-model," Frank quipped.

"I've made mistakes in the past but I've paid for them. That gold doesn't belong to you Vladimir and you shouldn't be the one who decides who lives and who dies from a world war two secret," Samir replied.

"How touching, I almost shed a tear. Now let's get on with it," Vladimir snapped as he moved towards the bomb.

Samir fired at the top of the well. The bullet ricocheted off of the metal walls and flew in the air above them before coming to rest on the floor next to Andre.

"Neat trick but I don't have time for theatrics," Vladimir said.

"Neither do we," said Alison as she slid a gold key into the bomb and turned it, leading to the entire display to light up.

"What the..." Vladimir began.

"You see, if you had been following me, you would have known that I met with Christopher Anderson and he gave me the ashes of Jack Walter Smith. In those ashes was a gold key. I never knew what it was for until a radiation expert saved mine and Alison's ass from being barbecued in the heat treatment unit!" Samir replied.

At that moment, Andre pulled his gun but Frank reacted first, hitting it out of his hands. Angela charged at Colin who headed for the exit. Blake launched himself at Vladimir, knocking him into the bomb and the gold bars. The small trolley that it was on rolled closer to the hole. Alison tried to grab hold of it but the gold bars began to tilt on the edge of the huge crater. Blake wrestled Vladimir to the ground as they rolled ever closer towards the huge crater.

"At least I'll have the pleasure of putting you out of my misery!" Vladimir said as they rolled closer to the hole.

"Don't count on it," Blake replied as he aimed a sharp fist to Vladimir's chest.

"It was beautiful Blake. Your grandparents on that beach. I took them out in two shots. Pop. Pop. One after the other. And now it's your turn."

Blake remembered the story he had been told by his own father, John Langford, of how his grandparents had been sat on Lepe Beach and had died together. Now, it suddenly made sense.

"You!" Blake cussed.

Vladimir nodded.

A fit of rage consumed Blake as he began pounding away at Vladimir's chest. Vladimir gasped for air as Blake's fists pummelled his chest relentlessly. Blood trickled from the corner of his mouth as his body went limp under Blake's raw fury. The others stood frozen, watching the brutal scene unfold before them.

"Blake, that's enough!" Angela finally shouted, rushing forward to pull him away from Vladimir's lifeless body. "It's done!"

Blake stumbled back, panting heavily, his hands clenched into fists at his sides. His eyes burned with a mixture of grief and anger as he looked down at Vladimir's motionless form on the ground.

"We need to get out of here," Samir said urgently, his voice breaking through the stunned silence that had settled over the group. "The bomb is still active."

Alison quickly grabbed the trolley attached to the bomb with the gold bars, pushing it away from the edge of the crater as they all made their way towards the exit. The sound of alarms blaring filled the air as they raced against time to escape. As they got to the exit, they heard a beeping like a timer ticking down. As they turned to look back at the bomb, they saw Andre entering a code.

"I thought the key deactivated it!" Samir gasped.

"Only the nuclear reactor part. There's still enough explosive to blow this place sky high!" Alison replied.

"Now she tells us," Frank said as he wrestled Andre from the control panel.

"It's too late, we all go down together," Andre laughed before grabbing Frank's gun and shooting himself under his chin.

Angela turned away in disgust.

"Saved me a job, where's that code?" Frank asked.

Blake touched his ear-piece. "Joe, are you still there?"

"I'm with you Blake."

"We need the code to deactivate the bomb."

"We don't even know if that's going to work."

"I've got two minutes to find out or this place gets blown to shit!"

"Okay, okay, it's ninety-eight, seventy-two, forty-six, seventy-nine, twenty-one. Now get the hell out of there!" Joe shouted.

Blake entered the code but the countdown continued. Sixty seconds, fifty-nine, fifty-eight, fifty-seven...

"Get the hell out of here, run!" Blake shouted.

"What are you doing?" Alison asked.

"I need to disarm the bomb!"

"It's gonna blow!"

"If it does, we're all dead!"

They looked at the display. Forty-nine, forty-eight, forty-seven, forty-six, forty-five...

They both looked at the gold bars.

"Are you thinking what I'm thinking?" Alison asked.

Blake nodded and they both pushed the trolley of gold bars over the edge and into the huge crater behind the bomb. With a loud clanking boom, the gold bars and the bomb disappeared into the crater. Frank, Angela, Blake, Samir and Alison all ran out of the main well and rushed away towards the exit. A few seconds later and a loud boom echoed around the refinery. In the distance, a huge plume of water rose up into the air creating a huge wave that engulfed the lower part of the oil refinery before receding back down towards the sea.

"How the hell did you know that would work?" Frank asked.

"I didn't," Blake replied.

"That was one hell of a water bomb," Samir smiled as police and emergency services arrived at the oil refinery gates.

Frank, Angela, Samir, Alison and Blake watched as the officers and emergency personnel swarmed the area. Even though the gold was gone, they had the knowledge that the bomb had been destroyed too.

"Next time you decide to trace back your ancestry, warn me first," Alison said as she led them out towards the village.

Blake smiled. "I wouldn't be very good at my job if I did."

As they adjusted to the aftermath, a reality set in that there would always be someone or something hunting them for the mistakes of the past. They would all need to lay low and stick together, at least for a while until the bodies of those involved were recovered. As Joe Knight pulled up in his car to pick them up, they knew their wishes for a simple life seemed as far away as ever. It was the nature of the job and no matter how much Blake didn't want to admit it, being a family man and working for Special Branch would always keep himself, his team and his family in the firing line.

When they arrived back at Southward Cottage, Michael came rushing out and wrapped his arms around his father's waist. Paula walked over and they held each other close for what seemed like an age.

"Is it over?" she asked.

"It's over," Blake replied as dawn slowly began to appear over the sea that was the backdrop to their family home.

"You missed something really cool Dad. About an hour ago, a huge wave came up and it soaked the back garden at the top of the cliff. It was awesome. I've never seen anything like it!" Michael explained.

Blake gave Alison and Paula a knowing look. "I'm sure it was great Michael, now how about we get some breakfast."

"Yeah! I'm making waffles!" Michael said as he rushed indoors.

"How's he still got the energy after being awake all night?" Alison asked.

"Oh to be kids again," Blake laughed as they all headed inside Southward Cottage.

Chapter Seventy-Five

Recover Your Soul
Monday 17th November 2008

Blake Langford entered the cemetery at All Saints Church near to Dibden Golf Club on the edge of The New Forest. He walked over near to the church where he found the grave of Mavis Irene Mary Langford and Edward George Ernest Langford. He placed a selection of artificial flowers into the rose bowl on the gravestone before standing in front of the grave and reading the inscription.

"We got him in the end, Grandad," Blake whispered to himself.

His mind cast back to kicking a football around in the back garden of Southward Cottage when he was seven years old. Using two metal bins as goal-posts, he would take shots at his grandad before enjoying homemade scones with fresh strawberry jam at the wooden picnic table.

As he was about to leave, he noticed a burgundy urn had been placed next to a white carnation on an unmarked grave in the shadow of the church alongside a wooden cross that had a remembrance day red and black poppy attached to it. Blake crouched down and looked at the urn. A gold inscription on the side read;

JACK WALTER SMITH
DIED: 21st AUGUST 1948
Aged 41 Years

Blake sighed. "Did they love you? I hope you made them happy even if it was only briefly," he said to himself.

As he stood up to leave, two robins hopped over the grass towards him. One of them flew up and sat on top of the gravestone next to the unmarked plot and looked at Blake for a moment before flying away. Blake smiled and looked up to the skies before continuing on his way back to his car. Alison was waiting for him in the passenger seat as he returned.

"You okay?" she asked.

"I think so. My father told me about how he felt cheated that his parents never had the opportunity to enjoy a retirement together. He'd searched for years to find out what really happened on that day at Lepe Beach."

"It must have been awful."

"When he came back here to identify them, the investigating officer at the time took him down to where it happened. He worked out that whoever had done it must have been standing near to the lighthouse at the top of the hill. If they'd just stayed on their own stretch of beach behind Southward Cottage, chances are they would have been all right."

"You don't know that for sure."

Blake nodded. "I guess. If Vladimir and Frances hadn't seen them on the beach they would have probably gone to the house."

"If you don't want to do this, I don't mind visiting the hospital alone."

"No, I need to have this closure. I need to know why," Blake replied as he started the car and drove into Southampton City Centre towards the hospital.

As they arrived at the hospital and walked along the glass corridors towards the Acute Medical Unit, Blake thought back to his father's last words before he died. He'd asked Blake to look after the family. To be the figurehead that for so long, John Langford had been. He'd sat at his father's bedside after rushing back from a Special Branch training course in Ireland to be at his bedside when he died. Now that the dust had settled following his mother's passing, Blake knew that he owed it to his father to keep the promise that he made to keep the family safe.

When they arrived at the Acute Medical Unit, Alison showed her ID to the nurse at the reception desk. She led them through the ward to a side room at the end of the corridor. Alison entered the room with Blake close behind. Machines beeped an endless monotone as they monitored the man laying motionless in the bed. The name plate above the bed read; Timothy John King.

"Timmy, can you hear me?" Alison asked as she sat on the chair at his bedside.

His eyes flickered momentarily before opening wide. He looked firstly at Blake before noticing Alison at his side. "Who are you?"

"I'm Alison Pearce, I work for Special Branch. We just wanted to ask you a few questions?"

"And who is he?"

"Blake Langford," Blake replied.

Timmy's eyes widened in recognition as Blake introduced himself. "Where is she? What have you done to my mother?"

"Your mother has sadly passed away, Timmy," Blake replied.

"You killed her!"

"No, she did it herself."

Timmy felt tears sting the backs of his eyes. "No, no, she'd never do that! You're lying!"

Alison placed her hand on Timmy's arm but he didn't respond to her. "Timmy, do you know Father Christoph Fischer from St David's Church in Lepe?"

Tears began streaming down Timmy's face. "I wanted to die," he cried. "My whole life has been one big lie. Mother would never let it go. My father had been alive the whole time and she lied to me. Her obsession with the Langfords consumed her." He looked directly at Blake. "And then you killed her!"

"She died with her first love. I hope you can find some comfort in that," Blake replied. "What do you know about Holbury Manor Timmy?"

He glared at Blake for a moment before answering. "It's a patch of woodland on the edge of The New Forest. During the war, the old Manor House was used to treat the wounded. They later turned the Manor House and the surrounding barns around it into a housing estate."

"Your mother believed that Jack Smith, the man who had robbed a bank in Portsmouth in 1938, had buried the gold within Holbury Manor."

"It was her inheritance and John Langford took it away from her. If I ever saw the bastard again, I'd kill him!" Timmy snapped.

"John Langford, my father, died of lung cancer in 1999," Blake replied.

Timmy didn't reply.

"He told me about his relationship with your mother when we used to fish off of Lepe Beach. How as soon as he left school, he helped her look after you and your Grandad. Your mother fell in love with him. They had a brief relationship but when it all broke down, she refused to accept it. She stalked him. She sent him letters. Thousands of them. Waited outside his house at Southward Cottage until he finished work and then hounded him constantly. Even when he moved to London she continued to send the letters."

"She loved him."

"It was through her letters that we discovered the truth about what had really happened all of those years ago. Mavis Langford, my grandmother and John's mother, signed over her share of the Smith gold to your mother, Frances King, on the understanding that she would leave John alone when he married my mother, Emily."

"And what a twisted family secret it turned out to be," Timmy snapped.

"Timmy," Alison spoke now. "You've spent your life hating and chasing a family that wasn't even related to you. All John Langford wanted to do was to help your mother after Christoph Fischer had left her alone with a young child and an ill father at a time where young single women had no support whatsoever."

"Christoph Fischer is dead to me. He was never there for us!"

"He is dead," Blake confirmed. "When he came face-to-face with your mother in Holbury Manor, he tried to help her. He wanted to help her to come to terms with the hurt and regret from almost sixty years ago. As he embraced her, she set off the suicide bomb vest that she was wearing and blew them both up. They died together. As it should have been. Christoph, who was a German soldier, should have been allowed to be with the mother of his child. If he had, maybe your mother would not have become involved with Vladimir Vaselievich. Maybe he would not have murdered my Grandparents, Mavis and Edward Langford, on the beach that day in 1984. Maybe, just maybe, if they had been allowed to be together, you wouldn't have jumped from that church balcony."

Timmy bowed his head. "They said I've broken my spine and I'm paralysed from the neck down. Oh my God, what have I done?"

"Your mind was poisoned by a manipulative and very mentally ill mother, Timmy," Alison replied. "The post-traumatic stress that must have put you and Dmitri through would have been immense."

"Where is Dmitri?" Timmy asked.

"He's been arrested and is going through the investigative procedure. We don't know for certain what the outcome will be," Blake replied.

"Thank you," Timmy said, looking straight at Blake.

"What for?"

"Being honest with me. It's been a long time since someone has been."

"You have a chance to recover your soul," Alison replied. "I know things may look bleak but you'll get through it."

Timmy smiled at Alison before closing his eyes once again. After a few minutes, Alison and Blake left the room and headed out of the hospital.

When they sat back into Blake's car, he let out a long exhale and ran his fingers through his hair.

"You okay?" Alison asked.

"I guess you never realise how much life can mess you up until much later when often it's too late," Blake replied.

"You seemed to have turned out alright though."

"Me? I'm a complete mess. I jump to conclusions. My anger management could do with some work."

"And you have a wonderful son and fiance who love you and if you didn't have those characteristics then you'd be a useless field agent. I know who I'd rather have watching my back."

Blake smiled as he started the car. "Thanks Ali. You're not too bad yourself."

"Believe me, you think your family has baggage, mine is a whole new level."

"Samir?"

"It's complicated."

"Meaning?"

"A sharp suit and a cute ass may be enough for some women but sometimes things need to go a lot deeper than that."

"Paula tells me that all the time."

"Does it cause friction considering your past with her sister?"

"If Rachael was still alive I think it would. As this case has shown, sometimes life doesn't always work out the way that we plan it. When Rachael disappeared in 1999, I thought I'd never see her again…"

"But you never gave up hope."

"Someone's been doing their homework."

"I like to know who I'm entrusting my life with."

"I followed that trail for eight years without so much as a glimmer and then Paula led me straight to her."

"So you can relate to the lost love that Frances experienced with your father."

"I guess. I never went out and killed people for Rachael though," Blake smirked.

"I know that but deep down, even after her disappearance and everything that happened, you still loved Rachael, right?"

"I did. I guess I still do. When she died, it felt like my whole life had been tipped up-side-down. Suddenly, I'd had a chance to be with the love of my life and then it was ripped away from me at the last minute. Then I found out I was a father to a son that I never knew for the first eight years of his life…"

"And now…"

"Now, I can't imagine a day without Michael or Paula. If you'd asked me three years ago where I'd be today, I'd never have predicted this."

Alison nodded.

"What are you thinking?" Blake asked.

"That, maybe, I guess, Samir deserves the benefit of the doubt."

"Only you can decide that."

Alison sighed deeply. "Why is love so hard?"

"That's what makes it worthwhile I guess. Where to now?"

"We need to catch up with Joe at Holbury Manor. Forensics would have hopefully finished piecing together whatever remains there were of the bomb that Frances had set off."

As the two friends travelled out of the city centre and back into The New Forest, Blake felt a renewed sense of purpose. The ghosts of the past had finally been laid to rest and he could focus on his family and his future.

When they arrived at Holbury Manor, blue and white police tape was surrounding the woodland whilst Joe Knight was directing police officers around the scene. He saw Alison and Blake approaching and walked over towards them.

"Glad you could make it," Joe smiled. "That bomb made quite a mess."

"That is what they're designed to do," Blake laughed.

"Have the police found anything interesting from where the trees were uprooted?" Alison asked.

"Nothing of note however, take a look at this," Joe said as he led them towards the third tree where the metal box that held the codes was found.

As he moved some of the mud and debris out of the way, he revealed a wooden handle. "Take a look at that," Joe smiled.

Blake reached down and pulled on the handle which released a knife with a six inch blade. "An old knife?" Blake asked. "Do I need to ask if it's Colonel Mustard in the Drawing Room?"

"Very funny. Look at the inscription," Joe replied.

"H. Boker and co." Blake read aloud.

"Boker was a rare knife maker around the time of the second world war. You're holding a museum piece there!"

Alison and Blake looked at each other. "Anything else?" she asked.

"Yes, down by the pond, this way," Joe replied as he headed down the mud path.

As Blake and Alison turned to follow him, they heard something growling behind them. Blake slowly turned around and saw two Staffordshire Bull Terriers growling and glaring at them.

"Don't move," Blake said as he slowly turned to face them.

"Amber! Mongo!" a man's voice called out.

Alison and Blake looked up towards the main path and saw a middle-aged man wearing grey shorts, a pale blue shirt and an orange hi-visibility jacket.

"Oh hi Blake, sorry about them, they're friendly really," the man called out.

"They look like it too," Alison quipped.

"Hi Steve, long time, no see. Are you still working at the local sorting office?" Blake asked.

"Not for much longer. I'm moving out to Boldre to enjoy some fishing and early retirement. The legs don't work as well as they used to," Steve replied.

"Excuse me Sir, you're trespassing inside a police corden!" One of the police officers called out.

"Sorry, just rescuing my dogs!" Steve replied as he attached Amber and Mongo to their leads and gave them a couple of biscuits each.

He handed some of the dog biscuits to Blake. "You'll probably need them if you're trawling through here. It's a dog walkers paradise."

"I'll keep that in mind, thanks," Blake replied as he watched Steve walk back up towards the main path.

"Old friend?" Alison asked.

"One of the local postmen I used to see around the area. Bristol City fan but nobody's perfect," Blake smiled as he followed Joe down towards the pond.

When they arrived, they found Samir crouched down on his knees with one of the forensic experts as they carefully dredged a fishing net through the murky water.

"What are they doing?" Alison asked.

"Removing traces of nickel and copper from the water. When that bomb went off, it sent shards of metal off in all directions," the forensic expert replied as he looked up at Blake. "You were lucky not to be torn to pieces."

"We found this too," Samir said as he handed Alison a small metal bucket.

Amongst the pieces of nickel and copper was a large gold and diamond wedding ring.

"It needs cleaning up but I'm sure somebody will want it back. It must have been worth a lot to whoever lost it," Samir continued.

Blake looked at the wedding ring and then checked his watch. It was just before quarter-to-three in the afternoon. He turned to Alison; "Are you okay to head back with Samir at the end of the day? There's somewhere I need to be."

Alison nodded. "Sure, is everything okay?"

"It will be, thanks," Blake replied before rushing off and heading back to his car.

Fifteen minutes later, he was parked outside Forest Way School. He walked through the side gate and up the slight incline of the path that snaked its way through the trees and hedges before walking past the school playground. He spotted Paula on the far side nearest to the entrance talking to another parent. As he walked over towards her, a teacher opened the door and allowed the children to run out of the doors towards their parents. Michael rushed over and wrapped his arms around Blake's waist.

Blake held him close as Paula joined them.

"Well this is an unexpected surprise," Paula smiled. "What brings you here?"

"A promise that I made to my father nine years ago that I intend to keep. Looking after my family first," Blake smiled.

"Dad, can we go over and buy some cakes from Mrs Prince's cake stall on the playground?" Michael asked.

Blake nodded and as Michael led them over towards the playground, he noticed three stalls had been set up selling homemade cakes, books that had been written by the children in the school and freshly baked bread.

As they looked at the stalls, Michael pointed out the book which had the poem inside that he had written a few months ago and explained how his class had used yeast and flour to bake twenty loaves of bread. Paula took hold of Blake's hand as Michael ran off to play briefly with one of his friends.

"This means a lot to him," she smiled as Blake held her close.

"I've spent too long rushing from one mission to the next. If mum's death has proven anything, it's that life is too short and I need to make the most of the life we have now."

"Michael needs you in his life right now. The transition to secondary school is going to be tough for him."

"Then we'll face it together as a family," Blake replied.

"You mean that?"

"When I proposed in London, you said yes. I hope that still stands."

Paula laughed. "Of course it does."

"Then let's do it. Let's book the church and make it official."

Paula looked into his eyes. "You're serious?"

"Never been more serious about anything," Blake smiled.

Paula held him close for a moment before Michael came running over towards them.

"Dad, can we get some chocolate cake?" he asked.

As they approached the cake stand, Blake recognised the lady standing behind the stall. "Hello Gloria, what brings you to the school?"

"Blake Langford, I haven't seen you in over twenty years!" Gloria smiled. "You haven't changed a bit!"

"Mrs Prince, can we have one of your amazing chocolate and marshmallow cakes please?" Michael asked.

"Of course you can. After all, everything's better with cake," Gloria replied.

As Paula and Blake continued to chat with Gloria and the other parents in the school playground, a navy blue BMW with a Greek number plate slowly drove along the road just outside the school gates. The driver waited for one of the parents to drive away before parking in their space next to the school gate. He picked up his binoculars and managed to peer through a gap in the trees towards the cake stall. He saw Paula and Blake laughing and chatting with a group of people.

"That's right Blake, play happy families for now. It's only a matter of time," a man said as he watched them for a moment.

"Excuse me Sir, is everything okay?" a lady carrying a large black and yellow lollipop asked as she approached the car.

The man placed his binoculars onto the passenger seat. "Everything's fine, thank you," he smiled.

"Does your child attend this school?"

"No, but my nephew does."

"And who is he, may I ask?"

"You seem very suspicious..."

"It pays to be when strange men are looking into a school playground with binoculars during school pick-up time. Do I need to speak to the headmaster about this?" the lady asked.

"That won't be necessary, I'm just going."

"Then may I ask who your nephew is?"

"His name's Michael. Michael Langford," the man replied before driving away.

BLAKE LANGFORD WILL RETURN...